The Night of the First Billion

MIDDLE EAST LITERATURE IN TRANSLATION
MICHAEL BEARD AND ADNAN HAYDAR, SERIES EDITORS

Other titles in Middle East Literature in Translation

The Committee
Sonallah Ibrahim; Mary St. Germain and Charlene Constable, trans.

A Cup of Sin: Selected Poems
Simin Behbahani; Farzaneh Milani and Kaveh Safa, trans.

In Search of Walid Masoud: A Novel
Jabra Ibrahim Jabra; Roger Allen and Adnan Haydar, trans.

Sleeping in the Forest: Stories and Poems
Sait Faik; Talat S. Halman, ed.

Three Tales of Love and Death
Out el Kouloub

A Time Between Ashes and Roses
Adonis; Shawkat M. Toorawa, trans.

Women Without Men: A Novella
Shahrnush Parsipur; Kamran Talattof and Jocelyn Sharlet, trans.

Yasar Kemal on His Life and Art
Eugene Lyons Hébert and Barry Tharaud, trans.

Zanouba: A Novel
Out el Kouloub; Nayra Atiya, trans.

The Night of the
First Billion

A NOVEL

◆ ◆ ◆

Ghada Samman

Translated from the Arabic by Nancy N. Roberts

SYRACUSE UNIVERSITY PRESS

First Edition 2005
05   06   07   08   09   10   6   5   4   3   2   1

Originally published in Arabic in 1986 as *Laylat al-Milyar* by Manshurat
Ghada Samman of Beirut, Lebanon. This translation follows the text of the
second edition of March 1991, also published by Manshurat Ghada Samman
of Beirut, Lebanon.

The paper used in this publication meets the minimum requirements of
American National Standard for Information Sciences—Permanence of
Paper for Printed Library Materials, ANSI Z39.48–1984.∞™

Library of Congress Cataloging-in-Publication Data
Sammān, Ghādah.
[Laylat al-milyār. English]
The night of the first billion : a novel / Ghada Samman ; translated from the
Arabic by Nancy N. Roberts.— 1st ed.
p. cm.—(Middle East literature in translation)
"Originally published in Arabic as Laylat al-Milyar by Manshurat Ghada
Samman of Beirut, Lebanon. This translation follows the text of the second
edition of March 1991, also published by Manshurat Ghada Samman of
Beirut, Lebanon."
ISBN 0–8156–0829–2 (hardcover (cloth) : alk. paper)
I. Roberts, Nancy N. II. Title. III. Series.
PJ7862.A584L3313 2004
892.7'36—dc22
2004020952

Manufactured in the United States of America

◆　◆　◆

To the champions of freedom in the land of Arabdom,
Both women and men,
Who have refused to drink from the wellspring of madness
Or the bogs of drug-induced numbness,
Whose sobriety is heroism,
Whose protection of democracy's compass is an adventure,
Whose lifetimes have become a gamble:
To them, wherever they may be, however they may be,
I dedicate this book.
For they are my people,
And to them I belong.

Ghada Samman, the author of more than twenty-eight books including the first two books of this trilogy, *Beirut '75* and *Beirut Nightmares,* has been called "the most prominent Syrian woman writer of fiction of the last century."

Nancy N. Roberts, who earlier translated the first two parts of this trilogy, has also contributed translations of works dealing with Islamic history, jurisprudence, mysticism (Sufism), and modern Islamic thought and practice.

Contents

Translator's Preface   ix

Sources of Incantations   xi

The Night of the First Billion   1

Translator's Preface

THE FINAL VOLUME of a three-novel trilogy revolving around different aspects of the ongoing conflict in Lebanon, Ghada Samman's *The Night of the First Billion* shifts its focus from the civil war that broke out in Lebanon in 1975 to a later, but related, development: the Israeli invasion of Lebanon in 1982 and its effect on the social and moral fabric of Lebanese society. In the trilogy's first part, *Beirut '75,* the author depicts the reality of the civil war at its inception, including its multiple societal causes, from the perspectives of five distinct but related characters,who fall victim to the tragedy of the war in different ways arising from their individual circumstances, stations in life, personal struggles, and points of view. *Beirut Nightmares* is also set in 1975, shortly after the war begins. In it, Samman presents a suspenseful personal account of the two weeks she spent immured in her house in Beirut as a virtual prisoner of war, trapped by the intensity of the fighting. However, rather than presenting the events of that short but intense period in diary form, as a personal daily chronicle, Samman recreates the experience as a series of vignettes—"nightmares"—from the perspectives of a range of characters, some real some fantastic.

Unlike the first two novels, *The Night of the First Billion* is set not in Lebanon, but in Switzerland. All of the book's protagonists, however, are of Lebanese origin, while its events occur against the ominous background of both Lebanon's civil war and the 1982 Israeli invasion. As the book progresses, we find that the moral and material corruption pervading Lebanese society, which both helped to bring about the war and was fueled by it, has not been mitigated by the characters' relocation from Beirut to Geneva. On the contrary, those who were beneficiaries of and contributors to this corruption in Lebanon—like billionaire Raghid Zahran and his right-hand man Nadim—pursue their unconscionable practices with even greater fervor and impunity and once they find themselves in the "safety" of the West. Similarly, idealists like Khalil Dar', who have fled from the political oppression and physical perils of the war, arrive in the "oasis" of Switzerland only to find that their desperation to eke out a living is drawing them mercilessly and inexorably into a morass of corruption and nihilism.

Raghid Zahran, the unrivaled villain of the story, is a soulless twentieth-century Midas who spends the better part of the novel wallowing (and glorying) in filthy lucre deriving from huge arms sales—sales that daily serve to multiply the death toll in his war-ravaged homeland. Zahran's ultimate demise, particularly the manner in which it takes place, shatters the complacency of the rich and powerful elite, who appear to have the material wherewithal to escape the war's nightmares by fleeing Lebanon to pursue their self-centered interests elsewhere in the world, even though it is their wastefulness and corruption that have in part brought about the war by aggravating class divisions. The fate of Zahran serves as an eloquent reminder that the nightmares caused by Lebanon's strife and turmoil threaten to destroy more than Lebanon's weak and disenfranchised (as in *Beirut '75*).

Samman also explores the theme of magic, embodied in the sorcerer Sheikh Watfan and symbolizing the universal desire to control one's fate or, at least, to protect oneself from its vicissitudes. Magic is woven powerfully into the intertwined sagas of the books' fugitive characters, who, each in his or her own way and to varying degrees, experience a gradual, increasing disillusionment with the "paradise" in which they now live. Eventually they realize that there is no such thing as complete safety anywhere on earth. Rather, the only genuine safety, in the most profound and human sense of the word, is to be found in the courageous willingness to confront, challenge, and seek to ease the sufferings that surround us.

Sources of Incantations

THE INCANTATIONS that appear in this novel were taken word for word from their original sources in Arabic folklore. Specifically, they were taken from the following books:

Al-Nur al-Rabbani fil-'Ilm al-Ruhani (Divine light on spiritual science), by 'Abdul Fattah Al-Sayyid al-Tukhi, general director of the Institute of Astrological Inquiry, The Folklore Library, Beirut, n.d.

Al-Jawahir al-Lamma'ah fi Istihdar Muluk Al-Jinn fil-Waqt wal-Sa'ah(Glittering jewels on evoking the kings of the jinn according to the time and hour), by the eminent professor Sheikh 'Ali Abu-Hayy Allah al-Marzuqi, The Folklore Library, Beirut, n.d.

Taskhir al-Shayatin fi Wisal al-'Ashiqin (Bringing demons into subjection in the communion of lovers), by 'Abdul Fattah Al-Sayyid al-Tukhi, The Folklore Library, Beirut, n.d.

Al-Lu'lu' wal-Marjan fi Taskhir Muluk al-Jann (Pearls and coral on bringing the kings of the jinn into subjection), author unknown, Dar al-'Ilm lil-Jami', n.d.

Al-Kabarit fi Ikhraj Al-'Afarit (Rare wisdom on casting out evil spirits), second printing, compiled and written by Professor 'Abdul Fattah Al-Sayyid al-Tukhi, general director of the Institute of Astrological Inquiry for Egypt and the Eastern Regions, The Folklore Library, Beirut, 1392 A.H. (A.D. 1972).

The Night of the First Billion

HIERASHE, HIEROSHE, HIEROWA, Hisha, Titoush, Titouash, Imarash Qiroush Mirnoulsh. Respond, O Nasour, and make yourself present to me in obedience to these names! Eiroush Brishe Jeryoush Dagharsh Hierarsh Waroush Zaliesh Matmarish. By the truth of these names, I call upon you, your helpers and servants from among the demons and sons of demons . . . by the right of Shayoush Barsh Barhoum Housayeh, answer me quickly in obedience to what you have heard, in the name of Atiesh Bartyouh Tuwwa . . .

"Roulsh Qimarish Izroulsh Hiariesh Houatiesh, in submission to these names . . . Hash-hashbish Mish-hibish, may they rebuke you and conquer you. Batar Haroush Houazies. Hearken unto my oath, smell my incense, and be present at this conference of mine. By the right that it claims over you I have determined and by these names I have sworn, whispering the urgent inspiration at this very hour . . .

"Ihtamoush Ajroukh Awtiesh Kinahiesh, and by the truth of a mystery which they have named in concert, return to the place from which you came without having to be banished. Be gone, O Nasour—you, your helpers and your servants with Milfaqoush Milyaqoush Qoush Hayya . . .

"I adjure you, all ye disobedient, fractious spirits and demons who soar away with the hosts of Iblis. . . . O sons of Shierah and sons of Silah, those who ride the winds, flying armed through the air . . .

"O ye who plunge beneath the dust of the earth, kings of heights and depths, sovereigns of air and land, fire and water . . .

"Commanders of earthquakes, givers of promises and companions of wrath. . . . Where is Maymoun the Blue, where is Burqan, where is Abul-Qasim, Master of the Earthquake, where is Taht, where is the Red One, where is Awf, Commander of Commanders, where is Abul-Qasim the Yellow, where is Abul-Wakir the Most Vigilant? I adjure you by the right of the One who created and subdued you and in the name of glorification. Aah, Umayya, Umayya Atish Atish, Allah created you, proportioned you, then determined your paths. Descend with your steeds and your men, your swords gleaming, your steeds snorting, and your fires ablaze. Go forth to him while the rhymes in his heart are still athrob. Set fire to his heart, drive him onward with the wind and the clouds, and bring him hence . . .

"If he partakes of food may it bring him no pleasure. If he drinks water, let his thirst not be quenched. And if he seats himself in the presence of others may he find no rest, peace, or spirit of perseverance as he calls upon the fire, the fire . . .

"O ye company of servants, pledge yourselves to fulfill this command, setting a thousand demons on his right and a thousand on his left, a thousand behind him, a thousand over his head and a thousand beneath him. If he sleeps, rouse him from his slumber, if he eats, cause it to lodge in his throat, and if he drinks, cause him to choke . . .

"In the names of Malakh, Dimlakh, and Burakh, Jawla Hila . . .

"I adjure you, O company of demons and Iblises, of satanic hosts and devils, I adjure you wherever you may be on the face of the earth, bring forth those who dwell in deserts, slaughterhouses, graveyards, markets, highways, byways, and towers. Where are the two Maymouns of the clouds? Where is Shamhawraq the Flier? Where is Burqan the Jew? Where is the August White Monarch? Where is the Most Venerable Crimson King? Where is the One with the Black Turban? Where is the Owner of the Coal-black Mule? Where is the One with a thousand heads, each of which has a thousand faces, each of which has a mouth with a thousand tongues, with every tongue praising God Almighty in a different language. . . ?

"Alkash Batat Lahawshal Muti'oush Yatfiryoush Batbatiqoush Mikshlash, inspiration, inspiration, haste, haste, the hour has come . . .

"Set him ablaze, O Maytatroun in the name of Tahitmighilyal and of the family of Shala' Ya'waywabay Bitke Bitkifal Bas'a Ka'a Mimyal by one who is obedient to me. As for you, O family of Jall Ziryal, burn . . .

"Burn, O rebellious giant who commits outrages against himself . . ."

◆ ◆ ◆

He knew they were trailing him.

He could feel them drawing nearer with the same intuition that used to clue him in to the fact that the prison guard was coming to take him to the confession room, or the room of amnesia, to the reopening of the wounds in his memory, or to their obliteration in a kind of involuntary mental cosmetic surgery.

He knew they were trailing him . . .

They'd been after him ever since they discovered that he didn't die in the cemetery that night, and they were determined to take him back there once again. Even when he wasn't seeing them through the hole in his bedroom drapes or through cracks in the window, he was conscious of their unseen, sinister presence. It was like the presence of ghosts in a house haunted by a stony gloom, exhaling icy breath in passageways filled with muffled whispers and moaning doorways.

Only now he wasn't in his haunted house or in the darkness of a prison cell. Instead, he was in his old jalopy on his way to the airport—in broad daylight, at 10:00 on a summery Monday morning, fleeing in terror from potential gunfire from all sides under the hot sun of June 7, 1982. Death hovered naked between the sea and people's gasps of distress, in the space between the heavens and his prayers of supplication. It was a savage, metallic death that came and went without the aid of gloves, masks, ghostly attire, or the wild costumes of real-life or imaginary vampires. No longer was it in the guise of a prison guard who had come to make him donate blood for the third time in a month on behalf of someone from the intellectual class (to which he didn't belong) and whose blood type happened to be the same as his.

He knew they were trailing him . . .

Israeli aircraft hovered overhead, and his pursuers were still behind him.

He was terrified, and as if his fear were contagious, his car raced along with a shiver like a horse gone mad, charged with a kind of life force that might unexpectedly malfunction or become aware of itself. As he fled from Beirut, everything around him seemed to be trembling: the charred remains of trees on either side of the street, the sea's bluish, motionless corpse, and the telephone poles lying prostrate on the bullet-riddled asphalt like so many slain giants.

He knew they were pursuing him even though he hadn't caught a glimpse of them yet. As they closed in on his panic-stricken being, subtle warning vibrations went coursing through his body. Once again he peered into the rearview mirror, its dusty silver surface having been transformed into a magic window through which he could see his executioner and his fate.

No one stopped him at the usual armed checkpoint on the way to the airport. In fact, he didn't come across anyone there, and no one looked him in the eye. Instead, all that remained were the sandbags which, stacked in tight rows, stared out indifferently with their dirt eyes at tanks with manholes shut tight and cannon barrels rising slowly skyward.

On a day like this, no one would be likely to stop you to ask you for your name, your age, or your identification papers, or to find out where you were coming from or where you were going. On the contrary, you could die wherever you liked or murder whomever you liked without being troubled by anyone—except, of course, by the Israeli fighter planes that for the last three days had been flying back and forth and bombing everything in sight: the living and the dead, widows and toddlers, sports stadiums, schools and ammunition depots, hospitals, prisons, prisoners, and prison guards, freedom fighters and murderers, law enforcers and lawbreakers and everything in between. A passionate rage blazed inside his head, making him forget his terror in a flash of bitter awareness.

(There are fools who blithely go on indulging in the luxury of playing tricks on the "politics" market, not to mention the betrayals that are so nicely justified for them—strategically and tactically, at least—by professional hired pens. Not for a moment does anyone stop to take notice of the metallic death approaching from on high to demolish the entire chessboard that Beirut has turned into—and to wipe us all out with it.)

Petrified, he wondered whether he'd end up being killed by an enemy shell or by a bullet fired by a so-called friend. He was so terrified he nearly lost his ability to recall anything, like someone with drug-induced amnesia. If it hadn't been for his wife's tearful prayers as she sat on the seat next to him and the coughing of one of his two little boys, he wouldn't have remembered even his family. He was like a tiny little beast running through the forest, followed by a horde of primitive birds with razor-sharp beaks and blood-curdling screeches. He could hear dinosaurs, snakes, scorpions, giant lizards, elephants, and oversized frogs creeping forward to put him to death. They were accompanied by vicious plants that reproduced behind him at an infernal speed, extending their plaited vines like nooses, then yielding fleshy blossoms with thorny, delicate teeth and mouths like open stomachs lined with crimson velvet. He nearly fell to the ground. Aah . . .

Then at last he saw them. Their images were etched inside the dusty silver rectangle of his rearview mirror. He felt a bit relieved as he eyed their black car, which was just the way he'd always seen it in his nightmares. It was gaining on him at a madman's pace. So, before long he'd be murdered by yesterday's allies and everything would be over: the sounds of drumbeats in the jungle and of wild animals' footsteps would be silenced. Gone would be the trees armed with bamboo rods and sharp wooden spears, and smoke would stop coming out of his eyes, ears, and mouth. The car kept coming closer until it was right across from his.

Not daring to turn his head, he let out a soundless scream. Then the car passed him and took off ahead of him for the airport as if nothing could have stood in its way.

"That wasn't them," said his wife Kafa, speaking to him for the first time since they'd left home. "It was just another family, scared out of their wits like us. Hurry, Khalil. For God's sake, hurry."

By now the airport had come into view, as had the Israeli warplanes. At the very same moment, an image of his pursuers flashed in the rearview mirror. It was then that he knew without a doubt that they had arrived. He caught sight of a machine gun being aimed out the window of a blue car that had been following him. He looked back at his two little boys, and for the first time in his miserable pacifist's life, he regretted the fact that out of allegiance to the principle of nonviolence, he'd never carried a weapon. The two boys were asleep. Typical kids, he thought. They do just the opposite of what you expect them to. Sleep had been an impossibility the entire night before, his ears filled with the sound of the shrieks he expected to hear at the dreaded moment of their execution, and his soul weighed down with grief and pity both for himself and for them. And now they were napping, and liable to die before they even knew what was happening.

The explosions kept coming, one after another. The black car that had passed him a little while earlier blew up before his very eyes and burst into flames. It had suffered a direct hit. So then, he thought, the Israeli planes are targeting civilian cars, too.

Maybe the fools who'd been pursuing him would change their minds now and run for cover. Or at least stop aiming their machine guns at him and point them instead at the hostile aircraft that came rushing toward them with their fiery scythes, mowing down everything in sight on the airport road, as well as the airport buildings and the creatures inside them. He could hear Rami and

Fadi whimpering softly. So then, the poor little guys had woken up. In the rearview mirror he spied another executioner aiming his machine gun out the back window. And he was firing in Khalil's direction, not toward the attacking aircraft.

His window shattered as he passed the black car, which now lay incinerating before him, along with everyone in it. Everything was happening so fast, it left him no time to be terrified. As for the blue car, it was still coming after him, and the armed man inside it fired again, heedless of everything around him.

By this time Khalil was overcome not with fear but with rage. He felt a crazy urge to stop in the middle of the road, get out of his car unarmed as he always had been, walk over to his pursuers and give them a piece of his mind. He'd tell them exactly what he thought of the stupid things they'd been doing. Then he'd grab the barrels of their machine guns and point them skyward, which was where they should have been aiming all along.

Give them a piece of my mind! He laughed aloud at the thought, a hysterical laugh that mingled with the screams of his two sons and the sobbing of his wife. Give them a piece of my mind! Wasn't that how he'd ended up where he was now—dying with his family, with all hell breaking loose all around them and fires blazing on either side of the road, with hostile Israeli aircraft flying overhead, and with yesterday's allies hot on his heels for trivial violations and mistakes as if blinders had been drawn over their eyes, preventing them from seeing things as they really are? By now he was on fire with rage, a profound, bitter, scornful rage. Sticking his head out the car window, he pointed to the most recently arrived Israeli aircraft and screamed at his pursuers like a madman, saying, "Look, everybody! Look, brothers . . . look, my country!"

He thought he could hear the man with the machine gun in his hand laughing. They probably thought he'd lost his mind. So be it, he thought. After all, who among them was still sane in this Arab theater of the absurd? Here he was face to face with his executioner. Someone had set fire to the gallows, while the executioner just went right on tying the noose and putting it around his neck. He didn't bother to turn around and look at the person who was coming to send them both up in flames, and his heart didn't so much as skip a beat at the sight of the truth lying naked before him in the June sun. So then, he thought, murder each other to your hearts' content, all ye brethren-turned-enemies! Sink to the depths of degradation with your petty resentments, and forget the deep wounds gone by and those yet to come.

Then, in a dreamlike flash, he realized that the airplane was attacking, firing, reaping its harvest. In the midst of the mad flurry of explosions, he saw the blue car blow up inside the dusty, silver rectangle of his rearview mirror. As its shattered remains went flying in all directions, the steering wheel momentarily escaped from his grip. He nearly howled at the top of his lungs, out of the depth of his silence and the quick of his wound, "Do you understand now?! Damn!"

His two little boys were screaming, and his wife was tongue-tied. As for him, some stranger who inhabited his body charged forward on his wounded steed. At last he came to a halt near the airport entrance. Then, dusting fragments of shattered glass off himself as he got out, he picked up his two panic-stricken children, holding them by the waist like a couple of lambs who've managed to avoid being slaughtered, and ran inside with them. Meanwhile, his wife had rushed inside ahead of the rest of them in hopes of finding shelter inside the airport's stony edifice.

Once inside, Khalil was surprised to find the airport bustling with people. After depositing his boys in a heap behind a marble pillar along with a number of other crying children, he took out a cigarette. But no sooner had he lit up than his wife said to him disapprovingly, "Hurry up and bring the bags."

He gasped. Then she added in that sweet, commanding tone of hers, "The raid is over now. Hurry up, Khalil, before they come back."

So he did.

◆ ◆ ◆

Half an hour's respite from the fighting, and the Beirut airport was back to normal. Seven years of having to coexist with death had taught people the art of carrying on with their daily lives without even stopping long enough to bury their dead or mourn their loved ones. Seven years had created a society that looked something like a community of ants being crushed under the feet of a giant ogre that paces back and forth, back and forth over their little home. Those who hadn't received a mortal blow went on their way laughing or crying, but they kept going.

It was in this sort of climate that people went about making travel arrangements. Would it be the airport tax, or the tax of the life to come? Public security, or the portals of heaven? Customs inspectors, or angels of judgment? Waiting for one's departure to another continent, or to another world?

However, the atmosphere in the glass-enclosed passengers' lounge was different. Airplanes sat parked outside in full view. So, would they carry people far away from this hell on earth? They saw a number of women weeping tearlessly. As for the woman next to them, she told them how the Israelis had occupied her village in south Lebanon at dawn the previous day, and how she had managed to escape with her children across the mountains. She was Lebanese, married to a Palestinian man working in the Gulf. There was something in her tone of voice that reminded Khalil of tobacco fields, so he took out a cigarette and lit up. Meanwhile, the woman carried on with her story, seemingly indifferent to whether anyone was listening. (Like me, she's trying to keep death at bay by listening to her own voice, to the terror inside her that still burns with hope.)

She had come to visit her family. The Israelis would see to it that her Palestinian children had their heads cut off. After all, she said, they were still small, and Begin's soldiers would prefer to slaughter them before they were old enough to fight.

She had decided to take her chances on the treacherous roads in hopes that she'd reach the airport safely and some airplane would carry her away. She'd arrived at dawn before the air battles had begun, and since then the airport had been closed and reopened twice. During the lulls between battles, some adventurous airplane would manage to get away, and the people left behind would be envious of those on board. She would have to wait until evening, which was when the flight to the Gulf was scheduled to leave. Finally, she decided to take her kids to the restroom for a few minutes and asked if they might be so kind as to keep an eye on a couple of overstuffed handbags that were obviously too big to be allowed on as carry-ons. Khalil could hear his wife Kafa replying uneasily, "No, we couldn't. It's almost time for our flight. You'll have to look for someone else," whereupon she proceeded to drag the entire family far away from the woman's bags.

"Why did you do that?" Khalil asked her.

"I don't trust anybody anymore," she replied miserably. "How do we know that somebody hasn't planted a bomb in her bags, with or without her knowledge? How do we know they won't blow up? And how can we be sure the woman isn't an impostor, or a dupe? How would we know?"

As Kafa spoke, Khalil felt a fiery blade of grief piercing his heart. And he felt ashamed. He too had lost his ability to trust anyone. He'd lost confidence both in those he loved and in those he hated. People's hearts had grown distant and cold, and where there had once been harmony, suspicion now reigned.

A voice came over the loudspeaker instructing passengers on the London flight to proceed to the boarding gate. Surrounded on all sides by envious sighs, the passengers concerned went rushing toward the bus that would take them to the airplane. One woman, laden with gold jewelry and plastered with cosmetics, insisted on boarding the first-class bus rather than the one used for economy class. Hadn't anyone ever told her that there's only one class for people going to their deaths?

A little while later they heard a voice coming over the loudspeaker again, this time announcing that the flight to Geneva was ready for boarding. At this, a throng of distinguished-looking men and fashionably dressed women came forward. As he walked next to his stylish wife, Khalil's unkempt beard and threadbare clothes made him look more fit to be her servant than her husband. He almost tried telling his story to the airline stewardess, explaining why he, the penniless Khalil Dar', would be traveling to Geneva bearing a red business-class card like the ones only the wealthy can afford. However, she took no notice of him. In fact, she didn't so much look at him as through him, as though she were talking to some sort of disembodied persona suspended above a broken ceiling light that had fallen to the floor.

"You'd better hurry," she said. "After all, there might be another air raid, in which case the airport will be closed again."

Wrenching his gaze away from the light's shattered remains, Khalil scurried off into the festival of terror.

◆   ◆   ◆

It seemed like some sort of farcical game of torture, as endless as the passageways of a maze in a nightmare. For the second time they boarded the aircraft and it began moving down the runway. Then, right before takeoff, the captain brought the airplane back to the spot where the passengers had boarded and asked them to get off, saying that the airport was being closed again. Fine. But he hadn't told them *why* it was being closed. One glance out the airplane window was enough for Khalil to be able to decipher the infernal line written on the horizon. He could see hostile aircraft and hear bomb blasts. It was war. So once again they all rushed to the waiting lounge as a fierce air battle took place before their very eyes. Most of the passengers stood in front of the glass wall of the lounge watching the blasts go off: in the sky, along the horizon, on the ground around the airport, in the hills, and toward the lofty mountains in the distance. One aircraft had burst into flames and was plummeting to the ground, while one of the blasts closer by had sent the shattered remains of glass windows flying in all directions, then thrust them like so many daggers into onlookers' necks and cheeks. Yet no one really cared. Even the children in the crowd squeezed themselves in between people's legs so as to get a long look at the blazing fireworks display.

What's going on? Khalil wondered. Is this the courage of the living, or the cold indifference of the dead? Have we grown so accustomed to death that all it arouses in us anymore is the urge to gawk and stare? Or have we actually developed such an appetite for it that now we seek it out, calling upon it to soothe our bloodshot eyes with the balm of its dusky gloom?

◆   ◆   ◆

Through the clouds of smoke; against the backdrop of silver MEA aircraft crouching on the ground; over the roar of explosions, people's gasps, madly screeching warplanes advancing and retreating, attacking and pouncing; and under Death's savage wing with its plumage unfurled over everything in sight till it obscured the blueness of the sky and the golden glow of the sun, transforming the world into a melancholy painting in shades of gray and black, Khalil caught a glimpse of a brightly colored paper airplane taking flight from a child's hand. In doing so, it launched an assault on the entire scene, intruding upon the morose panorama like a man stepping suddenly inside a painting. Colored red, blue, green, and purple, the paper airplane rose through the air, pursuing its remarkable ascent surrounded by hostile aircraft. As it was borne gently aloft by subtle, invisible winds the way snow creeps on tiptoe down the paths of the sky, its own secret sun seemed to light up inside it. Khalil couldn't hear the sounds of the battle anymore, and the instruments of death began to seem smaller and smaller compared with that colored paper airplane as it carried on with its delicate, soundless, sweet, majestic flight.

Had it been seconds? Minutes? All Khalil knew was that the air battle had come to an end, and that the airplane belonging to the unnamed youngster who had intervened in the fighting with his own "weapon" had begun growing larger and larger as it continued its mysterious, colorful journey. Like an audience discussing some exciting film during intermission, people began talking among themselves about what they'd just seen. Khalil was amazed that no one made any mention of the make and model of the paper airplane. After all, since so many people had been turned by the war into experts on weaponry and battle tactics, there was almost always someone on hand to offer a military analysis of sorts. Or was it just that he hadn't been listening well enough?

Ominously, Kafa asked, "What if they close the airport again? How will we get back home when the shooting and bombing are devouring all the roads in the city, and with the nearby Cocody district being one of the main enemy targets? We'll get hungry. So why don't we buy some sandwiches before. . . ?"

But apparently Kafa wasn't the only one who realized the potential tragedy that might await them.

For just at that moment, scores of people started heading toward the sandwich vendor, and Khalil found himself in a tumultuous sea of humanity that seemed to pulsate with the terror of hunger. With its untold numbers of outstretched hands, shoulders pressing up against other shoulders, feet treading heedlessly one atop the other, the crowd mutated into a single, huge, primitive creature engaged in a kind of unconscious self-destruction.

Then suddenly a cry went up, "There's no more bread!"

He heard the announcement as he took the last remaining sandwich from the vendor, who said, "This is all we've got left."

Besieged by resentful stares, Khalil shouted out a silent apology, "This is for my hungry little boy!" Then he slipped through the throng and fled back to his family. However, when he brought them the sandwich, the boys refused to take even so much as a nibble. Having returned to their remarkable calm, they just gazed about thoughtfully at the world around them, and even began to yawn. Khalil, though, kept growing tenser by the minute until he felt as though he were on the verge of a nervous breakdown.

For the third time their flight was announced over the loudspeaker. For the third time they headed toward Gate 5, trembling with fear and hope.

As if she wanted to pick a quarrel, one woman protested, "How can you let us take off when conditions are so dangerous?"

She was answered by a distinguished-looking man whom Khalil thought he'd seen before. "Nobody's forcing you to get on the airplane!" he shouted. "Whoever wants to stay here is free to do so."

◆　◆　◆

They all boarded the aircraft without a single refusal, and held their collective breath. Slowly the airplane began to move, then it came to a halt—for ten centuries, ten days, ten minutes, no one knew for sure. Then it took off madly down the runway. However, no one felt entirely reassured even when it left the ground and headed petulantly toward the sea, since just as they took off all hell broke loose again. As new explosions rang out, the people on board thought in dread about the possibility of either having to go back for another round of "airport torture" or taking a direct hit in the air, not to mention all sorts of other potential dangers, which they might not be able to name but which they could surely feel, as if the atmosphere itself were charged with peril. However, the captain stayed on course through what had turned into a kind of airborne minefield. No one breathed, and no one uttered a word. Now that they'd entered the battle for real, no one dared go on theorizing about it.

In spite of it all, Khalil stared sorrowfully out the tiny airplane window, trying in vain to get one last look at Beirut. Here he was running away like a coward as his homeland went up in flames. But, he thought, they chased me all the way to the airport. They left me no other choice.

By this time the airplane was flying over Cyprus. Now that the passengers actually believed that they'd made it to safety, they went into sudden fits of hysteria. One woman wanted to kiss the pilot, while another smooched a nearby woman who was a complete stranger to her. Meanwhile, everybody chattered away to everybody else as if they'd been transformed into one big happy family. Never mind that if the plane had happened to crash into the sea, they would have been at each other's throats within minutes, fighting over who would get out the emergency exit first. But barring such an eventuality, everyone was blissfully in love, with "humanity" being exuded by one and all and social niceties rolling off their tongues as the stewardesses made the rounds among them to crown their joy with a delectable repast and glasses of firewater.

The distinguished-looking man whom Khalil suspected he had seen before had begun to return Khalil's glances. Then suddenly a name flashed in his head. He really did know the man, after all. He was a neighbor of theirs who had emigrated quite some time earlier. Nadim was his name. Nadim Ghafir. Pretending not to have seen him, Khalil closed his eyes, hiding behind a mask of sleep. He wasn't as happy as he ought to be for a man who had escaped death several times in a single morning.

If only I hadn't listened to this woman's pleas and threats. If only I hadn't paid any attention to the apple in her hand and the tears in her eyes once she'd decided to use our two boys as a weapon against me. At the same time, I was fleeing oppression and being bombed by Israel. I'm riddled with the wounds inflicted on my homeland, and I'm exhausted. If only I'd stayed there. If only I'd stayed and been shot dead along with my fellow countrymen, or buried under the rubble left by some enemy attack. If I'd stayed, I might have found a chance to do something. I might have gone back to my village, where I was born and where I left my heart. But all roads leading back there were closed to me. In fact, the folks from my hometown managed to find their way to my house in Beirut this morning. They'd been forced to leave and were seeking me out for refuge. . . . The wounds of my homeland have sapped all my strength.

Suitcases . . . suitcases . . . a homeland scattered in all directions, its remains packed into suitcases . . .

Entire lives packed into suitcases, scurrying from village to city and from street to street, between barricades and lines of fire that pit enemy against unmasked enemy, from cars destroyed by explosions to buildings on the verge of collapse, and in battles among brothers turned enemies—under fire, in the rain, and in the profoundest shame . . .

Suitcases . . . suitcases . . . suitcases fleeing from south Lebanon to Beirut, and others in flight from Beirut to exile.

Suitcases gathered on the sidewalk in front of my house . . . and with all of us in a rush to be on our way, like thieves who've snatched their lives out of fate's back pocket and are making off with them as fast as their legs will carry them.

Suitcases, suitcases . . .

(They took the suitcases out of the car and brought them up to the house. Meanwhile, I was leaving the house with my own bags and getting ready to put them in a "getaway" car. As soon as I'd greeted them, I shouted, "Why didn't you stay there?!"

"And why don't you stay here?" they replied.

It was a long, long story—their story and mine, a story of the sieges that all of us had suffered, and of the family feuds that had made it possible for the enemy to hem us in. Consequently, we contented ourselves with a silent embrace. They didn't tell me about how no one had helped them to endure with anything but theories and pep talks. And I didn't tell them how I'd spent the last few years waging war against the very people I was supposed to be in solidarity with. Instead, I just bade them farewell, adding bitterly, "If you'd only stayed back there . . ."

To which they replied once more, "Why don't you stay here, too?"

And I might have done just that, if Kafa hadn't reminded me that the armed man who had fired at me and missed the day before had just come around a few minutes earlier to check out our balconies and windows, and that he wasn't alone. For all I know, my family's unannounced arrival from the south saved my life by camouflaging the bags I was about to flee with. Stuffed with the buds of some hopes and the corpses of others, with tears, hatred, memories, and protest—along with some bread and a few clothes—my suitcases had been piled on the sidewalk right beside theirs. Oh, I'm so weary of my homeland's wounds—so weary!)

He was roused out of his reverie by the voice of the stewardess, asking, "Tea or coffee, sir?" (Poison, Madame?)

But he ignored her and went on pretending to be asleep.

◆   ◆   ◆

Kafa sat back in her luxurious seat, feeling happy in a way that she hadn't for a long, long time. She knew her husband was only pretending to be asleep, which was just as well for both of them. Fadi and Rami were asleep by this time, having turned up their noses at the food they'd been offered. The airplane had left Beirut behind a few minutes earlier and was now flying her and her family off to a new life.

(A new life? Does such a thing exist? Is it really possible for me—or anyone else, for that matter—to bring my life suddenly to a halt and say, This isn't the path for me, and now I'm going to set off in a new direction, forgetting the life I've lived so far on the wrong path year after cursed year? Will I ever be able to forget my little girl Widad, her tender flesh scattered in all directions and mingled with the blood shed by Tuffah the street vendor and by all the other children who'd been playing with her? They'd been playing ball with a grenade they came across in a vacant lot, where it had been left behind after some damned dispute that had broken out between a couple of different local organizations. Can I really strip myself of my wounds the way one sheds some old, worn-out dress? Can bruises to the spirit be healed? Well, at least I finally have the chance to get out of the trap that I stumbled into as time went on. While my sisters were all living in the lap of luxury and safety with their husbands in this wealthy country or that, I was stuck in a city polluted with bomb blasts and violence, haunted by the ghost of hunger, and filled with worry, disappointment, shattered glass, the scattered remains of loved ones' mangled, decaying corpses, and caravans of suffering humanity. Then there was my loss of Widad, who's destined never to return, and my husband, who leaves one prison only to end up in another one without even knowing exactly why or where or who's against whom.

And why? Oh, I was so passionately in love with the fool, and now I don't know anything anymore. Once upon a time I fell madly in love with him because he was so wonderful, because he never said anything but the truth just the way his villager father had taught him. Little did I know that the very thing that I loved about him would become the thing that makes me miserable with him! All the catastrophes that have hit us have been on account of telling the "truth"—or at least, what he imagines to be the truth—wherever he happens to be and whatever the circumstances, demanding "the right to dialogue"! The idiot. Who has a dialogue with a barricade in the street? Who has a dialogue with the ringleaders of sadistic factions or experts in torture?)

She wasn't cut out for this sort of thing. However, what had happened, had happened. And now she was taking her first step into dreamland, sitting in the first-class compartment of an airplane headed toward Europe—toward Geneva, Switzerland, to be exact.

A cordial man seated behind her helped her get her handbag put away. As he did so, there was a gleam in his eye the likes of which she'd nearly forgotten existed, and which she missed. It was the glow of a virile man's admiration poured into the mold of gentlemanly courtesy. She was tired of Beirut and its coarse, barbaric, comfortless world.

(Rich people are so refined. They sleep well, they eat well, and as a result they have the time and energy to savor a beautiful woman like me and take proper care of her. The people I'd like to have around me and live the rest of my life with are the kind I find right here in this compartment with me.)

It was true, of course, that she'd sold the last of her worldly possessions in order to leave Beirut, including the expensive pieces of jewelry that she'd received as wedding gifts from her parents and well-to-do relatives (that is to say, who *had* been well-to-do before their fortunes were decimated by the war.) However, at least she'd managed to get tickets for her family, even though it had meant having to pay for first-class seats because all the tourist class seats had been booked up for weeks—ever since the night of the invasion. And she'd finally managed to drag her wayward husband onto the right track—the way of escape from danger—where he'd have no choice but to devote himself to his family and to building his future before it was too late. Thanks to the clowns who, taking him for somebody dangerous, had made up their minds to liquidate him, she'd finally been able to drag him and what remained of her family after Widad's death out of the "Switzerland of the East"— which was now on fire along with everyone in it—to the "Switzerland of the West" which awaited her with its stable tranquility.

(Oh, Widad! Do you suppose I'll ever get over the agony I feel over her— that little girl who was killed at the hands of another Arab, killed by an unforgivable act of sheer mindlessness? How can I even imagine forgetting or forgiving? Day before yesterday, or rather the day before that—Friday afternoon to be exact, and the day of the first Israeli raid on the Sports Complex— my neighbor Masa' came to me carrying the mangled body of her little girl, Nada. She'd been killed on the school bus along Khalda Road. I had a long cry with her. While she grieved over Nada, I wept bitter tears over Widad. I realized then that the sting of another person's death isn't always the same. After all, the death of a loved one at the hands of an enemy is a death with some sort of meaning. But when the death takes place at the hands of someone within one's one household, so to speak, it seems fruitless, absurd. Nada was a martyr, but Widad was a mere victim. I had to get out of that land of sorrows. If I'm determined to start a new life, I have to forget.)

And she was determined to do just that. She had set her mind on it with every beat of her young heart.

A handsome face was stealing glances at her from one of the front seats. It was a face she knew.

(Oh, my God! It's Nadim Ghafir! Nadim, that lucky rich man who manages to live in all the capitals of Europe at one time. Nadim, the neighbor I've seen coming to visit his elderly parents who insist on living in their old house in Beirut-now-turned-graveyard. How strange people are . . .)

Kafa smiled at him, remembering that she was a beautiful women blazing with charm. Something about Nadim reminded her of her forgotten passion for gold doorknobs, private airplanes, marble-floored living rooms and fur coats, diamond earrings, credit cards, caviar, crepes suzette, and lobster. She woke her husband, who, rather than really being asleep, was in torment over his disguised awareness of what was going on around him. In as much of a whisper as she could, she exclaimed, "Look who's with us on the plane! It's Mr. Nadim Ghafir!"

Meanwhile, picking up on Kafa's unspoken signals which, like a siren song, sent forth a summons charged with bewitching power, Nadim straightened up in his seat, ready to come over to her and greet her husband!

No sooner had he placed his enormous cigar between his lips than the stewardess came back into the cabin pulling a beverage-laden cart, thereby ruining the "blessed moment." However, after being passed hand to hand among a number of other "cordial" passengers, his calling card finally came to rest between Kafa's brightly manicured fingers. Printed in gold ink that lent it an aura of prestige, the card bore telephone numbers and addresses for a number of different offices, as well as a brief note in green ink that read: I would be pleased for you to contact me.

Khalil held his tongue while Kafa blushed with pleasure. After all, this meant that he'd taken them for wealthy people! Like him, they belonged to the genre of folks who travel first class, and who rightfully deserve to enjoy his hospitality. Khalil made a miserable attempt at a smile, but the best he could do was a grimace. If only Nadim Ghafir knew how poverty-stricken and terrified they were. The future that awaited them was little more than a black, drawn curtain. His two boys refused to eat the food not because they were dainty or spoiled, but simply because they'd never seen anything like it before. They'd never laid eyes on these ghastly looking black eggs called "caviar," which looked like a mound of expired ants, and they weren't devouring them—despite how hungry they were—for fear that they might bite! And as for Khalil's shabby clothes, he wasn't wearing them as a whim the way some rich folks might do . . . they really were the only ones he owned.

Khalil shut his eyes again, his eyelids a curtain that he could draw whenever he liked between himself and the rest of the world, then go wandering about through his private theater of sorrows.

(The people who ride in first-class cabins are the kind I hate to have around me, the kind I'd hate to have to spend the rest of my life with. But here I am, stuck inside the same capsule as Nadim Ghafir, a man whose amorality I utterly despise . . . the successful, wealthy man, the self-exiled rising star who would sell anything: arms, women, nations, airplanes, petrol . . .

Nadim Ghafir, whose parents' house is bombed along with my house and

everybody else's with the very weapons that he, his cronies and their support-
ers sell to anyone who will buy them.

Every passenger in this entire cabin has a face just like his. And this cabin
will just go on wandering aimlessly through space with us aboard in an eternity of humiliation for me. It's as though from the very first step I took out of
Beirut, I set my feet down in the wrong place, keeping company with the very
people that I'd once almost paid with my life for taking a stand against.)

Excitedly, Kafa cried, "Look, Khalil! We're flying over Mont Blanc, the
highest summit in the Alps!"

As he gazed out into the vast white expanse, he felt as though he were running alone through thick snow wearing nothing but flimsy, tattered clothing,
howling, falling to the ground and being buried by avalanches.

◆   ◆   ◆

"I've found an old woman who binds water to water and stars to the sky, who
binds the sea to its whales and the merchant to his scales. . . . Qatem, Latem,
by the truth of the One who said to the heavens and the earth, 'Come now,
willingly or grudgingly!' and to whom the heavens and the earth replied, 'We
have come in willing obedience!' I now bind thy organ, O Nadim Ghafir, from
all creatures male or female. I bind it with a knot of the Jews, the Christians,
and the Mazdeans, which no one can loose, neither male nor female, neither
demon nor human."

Dunya inhaled the aroma of the incense that burned in the room, and as
Watfan the astrologer mentioned her husband's name, a shudder of vindictive
glee coursed through her plump, aging frame. The place struck her as being
less like an ordinary room than like some cave straight out of a fairy tale, filled
with dark shadows and peculiar rock formations of the sort that make one's
imagination run wild. The impression was so vivid that when she came out and
shut the door behind her, she was astonished to find a number above the door.
She made her way to the end of the corridor and stopped in front of the lift,
which suddenly opened its doors wide. After the session from which she had
just emerged, she'd been expecting to be received not by an elevator, but by
mountains to be scaled and pristine forests to be traversed.

Before long she was back in the lobby of a posh Swiss hotel. When she
came out, she found herself on a street in Geneva. Across from the hotel there
stood the towering building where she had worked eighteen years earlier, be-

fore she'd become a millionaire's wife. That was during the days when she'd been studying and reading books, going to see exhibitions and listening to music, and counting her money several times before deciding to buy a new bookshelf for her library. Those were the days when she used to look in the newspapers for something other than the addresses of "spiritualists" and astrologers . . . when she used to rendezvous not with "cup readers," but with readers of books and imbibers of culture and learning.

She heard a voice calling to her from a nearby first-floor balcony. My God, she thought. How could I have forgotten that Layla Sabbak lives right here behind the hotel? Do you suppose she saw me coming out? What will I say to "Lilly Spock," as she's referred to by some people instead of by her real name?

Then Layla disappeared from the window. In no time she was standing beside Dunya, and in that special tone of hers somewhere between innocence and the epitome of malice, between sarcasm and feigned ignorance, she said, "I knew you'd be coming to shop in our neighborhood. I'll come along with you to the supermarket."

So then, thought Dunya, the bitch must have seen my car parked near the hotel, then started keeping an eye on it. After all, what else could I expect from a "friend" like her after a lifetime of feigned love and mutual ill will? On the other hand, is that really all she came to tell me—namely, that she'd seen me leaving the hotel? Or does she have something even more disturbing up her sleeve?

Dunya gazed at Layla with envy and a touch of ambivalence. She had to be at least forty years old, which would make the two of them about the same age. But if that was the case, then what made her look so damned much younger? Was it because she was divorced, happy, and loved? Was it because she was slender and elegant, and because everything about her seemed to dance with freedom, including her long hair and her nonchalant, almost mocking glances?

"Pardon me, but it seems you've come to our neck of the woods on some other sort of business."

"No, not at all," insisted Dunya. "Nadim is due back from Beirut this evening, so I came to pick out a few of his favorite things to eat and drink. Some of his friends are supposed to come by."

(I won't mention anything to her about the big party we're having at our house tonight. I don't want to invite her. I might feel jealous of her. I might . . .)

And was Layla being sarcastic when she said ever so seriously, "Love in marriage flourishes on the wife's tender loving care—and her food"?

In an attempt to change the tone of the conversation, Dunya asked with feigned concern, "And what have you been doing these days since you left your other job? I hear you've gone into the private sector—interior decorating, if I'm not mistaken."

"I've been working full-time for Raghid Zahran," Layla replied. "He's assigned me to oversee the preparations for the 'Night of the First Billion' celebration. You know what I mean . . . the decorations, food and drink, sending out invitations, that sort of thing."

Dunya gasped, unable to conceal her surprise. Yes . . . she did know what Layla meant. At least one million Swiss francs' worth of pure profit, not to mention expanded public relations with millionaires. The witch had done it, after all. At one time she'd thought Layla was chasing her husband Nadim in preparation for leaving Amir Nealy, and it had made her uneasy. Little had she known that Nadim was nothing but a storefront operation of sorts—a stepping-stone to get closer to Raghid Zahran. After all, why be content with a little tributary when you can have the fountainhead—the goldmine itself, Raghid the magnificent? That would really be hitting the jackpot. (So, Layla has done it, just the way my husband Nadim did it before her. But actually, Layla has always been a bit of a man in some ways—except where precious Amir was concerned.)

Not hesitating to deliver her final blow in the one weak spot she was sure of, Dunya asked, "What does Amir Nealy think of this new work of yours?"

It was obvious that the question had hit its mark, since Layla's only reply was silence, or what amounted to the same thing.

"Let's hurry," she said. "It's begun to rain and it'll be sure to mess up our hairdos."

Dunya knew quite well how little Layla cared about "hairdos" or anything else of the sort. She remembered how Layla had taken everyone by surprise by showing up at a New Year's Eve party in jeans where all the other women were dolled up and dressed to the hilt, decked out in silk and velvet, and sporting dazzling coiffures topped with jewels and tiaras. That night Layla had walked in alone, her luxuriant black locks combed by the wind and ornamented with nothing but raindrops. Over her jeans she wore a short black mink coat that was so shiny it fairly glowed, and which she quickly removed so as to show off the sports shirt beneath, her fingers as bare of jewels as those of a runaway schoolgirl. On her bosom there rested an antique coin with a hole bored through its center, and hanging from a delicate iron chain.

That was the night when Raghid Zahran first took notice of her. He seemed particularly interested in the antique piaster which she was wearing, and Dunya's husband—in his capacity as one of Raghid's right-hand men—volunteered to don a pair of reading spectacles and make an attempt at deciphering the half-obliterated words written on the rare coin. A number of other well-to-do folks in attendance likewise volunteered for the job, feasting their eyes both on the exquisite coin and on the luscious, well-endowed bosom on which it rested.

That despicable siren. Despite her relative indigence, she'd known just how to steal the limelight and dull the glitter of millions of dollars' worth of costly jewelry. Not only that, but she'd done it with a single, ancient coin whose cryptic inscriptions were so worn down, hardly anyone would be able to make them out in the romantic lighting of the distinguished celebration. And where had all this transpired? In Dunya's own house! Knowing that divorcees in relative financial straits are a necessity for aging men—whose wives invariably fall ill just in time not to go to a New Year's Eve bash—she had decided to invite Layla in hopes that she could help liven up the atmosphere. But then the bitch had gone and made herself into the star of the evening with nothing but a lousy piaster. ("It's luck, just luck, Shaykh Watfan. That's how she managed to snare Raghid Zahran, the biggest shark in the world of money, with a piaster!")[1]

My God, Dunya! Raghid wants to celebrate the fact that he's landed his first billion by inviting millionaires and billionaires to this party. And Layla is in charge of getting the thing ready, a service that no doubt will snag her her own first million. God, Dunya! To think that you were afraid of losing your husband to this woman, when in fact, Nadim was nothing but a mere sardine in Raghid Zahran's sea. And now it's Nadim's turn to be afraid—afraid of Layla as a fierce competitor. God, Dunya!

(The bitch has managed to get what she wants without going through a man to do it. She's a woman who knows how to capitalize on her mistakes. As

---

1. The irony in Dunya's words is intensified in the Arabic by a play on words based on the fact that the Arabic word for "piaster" (*qirsh*) makes up part of the phrase translated as "shark" (*samakat qirsh*).

for me, I placed myself in the service of a man whose profession Layla herself now practices. Rather than going straight for the fortune to be had, I contented myself with being Qays's handmaid. But no. . . . At the time when I married Nadim, I loved him. Then . . . then I don't remember anymore. It's as if I didn't mean to do what I did . . . as if my entire life has been nothing but a huge typo.)

As the two women reached the door of the supermarket, Dunya said suddenly, "My God! I forgot to pick up Picasso at the barber's. I've got to go back and get him. In any case, my chauffeur can come back later and pick up the things I need."

"Who's Picasso?"

"He's my new dog. Have you forgotten?"

Layla had enough insight to understand what was behind Dunya's flaunting of her wealth, her pampered dog and her chauffeur. After so many years of enmity disguised as friendship between one woman and another, every otherwise innocent word is transformed into a pinprick of sorts.

Returning the blow without hesitation, Layla took the opportunity to make sport of Dunya's flabby, overweight physique, saying, "Oh, my God! And I forgot my appointment at the Fitness Club!"

Before parting hurriedly in front of the supermarket entrance and going their separate ways, Layla delivered her coup de grace, saying, "Oh, and today's Monday, which is the day when Shaykh Watfan receives clients at the hotel. What do you say I go ask him for a good luck charm? Or perhaps you aren't a customer of his?"

So then, the witch did know that she'd been coming to see him! In fact, she'd come all the way down from her balcony just to make certain that Dunya knew that she knew. God, how she detested that self-important hussy, who prided herself on her freedom! And how she hoped to see some evil befall her.

Then, before the two supposed friends bade farewell, they kissed each other warmly several times on each cheek!

✦   ✦   ✦

He knew they were trailing him.

He could feel their hostile presence with the same intuition that warned him of a sudden drop in the price of this or that type of stock, or an unexpected rise in the value of gold, or the dollar or the yen or the baht or the mark or the dinar, or any of the other currencies on Planet Earth.

The car left his posh office in the heart of the Geneva business district and headed toward the suburb where his golden mansion was located.

He took no time to gaze at the magnificent Rhone River. He didn't stare out at the trees around the lake or its swans and boats. In fact, he couldn't stomach nature scenes.

He knew they were trailing him.

There was someone who wanted to kill him.

After all, it was only logical: a man with his kind of wealth, who in the next few weeks would be celebrating the occasion of having raked in his first billion dollars—who wouldn't be itching to assassinate him, out of jealousy at least?

Relaxing into the velvet upholstery of his Rolls Royce, he imbibed a glass of firewater before closing up the miniature, gilded bar. Scrutinizing his chauffeur, whose cap was tilted slightly to one side, he reprimanded him for not wearing the thing right. Then he turned his attention to his bodyguard's shaved head, but couldn't find anything to upbraid him for even though he had a yen to chew him out for something. There were plenty of people who would like to see him dead, including his chauffeur, his closest friends, and possibly his guards, and, without a doubt, the men he'd ruined on his way to the top. One by one he'd stepped on them like so many rungs on a ladder, leaving some behind bars, and others in mental institutions, graves, or poorhouses whose owners couldn't mention his name without breathing bitter curses against him. And the women . . . he'd forgotten them, too. There were so many of them, their faces had become superimposed on each other in his memory, like drawings done on layer after layer of transparent Plexiglas. All he could make out of the hideous mass now was a single face with untold numbers of now-forgotten eyes and mouths.

(Everyone detests me, even my guard dogs. Returning hatred for hatred, they loathe me secretly while I loathe them to their faces. Could love take any other form?

I take unabashed pleasure in hatred, and I glory in performing its base, despicable rights. I never married and I never had children so that I wouldn't have to pretend to love them. However, I regret that. I wish now that I'd had children, children I could have hated and been hated by in return without the slightest embarrassment. After all, as a well-to-do man, I can afford to be a beast without lecturing anybody on being humane, or immoral and licentious without preaching on virtue, or a scoundrel without boasting of my loyalty to never-ending friendships. The fact is, the difference between me and other folks isn't nearly as great as they might like to imagine. It's simply that as long I'm able to write checks in the amount of a billion dollars, it's easier for me to bare my claws than it is for most people.)

He wished he could find out the name of the person who was after his life. Time and time again he had begged Shaykh Watfan to read the person's name for him in his crystal ball. Time and time again he had brought him verdigris, green arsenic, cinnabar, camphor, Baghdadi spikenard, blue rooster's heart, oriental frankincense, sweet basil seeds, and incense in hopes of getting him to write down for him the name of his would-be murderer. But that confounded sorcerer—or the demon that held him in its possession—just mocked him, and wouldn't write anything for him but his own name: Raghid. Loving himself as he did to the point of adoration, he wouldn't have thought of martyring himself for anything on earth. So he hired a private investigations agency to make certain that none of the people in close contact with him had borne the name "Raghid" on his birth certificate.

By checking people's birth certificates, he'd managed to uncover the false names that had been used by virtually all his assistants, both previous and current, resident and itinerant, from Nadim Ghafir to Hani, Abdulghafour, Antoine, and even his butler Nasim and the sorcerer himself. He'd even checked out his current partner, Sakhr Ghanamali and his brother, and his former partners and potential future ones. But thus far not a single other "Raghid" had appeared on the horizon.

There was someone who wanted to kill him, but he wasn't going to make the person's job easy. He would have loved to be able to kill off the entire population of Planet Earth at the moment of his own demise. It was a desire he'd never kept a secret from anyone. However, nobody took it as anything but a great joke.

When a rich man says something inane, it's considered "original," and everybody laughs at his marvelous sense of humor. But when a poor man says the same thing, he's looked upon as rude, lacking in good taste, or even downright disgusting. God, how he loathed poverty!

(I may be a barbarian, but that doesn't change the fact that I'm the one who got them where they are!)

As the car penetrated deep into the forest surrounding his mansion, he could see Lac Léman glittering with the golden hue of a sunset that had set the treetops ablaze. The only times when he enjoyed nature scenes were when the sun had tinted them with the color of gold. He hated the lake, but adored gold. As for the trees, he detested them because, unlike grass, he couldn't walk on top of them or crush them underfoot.

(I ought to fire that damned gardener. He went and planted a tree in the mansion garden even after I'd explicitly forbidden the planting of anything in it that grows higher than grass. He claimed that the tree had grown up on its own, and that he hadn't had the heart to cut it down when it was still so small. He also maintains that in springtime the wildflowers sprout up in the grass of their own accord in spite of the pruning shears and other sorts of tools I've given him, not to mention all the other modern accoutrements I've supplied him with to make sure that the grass remains of pure stock, that is, the type that bows its head reverently when I step on it.

And that confounded Swiss chauffeur—one time I caught him sneaking a little boy onto the grounds and hiding him in the gardener's quarters. He knows very well that I detest children and that bringing them onto the premises isn't allowed. He told me the boy was his son, then he started talking about how it was the boy's birthday and giving other trivial excuses of the sort that ordinary, senseless folks resort to when they want to get out of doing their duties with the precision of a Swiss watch.)

Sighing in disgust, Raghid pressed a button to turn on the television in hopes of seeing something that could take his mind off people's stupidity. The first thing he saw was fires filling the screen. That was a pleasant sight. Then he saw bombing, air battles, death and terror, buildings being consumed by monstrous conflagrations and horrific explosions. Speaking sorrowfully about what was taking place in Beirut, the French newscaster announced the death of a colleague of hers who had been working as a photographer there.

(I knew I was selling them good stuff—an excellent product for everyone concerned. And now my clientele will increase even more. The arms business is better than the meat business. I used to think that nutritional products were more important than weapons. After all, I thought, everybody eats at least three times a day. But these days it looks as though they kill more than three people a day. At the same time, the number of people who only eat once a day is on the rise. So come, O Fate, I pray you, ignite war's flames under all the rallying cries on earth, and for all motives and all causes, be they virtuous or despicable, noble or ignoble! Ignite them wherever they may be found, and let their profits belong to me! The charred cadavers, the widows' moans, and the dark circles around the children's eyes will be transformed into glittering gold to be poured into my private swimming pool.)

He pressed the button again to silence the television, reassured that all was well as far as he was concerned. After all, he'd heard the newscaster announce the closing of the Beirut international airport after devastating battles had taken place overhead between Israeli and Syrian warplanes, and after Israel had bombed all the aircraft parked on the ground with the exception of the few that had managed to take off before and during the heat of the battle.

But damn. Did this mean that Nadim Ghafir wouldn't be getting back from Beirut tonight? And that the major deal he'd sent him there to work on would be delayed? If that wretch didn't swim back across the Mediterranean, he'd hang his scalp alongside all the other trophies in his collection.

Thinking about it made him start to feel short of breath. How would he ever be able to amass his second billion if things were going to drag this way? He pressed a button which opened the window to his right, then hurriedly closed it again for fear that a bullet might make its way inside, and hunkered down snugly in his bulletproof car. After a few minutes' worth of security measures, the doors to his mansion opened up, then duly closed behind him. The fences enclosing the garden around the mansion were electrified to keep animals off his private property, but the sight of the children who would sometimes get a painful, if not lethal, shock upon touching it was a pleasure indeed. The look of pained astonishment in their eyes the moment they touched the fence reminded him of the way beautiful women would look at him when, no sooner had the tremors of ecstasy overtaken him, they were ordered to evacuate his bed.

Once he was inside his golden fortress, he felt secure. He liked it just this way: with narrow windows, dimly lit, stuffed full of treasures and secrets, and resounding with the weeping of young virgins at the moment when the contract to purchase their maidenhood had been carried out, and the moment of their banishment. However, their numbers had been dwindling rapidly these days, so much so that virgins were becoming a rare commodity. For all he knew, he might have to start importing them before long.

He was received by his Lebanese butler Nasim, who said, "A Mr. Sirri Al-Din called—several times."

"And who is Sirri al-Din?"

"Don't you remember him? He's the student who donated his kidney to you about a year ago."

"You mean the one I *bought* a kidney from. . . . Why should I remember him? Do you expect me to remember every businessman I buy something from?"

"Pardon me, but perhaps you recall that he was poor, and that he sold his kidney so as to be able to pay for his university tuition and his mother's hospital treatment—not to establish a business. Now his money's run out, and even though his mother is out of the hospital, she's still suffering. For days he's been begging me to grant him even just a few minutes to talk to you. Sir, the cancer is eating his mother alive. It's very painful."

"I'm not a doctor. So don't go bothering me with this matter again."

"The poor guy's health deteriorated badly after he donated—uh, I mean, sold—his kidney to you. Once the operation was over, he didn't have enough money left to take proper care of himself. Then thanks to his mother's medical expenses and his university fees, he ended up poorer than ever."

Raghid seated himself in a chair with silk upholstery and armrests embroidered in gold thread. Then, sitting back in a near rapture as his fingers touched the lustrous, warm coolness of the gold, he replied indifferently, "That's none of my concern. After all, I'm not some charitable organization. Sirri Al-Din made a deal. And just as in any other transaction involving purchase or sale, suffering a loss is just as much a possibility as profit. As for this friend of yours, his business proposition turned out to be a loss."

"I'm afraid he might be forced to sell his memoirs to Charlotte Barnes— you know, that European journalist who specializes in publishing the Arabs' scandals. She's been trailing him for days now, and the newspaper she works for has been trying to entice him with a hefty sum. I'm afraid he might give in to the temptation, sir. And you must remember the negative repercussions from the article she wrote about Sakhr Ghanamali's life."

Dark clouds swirled about inside Raghid's eyes. However, his granite features didn't betray the slightest glimmer of unease—except, perhaps, for a quivering of the lips that looked something like a sardonic smile. Or was it a hateful grimace? Nasim couldn't tell. Even Raghid's voice sounded the same as usual: frigid and indifferent, devoid of all emotion.

"Don't worry," he said, "Trust me, and everything will be all right."

Without knowing why, Nasim was gripped by a vague feeling of angst. In vain he tried to bring back to mind the image of Raghid as a sick, laughable old man, married to his admiration for his private sorcerer, who would take his specially prepared diet meals alone in his luxurious, antique-looking dining room as a sort of sacred ritual, then steal by night into the kitchen where he would stand in front of the refrigerator gorging himself on delectable dainties. In horror he thought, the mere fact that the man is old, sick, and eccentric doesn't necessarily mean that he's harmless.

With this unsettling thought in mind, he inquired apprehensively, "What do you mean, sir?"

In reply, Raghid simply repeated slowly, "Don't worry. Trust me, and everything will be all right."

"Whatever you say . . ."

"Has Shaykh Watfan gotten back from the hotel?"

"He arrived a little while ago. He asked me not to disturb him, and to inform you that he'll carry out what you wrote in your memorandum. I handed it to him the moment he walked in the door."

"And is Nadim back from Beirut?"

"Mr. Nadim? I called to inquire about him about half an hour ago, and his wife told me he still hadn't arrived."

"Keep on calling him every half hour, and as soon as you find him, tell him to come immediately. Then follow me to the swimming pool. And don't forget to bring my blood pressure medicine the way you usually do."

"But I'm not the one who forgets. I bring it to you every day, and you forget to take it."

"Stay on my case about it, then. And whenever I forget, come running after me. Your job is to remember. Part of what I pay you for is the use of your memory."

"But . . ."

"Do we have to go back over this same conversation every evening? Go on now, get out of my face."

Remembering his poverty, his family, his city in flames, and his urgent need to keep his job, Nasim held his rage in check. Then, his voice booming like the exhalation of a volcano, he replied, "At your service, Pasha!"

At last he'd said it: "At your service, Pasha!" It was the first time he'd heard Nasim utter those words. So then, he'd finally managed to break him, crush him underfoot like so much grass, clip his prideful wings. The thought of it filled Raghid's heart with rapturous delight. What pleasure it gave him to cause pain to all the contemptible fools who detested him and mistakenly imagined that they could deceive him.

Getting up out of his chair, he headed toward the telephone. He didn't notice that Nasim was listening through the door. Nasim couldn't make out what Raghid said in the half-whispered telephone conversation. But it seemed to him that he'd heard the name Sirri Al-Din Mukhtar. Or had he just imagined it? He was gripped by an indescribable terror. After all, Raghid wasn't one to put anything off. And Nasim knew all too well the kinds of wicked deeds Raghid was most fond of perpetrating. On the other hand, he wondered, mightn't he be overly suspicious of the man? He was about to lose his senses in this solemn, gilded mansion, what with the sorcerer's spells and incantations in one wing, and Raghid's velvet-gloved brutality in the other. There wasn't a single child in the house, or even a woman in any real sense. The women who entered it were little more than pieces of merchandise that made their way one after another from the door to the bedroom, then back out the door, treading a path from horror to tears, from poverty to indolent covetousness. Nasim went scurrying about after everybody else, sweeping up the remains of tears, mascara, and unspoken words. Meanwhile, the odor of incense that clung to the corners of the rooms had transformed the place into a golden temple where human sacrifices were offered up in a barbaric, pagan ritual of worship.

◆   ◆   ◆

"I adjure you, O company of demons and Iblises, of satanic hosts and devils, I adjure you wherever you may be on the face of the earth, bring forth those who dwell in deserts, slaughterhouses, graveyards, markets, highways, by-ways and towers. Where are the two Maymouns of the clouds? Where is Shamhawraq the Flyer? Where is Burqan the Jew? Where is the August White Monarch? Where is the Most Venerable Crimson King? Where is the One with the Black Turban? Where is the Owner of the Coal-black Mule? Where is the One with a thousand heads, each of which has a thousand faces, each of which has a mouth with a thousand tongues, with every tongue praising God Almighty in a different language. . . ?"

With his eyes closed, Sheikh Watfan recited the incantations, which he had learned by heart from a number of ancient books after having practiced his profession for a period of time.

Had it been two years? Three? He couldn't recall anymore. As he called upon his followers and helpers, his voice grew alternately louder, then softer. Sometimes he would hiss like a snake, and at other times roar like a lion. With every moment that passed he felt himself drawing farther away from his earthly body and being transformed into something else: a creature of air, or of water, or of fire. In steady succession he cloaked himself in one form after another. He went leaping across plains, mountains, and oceans. He penetrated barriers of place and time. He released irresistible currents of spiritual, electromagnetic power that went coursing through the cosmos with the speed of light until they could break in upon some other spirit and bring it to ruin.

"Alaksh, Batat Lahoushal Mutee'oush Batriqoush Yatafrioush Batbatiqoush Makashlash, with urgency, with urgency, make haste, make haste, at this hour, at this hour . . .

"Burn him, O Mitatrouq, by the truth of Tahitamghilyal, and by the truth of the clan of Shala' Ya'ou Youbih Batkah Batakfal Bisa'a Ka'a Mimyal. By my servant who is obedient to you, O clan of Jall Ziryal, burn . . .

"Burn, O giant who hast wronged thyself . . . Burn . . . Bu . . ."

He didn't know what had come over him. Stammering, he tried in vain to utter the words, "Burn, O giant who hast wronged thyself, burn. . ." It was as if the opponent whom he intended to set on fire possessed a supernatural spiritual power that surrounded him with a protective shield capable of warding off the sorcerer's plot of destruction . . . as if he were indestructible. In vain he went on reciting his incantations, whose words no longer meant very much to him. They had become little more than musical notes that helped him to tune his own inner strings and adjust their rhythm, charging them with the speed and power necessary to bring their waves into harmony with each other and allow him to broadcast them in such a way that they could be received by other cosmic forces that might be brought into submission to him. But he tried without success to refocus his energies, to release his own forces and reduce this recalcitrant spirit to ashes. As he attempted to speak, the muscles in his tongue began to twitch, something that felt like thorns started growing on his vocal cords, and a shooting pain went through his eyes as he sought in vain to conjure a visible image in the crystal ball. Finally he wasn't able to go on any longer. And as if the physical pain had brought him to back to earthly, material reality, he covered his face with his hands in hopes of extinguishing the blazing firebrands that some unknown power had planted where his eyes were supposed to be. With a moan he asked his crystal ball, "What's this man's secret? Why does my magic have no power over him? This is the first time any human being has been able to resist it . . ."

The enchanted ball offered no reply. Instead, it went back to being a mere piece of glass, as lifeless as all the other objects in the room. This piqued the sorcerer's curiosity even more. How could this be happening to him? What was the secret? Who was it that had intervened between him and his intended victim? Who had sealed this superhuman being—this creature whom he had mistakenly imagined to be just one more wretched earthling—within such an impregnable wall of protection?

(Raghid gave me a man's picture and said, "This is my one greatest opponent. I want him wiped out." When I took a good look at the picture, I was quite surprised. It seemed to be a picture of an ordinary Arab man, no different from one you might meet up with in any Arab city or town. He had a familiar-looking face as if I'd seen him before, and there was nothing about his features that might have attracted one's attention. Yet at the same time he reminded me of people I'd known in my home country . . . schoolmates whose names I've forgotten, the roving vendor who used to sell sesame bread, the neighborhood shoe repairman, the janitor at the mosque, my brothers, my family, and my other relatives. . . . Then suddenly I was overcome with a feeling of sorrow and distress, and a man who'd been lying dormant inside me woke up and said, "No!" then went back to sleep.

"Who is this man?" I asked him.

"I don't know!"

Raghid Zahran had been acting a bit strangely that day. Why would he hide from me such a small thing? After all, he'd confided in me the names of rulers and princes whom he wanted to get out of the way of this project or that either by magic or by underhanded dealings.

"Who is this man, Pasha? What is his name?"

I called him "Pasha" as a term of affection, knowing that he liked this title despite the fact that he wasn't descended from a line of Pashas, and wasn't even Egyptian.

However, all he did was repeat the same answer, "I don't know. All I know is that he's my opponent."

"Well, as long as you don't know exactly who he is, why do you want to do him harm?"

"Because he's my archenemy. And one of us has to go."

"What do you know about him?"

"Everything, and nothing."

"Pasha, what is his name?"

"What difference does it make? Can't you see that I cut his picture out of a Beirut newspaper?"

"In that case, why did you cut out the picture without the news item that goes along with it? And why didn't you hold onto the name?"

"His name isn't important. He has millions of names, and millions of faces. Whenever we cut off one of his heads, scores of snakelike heads sprout in its place. I detest the man."

"What's his story?"

"The newspaper says he's missing!"

"A young, unknown man missing in Beirut. . . . Pasha, what's there to worry you about such a person when you're sitting safe and sound in your well-protected fortress in Switzerland? Maybe the poor fellow has been kidnapped. Or maybe he's been brutally murdered and the dogs have eaten his flesh. Maybe he emigrated to Australia without informing his family. Or maybe . . ."

"No," Raghid interrupted me. "People of his type don't emigrate, and they don't die. He's somewhere plotting evil against me. And even supposing he's emigrated, this is how he'd be spending his time in a foreign country. And he'll be back."

By this time he was starting to irritate me, whereas prior to this I'd never known him to be anything but brilliant.

So I said to him frankly, "You know that my magic isn't as effective unless I'm able to use astrological calculations to find out the signs of the zodiac that control the person's temperament and moods. So as usual, I need his name, his mother's name, and his birth date. A picture cut out of a newspaper isn't enough if I'm going to do a top notch job on this assignment."

I'll never forget the way Raghid's lips quivered and how his face flushed as he confided in me the name of his opponent. As for me, I was astonished. The name was quite common and ordinary. But his date of birth gave me a real shock. How could such a young-looking man have a birth date thousands of years ago?

When I first began performing my magic rites over the picture, I thought I was just doing Raghid a simple, passing favor. In fact, it seemed to be just one of his pranks.

However, I was soon to discover that this unknown young man who has so upset my equilibrium is being sheltered from danger by a supernatural force.

Oh, how exhausted I am . . . I'm short of breath, and there's a mysterious sort of dread sweeping over me. I'm afraid, afraid the way I used to be with people so long ago, before I became accustomed to the company of the jinn.)

◆   ◆   ◆

Feeling the golden waters envelop his body gave Raghid a rush of ecstasy the likes of which no woman had ever been able to arouse. For here he was making love to gold in the flesh, warm, watery gold, gold the panacea for all ills, the gold of which royal scepters are made, the gold with which he'd painted the inside of his swimming pool. His swimming pool was an architectural work of art that he had personally helped to plan, then watched grow and develop before his very eyes like a golden child to whom he'd given his single-hearted love and devotion. His engineer had wanted to design the pool in the shape of a starfish. However, Raghid had insisted that the engineer give it eight arms, not five, and make the pool convex.

(The engineer was afraid that the pool would look like a golden octopus. "That's exactly what I had in mind," I assured him. "I want a swimming pool painted gold in the shape of an octopus."

"But why an octopus?" he objected. "Why not a starfish, or perhaps a seahorse if you prefer?"

"Are you against romance?" I asked in reply. "This way, my guests who happen to be in love can enjoy my hospitality that much more. Two lovers can be alone together in each arm of the pool. Imagine eight pairs of lovers, and me in the center, looking out at their golden romances from the octopus's 'head' and pronouncing my blessing over them. Doesn't that sound lovely?"

A look of disbelief came over the engineer's face. He'd never known me to be a romantic, and he was skeptical. He had a right to be. After all, how was he to know that I'd even allow a woman to befoul my pool of gold? Women might be allowed to swim in the marble pool in the center of the garden on the other side of the mansion. But here in this one—no. And true, I might not have anything against having two mistresses in bed with me at the same time, but I wouldn't think of letting Sweetheart Gold be one of them. My passion for gold admits of no rivals. And I would never let another female, even if she happened to be Bo Derek or some other jet set beauty, lure me into betraying gold in full view of its magnificent, lustrous glitter. The engineer fell into a long, pensive silence. Then, barging in on my delightful reverie, he said, "But the disinfectant chemicals that we put in the pool water might eat away at the gold."

"Then we'll just repaint it every six months . . . or every day. No matter."

"What would you think of putting up some statues and objets d'art at the corners of the pool for decoration? Statues of beautiful women, children . . ."

"I don't want women, and I don't want children. I want statues of gold representing the currencies of the world. I want one of the dollar, another of the Swiss franc, others of the mark and the yen and so on . . . I want there to be eight of them, one for each of the pool's eight arms."

"And the staircase leading down to it?"

"I want it to be of pure gold. And I want the lighting to come from the bottom and sides of the pool in such a way that it gives the water a fiery luster and casts moving shadows onto the walls. The shadows should be so lively that they look like golden spirits whose presence I can conjure whenever I move my body in the water. As for the carpet around the pool, I want it to be gold also, and to have a pile as thick and shaggy as a grass lawn. The chairs between the arms of the pool should be gold-plated, and their cushions should be made of Damascene brocade embroidered in gold thread.

"Then around the chairs I want there to be gardens planted in flowers of gold, and I want the entire thing to be covered by a transparent glass dome. It should be bulletproof glass coated with a thin layer of gold spray so that when you look out, the whole world looks like an imaginary planet made of nothing but this dazzling, quivering metal that's captivated not only me, but millions of other people as well. And finally, I want a golden base for a statue which I plan to supply myself."

Flustered, the engineer said, "And how do you intend to protect this golden fortune from being stolen? This pool of yours will be as rich as Fort Knox!"

"Let it have a door like the ones they put on safes in banks. And I'll be the only one who knows the combination to the lock."

In jest, the engineer asked, "And would you like to have the door made of gold, too?"

"Yes," I replied, "I want it to be gold-plated on the inside.")

Raghid had spent fabulous sums to realize this dream of this. However, he had no regrets. For here alone—inside his golden-watered, golden-walled womb—did he feel safe from danger. Floating in the middle of the pool with only his head above the surface, the waters of the pool formed ripples and waves whenever his body moved, making the octopus look as though it really were alive. And at its center Raghid's eyes rotated in their sockets as he dreamed of his next victim.

He loved relaxing here. Here, he was no longer a stubby, half-flaccid body being ravaged by avarice and gluttony. Here he no longer suffered from high blood pressure, and his heart no longer threatened to stop functioning at any moment. In short, he was no longer Raghid Zahran. He was no longer sixty years old, he no longer suffered from diabetes or any of the other various diseases with which he was afflicted, and he no longer had eyesight on the verge of failing. He hadn't bought another man's kidney and wasn't living on borrowed organs. He wasn't in need of his long, stout cigar as a way of proclaiming his virility, or as a substitute for a billy club as he led his army of mercenaries, emasculated toadies, and loyal fools on their way to becoming full-fledged eunuchs.

Here there was no longer any time, or space, or history. Rather, he himself was time. He was space. He was eternity. He was no longer the clever son of the well-to-do, near-bankrupt merchant Sami Zahran living in terror of Gamal Abdul Nasser's nationalization laws, and whose ruin would have been certain had his son not stepped in to take over just in the nick of time. Here, he could go beyond everything to its true, inner reality: the all-encompassing grandeur of the cosmos that surpasses all of people's trivial concerns: from love, to pain, to sickness, to death. In this prayer niche of his, he could glorify the one thing that truly possessed him and held power over his being: hatred. It was a pure, unmitigated hatred for those who demonstrated by their foolish, senseless ways that they didn't deserve anything better than to be detested.

Here he no longer needed his sorcerer, and he wasn't even aware of the bald spot on his head. Nor was he conscious of his short stature, which normally caused him to surround himself as much as possible with right-hand men who were rather on the short side, and not to invite anyone to his soirées if he happened to be married to a tall woman. This even though the women he chose as bed partners tended to be veritable giraffes.

Here he was no longer a man who had left his homeland to flee from the looming specter of mass nationalizations. This pool had now become his homeland. From its safe haven he could vent his bitter hatred for Arab revolutions and his malicious glee over those of them that had failed. Here he was no longer Raghid the bachelor, since he was married to his pool and to his over-sized cigar. Besides, why would he want to marry when other men's wives—and sometimes even their daughters—were at his beck and call?

Here he didn't tremble at night in fear of the thunder and lightning, which, like all other powers that can't be bought or sold, remained free from the pull of his purse strings.

Here he didn't suffer from bad breath, and his wounds didn't begin to fester and putrefy before they had healed. Here he could reclaim himself, the self that had been wrested from him by a lawless, barbaric world that had raised him since he was a young child on lessons of harshness and cruelty. At the same time, though, he had learned his lessons well, having been predisposed to such things by an innate inward severity.

Here he was a fifth unique element alongside water, earth, air, and fire. Here he formed part of the most virile element of all, the one that had been manipulating the destinies of men since the beginning of time: gold . . . gold seated majestically atop the summit of all elements, with all others prostrating themselves reverently before it. Even Amir Nealy and his fellow radicals who had spent their lives proclaiming its evils and making known their hatred of it, even they were held captive by its constant presence, a presence whose influence and power were bound to be felt, whether negatively or positively.

(Oh, how I love this place! Here I feel completely safe and in utter, supreme bliss. Here I'm in absolute control, with nothing to fetter my perfect, infinite freedom. Here I know the blissful exhilaration of sailing over oceans of gold, a rapture the likes of which I've never known even in the ports of the most beautiful women or in their deepest, most uncharted waters. Here I feel the ecstasy of perfect, radiant health.)

Just then Nasim unexpectedly walked in, carrying a gold plate with a pill in the center of it.

Like someone who has just fallen out of a tall tree, Raghid shouted at him, saying, "Damn you! What are you doing here? Why do you harass me like this?"

"I've brought you your medicine, sir."

"What medicine?"

"Blood pressure medicine."

"Whose blood pressure?"

"Yours. You asked me to bring it to you."

"Get out of my face, you damned . . ."

Oh, how he loathed Nasim. And he loathed him more with every passing day, which was why he also grew more attached to him by the day, and increased his salary accordingly. Nasim, that miserable scoundrel who mistakenly imagined that he was outwitting him, not realizing that he had already figured out what he was up to. He knew, for example, that Nasim was studying secretly at the University of Geneva. He also knew that he was a follower of his despicable enemy, Amir Nealy. His informers apprised him of every surreptitious visit Nasim made to the university or to Amir, sneaking in and out under the illusion that his boss didn't know. . . .

If he only knew that he hadn't been kept on for his trustworthiness, nor for his refusal to resort to violence—something Raghid had learned of through a report by his informers. Rather, he had kept him in his employ because of his connection with Amir. Quite simply, he could use Nasim to pass on to Amir whatever he wanted to delude him into believing was a "top secret" piece of information. He could get him off track. How he detested Amir, that self-important son of a bitch in exile. And how overjoyed he had been when Amir survived an attempt on his life. After all, if he had died, then Raghid would have missed out on a chance to torture him again and again. This time he planned to hurt him through Layla. And the time after that, he'd find some other way to make him suffer. The important thing was for him not to die all at once, so that he could kill him over and over.

(His face looked like the face of a dead man. He was staring at the statue and reading what had been engraved on its base: the signature of his father, Mufid Nealy, the date of its completion, "Fall 1956," and the name of the statue: "Freedom Fighter." In addition, there was some other phrase that the artist had apparently written, then erased. I myself had dug up the story behind the obliterated phrase, and I knew that Amir knew it as well. But I wanted to hear it from his own mouth. I wanted to see the look on his face as he was dying of disappointment and defeat. So one day I invited him to visit me. I told him that I'd been wanting to put out a new Arabic magazine devoted to spreading "the truth"! When he first heard what I'd said, he made no reply, and I could picture the expression on his face as he sat at the other end of the phone line. Then his astonishment came pouring out through the receiver, and I knew he'd taken the bait.

He came, and I received him in my favorite lair: beside my golden swimming pool. It was obvious that he hadn't believed me. He hadn't believed that I, Raghid Zahran, would publish a magazine in the service of proclaiming the truth and make him its editor. However, he came to find out what exactly I did want from him. He looked around him in a sort of stupor that then turned to rage. He sat down on the gold-plated chair I'd offered him, and I took a seat opposite him. But before he'd had a chance to open his mouth, I rushed to start talking on his behalf.

"You'd like to tell me that this gold you see would be enough to feed and educate all the needy Arabs in the world, and that I have no right to hoard it for myself."

"Something like that."

"And you'd like to say that you don't believe my story about the magazine which I said I was planning to put out with you as its editor."

"Something like that."

"And you want to know the real reason for my inviting you here."

"Yes . . ."

"Especially in view of the fact that in everything you write, you take a stand against me and everything I represent."

"Exactly."

"Very well, then. I'm going to let you take a good look around this place, and then—if you really are as sharp as you seem—you'll discover on your own the reason for your being here."

Then, leaving him to himself, I took off my white hooded cloak embroidered in gold thread and got into the pool wearing my cozy, gold bathrobe. When I'd reached the center of the pool [the "eye of the octopus"], I saw him get up out of the chair where he'd been sitting in such a daze and begin slowly to make the rounds of the place like a trapped animal searching for a way to escape. I have to confess to his brilliance, and to the speed with which he managed to overcome the gold shock he'd just been administered. And despite the lighting being poured out on his face like a river of fire, he soon fixed his glance on the one thing that seemed out of place in the room, namely, the statue.

I'd asked my engineer to make a golden base for it, after which I'd brought it out of the prison where I'd kept it locked up for ages, namely, a chest in the hidden recesses of the mansion. Then the engineer enclosed it behind bars of gold, not simply to protect it, but to make it look like a prisoner in his own custom-made cage. As Amir walked around the statue, his face looked like a dead man's. I was so delighted with the spectacle, I started splashing around in an excited frenzy until the arms of the pool began to quake. He cast me a resentful glance, but didn't say a word. His ability to hold his tongue annoyed me. I wanted him to let out an agonized moan that would have made the encounter that much more pleasurable for me. So I decided to try getting a rise out of him.

"This statue was done by your father, wasn't it?" I asked.

"Maybe . . ."

"I think quite certainly. No one but he could have sculpted anything like it. And any half-baked art expert could assure you that it's the original."

"Perhaps . . ."

"What does this statue represent?"

"The Freedom Fighter. Isn't that what the sculptor wrote on it?"

"Yes. But you yourself know that it's a statue of Gamal Abdul Nasser. Any illiterate man off the street who took one look at it could tell you that."

"Fine. So what of it?"

"What are the words that were erased from the base? What is it that your father wrote, then thought better of it and scratched it out with his chisel?"

"I don't know."

"You do know, but you're pretending not to. Everybody knows the story. Your father had been an admirer of Abdul Nasser, perhaps even before he nationalized the Suez Canal in July 1956. But what's certain is that he did the sculpture and wrote a dedication of it to Abdul Nasser, then refused to sell it despite his poverty because he had decided to present it as a gift to coming generations."

"I wouldn't know."

"Surely you've heard the story. So why do you feign ignorance, covering up your wounds and the faults of your fellow 'revolutionaries'? Later on, your father was angered by Abdul Nasser's 'democratic' practices. He came to see that the revolution hadn't instituted freedom. On the contrary, it had inherited the same repressive practices which it claimed to be stamping out."

" . . ."

"So one angry, miserable night, he scratched out the dedication on the base of the statue. He did it in protest on behalf of a man who had been dismissed from his job, then taken into arbitrary detention by certain 'dawn visitors.'

"Your father fell into financial straits after being dismissed from the magazine staff and was nearly accused of being a spy, so he was forced to sell the statue in order to finance your education. And the person who bought it from him happened to be my father."

" . . ."

"Your father died in defeat and misery just a few months later. Then after his death he was awarded a badge of honor, which was hung on his tomb, of course."

" . . ."

"Your father did with Abdul Nasser what Beethoven did with Napoleon. In the beginning he'd been an admirer of Napoleon as a representative of the French Revolution. So much so that when he composed his Third Symphony, he dedicated it to him. However, when Napoleon later set himself up as emperor, thus going from being a revolutionary to being a tyrant, Beethoven came to hate him. Consequently, he withdrew his dedication of the symphony and renamed it 'The Heroic Symphony.' Napoleon never took revenge against Beethoven. However, Abdul Nasser did take revenge against your father."

"It wasn't Abdul Nasser himself who took revenge. Rather, it was the doing of certain government apparatuses, which concealed from him what they had done . . ."

"You know that isn't true. But the great one-sided thinker Amir Nealy would never acknowledge this bitter fact. Besides, even if it was Abdul Nasser's government apparatus that caused your father to end his days in wretchedness and poverty, that doesn't exempt Abdul Nasser from responsibility."

" . . ."

"Your slogans are lovely, and your practices are hideous. You play the role of bait for the masses, luring them to their deaths for nothing but illusions."

Amir's face flushed with rage. It was the first time I'd seen him really angry. It was obvious despite the golden lights being cast on his face. I said many more things to him, but I didn't manage to provoke him again or draw him into any direct discussion. The son of a bitch knew how to keep his wounds protected in a well of silence and secrecy . . .)

Nasim's reentry into the room deprived Raghid of the pleasure of recalling the rest of the story.

Furious, Raghid shouted at him, "What do you want, you bastard!?"

"The chef says that dinner is served. Would you like me to bring you your insulin injection?"

"Get out of my face, you damned . . . get out of here. You always show up at the wrong time . . . just like all the other folks of your class!"

◆   ◆   ◆

As Nasim exited, Raghid carried on with his tirade, screaming, "Scoundrels! Idiots! Rabble-rousers! None of you understands the first thing about good timing!"

(My father was a master of good timing the day he bought Abdul Nasser's statue. However, the statue didn't protect him from the slow but inexorable approach of the shadow of nationalization. He didn't buy the statue out of love for Abdul Nasser, but out of fear. And the fear didn't leave him even after he'd bought it. The fact is that Amir Nealy's father didn't sell it until after my father had expressed interest in it, and after he'd offered him a fantastic sum for it. Mufid Nealy had been in poverty since before Nasser's revolution. He hadn't been a patron of the royal court or a court artist, and even if he'd been Egyptian and been eligible for such a privileged position, he wouldn't have availed himself of it. Even so, the very people he loved oppressed him and caused him to die in misery and grief. And that's the mildest punishment that he and fellow fans of the revolution deserved.

As for me, I managed to put the statue to use at just the right time. While I was still just a young man working under my father's wing, I amassed my first million with the statue's help. The idea was simple: Given my father's fear of Abdul Nasser, it was only reasonable to suppose that all the other merchants and well-to-do folks were terrified of him as well. Accordingly, I got a second-rate artist to cast thousands of replicas of the statue. Then I sent a traveling salesman around to people, offering to sell each of them a copy of the statue as "decoration" for his office. There wasn't a single rich Syrian in the early days of the Union[2] who didn't end up buying a statue for an exorbitant sum and hanging it in some prominent spot in his office. No one dared turn down the offer. They thought my sales manager was working for Nasser's secret service, and that buying the statue was a sort of tax that had to be paid. And so it was that Nasser statues spread all over Syria, and I made my first million. When my sales manager and the man who manufactured the copies—may they rest in peace—were killed in a "mysterious" car accident, the secret died with them,

2. This is an allusion to the short-lived Egyptian-Syrian Union, which was formed in 1958 and lasted until 1961.

and no one ever caught wind of it until I told the story for the first time to Amir on that visit which I never tire of calling to mind. It's true, of course, that a concealed video camera recorded everything that happened. I've watched it so many times now I've gotten a bit sick of it. But somehow my own memory tape never gets old. Whenever I remember it I get a bigger kick out of it than the times before.)

◆   ◆   ◆

(I'm starting to get worried. What if he doesn't show up?)

Having just heard about the closing of the Beirut airport, Dunya made the rounds among her distinguished guests, carrying on as usual with her sumptuous rites of hospitality and being trailed by a well-trained team of butlers and maids.

(Do you suppose his plane took off, or will he stay there with his parents in the old house and die with them under a mound of rubble? Those two have gotten to be like a couple of ancient taproots that keep pulling him back to Beirut, but whenever he goes there he puts his life in mortal danger. All these risky missions that have to be carried out in Beirut—does Nadim really go on them out of materialistic ambition, or is it out of some inexplicable desire to hold onto the place he still secretly pines after? He vehemently denies that he has such a desire. But if that's the case, then why does he insist on keeping his presence alive among his friends and neighbors there? Why does he insist on surrounding himself with people he used to know in Beirut, arranging jobs for them there and sending presents to people who've stayed and refused to emigrate? He might send his favorite type of cigarettes to one, an electronic watch to someone who claims he couldn't find one in Beirut, baby clothes for the newborn of an old schoolmate, a ring as a wedding gift for some childhood buddy, or fancy clothes that his mother can show off in that ancient, poverty-stricken neighborhood of theirs. Everyone asks her where she got this or that, to which she replies proudly, "From my son Nadim!"

He wants his name to stay alive there, as if his life here were nothing but a borrowed existence.)

She gulped down a glass of firewater. She'd promised herself to stop doing that, at least in front of other people. The matter of her addiction had made her something of a laughingstock among fellow addicts who were more adept at keeping their vices under wraps. But tonight she was feeling especially distraught.

(Is it really Nadim's absence that has me so worried? Or am I worried about him coming home? Am I afraid for him, or of him? Was it my secret visit to Sheikh Watfan that made me aware of the depths to which I've fallen, or was it the sight of my old workplace? And that miserable moment, charged with the memory of all the times my life has seemed to disintegrate from the inside, like the collapse of a mine full of long-forgotten passageways. I just stood there in the middle of the street staring at the luxurious hotel on my right, the place which the sheikh makes his temporary headquarters when he leaves Raghid's mansion to provide services for the general public, and at another towering building to my left that reminded me of the days when I used to wake up at 7:00 in the morning (the way most people do) and rush off to another day of scrambling for a living. At the time I was a young woman, happy and full of hopes, energy, and ambition. Oh, what has success done to us? What is this frightening "fall to the summit," as it were? What is it that's destroyed me? After being a contented working girl who spatters paint on her fingers instead of her face, and who spends her salary on artists' canvases rather than fabric for new clothes, how did I end up as this envious, resentful, fearful woman who runs for protection to sorcerers and spirits? How could I have gone from standing on sidewalks waiting to go to work, to waiting on the sidewalk outside a hotel where I've arranged a secret rendezvous? What has the world done to you, Dunya?[3] What has wealth done to you and Nadim? How could you have let him put a bullet of gold through your fingers?)

Dunya made the rounds among her guests.

(But are they my guests, or my husband's—my husband, whose time is money? And speaking of time, he won't waste even a minute of it greeting me or asking me about my aching spirit. Instead, he'll go from the airport to bed, passing on his way through the cocktail party where he'll give me a passing glance as if I were some guest he's never seen before, and not thank me any more than he'd thank one of his house servants.)

The guests seemed particularly pleased with her this evening. The silent, smiling hostess was the ideal wife in this sort of milieu. Yet she had to confess: she detested them all. Oh, how she detested them! She'd spent the last years of her life with people not one of whom shared a single thing in common with her. She'd never once opened her heart to any of them. She'd never once said

---

3. There is a play on words here, since Dunya's name means "world" in the sense of the fleeting, material world as opposed to the enduring world of the afterlife.

to any of them a word she actually wanted to say, and not once had language between her and them brought about any genuine communication. Instead, she simply said what she was supposed to say in order to help Nadim collect what people owed him, and to ensure that his business deals got wrapped up. As for Nadim himself, it had been ages since she'd sat with him in a café on the shore of some moonlit lake. (I'm not really a romantic. What I miss isn't the cafés, or the moon, or the swans swimming in the lake, or the passionate kisses. What I miss is the conversation. We may still talk to each other, but it isn't what you'd call a dialogue.) Time had grown flaccid and obese, swelling up like a tumor, while she went scurrying here and there without accomplishing a thing. One day she might accompany some tycoon's wife to the market. Another day she might be off to the hospital to consult some famous physician or to see a real estate agent about buying a villa. Or she might invite some client for dinner with his family, his mistress, or some professional paramour depending on the client's mood and on the requirements of the business to be done. And now here she was living in this sumptuous villa of theirs (though it was modest by comparison to Raghid's palace). Set atop a hill inhabited by other, equally wealthy folks, the house overlooked quai Gustave Ador and the city of Geneva. Lac Léman lay at her feet, and deep inside her there lay a bird quaking in the throes of death.

As her guests spoke to her with avarice in their hearts, she nodded her head courteously like a painted china doll that can neither hear nor speak, her eyes fixed all the while on the painting that hung in the center of the wall behind them. A representation of herself before she'd met Nadim, it was the last painting she had ever done. After the manner of all the great artists whom she'd admired so much and sought to emulate during that time so long ago, she'd done a self-portrait in which she sought to embody how she saw herself, as well as the self she hoped to be.

What a difference there was between her face now and the face of the young woman in the painting. It wasn't merely a difference of eighteen years, but of eighteen centuries—eighteen centuries of decadence. What comparison could there be between the penetrating, fierce look in the eyes of the girl in the picture, so full of resolution and the determination to create, and the look in the eyes of the face she encountered in the mirror next to the painting—the look of a woman with nothing to do in life, a fearful, confused, disappointed woman hiding behind a veneer of hypocrisy, the hypocrisy of a motherhood that hadn't been enough to fill her life, and of a marital fidelity borne not of love, but of indolence and fear?

In a moment of tempestuous love, she had presented the painting to Nadim as a gift before they were married. It was during the days when she'd been a junior employee in that towering building, working her way through art school with her eyes set on her homeland and on the day she could return there. As for Nadim, he'd been an emigrant to Europe whose days were spent itinerating between Beirut and the West. His poverty, his charm, his feigned love of art and his exuberant youth had been tucked under his arm, and his eyes set on a fortune. On the occasion of one of their long-ago farewells, she'd taken the painting to the airport and given it to him as a token of her truest self. The next day he returned from Beirut to make her his wife. Yet not once since their marriage had he ceased his frenzied quest for the golden bird of opportunity.

(And now he's caught the bird, and lost me.)

Had it really been necessary for him to bring the painting back to her when he'd returned from his last trip to Lebanon? He'd done it to "make her happy," as he put it, and also because he'd been afraid it might be destroyed in a fire if he left it in Beirut. Yet from that day on there had been a fire blazing deep inside her. The girl in the painting spoke to her whenever she got tipsy, asking her what she had done to her and to herself.

(What have you done to the young woman you used to be, and whom you did this portrait of once upon a time?) Her face as it appeared in the painting and her face as it appeared in the mirror beside it were so different, it was as if they belonged to two entirely different women. Which of them belonged to the woman she really was? Or was she actually a third woman whom she didn't recognize?

She downed her fifth glass of firewater. Meanwhile, one of her most important guests was telling her about his greatness and immortality and about the stupidity of everyone around him, and how if it hadn't been for him, all work would grind to a halt, the entire city would go bankrupt, and Planet Earth would fall out of its orbit around the sun. As for her—the ideal, silent listener—she kept him happy with admiring smiles and nods of affirmation.

(Oh . . . I don't know anymore whether I love Nadim or hate him. Do I wish he'd come back, or that he'd die? Would my life be better without him, or have I grown so accustomed to the kind of mental laziness I live in that I've turned into part of this half-real, multihued, harried yet sleepy beast known to most as "high society"? It's a beast with a thousand heads. Each head is perfectly styled, oiled, and perfumed and has a face that emerges from beneath the fingertips of masseurs and cosmeticians. It comes out from under forked tongues that say what they don't mean and on whose undersides, if you examined most of them closely enough, you'd find hidden bags of poison. How I hate this mirror and the picture of me hanging beside it, where I see two different women without knowing which of them is me. Who am I anymore, really? And what would I want to do if I were free again? Would I be able to bear the choices that freedom brings with it, and the winding paths I might have to tread from then on? Do I still love Nadim? If I don't, then how am I to explain the fits of jealousy that come over me, even to the point of my going to sorcerers and other "peddlers of illusion," or of imagining that Nadim makes love to everybody and everything besides me—Layla, Raghid, our dog Picasso, the maid, his chauffeur. . . ?

And if I do, then why does my spirit burn with bitterness and disappointment whenever I shake off the numbing effect of this gilded crowd, whenever I'm alone with my sorrows and start thinking about this painting of mine? When that happens, it's as if there rises up in my spirit a determination to accomplish something I'd forgotten, a passion to rebuild the bridges between me and people I once loved but whom I never see anymore due to the fact that they're poor, whereas our household receives none but the well-to-do. Why is it that I fail every time I try to make some change in my situation, which sometimes seems so shameful to me? Why is it that whenever I decide to do something with this life of mine that's slipping away like rainwater running off a city street, I end up downing a few more glasses of firewater? With every glass I drink, my resentment against Nadim and what he's done to me intensifies all the more. Nadim—that dangerous man who knows how to play the unkempt, Gauloise-smoking vagabond when he's with the artist-bohemian set and the cigar-smoking, perfectly groomed tycoon when he hobnobs with the wealthy; who dons sandals and jeans when he talks to the leftists and totes a rifle for the benefit of his revolutionary comrades; who knows how to sing a mawwal[4] with his people's-class Arab guests, croon opera with his Italian business partner, talk about Herbert Von Karajan with a German factory owner, and devour

---

4. A *mawwal* is a poem sung in colloquial Arabic, often composed extemporaneously in a social gathering.

ketchup with his soup in front of his American client; who dons a turban and an Islamic cleric's robe with one group and recites "Our Father who art in heaven" with another, then chooses Saturday as his day off when he wants to wrap up a deal with a Jew. How am I supposed to know whether I love him or not when I can't even tell which of these "faces" is his, or what he's hiding under all his masks? Or is it that all these masks are actually a succession of incarnations of his one, true self, which has no independent existence apart from them?

Once I've finished the first bottle of firewater, I'm revived enough to lay out a plan for my life: to return to my roots, my people, my work. My plan consists of a number of resolutions, the first one being to kick this firewater addiction of mine. Then I go to sleep in peace. The next morning I wake up to the dizziness of a hangover and a splitting headache, I swallow a few pills to help me gather up the pieces of my body and stitch them back together like the remains of a rag doll that's been shredded to pieces by dogs. And once again I find that I'm nothing but a tiny screw in a huge, grinding, infernal machine . . . nothing but a rusty nail that, unless it goes on turning inside the same immense machine with all its interconnected parts, is bound to break. So I go on, and on. I float, and I sink. I remember, and I forget. I vacillate in confusion, then I become sure once again that I detest him. He's played games with both his life and mine. He's sold us to the golden idol, to the chief of the gods. And there's no salvation for me unless he disappears, or dies. Damn him. I hope he doesn't come back. I hope he burns to a crisp on board his airplane.)

Just then the door opened and in walked Nadim, beaming and radiating welcome to all his guests.

Rushing over to him, Dunya threw herself into his arms, saying, "Oh, I'm so happy you're here!"

Listening to her own voice, she didn't know whether she was lying or not. Nadim wasn't listening. He kissed her as routinely as if his mouth were a toothbrush being brought to her lips. And rather than look at her, he looked around to see the effect of the kiss on other men's wives. Then he began mingling with the guests, all the while bursting with stories about the adventures of his long day, the shooting, the closing of the airport and his rescue on the last plane out in a torrent of braggadocious charm.

◆   ◆   ◆

Nadim's arrival put life back into the party, his mansion a cluster of festive lights.

His Beirut adventures and fresh news brought excitement to his guests, who started one by one to calculate their profits or losses in light of the most recent events. The scale seemed to be tipping in favor of profits, the atmosphere was newly revived, and merriment was on the rise, touching most faces with its magic wand. This cocktail party was certain to be the talk of the town in all the elite circles.

There wasn't a single Arab tycoon in Switzerland who didn't attend. They came from Zurich, Gstaad, Montreux, Saint Serge, Montana, Interlaken, and elsewhere. They even came from areas of France along the French-Swiss border, which isn't more than half an hour away from Geneva . . . from Vernet, Anmas, Saint-Julien, Annecy, and on and on. The guests included former and future government ministers, former beauty queens, divorcees, wives, secretaries, and dreaming wayfarers.

There were retired political leaders with control over half their countries' treasuries, businessmen of dubious professional status and undisclosed incomes who'd been catapulted onto the shores of Europe by the waves of the petroleum sea discovered in the seventies. There were spongers and uninvited guests, there were men who'd gone bankrupt but whose plights hadn't yet become known and who were fishing for a chance to rescue themselves on the hook of the "anything goes" atmosphere of the jet set. There was a group who'd made a profession out of seeking exile for exile's sake in pursuit of wealth and prestige, and another that had resorted to self-imposed exile to escape from angry reprisals by people in their homelands. Then there were a number of celebrities of "literature" and "art," some rich and some poor, whose presence served as confirmation of the refined nature of this distinguished gathering and its wholehearted support of culture and intellectual life. After dinner had been served, they might all listen to a number of poetry readings, their thoughts wandering all the while to their own concerns. As for the women who'd been invited to serve as decor, they would come out periodically with exclamations of "Oh, my goodness!"—every one of them emitting her rapturous sighs for a thousand and one reasons, not one of which bore the slightest relation to poetry or literary criticism. Not to be found at the party, of course, were members of the poor working class, serious thinkers, or genuine freedom fighters—notwithstanding a few token revolutionaries whose claims weren't backed up with action but who'd decided to go along for the freedom-fighter ride as an excuse for practicing their own sorts of authoritarian, monetary, ritualistic, or even feminist acrobatics.

All of this came to Dunya in a painful flash as she looked around at her guests in bewilderment and dismay. The moment of awareness was so intense, it was like a lightning bolt that nearly split her head in two. It was as though she were seeing these people for the first time. As though she didn't know what she was doing here, and had just happened to fall into the house from some other planet.

(Amir Nealy, the first person ever to stand by me and encourage me as an artist, could never be invited to a place like this. The people I've truly loved and respected would refuse to come here even if Nadim invited them. And my husband is the perfect host—he would never think of causing discomfort to his guests by inviting someone whose presence would unsettle them in any way. Here just as in Lebanon, we Arabs are divided into "sons of the noblewoman" and "sons of the slave woman," with mixing between them considered undesirable unless it happens to reinforce the former's power over the latter. We have a neighbor who shipped his Rolls Royce all the way from Beirut to Geneva just to avoid being pestered by the poor folks at home. Here he feels safe, far from the claws and fangs of the untamable, hungry hordes. Oh, how did I ever get here? How did I manage to slip away from my old world? How?)

Nadim looked around proudly at his guests. (Just think, eighteen years ago the mere mention of these people's names would have been enough to send you into raptures. You used to pore over their pictures on the society page of magazines and newspapers. You used to loiter outside their doors. You asked some of them for work and were refused. And the ones who refused you back then would of course not remember your name or your face, which has filled out quite a bit since they saw you last. In fact, there are some of them who even come to you for favors now. You've betrayed, double-crossed, embezzled, bowed and scraped, and even stretched your body out on the muddy ground to be walked on by Raghid Zahran, Sakhr Ghanamali, and others of their ilk as they made their way from casino doors to their cars. You've abandoned every loser to attach yourself to his victor, and forsaken your loyalty to every friend slain so as to devote yourself to the ongoing work and to the slain man's murderer. After all, none of them ever gave a damn about you. So you learned the game fast, and stopped giving a damn about anyone but yourself. You did it, of course, without bitterness or hatred, and without either lasting enmity or lasting friendship. After all, the only thing that matters is lasting advantage. You left Sakhr Ghanamali behind to join the service of the man with the other billion, namely, Raghid Zahran, without hating the former or loving the latter. On the contrary, your main objection to Sakhr Ghanamali was that he still had enough heart left to sabotage the deals you were getting for him. As for Raghid, the heart removal operation he's done on himself appears to have been a smashing success. You're a big Arab businessman now, a key to Arab gold, and a servant to the cause of those who leave their countries in hopes of making their wealth and influence known to the West and staking out new territory for themselves.

You've joined the society of wealthy Arabs in Europe and elsewhere in the West, thereby aiding it in its onward expansion. You've become a member of a society that's united in the face of every attempt to make it doubt its independence from all the tragedies taking place in the Arab world—except, of course, when it comes to the effect they have on their fortunes. Two hundred million Arabs? One hundred fifty million? An 80 percent illiteracy rate? Or is it 90 percent? A declining average per capita income? People living in houses of tin siding, and in tents? Homelessness? Hunger? Such details might be of concern to a priest or a social reformer. As for you, though, you belong to the category of "businessman," which means that you deal with reality from a different angle— the angle having to do with secret bank accounts, stock market concerns, and the types of worldly pleasure that a man in such a demanding, highly qualified profession ought to be rewarded with. You're the Beirut native, from a family of moderate means that embodies the myth of excellence for your entire neighborhood. Thanks to the Arab fortunes you've managed to plunder, you've become a permanent guest on private airplanes headed for the lands of snow and blond beauties. From time to time you offer your condolences for the gold-plated sorrows and pampered concerns of those whose fortunes you've pillaged. And all the while the computer in your head is calculating the profits you can make by employing their suffering to your advantage.

The butler then enters, announcing in a half-whisper, "Raghid Bey Zahran requests your presence now."

The name "Raghid Zahran" rings out like the sound of gold ingots falling from the ceiling onto a marble floor: one thousand ingots for every letter in his name: Raghid Zahran. . . . Despite the fact that the butler's announcement is barely audible, everyone hears the name as loudly as if it were the sound of a storm blowing in, and is filled with humble reverence. After all, in the presence of Raghid Zahran, every one of them counts himself penniless. They, millionaires all, are reckoned as paupers. After all, they're the owners not of billions, but of mere millions. Moreover, he is the possessor of a billion dollars slated to multiply many times over. In hands like Raghid's, money has a way of reproducing itself at a rate rivaling that of the world's poor, without one knowing whence the heavens have rained this treasure down upon him. The interest on the balances of his frozen accounts has a way of doing the same thing, sprouting forth like the buds on trees in a tropical rainforest. His liquid funds soar on the fiery wings of stocks and bonds, ascending through the night sky like stars, then dotting the heavenly dome until none else can be seen.

Raghid Zahran . . .

They drop to their knees one and all in the presence of the name, while in the sky there appears a golden, soporific cloud.

In unison they sing, "Hallelujah!"

Raghid Zahran wants to see Nadim? What a tremendous honor! In such a situation he has no need to apologize to his guests, and he takes leave of them without bidding them farewell.

Meanwhile, all remain on their knees, singing, "Hallelujah! Glory be to him!" Even Dunya bends the knee, remembering with a miserable lump in her throat how she was his mistress for several nights. Do you suppose her husband knows about it, yet pretends not to? Is this part of the morality of the profession, a clause in one of the treaties governing this jungle of gold?)

❖ ❖ ❖

Khalil decided to crown his misery with a cigarette.

No one had said a word for several minutes, since the moment they'd met in the hotel room after their long, long day. As soon as they came in, everybody had collapsed onto a chair or a bed, then sat staring blankly at the porter as he set their bags down in a row and left the room. He couldn't believe that it had all happened in just one day. That very morning, they'd left their home in Beirut and fled from one death to another. Under bombardment by friend and foe alike, they'd passed through a gauntlet of their homeland's sorrows. Then they'd been flown stealthily to safety through the middle of an air battle as though they were actors in some half-rate, overdone war flick.

And the sun hadn't even gone down yet. The same sun that had been shining over all that horror, was shining now over the glorious splendor that looked in on him through the window. Over and over he repeated in amazement, "All this in one day . . . it's still the same day . . . Monday." Looking out the window without getting up out of his chair, he saw a lake possessed of an extraordinary magic and calm surrounded by gentle-looking flowers and greenery. Everything in sight seemed to exude tranquility.

Was it really possible for all these things to have happened in a single day? The date was still Monday, June 7, 1982. At the very same moment a week earlier, he'd been sitting in a communal jail cell preparing to meet his death after receiving news that a mass liquidation was in the offing due to insufficient cell capacity for the growing numbers of prisoners.

◆   ◆   ◆

Khalil decided to crown his dismay with a cigarette.

(Less taste, and more nicotine. That's what I need.)

He looked around in horror. The hotel suite they occupied was fabulously luxurious—too posh for a pauper like him.

All right, then. He knew he was basically a peasant, a village boy who knew nothing about classy Beirut hotels, not to mention classy Swiss ones. Kafa, on the other hand, coming from a well-established Beirut family, was a pampered soul who'd never tasted life's cruelties before knowing Khalil (and who now cursed the day she'd fallen in love with him). She, no doubt, knew how to choose things (if not husbands!). But . . . the hotel management was sure not to accept someone's family tree in place of payment. Numbers? That was all he'd learned in university. He'd studied business administration. However, he'd also learned quite a bit from adding up small figures, one piaster atop another, so as to be able to pay for tuition, books, a bite to eat in the morning, and the early morning cigarettes he used to top off his misery whenever he could afford to. And now, all he knew was that he didn't have a single piaster to his name. He didn't know how or why he'd ended up where he was, or where he was headed. Kafa had arranged everything: the passports, the visas, the airplane tickets. As for him, he'd been busy just trying to keep his head from being blown off in the middle of the red-hot, metallic spider's web that he'd fallen into in Beirut. He'd lived in constant danger of being cauterized in its flames and plunging headlong from one maze to another.

So he decided to top off his misery with a cigarette.

Kafa had stretched out luxuriously on the bed like someone who's just entered upon a pleasant dream.

Rami, sweet little boy that he was, had discovered the bathroom. A little

while after going in, he came out again carrying a glass of water, which he presented to Khalil in affectionate silence. Children's wordless ways of expressing
their love had a way of shaking him to his very core. He didn't like his wife's
direct style when it came to declaring affection, eloquent as it was. Ever since
he'd come back home in flight from death, both Rami and Fadi had been
showering him with love of the most extraordinary sweetness. They treated
him as though he were their baby boy. During the time when he'd been shut-
tling from one prison to another, he'd been kept awake at night by one dreadful thought: that he'd come home to find that they didn't recognize him . . .
and to hear them ask their mother indifferently, "Who's this man?"

The day he finally did come home, neither of the boys told him that he
loved him. Instead, they received him with the homespun, unadorned affection that one learns in the village. Rami offered him a glass of water, and when
he lay down exhausted, Fadi covered him with a Kleenex. They hadn't inherited any of their mother's ways, despite Khalil's fear of their being corrupted
by her social milieu, her well-to-do family, and the bribes offered by her chat-
terbox aunts in hopes of winning their little boy hearts. They hadn't inherited
a trace of either her physical or psychological features: the chestnut hair, the
blue eyes, the lily-white complexion. Looking over at her pensively, he
thought, what a beauty she is. He'd nearly forgotten.

He crowned his misery with a cigarette.

No one had said a word since they'd reached the hotel room after that
long, vast day that seemed to stretch the length of a horizon of suffering and
defeat.

As the boys recovered their usual vivacity, they began exploring the room,
including its two adjoining bathrooms, its enormous closets, the sitting room
and television, the small refrigerator set in one corner (the "mini-bar"), the
control buttons for the radio and the lights installed at the head of the bed, the
cords used to draw the curtains open and closed, the ultramodern, touch-tone
phone, the knotty rosewood that covered some of the walls and doors, and the
velvet-covered luggage carrier on wheels.

As Khalil began emerging from his nightmare, Kafa burrowed deeper into
her dream, tossing and turning on top of the sumptuous velvet bedspread. As
for the boys, they went into their usual jumping, hopping, and fighting phase.

He crowned his misery with still another cigarette.

The upholstery on his chair felt more like thorns than velvet, reminding him once again of his poverty. And despite the fact that he'd promised himself to hold his tongue on their first night, a peculiar-tasting fear filled his mouth as he looked over at their still unopened suitcases piled on one side of the room. They were all they owned in the paradise in which they'd arrived.

"Kafa . . . the hotel . . ."

"What about it?"

"It's quite beautiful," he said nervously, ". . . and fancy."

"Quite beautiful," she repeated in a tone of utter relaxation, "and fancy indeed."

He strolled over to the door, where a price list had been posted near the instructions for using the fire escape. No sooner had he read "1,500 francs per night" than a fire broke out in his head that nearly moved him to make a getaway down the fire escape right there and then. Where was he going to come up with what amounted to nearly three thousand Lebanese pounds a day so that they could rent an entire hotel suite? Had Kafa lost her mind?

The boys' altercation had gotten louder, and Kafa, emerging somewhat from her dreamy stupor, got up and went over to calm them down. Unable to keep quiet any longer, Khalil asked her again, "Kafa . . . the hotel . . ."

"What about it?"

"It's so ritzy . . . we don't have enough to pay for it. Tomorrow we'll have to find another place. Another room somewhere."

Seeing the frown that had appeared on her face, he tried to placate her, saying, "I mean, a small flat for the boys. They're going to go stir crazy in a closed-up space like this."

Replying with the composure of someone who's got a master plan up her sleeve, she replied, "Tomorrow the boys will be going to stay in a boarding school until we can get things worked out."

"A boarding school, in Switzerland? Have you got any idea what that would cost?"

"Of course. I've brought enough to pay their expenses for the summer. And in Swiss francs. I sold all my jewelry and got a loan from my sister's husband, and now I'm banking on you to come through for us. The boys will be enrolled in summer school so that they can adjust to the curriculum here and be ready for the coming school year."

So then, she really did have everything planned out. The fact was, for seven years she'd been planning for this very day. Ever since the war had broken out in 1975, she'd been begging Khalil to let them flee with everyone else.

He'd said to her, "I'm planted here like a tree. This is where I was born, and this is where I intend to die. I'm not one to emigrate. It was a bitter enough experience for me to leave my village for the big city. And even that wasn't my choice. It was my dad's."

And now here he was again, embarking on a pilgrimage that he hadn't chosen for himself.

"And what will we do in the fall when it comes time to pay more school fees?"

"Well, tomorrow you'll start your new job. Besides, we've got a long summer ahead of us, and God is gracious. He'll surely open up a way for us to make ends meet."

"New job? Where?"

"In the Restaurant of the East. I've brought a letter of recommendation for you from my brother-in-law. It's addressed to the restaurant manager, Shafiq Abi 'Ati, a close friend of his. You'll work as an accountant or as some sort of assistant to him until we can arrange something that suits us better."

So she'd chosen his profession for him, too!

Yet he didn't dare say anything to her. He'd spent the entire last week fleeing from one friend's house to another, biding his time until they could arrange for him to get out of Beirut. Kafa had done what she could. Of course, it did happen to be what she herself had been hoping to do for years. But this time he wasn't in any position to complain. After all, beggars can't be choosers.

Yet instead of thanking her, he was about to reprimand her. She'd spent everything she owned, including hers and her family's valuables, to bring him and her children out of danger. And he felt a sense of remorse piercing him to the heart.

◆　◆　◆

He went over to her and drew her into his arms. He'd forgotten the feel of her warm, delectable body. It had been a long time since the last time. In fact, it had been three years, or maybe even four. He didn't know what had come over him after that fateful night.

(As usual at the beginning of every week, I was changing the books in my shop's display window. I remember clearly how I was blanketing the floor of the display case with copies of the latest book by crusader Amir Nealy. All right, I admit, he's basically just a writer. But I think of him as a freedom fighter. He's genuinely on the side of the poor—not just the poor of a particular faction or organization. And he's straightforward about his bias in favor of "Arab identity"—not just that of Lebanon alone, but of all Arabs, some of whom boast of championing true Arabism, but don't practice what they preach. Nealy, on the other hand, advocates Arab identity in the most authentic sense of the word—not in the sense of some sort of police state or terrorism, or a dismembering of the land, uprooting people who live on it and cutting off their livelihoods as happens in some Arab countries. I myself have never had a knack for writing. But I'm an avid reader. And I refuse to sell any book or publication that doesn't show respect for my humanity, no matter how well I think it will sell or how popular it happens to be.

In any case, it was a marvelous autumn day—one of those days when Nature gives free rein to the wind and the rain after keeping them under lock and key all summer long, and the sky is full of clouds with a grayish-silver glow. It was one of those days when freedom's aroma seems to breathe in the air, and you feel nostalgic for all the slogans you use so often but are forbidden to live out in practice.

Two armed men walked into my bookshop. (Actually, it isn't much more than a tiny bookstall. But it is, after all, where I work, the place where I earn both my livelihood and a sense of dignity, and I would have ended up doing basically the same thing whether I'd been selling falafel sandwiches or books.) And I kicked them out.

The reason was that they tried to force me to sell a pamphlet they'd brought with them, insisting that I pay them in advance for the copies. I refused, and I told them to get out even before reading the name of the publication, who had issued it, or what sorts of ideas it contained. I've never been able to tolerate repression as a way of marketing an idea, even if it's the idea of freedom itself. I've never been able to accept fascist methods of spreading my own ideas or those of my allies and other folks I believe in. And it just so happened that the publication they were trying to force me to sell was in favor of some of my buddies. I—unlike Amir Nealy—can't put into words the sick feeling of humiliation that comes over me when someone violates my freedom. If someone were to ask me what I mean by my "freedom," I wouldn't know what to say. However, I always know when someone has done it harm or tries to take it away from me. I suppose that's the simple man's approach to freedom.

I told them, "I don't even want to know the name of this publication you're demanding that I sell and pay you for in advance, as if I owed you some sort of protection money. The fact is, I might believe every word it contains. But I certainly don't believe in forcing it on people. Besides which, the idea of paying protection money to my friends is even more unbearable than the idea of paying it to my enemies. I'd rather have my freedom taken from me by an opponent than by a so-called ally. So I reject the sort of path you're trying to drag me onto."

The minute I finished speaking, they started beating me mercilessly with the butts of their machine guns.

After the first blow, I screamed out something to the effect that these were machine guns that Arab peoples had paid for for the purpose of striking enemies, not friends. After that, the blows came even thicker and faster.

"The enemy is over there," I said, pointing over to a map that I kept on the wall. "They're over there. . . . I'll lead you to them if you'd like. It seems you've forgotten."

But they just went right on beating me until, by the time I'd made up my mind for sure to lead them to the enemy, we were on the sidewalk in front of my shop, as if I were somebody giving directions to a tourist who's lost his way. Then I collapsed on the pavement.

When I woke up in the hospital, it wasn't just my broken bones that were aching. Something inside me had been broken, too . . . something that was weeping silently and trembling inconsolably. And from that day on, I lost my appetite for life, for love, for the sun, and even for women. I didn't touch my wife after that. I didn't even notice her or any other woman. I also stopped spending time with the circle of buddies that I'd always gotten together with to talk about the homeland, freedom, and destiny and to plan how we could work for a better tomorrow, each of us in his own way. I stopped smoking the water pipe in the Rawda, a popular coffee shop along the seashore, and I no longer took any notice of the rising of the moon. I didn't enjoy music anymore, not even singing. There was only one thing that I couldn't stop doing: speaking the truth as I saw it. And I didn't lose my hunger for dialogue, dialogue that doesn't need to be accompanied by the blows of a rifle butt, or by burning cigarettes planted in my flesh by the people whose cause has been planted in my spirit for such a long time.

These things I couldn't stop. In fact, if anything, I became even more madly attached to them. I'd become addicted to carrying out my father's admonition, "Never speak anything but the truth." I was so determined to do what he'd said that I forgot that there were times when I could choose to remain silent. So I never did. I was no good at timing, or at choosing the right person to confide my inmost secrets to. Instead, I tended to say the same thing to everyone. I'd befriend whoever I considered to be worthy of my friendship even if he happened to be on his way to the gallows or smoking his last cigarette in front of his executioner. And so it was that I won friends that I didn't love, and made enemies that I didn't hate. I found myself associated with some organizations that I had no respect for, and rejected by others whose convictions I shared, but with whom I'd parted ways over their methods of operation. Consequently I ended up being transported from one prison to another, most of the time not even knowing who had put me behind bars, and trying to figure out what was going on from the executioner's tone of voice. The problem, though, is that all executioners speak a single language: the language of the mercenary, which makes it difficult to distinguish between one who works for your own people, and one who's in the employ of the enemy. So between one prison and the next, one argument and the next, one enemy attack and the next, one debate and the next, I'd meet my wife the way one checks up on a half-forgotten friend and kiss my children "hello" and "goodbye" at the same time. Then I'd rebuild my bombed-out bookshop and sell Amir Nealy's books until the next visit by those men who all look so much alike they might as well be a single person.

"Follow me," he'd say. So I'd follow him, and I'd hear the same old broken record again in still more unfamiliar dungeons: Who finances you? What group do you belong to? What activities are you involved in? Sabotage? Explosives? Thefts?

In vain I'd tell them that I still hadn't done anything to be either punished or praised for. They hadn't given me time to! And I started to understand what they were all about. It became apparent to me that friends and enemies all belonged to a single establishment with branches in various parts of town. They might use different slogans, but their mission was the same: to come up with so many accusations, trials, punishments, and executions that we wouldn't have enough time left to do anything of significance or value, or enough breath left to utter the words we'd once shouted out both in public demonstrations and in the isolation of our rooms. Of all those many protests, none remained in my mouth but a single word: Freedom . . . freedom!

Then one night, carrying out the bright idea of some genius who'd gotten fed up with transporting cadavers and dumping them into streets, under bridges and on top of hills, the executioner led us all away to the graveyard to put an end to us there. He'd decided to save both himself and our families a lot of trouble by executing us in the cemetery. After all, this way, there wouldn't be any need for them to gather up our severed limbs and carry them to cold storage rooms to be identified and wept over before being taken at last to their final resting places, or to transport the bodies in funeral processions that would just hold up traffic for the secret service men whose victims they'd been.

That night I really didn't know whose prisoner I was, why I was being tortured, what my tormentors thought I was, or why I was on my way to my death. I didn't know whether this was happening as part of some sort of collective "deal" to kill people from a particular faction, or to terrorize certain other individuals who were being prepared to carry out some mission or another. For all I knew, it might have been to create an atmosphere of terror that would raise the price of the dollar while someone in the higher echelons was wrapping up a lucrative stock transaction. All I knew for certain was that at the very same moment one week earlier, or the month or year or century before, I'd been shivering and half-blindfolded in a truck packed full of prisoners. Darkness had just fallen and the streets were deserted. The road we were traveling reeked of sweat and various other bodily secretions that fear tends to stimulate. Then the truck stopped and we all got out. Our captors didn't have to beat us to get us to take off running toward the cemetery. The fact was, we'd been longing for this moment. I spied my own grave in the darkness, and read my name written on its headstone in letters of dazzling light—or rather, in ugly, glaring neon letters of the sort you see on the doors of cheap cabarets. Then I collapsed and couldn't feel a thing anymore. I didn't even hear the shots that mowed down everyone around me. But when I came to again, I found them all dead.

Once I'd regained consciousness, I ran my hands over a body that had fallen on top of me. It was frigid and heavy, and I tried to push it off me. Meanwhile, terror had dug its claws into my neck until I began to choke. The body was semi-petrified. And as I tried to lift it off me, I suddenly recalled everything that had happened. Apparently I'd fainted before the moment when the execution took place, and fell to the ground before the bullets had begun to fly. So I'd survived. Or had I?

In any case, I took off running like nobody's business, stumbling over my feet, which had forgotten what it felt like to walk, much less to run. Fortunately for me, explosions were ringing out all around, and no one was in the mood to take notice of me. With everyone else busy trying to avoid dying himself in one of the periodic waves of erratic gunfire, even the sight of a blood-drenched ghost like me coming out of a graveyard wouldn't have been enough to arrest anyone's attention. I didn't realize how ghastly I looked until I reached home and knocked on the door only to find that my own wife didn't recognize me. She thought I was a burglar. And she would have screamed if I hadn't clapped her mouth shut with the last remnants of a strength that only God knows what demon inspired me with.

"Be quiet, woman!" I told her. "I'm your husband, Khalil!"

Then the neighbors started gathering around, led by secret service agents of various persuasions who'd been planted among us to pose as ordinary residents.)

◆　◆　◆

"I adjure you, O company of demons and Iblises, of satanic hosts and devils, I adjure you wherever you may be on the face of the earth, bring forth those who dwell in deserts, slaughterhouses, graveyards, markets, highways, by-ways, and towers. Where are the two Maymouns of the clouds? Where is Shamhawraq the Flyer? Where is Burqan the Jew? Where is the August White Monarch? Where is the Most Venerable Crimson King? Where is the One with the Black Turban? Where is the Owner of the Coal-black Mule? Where is the One with a thousand heads, each of which has a thousand faces, each of which has a mouth with a thousand tongues, with every tongue praising God Almighty in a different language?

"Alaksh, Batat Lahoushal Mutee'oush Batriqoush Yatafrioush Batbatiqoush Makashlash, urgently, urgently, with haste, with haste, at this hour, at this hour . . .

"Burn him, O Mitatrouq by the truth of Tahitamghilyal, and by the truth of the clan of Shala' Ya'ou Youbih Batkah Batakfal Bisa'a Ka'a Mimyal. By my servant who is obedient to you, O clan of Jall Ziryal, burn . . . someone . . . some . . ."

◆　◆　◆

"The bastard . . . I'll kill him!"

A silent scream rang out deep inside Nasim as he flung down the morning edition of *The Geneva Journal* newspaper. It contained a terse news item on the death of a certain Arab student by the name of Sirri Al-Din Mukhtar, who had reportedly been "run over by an unidentified automobile."

Around noon—that is, a short while before Raghid usually got out of bed—the same morning's edition of the *Geneva Tribune* arrived, containing a somewhat more detailed version of the event along with a picture of Sirri Al-Din's body lying mangled near the sidewalk. The driver hadn't stopped. According to his sick mother, he'd most likely thrown himself under the wheels of the car to escape from the financial straits and health crisis he'd been facing. Meanwhile, the police were searching for the offending automobile.

"God, what a bastard. He issued an order, and while they were murdering Sirri Al-Din, he was floating around contentedly in that gold-lined swimming pool of his. Somebody ought to murder the guy."

Meanwhile, like an obedient butler, Nasim got the tea ready, then went on arranging Raghid's breakfast on a tray that, like all the other dishes and utensils in the place, was made of gold.

(Why don't I just slip some bathroom disinfectant into his food? After all, isn't Raghid a filthy microbe? It should be a crime punishable by law not to kill him. Letting someone like him live should be grounds for suspecting those around him of criminal intent. Why do they go on making his breakfast the way I do, or keep him fed the rest of the day? Why do they run around carrying him on their backs, cleaning up his messes, picking up his clothes and his women off the bedroom floor, and bothering themselves with making arrangements for all his dirty work? Was Sirri Al-Din accidentally run over . . . or was he liquidated? If the former is true, then why did he happen to be killed in the same part of town as this golden fortress, on the street leading from the metro station to the mansion entrance? Had someone agreed to meet him at the mansion, then arranged for a hit man to lie in wait for him in the car that ran him down? Was it a traffic accident? Or was it a quick assassination carried out before the scandal could hit the press, then be snatched up by Charlotte Barnes to publish it or use it to blackmail Raghid, in which case she also would have been wiped out? Why is it that the people Raghid dislikes always end up dying in unexpected "accidents"?)

Nasim carried the golden breakfast tray to Raghid, not forgetting to include the morning newspaper or to spit on the yellow rose that Raghid liked to have in the middle of the tray and whose thorns always scratched Nasim's fingers when he put it in its little vase. It looked like a fierce little golden porcupine, as if the tiny but sometimes bloody wound it inflicted on Nasim every day was Raghid's way of saying "Good morning!" to the world.

Listen, man, he chided himself, you should ask God to forgive you for thinking this way. Maybe he didn't kill him. Maybe it was just a coincidence. Maybe Sirri Al-Din lost his senses and then, blinded by despair, rage, and humiliation, came by night to demand an audience with Raghid. Then, before he could reach his destination, he was run down by some drunk driver. As for you, go on playing the loyal butler until you can carry out your plan and finish your university degree. Remember the degradation you used to suffer with your brothers and sisters in Beirut whenever the landlord would evict you from his house. Remember who you are—the son of a family forced to emigrate from the Nab'a area, whose breadwinner couldn't even find a roof for his ten children and his cat to sleep under the first night on the road, and who by the seventh night went out wielding, not a sword, but a screwdriver for taking the nuts off car wheels.

(Using the nut loosener that he kept in the trunk of his taxi, my father managed to break open the door of a deserted house, and the whole family went in, trembling with exhaustion and shame. The day the owner got back from the Bahamas and demanded his house back, we were filled with chagrin. Even so, my father came back at him with a refusal that no doubt seemed totally illogical. All right, he told him. So you're the owner of the house. But why should your house lie empty while my family and I have to sleep on the sidewalk outside? And what sort of a country is it that would let people sleep in beds of mud in public parks while there are perfectly sound, empty houses that have been sealed shut with the wax of indifference and luxury cruises? So we're occupying your house. But you're occupying our right to a life of dignity. You're occupying my chance to make a living, when I should have the same opportunities that you do. Words . . . Words. . . . He responded with words still harsher than ours, saying, I'm a hard worker. I pulled myself up by my own bootstraps. Every piaster I own, I earned by the sweat of my brow, and I bought this house after long, hard years as a foreigner in a foreign land. Words . . . Words. . . . Some from him and some from us. But they all dissolved under the weight of the hateful stares we got from the neighbors, who resented the presence of our poor, homeless family in a building that had previously been occupied only by the wealthy. My younger brothers and sisters would romp around like little monsters, their shouts scratching the neighbors' velvet-soft ears. Day after day we were subjected to a degrading silent treatment. The only person who dared befriend us was the doorman, who was fired for his kindness, and the day he lost his job, our cat Filla died. Meanwhile, I'd go every day to the university, escorted by curses and nasty looks, then come home exhausted from my night job in a restaurant and try in vain to console my mother, who was being crushed by the weight of our having been turned into pariahs. After all, it was she who had always made it a habit to befriend our relatives, the other ladies in the neighborhood, and even the neighbors' children. We'd occupied the tenth floor, and my mother—despite her heart condition—was too ashamed to ride the lift. Even walking up ten flights of stairs was better than being surrounded on all sides by hostile glances inside a tiny closed box, exposing herself to vibrations of hatred and contempt for the period of time it took the lift to reach the ninth story, which was where the last neighbor lady got off. In the lift she'd be stared at all the way up as if her body were being pierced through with skewers of deadly malice. After all, in a lift you're about as close as you can get to other people, and it's impossible to rush by and pretend not to notice the other person the way you might if you were in the street or even on the stairs. In a lift, you're under siege. The day she first experienced it was when the rich neighbor lady on the ninth floor spit on her without uttering a word. Afterward my mother told me she'd felt a mysterious pain in her chest. She said it had seemed that instead of carrying her upward, the lift was taking her down, down under the ground into a bottomless pit. After that she didn't dare get on it again. After years of this sort of indignity and shame, I found her dead of heart failure on the stairs in front of the door leading onto the ninth floor . . . on the first step leading up to the tenth floor from the landing where the elevator is.

Year after year my father would make excuses to the owner of the flat. The first year he swore to him that he'd pay the rent and vacate the flat as soon as he could afford the price of a room. But then the owner waived his right to the rent, and even offered to pay us the equivalent of the rent if we would just get out! Yet the years kept passing, and the disasters went on multiplying, and poverty grew more intractable, and school fees kept on rising, and standards of living went on deteriorating. Then along come some armed vigilantes and stole my father's taxicab, saying they were going to use it to liberate a stolen homeland. When my father went to one of the militia leaders demanding his car back, the leader expressed his sincere regret, saying that the ones who had "done the job" were hiding behind slogans as an excuse for stealing people's cars, exploiting people's love for the cause to gain selfish advantage. He said he didn't know exactly who they were: Saboteurs? Murderers who'd managed to infiltrate the ranks of true revolutionaries? As for how to sort them all out, he didn't offer any solutions. It was after this that my father fell ill and collapsed. He'd work one day and be in pieces for two. He'd regain his energy for a day or so and be bedridden with grief for two years. Eventually he began to fade away. But like my mother, he didn't dare ride the lift. In vain we tried to find a way to leave that deadly tenth floor. Some people advised us to occupy another, fancier flat with a well and an electric generator on the first or second floor, especially in view of the fact that water and electricity were being cut off for the poor and the rich alike. Misery was spreading among one and all. Patrols were coming around in steady succession. Wars were breaking out one after another.

And then, half the floor we were occupying was destroyed by a shell. However, we were ashamed to try occupying another flat after having filched and sold what was left of the furniture in the flat we were in, the way others like us had done once morals became a luxury no poor man could afford. So we restricted our living space to the two rooms that were still intact. As injustice and inequality went on spreading their ugly tentacles, we stopped even trying to live lives of dignity. We forfeited our dreams of leaving poverty behind and finding justice for ourselves. But although we may have stopped dreaming, we couldn't seem to stop growing. In spite of people's nasty looks, we flourished and grew into a tribe of strapping, healthy giants. As for me, I became the head of the family and its breadwinner even before I came of age. And the first law I laid down in the household was: education. Every one of us would get an education. He could study in the university, learn a trade, whatever suited him. But one way or another, he'd end up with an education. Working as a mercenary in one of the local militias wasn't an option, although we could serve in one free of charge if we wanted to. It was likewise forbidden for any of us to join up with the ruling militia in return for a salary, and then when it was defeated to modify our beliefs and switch our allegiance to the newest militia to gain ascendancy so as to earn our salaries from them, and so on ad infinitum. I'd make good one day and lose out the next. We might eat one day and go hungry for several days thereafter.

Meanwhile, Beirut was choking to death, and sources of livelihood were shrinking by the day. When I finally graduated from the university, the only work I could find was my original job as a waiter. Everywhere I went in search of a job, I'd get laughed at when I told people I had a degree in humanities. Even Nadim Ghafir, a neighbor of a friend of mine, had a good long laugh at my major. It so happened that Nadim had been trying to convince a friend of mine to go to work as a cook and butler for some tycoon in Geneva, Switzerland, but my friend was determined not to leave home. Consequently, I begged him to let me go in my friend's place. That way, I could finish my education, have free room and board, and send my whole salary back to my family. I said this frankly to Nadim, and he replied, "All right, provided that you do the education bit on the sly. The man you'll be working for doesn't like 'intellectuals.' If he caught you smoking hashish, he'd laugh. If he found you snorting cocaine, he'd egg you on and maybe even join you. But if he caught you being a university student in the College of Arts and Humanities, you'd be a goner.")

Oh, no, he thought. The bell was ringing and Raghid's voice was thundering into the kitchen over the intercom, "Where's my breakfast, you. . . ?!"

Nasim reheated the tea and milk, then went scurrying off to Raghid's room. When he put the tray down in front of Raghid's face, puffy with sleep and overindulgence, he remembered the face of his classmate Sirri Al-Din in the picture he'd seen of him, lacerated and disfigured on the open road. He felt terrible remorse for having mediated the deal. He'd meant well by it, of course. He'd had no idea that it would lead to such a tragic end. He really was young, impulsive, naive, and inexperienced, just as Amir Nealy had told him he was. He stared over at Raghid with loathing and indignation. He was sixty years old, but he looked more like fifty what with his round, rosy face, a bald spot as smooth as the forehead of a pampered little boy, and his impish green eyes.

"Didn't any other newspapers come?" he asked. "What about *La Suisse?*"

Nasim screamed back in silence, "So you want to see a picture of the corpse in all the newspapers?! Isn't one enough? One of these mornings, I'm going to kill you. I'm going to strangle you in your bed, or in your golden swimming pool. I'm going to wring your neck. . . !"

However, all that came out of his mouth was, "I'll bring the rest of the papers as soon as they get here, sir."

"Have you taken breakfast to Sheikh Watfan?"

"He hasn't rung the bell yet. As you know, he doesn't wake up at any particular hour."

"Be sure to let him know when he does wake up that I want to see him."

(I'll let him know that I'm going to kill you, and that nothing will be able to protect you from me—not a sorcerer, not Iblis, not an angel of mercy. For people like you, there should be no mercy.)

Raghid rose to his full, squat stature, then proceeded toward the bathroom with his usual vampish gait looking nearly drunk with self-satisfaction. As he left the room, Nasim could hear a particular sound coming from the bathroom that nearly drove him insane. (It's Sirri Al-Din's kidney, still in the service of that son of a bitch. And now Sirri Al-Din is dead, and I'll never see him again. How in the hell will I face his mother?)

◆　◆　◆

Nasim went back to the kitchen and sat down beside his liege, the bell. A few minutes later he could hear the voice of the sorcerer, trembling like a ghost's over the intercom, "Nasim, come to my room."

Pressing the button to reply, Nasim asked, "Would you like to have your breakfast, sir?"

"No. I need something else. Come right away."

Through the long corridors of the half-darkened mansion, Nasim headed toward the sheikh's quarters. The corridor walls were covered with large hanging carpets that were decorated with old engraved pictures of European-looking faces and scenes of hunting, fishing, relaxation, and merriment against backgrounds of Swiss-looking forests, mountains, and lakes. They weren't ugly pictures. But they were alien to his world, and would have been better suited to a museum, or at least to some house other than the one he was living in. Besides, they made him terribly homesick. And the narrow windows that Raghid had covered with gold-plated iron bars were a constant reminder that he was little more than a prisoner—a prisoner to the necessity of earning his daily bread, besieged on one side by the misery of homesickness, and on the other by his miserable homeland, surrounded by degradation both here and there, and by loneliness, snow, wretched weather, and a longing for his brothers and sisters. Oh, when would he ever finish his thesis, get his degree, and be able to leave this insufferable golden fortress? No, he wasn't a saint. Once he'd thought of stealing one of Raghid's paintings, objets d'art, or gold water faucets so that he could sell it and use the money to pay for his and his broth-ers' and sisters' school fees—something far away from this daily torment. Raghid wouldn't have noticed, and he could have bought back two years of his life. But he hadn't been able to do it. He didn't know why, but he couldn't bring himself to steal. Apparently he really did believe in higher morality in spite of everything—and perhaps because of everything. He'd never once thought of resorting to anything but dialogue as a means of changing things—that is, until today when he'd seen Sirri Al-Din's picture in the newspaper. After all, he thought, strangling Raghid to death might be a shortcut to where he was try-ing to go. It might also bring a quicker end to the sufferings of the poor. On the other hand, as Amir had pointed out to him once, this Raghid would soon be replaced by some other Raghid, and the infernal wheel would just keep turning, pulverizing the bodies of the poor. Cutting off Raghid's head wouldn't do any more good than cutting off a chameleon's tail, which just grows right back. No, the entire "machine" would have to be put out of com-mission. But how? How? Most of the people who claimed to have been trying to do just that had ended up keeping the machine going once they'd taken it over themselves. And the result was that it went on crushing the unfortunate just the way it always had, but under new slogans. So, how?

He knocked on the sorcerer's door, then entered his room. He found him in bed. He was thin and pale, but relatively young, with a beard and a thick head of hair that hardly showed any signs of gray. He looked too tame to scare even a kitten—unless, that is, Nasim looked him straight in the eyes. And whenever he did that, a childlike shiver would course through his body. Sheikh Watfan had one brown eye and one green one. Or was he just imagin-ing it? He'd heard people say that no one dared look the sheikh in the eyes for very long. In any case, he wasn't planning to try it himself.

"Good morning, Sheikh Watfan."

"Good morning, son. Bring a piece of paper and a pen and get ready to write. I'm in need of a few things."

He always dictated to him the things that he needed. Never once had he given anyone a word written in his own handwriting. Was he afraid of some sort of countersorcery? Nasim nearly laughed out loud at the thought, but he didn't dare make the man angry. No, he wasn't afraid of his magic or his demons. However, ever since he'd been assigned the task of bringing the raw materials for the sheikh's sorcery, he'd found that it provided him with an extra chance to get out of the golden citadel either on the pretext of searching for the stuff, since some of the things couldn't be obtained in Geneva, or on the pretext of passing by the office of some private airline pilot or steward and asking him to bring them from abroad. And since he'd been placed in sole charge of expenditures in this area, he'd once been able to get a good deal on some celery seed and ginger, then send the difference by express mail to a brother of his who had enrolled in the Lebanese University at the beginning of the academic year. However, his conscience had bothered him so much over this embezzlement that he'd started having nightmares. And this despite the fact that it had been a paltry sum, and had rescued his brother from having to join a militia that he didn't believe in under the pressure of poverty and need. In any case, his mind had no rest until he finally promised himself in the darkness of the night that he wouldn't do that sort of thing again, and that he'd return the money as soon as God gave him the means to do so. He knew, of course, that Raghid's billion would hardly be affected by a few piasters or pounds, not to mention the fact that the entire fortune had been stolen in the first place. But still. . . .

The sheikh got out of bed, looking a bit terrifying. With his towering height and a cloaklike garment that cascaded down from his shoulders to the floor, nearly swallowing up his gaunt frame, he looked like a ghost that had just emerged from its coffin. And he really did have one brown eye and one green eye. However, this was merely a matter of biology, which in Nasim's view belonged to the realm of the ordinary, not to that of spirits and demons.

"I'm ready, sir," said Nasim.

"Write down the following: nutmeg, one ounce of black pepper, one ounce of white pepper, one ounce of ginger, one ounce of sparrow's tongue, one ounce of emblic, one ounce of 'ud qarh, one ounce of peony, one ounce of Baghdad spikenard, one ounce of red bahman, one ounce of oriental frankincense, one ounce of basil seed, one ounce of celery seed, one ounce of garden peppergrass seed, one ounce of radish seed, one ounce of onion seed, one ounce of black caraway, and pure bees' honey."

"Is that all?"

"Yes."

"Wouldn't you like to take breakfast?"

"Not now. I'll call for you when it's time."

"The pasha wants to see you."

"I'll call for him when it's time."

Nasim left the room. One ounce of sparrow's tongue. That was the only item on the list that would guarantee him a full day off. He'd tell them that he'd gone hunting for sparrows in order to cut out their tongues. Then he'd cut up some pig's rump into little pieces and call them sparrow's tongue. This way, he could spend his day in the university library and get some more work done on his thesis. God bless you, Sheikh Watfan! he thought. "Assistant Sorcerer" wasn't a bad profession for somebody like him who wasn't afraid of demons and spirits. Of course, he didn't dare rule out the possibility that there might be cosmic powers that science still hadn't revealed. But he wasn't afraid of "demons" in the popular sense. He'd become too familiar with them for that. In fact, they'd formed the backdrop for his entire life ever since he was a little boy. His mother used to threaten him by telling him that a jinni was going to come and strangle him to death. And his grandmother used to warn him that if he spilled boiling water on the doorstep, little devils would come around. (I was ten years old when my mother caught me pouring boiling water onto our only carpet. When she spanked me for it, I confessed that I'd been trying to pour water not on the carpet, but on the doorstep, and that the reason I'd done that was to get some little devils to come around so that they could play with me and my brothers and sisters. She uttered the name of the Merciful, then asked me in horror, "Did 'the lords' come? Did you see them?" But I didn't answer.)

Nutmeg, pepper, ginger, emblic, basil seed, celery, honey, etc. It was a concoction Nasim had become familiar with. Apparently Sheikh Sakhr had asked for it again despite the fact that it made his stomach ulcer flare up. After all, there was a certain famous lady singer performing for the Arabs of Geneva. Whenever she did a gig in Geneva, there was a huge run on this particular recipe, and as soon as she left, the clients who had ordered it would find their ulcers paining them again, and, as a result, their foreign doctors would find their bank balances flourishing nicely. Or did Raghid want a youth potion for himself in honor of some unfortunate young thing that had been sold—or had sold herself—to him for the afternoon? In any case, it was none of his business. And he had no intention of falling into the trap of playing hero on the sidelines. His first priority was to finish his studies and go back home. Education first. This was the law he'd laid down for himself and his little family, and he had to keep reminding himself of it constantly. He was just passing through this citadel of gold . . . through the sorcerer's life . . . through the life (and death) of Sirri Al-Din Mukhtar.

And Raghid . . . if only he could . . . if only he could restrain himself from killing the overindulged son of a bitch.

The doorbell rang. It was time for Raghid's daily bouquet of flowers to be delivered. Every day he had an enormous, beautiful bouquet sent to himself, since no one else seemed to love him the way he loved himself. He hated to have flowers planted in his garden. He hated them when they were alive. But he loved them this way, with severed necks and on the verge of withering and dying. Nasim carried the flowers to the study as he'd been instructed to do, then went back to his post in the kitchen to await further orders from his "masters," the bell and the intercom. At around the same time, the German chef arrived, cursing as usual in a language Nasim didn't understand. He was searched every morning, and never entered the mansion's royal domain without half of his clothes on and half of them in his hand. Raghid had made certain that Nasim didn't understand a word of German, and that the chef spoke nothing else. That way the two of them would never be able to have a conversation. After all, what two people could get together without plotting against him!

◆ ◆ ◆

Hammoush, Mudaqhir, Qahoush, Taheesh, Fannash Mahr See'y Hawl, O Spokesman, O Speaker, O Heet, O Leet. Distance thyself from him, shun him. Come now, O Father of Noukh Anoukh Bandakh. Receive your commission, O Spears, and you, O Morning. Answer, O Sham'oun and blind the eyes, you and your servants, O Maymoun the Flyer, by the truth of the Fire and the Light and the Shadow and Hurour by the Almighty God, the Most Forgiving. Respond, O Sham'oun and blindfold the eyes, you and your servants, O Maymoun the Flyer. Respond, O Sham'oun, and you, O Zaytoun, and you, O Maymoun. Do what I have commanded you urgently, with great haste, at this very hour. . ."

◆ ◆ ◆

The only room in the entire mansion with a huge picture window was Raghid's study. He hadn't had it placed there out of fondness for nature scenes, of course. Rather, he liked to be able to look out through the window's bullet-proof glass at the people around him to see whether they might perchance be thieves, conspirators, or murderers. No one was permitted entrance to his mansion but Nasim, the German chef, the chauffeur, and the maids. The maids, who were replaced constantly, worked individual shifts under close supervision by Nasim for "security reasons." There was another building for his guards and other employees at the far end of the garden, which was separated from the mansion by a deep, lackluster stream of water reminiscent of the moats they used to dig around ancient castles and fortresses in the Middle Ages. The moat was too deep and wide to be swum across with ease, and there was a narrow bridge joining the two banks with an iron, electrified gate which was kept locked at night and which could only be opened from the bank nearest the mansion. That way, the workers were sure to come not when they chose, but only when their "liege" so desired. The bridge was the only means of access to the mansion, which was guarded at night by a mute man who had a pack of terrifying, trained guard dogs that, from the way they bared their fangs, appeared to detest every member of the human race.

Nadim sat there poised for action, like a hunting dog waiting for orders from its master. He put out his own cigar in the presence of Raghid's, and as Nasim came in with the coffee, he imagined Nadim wagging his tail the way dogs do when their masters pet them in approval.

"I'm pleased with you," Raghid said to him. "You carried out the assignment more quickly than I'd expected."

Steaming with rage and suspicion, Nasim left the room as Nadim replied, "But I'm worried about my mother and father. Their house was hit by a shell fragment in the last raid."

"Don't worry," said Raghid in his familiar refrain. "Trust me, and everything will be all right."

Bitterly, Nasim wondered if they'd been talking about Sirri Al-Din's death. (Come on, man. Be reasonable. They might have been talking about his trip to Beirut or some other projects they've got cooking. After all, Raghid's got projects galore: corporations, hotels, investments, video companies, film production studios, airplane sales, contracting, banks, schools, tourist villages, you name it. So be rational, man. You ought to be ashamed of yourself.)

Nasim began muttering, "Say, I seek refuge with the Lord of mankind . . ." Then he continued, repeating over and over, "from the mischief of the Whisperer of Evil."[5]

---

5. These words come from the 114th and last chapter in the Qur'an, recited often in the five Muslim daily ritual prayers, and in situations where one seeks protection from evil.

He clasped his head in his hands as the image of Sirri Al-Din's mangled corpse blazed before his eyes. On the verge of collapse, he sobbed silently to himself. (I'm going to kill that son of a bitch. He's surrounded me on all sides with hatred and misery. Not a moment goes by without all the evils of the Arab world—my world—appearing before me in the mirror of his brutality. By forcing me to kill him, he threatens my life, too. I'm besieged on one side by my family's "exorbitant" poverty, and on the other by Raghid's "abject" wealth . . . besieged.)

◆   ◆   ◆

Despite his irritation at the man's tall stature, Raghid received Sheikh Sakhr Ghanamali in front of the mansion entrance with a handshake, then escorted him to his study. Nadim inched along behind the money monster as if he were trying to avoid bothering the other two men even by so much as the sound of his breathing or the rustling of his silk shirt, or as if he were swimming in deep, perilous waters next to a couple of sharks.

When the two men had settled into a couple of luxurious Chesterfield armchairs, Raghid drew out his cigar with the smug flourish of someone showing off his wealth and virility, while the other countered his gesture by unsheathing a Muslim rosary that fairly glowed with its jeweled beads and gold, diamond-studded threads.

In contrast to Raghid's frigid, hostile demeanor, there was something about Sheikh Sakhr's presence that radiated a warm, friendly merriment. His face was quite handsome with his ebony complexion, hawklike nose, and fleshy, sensuous lips. There was nothing about his comely, rounded cheeks that would have betrayed the fact that he was in his fifties or that he suffered from the pains of a stomach ulcer. And his masterfully dyed, coal-black hair glistened with vitality, especially when, like today, he was dressed in his European attire and didn't have it covered up with his kaffiyeh and 'iqal.[6] His fingers kept busy fiddling with his costly rosary beads, which, strung on a golden thread with diamond-studded ends, represented a small fortune all by themselves. Sometimes he would toss them into the air, then with the peculiar nonchalance of the well-to-do, catch them again by another bead. And when, with

---

6. The *kaffiyeh* is a large, square piece of fabric worn by some Arabs as a headdress, while the *'iqal* is a ropelike headband worn over the *kaffiyeh* to hold it in place.

the same nonchalance, he lit a cigarette with his gold-plated lighter inlaid with precious stones, he looked to Nadim as though he was about to throw it into the ashtray like some used-up match. Nadim gazed at Sakhr's merry eyes. No one but he knew that Sakhr suffered from color blindness. He couldn't distinguish either red or green—which meant he couldn't see the color of blood, trees, or oases. He'd escorted Sakhr on the day he went to the doctor, and had sworn himself to secrecy about the matter.

Revealing other people's secrets to Raghid, of course, wasn't a sin but a duty. However, at this particular moment he regretted doing so, because he'd almost begun feeling nostalgic for the days when he used to work for Sakhr. After all, Sakhr was jolly. Frank. Direct. Human. Dealing with him had been more comfortable and less complicated than dealing with Raghid, and never had he known Sakhr to hold a grudge against anyone. Nadim heaved a sigh as he looked pensively over at his former boss, and a moment of regret charged with memories flashed through his head like a bolt of lightning. There was no doubt about it. Life with Sakhr had been brighter and gentler. There'd been something novel about his anecdotes, his "mobile harem," and the mistresses and children he was always losing count of. As for his relationships with the foreign women journalists who were constantly trying to sniff out stories about his vulgar excesses in hopes of getting a cut of his small fortune, they generally came to a comical conclusion in Sakhr's bedroom. There had never been any violence or murder. Instead, life with him had been a constant stream of revelry and cheerful generosity in a climate of opulence and *la vie en rose.*

On the other hand, he thought, dealing with Raghid is profitable. Really profitable. Sakhr is a professional at life and a womanizer. And women love money. Likewise with Raghid, he loves and despises women at the same time. As far as he's concerned, they're all either wives or whores, and every one of them carries a particular price tag on the pleasure market. He doesn't even acknowledge the existence of the working woman or the woman who employs herself as a serious artist. Instead, all women are just potential members of his harem, and the rest is mere detail. As for working women who've made successes of themselves, they're more masculine than they are feminine, and consequently they have to be classified not as women, but as men.

Sakhr is basically a hedonist and a libertine, and isn't much given to worrying about landing an extra deal here or there regardless of how lucrative it might be. Raghid loves money for money's sake, and since I joined up with him I've multiplied my fortune several times over. He knows how to amass it, and he won't squander a minute on a deal if it doesn't guarantee him long-term profits. When he meets someone, he doesn't waste more than a few words on niceties or unnecessary preliminaries. Instead he gets right to the point, the way he's doing now with Sakhr.

"I want the airport," he said.

"My brother Hilal is against it," replied Sakhr.

"Why!"

"Because he hates you."

"But why?"

"You know why. He's got a thousand and one reasons."

"I can't think of one good reason for him to hate me."

"It's a long story. But he and I are constantly getting into arguments over you. After I gave you the permit to build that big school, as well as a lot of other things, he cut off communication with me for a long time."

"But why does he hate me?"

"He thinks you've corrupted me."

"I want this airport. I've promised mutual friends of ours that I'll get the permit, and I'll do a good job of it, as usual. You'll be proud of it, I assure you. And we'll share together in several hundred million francs' worth of profits."

"Hilal is adamant this time. He got here yesterday for treatment, and I don't want to get into another row with him. He's about to start hating me on your account."

"But . . ."

"He thinks you're the one who's dragged me down the path of women, wine, gambling, and all the forbidden pleasures of the world."

"But I haven't. You were that way to begin with. All I did was give you a few openings."

Laughing the boyish laugh that seemed never to leave him, Sakhr replied playfully, "You mean, the seeds of corruption were already there? Very well, then. But you've had a part in making them grow, for example, by watering them with a little booze now and then!"

Picking up on the hint, Nadim rushed to offer the sheikh a glass of liquor. He didn't refuse. Meanwhile, he started complaining like a beggar who's had his shoes stolen.

"As soon as Hilal got here, we made all the necessary adjustments. We hid all the atrocities in the cellar. The booze went into trunks, the women were packed away to hotels. . .''

Taking advantage of Sakhr's good humor, Raghid said, "By the way, here's the prescription you asked for. My sorcerer prepared it especially for you. Take it an hour before your rendezvous, and you'll have the strength of ten horses. It's the 'potency magic' prescription."

"Well, I need it, that's for sure. That good-looking journalist Charlotte Barnes is still on my tail. She plays the heartsick lover, and I play dumb. She wants material for a chapter she intends to write on wealthy Arabs, or a check in return for not mentioning me by name in it the way she did once in her newspaper. As for me, love is all I'm after. I'll never get over my passion for fair-skinned gals. Dark-skinned ones aren't allowed into my bed past the age of eighteen. As for blondes, they've got a green light with me till they're all of thirty."

"What do you think of Lilly Spock? Isn't she a good looker?"

"Is she even a woman? She works like a man, and she's turned herself into one, if you ask me. I can't stand her type. Besides which, work has made her old and decrepit. Every brunette past eighteen is retired, in my book."

As Sakhr imbibed, his cheeks took on a rosy glow, and Nadim took a few sips along with him out of politeness. Such were the requirements of good manners in dealings with his benefactors. As for his headache, it would have to be ignored for the time being. He could treat it later when he got back to the office by picking a fight with one of his employees or assistants.

Waxing eloquent on the subject of women, Sakhr continued, "My son Najm brought his girlfriend over one evening, and she was so luscious I borrowed her from him in return for letting him ride my white stallion. Oh, and my most recent wife, did you know she'd left me?"

"Does that upset you?"

"I don't know. I just miss the kids. She took them back with her to our country. You knew, didn't you, that she was my cousin's daughter?"

"Yes, I suppose I did. I mean, I thought that was the wife before last."

"Well, I consider her the last, since a wife who can't bear children doesn't count. And my oldest son by my cousin's daughter is still young. He's thirteen years old and is going to school back in Beirut—it's the school that you built. Do you remember? I was the one who helped you get the deal. I didn't realize at the time that I was winning a school for my son."

"Not to mention several million francs."

"And I spent it on Janine, and Gena Lulu, and Rita the beauty queen of the universe."

"A quarter of a century ago."

Laughter. Raghid wasn't one to waste his time for nothing. He'd be sure to pick up on this moment of relaxation and turn it into bait.

"Try to convince your brother that you'll cut off business ties with me, and that the airport deal is what you're asking of him in return. Then you'll let me go fair and square."

"I'll try," Sakhr assured him.

He looked at his watch, then got up suddenly as if he'd been stung, pushing the glass of firewater away from him in horror.

"It's time to pray," he said. "Oh, Lord, grant forgiveness to your lowly servant. If you'll excuse me, I need to do my ablutions. I'm not drunk. I haven't really had anything to drink yet."

Adding his fervent witness to what Sakhr had said, Nadim spread out the prayer rug on the office floor. Sakhr then adjusted it to point in the proper direction, aided by his Swiss-made gold watch designed specially for well-to-do Arabs with a built-in compass showing the direction of the qiblah. Noting that he was facing toward the servants' quarters, Sakhr asked Raghid in a vaguely reproachful tone, "How could you have built your servants' and employees' quarters in the direction of the qiblah?! Does your damned engineer want me to pray toward them? I'll go pray in a place that preserves my dignity!"[7]

He then took leave of the other two men rather angrily. However, by the time he reached the door he'd forgotten what he was so miffed about and had recovered his usual jovial disposition. Embracing Raghid, he asked Nadim for a favor, saying, "My son Saqr is in need of an escort and interpreter. Do you know anyone—besides yourself, of course—who could be depended on in this regard?"

Having asked the question with a tone of sarcasm in his voice, he burst out laughing with that special guffaw of his that could have filled the entire city. Then he suddenly fell silent while the other men were still laughing.

---

7. This passage is rife with irony, given the fact that Islam forbids the partaking of any alcoholic beverages whatsoever, not to mention Sakhr's extramarital exploits and his disdain for those of lower social status. *Qiblah* refers to the direction Muslims are to turn in prayer five times a day, namely, toward the Ka'ba in Mecca.

In a half-whisper, Raghid said to him, "A quick word before you go. I have a way to persuade Hilal regarding the airport."

Nadim knew then that he was supposed to withdraw and wait for them outside the door. It might be half an hour, an hour . . . what difference did it make? It was part of the job. As the two men left the room, Sakhr let forth his peculiar raucous laugh and said, "Hilal won't agree to any offer. Money means nothing to him. He lives just like a poor man or someone of the middle class."

Raghid bit down sternly on his cigar and didn't say a word. Nor did he join Sakhr in his loud cackling, which he kept up until he disappeared into the velvet-lined belly of his car. His solid gold license plate gleamed in the miserly Swiss sun, plunging its glistening knives into Nasim's eyes in a painful, shattering flash of light as he closed the door on the guest's departing cavalcade.

(Raghid and Nadim. Which of them should I murder? The mastermind, or the instrument of the crime? Do you suppose Nadim came to the mansion last night to oversee its execution?)

◆　◆　◆

Heaving a sigh of relief, Raghid brought Sheikh Sakhr's prayer beads out of his pocket.

"I've confiscated them!" he said victoriously, "and nationalized them!"

Nadim wasn't surprised by the theft. He already knew about this pastime of Raghid's, and had seen his sumptuous collection of rosaries, all of them stolen. In fact, he practiced the hobby himself when Raghid wasn't around. In Raghid's presence he didn't smoke a cigar, he didn't steal rosaries, and he didn't flirt with women. In Raghid's presence, his life was put on hold, and his entire existence was devoted to performing whatever service Raghid wanted performed. His dominion over him was absolute. When he was with Raghid, his one and only concern was to please him. He had no wife, no moral stance on anything, no nothing.

Sometimes he saw Raghid as a man of gold, and himself as someone who comes crawling behind him to pick up scattered fragments of ore. Meanwhile, he was getting richer, and richer. (Until the day I embezzled that huge sum of money. I got scared and really did intend to return it. But Raghid, who doesn't miss even the most infinitesimal irregularity when it comes to money, put his hand on the records just in the nick of time. Then he offered me the same sum as a "gift," holding onto the forged papers as a "memento of a golden friendship," as he phrased it.

Dunya warned me at the time, saying, "Give the money back to him and take the papers. Don't you see that he could have you thrown in prison at the drop of a hat?")

The moment he heard Raghid's voice, Nadim's brain reverted to a blank slate ready to receive new orders.

"Do you think we could provide facilities for Sheikh Sakhr's son?" he asked.

"Certainly, Pasha."

"Someone we can trust, but not them."

"Of course, Pasha."

"Someone who doesn't know much about financial deals."

"Of course, Pasha."

"I don't want him to take sides and complicate matters."

"Right . . . Pasha."

"I want him to be the type who could be fired in about a month, for example."

"We've got the type you're looking for . . . Pasha."

"And who can spy for us . . . I mean, who'll chatter away to us about things he's heard without him or anybody else noticing that he's our spy."

"Amazing . . . Pasha."

"I want to know what goes on between Sakhr and his twin brother Hilal, and between Sakhr and his family back in Lebanon."

"We'll find out, Pasha."

"I'm not confident anymore of his ability to make sure we get the contracts we're after."

"Ah. . ."

"His people don't respect him anymore. He's a spendthrift, he's got a big mouth, and his scandals have gotten to be public knowledge, which won't do for someone from a family like his."

"Definitely."

"Besides which, his people aren't as foolish as some would like to imagine. They're just less malicious and more honorable than some Arabs. And now, most of them have become aware of the scandals being stirred up by people in the West and in the homeland, as well as the wasted money, which makes our job that much more difficult."

"More difficult . . ."

"Now we've got to think of a way to placate Hilal, the righteous brother, and that's still harder. Unlike his twin brother, Hilal is a man who can't be bought. Not that Sakhr is for sale. However, he's so riddled with weak spots, it's easier to get through to him. Hilal's a harder nut to crack."

"A harder nut to crack, Pasha."

"We've got to think of a way to polish up my image where he's concerned—for example, by coming up with some humanitarian project for me to sponsor, and then drowning it in publicity. For example, I might come chivalrously to the rescue of some damsel in distress."

"We'll find her and rescue her."

"We've got to polish up my public image, too. On the practical level. For example, we might build a mosque and present it to them as a gift—say, a small mosque in the airport. It would be the first time an airport had its own mosque for praying folks to come to—not just a duty-free market, a restaurant, a bank, and other sorts of worldly accoutrements. Write down both those ideas."

"Got it."

"In order for business to keep booming, people have got to love me. As for corrupt men like Sakhr and his ilk, their days are over. From now on, we'll have to deal with people like Hilal, which requires that I get a new image for myself—the image of the popular, valiant altruist."

"People do love you, of course. And we'll make them love you even more, God willing."

"Shut your mouth, and stop flattering me!"

"Yes, Pasha."

"Every human being has his weak points, except for me, of course."

"Of course."

"And we've got to find those weak points in Hilal."

"Absolutely."

"Who would you suggest as a spy?"

" . . ."

"I want someone suitable right away."

"Yes. We have someone, Pasha."

"And his name?"

"Khalil. Khalil Dar', if I'm not mistaken. He's a Lebanese between thirty and thirty-five years old. A bookstore owner with a small-town background. According to what I've heard from his parents, he's a college graduate and a patriot, but not a party loyalist. He's poor and arrogant, and he has a lot of problems with his friends. However, of late he seems to have been trying to hobnob with the well-to-do. He travels first-class, but his worn-out clothes, his dirty, untrimmed fingernails and his cheap, old watch give him away. It's obvious that he's trying to mix with the rich in search of some type of break. When I first saw him with that well-dressed wife of his, I took them for a couple who'd gotten rich through the war. But then when the waitress brought the food and he didn't know how to pull out the tray hidden inside the arm of the chair, I realized that he was traveling first-class for the first time in his life. His wife is a bit shrewder than he is, since I heard her tell the stewardess in a loud, arrogant-sounding voice, 'Please pull out my tray for me. I'm afraid I might break my fingernails!' She's from a good family. If it weren't for her, I would have been afraid of the man. I would have thought he'd been planted on the plane to highjack it or something like that. Her father was a merchant of sizable means—Al-Baytmouni."

"Salim Al-Baytmouni?"

"Right. The late Salim Al-Baytmouni."

"Did the poor guy die?"

"Yes. The war came along and ate up his fortune, then he died of misery."

"Poor guy. I knew him. I advised him a long time ago to smuggle his money out of the country and leave Beirut. From the time Abdul Nasser came to power I started telling all my friends, 'This fellow means business. He's going to make a lot of mistakes. But he's got clean hands, and he's going to be hard to buy. He's like an earthquake that's going to spread from Egypt to Lebanon and to other countries and devour our fortunes. It's just a matter of time.' My father (may he rest in peace) sensed it, too. From the time he saw Nasser's picture and heard his speeches on the day he nationalized the Suez Canal, he started falling ill, and he didn't know how to work anymore. All he had to do was hear the man's name to have his blood pressure go up, start messing up his calculations, and lose deals. When I took over his business, it was on the brink of ruin. I fled with what was left of our money, and you know the rest of the story."

"I'll look for Khalil Dar', or for someone enough like him to fill the bill."

"No . . . I want Baytmouni's in-law, and nobody else. His daughter deserves the honor of attending our soirées, and our attention . . . and our care. Her poor father was a noble man. He wouldn't have hurt a flea. So of course, he ended up going bankrupt. I want you to contact him and his wife right away."

"I don't know their address. I only met up with them yesterday in the airplane."

"Find it out then."

"Yes, sir."

"That's all for now. By the way, have you brought me any new videos?"

"Yes, sir. We recorded them in your private studio with the help of the new photographer. Before I came, I saw a part that will bring joy to your heart."

"After Khalil Dar' has completed his assignment with Sakhr Ghanamali's son, we might transfer him to the video section. Who knows? He might have a bright future in store for him. Like yours. . ."

Nadim resented being compared to that good-for-nothing drifter.

"Will there be anything else, sir?"

"No. You can go now."

When Nadim reached the outer door his intercom beeped, summoning him back to Raghid. So he put out the cigar he'd lit and went back with drooping ears like an obedient hound.

"I forgot to ask you . . . are you still worried about your parents?"

(Damn. Why does he insist on turning his finger in a wound that I'm trying to forget?)

In a half-sarcastic tone, Raghid went on: "Nothing can touch them but what God has decreed for them! So set your mind at rest."

As Nadim left the mansion there was a bitterness in his mouth, like the taste of humiliation. But it soon melted into the taste of his fancy cigar.

◆　◆　◆

"Holy, Holy, Almighty God, Ajaliyyan, Jalina, Ashmakh, Talamakhta, Mahta, O Batmeenakh . . .

"Shamlah, Hamatmaheel, O Moukh Madoukh Qeematarkh Arkh Arkh Bayakhdha Ashmakh Hamouneen Yashtahoun Annareesh Matoush Youtoush Toush. O Allah, I ask Thee by the truth of these great names by which King Aseeya'eel, who was entrusted with the light, once spoke . . .

"We cast enmity and hatred between them until the Day of Resurrection. Whenever they light the fire of war, Iblis and his hosts shall ignite it. Go forth, O Iblis, and cast enmity and hatred between Sakhr Ibrahim Ghanamali and Hilal Ibrahim Ghanamali. Cause division between them by the truth of Shifshifi Shafan Shifa Dimlakh. He said, 'Would that you and I were as far apart as the East is from the West—urgently, quickly, posthaste—Raab, Ghanam, Hazeel, Musdaal, Shabeeet, Umayr, Salif, Qadaar, and Sim'aan, the Head of all Conspirators.' And naught are they but division and destruction."

◆　◆　◆

When Raghid left the sorcerer's wing, he headed for the video and television room, at one end of which there was a large movie screen. Nasim followed him stealthily. He'd never dared do such a thing before. But Sirri Al-Din's unexpected death had charged him with a hotheaded madness the likes of which his peace-loving soul had never known. What sorts of things were they filming for this overfed son of a bitch? His own private porno films presented by his assistants' wives, not one of whom hadn't made her way in and out of his bedroom on at least one occasion? Or perhaps by the young girls whose pristine forests he'd bought the right to explore before anyone else had passed through them? Or do you suppose they'd filmed the hit operations that he'd ordered to be carried out so that he could relish the sight of the victim's face as he swallowed the last, agonizing draughts of terror and death? Would they now see Sirri Al-Din's face as the car wheels struck the half-healed wound at the site of the kidney that he'd given to Raghid? Would they see him flying into the air, then dashed to the ground again like a puppet whose gig in the puppet show is over and has been cast into the night to be forgotten after having its strings cut by the theater owner? Would they see his face being lacerated and crushed?

Raghid was now settled into his royal seat, the videotape was turning, and images accompanied by sounds were appearing successively on the screen. Every now and then Raghid would let out a raucous laugh, and for quite a while he kept switching tapes periodically. Meanwhile, Nasim was panting on the floor, hidden behind the last row of seats. He could feel rushes of disbelief surging through his body until he was about to gasp.

Thinking that he'd heard something, Raghid turned to look behind him. However, by this time Nasim had torn out of the room as if he were fleeing for his life. He streaked to the kitchen, where he found the German chef bent over some sort of sauce as if he were preparing a medical prescription. Almost in tears, Nasim ran over to him and said, "I know you're not to going to understand a word I say. But I'm going to go crazy if I don't say something to somebody. Please . . . listen to me even if you don't understand. What difference does it make, anyway?"

Taking a brief break from his work, the chef gazed pensively at Nasim. His look betrayed no emotion and his features remained unchanged.

Then, with tears streaming down his cheeks, Nasim continued, saying, "Can you believe what sorts of things this man watches? He gawks at other men as they weep in defeat and poverty and talk about their disillusionments. They bring in refugees and misfits living in Europe, naive revolutionaries in exile, underage freedom fighters who've been defeated, exiled, overworked, and deceived and who are searching in vain for a fortune or at least a bite to eat. In other words, poor Arabs, students who've rejected oppressive regimes, are brought in, and every one of them tells his tale of woe in return for an enticing sum of money. In the case of those who refuse, they find other ways of getting them to talk, then film them without their knowledge. They catch somebody in a moment of weakness—either in a state of womanly emotion, drunkenness, or need for companionship—and the filming goes forward. The quality might be lousy, but they do it, anyway. That's what this lunatic does in his spare time. He enjoys gloating over the misfortunes of revolutionaries, freedom fighters, and Arab regimes, whether they be progressive or reactionary. And some of them, unfortunately, supply him with tasty morsels for his film crews. For example, he can revel in the miseries of brothers-turned-enemies, and of quarreling revolutionaries who kill each other off without turning around to see the approaching enemy. He takes pleasure in seeing the scandalous antics of people who boast of their lofty principles, then deliver their own people to bloodbaths so that they can go swimming unobserved in bathtubs of gold. He wants to prove that everything that's happened on Arab soil since the days of Abdul Nasser has been wrong simply because it caused trouble for his father and his big shot business buddies . . . and because it tightened the noose around the neck of modern-day feudalism.

"Amir had already told me all about it, but I thought he was exaggerating. And now I see he was right. This is a man whose sole pleasure in life is gloating over the misfortunes of others . . . of Europe's wealthy Arabs whenever he gets the chance, and of its poor Arabs, too . . . of Arabs living abroad and those still in their homelands, of Arabs everywhere. . . . They pick them up for him off streets, sidewalks, and prison doorsteps, in pubs, factories, universities, and hospitals. And there are plenty of them. Would you believe that just now he was watching Sirri Al-Din as he bargained with Nadim over the price of his kidney? I'm going to kill him. I swear to you, I'm going to do it. Would you believe that he keeps a statue of Abdul Nasser next to his gold-lined swimming pool? He talks to it, insults it, and gives it a day-by-day account of the tragedies being suffered by some Arabs while other Arabs look on unconcerned. He even beats on it, screams at it, and scolds it with a sort of gleeful malice.

" 'If you'd put your hand in ours, we could have ruled the world together. But instead you chose to throw in your lot with the fools, the poor, and the masses, and they killed you with grief and disappointment!' That's what I heard him shouting at it one time through that gold-sprayed glass dome of his. Another time I heard him reprimanding it because he hadn't mastered the art of repression, and didn't know how to use the police state to best advantage the way some of his successors had. Basically, Raghid would like to kill off every poor person on the face of the earth. He'd like to be able to rip off the bodily organs of every young man. To suck our blood. One of these days he's going to ask you to cook up my liver for him. After all, that crazy sorcerer of his might advise him to do just that. Who knows?"

Then, collapsing onto the chair, Nasim buried his face in his hands and began to weep. The chef rested his hand on his shoulder. What seemed like electrically charged particles of sympathy went coursing from his hand into Nasim's trembling frame, and he could feel the warmth of human contact. It was as if there were a mysterious sort of artery that extends every now and then from one person to another, connecting their two bloodstreams and making them into one. Something that goes beyond language, and that perhaps people experienced before language came to be. Something that can't be faked. An unnamable something that Nasim could feel coming from his comrade's presence through the hand grasping his shoulder. His features spotted with tears, Nasim lifted his face toward the other man. Then, picking up a filthy kitchen rag, the cook wiped Nasim's face with deliberate, unhurried solicitude. Then he went back to his saucepan.

◆　◆　◆

That night Nasim woke up feverish, and with tears streaming down his face. In a nightmare, Sirri Al-Din had come to him with his mother, his eyes dripping with blood. He said something that Nasim didn't understand, and when Nasim shook his hand, he was shocked to discover that his fingers were nothing but the bones of a skeleton.

He was still partly asleep when a wild madness exploded in his head: I'll throttle Raghid with these two hands! I can do it. No, I can't. . . . But I'll ask him about the truth, at least. And if I don't manage to murder him, I'll threaten to. I've got to do something. Anything . . .

He ascended the stairs without knowing exactly what he intended to do. When he got to Raghid's room, there was no light on. He turned the door-knob slowly, knowing even before he did so that he'd find it locked. Raghid was sure to wake up and get out of bed to check out the sound he'd heard. If he did, Nasim would have to respond accordingly. Even so, he went on turning the knob, and . . . it opened! At first he was just astonished. Then he was over-come with a sudden terror. So it hadn't been locked after all. His heart beating wildly as a drum in some primitive jungle rite, he proceeded toward Raghid's bed as quietly as a ghost. Finding the bed empty, he looked around him like someone wandering about inside a nightmare. He didn't see Raghid. After all, he would never have slept there without securing the room with all three locks. Leaving the room fearfully, Nasim wondered, do you suppose he sleeps somewhere else for fear of an attempt on his life? Does he spend his nights like a vampire in some underground passageway in this citadel of secrets? Or is he just paying a visit to his sorcerer?

He heard the sound of someone sobbing. Who, or what, could it be? The paintings on the corridor walls? The sorcerer? Barefoot, he followed the sound past Sheikh Watfan's room. The corridor in front of the sheikh's quarters was filled with the smell of incense and the echoes of his vague mumblings and in-cantations. But the loud, tearful wailing was coming from somewhere else—from upstairs.

After tracking the sound further, he found himself in front of the golden room on the top floor of the mansion, which was off limits to practically everyone.

Raghid had made known his desire to be buried in this room, and had de-voted his fortune as a bequest to all those who had paid it a visit, on condition that the visitor entered it barefoot and silent, with head bowed in reverence as one does when entering the tomb of an eminent, distinguished personage or some other sacred site. Nasim had thought he was joking when he first an-nounced his plan to mint a gold medallion with his own image imprinted on it, one of which would be awarded as a souvenir to each deserving pilgrim. In this way he intended to ensure that his entire, exorbitant fortune would be inher-ited by no one but the visitors to his tomb.

The door was ajar, and a ray of light could be seen stealing out through the resulting crack. Trembling, Nasim approached the door and peered inside. In the center of the vast chamber, he saw Raghid kneeling before the casket he had prepared for himself, while spotlights trained on the coffin of gold made it look as though it were on fire. The narrow, oval-shaped, marble-lined passageway which visitors were expected to file through when they paid him their respects later on was enveloped in near darkness. On one occasion he had heard Raghid talking with his lawyer and his physician about the way he was to be buried: lying down in the coffin, or standing up in a way that would make it look like a transparent, golden display case. He remembered the doctor saying something about the difficulty of preserving a corpse in an upright position and emphasizing the advantages of having it in a reclining pose. Raghid, for his part, insisted on being kept standing up so that he could look down at the people who'd be coming to see him. However, his lawyer finally managed to convince him that by that time he wouldn't be looking at anybody, and that instead it would be other people looking at him. Consequently, he said, the horizontal position would be preferable, since this way people would have to bow their heads when they paid him their respects at his grave.

And now here he was, weeping aloud in front of his crypt like a panic-stricken child. Every now and then he would climb into the empty casket and practice lying down inside it, then get out again and carry on with his wailing.

Nasim's hands froze at the sight. He couldn't kill a man while he was crying, or praying, or eating, no matter what a dastardly villain he happened to be.

Then Raghid rose and passed down the visitors' walkway, gazing at the coffin from a distance. It was as if he were going through a rehearsal of his own death in which he played the parts of the protagonist and the audience at one and the same time, choking all the while on his copious tears.

Now fully awake, Nasim headed back to bed in a state of shock, as wooden as a corpse and with the taste of madness in his mouth. As he wrapped the blankets around him like a womb, he wondered, would I really be capable of murder? Would I have been able to kill Raghid?

◆　◆　◆

"Burheeta Burheeta, Kareer Kareer, wait, wait. Burhush Burhush, Ghalmash Ghalmash, Khawtar Khawtar, Qalanhoud Qalanhoud, Burshan Burshan,

Kazheer Kazheer, Numoushalkh Numoushalkh, Barhayoula Barhayoula, Bashkaleekh Bashkaleekh, Quzmuz Quzmuz, Inghilileet Inghilileet, Qabraat Qabraat, Ghiyaaha Ghiyaaha, Kaydhoula Kaydhoula, Shamkhaheer Shamkhaheer Shamkhaheer, Shamhaheer Shamhaheer, Bakahkatouniya Bakahkatouniya. . . !"

Nasim tossed and turned feverishly in bed, trying to regain his composure and his ability to think. The ability to think—the mind—that was what he believed in. I've got to get out of this place before I murder him, he thought. I've got to reclaim myself. I remember the decision I made so long ago—to take a stand with my brothers and sisters outside a generation that's committing suicide with good reason, or drugging itself with good reason, or where brothers fight against brothers as if they were acting out some Shakespearean tragedy. It's a generation that sacrifices itself, but its sacrifices are in vain. Its victims' cadavers are piled one on top of another along hospital corridors, with the bodies of heroes and traitors, murderers and soldiers, thieves and thieves' victims, all lying side by side.

(Once I went to a hospital to identify the body of a friend of mine after a devastating Beirut street battle. All the bodies had been stacked on top of each other in the corridor, since the cold storage rooms were filled to overflowing and there were no beds left for the wounded, with the result that the hospitals could no longer accommodate the rivers of slain that kept pouring off the streets. I had to look a long time for my friend, since they were all in heaps, with the slayer next to the slain, or on top of him, or under him. And all those brothers-turned-enemies looked as though they were in a collective embrace. In death they'd embraced, become alike. It was as though some sort of dialectical connection bound the death of each of them to that of his enemy and even led to it as its inevitable result. Or as if there were some sort of unnamable malfunction that had caused them to embrace in death rather than reach mutual understanding in life. When I saw their pictures in the newspaper the next day, the same sense of absurdity came over me again.

Whether I'm stuck in my homeland or stuck here in exile, I've got to keep myself outside the circle of violence—outside a generation that's beyond reform. I don't want to be infected with its diseases, its schizophrenia, its sadism, its masochism, or its perverse mastery of violence born of futility and numbness. I want to keep myself outside an age that's about to turn me into a killer before my twenty-sixth birthday. But, can I do it? Is it possible to dig a trench, as it were, between one generation and another? One year and another? One age and another?

The important thing is to get out of this damned mansion before I kill him. If only I could . . . I hope I can't.

◆   ◆   ◆

(Why don't I just admit that I'm still in love with him? In spite of all the sorrows he's caused me, all the disappointments and catastrophes, my blood still runs hot at the memory of those passionate days we once knew. I'm still held captive by that rustic, village boy's body of his that knew how to go roving through my hidden caverns, running his fingers over their moist walls and boulders in the shadows of rapture. He was a master at tracking my secret estuaries back to their headwaters. Then with a single thrust, the boulders would shatter to pieces, hot springs would gush forth from the depths of the planet, and my subterranean grottos would tremble as though they'd been struck by a multicolored earthquake.)

Leaving her children in the care of the boarding school headmaster, Kafa left the College de Lemare in the Versoix neighborhood. She had hoped the school's headmaster would be Swiss, but discovered instead that he was Italian—a foreigner like herself.

In any case, she'd signed the papers and paid the fees, and when they requested extra documentation such as health certificates and the like, she'd promised to supply them. She'd also been taken aback by the atmosphere of the school. She'd imagined Swiss boarding schools to be oases of erudition and self-discipline, yet found to her surprise that the place betrayed signs of being rather chaotic, and of catering to the whims of the affluent. She rushed to the taxi, anxious to get back to the hotel where she'd left Khalil sound asleep. He hadn't been roused by the racket that Rami and Fadi made before leaving, nor by the bellboy when he brought in the breakfast or the noise she made taking the boys' luggage out to the taxi. And figuring he'd be seeing them again on the weekend, she hadn't woken him up to let him say goodbye to them. After all, he hadn't slept for at least a week, and it looked as though he might stay asleep for that much longer. She, on the other hand, had woken up bright and early, rosy-cheeked, full of energy and anxious to greet her long-awaited dream: taking leave of violence-ridden Beirut and living with what remained of her family in a cozy, safe place.

The taxi returned to Geneva by an extraordinarily lovely route. Kafa gazed out at the lake, dazzled by its beauty and wishing Khalil could be there to enjoy it with her. How she missed him. It might seem an odd thing for a woman to miss her husband. But this was what Beirut had done to her and to others like her. Between one imprisonment and the next, one kidnapping and the next, one argument and the next, years had now passed since "the last time." And she couldn't take it any longer. In fact, she'd told him so quite frankly before his last stint in prison.

(I'm on fire with that wild, reckless feeling which, as I see it, can't be gotten rid of with philosophy or academics. It can't be cured by raising oneself by dint of sheer will power to the plane of lofty aspirations, or by the type of "higher knowledge" that Khalil always preaches to me about as a way of distancing me from him! So once I lit into him like a wild animal. I was so furious, I started to shake, and I couldn't see straight. Then the feeling gave way to something else, and I succumbed to a wild abandon, throwing caution to the wind. And why shouldn't I? He *is* my husband, isn't he?

As if he were joking with me, he shouted, "Kafa! Kafa!"

I dug my fingernails into his shoulders, trying in vain to cling to the wondrous village boy I'd once known. Then I caught a whiff of burning oak mingled with wild thyme, lemon verbena essence, tobacco, cooking spices, and tropical flowers. Exhaling hot breaths, their crownlike buds blossomed with a tremor in the darkness of a night sweating with profuse, impassioned sighs.

Then, persisting in his evasive jesting, he said, "What are you doing? Are you trying to rape me?!"

But by this time I'd passed beyond the realm of words. I'd descended into the mouth of the volcano and was swimming through turbid streams of red-hot lava. Unable to reply, I just went on sailing toward the bottom of the volcano, where the lava boils at its fiercest and untamable elements are hurled in all directions.

Then, throwing me to the floor like a virgin struggling to defend her honor, he screamed furiously, "You don't love me!"

Frigid winds came blowing out of his mouth, as though his words had unleashed a violent ice storm. Bitter cold, freezing rain came pouring down on me and my face was pelted with hailstones. I lay there weeping in a jungle whose branches had been frozen stiff and its greenery burned with frost.

"It's true!" he went on. "You don't love me!"

"You moron," I replied, "If I don't love you, then what do you call my passionate advances toward you?"

"You might desire me, but you don't love me."

"So," I said, "we're back to the old 'speechology' to cover up our impotence! You're no different in matters of love than you are in politics. What did you want from me? A lecture on lovemaking?"

"You've said it yourself," he retorted, "that I'm no different in matters of love than I am in politics. But your words can be used against you."

"What do you mean?"

"I mean that gentleness and sensitivity are to love what democracy is to politics. And I've been denied both."

"Well, you may have been denied democracy. But you haven't been deprived of gentleness and sensitivity, or any other aspect of love, for that matter. It's just that you've rejected me."

"I reject your lust, if that's what you mean. But I'm hungry for your love."

"You're back to words and empty theorizing again, which is a convenient way to avoid doing anything. I mean, how is it that I desire you so passionately if I don't love you?"

"Love means understanding my wounds. It means running your hands tenderly over the places where I hurt. And it means being my friend, too. But lust means trying to possess me, dead or alive, miserable or happy."

"I don't understand."

"You and I are allies, but not friends. Our alliance was born of common interests: children, family, and so on. But our friendship hasn't been born yet."

"I don't understand."

"You've never loved me. Instead you've just desired me with a passion. You've wanted to own me and control me."

"I don't understand."

"You defied your wealthy family, your relatives by marriage, your father, and the entire Beirut business community in order to pull off your own sort of business deal, namely, to take possession of me. So you never really broke with them. Instead, you carried on their professional traditions by paying no attention to the welfare or opinion of anyone but yourself."

"You're out of your mind."

"I love you. That is, I go to the trouble to try to understand you, and I care about what you do with yourself even if it's for my sake. I feel for you on account of the fact that your father named you Kafa,[8] since you were the seventh girl born to a businessman who wished he could have even one male in the family other than his sons-in-law. I know that you grew up feeling half rejected. Your mother was supposed to have a son, and she blew her last chance to do it by having you. Consequently she was never terribly affectionate or generous toward you. After all, you were always 'the girl that should have been the brother that never was'—an unforgivable sin in your society. Poor village folks like us also get angry when a girl is born. However, they always end up saying, 'When a girl comes, her daily bread comes with her,' and then they love her as much as they would have loved a boy. Rich folks, by contrast, go on feeling miserable when they see their businesses flourishing and their economic empires growing if they don't have sons to inherit them. We poor folks go on feeling just as miserable, but in our case it's because all we have to pass on to our children is poverty and misery. So yes, I feel for you. I also feel as though I've been a battleground of sorts. After all, you wanted to defy your family, to prove that you were as tough as a male. But the fact is, you didn't really go against them when you married me. Instead, you just proved that you were able to rebel like a male, that you were as strong as a male. When I look at you, I see your father's face, the face of the great Baytmouni."

"And when I look at you, I see stupidity and disloyalty."

"You're a loser of the worst sort, since when you lose, you don't know how to own up to it. Your face these days looks the way your dad's did as he watched his shops going up in flames one after another."

"You're despicable. I gave up my family to be able to marry you!"

"That's not true. They showered you with gifts and jewelry after we were married. That's how they compensated you for the price of the flat they were supposed to give you as a wedding present the way they had with your six sisters. Not one of your relatives boycotted you. The only thing they boycotted was your relationship with me. So they used to come visit you when I wasn't around."

"You're really contemptible. Instead of being grateful to them for taking care of me while you were roaming like a hobo from one prison to another—out of work, neglecting your family, and depriving your children of support and safety—you rebel and complain!"

8. The name Kafa literally means, "That's enough!"

"You only claim to love me, and you play the deprived, mistreated wife. But have you ever once asked me how I feel about what's happening to my home-land? Or what I think about when I see oppression all around me? Or about the terror that grips me when I see the enemy devouring me, friends neglect-ing me and allies attacking me?"

"You know I don't like politics."

"This isn't politics. This is our life. These are the sorts of things that deter-mine whether our house will be blown up or not, whether you'll be able to find clothes for your children, and whether we'll have a homeland left tomorrow or will end up living in occupied territory. You're thinking about leaving, not about what happens to your country. The only thing on your mind is running away. As for me, I'm concerned about the future of my children. Under whose flag will they grow up to be young men? And will they have to go to the bat-tlefield the way we've been forced into the infernal internecine fighting that we're embroiled in now?"

"You know I don't like violence. In fact, I despise it in all its forms. But that doesn't mean that I don't love you. If I didn't, I could have left you a long time ago without being criticized by anybody."

"But you will leave me—once you've gotten the curse of my body out of your system, and when you're finally convinced that you can't just use me to fulfill your own dreams. I'm nothing but a means to an end as far as you're con-cerned. You don't love me for myself, but only for what you can do through me. You want me to be some sort of steed that can carry you to the land of pleasure and riches. It never even occurs to you to stop and wonder what it is that torments me, or who I really am."

"And you, have you ever thought about what it is that torments me?"

"What torments you is your craving to be off for the land of dreams. And what torments me is my desire to stay in my own country no matter what it costs."

"What a brilliant theorist you are. You're so dazzled by your eloquence and your ability to lay out the facts just the way you'd like them to be, you don't even stop to notice Widad's dead body—Widad, our little girl. I avoid even mentioning her so as to spare both your feelings and mine. But yes, I do want to be off for somewhere else, in hopes of keeping our other children alive. And I ask, is this entity that all you savage men claim to be recreating what you'd call a homeland? Your daughter was killed as a result of a feud between some of your buddies over the right way to liberate Palestine and Lebanon. Every one of them had his own viewpoint on how it should be done. And five-year-old Widad paid the price. Her death didn't serve the cause of liberating either Palestine or Lebanon. Instead, it happened on account of a useless argument over how to liberate them."

"Your grief over your daughter isn't anything compared to your vindictive glee over revolutionaries' misfortunes. You really are a product of your class."

"There you go again, withdrawing into your stronghold of words and theories. You're all just a bunch of frauds on the run. You run away from having to face the body of the woman you love, and from the enemy you hate. You flee from honesty and take refuge in rhetoric. Remember, Khalil. Our little girl was killed because you and your cronies don't know the meaning of dialogue except as a way of avoiding the facts . . . and distorting them."

"Don't turn my own weapon against me. And don't dig your fingernails any deeper into my wounds. You know the heartache I've suffered over Widad's death. You also know how I've suffered for the sake of achieving freedom and the kind of democracy that's based on open dialogue. Or rather, I've suffered because of the impossibility of having either freedom or democracy without real dialogue. You know that the main reason for all our troubles is my insistence on telling the truth as I see it."

"You're back to lecturing again. I was reminding you of Widad's death as a way of telling you that I don't want Fadi and Rami to be killed, too, especially in view of the fact that as long as you and I go on the way we are, we're not very likely to have any more children."

"First you belittle my pain, and then you insult my masculinity. All right, then. But it's your fault that Widad died. After all, you're the one who left her playing in the street when you went to the hairdresser's that day."

"How ridiculous can you be?! Do you mean to say that every woman who goes to the hairdresser should be dragged into court on charges of conspiracy to kill her children?"

"Whoever heard you talking would think you'd graduated from law school, not from a private girls' college for teaching home economics, languages, and piano to rich kids."

"The fact that I'm a rich man's daughter doesn't nullify my right to self-defense. No mother living in Beirut could possibly have kept her kids cooped up in the house more than I have. And why do we do it? To keep the streets clear for the grownups to 'play.' And they go on 'playing' for years without even cleaning up after themselves. Then our children come along and play with the remains of the big people's toys. That's all that Widad and the neighbor kids did. They ended up playing with a live bomb in the empty lot next door, and it exploded on them."

"You're just using her memory as a way to carry out your plans."

"Well, it's no sin to defend what children I have left. This city is no longer fit for children, or for ideas, or for fighting, for that matter. So it isn't a crime for me to wish I could leave with my family the way thousands of others have done. Now that you and your buddies have taken over my children's playgrounds and left mines among their toys, I'm not going to let you kill any more of them.")

By this time the driver had pulled up in front of the hotel.

Chiding her in a gentlemanly manner for her slowness to get out, he asked, "Is there somewhere else you'd like to go?"

She'd forgotten where she was and that she needed to get moving. So, taking the hint, she read the figure in the meter and paid him without saying a word. As she got out of the car, she hurriedly slammed the door shut in hopes of leaving her nightmare on the back seat. Otherwise, she feared, it might haunt her for the rest of the day.

◆　◆　◆

Khalil awoke to find himself stretched out on a bed in a lavishly furnished room. Where am I? he wondered. As the question flashed through his head, the answer came pouring forth in a cascade of horrific events.

He recalled the day before. The flight. The road to the airport. The shooting. The airplane. Geneva. Could all that have taken place in a single day? All he knew for certain was that he'd slept and slept. Then, as if in a dream, he'd seen Kafa get up and put on her clothes. He'd heard Rami and Fadi giggling at each other and watched them gobble down their breakfast. Suitcases had been packed. A porter had come in and a porter had gone out, both of them decked out in formal attire. As for him, he'd been alternately floating and sinking, seeing and not seeing. He would open his mouth to say something, then drift off again. Tossing and turning, he faded in and out, in and out, with every member of his body paralyzed by an overwhelming fatigue.

He looked at his watch. It was 12:30. Then he opened the curtain to find a coquettish sun peeking down at him from behind a translucent veil of clouds. Could he really have slept that long? And why not? After all, he hadn't slept for a full seven days. In fact, he hadn't *truly* slept for a full seven years. He got up sluggishly. Then, peering out the window, he let out an involuntary gasp at the splendorous sight that met his eyes. Before him lay a lake of awesome grandeur, and white swans floating atop its untroubled surface with long necks that made him think of question marks prancing across the water. The scene also included flowers and colorful, picturesque trees, an enormous fountain that seemed to break forth into the blue expanse beyond like a river emerging from an enchanted land and emptying into the heavens. He saw boats with multicolored sails, and on the opposite shore, lush hills with that distinctive composite hue that combines innumerable shades of green into one. The hills were also covered with buildings with red-tiled roofs. Do you suppose those houses are inhabited by human beings like me? he wondered. People with children? Folks who gaze out at the beauty all around them without having to catch their breath and without feeling guilty, terrified, or confused? As these thoughts went through his mind, he was overcome by an extraordinary sense of grief, a feeling akin to nausea in the face of a beauty so resplendent that it can neither be touched nor contained, or like a sense of pained covetousness in the face of the impossible.

The sight reminded him of Kafa's body, the thought of which made him feel ashamed and humiliated. After all, she'd been turning into the man of the house—taking the children to school and spending her own money on them while he lay sleeping in a posh hotel the likes of which he couldn't afford for even a single night. He felt about as respectable as a hooker who doesn't get up till noon. He was ending up just the way he'd feared he would: a destitute man being supported by his well-to-do wife. He'd tried pursuing a path of opposition, the path of resistance and the struggle for freedom. But his comrades had thrown him back on his own doorstep in a state of collapse, then shadowed him all the way to the airport.

He decided to get dressed and go look for a job. First, though, he'd top off the misery of his day with a smoke. When he went over to get a cigarette to devour, he found the letter in recommendation of his wretched person on the table. Kafa had left it where he couldn't help but see it: beside his pack of cigarettes.

He'd go to the restaurant without delay. He'd start work that very day. But was Kafa really foolish enough to think that a self-respecting accountant would be able to make a fortune anywhere in the world? Or was she trying to push him into doing the sorts of degrading side jobs that bring in the real money? None of the catastrophes he'd been through so far could even compare with the disaster of being supported by a woman, whether he happened to love her or not. So, her sister's husband had written the letter of recommendation? His rich, blood-sucking brother-in-law who'd gotten rich off the war by trading in glass, rice, flour, benzine, rubbing alcohol, Valium, gas lamps, and home electric generators—in other words, in all those things the horrors of war had turned into necessities for Lebanon's ill-fated citizens? In any case, he'd take this job even if it turned out to be the Devil himself who'd signed the letter. The important thing was to start this very day. Or night. And if the restaurant didn't need an accountant, he'd work as a waiter or a shoeshine boy. He'd do anything to keep from having to be supported by Kafa with Baytmouni money.

When he left the hotel he didn't see Kafa, who was walking with her head down in the direction of the lift.

◆　◆　◆

He got into a taxi and read the driver the address on the recommendation letter.

(So, here I am heading for a place I know nothing about in a city I've never set foot in before, to start a job on the first day after my arrival even before I've had a thing to eat. This must be what they call "tourism for the down-and-out.") Just then he was ravaged by a fierce hunger pang. He also remembered that he hadn't shaved, and that he was still wearing the same shabby clothes he'd had on when he fled from Beirut. Meanwhile, the taxi went sprinting down spotless streets as placid as a sleeping child. There wasn't a trace of refuse to be seen, nor of anyone who might be described as poor. Everything around him was enveloped in a translucent golden halo of opulence and relaxation. The elegance of the taxi driver, the evident well-being of passersby, and the skipping of the children, the polished beauty of the women and the supercilious glances of their pampered dogs, all exuded an aura of affluence and ease. And everyone could be seen reflected against the backdrop of sumptuous shop display windows that were so clean, they fairly sparkled.

The taxi sped over the Mont Blanc Bridge, moving along in tranquil silence with scores of other cars. He didn't hear a single horn screech, and people's faces weren't charged with nervous irritability. The River Rhone glided along its predetermined course, flanked on either side by ducks and swans, lovers and tourists, by flowers so vibrant they seemed to be sighing, and trees dotting the horizon. Everything in sight was bathed in the sun's blessing, and the city seemed to bare itself to receive the touch of its warm, golden fingers. Half-clad girls lounged on park benches, while older women lay stalking the sun's bronze blessing. When eventually the taxi emerged from this festival of the sun, it entered a side street and the driver pulled up in front of a restaurant with an impressive-looking entrance. Then, suddenly remembering that he didn't have a single Swiss franc to his name, Khalil froze in dismay. However, he reached into his pocket anyway as he prepared himself to explain his situation to the driver. And what should he discover but a fifty-franc bill!

(That woman—she thinks of everything. She doesn't miss a single detail when it comes to something that matters to her. For five years she played the helpless, submissive wife as a way of avoiding responsibility. And now, she's captain of a getaway ship who doesn't let a thing pass her notice. In this Napoleonic scheme of hers to invade Switzerland, she wouldn't let the slightest thing escape her.)

He pushed the restaurant door open and went in. Once inside, he was received by a waiter of German extraction who pointed to his watch and said, "We don't serve meals here after 1:30 P.M. Sorry."

He didn't *seem* terribly sorry. In fact, he seemed to make the announcement with a sort of vindictive, if well-mannered glee.

"I'm not here to eat," replied Khalil. "I need to see someone."

Then, taking the letter out of his pocket, he went forward into the spacious, dimly lit inner room. Illumined by nothing but candles on the tables, it was as dark as an air-raid shelter. Or was this what people termed, "romantic lighting"? He'd almost forgotten about that sort of thing. Instead, he'd come to associate candles with bombings, power outages, the misery of war and the wailing of young children. As for "romantic lighting," that would have meant bright lights the length of a ceiling that hadn't been ravaged by shells! He cast a sweeping, thoughtful glance around the place.

At one table a few patrons were sipping their coffee, while at another someone was asking for the tab. He headed toward the counter, where an employee sat behind a moneybox and an adding machine which Khalil figured probably didn't know how to subtract. The worker, who had Arab-looking features, was talking to someone standing beside him. The man standing up looked familiar somehow, and Khalil felt something flutter deep inside at the sight of him. A name almost floated to the surface of his memory, but then everything vanished like so many bubbles when the German-looking waiter caught up with him and said suspiciously, "What is it that you want, sir?"

Clinging to the letter as if it were a life buoy, Khalil was suddenly overcome by a sense of shame and humiliation. (Here I am: hungry, in a city I've never seen before, and looking for someone I don't know in order for him to give me a job out of respect for a man I detest along with his entire clan and everything he stands for!)

Gathering up what remained of his badly eroded courage, he recomposed himself lest his voice tremble when he spoke. However, not having uttered a word of French since his university days, nearly the only thing he could get to come out of his mouth was the name written on the letter: Mr. Shafiq Abi 'Ati.

"I want to see Mr. Shafiq Abi 'Ati," he said. "I have a letter for him."

The other three men burst out laughing as if he'd just told a hilarious joke.

Then the employee seated behind the moneybox added playfully, "That would be difficult now."

"Please . . . I've got to see him."

And they burst out laughing again. Khalil wasn't in any mood to join in. Instead, he felt gloomier than ever. Grief and helplessness gathered in his throat like clouds laden with salty tears. Joining the waiter in an attempt to humor him, the cashier said, "No one knows where he resides anymore. But you can try to find him if you insist!"

Gathering his strength again, Khalil repeated, "I would like to see Mr. Shafiq, if you please."

"That's impossible. But if you manage to do so and then make it back here again, we'll make you a millionaire!"

In polite desperation, Khalil repeated, "I have a letter for him that I must deliver in person."

Insulting him with equal politeness, the German-looking waiter said, "Go look for him, but don't come back here, since he won't be coming back."

Then, wanting to clear up the confusion and put an end to the fit of frivolity that had come over his two friends, the man that Khalil thought he recognized came up to him and said, "Mr. Shafiq is dead."

(The bastard. He died so he wouldn't have to do anything for a poor guy like me. I know what these folks are like. They're willing to die themselves if only they can make sure that you'll die along with them. And now what am I going to do? The hotel bills . . . the kids in school. . . .)

"He died a month ago," the man continued. "People die in Geneva, too. Even the rich ones."

"Dead . . . dead. . ."

"Are you a relative of his?"

"Do I look like it?" he asked, pointing to his threadbare clothes, now baggy on him from his days of imprisonment and his flight from the grave-yard execution.

"Why are you so upset about his death, then?"

(Because his death means my death, too.) Rather than say what was on his mind, Khalil simply apologized and withdrew. By this time the restaurant clientele had begun to leave as well.

So, bidding farewell to his friend sitting behind the moneybox, the man with the familiar face caught up with Khalil and asked him, "Are you an Arab?"

"Yes, I am."

"Would you mind if I spoke to you in Arabic?"

When Khalil heard these words, tears nearly came to his eyes.

"You'd be most welcome to, brother," he replied.

"Is there anything I can do for you?"

"Well, I was bringing Mr. Shafiq a letter of recommendation in hopes of his helping me find a job."

"I'm sorry."

"Thanks. But it's my problem, not yours."

"Everybody has some sort of problem, whether real or imaginary. But the problem of looking for work is a real one. Every time I'm between jobs, I suffer from it, too. Every time I get fired. . ."

Having stopped near the stairway leading out of the restaurant, they looked at each other thoughtfully in the candlelight, but neither could see very much. With the concern that weighed so heavily on him turning into a wordless cry, Khalil thought, I know this man. It seems I know him . . .

Then without forethought, he said, "My name is Khalil Dar', though I'm sure that means nothing to you."

"And my name is Amir Nealy, though I'm not an amir[9] of anything but poverty."

"Amir Nealy? You're Amir Nealy?"

"Most proudly, and most humbly. Which, of course, means nothing to anyone!"

(I've been beaten on this man's account. I've carried his words around with me from trench to trench and prison to prison. Like an addict or someone consumed by a single passion, I've made the rounds with his writings among brothers-turned-enemies, and I've nearly gotten killed trying to spread his message. I've spent more time studying his books than I have getting to know my wife's body, and I've been more moved by his torment than I have been by the wounds in Widad's dismembered corpse. He's wandered about in my home. He's visited me in prison. He's invaded my dreams. His words have come out of my mouth during nights filled with bombing and brokenness. He's shared my coffee and my food. His voice has cleansed me whenever I've had the good fortune to take a bath or sleep in a clean bed. Without realizing it, he's planned the most recent years of my life. Yet here I am standing before him as though he were just one more stranger.

What an ache it causes for a reader to love a writer who knows nothing about him. What a distressing alienation there is between two people when one of them knows the other with a thoroughness bordering on distraction, while the latter is ignorant of the former with a completeness as deadly as it is innocent. The one-sided human bond that develops between reader and writer is perilous, even devastating. A writer loves his readers wholesale, as though they were some imaginary corporate body with tens of thousands of faces. But the reader loves the writer with a passion, in the most direct, personal way.

I've been a fool. I'm in love with ideas which just happen to be associated with the name Amir Nealy, whereas they could just as easily have been associated with someone else's. I owe allegiance to the ideas themselves, not to this stranger standing in front of me.) Yet despite this carefully thought out conviction, Khalil's heart was filled with a childish bitterness and an inexplicable desire for revenge of the sort he might have felt if he'd been violently in love with someone to whom he couldn't declare his feelings.

9. The Arabic word *amir* means "prince"; hence the play on words here.

"You look upset," Amir went on. "May I treat you to a cup of coffee?"

Khalil nodded in acceptance. Once they were out on the sidewalk, he took a long, careful look at his companion. He was surprised to find that he was far younger than he had expected and more handsome than he appeared in his pictures. He'd imagined him to be in his fifties, only to find that he was in his early forties. He was simply dressed, youthful in his gestures and robustly built yet slender. He smiled easily and spontaneously, and when he did so, his even, symmetrically arranged teeth glistened, his eyes twinkled with the honeylike sweetness of a child, and his face glowed with genuine goodwill and concern.

(Here I am looking him over while he does the same to me. I haven't shaved, and he's sure to notice the dark rings under my eyes and the worry lines on my forehead. Yet I know he won't be embarrassed to be seen with me in these ratty clothes I've got on. After all, in his books, at least, he's a friend to people like me who don't stand out in any particular way. He identifies not with the people who are the most good-looking, successful, or powerful, but with those who have the most worries.)

They sat in the coffee shop looking at each other without saying a word. Meanwhile, Khalil crowned his misery with a cigarette. When the waiter came around Amir asked him, "What will you have to eat with your coffee?"

So then, he thought, I look hungry.

"I'm not hungry. Really I'm not."

"A cheese sandwich? Chicken?"

"I'm not hungry."

Speaking to the waiter, Amir said, "Four cheese sandwiches, and four chicken sandwiches. Four glasses of lemonade, and a cup of coffee for me."

Then both men burst into a long laugh, which was followed by an equally long silence.

Khalil lit another cigarette, anticipating the blessed arrival of the food. He didn't take notice of anyone in the restaurant or scrutinize the decor. Instead he was suddenly overwhelmed by hunger, which raised its banners high above all his other senses, as well as his thoughts, his worries, and his sorrows. When the food finally made its appearance several eons, or minutes, later, he proceeded to devour it without the least embarrassment. He preferred gobbling down his food like a savage in the presence of someone who understood his hunger to eating with silverware in the hotel restaurant, then having Kafa pay the bill with what remained of the Baytmouni fortune. When he'd finished his meal, the blood coursed anew through his veins and he regained his ability to love, hate, refuse, admire, and take proper notice of the people around him, including Amir who, although his presence was disconcerting, nevertheless refrained from asking him any personal questions. He didn't, for example, ask him, Do you read? Do you know that I'm a famous writer and a noted Arab intellectual? Have you read my writings? When are you going to bow down before me in admiration? Aren't you going to ask me to pose for a photograph with you, or to autograph a book or shirt, or to tattoo my name on your chest or your derriere? Are you going to tell me how wonderful I am, and what a thrill it is for you to be able to shake my hand—the hand that I write with?

Nor did the conversation take any other direction, one, for example, that would have led to talk about his "genius" and how much others admire him. For example, he didn't ask: So what's your story? Tell me about how you've failed so that I can tell you my success story—how I pulled myself up by my own bootstraps and achieved greatness and stardom. . . .

If Amir *had* asked him to tell his story just then, he wouldn't have uttered a word of the dialogue that for so long he'd imagined them having some day. As for that conversation, it would have gone something like this:

("Why?"

"I've become homeless because of you."

"How?"

"I refused to take your books out of my shop display window and replace them with 'their' newspapers and leaflets."

"Where?"

"In Beirut, where we've been fighting each other like wild beasts for the sake of peace. Where everybody represses everybody else for the sake of freedom and democracy."

"When?"

"Ever since extremists, adventurers and foreign agents exposed our inconsistencies as a way of achieving political or personal gain. Ever since we got so busy devouring everybody else that we were distracted from the real issues and forgot why we'd taken up arms in the first place. And until we reached the point of fighting against each other in the shadow of airplanes that bomb us all without exception, yet without our taking any notice of them."

"And then. . . ?"

"Then we did just the opposite of what you write about in your books.

Some people supported their actions based on misinterpretations of things you've said, practicing repression in the name of freedom and murdering in the name of liberation. They've sanctioned hypocrisy, discrimination, distortion of facts, tyranny, and suppression, stealing people's livelihoods and their lives as well under the pretext of tactical necessity. They've befriended the enemy and humiliated and abused friends in the name of strategy."

"And then. . . ?"

"Then we woke up. We woke up to find the barricades in the streets reaching inside us, and the battle lines stealing into our hearts. We'd become so barbaric that some people were sacrificing themselves on the altar of the past. Besides which, the shelling and bombing weren't our only tragedy anymore. By this time, we'd turned into shells being launched at some arbitrary target, then mortally wounding some loved one before even reaching the enemy. Every one of us had turned into a stray bullet, a bundle of explosives on its way to destroying a buddy, a live missile being guided toward destruction. As for the lovely ruin we'd hoped would be the beginning of an edifice still lovelier, it had turned into an all-encompassing, permanent wasteland."

"But . . ."

"The nightmares that we'd mistakenly imagined would give birth to a dream lost their power to deceive us, and we fell into a vicious cycle. The dream had given birth to a nightmare, and the nightmare to still more nightmares. The dream had been taken away from us and wedded to repression. And nightmares were their inevitable offspring.")

The two men sat together in silence until Amir asked, "Will you have a cup of coffee?"

"No, thanks."

Then, taking out a pen, Amir tore off a piece of one of the restaurant paper napkins and wrote a telephone number on it. Giving it to Khalil, he said, "Call me if you'd like. I have to be going now. I'm sorry about what's happened to you, and I wish you well," whereupon he got up quickly, paid the bill and disappeared into the crowds that filled the street.

Khalil stayed frozen in place. Had that really been Amir Nealy himself, or. . . ? Or had he been dreaming? Had he begun hallucinating? (He fed me without trying to impress me, or make me pay the bill as a way of flattering him or showing admiration. He didn't know that I know him, or that he owes me something.)

He left the coffee shop to find himself on streets he'd never seen before. How was he supposed to get back to the hotel? He could ask for directions and save himself the taxi fare by walking back. But how was he supposed to ask for directions when he didn't know the name of the hotel?

He felt panic-stricken for a moment. However, he calmed down when he came across the box of matches that he'd picked up in the hotel room with the hotel's name and address on it. Once he'd caught a taxi, he lit up a cigarette to top off his misery, pretending not to be able to read the "No Smoking" sign posted next to the ashtray.

The driver, of course, had the right to preserve his lungs for the fun things he planned to do over the weekend. As for himself, though, he was supposed to have died several weeks earlier, and the maggots in the graveyard should already have finished off his lungs. After being devoured by larvae, there wasn't much nicotine could do to them. Horrified, the elderly taxi driver turned back toward Khalil, pointing to the cigarette in his hand as if it were a machine gun. You'll live forever, friend! thought Khalil as he complied with the driver's wishes.

◆　◆　◆

As he walked into the hotel lobby, he met up with Kafa on her way back from the beauty parlor. She was looking extraordinarily gorgeous and affluent, with her chestnut colored hair now trimmed in a modern hairdo, the deep blue eyes she'd inherited from an Anatolian grandmother who was said to have been the daughter of a pasha, her towering, curvaceous frame, and her elegant attire.

He ran his fingers over his beard in chagrin, then rushed to the elevator over the sumptuous carpet that blanketed the lobby, the corridors, and the rooms. No sooner had he touched the elevator button than he jumped at an electric shock, which, light though it was, was still a bit painful, and more than a bit frightening. He thought, here you are in a place so beautiful and safe it could qualify as the entrance to Paradise. Then without warning, you get stung by an electric shock that's as painful as it is surprising. It's enough to spread an aura of terror over everything in sight. And you begin to wonder: what other shocks lie hidden inside all the velvet-soft, purple objects that you see everywhere? You might be sitting comfortably in some vermilion armchair, closing your eyes and enjoying your life of affluence, then get up to find your clothes spattered with blood.

"What happened?" Kafa asked him.

"I was insulted and kicked out ever so politely and respectfully."

"What do you mean? Didn't you get to see him?"

"It would have been difficult."

"Well, you'll go back tomorrow. Did you leave him the letter and your telephone number? He's sure to call you."

As they came out of the elevator he said, "He won't be calling, I won't be seeing him, and I won't get a job there. He's dead."

"Dead?" Kafa echoed with a gasp. "Damn him! How could he do this to me?!"

Khalil burst out laughing with a touch of vindictive glee. Rich folks! he thought. They look at death as something bizarre and inexplicable. On one hand they take a long pause in the face of death in rituals that I find revolting: special clothes, food, weeping and wailing. Yet not one of them is actually weeping over the deceased. What they're weeping over is the fact that they're mortal, capable of being annihilated. What they're really grieving is their own approaching deaths. And the reason they wail so bitterly is that they consider their own lives so precious.

Khalil unlocked the hotel room door, then turned the knob and pushed, only to start from a new shock. This time it was Kafa's turn to laugh.

"You seem to be allergic to static electricity!" she said.

"And who is 'Static Electricity'?" he inquired.

"The carpet generates an electrical field that your body absorbs as if it were hungry for it. Then when you take hold of something metallic, your body becomes like a conducting wire."

"What I'm allergic to is this entire place. Being in a foreign country gives me an electric jolt, just the way the executioners at home used to do!"

Kafa got a hot bath ready for him—a luscious, perfumed bubble bath.

"Why don't you just wash off all the years of your past?" she suggested.

"And what about the years to come? After all, I don't have a job."

"Don't worry. We'll work something out. The important thing is that we got out of that infernal death trap alive—I mean, we got out of Beirut."

Seeming truly overjoyed, she flitted about like a butterfly that's been set free from captivity. Khalil collapsed into the bathtub like a heavy rock that's been thrown into the water. He relaxed and closed his eyes. How long had it been since he'd enjoyed a bath like this? Feeling sorry for his body after all it had been through, he pampered himself, giving special attention to his face.

After shaving off his beard he stared at the face that looked back at him from the mirror. It was a homely face, familiar-looking but half-forgotten.

(Silly woman! How could she possibly find me handsome? I'm so ugly!) He could hear her voice in the other room where she was speaking on the telephone. There was a second telephone beside him in the bathroom. He thought of lifting the receiver so that he could listen to what she was saying and find out who she was talking to. However, his amazement over the mere existence of an extra telephone in the bathroom got the better of him. Those rich folks really know how to spoil themselves, he thought. They must be afraid they'll hurt their feet going all the way to the next room to answer the phone. As for him, he hadn't even tried to protect himself from being beaten on the soles of his feet as punishment for keeping Amir Nealy's books in his shop display window. Although actually, what he'd been most concerned about wasn't Nealy's books, but his own dignity. It had been a matter of principle. Everything in the end is a matter of principle. But Kafa would never understand that. In any case, he thought, why didn't you tell her about your meeting Amir? That is, assuming it really was him. All right, then. So you're afraid of her. You know she hates the man and considers him responsible for your ruin. She thinks he's poisoned your mind and spoiled your chances of climbing the social ladder to eminence and wealth. And now, are you going to contact him and ask him for help finding work? Who have you got besides him in this electrified paradise?

When he came out of the bathroom he found Kafa beaming with joy.

"Come on," she said. "Let's go buy you some new clothes!"

He scowled at the thought, but obeyed. He knew she'd inherited her mother's habit of searching her husband's pockets while avoiding any sort of direct interrogation. With her it would always start with an unexpected paroxysm of affectionate behavior. That was the carrot phase. However, if he didn't spontaneously confess to her what was behind a telephone number or unfamiliar address written on some stray piece of paper, she'd go on to the stick phase. He thought of asking her about the fleeting telephone conversation she'd had while he was in the bathroom. But then he was overtaken by a feeling of such indifference, he didn't bother. Maybe, as usual, she'd just been complaining about something: perhaps a button on the telephone receiver was stuck, one of the lights was too bright or too dim, or the iron knob on the window was hard to work. Details. She always took pause at tiny, frivolous details, yet never went beyond them to the essences of things. For all he knew, she wasn't even aware that there was such a thing as an essence. On one hand, that's why she was so content. Yet on the other, it made her susceptible to sudden fits of grief.

"What time is it?" she asked.

Looking at his watch, he replied, "It's 12:30."

"Ridiculous. Impossible. Your watch must be slow. Set it to the right time."

Ignoring the matter, he said nothing. As they left the hotel, he gazed out at the lake, while she stared over at the display window of the shop next door to the hotel.

"It's exorbitantly expensive," she said. "But it's right for you."

Once they were inside the store, he saw a rich Arab buying a dozen silk shirts, all different colors, and a dozen suits with a single wave of the hand. Meanwhile, he was being surrounded and cheered on by attractive, pampered-looking sales attendants.

Once Kafa had spent a small fortune to make Khalil look like the son of a tycoon, they left the store. He felt mortified to be walking around in a fancy silk shirt and velvet trousers, especially knowing that she'd decked him out with Baytmouni money. But he forgot all about the Baytmouni clan at the sight of the celebration of life with which Geneva greeted them. Before long they came to the same bridge he'd crossed on his way back from being kicked out of the restaurant a little while earlier. The bridge bore a sign that read "quai du Mont-Blanc." They crossed over to the opposite shore in the midst of a dazzling, lively display: scanty attire, bodies voraciously soaking up the rays of the sun, smiles exchanged by cheerful strangers, and glances overflowing with courtesy and goodwill. The comfort of prosperity seems to make kindness a way of life, as if kindness were simply people's surplus happiness flowing out toward others. He pictured people in a sidewalk exhibition carrying placards bearing expressions like: "I love you, Life!" or, "Roast my complexion, O Sun, and come forward, my darling!" or, "I'm rich and handsome—who'd like to come after me?" or, "Flatter me—I'm wonderful!" or, "Poor, young woman seeks rich, elderly man." Then there was a contingent of Arab women tourists dressed in their national garb and carrying posters saying things like, "I own $150 million—one dollar for every poor person in my Arab nation," or, "When will my father buy Geneva?" or, "Take my fortune and give me liberty!"

They then came to a paved area that widened into gloriously beautiful public parks, where warmth danced in the gaiety of half-clad young children and in the blooming of the flowers. And that over there—was it a dazzlingly beautiful young woman, or a creature of light flying through the air? She swept along like a breeze, with a translucent complexion and a head of hair that looked like a mass of serpentine luminescence. Wearing shoes with wheels on the bottoms, she glided in and out among the other people. She wore headphones on her ears, and a radio that must have been only too delighted to nestle close to her heaving, well-endowed bosom. Yet even without it she would have had her own music, while her dulcet, winged dance and her childlike freshness made her seem like some rarely seen sparrow. How lovely a woman can be when she's anonymous, still a child, and not one's wife! He thought of Widad and got a painful lump in his throat. She'd been playing with what remained of a spent bullet on the blanket of moss that overlay a garbage heap. She'd been playing to the rhythm of gunfire that was directed at the enemy only once for every thousand times it was aimed at friends. He'd longed to give Widad a homeland fit to grow up in. But instead she'd been blown up by a shell bearing the words, "For freedom and democracy"—words his beloved comrades had forgotten in the heat of their fruitless warring. He looked affectionately over at Kafa. He blamed her and didn't blame her. Or rather, he didn't know anymore whether he did or not.

"May I treat you to some coffee?" she asked, "Or Coca Cola? Or mineral water?"

Located in the paved area leading into the parks, the café was ringed with flowerbeds. They both took a seat, and his voice softened as he whispered, "I'll have whatever you order."

"Two bottles of Coke, please," she said in her refined French. As for him, he spoke the language with the accent of an Arab country bumpkin. Topping off his misery-laced pleasure with a cigarette, he drank his Coke straight from the bottle without touching the fancy glass the waiter had brought, and without regard for Kafa's reproachful glances. A tree with old, deep roots, he was bound to retain his uncouth manners whether he was in Beirut or in Geneva.

He could hear sweet music wafting toward them from somewhere in the distance. Apparently there was a band giving a free concert in one of the public parks. He gazed thoughtfully at the young children prancing about to the music and remembered his sons Rami and Fadi. Maybe Kafa had been right when she said it was his duty to provide them with a humane climate to grow up in.

But . . . was the climate of exile fit for growing up in, even if it happened to be cozy and luxurious? Had it been "humane" of him to cut his boys off from their homeland? On the other hand, would it have been any more humane to leave them there to be killed? A voice came from somewhere deep inside him as if it were Amir speaking: "Individual solutions won't lead anywhere. If you flee with your own children, then what about all the other children in the city, not to mention the villages, the country, and the rest of the Arab world?" Damn it. Why couldn't he relieve himself of responsibility for them the way tens of thousands of his countrymen had done? Why was he gripped with such shame whenever he managed to achieve some measure of personal liberation, however insignificant? The whole thing had begun with nightmares. Be patient, man, he'd told himself. These are the birth pangs that lead to the dream. But the dream had given birth to a whole new tribe of nightmares whose warriors went dancing about with masked faces in a frantic, savage carnival of theft, looting, terror, and factionalism—a carnival that nevertheless claimed to embody the dream and sought refuge in its slogans and bywords.

Kafa was saying something and laughing. He laughed along with her mechanically without listening. He'd grown accustomed to this sort of conversation with her. He gave her a smile, then went back to where he'd been before, that is, to the wild, brutal carnival. To slaying, theft, and bloodshed, to the oppression of the unfortunate and the innocent. And all of it was being done under the pretext of liberating them. How? he wondered. How could we have fallen into this vicious cycle? Nightmare. Dream. Nightmare. Dream. He would sink, then float, sink, then float. A carnival of nightmares. He and his comrades had hoped to create a celebration of life like the one now taking place before his very eyes. Yet the sight of it filled him with a wretchedness akin to the throes of death.

As he stared at the bottle of Coca Cola, he thought back to the demonstration he'd marched in following the June defeat.[10] Only eighteen years old at the time, he'd sworn on that day never to smoke an American-made cigarette or wear imported clothes, and his comrades had taken the same oath along with him. Their wrath had been terrible, the tragedy appalling, and "consciousness" their byword. So what happened? How could they have turned into a bunch of murderers so bloodthirsty that one of them would wipe

10. That is, the military defeat suffered by the Arabs at the hands of the Israelis in June 1967.

out another for no reason but that they disagreed over the way to achieve their aims? Why all this bitter, intractable conflict over the way to do things when everyone claimed to be headed in the same direction? How had he ended up a fugitive, an outcast, an emigrant drinking Coca Cola in a sidewalk café in Geneva, Switzerland, as his homeland went up in smoke?

Then along came a bee. It lit on the Coca Cola bottle and began to lick the mouth, hovering about the edges, then plunging suddenly inside the bottle as if it had been drugged or poisoned. It fell all the way to the bottom, and Khalil thought it had died. However, it got up again with a quiver and tried to take off. Then it cleaned off its wings and walked around as if it were exploring the bottom of the bottle. It approached the transparent wall in an attempt to make an exit, only to discover that it was now held captive inside a see-through prison. He could see it behind the words "Coca-Cola" written in large letters on the bottle. As it tried in vain to fly away, it would gain some height, then collide with the glass walls and fall back down. Yet it would keep coming back for another desperate attempt to return to the mouth through which it had entered. Staring at it like a soothsayer looking into his crystal ball, Khalil felt sad to see its successive falls. At the same time, he was amazed to see its heroic, death-defying attempts to fly again every time it failed, all the while making a buzzing noise that sounded something like moaning and cursing.

As Kafa paid the bill and they left the café, Khalil kept his eye on the bottle of Coca Cola. He could see the bee still flying around inside its glass prison, trying heroically to escape.

◆   ◆   ◆

"What time is it?"

"12:30."

"Your watch has stopped," she said, pointing in proof to the exquisite, golden clock in the center of the long, indoor walkway where they were seated. After a long trek around town, they'd stopped to rest in another sidewalk café located along the walkway.

It was 5:30 P.M., and the sun was still shining. Do you suppose the sun goes down in happy cities, too? he wondered.

"Set your watch to the right time," she told him, "and shake it. Maybe you forgot to wind it."

So then, it was 5:30 P.M. It was as if the hands on his watch had been so grief-stricken that they'd come to a halt at 12:30. Was that the moment when the airplane that had brought them into exile had taken off? Did he really believe that all those events had begun only the day before? Did he believe that only twenty-nine hours earlier (or rather, thirty hours if he figured in the time difference between the two continents) he'd had his feet still planted on home soil? Was he going to spend his time here counting not just the days, but the hours? He settled into his chair, fearful that his distress might put a damper on Kafa's bliss. Poor woman. What was she supposed to do with a man like him? Consumed by the desire to possess him, she'd clothed him in the raiment of her own dream. Then the dream had disintegrated, and nothing had remained but the children. And habit. They'd gotten married before the war broke out. But by the time she'd had Fadi and they'd decided to divorce, the war had begun and they forgot about their differences. Then along came Rami, followed by Widad. After that the fighting subsided and they went back to talking about divorce. However, with Khalil spending most of his time between one prison cell and the next, they hadn't been able to pursue the matter properly. She endured until Khalil's resources finally ran out and his world betrayed him, whereupon she picked him up and brought him to safety. To her kind of safety, at least. But what about him? She'd grown so accustomed to his long silences that only rarely did she try to engage him in conversation anymore. Or was she just too busy spying out her dream, which had now clothed itself in the garb of a city?

The festival of life continued exuberantly up and down the indoor walkway. Khalil gazed over at a young man in his early thirties. He was wearing shorts, and had his arm around his sweetheart as they looked together into a pharmacy display window. His face free of worry lines, he looked like the epitome of youthfulness and energy. It was as if the two of them weren't the same age—as if he were young enough to be Khalil's son. He and his girl exchanged a kiss, and none of the passersby even took any notice—that is, except for the Arabs among them.

Then he looked over at a shop whose display window was ablaze with the glitter of diamonds and gold. Just then the shop door opened to reveal a group of veiled Arab ladies. The women were being escorted outside by the proprietor and his wife, whose face glowed with delight. Shopping as they had been for diamonds, emeralds, and other treasures, they no doubt knew by heart the price of an ounce of gold or of a one-carat diamond. He wondered, do you suppose there's a single one among them who knows that the Israelis swallowed up south Lebanon in three days, and that just yesterday afternoon they were preying on the outskirts of Beirut and demolishing its airport? The reason he was being so silent was simply that he didn't dare let Kafa know what was going on in his heart. He could see the look of envy in her eyes. He knew she wished she were in those women's place, and that she hoped she'd never have to hear another word about Beirut, Lebanon or the Arab homeland. All she wanted to hear about were the prices of gold and diamonds, provided, of course, that she'd be able to afford them. It was true. She was "in love" with Khalil, but she didn't really love him. She found him extremely handsome, yet he knew he wasn't. She imagined him to be stern and dignified and used to chide him affectionately, saying, "You he-man, you!" Yet the fact was that his heart melted with sorrow over lots of things besides women. She dreamed of tasting the village-boy virility that she'd become so addicted to in their first years of marriage. And now it was as if she were trying in vain to restore him to his youth.

Bursting with vivacity and charm, every now and then she would respond to something with a gasp of admiration. She eyed what was going on around her with the greatest of interest. And men passing by eyed her back with equal admiration. (The fact is, she really is gorgeous. And you're really a blockhead. Take a good look at the festival going on here, and let yourself go with the flow. You failed to realize your own dream, so why not share in hers? Give it a try, at least. . . .)

So he ordered a glass of firewater and gulped it down. A warm feeling went coursing through him, and Kafa encouraged him to have another drink and another cigarette. However, she abstained herself—not out of virtue but rather out of fear that such vices might give her wrinkles. As for him, he began merging with the rhythm of the crowd, which seemed on fire with exhilaration. Now no longer a spectator, he heard the melodious sound of delicate bells. Turning his head to see where the sound was coming from, he saw the clock at the end of the walkway. As the clock struck six, one of its exquisitely carved doors opened, and out came a promenade of gilded figurines that glided over the surface of a narrow pathway. Surrounded by lights and music, the procession headed toward another door located on the other side of the artfully made timepiece, which extended the width of the walkway's end. The figures moved forward with the unhurried leisure of the affluent, then vanished inside the other door, which closed promptly behind them. As he took in the sight, Khalil felt as though he were a gilded doll in another festival, a festival whose figurines were human beings, and whose music was the chirping of lovebirds and their heartrending sighs of adoration.

The next thing Khalil saw was a caravan of young, backpack-toting European tourists hiking along with merry vivacity. When he was their age, the only hiking he'd done was to go marching in demonstrations.

As Khalil gazed at the young tourists, he was taken aback by a rare sight. Walking behind the tourists was a man dressed as they were—wearing a cotton shirt, shorts, and sandals, and with a Boy Scout pack dangling from his back, which most likely contained a sleeping bag, hygiene paraphernalia, and a mess kit. However, the man must have been at least seventy years old, and he didn't look the least bit deranged. (They've stolen our youth from us!) Khalil watched the elderly man with envy. The flesh on his aging legs quivered with every step, yet he seemed perfectly content, and took every step with gaiety, as if he were on his way to his grave! Khalil felt ashamed in the presence of this marvelous old man, so full of passion to embrace the innocent delights offered freely by the cosmos, and so determined to experience the pleasure of living until his very last breath. The infernal voice he knew so well nearly emerged from somewhere deep inside him to ask, "But what *is* the real pleasure of living?" But he silenced it with another gulp of liquor. Then he proceeded to devour his wife's lips in a ravenous kiss, with the voraciousness of a hungry man after seven lean years. His voice throaty with desire, he said, "Come on, Kafa. Let's go back to the hotel."

◆　◆　◆

Dazzlingly beautiful, stretched out over the blueness of the horizon, her breezes blew hot against his vessel. As he sailed along, white seagulls flapped their wings overhead, their cries sounding as though they were struggling for breath. And on he sailed. Ports where ivory and spices were to be found. Quarries of warm marble. Firm suppleness. The wind blew up, he unfurled his sails to embrace the horizon, and his boat picked up speed. Alternately rising and descending atop the waves, he went gliding along enchanted shores, past caves, through beds of seaweed. Moist and warm were the mermaids' songs and the sounds of their echoes against the cavern walls. Hurrying now, the boat rose and fell, rose and fell on its way to its port of destination. Ah, the port! Yet try as he might to drop anchor there, he couldn't. It was as if the chains used to let it down into the water had grown too rusty. Exerting his last ounce of energy, he broke into a sweat and his panting grew louder and louder. But he couldn't. He couldn't. He thought back to the port's delights, to the beating of the drums, to the fires of tender affection, and to the joyous earthquake at the rainbow's end. Yet he couldn't.

"Sorry . . ." he heard himself say in a sheepish voice.

He didn't dare turn on the light lest he see the disappointed look on her face.

"Try again," she urged.

As he took her into his arms, he could feel two masses of barbed wire protruding from her bosom and being plunged into his chest. Just then the telephone rang, but he didn't have enough voice to answer it. Instead, he just lay there defeated before the portals of her body-metropolis. Defeated before her delectable strongholds. Defeated, his wife now a cord of plaited barbed wire.

She answered the telephone with a calm that he found astounding. "Hello, Mr. Nadim!" she chirped. "Oh, yes. I asked about you but didn't find you. So I left you our address. Really? That's very kind . . . ah. . . . Oh, we went for a bit of an outing. What's that? Fine, I'll tell him. I'm sure he'll be pleased to meet you, too. And I also, of course. Tonight? Oh, I'm sorry, but that won't be possible. We have another engagement. Fine. Until tomorrow, then. Goodbye."

She hung up the receiver and, with the authoritative self-assurance of the stronger party, the promulgator of commands and prohibitions, she said, "That was Nadim. I tried calling him yesterday while you were taking a bath but he wasn't in. He'd like to see you . . . to see us. And before I'd even asked anything of him, he mentioned something about a job. You'll talk to him tomorrow. That's what we agreed on."

He made no reply. He was bathed in cold sweat as if he had a fever. Or as if he'd been running through a mine that was caving in on top of his head, trying in vain to pull his weary body forward with as much strength as a spent bullet inside a rusty revolver.

She turned on the light switch. Then she pressed another button that lit up the television screen. He looked at his watch, which still said 12:30. Then he looked over at the screen, which showed a picture of a clock that read 7:30 P.M., its second hand completing its orbit in repeated, silent twitches. So then, he'd left Beirut a day, a night and part of a day earlier to come to this "safe" place, where he'd thrown his children into some boarding school without a proper goodbye, and made love to his wife only to discover that he couldn't satisfy her anymore.

So he topped off his misery with a cigarette.

At 7:30 sharp, the clock with the silent, pulsating second hand disappeared, and in its place there poured forth a kind of high-strung-sounding music. Then a map of the continents of the world appeared on the screen, followed by the face of a news announcer. The announcer had a soothing, intelligent-looking face that bore no resemblance to the faces of his wife or of some female news announcers he'd seen in Lebanon, whose heavily made-up features and garish, dangly earrings reminded him of Christmas tree ornaments. Here was a human being that you could listen to rather than stare at her glorified face and wonder, how can she smile while the city's burning to the ground? And why does she act like a spoiled child crying over spilled milk when war and destruction are all around her?

The first news item was about Lebanon.

Kafa stayed relaxed in bed, while Khalil gave a nervous start. Then he drew the curtains back, letting the light from the long summer's day come pouring into the room.

The announcer spoke about the Israeli bombardment, which had begun on Friday, June 4, with the bombing of Beirut's sports complex and the Sabra refugee camp and which had now entered its fifth consecutive day. She then presented some rare documentary footage that had been shot by the Swiss station's representative. The same representative had been killed with camera in hand, and his assistant wounded. Thinking back to her neighbor's little girl who'd burned to death on a school bus on the afternoon of the same ill-fated day, Kafa thanked her lucky stars that she'd been able to bring her children out of that hellhole. And in her heart of hearts, she also thanked the nincompoops who had tried to murder her good-for-nothing husband (not realizing, of course, how good-for-nothing he really was). If it hadn't been for them, uprooting him and bringing him out of Lebanon would have been about as easy as pulling up the village oak tree with her bare hands.

Khalil got all choked up when he saw the footage, which showed Israeli bombs turning streets he knew and loved into charred ruins. Seeing a view of one side of the sports complex, he wondered, is that Burj Al-Barajneh, or the Shatileh refugee camp? And there's Bi'r Hassan Road, the Khaldeh Highway

and Na'imeh. He knew the Israelis had been launching attacks on civilian ve-
hicles. And he knew what it felt like. Sidon was now under siege and the
Shaqif Fortress had been occupied, which meant that the hordes were coming
closer and closer.

(What am I doing here? What have they done to me? What have I done
to myself? What did every one of us do to his buddies? How on earth could
our watchmen have fallen sleep when they should have been protecting the
vineyard?)

The news announcer confirmed that the Beirut International Airport had
been closed at 1:00 P.M. on the previous day—Monday—after a small number
of flights had taken off before noon. Kafa was overjoyed. So then, they'd managed to get out of that hellhole alive on the last plane.

Khalil said nothing. (So then, the airport's closed and there's no way for me
to get back. I ought to be there, not here warring in vain to stake out territory
on the slopes of my wife's body. We'd been making preparations for just such a
day as this. And here I am a prisoner in this electric utopia.)

The ever-forgotten cigarette between his lips was turning into ashes,
which began falling in stages onto the bedsheet, then strewing themselves
about like the charred remains of someone who'd been burned alive. And
without knowing why, he thought back to the frenzied flight of the bee he'd
seen inside the Coke bottle at the sidewalk café.

"Why do you insist on scattering your ashes all over the bed, the floor, and
everywhere?" Kafa asked reproachfully. "Here, take the ashtray."

As he took it, he imagined that one of the butts in it bore the image of his
face.

◆   ◆   ◆

"In the name of Qaher, Jalil, Halikh, Malkha, Mahloukhi, Mamloukhim. . . .
Respond, O Lord Tahitmaghilyal, in the name of the One to whom all necks
are laid bare, to Whom the most proud and haughty seraphs fall down in obei-
sance, in the name of the Living, Eternal God, Ruler and Sustainer of heaven
and earth. I beseech thee by the truth of these names and these holy verses to
bring the spiritual powers of Sakhr Ghanamali into subjection to me. Make
him putty in my hands, ready to do my bidding."

Raghid sat in the presence of his sorcerer like a little child. He believed in
figures, logic, and the untold numbers of computers he made use of in his of-

fices. He believed in videos, logarithm tables, telexes, and bribes, be they in the form of money or women. However, he still found comfort in the support he received from his wizard. His mother had always gone to the fortuneteller-astrologer in the lovely old Arab city where he was born. And so had his father, albeit on the sly. Government ministers and rulers had stolen to his house under cover of darkness in that age gone by. And he'd been told that although the old order had passed away and times had changed, the new generation still went to the astrologer. The clientele had changed, but the rituals had remained.

Without daring even to look into Sheikh Watfan's face, Raghid said, "I want you to tie the tongue of his twin brother Hilal. He wants to see harm come to me, and is preventing people from receiving what's best for them. I want to build them an airport, and he wants to keep them on mule and horse back. Please, sir."

"Please, sir . . ." were words that he used with no one but the sorcerer. Even in his meetings with emirs, revolutionaries, mercenaries, and heads of state he had no need for them. His sorcerer was the only person who struck fear in his heart and whose powers he actually believed in.

"Simm, himm . . . deaf, dumb, dumb, blind so that they see not. . . . O God, as you bound the jaws of lions to protect the prophet Daniel, bind the tongues of men who would harm Raghid Zahran.

"Shaqyoush Shaqyoush, Shardaloush Shardaloush, Lietoush Lietoush, Qatoush Qatoush, Shanyoush Shanyoush, Kielamoush Kielamoush, Mayenoush Mayenoush, Hiedaboush Hiedaboush, Sharnoush . . . Kharfiedous, Nariyoush . . . bind the tongue of Hilal Ghanamali with urgency, with haste, without delay . . .

"Hamattum 92119 and for him this day, seal their mouths, O God, seal the tongue of Hilal Ghanamali. . ."

"Please, sir, I want him to fall ill. And since he's present in Geneva right now, make him even more ill. He's come for treatment, but cause medical science to be of no use to him."

"Bring me an egg, some tar, and black ink, and an awl to bore a hole in the egg. I'll write on it what needs to be written either on Saturday or on Tuesday. I'll bore a hole in it and place it on three stones. As I place a spell on it thirty-one times, everything inside it will come flowing out. Then let Nasim bury it in a grave which no one ever visits."

"Please, sir . . . now. Please place the spell now."

"I adjure you, all ye spirits entrusted with illnesses, to afflict Hilal Ghanamali with disease. I adjure you by the truth of these names and by Qalafitriyat, by the right of some of you over others, by the truth of that which you obey, by the truth of Lajash, Louish, Shouish, by the truth of Ibki Lash Hallash, do what you have been commanded with urgency, with haste, without delay . . ."

"More, sir, more . . ."

"On Wednesday after the mid-afternoon prayer, bring me a piece of raw meat and the name of Hilal Ghanamali's mother. I'll write what needs to be written on the piece of meat, then place it in a fire that burns without ceasing. Remember to bring me the name of Hilal Ghanamali's mother."

"More, sir. More. . . . He wants to deprive people of knowledge, culture, and light. He doesn't want me to build the airport."

"Come see me again on Thursday at the hour of Venus or at the hour of Jupiter, and I'll write for you whatever is necessary to bind people's tongues and to attract clientele.

"Taghyab, Sighab, Salyoub, Hietoub, Tatyoub, Satyoub, Tatoub. . . .

"Ya Ahiya Sharahiya Adonai Asba'out, El Shaddai the Almighty, the Lord of Light Most High who, if the Angel Gabriel, the August King looked upon Him, he would bow in humble submission before the greatness and power of these names. So also let everyone who sees Raghid Zahran be brought into humble submission with dispatch, with dispatch, with haste, with haste, without delay, without delay. . ."

As the sheikh spoke, copious tears poured from Raghid's eyes. He wept like a child in the presence of his sorcerer as he had wept at the prospect of his approaching demise when it presented itself to him at his gravesite. Meanwhile, the sorcerer took a piece of special translucent paper that looked something like jerked human flesh and wrote on it the following, "This is a day on which they will not utter a word, nor will they be given permission to speak and they will seek excuses for themselves. None will speak but those to whom permission has been granted by the Most Merciful, and they will speak rightly . . ."[11] to the end of the verse. O God, I ask Thee by the truth of Sawsam Dawsam Brasam Trasam Krasam, by the beauty of Thy beauty, by the light of Thy face and by the stretching forth of Thy mercy, by the numbers 7 and 8 and their

---

11. From Qur'an 78:38.

unceasing mysteries which are from Thee and by Thy unrevealed Name, by Taha Yartah and by Kaha Barka', by the power with which the tongues of the dead and of beasts have been tied and the lions bound lest they bring harm to Daniel and Elijah for three years and seven months, and with which Thou withheld the rain so that it did not descend from the heavens to the earth. . . . I ask Thee, O God, to shield the bearer of these words, Raghid Zahran, from the tongues of all wicked people, male or female. By the chain in which their heads shall be arranged like mountains and their tongues like rows of packsaddles, keep them from speaking anything but good. O God, who silenced the evening with the stars and the stars with blazing meteors, I ask Thee to silence all creatures, human and nonhuman, male and female, lest they should speak evil of Raghid Zahran, the bearer of these words of mine. Let them speak nothing but favorable words, or let them hold their peace."

Then, enveloped in clouds of smoldering incense, the sorcerer folded up the piece of paper in a special way and handed it to Raghid, saying, "Don't open it and don't read it. But carry it with you wherever you go."

"One last question, sir. . . . Have you been consulted in the hotel by anyone who works for me? Do I know any of the people who've come to see you there?"

"Such matters are secrets of the spirit world which I am not permitted to reveal to anyone. All I do is meet people's needs. All I am is an intermediary between human beings and unseen powers. I have no way of knowing for certain whether those who come to me are in the wrong or in the right. All of them will be called to account by their Maker for their actions and intentions."

"Couldn't you possibly stay here in the mansion and stop going to your headquarters in the hotel? I'll pay whatever you ask. I'll bring you whatever you need. And you'll devote yourself exclusively to transforming base metals into gold."

"I'll consider it."

◆ ◆ ◆

Amir left the coffee shop and went wandering aimlessly through the city, having just left behind one more young man who would start going hungry within hours. One more young man who'd been catapulted out of the homeland into the promised Paradise. What was his name? Khalil Dar'? What difference did it make, anyway? Every day the homeland bled a few more, thrusting them into exile in a stream of futility. He definitely didn't belong to the category of the fugitive well-to-do who were fleeing with their treasures from the white heat of the revolutions they feared so much. Nor was he the son of a pasha. Do you suppose he might be one of those enterprising types that goes scavenging for wealth and adventure among the crumbs left on the tables of rich Arabs who've made Europe their refuge? The type whose homeland is money, whose passports are their checkbooks, and whose houses are the private airplanes that transport them from one bedroom to another all over the face of the globe? This was the type that gave no thought to any sort of public issue, or to any private one for that matter, except the matter of whether the rich would go on getting richer. So, had he come to hobnob with folks like them? Was he the type who might turn into a pimp for some third-rate dancer or singer? Judging from the dour look on his face, it wasn't likely. Besides which, thought Amir, he doesn't have the talent for that sort of thing. He hasn't got what it takes to make a good son of a bitch.

Or, he thought, maybe he's one of those people who've simply decided that there must be a better life in societies other than their own. He's educated, sensitive, and weak when it comes to facing life's cruel realities. He tried to change things in his country and failed, so he got on the first plane out and ran away.

Either that, or he never even bothered to try. Instead, he realized he only has about half a century left to live on this planet—which isn't long enough to change things in his country, but too long a time to spend in misery. Consequently, he went through a minor disillusionment that he then blew up into something major, after which he buried it in a grave somewhere, built a new Taj Mahal around it, and headed out West. Isn't that what crazy, dear Layla Sabbak did? Didn't she decide that the whole Arab world is tailor-made for men and that she, as an educated girl who'd graduated from one of the most elite universities in Europe, would never go back there again? After all, most of the laws in effect there treat her as a second-class citizen. Whenever she wants to renew her passport, for example, she, a university professor, has to be escorted to the police station by her mentally deranged brother—who spends his days being transported back and forth between his home and a mental institution—in his capacity as her legal guardian. And once she marries, she'll have to be escorted by her husband instead of her brother. She'll never even have a taste of success unless the males in her family agree to it. That's why she decided to marry a European and stay in the West. There, at least, she can inherit something from her husband in the event of his death rather than being driven out of his home if she hasn't managed to produce any male off-spring so that his male siblings can seize upon the benefits of the life they'd lived together.

Amir crossed the Mont Blanc Bridge, then continued on foot toward quai Wilson on his way to her house. As he walked along, he wondered why it was that he couldn't contemplate the beauty of the lake and of the girls passing by rather than drowning in the lake of his own thoughts. Why did he write non-stop, especially when he didn't have a pen in his hand and wasn't sitting at his desk, but instead was walking along some path so lovely and full of delights that it would have distracted most people from everything else? Why was he constantly writing inside his head, writing studies, articles, and petitions that would be signed in his name millions of times on behalf of millions of people who had been numbed into silence?

No . . . Khalil didn't seem like the same type as Layla. His decision to leave home didn't appear to be based on any sort of romantic existentialism. Rather, it was more as if he'd fallen by accident into that restaurant and coffee shop, like a typographical error that life had made at his expense. He remembered him being panic-stricken, and paralyzed with humiliation and anxiety.

Or, he thought, maybe he belongs to a third group, namely, those who've tried to survive in the homeland and to bring about change in spite of the scourge of repression, the forces that have made people flee their homes, and the harm done to people both in their livelihoods and their dignity. Has he worked in politics as a professional? It doesn't seem so. He might have just dared to speak his mind, which itself is an unforgivable sin. People who do that are shunned by the most repressed members of society for fear that they'll bring even worse repression on others around them. His own family would try to silence him even before his enemies did. Then society as a whole would im-prison him with ostracism, fencing him in, by its rejection of his perverse be-havior. He'd be closed in on by his family before the apparatus of repression had had a chance even to touch him.

Do you suppose he might have the makings of a freedom fighter? He's been wounded by disillusionment and killed by his hunger for democracy and freedom, which are being choked to death a little more with every passing day in most of the Arab world. So is it possible that he ran away, not out of greed for money or wealth, but rather, because he simply couldn't endure anymore? Did he despair of being able to change things for the better and decide instead to flee from the deluge, carrying his misery and his dream with him?

Or maybe he's a student who's come looking for an extra source of income. The tragic thing is that people of that sort don't go back home. Or at least most of them don't. Instead, they become Europeanized, marry European women, and have children who don't speak a word of Arabic. I've always tried to warn my followers against such a fate. But . . .

Could he have the makings of an intellectual who comes to work as a mercenary for whoever offers the best pay?

Or do you suppose he might be involved in some Arab intelligence-gathering network, and be trying to infiltrate the ranks of the Arab opposition? Has he been spying on me personally? Have they decided to try again after their last failed attempt on my life? If so, they've been clever in their choice of disguise for my new executioner: a burned out, penniless nobody.

On the other hand, he might be a former executioner who's lost his job, a mercenary trying to escape the wrath of his former clientele—and that of their children and grandchildren. What's driven him here? The need to eke out a living, or greed and selfishness? Repression, or the craving and lust born of affluence? Is he a freedom fighter on the run? Or an oppressor fleeing from the new oppression that's displaced the old? Is he the hit man who's been specially selected to be my executioner?

You can't be sure of anything anymore, he thought. He came to the La Perle du Lac Park, then turned and headed up toward the Intercontinental Hotel and the Boudet neighborhood, where he was suddenly attacked by a swarm of mosquitoes that felt like a cloud enveloping his head. He tried to shoo it away with his hands, but that only seemed to make it grow denser, so dense it threatened to cut off the torrent of thoughts running through his head. But the moment he stopped writing in his head, the cloud disappeared!

No, he thought. I don't believe that strange young man, Khalil Dar', is a spy or a terrorist. On the other hand, you can't be sure of anything these days. All sorts of surprises are possible. For example, who would have believed that a marvelous woman like Layla would agree to work for a son of a bitch like Raghid Zahran? Not only that, but he'd been told that she was doing her best to win Raghid's approval—she who had once despised the man and everyone like him.

Eighteen years earlier, she'd fled her home country to avoid having to marry a local version of Raghid Zahran. She'd dreamed of a different destiny for herself. So how was it that now she was trying to attract the attention of Raghid and others of his ilk? Amir hadn't yet broached the subject with her. He was waiting for things to take a more definite shape before he spoke. He had a long fuse, longer than his own lifetime. He had enough patience to last him decades, even centuries. Whenever he made plans for his homeland, he took the long view of things. So why couldn't he give Layla the coming year at least to decide her own fate?

He was assaulted by another cloud of mosquitoes, which encircled his head like a halo and got inside his nose as if they were trying to possess him. He nearly choked on them, then held his breath. He thought, why don't they take a picture of the mosquitoes around this lake and put *that* on their tourist postcards? And why don't people choke on them when they utter the name Geneva, licking their lips as if they were relishing the prospect of some luscious, impossible dream?

(Don't be an ingrate. Don't go looking for the flaws in every place that isn't your own country. Don't take a resentful attitude toward an amazing place like this, and then remember the mosquitoes at home with affectionate nostalgia. You can love your homeland without being prejudiced against other countries. If Geneva hadn't provided you with a tranquil refuge, the executioner from your own country would have cut off your head and eaten it for breakfast. And if it weren't so safe here, you would have had your throat cut by some traveling executioner, and you wouldn't have found anywhere you could write without fear. You keep writing and writing, and your publisher keeps begging you to lighten the dosage, editing some things and refusing to publish others. Even so, your books go on multiplying like Arab children. Besides which, you're not really a stranger here anymore, and in the homes of most of the poor you have a "heart hold" that grows with every book of yours they read.

He reached the tranquil Boudet neighborhood, which seemed to have been reserved especially for the Arab bourgeois class. Millionaires had another neighborhood of their own, while for the relatively poor there were neighborhoods like Servette, which was where Amir lived. It was as if Arab society here were a miniature version of what it was back home, a mirror image of old tribal divisions and loyalties. He walked up the stairs.

(Am I really coming to visit Layla's sick mother? Or am I just hiding behind social niceties that I've never cared the least thing about?)

Since she lived on the first floor, there was no need for him to climb into that wooden coffin more commonly known as a lift. How he missed this place. He rang the doorbell. He hadn't come around for a long time. He rang the doorbell a second time. They hadn't had an argument. However, they'd both retreated into their respective shells. They'd reached the point where even the slightest bit of conversation was bound to lead to a breakup, so they both tried to avoid talking. He rang a third time. Layla opened the door, looking distraught. Then she ran back inside, saying, "Excuse me. Mother. . ."

He stepped inside, then headed toward the mother's room. He knew the place well. He found Layla's mother in bed, pale and motionless, and her granddaughter standing in front of the window, flustered and nearly panic-stricken.

Addressing her in French he asked, "Miriame, what's happened?"

"I don't know," she said. "My mother hadn't come home yet, and my grandmother called to me. She was pale and was having difficulty breathing. So I took her into my arms, and she started saying all sorts of things in Arabic. Well, you know I don't speak a word of Arabic, and she doesn't speak a word of French. In any case, she seemed to be in pain, so I tried to run to the phone to call either my mother or an ambulance. But she grabbed hold of me so hard that she nearly injured my hand. Meanwhile, she kept on talking and talking as if she were in such torment, she'd lost her senses. She seemed to be scolding me for something I'd done wrong, but I didn't know what it was. She kept shouting in my face as though she were angry with me, or as if she wanted me to relay some sort of an order or a curse to my mother. I heard her saying my mother's name, my name, and lots of other names that I didn't know. Maybe they were the names of people in her family back in her country. Then she collapsed in my arms without saying another word. Right after that, my mother got here. It all happened in a flash, just a few minutes ago."

Amir leaned over the grandmother's bed. Her face was still as wax, she didn't utter a sound, and there was no glimmer of recognition in her eyes. The wrinkles in her face were in total repose, and the look in her eyes was like the glow of a lamp about to go out, or like the gaze of someone who has retired to some secret inner chamber. Could she have died?

He took her hand in his to feel for her pulse. In doing so, he saw the blue tattoo on her arm. It was the first time he had noticed it. It was as if it were a message from the Bedouin in the heart of the desert, which nothing had been able to erase. Layla came in and whispered, "The doctor's on his way. I've called for an ambulance, too."

Amir kept hold of the lifeless hand. It hadn't grown cold yet, but the life had gone out of it. However, he didn't dare say so. Layla may have sensed it as she ran her hand over her mother's tepid, expressionless face. He kept staring at the blue tattoo. He remembered that Layla's mother had never once visited or even spoken to anyone here, nor had anyone visited her. Instead, she'd struggled desperately to deny, or at least ignore, her life in exile. She'd never left the safety of her house, refusing to speak to salesman and neighbor alike and never so much as venturing out into the street. She didn't befriend French women because she didn't speak their language, and she didn't befriend Arab women because she didn't want to acknowledge that like them, she was a foreigner. In mute anguish she attached herself to her daughter, and took responsibility for raising her granddaughter Miriame until Layla and her French husband were divorced, at which time Miriame was two years old. The strange thing was that Miriame grew up not speaking a word of Arabic, since she lived in Paris with her father until she was a teenager, and had only come back to live with her mother after his death a few months earlier. That's how Layla was—strong-willed and indifferent to her emotions if they conflicted with her convictions. She hadn't wanted Miriame to grow up divided the way she had. She hoped she'd turn out to be "pure French" like her father, not wanting to bequeath her either her grandmother's tattoo, or the agony of exile and nonbelonging that plagued her own heart. Consequently, she left him free to raise her with a single homeland.

The ambulance arrived. One of the medics placed his hand on the patient, examined her eyes with a small flashlight, listened to her heart, then shut her eyelids with routine indifference and covered her face.

Miriame went running out toward the street and was pursued by Frederic, her Swiss boyfriend who had been sitting in the living room in well-mannered silence.

"Miriame!" he called out to her. "Marie!"

Amir caught a glimpse of the fleeing girl's face as she was swallowed up by the darkness beyond the door, and imagined that he saw a blue tattoo like her grandmother's on her arm.

He approached Layla to offer his condolences.

"I'm the one who killed her," she said sorrowfully, as if she hadn't heard him. She kept repeating the words over and over as he uttered half-inane, worn-out platitudes.

"May your own well-being compensate you for your loss."

"I'm the one who killed her."

"All of us are headed for the same fate."

"I'm the one who killed her."

"I'm sorry. I don't know what to say."

"I'm the one who killed her. I killed her."

Then she burst into tears, uttering the same statement over and over in a kind of frenzied delirium.

(I brought Layla home after an enjoyable evening together. She got out her key, and before placing it in the lock, whispered lustily, "Kiss me. Now. Take me, right here on the stairs."

As for me, I got flustered. I'd never kissed a woman in front of her house before. I used to see that sort of thing in American films, where two lovers exchange impassioned kisses on the front step as the taxi driver waits with his eye on the meter to whisk the man away and as the father looks on with indifference. I personally can't feel comfortable being intimate with a woman in an unintimate place. However, with childlike petulance she insisted, saying, "Please, kiss me now!"

So, taking hold of her by her long black hair, which seemed to span the farthest reaches of the night, I went sailing over her mouth to islands of sultry delight. Then quite unexpectedly, her mother opened the door. I stepped back as if a bucket of cold rainwater had been poured over my head. I was filled with such an acute, terror-stricken shame, it was as though I'd suddenly reverted to adolescence. Layla appeared unfazed. Her mother didn't say a word. However, she cast her daughter a glance filled with bewilderment, the bewilderment of a sorrow-stricken child, like a young girl who's just discovered that the mother she adores is a harlot. Layla appeared mature, calm, and self-possessed, whereas her mother seemed as perplexed and distraught as a little girl.

The mother stood frozen in place for I don't know how long. It might have been seconds, or years. I muttered a few words in reply. I might have said, "We're going to get married. Pardon me. Sorry," or some such thing.

As for the mother, she withdrew. Layla then closed the door and drew me away by the hand, whispering, "Come on. Let's walk for a while."

So we went back out into the night, to the streets and sidewalks, to the Swiss moon in all its obscene beauty and the incomparable views it makes possible of the earth below.

In a half-sarcastic tone Layla said, "When I decided to leave home and come work here, my mother escorted me all the way overseas to preserve our reputation."

"An understandable reaction."

"She said I suffered from a superiority complex, that my yen to live in Europe was just a passing caprice, and that once it had run its course we'd come back home without any scandals."

"Well, that was one way of looking at it."

"But as you know, I married a Frenchman. And she found herself in a situation where she couldn't decide where she fit in or what attitude to take toward things. So, in short, she rejected it. She rejected it with a kind of unthinking arrogance. She imprisoned herself in this box called a house, living for the day when she could go home. She also refused to become a part of the so-called Arab overseas community here, considering herself to be a mere transient on her way home and not wanting to admit otherwise."

"Like me . . ."

"She held out for a long time inside the shell of her miserable isolation and estrangement. She wouldn't leave the house for anything except to go to the park, where she'd spend hours feeding breadcrumbs to the sparrows and not uttering a word to anyone but them.

"She disliked my husband simply because he wasn't an Arab, and she was quite happy about our divorce. Then when Miriame came back to live with us, she had a long cry when she discovered that Miriame didn't know Arabic anymore, and it was miserable for me to have to play the role of linguistic go-between for my mother and my daughter. Then one day she announced that she was going to take Miriame for a visit to Lebanon during the summer vacation so that she could meet her uncles and the rest of our family, adding that she might marry an Arab. When I translated this part for Miriame, she scoffed at the idea right in front of her grandmother and announced her intention to marry Frederic. Fortunately, of course, my mother didn't understand what Miriame had said. Or do you suppose she really does understand French and pretends not to?"

"I don't know. But I'm really embarrassed by what happened."

"Why's that? You should have seen the look on her face the day Miriame went to spend the night at Frederic's house!"

"And what about you? Did you let her?"

"Why shouldn't I? Do you want her to be torn the way I have been, being part Arab and part Western and with the two parts fighting it out all the time? She's French. So let her live as the French do!"

"I'm really embarrassed. I don't know how I'll face your mother after what happened."

"You silly Arab! She knows you and I are lovers and that we kiss each other. So why is it that disaster strikes only if she actually sees it happen? Why don't they impose mandatory solitude on us?"

"You're oversimplifying matters."

"Of course I am! But you do the same thing. Like when you told her we were going to get married."

"Sorry. You know about my marriage and my five children. But she'll think I'm just playing games with you."

"I know the old refrain: Your wife is like a friend to you. There isn't any passion or mutual understanding between you, but you feel indebted to her because she's such a virtuous woman, because she does such a good job of raising your children, because she puts up with your vagabond lifestyle since she wouldn't want to hurt the children by divorcing you, etc."

"Please, Layla. It was an incredibly sweet evening. So don't go ruining it with your exaggerations. After all, isn't it an exaggeration to consider your mother a symbol of everything you detest back home?"

"You're constantly asserting that I'm 'an intellectual without a clear sense of belonging,' that I'm torturing myself and destroying my life, and that a sense of belonging isn't a luxury, but a necessity. Don't you see that you're a married man without a clear sense of 'conjugal belonging'?"

"Are you really serious about wanting to marry me?"

"I'm serious about wanting *you* to want to marry *me!* And after that, I might kiss you, or I might refuse to."

I held my tongue. Meanwhile, my children's faces twinkled inside my head like stars in the moonlight, and we didn't exchange another word until I'd escorted her home for the second time.

Then, just as peevishly as the first time, she said, "Kiss me. Here. Now. In front of the door. My mother won't do what she did a second time."

"Sorry, I can't. I also won't do what I did a second time!"

Then I fled, trailed all the way by her peevish laugh and paralyzed by the look in her mother's eyes.)

Layla kept on sobbing and repeating the words, "I'm the one who killed her. I'm the one who killed her!"

Amir didn't leave her side for several hours, after putting her to bed like a little girl and filling her stomach with sedatives. Before leaving, he listened with her to the music of Grieg, Schumann, and Brahms, which she loved so much. He'd heard Layla scoff at Arabic music so many times, he didn't dare put on any of the Arabic music tapes he came across. (Maybe somebody left these here by accident.) Then he stole away on tiptoe. He had a feeling Miriame wouldn't be back, since she and Frederic had lived together for weeks as a way of deciding whether to get married.

As he walked slowly down the stairs, the grandmother's blue tattoo danced before his eyes, and the feel of her withered hand, as frigid as desert sands on a winter night, lingered on his skin. Once outside, he paused under a tree to catch his breath. He gazed up at the stars, which looked like luminescent apertures in a night without end. Then he looked up at Layla's window and was surprised to find her light on. The sound of the Bach recording he'd put on before leaving then came to a sudden halt. So Layla hadn't really gone to sleep after all. Instead, she'd retreated as usual into silence. He froze in place. Then before long he heard the sound of Umm Kulthoum singing an old, heartrending melody. Who would have believed that Layla had kept Umm Kulthoum's records and listened to them in secret?

He still had so much to say to her, about their relationship, and in particular about her relationship with Raghid. But her mother, at least, had said everything she had to say tonight . . . in silence, with a single stroke of her tattooed hand. Would her hand be buried in Grand-Saconnex Cemetery? Would her bones find repose there? And would people go on wondering after this why the ghosts of the dead buried in their tombs don't just rest and leave the living in peace? Perhaps it's because the living didn't let them die in peace. Do you suppose a dead person's ghost is simply the guilt-laden conscience of the murderer, etched onto the victim's tombstone in a kind of television of eternity?

Would that aged hand go on pummeling Layla in her dreams, with the blue tattoo glowing through horror-filled nights?

Would her ghost emerge every night from the Grand-Saconnex Cemetery, screaming in Layla's face and demanding that she go back to the desert? Had her death been a "wedding present" for Miriame and Frederic? And even if he managed to forget his deep love for fickle, fiery Layla, would he ever be able to forget that infernal triangle: the grandmother, Layla, Miriame?

Would he be able to keep from wondering: What did the grandmother say in Arabic to her granddaughter who understands nothing but French? No one will ever know.

And Miriame, could she go on with her life without wondering what her grandmother had shouted in her face as she extended her tattooed hand and pointed at her so accusingly at the moment of her demise?

◆ ◆ ◆

Kafa got herself ready for the "intimate dinner" that Nadim had invited them to attend. She passed by the beauty salon to have her hair redone, then put on a blue dress that showed off her bodily charms and brought out the blueness of her eyes. Whenever she put on this particular color, Khalil knew she was out to snag a man on her blue hook. That was what she'd done when she started frequenting his bookshop until she managed to reel him into her territorial waters on a blue fishing line. Khalil was still trembling with defeat and humiliation from their compulsory visit to the boutique to buy him formal, contemporary attire for their evening out. Kafa had decided that his old clothes wouldn't do for someone on his way to becoming rich and making a new start in life with respectable people who'd made it to the top.

There was something else tormenting him also as the taxi carried them to Nadim's mansion. According to Kafa, it was now 7:45 P.M., which meant that he'd missed the 7:30 news broadcast on the Suisse Romande channel, and that he'd also miss the news at 8:00 P.M. on the two channels from France. It was true, of course, that he'd spent the entire morning combing the papers for every news item he could find about Lebanon and making sure when the TV news broadcasts would come on. He'd also managed to catch the 1:00 P.M. "news flash" in spite of Kafa's insistence on their getting to Le Bateau lakeside restaurant before closing time. It was a meal she'd dreamed of for so long, she didn't want to miss it. Even so, he was burning to hear news from home. It was as if he'd left his soul there, and was running to and fro in involuntary exile inside a lifeless corpse.

His main concern of the evening was to get back in time for the 10:30 news. Had they really managed to occupy southern Lebanon? Khalda? And what were they after?

(It's ludicrous of me even to ask such a question. They've made it quite plain what they're after. Meanwhile, Begin reaffirms it every day with letters written in the sky by warplanes flying in formation. Could anyone but he claim that the massacres of the past and those yet to come are the result of a mere "misunderstanding"?)

He felt distressed and ashamed to be taking part in this glittering evening or enjoying long days bathed in luxury and ease while his people were being massacred back home. Had his village been occupied? Had the old oak tree been blasted away? And what about his buddies, his world, his bookshop, Widad's and his mother's graves?

And here he was going to the house of a man who was envied—albeit not respected—by everyone in the neighborhood, in hopes of landing a job for himself so that his two boys could stay in a fancy Swiss boarding school and so that Kafa could buy herself a Piaget watch, a Cartier cigarette lighter, Ted Lapidus suits, Yves St. Laurent makeup, Charles Jardin shoes, and all the other luxurious atrocities that she liked to spend her days drooling over in shop display windows, dragging him along with her and planning their future together—hers and her luxuries' future, that is! As for him, he was too dazed to be mindful of any of it, like someone who's escaped from one trap only to fall into another of a different kind.

They arrived at the Jewel Mansion.

A garden. A marble staircase. A front door of carved woodwork suggestive of the elegance to be found inside. Kafa rang the doorbell, which had the sound of melodious music. The door opened to reveal a maid wearing a special uniform and a world of exquisite objets d'art. They stepped inside, neither of them looking at the other. Gazing at the Persian carpet, the brightly colored, luminous Galle ceramic pieces shaped like mushrooms, the artistically carved and varnished wooden chairs, the crystal chandeliers, the elegant Sevres planters, the gold doorknobs, and the velvety wallpaper, Kafa let out a gasp of longing, envy and distress. To Khalil her voice sounded like the hissing of an adder. But he paid no attention to her. From the time he entered the house, he'd been drawn to the eyes of a woman in a painting that hung in a prominent spot on the wall. He walked toward it, oblivious to everything else around him. It was an oil painting representing a young woman in her early twenties. She had lovely features, and in her eyes there was a look of determination, defiance, and hope. At the same time, her face was free of tension, harshness, or coquettishness. It was a face with an intensely human presence, a presence that the artist had highlighted by painting the neck and shoulders a misty, creamy hue that brought out her positive, vivacious spirit and an absence of carnal worldliness. He stared at the lips and wondered, is that a smile of naive optimism, or of the sort of realistic self-confidence that goes beyond mere romantic idealism?

After a few moments had passed, Nadim came in. It was as if he liked to give his guests a bit of time to catch their breath and to admire this miniature museum of his properly before gracing them with his presence. He was accompanied by a woman who appeared to be around forty years old. She wore a black dress adorned with diamonds that glittered on her bosom and around her neck, and still more diamonds on her ears and fingers.

He introduced her to them, saying, "My wife, Dunya."

Ogling Dunya's jewelry with covetous admiration, Kafa greeted her with a warm squeeze of the hand. As for Khalil, what arrested his attention was the sorrowful eyes in her half-withered face. He pictured himself picking her up tenderly, then whisking her away, placing her head in the shower and washing away the layers and layers of makeup that had accumulated on her features. After this he brushed her hair away from her forehead and took her cheeks in his hands. As he did so, he saw the distinctive face of the young woman in the painting before the storms of time had passed over it, leaving their fingerprints on everything they touched: her cheeks, her lips, her eyes. Even the look of spunk and vitality that he'd seen in the painting had turned into a remorseful, shadowy glow too deep to fathom. Yet nothing had truly changed. Meanwhile, he shook her hand quietly, saying, "Hello, Madame Dunya."

Not being one to waste time, Nadim addressed Khalil while everyone else froze in rapt attention, saying, "The reason I invited the two of you earlier than the other guests is that there's some business I'd like to discuss with you in private."

Kafa piped in, saying, "You said it would be an intimate dinner."

Dunya replied, "That means that there won't be more—or less—than twenty guests."

Everybody laughed at her statement as if it had been a joke. Then they all began looking warily at each other like a bunch of street cats who've met up under a tree, with everyone sizing up everyone else as they remained seated ever so politely in their chairs. Kafa stared enviously at Dunya. (How lucky she is. She's so elegant and so rich. Diamonds. A successful, well-dressed husband with looks fit to kill. A house so lavish it could pass for a museum, and security and stability in the world's most stable, secure city.)

And Dunya stared enviously back at Kafa. (How young she is. And she's so vivacious and beautiful. She might still be in her late twenties. Her husband is a good-looking young man who seems like a sensitive person. And they've both still got all life's possibilities open to them.)

Khalil looked over at Dunya, who was seated elegantly in her chair, then at the painting that had attracted his attention on the wall behind her. (She's the young woman in the painting, all right. Or rather, she is, and she isn't. I could have fallen in love with a girl like that—a serious, tender girl who takes a thoughtful view of things. But the sun snatched her away and the earth made ten revolutions on its axis before it could get her back. And all of that happened before I was even born. I've been betrayed! If she were only ten years younger and about ten kilos thinner.)

"Come with me, Khalil," said Nadim. "Let's go out onto the balcony. The weather's nice. We'll have a chat."

Then, turning to the two women and bowing his head with a debonair refinement that enchanted Kafa, he said, "Now if the two ladies will excuse us . . ."

As the two men walked away side by side, Kafa followed them with her gaze. (What a contrast! There's Nadim with his huge cigar, erect as a spear, and my husband with his ever-forgotten cigarette hanging limply out of his mouth like the half-charred flag of a defeated army. Nadim is more sophisticated and has better social graces. Of course, he *is* a bit shorter than Khalil, but the way he carries himself is different. He walks as though he were carrying a bouquet of flowers in which he takes great pride, whereas my husband looks as though he were walking through a graveyard with a shovel and a pickax in his hand. Nadim struts along in his clothes. His body seems to be in harmony with the silk of his shirt, and his skin seems at ease inside its costly cocoon. As for Khalil, he looks as though he's doing battle with his fancy clothes.) She watched Khalil as the men made their way toward the balcony. One minute he was rolling up his sleeves in irritation, and the next minute he was putting his fingers inside his shirt collar to get it off his neck. (Damn it. He's just an uncouth boor, but I'll try to polish him up. When we were buying him his fancy clothes the other day, he didn't appreciate what I was doing. He didn't know what it meant for me to be spending my own money on clothes for him when

I could have been buying things for myself. And as usual, he turned all the care and attention I'd been showering on him into an accusation, saying, "You aren't really buying clothes for me. You're buying them for yourself. That is, you buy them and then force me to wear them so that my looks will fit the role you want to play in life. You're just using your money to change the way I look in hopes of profiting from it yourself."

"I know I'll never hear a word of thanks from you no matter what I do for you. What do you think of this necktie?"

"You know how I hate neckties. I don't know why this piece of cloth means so much. . . . It's as if the ability to keep an expensive, clean rag around one's neck were some sort of legal proof of one's loyalty to the pack.")

As the two men disappeared through the door, Kafa heaved a sigh, and Dunya sighed with her, each of them harboring worlds of passions and secrets in her heart.

When the guests began to arrive, Kafa glowed with pleasure to be meeting people from the upper crust, whose genteel company she had been deprived of since she took leave of her father's household to go live with Khalil.

("It's a mistake. This marriage is a huge mistake!" That's what I remember my father shouting before the wedding. I was standing behind the door and eavesdropping on him and my mother. She said, "She's the spoiled baby daughter. You hated her when she was first born. You were so sick of us having daughters, you named her Kafa. But then you fell madly in love with her and spoiled her rotten. She's gotten bullheaded and insists on having everything she takes a fancy to."

"Once the marriage has been consummated, poverty will come creeping in the door, and love will fly out the window."

"On the other hand, he's young and educated, and we could help him. He could go into business with you and amass a fortune. Our third son-in-law wasn't any better than him in the beginning, and now he's a top-notch businessman."

"But Khalil wouldn't turn out the way our son-in-law has. He doesn't seem like the sort who could be cultivated. He's poor and arrogant at the same time. Haven't you noticed how rude he always is to us, when he ought to be groveling on the carpet for our having deigned to receive him in our home?")

After some time Nadim and Khalil came back in from the balcony. What do you suppose they'd agreed on? What kind of job would it be? How much would he get paid? Would his salary be in the form of profits? Commissions?

Nadim appeared unruffled, even brash in the self-satisfied nonchalance that bewitched Kafa so. As for Khalil, he looked tense and red in the face. But as she chatted with the high-class guests, she forgot about him, winning the admiration of the new arrivals one after another with her svelte figure, her blue eyes and the oriental features that made the blueness of her eyes all the more stunning and exotic. Not to mention her refined, polished charm, her stylish hairdo, her chic dress, the stockings, and the shoes. After all, she wasn't simply beautiful. She was also a woman of distinguished lineage who knew how to address people according to proper rules of etiquette, and who thereby deserved to be received into their secret society as a member in good standing. One of the guests also happened to have known her father, the late, great Salman Baytmouni, which elevated her status even further and crowned her queen of the soirée. Khalil found a place to sit down and didn't utter a word, an act of virtue that endeared him to the chatterboxes in attendance and on account of which he became a celebrity of sorts in his own right. Each of the other guests came up to him and, standing in front of him with a glass in hand, kept up a steady monologue as if swarms of flies were coming out of his mouth. Khalil would sit there in frozen silence with a half-smile on his face while his interlocutor asked all the questions and answered them himself, then withdrew after telling Khalil how delighted he was to have made his acquaintance and how much he'd enjoyed their conversation!

And he was a favorite with the women, too. After all, he was young, handsome in a rugged sort of way, quiet, calm, and sophisticated-looking, and had a mysterious look in his eyes. Besides which, he was a stud! That, at least, was the impression he'd given a certain tipsy, well-to-do lady who kept telling him dirty jokes that she laughed at herself, taking hold of his hand after each one. Kafa looked over at the two of them with pleasure and satisfaction. Here was her husband, learning at long last how to conduct himself in the company of high society. Then she looked over at Nadim. Oh, Nadim! He's so good-looking!

Khalil suddenly began to feel weak and vulnerable. (I used to be an impregnable fortress. Other people tried to penetrate my armor, but there was a small, clean place inside me that I always kept to myself. There are people who want to take that away from me, too, and Kafa is in league with them. She knows my weak spots and the times I've fallen prey to temptation. Then she uses them to her advantage and calls it love!)

Another lady came up to talk to him. Glasses came and went. Faces floated to the surface, then were submerged once again in the crowd. The painted, lust-tinged faces of the women here all looked alike to him. Without knowing why, he imagined that all of them had exactly the same face and bore the same expressions, with minor modifications here and there. The whispers, the music, and the laughter began getting louder, the scents of perfume wafted in his direction, and the glitter of jewelry grew steadily brighter. A circle of ad-mirers had gathered about Kafa, and he could hear her scintillating voice as she recounted the story of how they had escaped from Lebanon on the last flight out of Beirut. Yes, indeed, the last flight . . .

"And it was in the first-class cabin that we met Nadim!"

She didn't forget to place special emphasis on the part about their being in the first-class cabin. Meanwhile, the other guests recapitulated her story with gasps of horror and admiration:

"Ah. . . !"

"Ooh la la!"

"Beirut? What a savage, brutal place! How did you manage to survive there all this time? A cultivated, refined, beautiful lady like you living among the beasts in Beirut? Ooh, la la la la la. . . !"

No one appeared to be concerned about the fate of Beirut itself, or of its children and all the other people living there. With a miserable lump in his throat he wondered, don't other Arabs have children, too? I mean, maybe they don't give a damn about Palestine or about whether it's an Arab nation or not, and maybe they can say, "To hell with Lebanon. Let it pluck the thorn out of its own side!" But is it possible for someone who's washed his hands of Arabs and their concerns to wash his hands of all humanity as well?

(I stood up on top of the grand piano. I took off the fancy shoes that hurt my feet and the necktie that was about to choke me. Then I broke a Galle lamp on the edge of the piano and, brandishing it like a billy club, I screamed at everyone, "You talk about Beirut as if it were no concern of yours, as if you had nothing to do with what's happening there! You've all been part of the move-ment to exploit our hunger for food so as to take away our freedom, and our hunger for freedom in order to take away our ability to earn our daily bread. You've helped to destroy Beirut so that you can hold it up as an example to your own peoples, saying, 'Look what happens to people who use their brains and meddle in politics! Look what happens to children who turn into troublemakers! So hurry back to your petty concerns and to your wives' arms. Leave it to us to protect you. Otherwise, you'll end up no better off than the people of Beirut.' ")

No one heard him, though, since he didn't utter a word of what he was thinking. Instead, he just went on smiling politely whenever the lady stopped talking, and laughing out loud whenever she did. The sense of self-mastery that he'd always enjoyed had been suddenly shattered. When he gazed out into the inky darkness beyond the windows, he was seized by the fear that there was a bomb inside him, a bomb that might explode at any moment, sending his disfigured remains flying in all directions and sullying the clothes and faces of the other guests.

"Dinner is served."

Kafa, now the guest of honor, glowed with pleasure, and took her seat like someone who had returned to her own kith and kin after a long absence. Khalil sat down in chagrin, fearful of the hosts of silver knives, forks, and spoons that surrounded his plate and not knowing which of them to pick up first lest he appear uncivilized.

(I hurl the silverware off the table, roll up my sleeves, and grab the delectable-looking chicken off its huge silver platter. Then, holding it with both hands, I bury my face in it like a gluttonous ogre. I munch, I swallow, and I pant, not raising my head except to spit out the bones onto the sumptuous carpet, onto the plate of the lady sitting next to me, onto the diamond necklace she's wearing, or onto Nadim's cigar.) Picking up the outermost spoon in the queue of silver soldiers that flanked his plate, Khalil dipped it into the soup as he'd seen Kafa do, then swallowed its contents, being careful not to make any noise. He burned his tongue in the process. However, smiling ever so politely through the pain, he said to Dunya, "This soup is delicious, Madame. You're quite a cook!"

Smiling with what ended up as a grimace as miserable and phony as Khalil's, she replied, "Thank you, sir. It's kind of you to say so." (Poor man. He thinks it's his duty to compliment me, but he doesn't do a very good job of it. Doesn't he know that "society ladies" like me don't cook even for their children, much less their guests? He should have gone to the kitchen to kiss and thank the chef. So why don't I have the guts to tell him so? How did I turn into a tape recording that spouts the traditional, "proper" lines, but doesn't express what's inside me? Poor Khalil, with his wife who's so dazzled by our social status. One more couple that Nadim's brought home in hopes of adding some young blood to this rapacious but dwindling clique of ours. New blood. A new scandal. A new adventure. And both of them are liable to get burned. But it won't be long before they've been consumed, and then they'll be spit out of everyone's mouth. When they're on their way to the lunatic asylum, the hospital, or the airport, they'll be ignored as if they never existed. Only a few end up being more rapacious than those around them. They're the ones who manage to amass a fortune that guarantees their entry as permanent members into our "Merry Murder Club." Kafa might make it. She seems to really enjoy all our refined yet vulgar practices. Or do you suppose she's just still in shock, blinded by the thrill of discovery? As for Khalil, it's hard to be sure just what he's hiding behind that calm, silent exterior of his. But he seems like the sensitive type. And that's an unforgivable weakness in our world. The day will come when he'll break, just the way I've begun to.)

After dinner, the evening's gathering was honored by the presence of Sakhr Ghanamali and his son, Saqr, who passed by for a cup of coffee on their way to another engagement. When Nadim introduced Khalil and Kafa to them, both men were impressed with Kafa, as evidenced by the admiring gleam in their eyes. But they took little notice of Khalil. And they didn't stay long.

As Nadim escorted them to the door, Sakhr said to him, "He'll do. But are you sure he isn't a spy, and that he's 'clean'?"

"Too clean, if you ask me."

"And his wife is too beautiful—for a man like him, at any rate."

"My dad's right," said Saqr in affirmation.

So then, Sakhr Ghanamali was taken by Kafa. When Nadim rejoined the guests, he took a closer look at her. Their eyes met. Kafa felt a hot, stormy urge to squeeze him, as if she knew she was going to fall in love. Or as if she already had. (I've never cheated on my husband before. After all, that would have been difficult in Beirut, which is crawling with poor, longhaired men who leave something to be desired when it comes to personal hygiene and knowing how to dress. But ah, Nadim! Those polished good looks of his, and that luscious smile. His body holds out the promise of pleasures to come, and that black mane of his is flecked with tiny silver hairs that make him all the more alluring. Here's a man who's experienced life, and who knows the keys that can unlock the secrets of a woman's body. Dunya is so lucky to have a husband like him. But she doesn't appreciate him. In fact, she outright neglects him. The poor man needs the tender loving care of a woman like me. Not once since the party began have I seen his wife smile at him, caress his delectable face, or put her arms around his neck and plant a kiss on each of those two dimples of his, letting herself be set on fire by his breath, by the aroma of his cologne, and by the feel of his arms around her. If only *I* were his wife instead of her!)

As Kafa contemplated Dunya with envy, Dunya was out on the balcony talking to Kafa's boring husband, Khalil . . .

But Dunya didn't find him boring. She found him to be the sensitive type, just as she'd suspected she would. He casually lit a couple of cigarettes and offered her one of them, saying, "Maybe you smoke another brand."

It had been a long time since anyone had offered her a lit cigarette after the manner of artists and simple folk who care nothing for the "proper" way of doing things, and she felt a kind of intimacy developing between them. Inhaling the smoke as if it were a fiery passion out of the past that she longed to relive, she replied, "I smoke any brand when I'm in need of a cigarette—which is all the time!"

They both laughed.

"That's an incredible painting," he said, "I mean, the picture of the young woman."

"It's a picture of me eighteen centuries ago. I painted it myself."

"So you paint, too?"

"Unfortunately, I don't anymore. It isn't possible to paint 'too.' You either paint, or you don't paint. And if you do paint, you don't do anything else. There isn't time enough in a lifetime to paint and to do other things, too. And that's why I haven't painted since I got married."

"That's really unfortunate."

"In your opinion, perhaps. But as most people see it, I was rescued from the trap of art by a prosperous marriage!"

She said it with bitter irony. As she spoke, there flowed between them the warmth of friendly candor, the sort that rarely develops except between strangers seated next to each other on an airplane, in airports, or in the duty-free zone, where you can pour out your heart to a stranger or tell him your life story without embarrassment.

There welled up in Khalil a love for something about her that he couldn't quite name.

He said, "What's even lovelier than the young woman in the picture is the hand that painted it. The girl in the painting might fade, but creativity endures. A woman might shatter against time's unyielding surface the way a fragile bottle or glass breaks on a hard tile floor. But the power to create can flourish as time goes by. So it's too bad you gave up painting, whatever the reasons for it."

As they talked, Dunya felt a happiness she'd forgotten existed. Here was someone who genuinely cared about seeing a painting, without thinking of buying it or asking how much it cost. Instead, he was thinking about what had happened to the person who had brought it into being. How she missed this sort of person. He was like the folks she'd kept company with before she married. (Nobody in Nadim's clique noticed when the painting first appeared on the wall except that someone made fun of the look in her eyes. He said it scared him in the dark because she stared out at him like a witch. When I got tipsy and told people who'd come for the evening that I was guilty of painting it myself, some woman let out a phony gasp of admiration that dripped with indifference and said, "Really, dear? How nice! Are you good at needlepoint, too?" Another woman said, "The collar on the girl's dress is pretty. Did you know that this type of collar has come back in style?")

She and Khalil were talking as if they'd known each other for ages. She gazed down at Geneva, which glittered in the valley below like a meadow full of stars.

"We don't always fulfill our dreams," she said bitterly. "There are winds that blow and take our lives wherever they please. Don't you believe in fate?"

"I do. But I also believe that we need to resist it as much as possible . . ."

"Are you really capable of doing that? Or are you just repeating something Amir Nealy has said?"

"Do you know him?"

"He was the first one to come out in support of me on the day I opened the exhibit that caused such an uproar way back when."

"My God, how could I have forgotten? I remember reading something about that a long time ago. So you're Dunya Thabit, the one who opened an art exhibit that featured paintings and sculptures of naked men. You're the rebel against tradition who can't understand why it is that when men paint pictures of naked women, it's considered art, whereas if a woman paints pictures of naked men, it's a scandal."

"I am, and I'm not. It's as if being married to Nadim is also a kind of profession. Perhaps all marriages are that way . . . a profession more than an emotional bond."

She seemed sorrowful and fragile, and he felt an urge to tell her his own story . . . to get close to her. He wished they could hold each other in the dark and tremble in horror at a world that was crushing them without mercy, ridiculing their weaknesses and holding them up as examples for others not to follow.

Through the glass door of the balcony he could see Kafa glowing in the light inside. Blissful and dazzled, she cast the other people in the room a look of collective affection.

"I know exactly what you mean," he said to Dunya. "It's really horrible if a person doesn't like his profession."

"Are you happy about your upcoming job with Sakhr Ghanamali?"

Khalil began to stammer. But before he could get a reply out, a handsome boy came onto the balcony and said something to Dunya in French without looking at Khalil. Then he withdrew.

"That's my son, Bahir," she said. "Unfortunately, like my daughter, he doesn't speak Arabic. Both of them were born and raised here."

"Don't you take them home on visits?"

"We haven't got time for anything but work here, and we usually spend the summers in Palma de Majorca or Marbella depending on how much we've got to do. And sometimes we go to Nice or Cannes."

"Doesn't he have a grandmother or uncles that you could let him stay with there?"

"I was late in realizing my mistake—that is, Nadim's and my mistake. The constant demands of his work were cheating us out of all our time. So two—no, three—years ago, I took him there. He hated the place. It started from the moment we arrived. First he was appalled at how filthy the airport was, and by the way we were assailed by porters desperate to eke out a living for themselves. Then when we got to Beirut, he hated the garbage in the streets, the people's ill temper, and the crazy fighting. Those of us who know the city the way it used to be hold onto the Beirut of our dreams, and consequently, we love it no matter how dreadful it gets. As for young people like him, the only image they have of their homeland is based on the ugly situation they see there now."

He almost said to her, "But the two of you are responsible anyway. After all, in the end your son will go on being an alien without a country to call home."

But then he thought better of it. After all, wasn't he doing the same thing to his own children?

Then she went on, saying, "My son Bahir lives in a world of machines. His father is the television and his playmates are electronic games—Intelevision, Atari, and the like. Playing for him means spending his time making war in his bedroom. The battles take place on the screen, and he controls things with buttons while he sits safe and sound in his chair, far out of death's reach."

He nearly replied, "Isn't a boy his age supposed to speak the language of his country? And shouldn't he be expected to enter a real battle after some years have passed, like any other young man whose country is going up in flames?"

But then he remembered that Bahir's present promised to be his own children's future, and he held his tongue. The thought of it filled him with dismay. However, his ruminations were interrupted as Nadim walked out onto the balcony. With a note of reproach in his voice, he said to Dunya, "The guests have started leaving. Hurry out and say goodbye to them."

At that point, the two of them fell into what seemed like a deep abyss. She rushed inside while Khalil stayed on the balcony. And without knowing why, he thought he glimpsed the girl in the painting running through a dark jungle.

◆   ◆   ◆

As they got ready to leave the party in Nadim's elegant car, the chauffeur tipped his hat to Kafa as he opened the door for her.

"Ah, this is the life!" she said ecstatically.

"This is death," he whispered gloomily.

He remembered the bee that had fallen inside the Coke bottle in the coffee shop. As he thought back to its desperate struggle to exit through the bottle's narrow neck and how its wings started to break against the hard glass walls, his ears were filled with its buzzing, which sounded like human cries for help.

◆   ◆   ◆

He woke up to the chirping of sparrows. It was the first time it had happened to him in ages, since the times when he used to go stay in the village with his grandfather as a child. He looked at his watch. It still said 12:30. According to the clock in the hotel room, it was 6:00 A.M. He sat down in front of the window and drew back the curtain slightly, enough for him to be able to see out without letting in so much light it would disturb Kafa. He didn't want her to wake up yet. He wanted to be alone for a while so that he could think about his predicament and come up with new solutions.

A mechanical sweeper was moving down the sidewalk and cleaning it with soap and water, while a second cleaning truck moved alongside it in the middle of the street. He thought forlornly about the stench given off by the garbage bonfires that filled the sidewalks of Beirut. This was how he hoped his own country would be some day: immaculate, tranquil, a place fit for children and sparrows to live in. But what had happened had happened. No longer was it the sweet scent of the ocean that wafted through Beirut by night.

Turning over in bed, Kafa asked him, "What are you doing? Come back to sleep. It's still early."

"I'm not sleepy. I'm going out for a short walk."

"I'm not letting you out for a long walk or a short one. You'll find yourself another Arab, then the two of you will start talking, you'll get into an argument and we'll be in trouble all over again. Go back to sleep so that you'll be on top of things when you start your new job."

" . . . "

"You didn't tell me anything about what you and Nadim agreed on yesterday."

" . . . "

"Why did you get angry and boycott me in bed?"

" . . . "

"Is it because I turned off the television? I did it to give both you and me a break from looking at scenes of destruction in our country. Aren't you tired of scenes of violence, devastation, and dead bodies? We're through with all that forever. So why don't you rest and let others do the same? Just like every other mother, I despise violence, destruction, and killing. We left the city to you all in hopes that you'd do us the kindness of liberating Palestine. Then you proceeded to liberate it from its inhabitants, its means of subsistence and even its buildings. And now Israel is finishing up the job!"

She'd finally managed to get a rise out of him.

"That's not exactly what happened!" he shouted. "But it's what some people wanted it to look like, so that some moronic woman like you would say what you're saying!"

"Speechology. . . . That's all I ever hear from you. Meanwhile, the corpses keep piling up and there are people who try to convince us that the road to

Jerusalem should pass through Beirut, Tripoli, etc. And that it should pass over our mangled corpses. Just let us live. . . ! But you and your kind aren't really serious about your so-called cause."

"Well, unfortunately, you and your kind *are* serious about your so-called cause, which is to keep on exploiting us or destroying us by every means possible—and that includes driving a person to kill his own brother, or driving both of them to suicide."

"Speechology. I'm sick of all your talk about the struggle for freedom, peace, and prosperity when every day they bring home one more dead young man to be mourned by the womenfolk."

"People's futures aren't built in ten days, or in ten years, for that matter. What I'm talking about might only be realized for our children or our grandchildren. But it will never happen if we don't do anything. Perhaps we've used the wrong tactics. But the struggle itself and its basic strategies can't be blamed."

"Speechology: 'Tactics.' 'Strategies.' 'Struggle.' I say: Let your children grow up in a humane place. And let's have done with damned Beirut and all its despicable memories."

"They aren't 'despicable memories.' They might be painful, and shocking, and full of mistakes. But let's learn from them rather than use them as an excuse to shirk our responsibility toward our country."

"Speechology . . ."

"The struggle for freedom isn't like doing your hair. It's like agriculture. What I mean is: we plant a seed. Then the winds might be favorable, and the storms might blow. It might rain 'coolness and peace,' or a frost might come and nip it in the bud. One seed dies, and another survives. One gets accidentally trampled under foot, another gets blown up, and still another gets killed either by the elements of nature or by human negligence. But what matters is to plant, and to keep on planting. The day is bound to come when the efforts of the thousands of good-hearted, sincere people who've suffered and possibly even been martyred finally bear fruit."

"You're so tiresome! You and everybody else of your type. When you talk, you sound like a tape recording that's all cliches. I've seen you all picking up your hoes and turning pasturelands into graveyards. So don't give me any more of your speechology, please."

"You'll never understand what I'm saying because you don't listen. You've got your point of view, and I've got mine."

At which point he got back into bed in hopes of avoiding any further discussion, and pretended to go asleep.

"What did you agree on with Nadim?" she asked.

She was the persistent type who didn't give up easily. All right then, he thought, I'll tell her.

"I'll be working as a secretary for Sakhr Ghanamali's son. The salary is reasonable. Nadim says it all depends on how enterprising I am, and that there's a chance of making big commissions."

She didn't look surprised. It was as if she already knew. As though she'd had a telephone conversation with Nadim that he didn't know about—from the beauty salon, for example. As if she was siding with "them."

She didn't say anything. He'd noticed a bit of lukewarmness creeping into her behavior toward him. He'd gotten used to having her pamper him, cry at times, get angry with him, then warm right back up again. He was shaken by her nonchalance, which worried him. It made him wonder whether he cared more about her than he liked to admit to himself.

Taking her into his arms, he gazed at her fresh, youthful beauty as she lay there awash in the light that was stealing in through the opening between the curtains. In the room's relative darkness, she looked as though she were made of sparkling crystal.

Stroking her hair, he whispered, "Please, let's not fight now that we've left home. Can't we be friends?"

"And have we been more than that?"

She said it spitefully, with the kind of suggestive tone that women are so good at using when they're out to insult their men's virility.

The pain went through him like a knife, and he could feel tendrils of black hatred growing up around the wound. He thought of taking the wedding band off her finger, then rushing off to bring his sons home from the boarding school and take them back to Beirut. On the other hand, he wondered, is she still even wearing that cheap ring I got her, or is she ashamed of it? He looked over at her limp hand . . . and didn't see the ring. Instead, he found another ring—a diamond ring—in its place. He was stunned.

"Kafa . . . where did you get this ring?"

"I lifted it!" she replied with a frivolous laugh.

He started as if he'd just been stung. "You're kidding."

"No, I'm not. I stole it."

"Where?"

"From the guest bathroom at Dunya's house."

"How?"

"I think she forgot it. I went in after her to wash my hands and found it. I kept it hidden in my bra for the rest of the evening."

"Weren't you afraid of being punished for it?"

"Of course I was. But I enjoyed it. My heart was beating like crazy, and it gave me a great rush."

"That's disgraceful! We're going to take it back to her right now."

"If she were in need of it, she would have missed it by now. Look at how beautiful it is. And the diamond is so huge. It's like the solitaire that my sister Manal got from her husband."

He got up and put on his clothes, then headed out of the hotel as if he knew exactly where he was going.

"Would you like me to call a taxi for you, sir?" asked the smartly uniformed doorman.

"No," he replied, "but could you please direct me to the station?"

"Ah . . . the Cornavin. That's easy. It's just a few minutes' walk away. First you go down this street, Alp Street. Then after a few minutes of walking you'll find yourself in Cornavin Square. The station's in the center of it."

As he started walking, the cool morning air helped to cool him down. He passed Jardin Brunswick, then crossed Paquis Street on his way up Talberg Street with a magnificent flowerbed to his left. He took long, deep breaths like someone discovering his lungs for the first time, then rushed to light a cigarette as if he weren't accustomed to such clean air. On the sidewalk across the street he saw a small carlike vehicle with a giant broom at its base. Water came gushing out through the broom as it rinsed and polished the surface below. Once again he thought back to the piles of refuse and cadavers that filled the sidewalks in Beirut, and was filled with anguish. As he came to the station, he noticed the precise timing of the traffic signals and the special courtesy shown to pedestrians. (This is a city where a person can stop to think without being run down by a car or killed by a stray bullet because of some argument that turned into a battle, and without getting shot at for "insubordination" because he got distracted and went rushing accidentally through an armed checkpoint.) He had to admit it. It really was a marvelous country. Its only fault was that it wasn't *his* country. It was the fruit of effort, labor, and wars just like any other homeland. But he couldn't simply choose the safest country on earth to spend his life in, running away from his own country because it didn't happen to be democratic, free, and humane. That's what he'd told Kafa time and time again. He'd told her that the Nazis occupied most of Europe for at least five years, between 1940 and 1945, but that the people in Holland, Belgium, and France didn't turn into professional refugees. Instead, they practiced resistance. And Germany bombed London for months, but the people there didn't go rushing off by land and sea to Beirut, for example. Instead, they went down into bomb shelters. So how had he ended up here? He remembered with dismay that when he came to Switzerland, it wasn't Israel he'd been running from. He'd already been fleeing from something else when Begin's soldiers attacked.

Driving him and thousands of others like him out of Lebanon—wasn't it part of a plan to empty the country of those who would defend it, scattering them abroad and distracting them with petty disputes in preparation for bringing the country down and making it that much easier to swallow up? Past offenses might be forgiven. But would it be possible after this for an Arab to take up arms against another Arab? Certainly not. It was unthinkable.

He bought a ticket to the Versoix district. The train was due to leave at 7:02 from Platform 4. He was amazed that the timing could be so precise, and thinking about it awakened in him his long-felt passion for punctuality in public services as a way of showing respect for the ordinary citizen. A quarter of an hour later, he got off the train in a suburban station. The place was filled with flowers in lovely planters. Rather than being restricted to the mansions of the wealthy and prestigious, they were here to be enjoyed by any passerby.

He asked for directions to the school and someone told him how to get there: after a ten-minute walk up a road leading through a wooded area, he'd take the third turn on the right. Soon he found himself walking through a veritable paradise. The fantastically beautiful water of the lake could be seen below. Sometimes the foliage was a translucent green, and other times blood-red. The place was filled with a wondrous, silent tranquility, not at all like the sepulchral stillness that used to fall over Beirut following long hours of shelling. Rather than being a prelude to the next barrage of gunfire, this kind of stillness was a transition to something still more lovely. At last he could see the school's playgrounds and buildings with their graceful, cozy-looking tile roofs and their pleasant verandas and windows.

He took a long look at the football field, the likes of which his two boys had never seen before except on television—during the rare intervals in which there was broadcasting between one power cut and the next. Yet football was their favorite sport, and for a long time they'd resorted to playing it with the remains of bombs, ball-shaped pieces of shrapnel and empty tin cans. So who was he to deprive them of this clean, safe football field? It even had newly painted lines on it, evidence of the special care devoted in this place to every last detail. The children came pouring out into the school courtyard like a collective bundle of energy and raucous, spirited laughter. Seeing them clad in their clean white shorts and sports jerseys, he wondered if the weather wasn't a bit chilly for them not to be dressed more warmly. Appearing not to share his opinion, the children darted about like lovable imps while their young physical education teacher went dashing around with them. As the ball went flying from foot to foot, a minor skirmish broke out. The teacher blew his whistle and declared time out—no, a free shot for one of the teams. Khalil scanned the field for his two boys. The goalie would have to be Fadi. That was his favorite position. And his other son loved to play defense. That one's my boy, he thought. No, that one. No. . . . What a fool I am. What makes me think my boys are necessarily out there on the field today?)

Standing near a towering tree along the narrow country road and leaning up against a barbed wire fence, he gazed for a long time at the charming, intimate morning scene of children playing without fear in a place where they were allowed to grow and develop freely. After this he intended to head toward the reception building to inquire about his sons. However, just then the ball rolled in his direction. Panting and grinning, a young boy came running after it until he reached the edge of the playing field. He grabbed the ball, licking his lip victoriously and raising his head. As the boy looked up, Khalil got a good look at his face. It was his son Rami. Khalil froze in place, the barbed wire pressing into his flesh. He wanted to call out to him, but he couldn't get anything to come out of his mouth. Instead, he hid behind the tree lest the child catch a glimpse of him. Too preoccupied with the ball to be distracted by anything else, Rami ran away with it to where he'd come from. Hugging the barbed wire as if it were a fellow sufferer, Khalil burst into tears. He wept as he'd never wept before in his life. He wept because he couldn't bring himself to snatch his children away from this heaven on earth. He knew, of course, all the arguments one might use against this sort of position: There's no such thing as a "paradise" outside one's own homeland. We've got to create paradise for our children with our own hands the way other people before us have done. As for this place, it's nothing but a secondhand utopia that we don't deserve to enjoy simply because we've paid to get in with money taken from the rest of the poor in the Arab world. What you're talking about is an individualistic, subjective solution, and therefore it's unacceptable. . . . At the same time, he knew that if he left his children here, he would be leaving them in a safe place, even though not having been true to himself would torment him for the rest of his life. He knew that for the first time ever, he'd agreed to do something that was inconsistent with his most deeply held convictions. So was this what he'd heard described as the servility that comes with being a parent? Or was it simply that at some point, even the strongest of men weakens? (I used to be an impregnable fortress. And now it's been penetrated.) He wept bitterly, in defeat and humiliation. He wept in the tree's arms. (I haven't cried like this since my divorced mother died. She was in the village when the Israelis came to blow up the neighbors' house in retaliation for harboring Palestinian fedayeen. The neighbor lady collapsed, and everyone in the neighborhood rallied around to comfort her. My mother ran to get out the water pipe and tobacco for her. However, the Israelis had forbidden anyone to go near the place, and had placed a quarantine on the house to ensure the "safety" [!] of the people in the village. No one knows how my frail mother managed to pass through the gauntlet of Israeli rifles to take the lady her water pipe. But no sooner had she stepped inside the door than the house exploded, and she was lost among the dust and debris while everyone stood watching.)

◆　　◆　　◆

When Khalil got back to the hotel, Kafa was having breakfast and looking out at the lake and the swans with the diamond ring still glistening on her finger. She didn't ask him where he'd been. Instead, she announced, "Nadim Bey called to tell you that Sheikh Sakhr and his son are waiting for you. Call him now so that he can pass by. Oh, and by the way, we're invited somewhere for dinner this evening . . ."

" . . ."

"Please, Khalil, let's enjoy life. I beg you! Let's forget Beirut. I hate violence. I detest all those armed vigilantes and wish something terrible would happen to them, like what happened to me because of them. Even the mothers of soldiers pray for God to deliver their sons from the fate of dying on the streets of

Beirut rather than in the land of Palestine. So how can you expect me not to be delighted that I've left Beirut, the biggest cesspool of violence on planet Earth? Please. . . . It's enough that we lost your mother."

"You didn't like her."

"And our daughter Widad."

He was too dejected to respond. He could have said to her, "You're a thief. . ." But he couldn't say she hadn't loved her daughter, or tell her how much she'd changed since Widad's death. But she'd changed a lot. The woman he married hadn't been like this, though some of the seeds of what she was now had been there. She'd been standing at a crossroads. Then when Widad died, she abandoned him and went running like mad in the opposite direction.

"What's that green paint you've got all over your new clothes?"

"It's green blood . . . or tree tears. What difference does it make, anyway?"

"Well, it doesn't make any difference if you change them now and go start your new job!"

When he changed his clothes, he didn't forget the paper napkin with Amir's telephone number on it. He kept on switching it from one pocket to another as if it were his own special good luck charm . . . or his last shot.

This time he stared at the number and recorded it in his memory. He was sure he wouldn't forget it as long as he could remember his own children's names.

Countless times he'd thought of calling Amir only to change his mind. After all, the mere fact that he was one of the man's admirers was no reason to ask for his help. Besides which, he was sure to have his own worries and sorrows. It was no secret, for example, that the authorities back home wanted his head, that his family was forbidden to leave the country and that he hadn't seen his children for years. The fact that Amir was famous didn't mean he was public property, and the fact that Khalil admired him so much didn't put Amir in his debt. He felt a great need to talk to him and to ask for his advice. But what made him think that his favorite author would necessarily be a good shrink? For all he knew, Amir might suffer inner anguish that other people wouldn't be able to bear and which no one else could even fathom. Do you suppose he'd become a writer because of having had to suppress things for so long? If so, then when he wrote he'd have to take care to conceal the greater part of the iceberg of which only about one-tenth appeared above the surface of his deep, opaque waters.

Besides which, he thought, everybody else emigrates in search of sustenance and safety. Why is it that I'm the only one who's so guilt-ridden over it?

(I walk down the world's highways and byways, carrying a globe on my shoulders that's bigger than I am. The globe is dripping with blood, and leaves a red trail on the asphalt—the red hue of torment. The only person who pays any attention to me is my wife, who spits in my face. I walk and walk until I reach the College de Lemare where my two boys are staying. I've come to take them with me on my tormented, circuitous voyage. I stand behind a huge tree that reminds me somehow of a mother's breast. Then I lie in wait for them like a rapacious wolf, preparing myself to snatch them away from a football field that's carpeted with cotton and sterile gauze and smells like rubbing alcohol. As the two boys run around giggling, the referee blows the whistle. At the same time, the tree keeps growing larger, and hanging from its branches I see pieces of barbed wire that come between me and the boys. I look at my hands only to discover that they've turned into barbed wire. Defeated, I take the globe down off my shoulders and roll it into the middle of the street, where a huge truck comes along and crushes it beneath its wheels. I start to howl like a grief-stricken wolf and take off running toward Sheikh Sakhr's mansion to start another new job—a job other than carrying Planet Earth on my shoulders night and day.)

◆　◆　◆

Madame Anbara shrieked in terror, "My little boy, Oh Sheikh! I beg of you!"

"What do the doctors say?"

"They don't know. That's what they said after a month of transferring him from one X-ray machine to another. What with stretchers, colored needles, brain scans and heart scans, his fragile bones have been broken, and he's only twelve years old. . ."

Sheikh Watfan looked pensively at the boy lying prostrate before him. Despite the fact that his face looked prematurely withered, he was beautiful like his mother. And before long he fell into a near-swoon.

"Where was he the first time he fainted?"

"At the boarding school in America. His father sent him there because it's one of the best schools in the world—or so they say. Most of his older brothers and sisters attended the same school—I mean, his brothers and sisters by the sheikh's other wives. He's the youngest, the spoiled favorite child."

"Were you with him the day he had this attack?"

"No, I was in Geneva."

"When you spent vacations with him, did you notice anything?"

"I've never spent a vacation with him. His father wants him to grow up as a modern young man, to discover the world from the time he's young and meet people. Consequently, he spends his vacations in far away places, like Colonie de Vacance. Last time he went to the Isle of Man."

"And have the spells started coming over him again?"

"Sometimes his condition improves, and other times he collapses."

"I need the incense burner. Tell them to get it ready."

"It's ready now."

"Taking the censer, Sheikh Watfan placed some incense, coriander, and oriental frankincense in it. Then he took the young boy's hand gently in his and began reciting verses from the Qur'an: the *Fatiha*, the "throne verse" and a number of traditional prayers of supplication. He kept reciting for such a long time that his voice started to grow faint, as though it were coming not from his gaunt frame, but from some distant cavern. Sometimes Anbara could hear him, and sometimes she couldn't. And when he'd finished his Qur'anic recitation, he began chanting mysterious incantations:

"Aqish Aqish, Qishyamous Qishyamous, Chiyamoush Yarqash Yarqash Yarqash Arqash, it is from Solomon . . . by the truth of the One who was revealed to the mountain, leveling it to the ground, and before Whom Moses fell upon his face as though smitten by lightning. . . .

"Obey, O Maymoun, O Father of Noukh. Enter into his hand and signal with his fingers . . .

"If he is afflicted with the evil eye, raise his little finger for me. If he is in rapture, raise his middle finger. If he has been afflicted by magic, raise his forefinger. If he suffers from an intestinal disturbance, raise his thumb. If he is possessed by a spirit, place his hand upon his head and wrestle him to the ground. May God's blessings be in you and upon you. . ."

Anbara thought she saw her son's hand being raised toward his head. Or was he just trying to wave the odor of the incense away from his nose? Then the boy began to yawn. She thought he'd gotten drowsy on account of the darkened room and the sheikh's monotonous voice as he kept reciting and whispering. However, the sheikh said that the boy's yawning indicated that his malady was caused by spirits, which would have to be exorcised. Then the boy's voice began coming from deep inside him and sounded somewhat different from usual. The sheikh said it was the voice of the spirit that had possessed him. But was such a thing possible? Or was the boy just so terrified that his voice had changed? He moaned and sobbed, calling for his mother and saying that he wanted to stay with her.

"I'll cast it out of him," the sheikh told her. Then he wrote a few cryptic phrases on a piece of paper and burned it with the incense, saying, "Hasis hasis, 'asis, 'asis, shilshal shilshal . . . come out, O spirit—evil, the horseman, the pain that knocks at the heart, the eye and the glance—from the corpse of Burak, son of Anbara. . ."

"Please, Sheikh Watfan . . . give me some reassurance."

"He will recover from the 'earthly winds' and be restored to perfect health, God willing . . . Dimliekh . . . Al-'Afoush . . . Where is Maymoun of the clouds? Where is Maymoun the Swordsman, the Robber, the Red One? Where are the ones with eyes beneath their wings?

"Answer with haste, clothe yourselves in his hand and signal with his fingers. Raise his hand to his head and bring to the ground the spirit that wrongs itself and stirs up mutiny against this lifeless human body. Yet do so without causing harm or disturbance. Make haste, make haste, immediately, immediately, at this hour, at this hour, at this hour. . ."

Just then the boy's body jumped, and the sorcerer rushed to write an inverted *nun*[12] between his eyes, muttering, "I have imprisoned you with the letter *nun*, with the pen, and with that which they write."

Above the *nun* on the boy's forehead he wrote, *"Dham Abhar.* Bring them to a halt, for they are responsible."

Then he wrote on the back of his hand, "Bloodhish Bloodhish," and the same thing on the soles of his feet.

"Don't be afraid," he whispered to Anbara, "I'm going to make the jinni speak."

Then, addressing the spirit he said, "What is your name? What is your tribe? Your religion? Why are you harassing this member of the human race?"

"Mother! Help! Let me run away!"

The boy's voice sounded peculiar, as if it were the voice of some other creature that truly was occupying his body. Or might it just have been that the

---

12. *Nun* is a letter in the Arabic alphabet, corresponding to the English letter "n."

smoke from burning the frankincense, coriander, and paper with black ink on it had stopped up his nose and changed the tenor of his voice?

"You have to be made to speak before you can be released."

"Please!" cried out the boy, "leave me alone!"

"I won't leave you alone until you've spoken, saying, 'I declare the truth of His words: And they will say to their skins: 'Why bear ye witness against us?' They will say: 'God hath given us speech, He who giveth speech to every-thing. . . .' " [13] He also caused Jesus to speak in the cradle as an infant, where-upon he spoke in the name of Ashmakh Shammakh the Exalted One concerning the 'burakh' of God Almighty. He spoke in the names of Bahsh Hansh Hieloush Armyoush Shalha Shiet Tahsh. If you are a Muslim, then say *Al-salamu 'alaykum wa rahmat Allahi wa barakatuhu.* [14] If you're a Christian, then say *Hayyakum Allah.* [15] If you're a Jew, say, "Salam 'ala khaym," and if you're a for-eigner belonging to none of these faiths, then say, "Light upon light." Speak and fear not. You are protected from all danger. . ."

The sheikh then went on repeating, "You are protected from all danger" over and over again.

Finally the boy screamed, "Please, leave me alone! I'll never do anything again. . ."

"Do you relinquish this afflicted soul to me?"

"I do." As the boy spoke the words, he was panting like someone with a heavy weight resting upon his chest. And he went on repeating what he had said again and again as though he wanted to be rid of the sorcerer and his in-cense at any price. Or, Anbara wondered, had the words actually been spoken by a jinni who now occupied his body?

"Promise me never to return again," intoned the sheikh.

"I promise."

Placing his hand in the boy's, the sorcerer droned, "Recite the words of the covenant and learn them by heart: The covenant of God and His sacred oath constrain me. Moreover, by the trust and the pledges which were received by God's prophet Solomon son of David from all spirits and kings, by the names of God Most High which were engraved on his signet ring and by what you

---

13. Qur'an 41:21.

14. That is, "May peace be upon you, and the mercy and blessings of God."

15. That is, "May God give you life."

owe to the Lord of the Worlds, you shall not return to this human being, Burak son of Anbara. No longer shall you harass him outwardly or inwardly, by night or by day, waking or sleeping, eating or drinking, walking, standing or sitting, in speech or in silence—neither you nor your family nor anyone else among your soldiers or your clan. And if you should rebel and violate this covenant . . .

". . . you shall be banished from among the tribes of the jinn, and a curse shall rest upon you until the Day of Judgment in the names of Tanghour Taghmur Tiethatur Taasa Tasha Tahshurh Hanjarousha. And if you should return in defiance of these names, you shall be put to death and burned.

"Bear witness, all ye kings of the Earth in attendance here. . . . Then repeat after me, 'By the truth of Ouf Ouf.' "

Bathed in perspiration, the boy repeated, "By the truth of Ouf Ouf."

"Oush Oush, I shall never return."

However, this time the boy remained silent.

"Repeat after me, O evil spirit, else I shall punish you with severe affliction. Say, 'Oush Oush.' "

"Oush Oush."

"I shall never return."

"I shall never return."

At this point the boy burst into tears and fled to his mother's arms, while the sorcerer opened the door and the windows to facilitate the spirit's departure!

Burak heaved a deep sigh, then fell into a deep sleep.

Sheikh Watfan left the room and was followed out by Anbara.

"He'll sleep peacefully," he said to her. "It's over."

"Will the spells come back?"

"I don't think so. But as a precaution, would it be possible for you to stop sending the boy to a boarding school?"

"Of course. But why?"

"I want him to stay by your side for as long as possible. The mother's presence casts out evil spirits. Don't leave him in the care of nannies, and spend the vacations with him. Make sure he has friends whose parents are virtuous people. And oversee personally every detail of his life."

"There's nothing that would make me happier."

"Tell his father that this is what the sheikh advised you to do, and that otherwise, you'll lose this child companion of yours."

"I'll do that. In any case, this is what Sheikh Sakhr Ghanamali's wife did. She picked up her children and took them back to their own country. They're enrolled now in schools there, and she says their condition has improved since going home again."

"This is my advice to you also, my daughter."

Presenting him with a small bag made of olive green velvet, she whispered gratefully, "I hope you'll keep this as something to remember me by."

"Oh, no, Madame Anbara. You're too kind. . ."

"Please, Sheikh Watfan . . ."

"If it weren't for you, I wouldn't be here. You're the one who sent for me from Beirut. I owe you my safety, even my life."

"Please. The reason I sent for you is that I'd come to know the godliness of your family from the time I was a little girl. During the days when it was still possible for people to spend their summers in Beirut and the surrounding mountains, my mother used to pay visits to your late uncle. I used to come along with her, and I'd often see you. Don't you remember me? I'm the daughter of a sheikh and my mother is Lebanese, from Beirut. I was named after my grandmother Anbara. Do you remember? I grew accustomed to you and your uncle over the years, so when it got to be dangerous to come see you, it delighted me that you were kind enough to accept my invitation, and that your kindness extended even to my family and friends."

(Do I remember you! How could I forget you? How can a man forget the only woman he's ever loved in his entire, barren life? How can he forget, even if he does happen to be a sorcerer?)

"You're a blessing in our lives. I wish you'd stay to have dinner with us."

Sheikh Watfan kept his composure. Making a superhuman effort to sound calm, he said, "I can't. I have to hurry back to the hotel. There's a reporter waiting for me there—I prepare the horoscope for his magazine."

"How about tomorrow? Can you have lunch with us?"

"I'm sorry, but I'll have to get back to Raghid Zahran."

"I've heard that you divide your time between his mansion and the hotel."

"He's unmarried and alone."

"He has no confidence in anyone but you. That's what I've heard."

"People's confidence is a gift from God. Goodbye, Madame. And don't forget my advice. Your son needs you, so don't deprive him of your company, or he's certain to be possessed again."

Anbara escorted him to the car. As he got into the posh Rolls Royce, he heaved an exhausted sigh, while Anbara stood there looking intently at him as if she were waiting for him to say something else. (Can't one simply tell a mother, "Your son is sick due to family negligence?" Is it necessary to cast out demons and burn incense to get her to understand this simple fact?) But how could he, when he wasn't actually convinced that demons *didn't* exit? In the beginning he had been . . . but as he continued to call upon them, he started imagining that he really did see them and speak to them. He'd begun to live with them, yet at times he was as uncertain about their reality as his clients were.

It happened quickly.

Anbara was still standing in front of the open car door, and the chauffeur had stepped back to let her approach. As she thanked Sheikh Watfan, she slipped something small and velvety into his hand. He shuddered when her delicate hand touched his fingers. No. He didn't want any sort of payment or reward from her. He owed her his love for the way she had taken care of him. She was the only person he would have done something for without asking anything in return. He would have plucked out his very eyes and given them to her. In fact, to protect the well-being of her son or that of anyone else she loved, he was even willing to engage in strictly logical thinking without regard for the world of spirits and demons.

He tried to free his hand from her tender grip and return the velvety thing that she so wanted to give him. She obliged him to receive her gift. Then she unexpectedly bowed her head and planted a kiss on his hand. She kissed it only once, yet it was a long, feverish kiss like an extended sigh or moan, and the touch of her lips to his hand felt like a live coal.

He had kept her childhood love hidden deep inside him, shrouding it in dust, long distances and cryptic spells and charms until he'd nearly forgotten it. And now he'd grown accustomed to the forgetting, and to restricting his place in her life to the tepid role of sorcerer.

But that unexpected kiss had set his hand on fire, awakening in his breast a man he thought had died.

He was also taken unawares by the tears that gathered in his eyes with the speed of tropical clouds—he who hadn't wept for ages. And it all happened with lightning speed, the way things happen in dreams. Then Anbara shut the car door and the chauffeur whisked him away while she sped back into the night. He let his tears flow silently in the darkness, pouring down onto his lips and his beard.

As he sat enveloped in the embrace of his velvet and silk upholstered seat, it felt like a field of prickly pears. The kiss she had placed on his hand was still burning, caustic. (Did she kiss me out of gratitude, or does she feel toward me some of what I feel toward her? Has she ever loved me? Has she loved me in silent brokenness, with the love of a young beauty pledged to marry an aged tycoon without being given any say in the matter? Did she ever take notice of the young man hiding inside the shell of a sorcerer's apprentice, or the lonely man tormented like an ant on the ground beneath the feet of fighting dinosaurs?) He wished she were with him now . . . perhaps he could find the courage to ask her what she had meant by that unexpected kiss that seemed to come pouring out toward him from the depths of the past. But her timing had been such that just as the fleeting kiss had been delivered, he was left alone with his bewilderment and dismay, and with the velvet bag that she had slipped into his hand. He opened the bag and removed what was inside. In the dim street light, there appeared a large emerald. Its greenness sparkled as though entire forests had been distilled into a single jewel. Grasping it between his fingers, it stung him as though it were a live coal, not a gift or a treasure. In fact, he was deeply pained. So then, it was nothing but an expression of gratitude. And the kiss had been as well. Yes. No. Oh, he didn't know. . . . When it came to women, he didn't know anything. All he knew was that this emerald brought profound, burning sorrow to his soul. (What's come over me? Three years ago I couldn't even make ends meet. And here I am today, going from silk to silk to emeralds to diamonds to a fortune in the bank, and from mansion to mansion to hotels as luxurious as palaces. And it's all because I finally bent the knee to the king of the demons and agreed to be transformed from a poet into a magician. I gave up my dream and was married to my limited possibilities. I forgot about the bride of poetry and about Anbara, too—or so I thought—and instead took a bride from among the jinn. But what did they do then? They burned up everything. They set fire to everything around me, to everything I'd loved and everything I'd hated, leaving me no choice but to devote myself to old, yellowed books.)

The car pulled up in front of the hotel entrance. The chauffeur got out and respectfully opened the door for him. He found the reporter waiting for him with baited breath.

"We're about to finish up this issue," he said. "Please . . . the editor will have my head. Our sales have gone up since we started consulting the stars about what will happen to people according to their 'signs.' It's all the rage now, even in Europe."

"It's an ancient craft passed down from generation to generation and which I inherited from my ancestors. After my uncle, I'm the last one in my family to practice it."

"And your father?"

"He did something else. He went out with the rescue army in 1948 to liberate Palestine. He was killed there and never came back. And neither did Palestine."

"And your brothers?"

"My brothers also did other things besides practice magic. Burqan, Kan'an, and Ghilan . . . all of them did other things."

By this time they'd gotten into the crowded lift, so they both fell silent. Something about her kiss had taken him back to his past, to his family, and to his true self, and he felt a need to talk about them. Perhaps it was to confirm to himself that once upon a time he'd been another person, that he had a family, a past, and a heart just like everyone else and that like other people, he could feel pain and torment. Disturbed by the silence on the lift, he turned into a baby wolf howling in sorrow. But the other people riding the lift took no notice of him and neither did the reporter. He went on howling, and under the force of his gaze, the iron walls of the lift melted away. So he stepped out and jumped over the moon, a lone wolf letting forth its cries and running aimlessly about in the heart of the darkness, in the heart of the wind, in the heart of anguish and forgetfulness. He was miserable, alone, and frightened. Deep inside there lived the torments of confused, anxiety-ridden years now shrouded in oblivion, but which Anbara had awakened with her kiss. He had loved her in mute silence as she came visiting with her mother long ago. And he had suffered when she, like her mother, married a well-to-do man. Yet he hadn't uttered a word, because he was weak. Ever since he was a child he'd been weaker than any of his five siblings. Even his sister, Wad'a, had been blessed with a hardier constitution than his. So what was left for him to do but turn back into a baby wolf, jump off the moon onto icy hilltops, weep and howl in the face of the storm and strike terror in the hearts of his fellow travelers?

The lift came to a halt and they got off.

They entered the sorcerer's private suite, and by force of habit, the reporter went back to asking questions without really expecting answers or taking any interest in Watfan himself. After all, he personally didn't believe in astrologers. But in the business of journalism, the reader is king, and the mail from one's readership has the final say in what one does.

"And your brothers? Your brothers who tried doing something else? What happened to them? Where are they now? Where is your family? Who are you, really?"

Saying nothing, Sheikh Watfan knit his brow and sparks came pouring out of his extraordinary eyes, the right one green and the left one brown. A rush of childlike fear coursed through the reporter's veins, and he fell silent.

Then suddenly Watfan replied, saying, "I used to have brothers. But they've all died, along with their children."

After this the reporter didn't dare ask any more personal questions. During the following half hour he said nothing but "Fine," "Yes," and "Goodbye," after which he went his way, horoscope in hand.

◆　◆　◆

The reporter had left him, but the question still hung in the air around him: "And your brothers? Don't you have any brothers?" (I left the world of human beings and fled to the world of magic in hopes of forgetting. But there is no forgetting, it seems.

Why didn't I answer him? Why didn't I weep a bit and tell him my story? It might have provided some relief. Why didn't I tell him, "My father died in the military," and go on repeating it until I was blue in the face or until I'd passed out? Why didn't I break into sobs and recount to him how all of us tried to do something other than sorcery, and failed? It seems I haven't forgotten after all. It's as if, even though I'm walking down the paths of the jinn, my bleeding heart is still suspended like a ghost over the door of our charred home in Beirut. I run with goblins and sprites, while my own spirit still wanders aimlessly in a time gone by.

I still seem to remember the argument that broke out between my grandfather and my father before he went to fight in Palestine. I was less than ten years old. Or was it my mother who told me about it and my childhood imagination that filled in the details?

My grandfather slapped my father and screamed, "Damn you, Bahjat! You weren't born to be a soldier! You were born to practice sorcery. So why are you being so bullheaded?" My grandfather commanded not only the obedience of spirits, but of humans as well. My father received the blow without saying a word. Meanwhile, my grandfather went on, saying, "Look at your brother Najdat. You're the eldest son, but he's the one who's my apprentice. As for you, you mock this sacred profession of ours and spend your time unemployed while we support your family. You've got four sons and a daughter—Ghilan, Burqan, Kan'an, Watfan, and Wad'a. Who's going to support them if you die?"

"I'm not unemployed."

"Anyone in our family who doesn't practice sorcery might as well be un-employed. It's the profession that we've passed down from one generation to the next, and that's how things are going to stay. But you read all the books in the world except the ones you've inherited from your ancestors."

"You mean those old musty ones? I can't read them. I don't believe they do anybody any good."

"What we practice isn't just magic. We serve God and people."

"And I also serve people."

"You're a fireman. Aren't you ashamed of your profession?"

"Some people set houses on fire. So there's got to be somebody to put the fires out. Besides, you've always said that the fiery signs of the zodiac threaten our family, and that enemy spirits are conspiring to burn it up. So here I am ready to be of service as a fireman!"

Ignoring the sarcastic tone in my father's voice, my grandfather kept up his angry rebuke, saying, "And your wife and children?"

"What I do, I'm doing for my children's sake. If I don't fight now, then my children will be obliged to later on. And if they don't fight, then the task will fall to *their* children. There's no escaping it, dad."

At the moment the two of them said goodbye, did my grandfather get teary-eyed out of anger, or sadness? We didn't know. But my mother embraced him and wept, and we wept with her.

I remember. I remember and my heart shows me no compassion. I remember that I myself didn't see that teary-eyed look until the day my grandfather informed us of my father's death.

"Your father has been killed in Palestine," he said, "and your mother will marry your uncle, Sheikh Najdat. This is the best solution, since this way we'll go on living together and not be at the mercy of angry spirits or of people who like to gossip." My mother made no objection. However, I believe she was miserable, and that she hated my uncle Najdat with his wicked-looking green eyes. Even so, she didn't object. She didn't dare. My grandfather said, "This is best for you and for the children." However, it wasn't really "the best solution." Without knowing exactly why, we hated our uncle. It may have been that we sensed our mother's dislike and fear of him. In any case, they had no children. In the beginning he used to beat her when the two of them would argue, and his eyes would gleam with a dark, sinister-looking greenness that reminded me of the plants that grow up around tombstones. She used to weep over my father, whom my uncle described as a no good drunkard. There's no doubt that she loved my father. She kept a picture of him that showed his big brown eyes and his moustache that was so thick a hawk could have perched on top of it.

But why do I torture myself with memories?)

Sheikh Watfan got up and stood in front of the window. He gazed out at the beautiful lake, and then at the windowpane. It was no use. There were nights when he was assailed by memories without his knowing what had provoked them. For all he knew, they might have been triggered by the first summer breezes. Perhaps the sudden warmth came as a kind of assault to a sorcerer who'd grown attached to the chill of ghosts and the icy feel of tormented, living cadavers. However, he had to admit that what had really brought the memories back was the encounter with the lovely Anbara, who two or three years earlier had brought him out of the hell in which he'd been living before. His house had burned to the ground and his neighbors had taken pity on him and given him shelter in their homes for a number of days while he recovered from the shock of his loss. It had come as the crowning blow after countless other disasters that had befallen his family: the death of his three brothers, his mother's suicide, and finally the destruction of his home along with the remaining members of his family. The neighbors who had taken him in were poor, and had has many troubles as he did. But they'd been neighbors ever since their troubles began.

(I got home rather late that night, and I knew my uncle would give me a tongue-lashing since as far as he was concerned, I was nothing but a slave who had no right to stay out all day long. I'd gotten together with a poet friend of mine who only rarely left his village to visit Beirut. He lived in a mountain village where he worked as a teacher and wrote poetry and literary criticism. Like most people who know Beirut, he both hated the city and loved it. He was the only person in the world I could confide in. I used to tell him how much I loved poetry and how I loved Anbara, who some years earlier had married a wealthy Arab just as her Lebanese mother had done. That night my friend bid me a final farewell, having decided to stop writing poetry and leave Lebanon for good. When I got back to our neighborhood I found a number of men forbidding people to go near a certain area. I thought I heard the sounds of explosions in the darkness. The smoke was coming out of our house, and some of its walls had collapsed. I begged the men to let me pass. "That's my house!" I told them. "That's where I live!"

"Are you carrying a weapon?"

"No. My name is Watfan Hisrim, and my house is at the end of this side street."

They searched me and found nothing on me but a few poems and sighs. Even so, they refused to let me pass.

They said the area had been cordoned off due to armed clashes in the neighborhood, and that sniper fire would bring me to the ground before I got to my house or even to the other side of the street. So I went wandering aimlessly through the city, being driven by the rain from one sidewalk to the next. Then, chilled to the bone, I sought shelter in the entranceway to some building alongside a mangy dog. I don't know why it didn't occur to me to take refuge in a hostel for the night. Every time I managed to regather what little strength I had left, I'd go back again in hopes of finding a way to get through the blockade. And every time, the vigilantes would chase me away while letting other people pass through in heavily armed cars. An entire day passed this way. Then the next afternoon the clashes died down and the fighters withdrew. Heads began popping out of windows and the wailing of ambulances could be heard. I felt the urge to run away and not go see what had happened to my house after all. I didn't know why, but in a moment suspended between dream and reality, it had appeared to me in a kind of vision as it went up in flames. Nothing like it had ever happened to me before. It was the first time I'd been possessed by a certainty that what might seem like nothing but a chimera passing through my mind was actually a supernatural prescience that went beyond my cold, logical understanding of things. So I began to think: Maybe I really *am* descended from a family endowed with special perceptive capacities—a phenomenon that even modern science doesn't deny and that simple folks call "magic." There wasn't time at that moment to ponder the mysterious powers of the human brain. Instead, I forced myself to go home, and unfortunately, the vision was confirmed. The house had been completely consumed by the fire, and the rain was falling in a savage, eerie way onto its remains. I realized then that everyone inside had been burned to death without anyone informing me. The images were pouring out through a secret hole inside my head that I hadn't been aware of. When I approached the house, I didn't *find* the door so much as I felt where it was. I went frantically through the charred rubble from one room to the next. Everything had gone up in flames. Not finding anyone in the house, I rushed over to our semi-secret iron safe, which had been covered with piles of wood to make it invisible to would-be thieves. But the wood had been consumed by the flames. To get to it, I had to keep digging for a long time through debris, ashes, and fine dust saturated with rainwater, like someone excavating a hill built up through the accumulations of ages past. When at last I reached the bottom, I found the safe closed, but not locked. And there was no money in it, either—not even so much as a piaster. All it contained was a pile of old, yellowed books on sorcery. I looked around me and saw nothing in the entire, incinerated house but dust and debris. Nothing but old, musty books. I despised books on magic, but for some reason I didn't tear them up. Instead, I picked them up as if they were some sort of lifeless corpse and rushed away with them, knowing that they were all I had left. Then a horrifying thought passed through my mind. Do you suppose they really *were* all burned to death, just the way they were in the vision? I knocked on the neighbors' door and found it open. As I stepped inside, I found them all looking at me apprehensively: "Were they all burned to death?" I asked.

"Yes, son. May they rest in peace. Not one of them survived—your uncle Najdat, your sister Wad'a or any of your brother's children. It's an old house, and the fire spread quickly. Everything happened with unbelievable speed."

And I collapsed.

When I came to, I found that they'd laid me on a bed blackened with soot. One of the neighbors said apologetically, "The smoke from the fire has blackened all the houses in the neighborhood, son. You can't even find a pillow that isn't grey."

"What happened?"

"As usual, there was a difference of opinion among the fighters. It's said that when they were on their way toward the south, one of them insisted that they should go right, while another one insisted that they should go left. The boy who works in the corner store claims he heard the argument. He says he told them that whichever way they turned, they'd get where they were trying to go as long as they kept moving. But they weren't convinced. In any case, they kept on arguing amongst themselves without any of them knowing exactly why. Finally one of them fired a shot. Then somebody else launched a shell that missed the car it had been aimed at and hit the house instead. And it went up in smoke in no time. It seems your family was on the second floor, and the whole building collapsed in flames. The people in the neighborhood who tried to rescue them are still suffering from burns on their hands and faces. And they weren't able to approach the house very quickly because the fighters were going right on with their feud. So in the end, we all fled to the shelters."

"And the culprits?"

"As usual, they went on fighting all night long. After that, reinforcements reached both sides. So, after demolishing all the houses in our neighborhood, breaking all the glass, shooting our nerves apart and keeping our children from sleeping, for all we know they might be trying to hunt each other down in some other neighborhood now."

"Damn. . . . They burned up my brother's three orphaned children after he'd died for their sake. Poor Burqan."

" . . ."

"Damn! Every time one of us tries to do something other than sorcery, he's killed—and not by his enemies, but by his friends!"

"Fear God, son, and calm down."

"And my poor sister Wad'a, what had she done to deserve such a thing? She was burned to death. Damn! I swear I'll be a sorcerer. And from now on I won't try to do anything else."

"Relax, son."

"Our family has seen enough victims. And to think that I used to fight with my poor uncle to be able to join their ranks."

"Go to sleep, son. Things will look better in the morning."

But things didn't look any better in the morning. On the contrary, the next day brought nothing but torment. At dawn I woke up to the sounds of shelling, and my heart was filled with loathing for all the violence in the city. In fact, I was filled with loathing for everything that moved . . . fighting . . . fighting . . . death . . . destruction . . . corpses.)

◆   ◆   ◆

The sorcerer put his head under the water faucet, his heart pounding and swelling until it filled his chest and was about to bulge out through his throat and gag him. (Then Madame Anbara sent a messenger to the house, but all he found was a charred ruin. The local ironer said to him, "The poor fellow is living in the baker's house. His family were kindhearted folks, serving people for practically nothing." And I decided then and there not to repeat the mistake that my kindhearted, foolhardy family had made. I decided to spare myself the wretchedness and misfortune they'd known both as magicians and as freedom fighters. I'd be heir to all the ugliness that they'd planted in my heart for no reason but that I was peaceable and weak. I'd flee from fear by resorting to the use of power.)

When he brought his head out from under the cold water, it was so heavy he had to support it with his hands. Then he sat down at the table, where his crystal ball lay before him. He tried to avert his gaze from it, but he wasn't able. Inside it he saw his older brother screaming, and his mother in tears. That was in 1968. And all he could do was stare at them inside that magical, translucent ball.

("Ghilan, please don't go! I went through enough when I lost your father. We've offered one martyr to Palestine, so we've done our part, and that's that!"

"The fact is, we haven't even begun doing our part. Please, Mama, I need your blessing."

"Your uncle will be angry."

"Even if he took a whip to me, I wouldn't listen to him. I'm going. So let me say goodbye to you with joy, not with tears."

Just then my uncle walked in.

"So you're joining the fedayeen?" he asked irately. "We'll see what your grandfather says!"

Then he stormed out. As for my grandfather, he didn't say anything. But the next morning they found him dead of a heart attack.

So Ghilan left. Later on we were told by some that he'd died a martyr's death, and by others that he was still alive and might knock on our door any day. As for my mother, she didn't cry. It was as if she'd exhausted her supply of tears.

After Ghilan went away, she didn't cry for joy again until the day of Burqan's wedding. But when Burqan was blessed with children, she showed no concern, as if she'd washed her hands of the whole ill-fated family. And when she discovered that he was corrupt just like my father and my brother Ghilan, that he was working in politics, and that he preferred his job as a taxi driver to practicing the profession of his wizard forefathers, she didn't say a word. By this time my uncle was getting up in years and we no longer felt afraid of him the way we had before. I was working grudgingly as his assistant. His relations with the jinn and the neighbors were as cordial as ever, and he went on supporting the entire family just the way he'd done for so long. Meanwhile, my brother Burqan kept bestowing on us a new mouth to be fed with every year that passed. Every now and then he'd come around wounded and drunk with his machine gun in his hand, until finally his wife ran away, leaving behind three children for my sister Wad'a to adopt. We were told that he was confused and quarrelsome, joining then leaving one organization after another, and that he'd lost sight of the goal and fallen into a life of contradictions. He was wretched and wild, but I loved him, and he and I used to talk to each other on the sly. Once he tried to persuade me to join some organization with him. I told him I wasn't sure where I stood, and he confessed to me that he also didn't know what he believed anymore. I told him I was a coward, that I was afraid, that I was trying to find my own personal deliverance through poetry. And he laughed at me. That evening he came back after having gotten into a row with his buddies, and said he'd be changing location. Then he fled the house and disappeared for several days, at the end of which we found his bullet-riddled body draped over the top of his taxi in front of the house. His "buddies" had been waiting for him and executed him on the spot.

His body was still warm and dripping with blood when some noble, generous folks picked him up and carried him away. They brought him inside the house, and my mother heard one of them saying that he was dead. I was standing not far from her when she struck her head with both hands, then kept them there on top of her head as if it had been severed from her body and she was afraid it might roll off. Then I heard a lone shriek, like the sound of an animal about to breathe its last. It wasn't a human shriek. Rather, it was a muffled, wounded scream that seemed to come from somewhere far, far away. My brother Burqan's face was mangled, torn to shreds by the bullets. The sight of his corpse was enough to make one's heart bleed. My mother sat staring into space without uttering a word, with a mute scream on her lips that seemed to have been suspended in midcourse.

A terrible silence hung over the place as the men stood awkwardly before her, bearing the lifeless body of her child now become a man and waiting for her to shatter the solemnity of the moment with a womanly outburst of mourning. However, she didn't even weep. It was as if, fearful for her sanity, she had decided not to let her heart grasp what her eye had beheld. Or had she become so conscious of the absurdity of things that she was paralyzed? The place was charged with a grief so dreadful, it went beyond voices or sounds. It was as if the women of the city had exhausted their supply of tears for centuries to come, and no longer enjoyed the luxury of public displays of sorrow. As I came up to the men I was sobbing openly. But my mother remained as unmoved as a pillar of salt. The contagion of her broken dignity spread to the men bearing the corpse, who bowed their heads as if they'd grasped the essence of death for the first time.

How could I ever forget the look in my mother's eyes?

After several awful moments of stark, gloomy silence, a look of chagrin appeared on the faces of the men who were carrying Burqan's body. It was as if they had killed him themselves, or at least had played some role in his demise. As if every living creature in all Beirut were a criminal in some sense. The look in my mother's eyes wasn't a hostile one. Even so, the pallbearers looked as though they suffered from a vague sense of guilt mixed with the urge to flee. It was as if Burqan's body had become heavy, ever so heavy—as heavy as the corpses of all the slain who had fallen in Beirut.

Then, as they moved to lay his body on the bed in preparation to escape from an atmosphere that went beyond that of ordinary mourning, my mother opened her lips and said something to them in a soft voice.

We listened carefully, expecting to hear the quiet prelude to a frenzied symphony of tears. All we wanted was for her to scream a bit and cry the way women have always done so that death could take its usual, repetitive, half-monotonous course. But instead she surprised us by doing something that none of us would ever have expected, and which never would have happened anywhere but in Beirut. Still holding on to the cleaning rag that she'd been using before their arrival, she said to the men, "Can't you see he's bleeding? You're going to get the bed all dirty. Put him out on the balcony." I'll never forget the peculiar look in my mother's eyes. It was a blank stare that seemed to retreat inside her, either to utter emptiness, or to the silent unknown.)

◆　◆　◆

Oh . . . night's approaching, and I'll be alone. Then all those images will attack me again, unless I settle things by performing the nocturnal rites that will take me away forever to the land of the jinn. But do I dare? Why did Anbara kiss my hand? When she put her lips to my skin, she broke the spell of forgetfulness.

In my early days as a sorcerer, whenever my clients left I'd begin trembling with horror and fright. I'd know that the night was approaching again and that I'd be alone. And once I was by myself, I'd remember and remember, and my heart would show me no mercy. I would stare into my magic ball, and in it I would see my poor mother—the mother that all of us had made so unhappy, the woman who'd been subjected to slow torture until she'd decided to withdraw from life altogether. As for me, I used to flee for refuge to the "jinn bride," immersing myself in the pleasures of her world. Every time I went to her, she would clothe herself in the body of a different woman. So why did Anbara have to come and sow discontent in my spirit all over again?

(After the death of my brother Burqan, my mother didn't utter a word to anyone for an entire week. And no one could rein in the wandering, distant look in her eyes. Not even my brother's children could arouse a response in her face, which was as rigid and blue as that of a corpse. She looked as though she'd died and left her spirit behind to go wandering aimlessly through worlds less miserable than the one she had known. And now all that remained was for her to rid herself of the body, which had become a barrier that stood between her and her final escape.

The people in the neighborhood said she'd lost her mind. And nobody blamed her. After all, she'd suffered terribly with the loss of her three sons and her husband. When Burqan was killed, only a few years had passed since the death of her newly wed son Kan'an. He'd gone with his bride to visit her family in south Lebanon when the car they were riding in was run over by an Israeli tank. And because his flesh was so riddled with iron splinters and disfigured by the marks left by the tracks of the tank, they didn't even send us his remains. As for the cause of the incident, the tank had run them down just because it had a schedule to meet in the Israeli invasion of south Lebanon in 1978.

My uncle claimed that she was possessed by an evil spirit and that the deaths of my father and my three brothers Ghilan, Burqan, and Kan'an weren't enough to explain the state she was in. He said he was going to force the spirit to speak even if he had to take a whip to my mother. So he set about preparing the incense he would need for the session. Some of the neighbors got ready to attend the event, but others said that the successive calamities that had befallen us were divine retribution for our having meddled in the realm of unseen powers.

The next day at dawn, we heard my mother scream. At the same time, we smelled the odor of kerosene and burning human flesh: my poor mother had set herself on fire. When I saw her face through the flames, it had regained the tormented, human expression that had disappeared during the final years of her earthly life. And then it was transformed into charred remains.)

Have mercy, O night! Have mercy, O ye spirits that emerge from the chambers of the past. Have mercy, O ye ghosts of loved ones lost. Leave me in peace. Come out of my crystal ball. Remove yourselves from my bloodstream, from my mortal eye. Have compassion on a poet forced by life's cruelty to play the sorcerer, and who then became so consumed by his new role that he lost confidence in his ability to face himself. I've stepped inside the mirror so many times, I've lost the ability to step out again into the world of human beings. It's as if I've begun to evaporate in a cloud of incense. Have mercy, O Anbara, thou who hast emerged from my old, tattered dreams. Allow me to forget that I once belonged to a family, that I was a young man, that I was a poet, or that I was in love with you. The fortune I've amassed in a mere two years, I don't know how to enjoy anymore. It's as if the mirror has taken me captive. And now the only choice before me is to go deeper and deeper into the land of the jinn, who've abandoned me like a tattered rag on the shore beside a sea of fire.

What use is it to have fame, authority, and power when I'm miserable, terrified, and lonely, uprooted from my own soil and wandering aimlessly with my incense through an empty expanse ruled by the jinn? The night is coming, and I'll be alone again . . . paralyzed with fear. The most powerful men on earth tremble in my presence, the most beautiful women beg for my blessing with tears in their eyes, and rulers and governors bend the knee before me. But when night falls I revert to being alone and afraid, so afraid that I quake at the sound of a butterfly's footsteps, and I fall apart at the sound of the approaching darkness. I flee for refuge to the first female whose body can serve as the jinn bride's earthly veil. I go to Berne Street in partial disguise to pick her up off the sidewalk. Then I plant my sorrows inside her body and leave her in silence, or I beat her in hopes of driving out of her body the spirit that's entered her for my sake. But tonight I won't be able to go out on my usual nocturnal foray in hopes of numbing myself. I'm besieged on all sides by Anbara, who captured me with that innocent, furtive kiss in the heart of a mournful, never-ending twilight.

◆　◆　◆

Nasim walked along, stung on the outside by the chilly Geneva winds, but on the inside, a volcano. (Every night before I go to sleep I swear I'm going to kill him. And every morning I go on waiting on him hand and foot like some bootlicking dog. When are my fangs and claws going to grow enough for me to destroy that beast known as Raghid Zahran, who has thousands of faces and lives in thousands of mansions and controls the livelihoods and destinies of people from one seashore to another? He humiliates me in my work, he tramples on my dignity, and he does the same to others. He knows I'm weak because my country is falling apart, so he takes advantage of the situation by grinding me a little further into the dust. But I'll never be able to do what I intend until I've finished my degree and gotten myself and my family on solid ground. You're really laughable, Nasim. You're the head of a family with ten mouths to feed and school fees to pay when you're not even twenty-five years old yet, and you say you want the head of Raghid Zahran! But you wouldn't be satisfied with the head living in this mansion. No, you'd want all his other heads, too—the ones that take up residence in fortresses all over the globe, and with features, names, and masks that differ to suit the locale.)

Nasim went speeding down one of the walkways at the University of Geneva, then turned a bend and began heading toward the library. Just then he spotted Dr. Amir Nealy, who didn't see him. Rushing to catch up with him, he shouted with genuine enthusiasm, "Dr. Amir! Good morning! I'm so glad to see you!"

"Hi, Nasim. How did you manage to escape from your golden spider's web this time? And in the morning, no less!"

"I managed thanks to the sorcerer. His orders have been multiplying, which gives me more chances to get away to attend a few lectures and collect references for my thesis."

"How's the writing going?"

"Slowly. The golden spider is getting crazier and crazier."

"The important thing is for you to get your thesis done before it swallows you up."

"I nearly murdered him with my own two hands the other day. Imagine . . . Nasim, the cool-headed, logical, rational man who loves nothing more than a debate where he can play the devil's advocate, was about to turn into a club-carrying savage straight out of the jungle."

"Would you like to tell me what happened?"

"Not now. You've got work to do. And I've got to hurry and get something done in the library."

"Great. So then, your work is flourishing. And all the rest is mere detail."

"Well, the sorcerer's work is flourishing, at least. And it looks like he's switching from burning incense and preparing potions to preying on live victims."

"What do you mean?"

"He wants a kind of sparrow that's blue and has a crown. Or rather, he wants a blue dove for his rites. I came to look in the library for the name of a bird that fits the description, if one exists. Where am I going to find a small blue bird with a crown?"

"Why don't you go get a white dove, then the two of us can dye it blue?"

They both laughed, and Nasim could feel himself being infected with a bit of Amir's unaffected gaiety.

"In any case," Amir went on, "I hope you can finish your thesis before he graduates from animal and bird sacrifices to human ones. After all, the demons might choose you to be their next victim. . . !"

This time they had a good long laugh. However, Nasim was dreading the prospect of having to pass on news about Layla. He knew the laughter would die on Amir's lips as soon as he'd heard it. But there was no avoiding it . . .

Whispering like a spy, Nasim said, "I'm sorry, but I have something to tell you about Layla that might upset you. I don't want to play the tattletale. But I know what confidence you have in her and how much you've loved her. She's been coming around constantly. I mean . . . to see Raghid. There have been several telephone calls a day."

"Strange. She's never told me anything about her connection to Raghid."

"And you . . . have you ever told her anything about me? Have you told her that I'm your student and that I spy on people for you? I'd lose my job if Layla let Raghid in on this secret of mine."

"Layla already knows about your connection to me, since she's seen you in my house so many times. So if she really has joined up with Raghid and his gang, you may in fact lose your job, friend. I'm really sorry. I don't trust women generally, and it looks like I'm no different from any other careful man: a total fool when it comes to love."

"Well, whatever happens, happens. In any case, I won't hide anything from you. During her last visit to Raghid, something odd happened. She sold him a coin that's worth a fortune. It's an antique Palestinian piaster. Can you believe it?"

"Go on."

"They talked about various joint ventures, one of them being a huge bash that Raghid is planning called The Night of the First Billion, in celebration of his having amassed his first billion dollars. And Layla's responsible for planning the whole thing. Raghid's interested in the service agency that Layla's set up, so he's been supplying her with some rich clients, including Ghanamali. And he's promised to send others her way as well. He started recommending her services to them some time back, apparently. He seemed as excited as a little kid over the antique coin, and when she left, he picked it up and took it into where his golden swimming pool is. You know the one. Well, once he'd taken it inside, he started ranting and raving as usual at the Freedom Fighter statue. And then he did something really bizarre. He tried to force the statue to swallow the coin! I wasn't trying to spy on him. But I happened to be bringing him his medicine when I saw him do it. Is it really possible for somebody to spend a small fortune on an old coin just so he can use it to get a rise out of a dead statue?"

Both men remained silent for some time. Amir nearly said, "The coin is still new," and "The statue is still alive," but he held his tongue at the last minute.

He hated ending his statements with melodramatic turns of speech, even if they happened to be true. As for Nasim, he began stammering and repeating himself.

"This fabulous Night of the First Billion . . . Layla's going to get the whole thing ready."

"You already told me that."

"He flirted with her, and she played hard to get but in a very nice way, as if she was putting him off for a while but not really rejecting him."

"That's strange. He usually only has dealings with virgins and young girls—that is, unless they're the wives of his employees. As for Layla, she's forty years old."

"I suspect she brings out his lust for control—over men, that is! This lady conducts her affairs like a male, you know."

" . . . "

"One of her clients is Sakhr Ghanamali. Supposedly she put together some sort of decorative objet d'art for him and Raghid. I didn't mean to eavesdrop. But unlike eyes, ears don't have lids that you can close when you don't want to see something."

"Go on."

"That's all."

Keeping his composure, Amir said in his usual merry, lovable tone of voice, "Fine. And I've got some information that might be of interest to you and your sorcerer. There really is such a thing as a blue-crowned dove. It's called the crowned Queen Victoria dove. It's a brilliantly colored bird, and on top of its head it has an exquisitely shaped tuft of blue feathers whose outer edges look like white lace. It's indigenous to New Guinea. So you can go to the library and do two hours' work on your thesis, then take this information back to the sorcerer after making a quick call to the airlines to find out how much it costs to fly to Australia, which is where your bird lives. Then you can disappear for a whole week on the pretext of going there to bring it back with you. And in the meantime, I'll round one up for you here in Geneva. I've got friends who raise birds professionally and who know how crazy I am about them."

"Getting away from my golden spider's web isn't easy. Before he allots me a single franc of my salary, he'll look for the entry visa to Australia in my passport. He's an incredible miser and an incredible spendthrift at the same time. He's a tightwad with the poor, and just the opposite with the well-to-do. Besides which, I'm afraid of the man. There are moments when I get the feeling I'm being watched, and that he knows everything: that I'm in contact with you, that I'm a student in the College of Humanities working on a thesis on 'Arab Human Rights,' that I'm a graduate of the Lebanese University with a major in political science, and that I hate his guts. Oh, if only I could concentrate all my energy on my academic work for one solid week. Sometimes I have to return books to the library before I've finished using them. They come due before I've had the chance to read them the way they need to be read. Being a student when you're poor and living abroad is torture. When you're in your own country, you feel stronger, maybe because you don't need so much money."

"Write me a list of the books you need, and I'll take them out in my name."

"I'd appreciate that a lot. I don't know how I can ever repay you. If it weren't for you, I wouldn't be able to keep going."

"You all are my comrades and my sons. And gratitude is the sign that one is merely a pilgrim passing through this world."

As soon as Nasim was gone, the smile disappeared from Amir's face, and he took off wandering without knowing where he was headed. He walked for a long time through the trees around the lake. He was always this way. He always thought better when he was walking. And if he could have, he would have spread his wings and taken off flying like the sparrows that he loved so much. After all, to him walking was just a poor substitute for flying. He thought about her—about that precious woman Layla. What was she doing to him and to herself?

What had come over her since that failed attempt on his life? Instead of getting more attached to him and rejoicing over his having survived, she'd begun acting as though he'd actually died. Women are really strange, he thought. They hold on to you for reasons that to you seem more like justifications for leaving, and they leave you because of things that you would have expected to fuel the fires of passion.

("I'm married."

"I love you."

"I have children."

"I love you."

"And I love them all."

"I love you."

"I'll never be able to marry you. I couldn't betray the mother of my children, the one who's stood beside me through thick and thin and taken care of the children the whole way through. I'm indebted to her. And I respect her."

"I love you. And trivial things like these will never come between us.")

The events passed before his eyes as if they were happening right then and there. He could hear Layla's voice, on fire with a passion the likes of which he'd never known before, the type that casts care to the wind. The type that comes from a curious mixture of maturity and puppy love. With her he'd forgotten his poverty. He'd forgotten his misery. He'd forgotten the bitterness of living in exile. He'd had more energy for his work. He'd written his best books. And now . . . what had happened?

The antique Palestinian coin he'd given her was the most valuable thing he owned. It was a piaster that had been given to him by a partner in his political struggles. On the day his buddy fled from Palestine as a little boy, he'd brought it with him, along with a number of other coins that were lost on the way. Rusty and with a hole bored in its center, it had "Palestine, 1946" inscribed on its face in Arabic, English, and Hebrew. And on the other side its value—ten mils—was written in the same three languages. However, it was worth far more than a mere ten mils. He'd carried it with him year after year as a good luck charm . . . in the bitter cold of detention camps and the places he'd made his homes away from home, he'd clung to it like someone who's holding his heart in his hand.

The name "Palestine" inscribed in Arabic, English, and Hebrew on the face of the coin, which was now nearly worn smooth, burned like a live coal, searing his hand, his spirit, his entire being. He'd grown up hearing Arabs refer to Palestine as "so-called Israel," while most events of late seemed to warn of the pending collapse of the "so-called Arab countries." But he'd never lost hope. And he never would.

So, Raghid had flirted with her? And he was surprised? Perhaps she'd been surprised herself. Poor woman. Little did she know that her body had turned into a battlefield between him and another man. Perhaps she didn't realize that his sculptor father, Mufid Nealy, was the person who had done the statue beside Raghid's pool . . . and that after buying the sculpture, Raghid had tried to buy the sculptor's son, but without success. And now here he was buying the woman he loved. And the piaster he'd given her. She must have told Raghid that she'd received it as a gift from him, in which case he had bought it not to honor Layla, but to hurt the person she'd received it from. He'd heard about the New Year's Eve party where she'd used the coin to create a stir.

(I was wrong. I should have told her about the details of my relationship with Raghid, and about the nasty motives that control the huge, golden chess game in which he's about to turn her into one of his pawns. I should have told her the details of that visit I made to Raghid, and how I declined to become the editor of the journal he was planning to put out as a vehicle for taming destitute Arab intellectuals in exile who might be forced by the curse of having to make a living to lick someone's boots and come out in defense of irreconcilable opposites. It was going to be the first stage in a process of transplanting tribal and sectarian disputes from where they'd first begun to the Arab community abroad.)

But he, the destitute, fugitive, outcast refugee, hadn't wanted to appear conceited by bragging in front of a woman, saying, "Raghid Zahran, the billionaire, hates me so much he's afraid of me. And the only thing that will make him comfortable is to be able to 'buy' me. The reason is that in his view, I'm not just a single man. Rather, I'm a current that could become so powerful that it sweeps him away. This sort of thing has happened many times before, and it could happen again. Men like him refuse to engage in dialogue with me or even to acknowledge my humanity. The only thing that will relieve their discomfort where I'm concerned is to buy me at any price. If they could, it would guarantee that I'd become one of his devotees, so to speak. A very costly one, or a very cheap one. It makes no difference. These things are merely quantitative differences, not qualitative ones. Men the likes of Raghid aren't satisfied even if someone praises or compliments them—as long as it's done free of charge. After all, if there's no price tag on it, then the other person is still free to think as he chooses, and consequently, he's free to change his mind and renounce him later on once he finds out what the man's really like. Everyone has to be bought, friend and foe alike."

However, Raghid had found him unyielding. So he tried to vanquish him by buying a part of him: Layla. And in doing so, he stabbed him in the very heart.

(Really. I should have told her.)

So why not go see her and tell her frankly about certain things so that they could talk them out?

Once the attempt had been made on his life and Layla had started cooling off toward him, he didn't dare broach any painful subjects with her. And now he'd begun to feel her elderly mother's tattooed hand reaching out in front of him, as if to prevent him from harassing her or bringing up any more of her sorrows. Fine, then. He'd go see her at her new office on Rhone Street and congratulate her on her new job. Then if the mood seemed right, he might invite her for lunch and they could have a frank talk. But no . . . he wouldn't be able to invite her out. His pockets were nearly empty, and he didn't have a franc to spare. He'd recently helped a friend of Nasim's who didn't have enough money to pay his tuition. These poor Arab students were struggling to educate themselves, while others were struggling to fritter away his money. At one time he'd thought that Layla understood all this. So how could she have turned against him this way? That young woman who'd been like a living cry of dissent, who used to go out and join any protest demonstration she saw in the street without even asking what it was about . . . whose sole calling in life had been to reject and refuse . . . how could she have changed so completely? He'd made a special effort to bring her out of her subjective, existential, floating alienation and to make her realize that the true roots of her alienation lay in her loss of a homeland. There was a sense in which she had brought about her own alienation by westernizing herself, and the West was where she felt she belonged now. She'd replaced a concrete struggle with her own people aimed at changing the painful reality in which they were living, with a phantomlike, existential struggle against the fog of European cities. He'd fought against her propensity for the traditional, romantic sort of disaffection by bringing it back down to earth . . . the "earth" of her homeland. He'd taught her to give a real-life focus to her floating hostility and her penchant for rejection and renunciation, and helped her to understand the priorities of a freedom fighter: that it's more important to struggle on behalf of the children in her homeland than on behalf of baby seals, that warring against Menachem Begin and his ilk matters more than warring against obesity, and that as an Arab woman, the most authentic thing she could do was to march on behalf of the Arabs being slaughtered in the occupied lands—not to go out protesting the maltreatment of canines in some "dog hotel" in a Geneva suburb the way she'd been doing the day he first met her. He used to think he'd won her—that she'd won herself. He'd done his utmost to see to it that her creative energies weren't poured out in vain into the cups of the inebriated. Time and time again he'd stood by her side openly and exposed himself to ridicule in hopes that the cause would win over a scattered rebel like her.

So what had she done?

She'd put on the fur coats that she'd refused to wear in the past. She'd gone to celebrate the attempt on his life. She'd prostituted the coin he'd given her as a symbol of his raison d'être. She'd curried favor with the man who embodied the interests of the slaughterers of his people and those who sought to take his life. And now she was vying with the likes of Nadim to become one of his assistants.

He paused in front of the posh building where her office was located to gaze at a chess set in a jewelry-store display window on the first floor. It consisted of a gold, diamond-studded board and playing pieces of silver and gold. How could she afford to rent an office above such a luxurious shop? He went on staring at the chess set and thinking about her. He wasn't surprised to glimpse her inside the store—lovely Layla with her long raven hair, now transformed into a golden pawn.

When she saw him staring in at her, she raised her hand and waved at him, shouting, "Bonjour, Amir! Haven't you died yet? If not, you're as good as dead. As for me, I've gone with the winner!"

He almost said to her, "Well, if he wasn't a winner to begin with, your choice of him will make him into one. How could you have weakened and sold him that priceless coin?"

But he didn't say it. For one thing, he was afraid she wouldn't be able to hear him through the window. And secondly, he was afraid that passersby would think he was some crackpot who'd started having conversations with chess pieces. And that would be a bit difficult to explain to the ever-vigilant Swiss police!

He was anxious to go up and speak with her. But without knowing exactly why, his feet betrayed him and took him instead to the coffee shop across the street. (I love her more than I realized. I'm afraid of making her angry, and I don't want to do something rash and lose her forever. So it's better to sit here for a while and get my thoughts in order. What exactly do I want to say to her? Have I come to try to drag her into an argument? If so, what good would that do? Calm down, you foolish heart, and let logic and reason write an article or dissertation on love and betrayal.)

He was always making fun of himself. It made him feel better. Since she'd left him, some of his hardness had been broken. But he hadn't lost his composure.

("Slap her!"

Bassam said it quite matter-of-factly, then continued, "Stop thinking logically about the reasons she left you. It's useless to use common sense with women, since they haven't got any. So just slap her, and she'll fall on her knees."

"It would be nice if you'd confront your life the way you tell me to confront Layla. You, Bassam, are running away from everything. Never once have you slapped life in the face with a single solid decision. And now you want me to slap Layla?!"

"What do you mean?"

"What I mean is that the work you've been doing on your Ph.D. ever since the civil war started in Lebanon is nothing but an excuse to run away. And you know it. Imagine—a successful, mature lawyer like you with ten years of experience in his profession, dropping everything just like that the day the war broke out in 1975, claiming that he wants to go on for a Ph.D. Isn't that running away? Is that the way you slap the civil war in the face? And the tragedies going on in your country? Or is it only women we're allowed to slap?"

"I'm free to do as I please. So I decided I wanted to finish a Ph.D. at Cambridge. . . . All my life I'd dreamed of studying there."

"Four years at Cambridge, and you still haven't done what you came to do. If anything, you're farther from being finished now than you were when you first went there. Instead of doing what you said you'd come to do, you started hopping from one university to another, spending all your savings, and being afraid of getting your work done lest you have to face the moment of decision: whether to go back home, or to live in self-imposed exile. You prefer to wallow in procrastination!"

It was pouring down rain. And with the rain my rage and sorrow came pouring out like a flood with nothing to check its flow. Only rarely do I lose my temper with someone I love. I don't know what came over me when he advised me to slap her. But I could feel the anger rising in my throat and turning into harsh words: "Listen, Bassam . . . you only want me to slap her because you're a coward. You run away from marriage for fear that your wife would cheat on you. You run away from love for fear of the responsibility it would bring. You run away from sex for fear of disease. You run away from life for fear of dying. You run away from Beirut for fear of being killed, kidnapped, or hit by sniper fire. Yet you fail to notice that in the meantime, you've joined the ranks of the living dead. You're under the illusion that people are watching you and want to murder you simply because you're one of my friends and because you attend some of my seminars and gatherings. You're terrified. You've stopped engaging in any kind of activity for the past eight years, and the world has forgotten you. So, instead of asking me to slap Layla, why don't you come to terms with your own life?"

Bassam started gathering what few clothes he owned and putting them in a small suitcase, and I knew he was leaving. Feeling incredibly ashamed, all my anger turned into sadness and regret.

"I've been a burden to you by living with you," he said gloomily. "The reason you're overreacting like this is that I bother you by being here. I apologize. And I'm leaving."

"Don't go!" I begged him. "Please accept my apology!"

"You're being hard on me because it was after I moved in that your relationship with Layla went on the rocks. I know I'm a dimwit, bankrupt and good for nothing. But I didn't mean to come between you two. You don't have anywhere to meet anymore. You're afraid of her mother, and she doesn't like to have me around. You aren't teenagers who'd be content to take their love affair public in bars and nightclubs. I've ruined everything, and I've got to go."

"You haven't ruined anything. These are hard times, and things were already starting to go to pot all by themselves. After all, Layla isn't the only one who's changed. Rather, she's more like a symbol for a whole world that's changing. A symbol of the betrayal of causes. I respect you for refusing to work for Raghid when he tried to get you to sell yourself out the way he did with me. As for her, she did an about-face, just like so many others that we've known and loved. So I don't think I'm hurting over her alone. Rather, she reminds me of all of them at once. She reminds me of a certain unbiased writer who held out for what seemed like an eternity against the political line held by some king. Then about a year ago he starting speaking highly of "His Majesty," and wrote an article in which he referred to "His Majesty" no less than twenty-five times. She reminds me of a young man who used to be so devoted to our cause he would have laid down his life in our defense. He was like a coat of mail over our hearts, only then he turned around and became an informer for the other side. Or the journalist that was against a certain president, then turned into a press attaché in "His Excellency's" entourage. And the magazine that used to devote half its time to combating a certain figure and everything he stood for, and the other half to proudly publishing the man's memoirs. . . . This is painful. What good would it do to slap Layla when treachery slaps us in the face every single moment? Everything changes, and we're falling like dominoes.")

However, as he sat there in the coffee shop dripping with sorrow and humiliation, he really did wish he could slap her. He wished he could go right upstairs, strike her on the cheek, and leave. So was he beginning to change, too?

❖   ❖   ❖

Once in the study, Khalil relaxed, and for the first time he felt some semblance of safety. The Ghanamali estate was a world of uproarious contradictions.

It was true that Sheikh Sakhr had treated him kindly since he began his job a few days earlier. And his son Saqr seemed as delighted with him as a little boy with a new toy that he still hasn't managed either to figure out or to break. Even so, ever since his arrival at their extraordinary mansion on the shores of Lac Léman, he'd been haunted by a vague feeling of discomfort. One reason was that the men who worked in the garden were cutting down all the trees in the mansion's front yard. Then once the trees were cleared away, trucks would bring loads of sand and dump it out over the grass and the tree stumps. Sheikh Sakhr felt homesick and wanted to create a desert for his she-camel. He was also thinking of pitching a tent outside not far from the mansion. But the budding features of his mock desert looked rather pitiful against the backdrop of greenery, water, European summer rain, and miserly Swiss sunshine. As for the camel he'd had flown in on his private airplane—since he was accustomed to drinking her milk—she looked miserable, withered and lost. They said it wasn't the first time something like this had happened. The first camel had kept getting sick, so they'd brought in another one, which died. Then the one that died was replaced, and so on it went. It was after this that, in a moment of caprice, the sheikh had decided to make a desert for himself and his camel.

His twin brother, Sheikh Hilal, appeared to take a dim view of what was going on.

"Don't you fear God!?" he would shout reproachfully. "What is this waste? I won't stand for any more of it. This mansion ought to be sold, and you all ought to gather up your scandals and your harems and head back home. God have mercy! Are these the only interests you've got? Don't you give a damn about what's happening anywhere else? Have you heard what's going on in Lebanon? Aren't you afraid the conflagration there will spread?"

These were the first words Khalil had heard as he sat in the hallway that morning waiting for Saqr. First, his father Sakhr had walked in unexpectedly, laughing with delight like a little boy being scolded by his daddy. Then Sheikh Hilal had passed by, staring at Khalil contemptuously, as he did every day, yet refusing to speak to him. Saqr received Sheikh Hilal cheerfully, saying, "Welcome, Uncle Hilal! This is Khalil Dar', my new secretary from Lebanon."

The uncle didn't shake his hand, contenting himself instead with a nod of the head.

(How can I blame him? He thinks I'm just like them. I'm the Lebanese secretary who's going to set up drug deliveries, arrange liaisons with women, and get places for them at gambling tables in places where people go to numb themselves against reality. But am I not on the way to becoming the way they are? Am I like the hypocritical virgin who gulps down the glass of liquor pretending not to know what it is, then bemoans the loss of her chastity the next morning? Am I secretary to Amir Nealy, or to Saqr Ghanamali, a Don Juan in love with the high life, as Nadim gave me to understand as tactfully as he knew how? I mean, do I think this man needs me to help him translate the *Encyclopaedia Britannica* and the Webster's and Oxford dictionaries into Arabic, or have I come of my own free will to take a job that I wouldn't want to be accused of doing?)

It was only when he found himself between the four walls of the study that he felt some semblance of peace come over his soul. Here he was in the midst of exquisitely bound volumes full of treasures for those who read them, with their titles engraved in gold letters on their spines. He read: *Al-Kamil* by Mubarrad, *Diwan Al-Hamasa*, *Al-Aghani* by Isfahani, *Deliverer from Error* and *The Downfall of the Philosophers* by Al-Ghazali, *Al-Muqaddimah* by Ibn Khaldoun, *Pastures of Gold* by Mas'udi, *Sultans' Rulings* and *Ministerial Laws and Royal Policy* by Mawardi, *Delight and Conviviality* by Abu Hayyan Al-Tawhidi, *Orphan of Time* by Tha'alibi, *Lisan Al-'Arab* by Ibn Mansur, *Classes of Nations* by Sa'id al-Andalusi, *Extraordinary Creatures* by Al-Qazwini, *The Rare Necklace* by Ibn Abd Rabbih, *The History of Damascus* by Ibn Asakir, *The Pillar* by Ibn Rashiq, and other titles. . . . They were lovely, valuable books that he'd read in the past, at least in part, and he had loved them. He'd felt a kind of intimate familiarity in their presence. Perhaps Sheikh Hilal had given them to his misguided brother and his family in an attempt to educate them. It was unfortunate that Hilal despised and hated him before they'd had a chance to get to know each other. Otherwise, they might have been able to have some good conversations. A wave of enthusiasm came over him for a moment. Oh, what wonderful books. . . .

Holding onto to one's heritage is a basic necessity. However, he could also give them some books by Amir Nealy, as well as some other contemporary works the names of which he couldn't recall just then.

Noticing that Khalil was spending a long time looking at the books, Saqr had a sudden urge to give him a shock. Stepping up to the large bookcase, he pressed a pen into the hand of a small statue of some man of letters that had been placed on the shelf for decoration. At the touch of the pen, the entire wall lined with books began to move, slowly opening to reveal a bar stocked with countless bottles of liquor. As for the volumes arranged on the shelves, they were nothing but a decorative veneer fixed to the bar's wooden door. Nothing but book covers and titles! And no sooner had the door opened than the entire bar lit up. Its inner wall consisted of overlapping triangular mirrors placed together in such a way that the reflection of a single bottle looked like hundreds of crystalline containers of firewater. Yes, he'd succeeded in shocking him. Khalil had had no idea that such splendor was even possible—whereas in fact he hadn't seen anything yet.

"I've never seen anything like this before . . . it's amazing," he said simply.

Giggling with delight, Saqr said with an air of confidentiality, "My dad saw it in one of Raghid Zahran's offices. Then Lilly Spock designed one like it for him in secret. She's got all sorts of talents—that woman-man. And Raghid Zahran speaks highly of her."

"And who is Raghid Zahran?"

This time Saqr guffawed until he collapsed onto the velvet-upholstered armchair.

"You've never heard of Raghid Zahran?" he asked. "My dad will have to hear about this! He'll be really happy for you. He'll like you just because you've never heard of Raghid Zahran. In any case, Raghid Zahran is the person who arranged this job for you. He put in a good word for you with Nadim."

"Fine. And who is Lilly Spock?"

"You haven't heard of her either?" asked Saqr with another guffaw. "Where have *you* been living?"

(I get up out of my chair and I slap that twenty-year-old Saqr on both cheeks, saying, "I've been living with my people in the heart of a wound. And you, where have *you* been living?")

Khalil didn't move, and he didn't reply. Instead, he began speaking the truth just the way his father had always advised him to do, yet without words.

Then Saqr went on reproachfully, "Lilly Spock is an old woman, around forty years old. And she's the only woman who collects money from Nadim and Raghid without either of them touching her. After all, she's really a man, even though she might seem like a woman at times. She's got some sort of service agency that she set up herself during the last few months, and it's been quite a success. She's really energetic and she's got her own contacts here. When you ask her for something, she comes up with it right away and exactly according to your specifications. She studied law and got a job in the United Nations, then decided to go into some other line of work. People say she's of Arab origin, but I don't think so. She's got too much going for her to be an Arab. She's got to be European. However, it's a good thing she understands Arabic, since this way, I don't have to speak to her in French or English. If I did, it would be embarrassing, since I'm not all that good at foreign languages. Did you know I was a graduate of all the universities in Switzerland—by expulsion?"

Whereupon he burst again into his peculiar laugh, which generally ended with a sort of gasp that made him sound as though he were being choked, and after which it would come to an abrupt halt. Khalil laughed along with him. But oh, if only his father had been able to afford to help him complete his education, he could have studied in the best universities. He'd always been obliged to work his way through school. And when he graduated in Beirut, he felt as though he was coming out of a marathon race. Even so, he'd clung to the hope that one day he'd be able to go on with his studies. And now here was this kid bragging about having been expelled from school. But he kept quiet. Then Saqr laughed again, only this time for a reason known only to himself, and said, "You don't talk much. And I like that. The only voice I like to hear is my own. I'm actually quite taken with myself, with my words, my laugh. And don't you think I'm good-looking?"

(I punched him and told him he was a conceited jerk who ought to be packed off to a military training camp where he'd have to memorize the map of the Arab world and find out about the rising percentage of those who suffer from hunger, poverty, disease, oppression, and illiteracy there.)

Khalil continued not to say a word. Meanwhile, Saqr went on smugly, "I'm in excellent health, and my eyesight is keen as a hawk's. Besides which, I'm not color-blind like my dad."

Khalil laughed dutifully. Then he continued, saying, "I'm not kidding. We noticed that he couldn't distinguish colors very well. For example, a dancer would come in wearing a red dress, and he wouldn't know what color it was. So we took him to see a well-known doctor, and he diagnosed him as having color-blindness."

(You don't need a doctor to figure that out.) Khalil went on holding his tongue as Saqr added, "That's why we canceled our trip to Spain. What would be the use of watching a bullfight if my dad couldn't see the color of the bull-fighter's cape? But then we found out that the bull can't see red either, and that what gets him excited is the matador's movement, not the color of the cloth he's carrying. Did you know that?"

"No, I certainly didn't."

"Very good. I don't like people who know more than I do. Do you know how to snow-ski?"

"No."

"Great. You'll escort me to our winter mansion in Gstaad this year and I'll teach you how. Then we'll make the rounds of our chalets in St. Moritz and Cartina for the rest of your skiing lessons!"

"I thank you."

"Do you know how to water-ski?"

"No."

"Wonderful. You'll go with me to our summer place in Montreux, and I'll show you."

"I thank you."

"Do you know how to ride a horse?"

"No."

"Marvelous. We'll go to our estate in the Wentworth district near London and I'll show you my horses and stables there and teach you how to ride."

"I thank you."

"Do you know how to fly a helicopter?"

"No."

"I'll teach you right now."

"No, please. . . . I'm afraid."

"That makes it all the more enjoyable for me. Do you know how to satisfy an entire harem in one night?"

"No."

"With God's help, along with some of Sheikh Watfan's potions, it'll be easy for you. My dad's fifty years old though he claims to be forty, and he claims he can do it as if he were just twenty."

"Good for him."

"And we used to think he really could, until his ulcer started bleeding on account of all the drugs he'd been taking."

"I hope he gets better soon."

"Do you know how to play poker?"

"No."

"What *do* you know how to do then?"

"Well, I know how to smoke. Would you allow me. . . ?"

"Go right ahead. Here's a joint of hashish—made in your country."

Khalil took it from him in astonishment. He'd never tried that before.

Saqr was pleased. The previous secretary had been fired when he refused the same offer. Nadim had supplied Khalil with this bit of information and others as well, and since he'd begun the job he'd been expecting a lot worse. In any case, there was nothing else he could do.

Said Saqr, "I'll take you to the house where we keep the harem. My dad and

I used to keep most of them here. We'd share them between us, and also with some of my brothers and our guests, since we believe in nationalization and socialism. But when my uncle Hilal got here we had to move them fast. So we rented them a hotel and a few furnished apartments. It was a big hassle for us. Our life is really rough! Rough and tiring. If it weren't for saunas and massages, I'd collapse!"

"I feel for you."

Just then Sheikh Sakhr came into the library. Khalil withdrew automatically toward the balcony and was followed by a laughing, mirthful Saqr. Meanwhile, Hilal followed his twin brother into the library. The two men appeared to be continuing an argument begun earlier, and the gray hair on Sheikh Hilal's temples glistened as he said, "How long will this perversity go on? The whole country knows that you dye your hair and your moustache, and that you gad about with your mobile harem and your various and sundry mistresses. That European journalist, Charlotte Barnes, has published your scandals in the newspapers. And our ruler is really furious. You know very well what an upright man he is and how strict he is when it comes to morals. And there are people who translate for him what Charlotte Barnes and others write about your prodigal ways."

"It's just because I didn't pay her."

"I know that. She's despicable. But that doesn't justify your own despicable actions."

"Well, I pay the zakat, and my taxes. But beyond that, I consider myself free to spend my money as I please."

"You're not free to hurt society. And your method of spending money is a kind of mass murder!"

"I'm free as long as I'm not breaking the law."

"You're violating the spirit of the law. And people will change the laws to catch up with people like you."

"I *am* free."

"No, you aren't. The offenses you've been committing hurt both you and others."

"God is forgiving and merciful."

"But people are neither forgiving nor merciful. They're fed up with people like you. And if we don't manage to straighten you out, then they'll do it. You've disgraced the Ghanamali name!"

"Hold your tongue, brother! You and I are twins. But I'm content to let you treat me this way in your capacity as older brother, since you came out a few seconds before I did."

Then, as usual, Sheikh Sakhr forgot the reason for his anger and went on jokingly, "The fact is, I tell my lady friends that you're ten years older than I am. You look like it, at least."

Then he burst into laughter reminiscent of his son Saqr's jolly hysteria.

As Khalil and Saqr sat calmly smoking their joints on the balcony, the argument sounded as though it were taking place in some deep, distant well.

Hilal exploded, saying, "You can't go on this way! You can't turn Switzerland into a desert just because you happen to be homesick! Go back home, brother. We've had enough scandals. And let the rest of your children enroll in schools and universities."

"Why do you call them scandals? The women I want, I marry according to Islamic law. Women in this world are all either virtuous wives or whores. And I treat each kind as she deserves to be treated."

"Don't blaspheme. Don't hide the heinousness of your acts behind things sacred. Why are you trying to dodge the issue? There isn't anyone anymore who doesn't know what you're involved in—your deals, your wealth. . . . The government is concerned about what you're doing. And it considers you to be one of the direct causes behind popular discontent. Western newspapers are filled with news of your outrageous behavior, and my sons studying at Cambridge claim they aren't related to you—that the similarity between your name and theirs is a mere coincidence. Even your nieces and nephews have started feeling ashamed of the way you act. Your own oldest son refuses to visit you, and after every prayer he performs, he asks God to guide you back to the right path. Everyone's eyes have been opened to the real nature of the shady deals you've been making with that partner of yours, Raghid."

"And that wonderful school that Raghid Zahran had built—don't you consider it a kind of extenuating factor? I mean, I can understand why you hate our getting involved—that is, *his* getting involved—in arms deals and that sort of thing. But what about all the humanitarian services we've provided, the school being one of the most noteworthy?"

"The fact is, even that deal aroused a lot of suspicions. The workers employed on the project say some serious fraud was going on in connection with the materials used in the school's construction and in the specifications for the iron and concrete buttresses."

"I swear I had nothing to do with such a despicable plot! Some of my own children are attending that school, including my son Abdullah!"

"Now, I realize that you're innocent and I believe what you're saying. But I'm afraid it may have happened without your knowledge. You're a scoundrel, but you're just a small-time one, and I haven't given up hope of being able to reform you without having to cut off your head to do it."

"Are you against the airport for the same reason—that is, on account of rumors being circulated by people who are just out for their own interests?"

"It's one of the reasons. But it's quite an important reason. Imagine an airport that collapses on the heads of all the people inside, or a runway so flimsy it collapses under the weight of the airplanes."

"You're exaggerating. Nothing of the sort has happened to any of the projects we've funded with Raghid. He's quite adept when it comes to calculating potential outcomes."

"He might, for example, be counting on the airport not collapsing for several years. That way, he could put the blame on a lightning bolt, a storm, a minor earthquake, negligence on the part of an investor, or something like that."

"You're exaggerating."

"I have a deep concern for my homeland and the people who live there or come from there. And you used to be like me. But since 1973, you've changed. The wealth came and Lebanon's summer ended. That was where you used to hide whenever tribulations came on account of your waywardness. But in Europe your veil of modesty fell off. I'm against wasting Arab wealth. It's meant to be for everyone, brother. You're stealing money from the poor."

"I'm not stealing. I'm just spending what God has provided."

"Wastefulness is theft. So don't drag God into your own misinterpretation of what it means to make an honest living!"

Changing the subject, Sakhr said, "Tell me, how's your health?"

"It's getting better, thank God. I'm thinking of going for treatment in a hospital back home. It seems our Arab doctors are more competent than we used to think. I paid a fortune at that British doctor's clinic and then at the hospital where he practices, just for him to end up telling me the same thing an Arab doctor had told me the first time I was examined."

"God bless our countrymen."

"Oh . . . I just remembered something. I want to transfer one million British pounds to the hospital where I was treated in London. And it wouldn't be a bad idea to transfer another million to the London municipality for them to improve the park next to the hospital. Do you think that's enough?"

"Of course not. Do you want them to say that Arabs are tightwads? What about the legendary generosity that we're famous for?"

"All right then. Let's double it, then wire the money to them in pounds."

"Khalil will take care of it. He's my son's new secretary."

As Khalil heard him, a mad thought occurred to him. (I'll transfer the whole thing to victims of the war in Lebanon, the war most Arabs have managed to run away from so far.) By this time the last joint was gone, and so was Khalil's sobriety. His ears had become so sharply tuned they picked up every word spoken, and his head was floating through midair spying on people in the room.

"London," said Saqr, "I just remembered that I have an appointment to keep there. We'll travel there right away, Khalil."

"I can't. I don't have an entry visa."

"Another joint and you'll forget all about the visas."

"Save it for the police officer at the airport when we go in, and he'll forget I'm even there."

Saqr laughed and said, "We'll make sure you get it. Contact Lilly Spock at her office and tell her that I want visas."

"I don't have a residence card in Switzerland. I came in as a tourist and I won't be granted a visa easily, since I'm Lebanese. Nobody wants me in his territory. Every embassy that sees a Lebanese passport just throws it back in our faces. They think we're all terrorists or hashish smugglers. But . . ."

"You're not Lebanese anymore, or even Arab. Now that you're my secretary, your nationality is Jet Set."

"And does the country of Jet Set issue passports?"

Letting out a long, jolly, hashish addict's guffaw, Saqr said, "This country owns the whole world. Come on now, call Lilly Spock and let her arrange your residency, your work permit, and entrance visas for all the European countries we want to visit. We'll be touring around for a while. But it would be best for you to go see her yourself, since there might be some papers you'll have to sign. This is her address on Rhone Street. Get going right away, and I'll call her and let her know you're coming. Tell me, have you ever been to these countries before?"

"No. This is the first time I've traveled outside Lebanon. I mean, I've visited other Arab countries before, and I've been on guided tours of places like Bucharest, Moscow, and Leningrad."

"Well, the trips you went on before weren't real entertainment. They were nothing but poor folks' tours. But I'll be your guide to the land of bliss and delight. Now, take down the names of the countries we'll visit first. By the way, why don't you bring along that lovely wife of yours?"

"Because she's . . . because she's pregnant. In her second month."

It may have been the first time he'd ever lied in his entire life, and he didn't know what made him do it.

"That wouldn't bother me in the least," replied Saqr.

"Well, it might bother the baby!"

"Here. Take this with you to pay the bill."

Whereupon he handed Khalil a sum the likes of which he'd never laid eyes on all at once before.

Khalil left the place quickly, passing on his way out through the artificial desert where the job of the workers was to keep the grass from growing. In the distance he could see the she-camel, which looked like a brown, dead spot on an otherwise green leaf.

Amir didn't see Khalil as he got out of a Ghanamali Rolls Royce on Rhone Street. And if he had, he wouldn't have been surprised, since he was past the point of being shocked by anything. Had the restaurant orphan, the underfed, ragged coffee shop vagabond been transformed within days into a wealthy-looking man complete with a chauffeur who tipped his hat as he opened the door for him? "Everything changes. And we're falling like dominoes." Repeating the words to himself over and over, Amir didn't see Khalil as he paused in disbelief in front of the fantastically luxurious jewelry shop display case with equally fantastic prices, then went rushing up to the office of "Lilly Spock" (as she was called on the copper door plaque) as if he were fleeing from the golden chessboard in the display window.

As he sat in the café sipping his cold coffee, there was a painful sorrow weighing on the left side of his chest, a pain that was growing steadily more severe and spreading in snakelike fashion to his left shoulder and arm.

Could Layla really have done such a thing? Could she of all people simply have turned herself into "Lilly Spock"? It was an ominous sign that a genuine, sincere person like her, indifferent to wealth and appearances, would give up his antique piaster in return for an offer of money. So then, the well-constructed plan to make people lose faith in the things most sacred to them had begun to bear fruit. Next would come the phase of miserable surrender to the outward reality of things without any understanding of their true nature. And this was exactly what distressed him so much. It was as if it wasn't Layla he was grieving over, but the untold numbers of other people who, like her, had turned away from the cause. It wasn't easy to justify taking the methods of oppression employed by the right and adapting them for use by the left, or the suppression of freedoms being practiced by most of those he'd once defended and whose theories he'd sketched out for them. Consequently, people had lost faith in what they were doing and fled as renegades: this one to magic, another to money, and others to life in voluntary exile or to numbing themselves against reality in various and sundry ways. Beirut wasn't the only place where one could find snipers. No, they were here also, lying in wait for the chance to send an invisible bullet through the heart of every Arab who had the misfortune of betraying some weakness.

As for him, he wasn't going to let despair creep into his writings. He wasn't going to let them work their wicked magic on him—the type of magic that turns brother against brother based on some laughable disagreement or groundless hatred. The type that makes Cain kill Abel and then himself. The type that makes an enemy feign moral outrage at the barbarity of events in loose verbal pronouncements that neither deter nor hinder.

With the darkness this thick, he had no choice but to reinvent electricity. He'd been accused of being overly optimistic, which really wasn't true. However, he'd discovered that optimism is a serious occupation that requires a lot of hard work. And this was the occupation he had chosen.

He'd decided to try to talk to Layla with the same good will and affection they'd always known. It was true, of course, that he wished he could slap her, but what good would that do? Wasn't that just the way his enemy Raghid would like to see him behave? No. He wasn't going to let hurt feelings or base desires for revenge get the better of him. And if he ever did kill somebody, it wouldn't be Layla or any other former ally. Rather, he'd strike at the real enemy. Nor was he going to let the psychedelic lighting or dramatic events on the Arab stage distract him from the foe, his original target and—as he saw it—the fountainhead of all evils and sorrows.

There he'd done it again. He'd gone back to writing a chapter in his latest romantic, sentimental work on politics, or a page in some magazine. Writing inside his head was a bad habit, but it helped him relax a bit, at least, and relieved the ache on the left side of his chest and in his left arm, which was the one he wrote with.

All right now, you Arab Hamlet, he said to himself. That's enough rumination for the day. Go up there and face Layla Al-Amiriya. Don't be weak like Qays, and don't go asking for fire.[16] Instead, ask for clarification. Why did she change this way after the attempt on your life? It's true that the people who tried to kill you weren't your original enemies. Instead they were recently acquired foes that you agree with on questions of strategy but differ with when it comes to tactics, insisting on democratic freedom as a basic condition for every new step that's taken. But what does any of that have to do with her leaving you? Her sweetheart was nearly killed and survived. That's all. No, that's only part of it.

(Here I am sitting around theorizing about why she left me, even though it's been months now since her ship left my shores, so to speak. Maybe Bassam was right when he advised me to go and slap her. He surely didn't mean it literally. But he was drawing my attention to the importance of getting past the stage of theorizing and moving on to action. I do have a tendency to focus on the theoretical side of things, which is an unforgivable sin when the enemy is getting things done while I sit around and rot. I misunderstood Bassam and I was unfair to him. I may talk a lot and I may even be eloquent, but I don't have any more to show for it than he does for his silence. He's fallen into silent passivity, and I've fallen into repeating myself like a parrot. When Raghid offered Bassam the same position he offered me, he turned it down. He refused despite his poverty and degradation, and in spite of the ridicule that he puts up with from friends for staying in my house without doing any kind of work except memorizing the *Encyclopaedia Britannica.* "Go slap her." It's as if the poor guy was alluding to an actual fact, namely, that I'm strong on theory and weak when it comes to practice and consequently, I'm not being effective in the times we're living through now.)

16. This is an allusion to the story of Qays ibn al-Mulawwah and Layla Al-Amiriyah. Qays, who was madly in love with his paternal cousin Layla but could not marry her because he had besmirched her honor by declaring his love for her publicly in a verse of poetry, used to go to Layla's house in the hope of seeing her. However, since he did not dare state the real purpose of his visit, he would come asking for a firebrand with which his family could burn their firewood.

When Amir walked in, he was taken aback first by the luxuriousness of the decor, and then by the fact that the secretary tried to prevent him from going into Layla's office. The reason, she said, was that Madame Layla had an important guest and didn't want to be disturbed. When the "guard secretary" left to take care of something in another room, he couldn't resist the urge to open the door ever so slowly, devour the place with his eyes, and take a long look at Layla's face. He noticed that she wasn't dressed in mourning for her mother—although that didn't necessarily mean anything—and that her face was coated with layers of garish makeup. It was the first time he'd see her this way. Prior to this he'd never known her even to touch cosmetics except for a bit of mascara. Her hair was dyed a reddish, chestnut brown, which was the latest style, and he hardly recognized her. Too busy to notice him, she was engrossed in writing something on a piece of paper. He looked over at the "guest," and who should he see but the "restaurant vagabond" himself. At that very moment, as if by some mysterious sixth sense, Layla looked up from her papers and saw him. Not moving from her place, she said tepidly, "Amir. Hi."

"Hi, Layla. I just happened to be passing by, so. . ."

Then she went on sarcastically, "I see. You thought of 'happening' to pass by so that we could 'happen' to discuss an important matter. But as you can se, I'm busy. Your visit is accepted, but the discussion will have to be postponed."

Khalil was stunned—not so much by Amir's sudden appearance or by the exceedingly familiar way she and Amir related to each other as by the fact that "Madame Lilly" spoke fluent Arabic, and that she wasn't a European after all, despite her having received him and gone on speaking to him in such impeccable French that he had spent the last several minutes struggling to concentrate on improving his language so that he could keep up with this clever Swiss lawyer. Saqr had claimed that she was a Swiss woman of Arab origin who had learned the language well.

Introducing Khalil to him, Layla said, "Mr. Khalil Dar', secretary to Saqr Ghanamali, son of Sakhr Ghanamali."

Amir shook his hand cordially. "Hello, Khalil. Do you remember me?"

Then, as if the surprise of seeing Amir had loosened his tongue (or was it the residual effect of the hashish he'd smoked?), Khalil said, "Remember you? How can someone forget the cause of his ruin? All my problems began the day I first read your work and was impressed by your ideas. And they multiplied the day I refused to take your books out of my bookstall's display window and replace them with the *Rifaq* newspaper. When I did that, I was trying to apply what you say about democratic practices. Then I really went into a crisis because I took things even further by trying to live by my father's motto: Always tell the truth no matter what it costs. He lived by it and as a result, he ended up being divorced by my mother and by two wives after her. I've lived by it too, and all sorts of repression have been practiced against me. Do I know you? You're the bane of my existence, so how could I possibly forget you? My wife found your telephone number in my pocket, and I didn't dare admit to her that I'd seen you. She wouldn't believe that such a coincidence could have taken place."

Amir and Layla laughed, and Khalil was taken aback. He hadn't been trying to be funny. He'd meant what he said. Amir decided to interrupt Khalil in an attempt to bring a halt to his outpouring. It was obvious that he knew nothing about Layla, Raghid, and Sakhr and their intellectual and political leanings. He didn't know that Layla was a former ally who had moved over to the enemy camp, and that he could lose his job because of the information he'd just revealed when he passed it on—as no doubt she would—to Raghid and Sakhr.

Saying the first thing that came to his mind, Amir replied, "Oh, your wife—I know. She called the number in your pocket and asked whose number it was. Then she asked me if you were there. I told her I'd never seen you and didn't even know you, and she called me names. It happened early one morning—maybe this morning, in fact."

With genuine affection, Khalil added, "So your beloved curse follows me all the way here! My wife will try to assassinate you, just like those others have tried."

"Do people in Beirut know about what happened?"

"The fact is, Beirut is the only place these days with open ears, open eyes, and an open wound. As for most other Arab cities, they've been snoring away for ages, and their slumber is perpetuated by the media."

Interrupting, Layla said, "Please, I don't want to hear any political talk. I've graduated from that college of torture, and I've declared my withdrawal from the labyrinth."

It's not enough for you to want to withdraw," said Khalil excitedly. "The labyrinth won't withdraw from your life. It's been imposed upon us. If we don't struggle against it, it will swallow us up."

"Well," Layla replied in a distant, mesmerized sounding voice, "it seems to have swallowed up the two of you for good. As for me, I got out before it was too late. And you, Mr. Khalil, appear to be one of Amir's zealous disciples. You've apparently memorized his words, since you borrow them all the time. And now, why don't the two of you carry on with this speechology party of yours at his house?"

"You seem to have borrowed my wife's phrase to make fun of us. I've come to a rather shameful conclusion: that beautiful women aren't fit for the struggle, since they think of it as nothing but another kind of adornment. Arab women still haven't matured enough to engage in any sort of serious work."

"A little while ago you were sitting politely here in front of me because I'd fooled you and others into thinking that I was European. And now that you know I'm Arab, you've been inspired by the presence of your professor to attack me and start making generalizations."

"I apologize. I was thinking of my wife."

"Is she that bad?"

"I don't know, really. Maybe she has an excuse."

Amir suddenly lost his interest in a tête-a-tête with Layla, perhaps because he realized that his presence might cost Khalil his job, and perhaps because Layla wasn't herself anymore. She'd begun casting aspersions on her mother tongue, her ethnic origin, and the Bedouin tattoo that he'd never forget on her mother's hand. He wanted to run away from her bleached hair, her makeup, her new appearance, and the inexplicable part of her that bristled with cruel indifference.

"Pardon me," he said quickly, "I've interfered with what you two were doing. I'll see you some other time."

Then he hurriedly withdrew.

Layla said casually to Khalil, "You can stay if you like."

However, he followed Amir out to the secretary's office and asked him in a whisper, "I don't know what's going on between the two of you, but would you like me to leave?"

"No. I'm the one who should be leaving."

"Are you tired? Sick?"

"No."

"You look as though you're one of the two."

"I just look that way. Tell me, are you happy with your job?"

"No. Not unless pampering a twenty-eight-year-old little boy is considered a profession. I've become the secretary to Saqr Ghanamali, as Layla mentioned to you. Do you know both of them?"

"Yes, unfortunately."

"What do you think of my job?"

Amir didn't reply. His silence seemed to last forever, and Khalil would have felt ashamed and insulted if it hadn't been for the way he went back to sounding like his cheerful, witty self again as he said, "Let's just say you've found a job as a nanny!"

Then he went his way, muttering silently the phrase from Keats, "Everything changes, and we're falling like dominoes."

◆　◆　◆

There was a fire coursing through her body, caustic and ominous. (I can't take it any longer. Don't men know that this happens to us, too?)

She was at a loss. What was she to do—an attractive woman like her consumed with desire and bursting with vitality—with a husband who hadn't been able to satisfy her needs for five years straight?

What's any woman to do when she's starving for love and her husband's body is a famine-stricken wasteland?

Is there any man who would declare a sexual fast simply because his wife's mental condition happens to have rendered her unresponsive? Hasn't the male-dominated society we live in created a veritable supermarket offering whatever sort of flesh one might desire: white flesh, dark flesh, rosy flesh, black . . . to allow a man to satisfy volcanic desires like these without being punished or blamed?

And she, what was she supposed to do? The life of luxurious indolence in the posh Swiss hotel had ignited her passions anew. The bed took up more than half the hotel room, and when her husband slept beside her he seemed to shrink up like an ant hiding under the pillow, wed to his political worries and concerns.

So how could she help but fall in love with Nadim, that marvelous, luscious man with ages of experience, with that captivating, endearing smile of his, and with a flaming vitality that brought back memories of a forgotten intoxication?

The day Widad died, she felt she'd died herself. And perhaps she had. Then when Khalil became a perpetual guest in the prison cells of friends and foes alike, she thought her body had turned to ice and ashes. But life seems to be like a wheel that's been set rolling down a hill by a small child. It just keeps on rolling, colliding sometimes with boulders and other times with flowers. But it doesn't stop until death. And neither do one's passions and desires.

With Nadim's furtive glances and whispers over the telephone, she'd turned from ashes to live coals, and the wound of pleasures denied was re-opened and reinflamed.

From the time they met on the airplane, he'd captured her admiration. Of course, even before this she used to envy his family from a distance for their wealth and position the way one envies an abstract idea. On the airplane, the idea had taken on flesh, flesh, of the sort that gave her the urge to let out a long, impassioned, throaty moan, like the nocturnal howling of alley cats in the mating season. He was a man with strength and authority, and that was the type of man she liked. There was something about the physical presence of a man like him that filled her with the exhilaration of power. It was as if, by possessing such a man, she was taking on some of his strength, participating with him in the thrill of grasping the scepter of influence and prestige.

When she fell in love with Khalil, he'd seemed as strong and impenetrable as a fortress. At first he'd tried to avoid her and treated her rather indifferently, which fueled her desire to tame him. She surrounded his fortress with her eyes' blue banners, then moved in and occupied it. Once inside, she found him to be a wild stallion roving the steppes of bliss. But then he'd changed. Sometimes he would be a barren desert of sorrows and disappointments, and other times a flaming mass of excitement. Yet it was an excitement that was poured out fruitlessly in distant, public realms. And since Kafa was in the private domain, so to speak, her pleasures were sealed in red wax and everyone—she especially—forgot about anything having to do with her enjoyment or her body.

But now her spirit had declared itself in rebellion. Her memory had flung off the robes of amnesia, reminding her anew that she was, and always had been, a woman made for love, and for love alone.

So when Nadim called to reassure her that her husband was persevering in his new job and to tell her that he might not be home till late that night, how could she have possibly said no when he asked if she might like to have lunch with him? He didn't mention whether his wife would be with him or whether the invitation was to their home or somewhere else. And she didn't ask.

All she said was, "Yes." And that's what she would have said whatever the question happened to have been.

He passed by for her at the hotel. But no sooner had she gotten down to the lobby than who should walk in but Khalil. Damn him. He'd been sent back by Layla Sabbak to fetch his passport for the visas and his residence and work permits.

Maintaining perfect composure, Nadim said, "Raghid Zahran has sent me to inform the two of you that you've been invited for dinner at his home this evening. He'll be expecting you at 8:30 P.M. I would have left you a note at the reception desk, but then I happened to run into Madame Kafa in the lobby. See you this evening."

Then he departed without so much as batting an eyelid. But Kafa was trembling. Do you suppose Khalil had believed his lie?

"What kind of invitation was that?" Khalil asked. "It sounded more like a subpoena than a dinner invitation!"

As for her, it thrilled her just to think about it, so much so that she forgot all about being afraid of her husband. And perhaps she didn't really care what he thought anymore, anyway.

"We're going to see Raghid Zahran, and you're complaining? Haven't you heard of him? There wasn't a single person at Nadim's party the other evening who didn't talk about the man. He's the greatest! As for you, you really are strange!"

Then without knowing why, he thought of Amir. Maybe it was because if he was "strange," then Amir was more so. Amir was a man who made no compromises and who didn't bend with the storms. He didn't dare tell Kafa how he'd met up with Amir, just as she didn't dare tell him how she'd met up with Nadim. But he was no fool. Nadim wasn't the sort who'd go around delivering other people's messages for them like some lowly servant. After all, he had untold numbers of underlings he could send on this sort of trivial errand. So was it possible that. . . ?

But then something went off inside his head. And he was convinced, as most men usually are, that such a thing was unthinkable. Maybe Nadim had been passing by on his way somewhere. Or maybe he really was in the habit of delivering Raghid Zahran's invitations in person after all.

Of course! "That" sort of thing surely couldn't happen, he reasoned to himself. Or if it did, it wouldn't be that "the husband is the last to know," but simply that he doesn't want to know or believe.

And that sort of thing, of course, happens to other men. Not to me.

◆　◆　◆

"I want to tell you something confidential, Sheikh Watfan."

"Tell me what's on your mind. Your secrets are safe with me."

"Well, the day I bought this mansion-fortress, I was told that there were golden treasures buried underneath it, in the garden or in the cellars. It would be a terrible shame and ingratitude to God to leave the gold where it is and deprive people of the benefits it could bring. I've done everything I can to locate it, but without success. So could you help me?"

"Certainly."

"And would you honor me with your presence at my dinner table this evening? I've invited a small number of friends, all of whom you know, as well as a Lebanese man and his wife. His name is Khalil Dar'. I'd like you to find out his sign for me, which will make it easier to keep him in line."

"I'll need to know his mother's name and his birth date in order to find out whether he falls under the fire signs, the earth signs, the air signs, or the water signs."

"I've got the information written down on this piece of paper. But the lawyer got it from his passport. I hope it's correct."

"We'll see."

"And about dinner?"

"I may join you all later on."

◆　◆　◆

"Respond and be present, O storm of the winds, O sal'alah of the earth, O Tawus, O Karakil, O Maymoun, O Shamroul the Winged One, O Jaljya'il, O Thou who hast built and populated this place. If there is gold or silver concealed or hidden here, reveal them by the truth of the Almighty, the All-encompassing One, the Lord of Hosts.

"Reveal the wealth which is in this place, with a curse upon every tongue-wagger who has amassed wealth for himself. Gather the riches here by the truth of the letter *nun* and of the pen and of that which they write. I adjure you by the Day of Gathering and Resurrection to cleave this earth, or the wall, or the pillar, or the clay oven. Reveal the wealth that is in this place. Respond, O storm of the winds, O sal'alah of the earth, O Tarish, O Karakil, O Maymoun,

O Shamardal, O Jalya'il, O Thou who hast built and populated this place, by the truth of the letters *kâf, hâ, yâ, ayn, sâd, hâ, mîm, ayn, sîn, qâf,* by the truth of Surat al-Taghabun,[17] by the Day of Gathering and Resurrection, I command you to rend this earth asunder, or the wall or the pillar or the clay oven, revealing any hidden or buried treasure, be it silver, gold, or copper. Accomplish that which you have been commanded by the truth of these names and their authority over you. And should any of you rebel against our command, we shall cause him to taste of the torment of the searing flames.

"Respond before tongues of fire and splinters of copper are rained upon you, causing you to be defeated forevermore, and lest we curse you as we cursed the companions of the sabbath. The command of God shall be brought to pass immediately, with haste, at this very hour."

The room was filled with the fragrance of incense: oriental frankincense, raw wax, sandarac, Indian sakhatir, and safflower seed. Meanwhile, the sorcerer stoked his candle with hoopoe hairs and swine bristles.

Nasim, who had come in carrying a tray with jasmine tea on it, got a stuffy nose from the smell. He'd just seen the news broadcast on television. As Beirut went up in flames, this sorcerer was seated before his translucent magic ball staring into it so calmly he might have been hypnotized. Nasim felt a terrible urge to smash the crystal ball, grab the sorcerer by the beard, and drag him over to the television screen to look at a homeland on fire and human beings being destroyed and oppressed. His brothers and sisters—what had become of them? And this sorcerer—didn't he have a family? Brothers and sisters? A homeland? Did he really belong to the world of the jinn? Were his brothers and sisters ghosts and spirits, while he played the fool for Raghid Zahran "to serve people" as he imagined himself to be doing? Wasn't he a human being of flesh and blood? Didn't he have a birthplace, somewhere his heart could call home? Wasn't there a single tear in his eyes? A gasp in his throat? Passions and desires in his heart? Wasn't he beset by nightmares sometimes? And did he ever dream?

Just then the sorcerer looked at Nasim out of the corner of his eye as if he'd been reading his thoughts. Angrily Nasim thought, all right, all right, I do believe in mental telepathy, and that some people have the ability to read other people's minds by means of a sense that goes beyond language. Maybe this

17. Surat Al-Taghabun ("Mutual Loss and Gain") is the 54th chapter of the Qur'an.

man has such an ability, and maybe not. But whether he does or not, this sort of sense ought to be placed in the service of science, not be driven by inherited superstitions.)

In a voice that sounded like the rhythm of autumn winds, Sheikh Watfan said, "Son, your heart is filled with storms. I'd advise you to pray before you sleep."

A chill went through Nasim's whole body. (He really can read minds. And he really does possess powers that seem to be supernatural. But science has explained some of them, and is working on the others. Capacities like these are tens of thousands of years old, while the science of parapsychology is still so young it's just barely begun to crawl, so to speak. And until all the mysteries are explained, I'll go on trembling from time to time, whenever my spirit is touched by those cryptic vibes of his. They're like electrically charged particles that I can feel going right through me, plumbing the depths of my soul and stripping the protective veil off even my most private thoughts.)

Repeating himself, Sheikh Watfan said, "Nasim, your heart has been full of storms for days now. Beware of violence, son."

And with that, a quaking Nasim fled from the room. (Could he possibly have sensed my desire to murder Raghid?) He felt lonely, beleaguered and in need of warmth and affection. And without knowing quite why, he thought of his mother.

◆　◆　◆

Kafa was tongue-tied at the sight of the golden fortress. And even Khalil fell into a stunned, indignant silence. Compared to this place, Nadim's house seemed positively bare. The security measures to which they were subjected upon entry created a solemn atmosphere which was spoiled only by the curses and insults flung out by the taxi driver. Next they came to a vast garden where the grass glittered like gold beneath a special, breathtaking lighting, followed by a huge, gold-plated gate heavily ornamented with statues. At the entranceway there stood two butlers, each of whom held a wet, perfumed sponge in his hand to wipe off the shoes of those entering, thereby rendering them worthy to touch the sacred golden temple. Bewildered, Khalil wondered why it was that the two attendants stood there bowing in such ridiculous looking attire. Nadim directed Kafa to lift her foot so as to let one of them wipe off the bottom of her shoe. When it was Khalil's turn, he made a move to try to escape, but the other attendant lifted his foot for him. Noticing how flustered he was, Nasim heard him saying to one of the two attendants, "For God's sake, brother, I'll do it myself if it really has to be done!"

Irritated with her gauche husband, Kafa eyed him in disdain as he took off his own shoe with a look of disgust on his face, thereby ruining the sublimity of the ritual by taking part in the operation. As he observed Khalil, Nasim felt a delightful closeness to him. Their eyes met in a flash of mutual understanding as if they'd met years before—like a warm, friendly handshake.

Kafa forgot about him again as she stepped into her dream, like someone stepping into the sumptuous make-believe world of a cigarette ad. Inebriated with pleasure, she looked around her: Is this a house, she wondered, or the Louvre Museum? Is this a mansion, or some imaginary citadel constructed by the genie of Arabian Nights? Are these rooms, or gold mines? Plunging into a whirlwind of fabulous luxury, she began running her hands dreamily over the silk curtains, and didn't wake up until Nasim led her over to a group of people which included the owner of the mansion and the other guests: Nadim and Dunya. She lowered her glance demurely at Raghid's crafty smile. With green eyes the color of dung in a cemetery, he announced proudly, "I'm Raghid Zahran. Welcome to my humble abode!"

Khalil felt as though he'd landed by accident in the cave of the mythical *rukh* bird, which might devour him at any moment. By this time he'd come out of his initial shock and disbelief. But before he could enter the phase of outright nausea, Raghid pressed him to take a glass of liquor. And who would dare refuse something from the hand of Raghid Bey, even if it happened to be poison or bitter colocynth?

Nasim came in and served a third drink to each of the guests. There were times when Raghid avoided alcohol, not on account of his diabetes, but because he wanted to stay sober while everyone else got drunk. Nasim and Dunya looked at each other. (Don't worry, Madame. I won't reveal your secret to your husband. It's true. I did see you coming out of Raghid's bedroom. But that makes no difference to me, and your husband may know about it, anyhow. But what I don't understand is that I also saw you coming out of Amir Nealy's house. So, what's your story? They belong to two different worlds, so are you confused, or are you a spy? Why do you try to build bridges between irreconcilable opposites? So will you choose, or will you collapse?)

Nasim handed a glass to Kafa. (How lovely you are, Madame. No doubt we'll be seeing you in Raghid's bedroom before long. The other employees' wives have got themselves a rival their own age now. They're the only older women who grace his bed, if not for passion, then for power. He takes possession of other men and of their women as well.)

He offered a glass to Nadim, then to an overwhelmed looking Khalil. (You unlucky Lebanese, what winds blew you here? What are you and I doing here when our homeland is going up in flames? Unlike Nadim, you don't look like the type who can relax and enjoy himself. Was it the curse of having to eke out a living that drove both of us here?) After the third glass, the remaining guest arrived—Layla Sabbak. She always knew just how to time her appearances.

Kafa looked radiant as Raghid praised her beauty, telling her how delighted he was to meet the daughter of his late friend, Baytmouni. However, he didn't seem particularly glad to make Khalil's acquaintance, since Layla had wasted no time in ringing him up with information on Khalil's allegiance to Amir Nealy. (Nadim doesn't know about it apparently. Women are better than men at spying and digging up secrets.) And, not being one to miss a single detail when it comes to diamonds and gold, he complimented Dunya on the new ring she was wearing.

Apologetically she said, "The ring you gave me was stolen. It was taken right out of my own house during a dinner party."

Letting out a gasp of surprise so convincing that even Khalil was amazed at her theatrical abilities, Kafa said, "The marvelous ring you were wearing the night of the party was stolen?!"

"Yes, it was."

"Who do you think took it? One of the maids?"

"I really don't know. I'm going to ask Sheikh Watfan."

"Who is Sheikh Watfan?"

"Haven't you heard of him? He has truly extraordinary powers. Everyone who's dealt with him is convinced of it."

"Some people really do have psychic powers," Khalil piped in. "Science has proved their existence. It's also been shown that they have nothing to do with charlatanism or so-called magic. Instead, they've all been classified under the heading of a new science called parapsychology. The fact is, every one of us could exercise special powers if we concentrated on developing them. Bookstores and libraries are full of books on the subject, with logical explanations for bewildering phenomena that people used to attribute to magic. I used to always make a point of promoting them in my bookshop, but I refuse to sell books on magic."

Unimpressed by Khalil's scholarly discourse, Nadim broke in, saying, "Sheikh Watfan spends most of his time here at the mansion. The pasha believes in his powers, and you'll see that he's able to identify the culprit."

His words sent a shudder of horror down Kafa's spine. All her life she'd believed in astrologers, along with her family, their neighbors, and their ancestors.

Speaking to Dunya, Raghid said, "He'll be joining us after dinner, but he's busy right now unearthing some treasures. As for the ring, it isn't worth getting upset about. In fact, its being stolen gives me an occasion to get you something new."

Dunya was pleased. Kafa was so overjoyed she nearly leaned over and kissed Raghid's hand. Layla, by contrast, remained so silent and calm, you'd think she'd been mesmerized or bewitched. In fact, she seemed like some sort of bionic woman who'd programmed herself to do nothing but destroy. She didn't seem alive like Dunya, or happy and starry-eyed like Kafa. What's this woman doing here? Khalil wondered. And what is she doing in Amir's life? Thinking back to the intense pain that Amir had been concealing with such difficulty in her office and the indifference with which she had treated him, he was filled with such hostility toward her that he ignored her when she asked him when he planned to travel with Saqr. However, when she repeated the question, Raghid heard her and turned in her direction, causing everyone to fall silent, so he had no choice but to reply.

"That depends on you," he said, "and how fast you get the visas ready."

"Oh, "she replied sarcastically, "are you anxious to leave?"

"I don't know."

"And how could a man with a wife as charming as Kafa be anxious to leave?" chimed in Nadim.

"It's all right with me, if that's what his work requires," Kafa said, her bosom swelling with a kind of luscious nonchalance.

"How do you like your job, Khalil?" Raghid asked him in a disinterested tone of voice. As he spoke, he unsheathed a gargantuan cigar, while Nadim hastened to put his out.

"It's all right. Saqr is a good-hearted young man." (He didn't go on to add, "He's also a spoiled jerk and a drug addict.")

"I don't think the two of you will be able to travel until Sheikh Hilal has left," said Nadim. "Do you know him?"

"Yes, I do," replied Khalil. "I saw him this morning, and he was having an argument with his brother. I didn't mean to spy on them, but Saqr and I were sitting on the porch, and they didn't realize we were there."

Pleased with the information as well as its speedy delivery, Raghid encouraged Khalil, saying, "Continue, friend. You don't need to feel embarrassed because you heard what you heard. Sheikh Sakhr and Sheikh Hilal are dear friends of mine, and I'd like to do whatever I can to promote good relations between the two of them. I don't like to see brothers at odds with each other."

"You're right to feel that way. Only, you were what they were arguing about."

With the feigned good will of a dictatorial patriarch, Raghid put his arm around Khalil's shoulder. Khalil stood up almost reflexively, and Raghid took leave of his other guests, saying, "Carry on, and don't worry yourselves about work-related concerns."

As for Nadim, whose primary function was to carry out Raghid's orders, he was pleased with his success in putting his spy to use so quickly and even getting him to deliver a report on one of his first visits to Raghid. And the delight he felt turned into a flood of benevolence and good will, which he duly poured out upon Kafa.

"You look lovely this evening, Madame Kafa. Don't you think so, Dunya?"

"Yes, she certainly does," she said, having already noticed Raghid's interest in her. (Her eyes are pretty, but they're dripping with stupidity—stupidity mixed with a bit of womanly guile. She's a delectable little sardine, and she's sure to be gobbled up in no time in this world of ours.)

When they all sat down at the dinner table, protocol required that Khalil sit beside Dunya, which pleased him. There was something sorrowful about the woman that drew him to her, something broken and alienated with the taste of ashes and disillusionment.

For the first few moments of the meal, Kafa sat in stunned silence, having discovered that all the table service was made of almost pure gold. Behind every guest there stood a butler to attend to the guest's every need—or was it to keep them from pilfering any of the golden spoons as souvenirs? In the lavish, passion-titillating atmosphere, she and Nadim exchanged admiring glances and love birds flew from her eyes to his in the gold's feverish glow.

When he offered her a cigarette between courses, she felt herself stepping once again into that sumptuous cigarette ad. Taking the place of the girl in the ad, she'd clothed herself in elegant finery and was casting amorous glances in the direction of her male companion—who had to be Nadim. As they prepared to exchange a kiss, a helicopter hovered behind them against the background of some European capital, where city lights twinkling in the valley below held out the promise of worldly delights. She decided to switch to that brand of cigarettes so that from then on she could always be his pampered, cherished sweetheart and the star of high society. Then an evening breeze blew in the ad so that she had to straighten her hair!

The chef had taken care to prepare special dishes for Raghid on account of his diabetes and high blood pressure. Even so, they looked more delectable than the ones being served to his guests. Once the food had been brought to the table, Raghid dug in with a vengeance. And since the host had fallen silent while he savored every morsel, devoting himself entirely to his gastronomic enjoyment, a pall fell over everyone present for most of the mealtime with the exception of a few side conversations that some people dared to exchange.

Layla was feeling resentment, which she skillfully concealed. The information she'd passed on to Raghid about the connection between Khalil and Amir had become useless now that Khalil had succeeded in the "secret agent" mission for which Nadim had recruited him. Just minutes earlier he had disclosed some secrets that Raghid had been dying to know about. She began to think again of some job that could help her defeat Nadim. There was a war on between her and him as well as between him and the rest of Raghid's employees. And it was a war whose fires Raghid deliberately kept ablaze in keeping with the principle: Divide and rule. He couldn't feel comfortable unless there was an "apprentices' war" going on among them, and whenever it began to cool down he'd fan its flames anew. After all, if they didn't stay busy hating each other, then they'd have time to hate him. Besides which, fostering an atmosphere of competition would make them work harder, since then they'd be working not just for the salaries he paid them, but also to satisfy their mutual petty resentments. Raghid even liked to stir up political and sectarian conflicts in hopes of seeing his workers as divided among themselves as the Lebanese people still living at home. She'd seen the game being played as an outside observer, but now she'd fallen captive to it herself, like someone slipping slowly but surely into a bog of quicksand.

Khalil was revolted by all the wanton consumption he was seeing. (History will never forgive this sort of ostentation!) He thought about the poverty in his home country and the food embargo being imposed on it, then about the famines being suffered throughout the world, and choked on his food. However, given the constraints of the present situation, he did his best to be polite. In an attempt to make a bit of conventional table conversation, he said to Dunya, "The weather is lovely, isn't it?"

"Yes, it is. Geneva is marvelous this month. It tends to be pleasantly warm in the summers, but it's unbearable in the winter. The cold is beastly."

"And your children, have they gotten used to it?"

(My God! How could I have said something so stupid? She told me once that her children had lived all their lives here. So why am I speaking to her as if she were a foreigner? I'm dying to leave this golden mansion with her and go somewhere we could say something from the heart. I need to pour out my sorrows to someone who would really understand—to a tenderhearted female who knows what it's like to suffer pain and alienation. And that's the kind of woman she seems to be. Not like my wife, who's perfectly content in this grief-laden pavilion of pomp and circumstance. If she weren't tolerant, sensitive, and in pain, she wouldn't have opened her heart to me the way she did the other day.)

Then, like someone baring the tragedies of her soul, she whispered, "I've never given birth here in the truest sense of the word. Both of our children were conceived in Beirut. During the first two years of our marriage we were still making visits there, and it was as if we had brought both our son and our daughter with us from Beirut. It's true, of course, that they were born here. But that was just a geographical coincidence, you might say. Only rarely after that did we visit home. And the strange thing is that from then on we were never blessed with any more children. We became sterile. First we went to doctors, and then to sorcerers, but none of them could do anything for us."

By this time her voice had grown very faint.

"That's odd," whispered Khalil.

"Actually, it isn't. Most of our friends abroad have had the same problem."

At this point he almost told her his own secret: that when he was attacked and had his freedom forcibly wrested from him like a bird that's been captured and put in a cage, he became impotent even though he was still at home in Lebanon.

But instead he said, "At least God gave you two children. That by itself is a blessing."

They were both whispering, and other hushed tête-a-têtes were going on at the same time. Consequently, no one took any notice of them. Nadim was busy making eyes at Kafa, and Raghid was interrogating Layla about the name of Khalil's mother and the sign he'd been born under to make sure that there was no mistake in the information he'd passed on to his sorcerer. After looking around and reassuring herself that everyone else was too preoccupied to overhear her, Dunya continued, "Our children are strangers to us, maybe because we never found enough time to be friends to them. From the time we were first married, I got busy helping Nadim in his work. I didn't really take thought for my children until after I'd made sure of Nadim's success in his career. But by that time, I'd distanced myself so much from them that they were more attached to their nanny than they were to me. I'll admit to you, I was so envious of her that one day I just fired her, even though she'd been perfectly reliable!"

"What do you mean?"

"They'd come to love her as a mother. As for me, I thought it was because of her that they hated me, so I fired her. Well, after that they hated me more, and were even more distant than before. Imagine. Last night my sixteen-year-old daughter told me that I envy her because she's young and beautiful, and that she's going to marry a man she loves . . . just because I opposed the idea of her marrying an Arab classmate of hers that isn't very well off. His father is an ordinary employee in the United Nations. You know as well as I do that marriage isn't built on love alone."

"It also isn't built on convenience alone."

"When I told her that I was the one who'd given birth to her and asked her who in the world besides me would be more interested in her welfare, she said, 'As far as I'm concerned, you're nothing but a baby-making machine, and your job was finished a long time ago.' In fact, she even said she preferred to marry young rather than start having sexual relationships outside marriage the way her friends do, and she blamed me for not having taught her her mother tongue. She said she admired Arab culture, and that I'd turned her into an Orientalist rather than an Arab citizen. This girl causes me so much suffering. But she's still so young, how can I let her marry some poverty-stricken Lebanese when Lebanon could blow up at any moment?"

". . ."

"That conversation really hurt me. But we were getting ready to leave the house to come here, so I had no choice but to keep quiet and go on getting dressed. Her boyfriend is making a rebel out of her. He's a twenty-year-old university student who, as she puts it, is teaching her love and the Arabic language at the same time. She says she has no roots here. I say he's poisoning her mind, and that she's just a child who's playing games with her own life."

Khalil almost told her, "We're all playing games with our lives." But he was too busy worrying about what she'd said. He'd never stopped to wonder before what his relationship with his boys would be like now that they were in Switzerland. First he'd been too busy for them because of his political involvements, and now he was too busy for them because he was working night and day to pay their school fees in a foreign land. (This conversation is bringing me closer to her, maybe because it's bringing me closer to myself and to the wounds I carry around on the inside. This sallow, chubby woman possesses a wealth of experience and feelings. Besides which, she isn't as fat as I'd imagined at first. And she isn't old and flabby, either. She looks younger to me now, and of all the customers in this market of gilded sorrows, she's the only person whose company I enjoy. But why do the rich complain more than the poor?)

After dinner, Raghid issued orders for the coffee to be served around the golden swimming pool, beneath the gaze of the Freedom Fighter statue.

After Layla told him about the intimate conversation that had taken place between Khalil and Amir Nealy, Raghid became all the more interested in both using Khalil and causing him pain. Layla was the first to speak.

"Have you decided when you'd like to hold the 'The First Billion' celebration?"

Kafa didn't hear her. She was too busy gawking in disbelief at the golden, octopus-shaped swimming pool.

Seeing her reflection in the golden pool, Dunya wondered miserably to herself, which one is the real me—the woman sitting here, or my reflection in the water?

As for Khalil, the first thing he noticed was the Freedom Fighter statue, which looked out of place alongside the host of golden statues that filled the place.

"Yes, I have," replied Raghid, "It will be quite soon."

"What would you think of appointing Kafa as my assistant? Since her husband is going to be away, she might find the work interesting and profitable."

(Why don't they leave my stupid wife alone? And who is this Layla, anyway? What could a woman like her have in common with Amir? I've got to ask Dunya.) If Layla hadn't been confident that Raghid would be pleased with the idea, she wouldn't have suggested it. And the reason for her confidence was the furtive looks of admiration she'd seen him aiming in the direction of the high-society girl, the daughter of the late Baytmouni. Perhaps the secret behind Raghid's enchantment with Layla was that she knew how to read his thoughts and fulfill his wishes before he even voiced them. He hadn't been attracted to her merely as a weapon against Amir, but because she truly was useful to him.

Nadim was furious. (Now it will be harder to see her. That nasty Layla rushed to recruit her before I got the chance myself. She's starting to look like a pretty formidable rival, and she has the advantage of being able to read minds. She's got something of Sheikh Watfan in her—something mysterious that Raghid loves. In addition to which, she's determined to succeed. Since she left Amir, she's changed completely. We used to invite her to our soirées so that she could keep the older men entertained with her wit and her unconventionality. And now she comes up with this new "businessman's" talent that we didn't know about before. She single-handedly snagged contracts with both of the "giants" Raghid Zahran and Sakhr Ghanamali—something nobody's ever managed to do before. And Sheikh Sakhr's got a thing for her, but isn't sure how to handle her. Sometimes he thinks she's a foreigner formerly married to an Arab, and other times he thinks she's an Arab who used to be married to a foreigner. As for her, she affirms nothing, and denies nothing. Very well, then, I'll make a strike of my own. And I'll prove to Raghid that he can't do without me.)

Taking a newspaper out of his pocket, he said to Raghid, "Now here's a rare find. It's a Beirut newspaper that was brought to me by someone who fled the country through Cyprus and arrived this evening. It contains some news items that might be of interest to you."

"Nothing about Beirut interests me, except the shipments of reinforcements of which you're aware."

"How kindhearted you are!" burst in Kafa. "Are you sending humanitarian aid to the people there?"

Dunya shot her a meaningful glance. But Raghid looked pleased. After all, he loved to be complimented and flattered, and he knew Kafa wasn't smart enough to resort to sarcasm. No, the vapid woman had meant what she said. (Here's a woman that most smart, rich folks would love to have at their parties, since she'd save them the trouble of having to watch out for snide, offensive remarks. She'd be sincere in her admiration of their gold and their treasures, and even attribute virtues to those who possessed none. Raghid loves to look like a hero.) Then he looked over at the statue of Abdul Nasser. Attuned to every blink of his eyes and eager to satisfy his every whim, Kafa asked, "Why do you keep this statue here? It isn't made of gold like all the others. Do you like him that much?"

Nadim cringed, and Dunya seemed to shrink visibly inside herself. Both of them knew how much Raghid despised the man represented by the statue. Layla stared down at the golden floor as if she were embarrassed, while a pi-aster with a hole in the middle seemed to hang suspended before her eyes.

Jubilant, Raghid replied, "Of course I do, Kafa. You were very young at that time, or perhaps you hadn't even been born yet. But I love him because he's one of the primary reasons for my happiness in life: that is, for my success and my wealth. It was thanks to him that I amassed my first million dollars. It hap-pened during the final days of the union between Syria and Egypt. He an-nounced his intention to unite the entire Arab world, and he began with Syria. My father said that people's fortunes and the property that remained there had all vanished, while the specter of nationalization hung over everything. I tried to reassure him that all was well. As it happened, he had bought this statue from a penniless Arab sculptor by the name of Mufid Nealy. Have you heard of him?"

"No. But I've heard of someone else from the Nealy family—Amir Nealy. And I don't like the man."

"That's good. And have you heard of Gamal Abdul Nasser and the Egypt-ian-Syrian Union?"

"I think so. But I'm not fond of him, either. It's said that he was a dictator, and that he ruined people's businesses and livelihoods. Did he force Mufid Nealy to make a statue of him?"

"No, he didn't force him. The poor man sculpted it in 1956 out of genuine love for Abdul Nasser. That was during the period when he'd fooled just about everyone except for folks like us. When my father bought the statue, he did it out of fear, not love. In any case, it became our property, so I took it with me to Damascus, where I rented a small house in the Seven Seas neighborhood near Baghdad Street. Then I brought in an artist of another sort and asked him to cast a mold from the statue and make a large number of copies from plaster. It didn't matter whether the material they were made of was durable, since I didn't expect the Syrian-Egyptian Union to last that long, in which case the statues wouldn't have to last long, either. Then, making use of Nasser's own apparatus for oppressing people and depriving them even of the chance to complain, I started selling the statues. My sales representative would go around to the offices of major businessmen and other wealthy folks and suggest that they buy one, but for an exorbitant price compared to the costs of production—$1,000 per statue. He didn't hold a gun to their heads, of course. However, he made it clear to them in a roundabout way that there was a desire on the part of government officials to see such statues in their offices, and that it was an expression of good will that wouldn't go unnoticed by the authorities. Before the government got wind of what we were up to, we'd sold fifteen hundred statues for a grand total of $1,500,000—with a net profit of more then $1,000,000 just for me. Merchants were upset about it, of course, but none of them dared complain. In fact, they pretended later on that they'd been the ones to go looking for this sort of statue out of love for Nasser! What happened increased their fears and resentment, but what fault was it of mine that they'd gone along with the idea? Besides, business depends on personal wit and enterprise, doesn't it?"

Kafa laughed with delight. "Really!" she exclaimed. "My father used to say the same thing. You tell such good stories!"

Nadim didn't dare yawn as Raghid spoke, even though he was hearing the story for the thousandth time.

Raghid continued, "Ah. . . . May he rest in peace, our friend Baytmouni."

Sounding tense and defiant, Khalil asked, "Was the sculptor Mufid Nealy the father of Amir Nealy?"

"Yes, he was. Do you know him?"

"Yes, somewhat," Khalil replied. He didn't know why he hadn't rushed to deny the charge.

Then a thought occurred to him: Might Layla have told Raghid about their encounter in her office and about what he'd said to Amir? He looked over at her, but she'd donned a poker face as opaque as a closed door.

Then he got up and headed over toward the statue. When he'd gotten closer, he noticed a rusty coin with a hole in the center inside the statue's golden cage. On the face of the coin he read, "Palestine, 1946" in Arabic, He-brew, and English. Without asking Raghid for permission, he reached in and picked it up, then turned it over to see what was written on the other side: "Ten mils."

"This piaster is priceless," he said. "What's *its* story, Raghid?"

Layla started with alarm when the Pasha opened his mouth to speak. But he said, "That story will have to wait till the next party. There's a pleasant tid-bit for every get together. And the series never ends!"

Layla's thoughts began to wander. (Why does Amir blow things out of pro-portion? He turns an ordinary old coin into an "issue," then comes to see me in my office looking so dejected you'd think he was Othello the day Desde-mona's scarf was delivered to him! When is this game of silence and mutual re-sentment going to end? And how can I tell him that I've become another woman? Doesn't he understand?)

Nadim made another attempt to pick up the thread of the conversation that he'd lost when he'd first unsheathed his newspaper like a sword in the "war of the apprentices." He'd done it in hopes of striking a blow at Raghid's grow-ing satisfaction with Layla's modus operandi.

"Pasha, look at this picture in the Beirut newspaper I told you about."

"Pasha?" exclaimed Kafa in adulation. "That title suits you so perfectly!"

Khalil lowered his glance in embarrassment at Kafa's behavior. Taking out a pair of gold-rimmed spectacles, Raghid stared at the newspaper and read a few lines. As he looked up at Nadim, sparks of unspoken understanding passed between them. It may have been a product of their many years together, as well as Nadim's desire to please his chief at any price.

"Bahriya Zahran," intoned Raghid.

He uttered the name, then paused for a few moments as if to test out its musical effect. No one said a word, but their eyes were full of curiosity, as if they were looking to see what was written in the newspaper about a woman or young girl by the name of Bahriya Zahran whose welfare appeared to be of concern to him, and whose name indicated that she might be a relative of his.

Raghid continued, "'Bahriya Zahran is a destitute young woman who has been forced out of her home. The building in which she and her family were residing along with hundreds of other homeless individuals was struck by a bomb. The entire edifice collapsed on the heads of those inside as if a giant ogre had trampled it under foot. This girl alone survived. She appears to have been outside the building, coming to take refuge there or returning to her house, and to have witnessed the demolition of the building as it occurred. She was found running frantically to and fro through the rubble. The unfortunate young woman is said to have suffered a nervous breakdown and lost the ability to speak, having lost all the family she had in the world.' That's all the newspaper has to report. Do you think she and I are related?"

"It's possible. In fact, you must be. Look at this picture of her."

"I've got to help her, then. I'll bring her to Switzerland to be treated for her nervous breakdown and muteness."

"Oh, what a noble, big-hearted man you are! God bless you and those like you!" Kafa cried admiringly.

Raghid was supremely pleased with her. This was exactly the impression he wanted to leave in the minds of the mediocre-minded majority—that is, in the minds of people like her. So then, the idea of polishing up his public image by making use of the media wasn't a bad one. And it might help to provide a suitable climate for the contracts and projects he wanted to carry out. But, would Hilal fall for it? He could try at any rate. He had nothing to lose. So he'd try.

Kafa looked thoughtfully at the photo of the girl and said, "She's gorgeous. I mean, after suffering from the shelling and going hungry and being without makeup or a proper hairdo, it's amazing that she can still look so pretty."

"I'll take responsibility for her," said Nadim. "I'll send a messenger from our office in Cyprus or Athens to bring her."

Interrupting, Layla said, "I'll do the paperwork for her visa to Switzerland. As you know, the Swiss embassy in Beirut is closed at present, so I might have to arrange an adoption of sorts, which could be nullified later on, of course."

Irritated to have her snatching the ball from him, Nadim said, "I did all that this morning. Her passport is waiting for her in Cyprus with a stamp on it indicating her departure from Lebanon, as well as a tourist visa to Switzerland. She's eighteen years old, so she isn't a minor and couldn't be adopted."

"My poor orphaned relative, Bahriya Zahran," said Raghid.

As he repeated the words, his voice quivered as if he actually believed his own lie.

"Oh, you generous man," said Kafa, her eyes moist with tears.

Delighted by her words, he felt intoxicated with his own glory and magnificence. He reassured her that he would host a gala affair in celebration of

Bahriya's arrival, and that (being the marvelous, great man that he was), he wouldn't abandon the cause until she'd fully recovered.

Then, his heart ablaze with renewed hatred for the changes in the Arab world that had nearly toppled his fortunes, and overcome by a wave of self-pity mingled with malicious glee over others' bad luck, he said, "Those who claim to love Lebanon and to be mourning over its sad fate—they're the true causes of its calamities!"

With the gleam of hand plows shining in his eyes and redolent with the fragrance of wild thyme and tobacco, Khalil said sadly, "Israel has occupied south Lebanon, Sidon has fallen, and . . ."

"The people of south Lebanon have suffered for a long time from the expanding Palestinian presence there," interrupted Raghid, "and in Sidon in particular, the people have suffered from heinous violations of their rights. The Palestinian fighters have enslaved south Lebanon in the name of liberating Palestine. So now the Lebanese people will be rid of them."

Ignoring what Raghid had said, Khalil continued, "And now Israel is bombarding Beirut like mad, apparently in preparation to occupy it."

"Beirut is the pawn of the armed Palestinians and their allies. There's nothing the people of Beirut long for more than to be delivered from the Palestinian mafia that goes around armed to the teeth. Nadim tells me that you two left on the last plane out. Well, you're lucky."

His blood boiling with rage, Khalil made up his mind to stand up to Raghid no matter what it cost.

"Your logic isn't correct," he replied, "and the picture you're painting isn't accurate, since it's based on generalizations."

"Beirut is a hellhole," broke in Kafa. "I still feel amazed whenever I turn on a light switch and it actually works, or whenever I turn on a water faucet and what comes out is real water rather than ants. I'm still amazed when I see people walking out in the streets here at night. We'd forgotten what it feels like to live in peace. Even in the bomb shelters they wouldn't leave us alone. One time when the bombing was shaking everything in sight, two armed men came into the shelter and robbed everyone of everything they had with them. They robbed us, too, and with the shelling and all, there was no way for us to resist or fight back. It was a laughable sight. But nobody laughed."

Ignoring her, Raghid went on spitefully, "The armed vigilantes and their helpers set up heavy weapons on the roofs of people's houses, and on top of mosques, churches, and schools, as well as hospitals and schools filled with unfortunate people who've been forced out of their homes. They even set them up near orphanages and nursing homes for the elderly. Their behavior shows total disregard for the people who've done so much to help them, not to mention the heavy price the people of the city have had to pay on their account. In the end they'll leave Beirut a charred ruin, which is what they'll do to every city that takes them in. Mark my words."

By this time Khalil was so angry, he was red in the face. He opened his mouth to reply, but before he could say anything he was surprised to find Nadim, Layla, and Dunya all looking at him in a way that told him he'd better be careful. Nasim, who was serving coffee to the guests, added his own cautioning glance to theirs. He'd just happened to enter the room as Khalil was uttering his first objection. Given Nasim's collusive look, Khalil was convinced that the warning was in order, and he fell silent.

(I throw Raghid into his golden pool. Then I jump in on top of him for the pleasure of strangling him slowly to death. I press his head down to keep it under water as I scream, "And what about the fortunes that people like you spend to keep our conflicts alive and well, to revive sectarianism and clan rivalries, and to create a spirit of prejudice and discrimination to make people think they have a reason to fight each other?"

His head comes up out of the water and he screams back, "You see? You're all terrorists, and you don't even know how to have a decent conversation! Why don't you offer some reply to the things I said? Instead, you try to choke me to death after putting one individual on trial, after which you decide that I'm a traitor and execute me single-handedly. To people like you, everyone's either a traitor or a hero, either a martyr or some scoundrel that deserves to be killed. You all preach democracy, but on the condition that you get to put a gun to your opponent's head while you have your dialogue."

"And what about the original sin that was committed in Palestine? Banishing a peaceable people from their homeland, making a million people homeless, and then abandoning them? Then nominating the Arab countries one after another to be another Palestine to be swallowed up later by Israel? What do you want us to do? Treat the things most sacred to us as merchandise that we can trade in so as to amass our first million? Then emigrate and go wandering around the world with our homeland stuffed in a suitcase so that our children can sprout up like moss on a stone, strangers and aliens without roots?

What can we do but resist? Mistakes? Backward folks that we are, it's only natural for there to be mistakes as long as we're doing something. But we won't put up with some spiteful person who just wants to gloat over our misfortunes. We'll accept criticism that comes from a fellow patriot, but not from a traitor. We'll accept it from Amir Nealy, but not from Raghid Zahran."

"The Palestinians have turned Beirut into a city of misery, and they delight in the control they wield over it. They've taught you to despise democracy and freedom of expression until it's become second nature to you to sell out to whoever comes along, both in what you say and in what you write."

"The Palestinians didn't choose Beirut. It just happens to be where they found themselves. Besides which, generalizations won't do. They didn't make it miserable. It was already that way before they got there. Do you know anything about the hundreds of thousands of destitute people there, and about the wretched suburbs that ring the city's wealth-surfeited interior? Besides which, we haven't sold out to anyone, either in what we write or what we say. At least most of us haven't. We really meant what we said, and we still do."

And here you are trying to kill me just because I expressed an opinion different from yours. Isn't that against the principle espoused by your prince, Amir Nealy?"

"Well, maybe I was wrong to try to kill you. On the other hand, maybe I was wrong not to go through with it. I'll have to think about it."

"Isn't this the way you and your friends deal with each other? I'm not angry with you, though. I know this is the only way you know how to have a dialogue."

"Don't ask us for dinner table conversation when you're in the business of wiping us off the face of the globe."

I feel so defeated, helpless, and irate that I dunk Raghid's head into the water again after every sentence. Finally I shriek, "So you've chosen a fine time to gloat over me, now that I'm homeless, weak, and defeated and my country is being overrun by the enemy! I'll kill you. There's something about you that brings out all my violent, destructive impulses. I'll kill you right here in this golden pool of yours, right in the center where the octopus's head would be, in plain view of your beloved gold and your statues, including the one imprisoned in a golden cage!")

Khalil didn't say a word. Instead, he just sat there beside the pool, looking into the water and imagining himself wringing Raghid's neck. Meanwhile, by way of apology for the objection voiced by her husband—who had dared to deviate from the views of the Pasha, who of course is always right—Kafa was telling the story of how her little girl Widad died. The atmosphere in the place was electrified, as if Raghid knew what was going on in Khalil's head. He wasn't wet, he hadn't fallen into the pool, and he wasn't about to choke to death. In fact, Khalil hadn't even raised his voice at him. All that had happened was that his breathing had accelerated. But that was enough for Raghid to pick up on his wave length and to feel the delightful rush that he got whenever he had the chance to revel in someone else's pain. (So, here's another revolutionary with a broken heart and broken wings. So turn your knife in his wound, Raghid. Insult him and enjoy the bliss of hatred! It has a taste even more savory than the adulation you've been feasting on off the blue "dish" of Kafa's eyes. The pleasure of hatred is a spicy morsel indeed. It reminds me of the taste of the aphrodisiac that I get from Sheikh Watfan, and both have the same effect. It energizes me and polishes up my practical skills.)

When Layla saw the look of euphoria that had suddenly appeared on Raghid's face, she went rushing after it like a ball that's left the playing field, then picked it up, brought it back and tossed it to Raghid.

"So then," she said, "Kafa will be joining the preparation crew for the great celebration, the Night of the First Billion."

Remembering the billion dollars that he owned, Raghid went into raptures.

"I'd be delighted to have Kafa participate. And who knows? Bahriya might be able to lend a hand, too. And if Madame Dunya had time to lend a hand, that would be lovely."

"Of course," replied Dunya curtly.

This will be the night of a lifetime, Pasha," added Layla. "It will give people an occasion to laud your great accomplishments."

"We'll build both a mosque and a church for the occasion, Pasha," said Nadim.

"The well-to-do will come from all over the world, provided that they're at least millionaires. Although we might invite some poor folks with just hundreds of thousands, for example."

"Of course, Pasha," repeated the chorus.

"And I'll also invite other poor people, such as writers and thinkers who've had to flee from countries that don't realize their true worth. Like Amir Nealy, for instance."

Khalil trembled with rage, but said nothing. (Yeah, you'll invite him to gloat over his poverty. You really do bring out my violent side!)

"But there won't be enough room in the mansion for all the guests," said Raghid. "What shall we do about that, Lilly?"

"I've reserved the entire hotel next door for five days, Pasha."

"You're a genius, my dear. I'll leave all the details to you."

"The food will be brought in on private refrigerated airplanes. The fruit will be imported from all over the world."

Breaking in with childlike enthusiasm as if she were planning a birthday party for one of her children, Kafa said, "Oh, Pasha, we'll decorate the house with colored paper and flowers and balloons!"

Raghid Bey is allergic to flowers," said Layla. "The dust they bring in makes him cough. So I've ordered one thousand gold flowers to be custom-made for the occasion."

"That's a marvelous idea. You know how I love the color gold."

Then suddenly in walked the sorcerer. And with that the vociferous bidding for the Pasha's approval came to an abrupt halt.

Kafa felt a bit frightened when she shook his hand and he looked into her face with those peculiar eyes of his, the right one brown and the left one green. She'd never seen anyone like him before, with eyes of different colors, and with a towering, ghostlike frame that seemed to disappear beneath his long cloak. It was as if there were winds, sighs, and specters careening about inside it.

"Your blessings, Sheikh Watfan."

Khalil shook his hand and looked intently into his face. For some reason, he didn't fit the conventional image of a sorcerer. Instead, he seemed frightened, even terrified. He and Khalil exchanged a long look that convinced Khalil that what was being emitted by the sorcerer's eyes was nothing less than sheer terror. He kept on looking at him, trying in vain to penetrate the mask created by his beard and to get through to the mysterious man behind it. He was like a solid wall with neither windows nor doors.

He was sure he'd seen him before, though he couldn't remember where. Whenever his memory was about to seize upon an image from the past, it would slip away like some sort of mercurial fish.

Dunya, and even Raghid, rose to their feet when the sorcerer entered the room. Dunya was confident that he wouldn't reveal her secret to her husband, that is, that she'd come asking him to prevent her husband from making love to any other woman. He wasn't a man to break a confidence. But one thing was clear. Everyone was afraid of him. Everyone without exception. Khalil was the only one who, in addition to feeling afraid, felt a kind of bewilderment in his presence. He'd just met someone he didn't know, yet he'd seen him in his dreams many times before. He had a powerful desire to know more about the man, especially after having heard people talk about his legendary feats. Was it possible that he really did know him? Where had he seen him before? He was sure that he had, perhaps dressed differently than he was now. But where? Where? Where?

Everyone sat for a while in a kind of reverent silence. Then the sorcerer apologized for not being able to stay long since he was tired. He said he'd come to greet the guests who'd arrived from Lebanon and that after that he would have to be on his way.

(How could Raghid have failed to notice that his guest Khalil is the same person whose picture he once showed me, asking me to destroy the person in the photograph, and whom I couldn't do a thing to? There's some powerful, mysterious magic protecting this ordinary, nondescript-looking man.)

The sorcerer bid them farewell ever so politely, then departed, leaving a frigid, frightening presence on the chair where he'd sat, as well as obscure answers to the questions Kafa had asked as a child.

"What is magic really, sir?" she'd asked.

"Magic is real as long as you believe that it is. And I'm a magician with powers as long as you believe in my magic. What's my secret? You're my secret."

"The Pasha needs to rest," said Dunya. "We've stayed quite late."

Raghid bid the guests farewell with a special send off for Kafa. Then he whispered to Nadim—as the one who would be bringing Bahriya from Beirut, "Why don't you arrange a new series of car explosions? They're proving to be quite effective. Every time a car blows up and kills hundreds of victims, weapons orders go up from all the groups involved in the fighting, since every group thinks the others were responsible for booby-trapping the car!"

"Right away, sir."

As the guests left, Khalil took note of the tight security procedures they had to pass through on their way out just as they had on their way in. After the one-sided conversation he'd had with Raghid, it didn't surprise him. He didn't feel like stealing anything, but like others, he would have loved to murder the man with his own two hands from the first moment he laid eyes on him.

On their way home, Kafa's passions were rekindled as she contemplated Nadim's speedy new car, which hummed smoothly along in a noiseless world of ease and luxurious tranquility. Then she thought back by way of comparison to her husband's noisy old rattletrap. She got a lump in her throat as she watched Nadim with one hand on the steering wheel and the other on his cellular phone.

Wealth and influence brought a whole new life with them. And it was a life she loved as much as she hated the life represented by Khalil's rickety old jalopy. Nadim and his world were so marvelous. What vitality and potency. She was in love with him. In love, delighted to be near him, and delighted with the telephone in his car!

"The television is in front of you," he told her with a note of pride in his voice. "Feel free to enjoy it if you like. And the bar is next to it."

Unhappily she thought: Dunya is such a lucky woman to have a husband like him. But she obviously isn't aware of it. If only I were in her place.

She pressed the button to turn on the television, and a blazing Beirut appeared on the screen. She didn't turn up the volume.

As they went speeding down Switzerland's safe, well-lit streets, Kafa looked away from the picture on the screen and out the car window, contemplating the delights of Switzerland and trying to imagine what share she might have in the happiness she found all around her.

Khalil's gaze was fixed on the television screen. Tears of humiliation found their way from his throat to his eyes. He wiped them off in the darkness in stifled silence.

"What time is it?" Kafa asked him.

"Twelve-thirty," he said.

"When on earth are you going to fix your watch?"

Pressing his lips shut, he replied silently, "I'll never fix it. I'm sure it must be right."

Ignoring him, Kafa turned to Nadim and said, "What a scary man that sorcerer is! Don't you think so?"

"He certainly is," he muttered. "Frightening."

❖   ❖   ❖

(Oh, I'm so frightened. I'm scared to death. Dread is about to eat me alive. Things are happening to me that I can't understand. I've lost control of my senses and my brain. There are moments when the threads start to unravel and when I lose my grasp completely, like when I saw Khalil.)

Watfan the sorcerer stared out the window. The guests' car was leaving, and he was beginning to calm down a little. (I feel as though my enemies have followed me all the way here. They put on familiar faces and possess people that I love just so that they can bring me down. Oh, what's happening to me? I've amassed a fortune, and I don't even know why anymore. What's the use of money when I'm living in exile in the world of demons? I was happy at first, when I was still just an impostor. But then they took me by surprise. I'd tampered with some graves where some "presence" lived, and I came face to face with them. Then I lay with the women of the jinn. So what's come over me all of a sudden? Is Anbara a demon from an enemy tribe who's come to mock me, clothing herself in the body of the woman I loved long ago? Why is it that ever since she slipped that evil, bewitched green stone that looked like an emerald into my hand, my nightmares have come back?

And if Anbara doesn't belong to the world of demons, then how did she disappear so fast?

I mustered all the courage I had left and called her house, but I was told that she'd left the country. I called a second time and there was no answer. So I went there myself, only to find the place all shut up, with dust piled up on the windowsills and doorknobs. I saw infernal-looking spiders reproducing and multiplying before my very eyes, and in a matter of minutes, nothing was left of the house but a colony of gargantuan spiders, adders, worms, and scorpions. I took off running and the gargoyles came running after me, roaring like lions. Then today, my diabolical foe hid behind the face of a poor, ordinary-looking fellow by the name of Khalil. It's as if the spirit that intends to destroy me has occupied my memory.

Oh, I'm so frightened. I'm scared to death.)

◆　◆　◆

Somewhere between sleep and wakefulness, Dunya heard a voice calling to her. She strained to hear what it was. (I must be imagining things.) Then, no sooner had she dozed off again than the familiar woman's voice called to her once more.

She got out of bed. Her husband was asleep in the adjoining room. For a long time now they'd slept apart. She looked at her watch. It was 4:20 A.M.

The voice called to her a third time, in a whisper that made it sound as though it were coming from a deep well. She stepped forward over the sound waves like a somnambulant until, catching up with its echo, she found herself standing before her painting, the picture she had drawn of the young woman that she once had been.

"Dunya," said the girl in the picture, "your sleep has gotten heavy. You used to wake up at the drop of a feather."

"   . . ."

"It seems you've had too much to drink, as usual. I don't remember your ever even tasting alcohol before."

"   . . ."

"Your body is out of shape. Why don't you work out the way you used to?"

"   . . ."

"What are you doing to yourself, and to me?"

"   . . ."

Dunya's only reply was a blank, bewildered stare.

Could her painting actually be talking to her? Or was she dreaming? Was she entering the stage of hallucinations and nightmares? Was this what happens to alcoholics in the end?

There was a painful, tingling sensation in her knees. They weren't strong enough to bear her weight anymore, and she collapsed onto the chair opposite the painting. Feeling as though she was about to choke, she reached up and took off her diamond necklace with the delicate gold chain and placed it beside her on the table.

"Dunya," called out the girl in the painting, "have you gone back to sleep?"

"No. But I don't believe what's happening."

"Do you think you're either asleep or insane?"

"Exactly."

"Well, you're not asleep. In fact, it's the first time in years that you've been awake. And you're not insane at this moment. But you've been insane for years now, ever since the two of us parted ways."

"This is a bad joke. Who is it that's trying to make me believe that a painting is talking to me?'

She looked all around her. Perhaps her daughter, who'd announced quite plainly that she hated her, was playing a trick on her. She went upstairs to her children's rooms, then passed by her husband's bedroom. They were all fast asleep. Then the painting began calling to her again, so she went back to where she had been standing. As she stood there looking at the picture, the girl's lips and features began to move and her eyelashes fluttered. Meanwhile, her hand was pointing menacingly outside the picture frame.

"All right then," said Dunya. "What do you want? Let's suppose that you really are the one speaking to me. Why are you harassing me?"

"Harassing you? You destroyed my life, and you blame me for harassing you?"

"So I've destroyed your life? How?"

"When I was young, I was free and alive. I was full of hopes. It was talent that flowed through my veins, not alcohol. Look at what you've done to me. Look at the slavery that I strain under now. Look at what you've done to the young woman that you were once upon a time."

"What do you mean, what have I done? We used to be poor, and now we're rich."

"We weren't poor really. I was able to work and support myself. I was planning to do a type of work that I loved and could feel proud of. That's what life is all about."

"But I do work!"

"I was hoping that my profession would be knowing and serving the truth. But you've used me to bury facts, destroy honesty, and raise high the banner of falsehood wherever you go."

"That isn't exactly what happened. I got married . . ."

"Do you call what you have a marriage? You're an employee in a financial establishment that you call marriage. You're a receptionist, a public relations secretary."

"That's not true. I'm the mother of his children. We're a family."

"You were a baby making machine, just as your daughter told you this morning. You were his way of getting children, and that was the end of it."

"My daughter's spoiled. I've never deprived her of anything."

"You deprived her of your company when she was a little girl, and of your friendship when she was a teenager. So she's come to hate you. As for your son, he neither loves you nor hates you. He lives inside his television set. He's taken up residence in his own little fantasy world: Intelevision, Atari, and the like. The collections of robots that he takes such pride in are closer to him than you are. They're his real family."

"But I'm busy and exhausted. I haven't got even a moment of free time."

"You're exhausted because you're doing what you hate. Do you honestly feel fond of the people who are all around you?"

"No. There isn't any real communication between us."

"Even so, you devote your time to pleasing them. You wear the clothes they like, you buy jewelry that they'll envy you for having, you spend half your day at the hairdresser to turn your black hair another color because the color black isn't in style this season. You choke on the fumes from the chemicals they use to bleach your hair just so that you can please your peers."

"I have to adapt myself to the environment I live in."

"The problem is in the environment that you chose."

"I didn't choose it. This is how the rich live."

"The mistake is in your not choosing the world that's consistent with who you really are."

"I've stood by my husband, and this is his world."

"You've encouraged him, and as a result you've lost him. In this world there's no such thing as friendship or love. There's nothing but emptiness—a frightening emptiness."

" . . ."

"And instead of fleeing to your work, to what you really are, you kept on plunging ahead—into alcohol."

" . . ."

"You feel lonely and homesick, and deprived of genuine love and affection with your husband, children, and friends. And if you do find a friend that you feel comfortable with like Khalil, you find no time for him in the marriage madhouse you've gotten yourself into."

" . . ."

"Divorce him."

"It's too late. I've gotten used to this life of indolence mixed with rushing around all the time. Or, let's say I've gotten used to being rich."

"Divorce him. Haven't you ever heard of making a new start in life? People may envy you, but you're a failure. You despise this life of yours. So change it."

"I can't. A person can't just conclude that he took the wrong path eighteen years earlier, then go back to the point where he was when he made the mistake and put his life back in order."

"Divorce him."

"I can't. I'm not young enough to start all over. And I'm not old enough to forget."

"Divorce him."

"Okay, then. So what if I did divorce him? Could I strike my children's names off the birth register and say: They were just a typographical error? Could I take an eraser and wipe out eighteen years of my life, including a husband and two children, the way an artist erases a pencil mark that he's made on one of his drawings?"

"And are you saying there's no hope for us? Can't we backtrack even a little?"

"I don't think so. So just leave me in peace."

The girl in the painting pressed her lips together, and a lone tear came flowing down from her left eye. It was just the way Dunya had always cried as a young girl. Many were the admirers who'd been charmed by that single, comical-looking tear flowing out of one eye, as if her other eye had been hewn out of stone. Then she drew her hand back inside the frame while her fingers relaxed once again into their original position.

Dunya got up and went back to bed, turning her eyes away from the rays of the early summer dawn. When she was young, she had loved the early morning rather than loathing it as she did now, and she'd loved to examine things in the light of day so as to see them as they really were. If a sweetheart danced with her in some nightclub, for instance, she used to go back to the place the following morning and try to "see" him in the sunlight. (Wadi' took me out dancing once. He was a penniless poet and destined to stay that way. In any case, I went soaring with him over a pink cloud and reached out to touch the stars. When he picked them out of the sky for me and sprinkled them in my hair, I felt as though I'd been crowned the princess of passionate love.

The next morning I went back to the place he'd taken me to dance. The door was locked. I sat down in front of the door and stayed there until noon, at which point a janitor came along to unlock the place so that he could clean it. I told him I'd forgotten a book inside, and that I needed it urgently because of a test I had to study for. I begged him to let me go in and get it. He asked me where I'd been sitting and said he'd bring it out to me, but he refused to let me go in myself.

So when he went in, I snuck in behind him. As he opened the drapes, sunlight poured in like iridescent rain, washing away my illusions. The armchairs which the night before had looked like beds of flower blossoms now appeared as they really were—old and stained with liquor, vomit, and other things reminiscent of a hooker's bed. As for the colored, psychedelic lights that had looked like stars dancing in a cosmic festival, they were coated with dust along with the unsightly wires that hung suspended in the former cosmic outer space. When I glanced over at the seat where we'd sat the night before, I saw cockroaches scurrying across the words of poetry that had come falling from our lips and out of our pockets. I took off running like crazy while the janitor shouted angrily, "There aren't any books here, Miss! I didn't find a thing!"

As for me, I'd found something, and lost it. I decided that a love that could survive only in a disco, surrounded by artificial lights and the fog of illusions, wasn't really love. After that I refused to see Wadi' unless it was somewhere outside the disco. So he left me and wrote a marvelous poem, and I did a good painting. And that was that.)

I used to love to look at the truth no matter how painful it was. So why is it that now, I don't dare look at the way my life has turned out or at what I used to be?

Dunya awakened to the feel of someone's hand shaking her. It was Nadim, who had gotten dressed and was on his way out. She got up exhausted.

He said, "I forgot to tell you yesterday that we've got guests coming this evening. Six people for dinner at 8:45."

"You also forgot to say 'Good morning!' " she shouted.

"We stopped doing that a long time ago, to save time. Have you forgotten?"

"Do you think I'm running a restaurant here?"

"Of course. That's part of our partnership. What's changed?"

"Don't I have a right to know the names of the guests?"

"What difference would it make? They're coming on business."

"Haven't you noticed that we don't have any friends? I mean, friends whose company we really enjoy, not friends that we 'benefit' from."

"It's one of the drawbacks of the profession. When we decided to amass a fortune, we knew that."

"But I didn't know how hard it would be. What if we were to get sick? Or suffered some catastrophe? We wouldn't find a single true friend to support us."

"There's no such thing as a true friend. In any case, we'd be supported by our wealth."

"I can't stand to go on this way any longer. I've begun to hate you, and to hate myself."

"You've hated me for a long time. Ever since you hired a secret agent to follow me around and found out that I was cheating on you. So why make a big scene over it now when I'm busy?"

"You've driven me to despise myself."

"You mean, because you visited Sheikh Watfan in the hotel to get him to hurt me? Does it surprise you that I know about it? I hired a spy to follow you around, too. That's part of our lives as wealthy folks. And now, I'm out of here. Be ready at 8:30 in case some of the guests arrive early."

"You don't give a damn how I feel."

"Dunya, what's gotten into you? You're acting as if you were Rabi'a Al-Adawiya after someone had tried to tempt her to evil.[18] Or as if you'd reverted to childhood. The day you decided to divorce me thirteen years ago then changed your mind for the children's sake, as you put it, we didn't have a conversation like this."

"You mean, after you begged me to come back. Don't you remember how you cried?"

"What difference does it make? All that is part of a past that's long gone. You're forty years old now. Have you forgotten?"

"Our tragedy is that we're allies without also being lovers, or even friends."

"We know each other too well, so well that love has become impossible. We're both obnoxious."

"I'm not that obnoxious."

"You're worse than I am. You got the wealth you wanted, and now you're trying to get out of having to pay the price that comes with it."

As he said it, he left the room angrily, slamming the door behind him.

No. She wasn't going to give in. She might not be able to start her life all over again, but she was going to try to reform her ways to some extent. That much, at least, is possible, she thought. No, it isn't. Yes, it is. No, it isn't. Why had she picked a fight with her husband? What good would that do? It was the dream she'd had. All of a sudden it came back to her. That painting. When it first came into the house, she nearly destroyed it. Then it had begun stealing into her dreams, turning her into a hostile, aggressive woman who liked to start an argument with her husband whenever she got the chance. What a

18. Rabi'a Al-Adawiyah was a Muslim mystic saint (d. 185 A.H.) well known for her piety and devotion to God.

dream it had been. She'd begun talking to paintings in her dreams. It must be the beginning of the road to insanity.

Just then the maid walked in and said to her, "I found this necklace of yours on the table in the living room, Ma'am."

As she took the necklace, she felt as though she'd been struck by a bolt of lighting. Distraught, she got out of bed. As she walked down the hallway, she passed her daughter, who hadn't said, "Good morning" to her since the time she fired the nanny. She generally avoided running into her mother. So why was it that this time she seemed to have deliberately come out to see her? Then, with a fearful, sad expression on her face, she took her mother's hand and said, "I'm not the one who fooled with your painting. I swear. I know you'll accuse me of it, but I didn't do it. That painting is the only thing that belongs to you that I really love."

"What about it? What's happened to the painting?"

"Somebody's painted a tear under her left eye. It isn't badly done and doesn't mess up the way the painting looks. But . . ."

"What? What are you saying?"

"I swear to you. I didn't do it. If I had, I'd admit it, since I don't care that much about your feelings. But I'm telling you the truth. You know how important it is to me to be honest. And maybe that's why I hate you sometimes. But I don't hate you enough to vandalize that choice painting of yours."

Without saying a word, Dunya went into the bathroom and locked the door behind her. Once alone, she heaved a sigh of relief despite her splitting headache. As she washed her face with cold water she thought, that damned booze! And these damned hangovers. And this wretched feeling of fatigue and nausea. And these headaches that have me on the verge of collapsing. She wished she could put her whole head under the stream of cold water, but with guests coming that same evening, she was afraid of ruining her hairdo. The hair salon was always at its busiest on the weekend. So she contented herself with washing her face with cold water. (All right. Maybe it wasn't my daughter who tampered with the painting. Maybe I was drunk and did it myself. Or have dreams begun crossing over into reality in this split life I lead? No. It's impossible that all those things could have actually happened. My daughter's been playing tricks on me. But, how did my necklace get onto the living room table? Did my daughter steal it from inside my dream to put it there? Or did I really go sleepwalking and leave it near the painting without realizing it?) As she searched for a logical explanation for things, a thought occurred to her: Perhaps the events of the day before really had taken place, yet without her having gotten out of bed, and maybe she'd forgotten the necklace on the table some time before that. She wished Khalil were nearby so that she could tell him what had happened—either Khalil or Amir. Or, for that matter, any friend that could feel with someone whose spirit was full of holes. It was strange, indeed. But, she wondered, isn't it possible for such things to happen in our world?

The most amazing thing of all was that she found her cosmetics case opened and in disarray, even though she couldn't remember having touched it. But hadn't she believed for some time in the existence of unseen human powers—the ability to speak to plants, for example, or possibly even infuse inanimate objects with life? Had she actually caused the paintbrush to move with an energy generated by her torment and misery? And had the tear painted itself on such that if someone had seen it happening, he would have thought that a ghost was moving the brush? Was this the kind of thing that happened with Sheikh Watfan when objects would move under the force of his gaze? Is this universe really nothing more than what we perceive when we take a transient, hurried, superficial view of things? Are we all just in a race for riches, running like donkeys after a golden carrot?

Oh, what a headache she had. But she had to get the menu ready for the evening. There was no time to be thinking about such things. There was no time to feel. No time for anything. (Where are you, Picasso—my sweet dog, my only friend? Picasso, come, dear. Come to the health club with your friend who's being split in two. She's still busy trying to shrink her derriere, where she carries the weight of the world's cares and unsolved mysteries. After that we'll go to the barber, yours and mine, then to the tailor, then the coffee shop, then the masseur. There's no time to be sad, or to be happy, for that matter. There's no time to stop and reflect on things, or to make friends, or to remember. There's no time for death. There's no time for anything. Hurry, Picasso. Hurry!)

❖   ❖   ❖

Saqr took a gold box out of his pocket, opened it, and removed a small bag along with a hundred-dollar bill. Khalil looked on curiously. However, Saqr made no reply to Khalil's silent questioning except to laugh his usual hysterical laugh, followed by an abrupt silence. Then he poured some of the contents of the bag onto the newspaper. Staring at the newspaper, Khalil saw a news item about Beirut. He saw a photograph of some of the destruction and a small mound of white powder atop the flames in the picture. Saqr divided the powder into two parts, then into four. Then he tore the bill into pieces and rolled part of it up in the shape of a tiny tube. Drawing his face near the newspaper and placing one end of the tube over one fourth of the white powder, he inserted the other end in his right nostril, then inhaled forcefully with a loud snort. He repeated the procedure with the second pile of powder, only this time he inserted the tube into his left nostril. Then he rubbed his nose vigorously and blissfully closed his eyes.

"Have you ever done cocaine before?" he asked Khalil.

"No."

"Great. I love your ignorance. I'll teach you and sophisticate you."

"But . . ."

"Come on, snort the rest. Here . . ."

Khalil nearly threw the vile stuff in Saqr's face and ran away with the newspaper to read about Beirut. But then he remembered his sons' school fees, the sky-high rent he had to pay for the hotel suite, and the fact that Kafa's money was about to run out. He also remembered that on this particular day he'd decided to wait for an opportunity to ask for an advance on his salary. So he obeyed Saqr's orders and snorted. Bothered by the strange substance in his nose, he started to rub it.

"Be careful not to sneeze," Saqr told him.

Khalil fought off a terrible urge to cough and sneeze, which soon gave way to a numbness in his nose and then in his throat. A feeling of distress came over him as he swallowed his saliva along with his unspoken objections.

They sipped their coffee in silence, and within a few minutes Khalil had begun to feel in fine health indeed. He felt happy, strong, and full of energy, as though he'd taken off in a time machine and headed backward until he was no longer thirty-three, but twenty-three instead. Filled suddenly with a friendly hilarity, his heart started to dance in his chest like a sparrow thrilled with its ability to fly.

"Can you get off on this much, or do you need some more?" Saqr asked him.

"I'm already flying."

"I can't take off on this amount anymore."

"This is my first time. Don't forget that."

Saqr treated himself to another fix, then rang the bell and ordered another cup of coffee.

As Khalil stared out the window, he saw the tree outside as if he were seeing one for the first time in his life, with its exquisite trunk and its green leaves that seemed to blink on and off beneath the rays of the sun like thousands of tiny mirrors sending signals to other planets.

Taking hold of the gold box from which Saqr had taken the white forgetting powder, he turned it in such a way that it reflected the sunlight and began casting its rays back onto the ceiling and the wall.

"What are you doing?" Saqr asked him.

"I'm sending messages in code."

"What are you saying?"

"Help!"

"And what else?"

"O ye residents of other planets, I'm on my way. Prepare the banquet!"

This time they laughed together, and Saqr appeared to quite enjoy Khalil's company. He also seemed to be less under the influence of the joy powder than Khalil was, since without warning, he dragged him back down to earth, saying, "You seem younger now. Less than thirty years old."

"I'm immortal, eternal, without beginning or end. And I stay twenty years old for all time . . ."

"Do you really have children?"

He nearly slapped him. Was this the time to be talking about children? Then he remembered something. Suddenly feeling capable of being tactless, brazen, and even violent, he replied, "Yes, I do. And that reminds me, I'm in need of a salary advance. I haven't got a single Swiss franc to my name."

With that, Saqr took a handful of bills out of his pocket. Focusing his gaze with difficulty, Khalil made out the number "one thousand" on one of them. There were ten, or perhaps twenty, thousand-franc bills. He reached out and took them, saying, "I need the whole amount. Don't you have any more on you?"

Laughing his hysterical laugh, Saqr emptied his pockets of everything in them, and Khalil took all the money he offered him without hesitation. Taking the golden box also, he returned to Saqr the small bag filled with the white powder, a bunch of keys, and a bottle of medicine, and kept the rest.

Just then Sakhr walked in.

"Please, Dad," enjoined the son. "I'm broke. Help!"

"You were broke yesterday too. And I helped you."

"Help me some more, Dad. Help me some more!"

"That's all anybody ever says to me. My women, my children, my friends, they're all the same. Nobody asks me for anything else. Nobody would want to take my ulcer from me, for example."

"Why don't you try Sheikh Watfan?" offered Khalil jokingly, and with a brashness he wasn't accustomed to seeing in himself.

"It's Sheikh Watfan's potions that gave me the ulcer in the first place."

Following Sakhr into the room, Hilal heard the name, "Sheikh Watfan."

Addressing himself to Khalil, he asked, "Is he really what people say? Able to cure the sick? You're a modern, educated young man. What do you say about it?"

"I say what he said to my wife: 'I'm capable as a sorcerer because you all believe in my sorcery.' "

As he said the words he mimicked the voice of Sheikh Watfan. Everyone burst out laughing except for Sakhr, who said, "Nothing's sacred to this generation."

Hilal interjected, "The astrologers lie even when they speak the truth."

"That isn't a Qur'anic verse," said Saqr defiantly. "The phrase 'the astrologers' isn't mentioned anywhere in the Qur'an."

"The Qur'an contains numerous references to sorcery," Hilal insisted, "Remember to supply me with them, Khalil."

"Yes, yes," he muttered.

Whereupon Saqr withdrew hurriedly, followed by Khalil. Once the two of them had left the room, Saqr said, "So, it really is your first time on star dust. Now I believe you. How did you have the audacity to imitate Sheikh Watfan?"

"Well, I was about to imitate your dad's voice, too . . . and your uncle's, and your ancestors . . ."

"Come on, let's get out of here before you cause me a scandal."

Then, taking a bottle of medicine out of his pocket, Saqr swallowed a pill without water and gave another one to Khalil, who said, "Thanks a lot. But I'm not sick."

As they pulled out, Saqr insisted, "I'm not sick, either. Just swallow it."

So he swallowed it, repeating, "I'm not sick, either."

"All right," said Saqr, "I'll admit, I am sick. I'm lovesick. I'm smitten with love for life. And this is my cure. It sets life on fire in my body."

"But you'd be that way anyway. I mean, you're only twenty-three years old, if that."

"That isn't enough. Uppers do to you what you do to a car when you expand the valve that releases gasoline into the combustion chamber."

Khalil took a long look at his hand, and was surprised to notice how his veins protruded and how blue they were. Thinking that some insect was walking between his veins and the surface of the skin, he tried to drive it out, then forgot about it.

Saqr was driving like a speed demon, but rather than feeling afraid the way he normally would, Khalil felt high—he, the one who hated people who turn city streets into race tracks. In fact, he even wished they'd be stopped by a policeman so that he could taunt him and maybe even beat him up. Was this what the drug had done to him?

"Are you hungry"? Saqr asked him.

"No."

"Well, it's lunchtime, so let's go to some restaurant and just not eat anything."

They went to the same Arabic restaurant where Khalil was supposed to have worked as an accountant but got kicked out instead. The waiter who had been so haughty before forgot his self-importance when he saw Saqr's fancy car. Instead he received them with the utmost deference, opening the door for them and extending his palms as if to say: If your shoes aren't satisfied with the feel of the carpet, walk over my hands instead! He didn't appear to remember Khalil. And why should he? He'd just been one more hobo begging for a free meal as far as he was concerned. Khalil felt sad and belligerent at the same time. (Why do people from the poor class treat each other like dirt, then treat the rich with a respect that they don't necessarily deserve? Or is that the function of the poor in consumer societies?)

They drank what they'd ordered from the bar, then ordered food that they knew they wouldn't eat since neither of them was hungry. Even so, Saqr scolded the waiter when he was late bringing the meal, then sent him away and said he'd decided to buy the restaurant so that he could fire him. After a while they started to get bored.

"What do you say we break into somebody's house?" Saqr asked.

"Great idea."

"And rape some married woman?"

"I'll leave that part to you."

"But you'll watch, won't you?"

"I'm not in the habit of spying on people."

"Oh, please do. I'd enjoy it!"

"Well, all right—if it's part of my job."

"What if the woman happened to be my girlfriend? She's a French dancer, and I rent a posh apartment for her and a friend of hers."

"Somebody you know would be better than somebody you've met for the first time."

They both laughed.

"Do you really mean it?" Khalil asked him.

"You'd better believe it. I'd get a kick out of it. The idea of rape turns me on."

"But you know her. And she knows you."

"She won't know me when I've got on that Mexican mask of mine. And she wouldn't dare remember you afterward. We'll have ourselves some fun."

When they left the restaurant, Khalil noticed that his hands were trembling as he paid the bill, and his heart was pounding like a drum in some African jungle. The city had turned into a jungle as far as he was concerned, and he wished he could pick up his spear and go running through the trees to the riverbank. He'd kill the lynxes, cheetahs, and panthers that he met up with on the way, then ride over to the opposite bank on a crocodile's back in search of apple trees and vipers to dance with. He'd squeeze the juice out of an apple by hand, ferment it in the scorching sun, and give it to his blue-eyed, smooth-tongued adder.

Saqr pulled into a parking garage on the lower level of a posh building that Khalil had passed by numerous times before, always wondering who would be worthy to live in it and look out its windows. And now, he himself was living in it. In fact, he owned it personally. Moving toward the window which he'd lusted after those many times, he opened the silk curtains and looked out to ponder the sight of the lake with its swans, boats, bathing beauties, birds, and flower-studded verdure. How beautiful and exciting life was now.

Before they went up, Saqr opened the trunk and brought out a devil's face-mask. He put it on and gave another one to Khalil. Then he brought out a knife and a revolver, the sight of which made Khalil start with fright. No sooner had he gotten them out than he stabbed Khalil in the chest, right in the spot over his heart. But instead of going in, the blade went back inside the knife handle.

"It's a toy!" laughed Saqr. "They use it in the circus. Instead of going into your chest, it goes back into its sheath." (Most of the knives the enemy attacks us with are the same way—pseudo-weapons wielded by men who are nothing but a bunch of buffoons.) He nearly drowned in sorrow as he thought about it. But just then Saqr drew the revolver on him. When he pulled the trigger, Khalil's face was drenched with water. It was so refreshing, his childlike spirit was revived and he burst out laughing.

"This one's a toy, too," said Saqr. "Come on, let's play. What do you think of this other pistol?"

As he spoke, he brought out a second gun and fired. The loud noise made by the shot and its echo against the walls of the parking garage were deafening, and Khalil nearly fainted from fright. He looked down at his chest where he'd been shot, but all he saw was a black, scorched spot that wasn't bleeding. And he let out another long, delighted laugh.

"It's nothing but a sound pistol," Saqr said. "Now let's get out of here before the police or somebody else shows up."

As they headed for the elevator Khalil put on his mask, hoping that the elevator wouldn't be empty. He had a playful urge to scare the living daylights out of some normally rational person (or someone who considered himself to be so) and have himself a long laugh. Unfortunately, they didn't meet up with anyone either in the lift or in the corridor.

With the composure of a thief, Saqr opened the apartment door with his own key and they slipped inside.

Marilyn was on her way to the living room when Saqr came upon her. He clapped his hand over her mouth while Khalil tied her hands behind her back with the sash of her house robe, which opened in front to reveal orbs of fair-skinned beauty, like translucent, succulent white grapes just about to be picked. Then he took the scarf that she'd had her hair tied back with and secured it over her mouth. Khalil couldn't believe he was doing what he was doing, but he was performing the task like a pro. It was as if the white powder had turned him into two different men, one of whom had come out to play like a rowdy little boy while the other looked on as if he were watching an amusing film.

When Therese heard the commotion she came out of the corridor, and Khalil pointed the revolver at her head. Meanwhile, Saqr was threatening his girlfriend with his knife.

Calmly, Therese said, "What do you want? Don't hurt us, and we'll give you all we have."

Neither of the men said a word.

Without turning to look at Therese, Saqr slapped Marilyn and dragged her by the hair toward the other room. She shrieked in pain, her voice muffled by fright.

Khalil didn't feel any pleasure when he saw the look of sheer terror in the two women's eyes.

Meanwhile, Saqr disappeared with Marilyn into the other room and left the door open. Khalil saw her lying helplessly on the bed, a citadel of petrified whiteness. She resisted, but to no avail, and before long her walls collapsed and her gates were opened to the invaders. He kept his water pistol pointed at her panic-stricken roommate's head, and when she tried to escape, he slapped her. (I've never slapped anybody in my life before. What sort of monster lives inside me that needs only a couple of specks of white powder to awaken from its slumber?) Then suddenly he was overcome with fear, of himself and of her. What if she really did get away and called the police? Is this what you've come to, Khalil? Is this how your long resistance is going to end?

A thousand years later, or perhaps one second, when Saqr was out of gasps and Marilyn was out of tears, he took off his mask and exploded with laughter while the two dancers burst into hysterical tears. And despite his delight over their weeping, Saqr shouted reproachfully, "You idiot! Didn't you recognize my style? I don't want you anymore!"

Then he turned to Khalil and said, "And now it's your turn, if you'd like."

"I thank you. Some other time. I'll be leaving now."

Laughing that wild laugh of his somewhere between a gasp of delight and a death rattle, Saqr said, "I like a man who knows when to step back. But we'll carry on with our fun a little while longer. After all, Therese has to get her share before I'm finished with these two. Imagine. Marilyn didn't recognize me. As for you, Khalil, I won't be needing you for the rest of the day. Come early tomorrow, at around noon."

So he took off his mask, put down his pistol, and left.

As he looked at himself in the elevator mirror, he thought he saw the mask still covering his face. What he saw was a devil's face, and he even heard him laugh. Then once again he felt those tiny black insects scampering around under the skin on his hand.

He rushed away from the building in a terrible fright, feeling somehow that he'd lost the most precious thing that either a man or a woman can lose. Just then a car sped by, and in it he glimpsed his wife Kafa sitting beside Nadim. He tried to get a closer look, but the car was already out of sight. Was it Nadim's car? He wondered. Or a cocaine-induced hallucination?

◆　◆　◆

Kafa sighed coquettishly, like a branch that's growing weary of bearing the weight of its fruit and longs for the touches of the harvester—for the wild winds, the playful rain and the storm's embrace.

(Is it really necessary to waste all this time sitting on the veranda, devouring food and drinking cocktails for the sake of creating the right atmosphere?

Doesn't he realize that I've been ready for the past five years, that I've been waiting for him ever since Khalil abandoned my body, never to return? Sometimes I'm inundated by a flood of longing for plows, planting, and fresh ears of corn, for nights of harvest and for the sweetness of a gasp on the blade of love's sickle. If he'd taken me by the hand on the airplane and dragged me back to some empty seat in the rear, I would have thrown myself into his arms, a city without walls ready to welcome the conqueror.

It's true, of course, that the food is scrumptious. And the balcony of the Belle Vue Hotel is perched atop the waves of a fantastically beautiful lake. It's true also that a little booze can facilitate matters, as can pleasant conversation and those "little sweet nothings" whispered in the ear that tickle one's pride. But I'm tired of mobilization and preparatory maneuvers. When are we going into battle with live ammunition?)

"When is your husband coming back?"

"I don't know."

"What are you going to say to him?"

"I don't know."

"Are you going to tell him the truth?"

"Maybe."

"Please don't. You see, he's working with us now—I mean, with the Pasha's partner Sheikh Sakhr and his son. We don't want to let emotional matters interfere with business."

"All right then. I won't."

So, here he was beating a possible line of retreat. He'd stuck his head out from behind the barricade, then thought better of it. What was he afraid of? Would she have to drag him out of the slough of details and on to the heart of the matter? When would he finish writing his tedious marginal glosses with fruit, pastries, and coffee and start penning the phrase that had reawakened in her heart so fresh and full of life? It was as if she'd slept for years, then awakened to the rhythm of his breathing. Was he really flustered, or was he just pretending to be for her sake? Was he feigning innocence to make her think that she was the first and the last woman he'd approached in this way, that this was a unique happening in his life that he would never forget? Whatever the case might be, she was on fire, burning up on the inside, and wasn't about to interrogate the fireman about his emotional life. It was enough for him to put out the blaze.

An hour and a half later, she left the luxurious hotel room with her fires raging more furiously than ever. Nadim was a man of cotton. His fingertips were adept at plucking the strings, and he knew just how to make her sirens go off with his breathing. But she needed something else, which he no longer possessed. She still loved him and didn't want to lose that exquisite feeling, so she planned to give him another chance.

She loved the image that she had of him in her mind, and she'd expected him to live up to it. But . . .

When Nadim let her off at a spot where she could catch a taxi back to her hotel, he breathed a sigh of relief. This bombshell of a woman would need an entire work team to satisfy her. There was an all out famine in her body, and his own resources were spent. She was still a jewel in the rough. With her, even the experience he'd gained over the years hadn't been enough to compensate for what the years had taken from him. For the first time he'd been made aware that he really was getting older, and that it was no longer possible for him to satisfy a woman about to enter her thirties with wild gusto.

Even so, his desire for her had increased several times over. He wouldn't be defeated in the face of her marble walls.

So, had the time come for him to seek help from Sheikh Watfan as others had done?

◆　◆　◆

As Khalil stretched out on the park bench, dusk was beginning to descend over the city, and the blood had begun to grow calmer in his veins after having raged for hours through those poor little vessels like a stormy sea in a strait. The phase of high flying, potency, and excitement had come to an end, and the waters were receding from the boulders, shores, and straits, leaving behind a clutter of shells, lifeless seabirds, and ships' remains.

He'd spent a long time wandering around the city. With a feeling of super-human strength erupting from deep inside him and a special sort of intoxication that enveloped his whole being, he'd taken a walking tour of Old Geneva and its pleasant side streets. He'd gone as far as the Athens Museum, then hiked another long stretch, moving from one museum to the next and from one garden to another. He'd gone into an art exhibit where he enjoyed listening to the voices of the statues and the rustling of the leaves on the trees as the breezes blew through the paintings. He had walked and walked until he'd found himself in this particular park. He'd roamed around among its beds of rare roses, each labeled with a sign. Then he'd remembered the nameless corpses piled in the streets of Beirut to be buried in mass graves, not one of which covered an area greater than that designated for the flower bed labeled "Maria Callas Rose." So he had cursed the world, where some places build houses for roses, enclosing them with glass lest they catch cold, while in other places the dead can't even find a decent grave to be buried in nor the living a roof to cover their heads. And all these things were taking place on the same planet.

At that moment, he had suddenly begun coming down from his high. The sun was singing a woeful swan's song after another day of witnessing violence and affliction all over the world, and dust was casting its ashen cloak over joys and sorrows alike. Without warning he'd felt cold and empty and begun to tremble. He had left the park, which was closing for the day, crossed the street, and flung himself down on a bench on the sidewalk that ran along the lakeshore. He'd been escorted out of the park by a couple of charming squirrels, chasing each other through a tree so tall that, like the trees one reads about in fairytales, its upper branches seemed to reach into the heavens.

But now he was hungry and exhausted. Shaking from the cold, he felt a desolate void deep inside him and a raging thirst. As he reviewed the events of his day, a feeling of terrible shame seemed to wrap itself around his chest. Could he really have done all those despicable things? He felt for the money in his pocket, and found it. So then, he really had done what he'd done. Damn!

He went into a telephone booth for the tenth time since noon. This time he finally managed to remember Amir's number. (Please, God, let him talk to me. Let him be at home. Let his telephone not be out of order. I hope I can get a line. You dimwit, this is Geneva! Telephones work here, you know.)

When he heard Amir's voice, he collapsed like someone who's just put his head and shoulders through a lifesaver and can now allow himself the luxury of falling into a swoon.

"Please, Amir. May I come over?"

"Of course. I've been expecting you."

"Are you alone?"

"There are no strangers here, at least. Take down the address."

So, after a taxi ride through the streets of Geneva and a trip upstairs in a lift, he found himself at Amir's door. He rang the doorbell several times before he noticed that the door was wide open. Meanwhile, a voice was shouting, "Come in! Come in!"

◆   ◆   ◆

"Khalil is late."

Kafa paced anxiously around the sumptuous hotel room. Their money was about to dry up, and after what had happened earlier in the day, there was no hope of getting any help from Nadim. There would never be any romance between the two of them now. Her womanly instinct told her that a man like him would never forgive her for not having enjoyed herself. She hadn't even pretended to.

She'd stood him up against the wall, so to speak, like a lazy schoolboy who'd failed his lesson in love. She surprised herself with her own unseemly behavior. But after five years of famine, she hadn't been able to hide her disappointment over what his table had to offer. She'd expected it to be filled to groaning. Unfortunately, though, it had been filled with everything except food.

And now she was broke. She'd been reminded at the hotel that same day, ever so politely, of the necessity of paying the bill. Or rather, they'd left the bill with her room key, accompanied by a note to the effect that, "Either you pay, or you go to prison." So she paid. And not much was left. It wasn't even enough to pay for four more nights. (The party's over.) And what made her even more nervous was that after her disappointing return from "Planet Nadim," she'd taken another disappointing trip. She'd been thinking of selling the stolen ring and using part of the money to help cover the hotel bill. As she presented it to the jeweler, her heart was pounding so hard she thought it would come out of her chest. She claimed that she'd received it as a gift and that she wanted to know its approximate value so as to be able to reciprocate with something comparable. He examined the ring under his magnifying glass. When she saw him frown, she was afraid she'd made a terrible mistake, that he was going to rush out into the street shouting, "Thief!" and call the police to come and take her away. However, all he said was "This isn't a real diamond. It's a special type of glass—a synthetic diamond known as dimilite with no value to speak of. It has the appearance of diamond, and the value of crystal."

So then, her last line of defense was gone. They'd go hungry now, and when the six weeks remaining in the school term were over, the school would demand ten thousand Swiss francs in tuition—either that, or throw her two sons back in her face.

"Khalil is late."

A feeling of terror began to come over her. She'd nearly forgotten all about him over the past several days. She'd been intoxicated. Her pocketbook had been bursting and her heart full to overflowing with the wine of new love. But today the wineskin had burst and she'd emptied the pocketbook. Besides which, she was overwhelmed by a sudden urge to see her two boys.

She called the school and asked to speak with them. The operator refused her request, saying, "Life here is strictly regulated, and there's a specific time when parents can call their children—after lunch, between one o'clock and two o'clock in the afternoon."

Damn it all. She'd never been denied access to them before. Something had been set on fire deep inside her, and she burned with longing for her children, and for Khalil. She apparently didn't hate him as much as she'd thought. But she did hate the world he belonged to. She hated his world, his impotence, and the way he'd let her down. She hated his unwillingness to risk picking and enjoying life's delectable fruits, which were passing her by for good, never to be offered to her again. He'd kept her waiting so long, she resorted to turning on the television. The news was on, and Lebanon was the first item. She never wanted to see that playing field of violence ever again. She hated what had been done to it by its own people, by the Arabs, by the West, by the East, by the North, and by the South. Any fate, as far as she was concerned, was preferable to going back to that hell on earth, where even children are killed for no reason. Her mind was assaulted by an image of Widad, so she fled from it by switching to the hotel's video channel, which showed nonstop movies. This was a sentimental one, with Alain Delon kissing Catherine Deneuve as they rode in a car down the lovely, well-lit, immaculate streets of Paris. Why couldn't she live in a city like that, and with a man like him? So she decided to throw Catherine Deneuve off the screen and take her place. Now it was she who was seated beside Delon in the car, who was embracing her and telling her that he loved her. As the film continued, she accompanied him to the George V Hotel. He slapped her. She slapped him back. He kissed her. She kissed him back. Then they made hot, impassioned love, not the wilted, insipid type she'd been treated to by Nadim in that other hotel room. Then the bad guys came to kidnap the two of them. What did she care so long as she was with her beloved? The kidnappers tried to murder him. She grabbed hold of the iron poke next to the fireplace and dealt a blow to the villain. She was a heroine, and the object of someone's passionate love.

Then suddenly the maid walked in.

Leaving Delon on the set to face his destiny alone, she received the maid with angry words. The latter apologized, saying she hadn't seen a "Do not disturb" sign on the door, then left. When she got back to the video, she didn't find Delon waiting for her. He was gone. She thought about her husband. For all she knew, he was the only person in this entire city that she really mattered to. He wasn't as bad as she made him out to be sometimes. But he was a weak man. And she'd grown weary of weak men in a city full of cruelty and brutality, a city that had taught her to love men with power.

Khalil was broken, like a skiff that's been cast ashore by a tempestuous sea. She imagined him coming back to her laden with a bundle of banknotes and passionate desires. She loved daydreams. (I shower him with affection. He gives me the money and tells me it's "dirty." My desires inflamed, I cover my breasts and shoulders with the bills. He starts with alarm, then runs away from me by going to sleep.) Ah. . . . If only he'd come home early tonight.

She was terrified of what awaited the two of them. She wanted to talk to him about the phony ring, Raghid Zahran's gift to Dunya Ghafir, and lay on him the big surprise: The stone in the solitaire ring was made of synthetic diamond! She knew, of course, that it wouldn't really surprise him, though he might feel a bit of vindictive glee. Even if she woke him up to give him the news, he'd just go back to sleep. He wouldn't jump up and down or reel from the shock the way she had. Instead he'd just say indifferently, "So does that surprise you? What do you expect from people like them?" and close his eyes again.

She was shaken. She'd heard the first warning siren going off inside her head, and the ground didn't feel solid under her feet anymore.

She'd been thinking that at long last she was safe again, that she'd found the people she truly belonged with, good folks from respectable families.

And now she was finding out that they were . . .

She'd thought that after all her suffering, she was finally taking hold of her dream.

But instead, she was discovering that her dream, too, was frightening, as if it were nothing but a new kind of nightmare.

So then, these people also . . .

She fell into an abyss of unspeakable dread. For the first time she'd come to realize that even here in Switzerland, she was walking through a minefield, albeit not the sort she'd known before. She knew now that she'd fled from the nightmares in Beirut only to be faced with the nightmares of life in a foreign land.

(She heard a voice somewhere deep inside saying sarcastically, "But you stole the ring! Have you forgotten about that?")

Perhaps Raghid Zahran had reasons of his own for giving Dunya a phony ring. And perhaps Dunya knew that. (In any case, that's a personal issue between the two of them. What business is it of yours? And if you think they are evil, then remember that you're the worst one of all—so far.)

✦   ✦   ✦

The door to Amir's flat was wide open, like two wooden arms outspread to welcome whoever might come through them. There were no security precautions or even guards, despite the attempt that had been made on Amir's life.

Khalil entered hesitantly. The place looked something like a white hotel, and with the men seated in a circle on the floor, it reminded him of his grandfather's house in the village where he grew up. He tried in vain to focus on the faces of the people present. He was in a state of utter exhaustion, feeling as crushed as a clove of garlic in a mortar. Suddenly overcome with panic as his timid nature reasserted itself, he turned around and thought of fleeing. But then he felt Amir's welcoming hand on his shoulder, pulling him back inside.

When Nasim's face greeted him, he was neither surprised nor upset. He saw another face that wasn't familiar, a round, sensitive-looking face mounted atop a round, exceedingly plump torso. He heard someone addressing this mass of flesh as Bassam.

Before long he'd gone from utter terror to absolute tranquility. Amir was there, and Amir's friends were his friends, too.

At the same time he was flooded with a profound relief, as if he'd come home somehow, and he sank into a rather secluded seat to which Amir had led him in one corner of the room. He looked around. There was no furniture other than the bookcase and the mats on the floor. Yet the walls were white and clean, and try as he might, he couldn't seem to focus his eyes on the map that hung opposite him. For some reason his senses were betraying him, as if they were ashamed of him. Through an open door he glimpsed a bedroom that contained a mat spread on the floor. In fact, there was a collection of mats, like what one finds in hostels for the destitute. He thought back to his grand-father's house in the village and closed his eyes.

"You look like you're in bad shape."

The obese man brought him a glass of water and said with a frown, "I'm Bassam—Bassan Dam'a."

"Thanks. Uh, I mean, nice to meet you."

He downed the glass of water in a single gulp, which made him feel a bit fresher. Bassam Dam'a. The name was familiar.

With the smell of alcohol on his breath, Bassam asked, "Have you heard of me?"

"Yes, I have."

"Do you remember where?"

"No. But I think you wrote some book . . ."

"You see? People remember me the way they remember some writer who's been dead for years! Like I told you, I'm dead and that's that. But nobody wants to believe it."

"Pardon me, but if you'd asked me at some other time, I might have re-membered."

"No. You were just a teenager when I died. You don't belong to the genera-tion that knows my story. Besides, I've spent the last ten years in Cambridge University and elsewhere."

"He was preparing his doctoral dissertation. He's a brilliant lawyer, too," interjected Amir.

"I wasn't preparing anything, really. I'd run away, and was waiting for a bet-ter time to come along. Young men come along one after another. They grad-uate and scatter all over the globe to do good or bad, while I go on waiting for a time that's right for me—an age that suits my mood."

"That's enough, Bassam," said Amir sternly.

"I want to find out for myself," Bassam went on with drunken obstinacy. "I've been a fugitive from the Arab world since 1967, ever since I published my book *Critique of the Fundamentalist Mind.* And I've been on the run from Lebanon since 1975. I like to engage in freedom fighting by correspondence, not because the circumstances require it but because I'm a wimp. I write letters to my friends and tell them about how rough the struggle is in England and Switzerland, and in the meantime I capitalize on the glories of my ancient book, *Critique of the Fundamentalist Mind!*"

He reached out to pour himself another glass of wine, but Amir signaled to Nasim to take it away from him, which he did.

"You're exhausted. Why don't you try to get some sleep?"

"I'll go do some work on my latest book. Haven't you read my first one— and my last? Ah . . . I forgot that you were just a little boy when it came out. Damn. You all grow up so fast."

Taking him by the hand, Amir dragged him to the adjoining room.

Nasim said, "He's been staying here as Amir's guest for a year now. He's a kindhearted drunk, a wasted thinker."

Khalil said nothing. He felt wasted himself, like a seagull that's flown through a thunderstorm and gotten its wings singed by lightning.

"What's wrong, Mr. Khalil?" Nasim asked.

"As you can see . . ."

"Would you like some more water?"

"Please."

Just then Amir came back into the room and said, "Nasim is a courageous young man. He's preparing his thesis in secret. Please don't let Raghid know about it. It wouldn't be a good time for him to lose his job. His family has been driven out of their home, and he's the sole breadwinner."

Like someone defending himself against a damning accusation, Khalil replied, "What? Me report Nasim to Raghid? I'd die of starvation first!"

"I know you wouldn't," said Nasim as he handed him another glass of water. "When I heard the way you answered back to Raghid the night of the dinner party, my hands started to shake as I was serving the coffee. I even told Amir about it, and about how you defended the Palestinian cause in spite of everybody else's disapproval because you'd put 'Raghid Pasha' in a bad mood."

Khalil smiled wanly. He would have liked to tell them about how he murdered Raghid in a waking dream, but it seemed so complicated, he didn't know how he would explain it. He wished he could convey to them the silent conversation that he'd had with Raghid that night. But . . .

"What's with you?" asked Amir. "You look as though you've just come home from your first day at work as a porter at the Hong Kong harbor."

"I wish I had. I really do."

"What happened?"

Sensing that Khalil was hesitant to speak in his presence and that there was some secret he didn't want him to know about, Nasim excused himself, saying, "I've got to be going now. . ."

"Are you on vacation?" Khalil asked him.

"No. But in my capacity as sorcerer's assistant, I've been getting a bat ready for Sheikh Watfan. I bought it during the day. Then I remembered that I could claim that bats can only be rounded up at night. So I took this chance to come over, the way I always do whenever he asks me to bring him a bat, a rat, or a porcupine. If it weren't for the sorcerer, I'd be flunking out."

"Why a bat?"

"He's going to need it to treat Bahriya, some relative of Raghid Zahran's. When her family all died in the war, she lost her ability to speak and, basically, went out of her mind. Raghid's bringing her here to adopt her. He's an angel, as you can see!"

"He's a liar," said Khalil. "Bahriya is no relative of his. There just happens to be a similarity between their family names, and Nadim wants to take advantage of it. He and Raghid discovered her in some newspaper. And God only knows how they're going to exploit her."

"For starters, Raghid wants to use her to polish up his rotten public image. Then after that he and Nadim will put her to use in whatever other ways they can."

"Damn it all."

In parting, Amir said to Nasim, "So then, we've agreed on a time for the beginning of the demonstration. You all start doing the organizing. Make whatever contacts you can. Then tomorrow when Bassam is sober, he may do his part. I'll talk to Khalil about it. I think he'll help us."

"He's one of us now. I'm sure of it."

When Nasim was gone, Amir came up to Khalil and asked him abruptly, "What have you taken? You're coming apart at the seams. What have you done to yourself?"

"Cocaine. And some kind of upper, but I don't know what it was. I've got a pain in my neck that makes me feel as though I'm choking. From the first snort, I felt paralyzed in the neck, and I couldn't even swallow my saliva."

"Was this your first time?"

"Yes."

"Did you get yourselves in trouble with the police?"

"No. Saqr raped his girlfriend after breaking into her apartment, and I helped him threaten her and her roommate with a knife and a handgun."

"That's serious."

"The knife and the gun were both just toys. He was wearing a mask, or rather, we both were. He just wanted to have a good time."

"Did you participate?"

"I couldn't."

"Did he fire you?"

"Actually, he was pleased that I didn't. It made him look that much more macho. He was quite generous with me."

"Cocaine. Do you realize that this is a very serious matter?"

"I'm spent."

"We've got to find you another job."

Taking the money out of his pocket along with the golden box, he heaped it on the floor in front of Amir—a small fortune.

"What other job would bring in this much in one day?" he asked.

Amir rushed to cover it up before anyone else could catch a glimpse of it. Fortunately, the others in the room were too distracted to notice, being engrossed in a lively discussion that grew alternately louder and softer.

"Do you need it?" Amir asked. "Do you want to be rich like Nadim?"

"It wouldn't bother me to get rich. But not this way."

"And what do you need money for?"

"For my kids' school fees. And my wife: her clothes, her hairdresser, the fancy hotel. . . . I'm going to end up in prison if I don't get it."

"Calm down a bit. We'll work it out."

"If only I could find a humble flat somewhere and quit working for those people."

"That would be difficult. In Geneva they only rent unfurnished apartments to people who have work and residence permits."

"So what can I do?"

"I'll think of something."

Then, noticing how undone Khalil was and how impossible it would be to carry on any sort of logical conversation with him about his future just then, Amir said, "By the way, how about you and your family spending the weekend with me and Bassam? We could take a train or a bus to some quiet village."

"If Saqr gives me the time off. Nadim told me that our 'vacations' were restricted to the times when our bosses are asleep!"

"Listen, Khalil. I want to help you. But in order for me to do that, you've got to stop taking cocaine. Pretend to be taking it with him, but don't. Meanwhile, I'll find you another job, something honorable, even if it doesn't bring in nearly as much money."

"I'll try to convince my wife that this would be better for us. But I'm not sure she'll understand. Oh, and there's something I forgot to tell you about: I think I saw her riding with Nadim in his car today. I think she's cheating on me."

"Did you see her before or after you took the drug?"

"After."

"In that case, you might have been hallucinating. Besides, you're exhausted. Go to sleep, and let me take care of it. Just don't touch cocaine and don't swallow any of those pills. If you're lucky, you'll only end up in some sanitarium—that is, if you can afford it."

Amir turned on the television and continued, saying, "We're organizing an Arab demonstration in protest against the Israeli invasion of Lebanon. The silence on the part of the Arab masses is a real disgrace."

Without knowing whether any sound had come out of his mouth, Khalil murmured, "Some have gone numb, while others are so oppressed, they don't have any way to express their opinions."

As the final news broadcast of the day began, Khalil felt himself sinking into a bog of quicksand, then floating to the surface again, sinking, then floating, sinking, then floating. At the Beirut International Airport he saw airplanes bearing the familiar "Mideast Air" logo going up in flames. He remembered having seen two of these very airplanes parked at the airport when he took off on the last flight out. He remembered the shelling and the chase, and a profound sadness came over him. In a breathless, staccato voice he recounted to Amir what had happened. He told him everything from the beginning, or one of the beginnings.

"It's a plan," Amir replied, "to keep us on each other's tails so that they can go on swallowing up both the slayer and the slain."

As he was pulled under by the quicksand once again, he heard Amir calling for a taxi.

"I prefer to walk," he said. "I feel as though I'm under siege. I'm about to suffocate."

"How do you intend to walk when you're not even strong enough to stand up? Get in touch with me tomorrow after you're sobered up, and we'll talk in detail about the demonstration."

"I will, for sure."

"You don't have to . . ."

"Yes, I do . . . if I don't want to forget who I am."

❖   ❖   ❖

Raghid had his breakfast in bed. He began with the egg that Nasim had brought to him from his sorcerer, and several chickpeas. The egg was boiled and had some expression written on it in cryptic characters that he didn't try to read lest he ruin its magical effect. He had asked his sorcerer for a potion to break magic spells. After all, he figured, as long as he was having magic spells cast on his enemies, why wouldn't they be doing the same thing to him?

He'd voiced such fears once to Sheikh Watfan, who reassured him that he had no cause for concern. But as a consequence, Nasim's troubles multiplied, since it was he who had to bring the chickpeas to the sorcerer's chamber every day along with a lead container. The sorcerer would write some magical combination of words on the bottom of the container and then soak the chickpeas in it. As for the boiled egg, on the first day he wrote the words, "They bewitched people's eyes with a mighty deed, then truth descended and their works were brought to naught," and Raghid ate it with great gusto. On the second day another egg was similarly boiled and on it he wrote, "Have not the unbelievers seen that the heavens and the earth were in one piece, and We rent them asunder?"[19] And on the third day, "God has decreed: It is I and my apostles who must prevail. For God is the one full of strength, able to enforce His will."[20]

The container in which the egg was boiled had to be taken to the sorcerer so that he could write various incantations and things in the bottom of it. Consequently, an exhausted Nasim was kept running back and forth between the

19. Qur'an 21:30.
20. Qur'an 21:30.

kitchen and the sorcerer's wing. As the fire blazed beneath, as the water bubbled and frothed, and as the egg jumped about in fright, he would stare intently into the bottom of the pot. He used to imagine that there was a chick inside the egg crying to be released from the hell it was in. Sometimes he would feel as though he himself was the one imprisoned inside the egg and that the tiny little chick had his face. And through the steam he would read in the bottom of the pot: "I have averted its power from you by one, and that which is done against you by two, I have averted by two: the night and the day. That which is done against you by three, I have averted from you by three: Jibril, Mika'il, and Israfil. And that which is done against you by four, I have averted from you by four: The Tawrat, the Injil, the Zabour, and the Great Furqan."

Nasim was worried about his family in Beirut. He hadn't received news of his nine brothers and sisters, and he didn't know whether they were dead or alive. Meanwhile, he went running back and forth down the corridors of a golden fortress straight out of the Middle Ages carrying out bizarre orders. Whenever he went into the sorcerer's chamber he would look away from the cursed crystal ball, since it reminded him of a glass television screen with his homeland burning up inside it. Before Raghid left to go anywhere, he would ask Nasim to help him don his heavy bulletproof vest and to hang untold numbers of charms, amulets and prayers for protection—prepared for him by his peerless wizard—around his neck and on his chest.

Could this really be happening in our day and age, he wondered? It had bewildered him for a long time now. In the beginning he'd thought it was a joke. But according to Amir, the sorcerer's patrons came from all walks of life and all strata of society: politicians, leaders and statesmen, revolutionaries and reactionaries, rich and poor, geniuses and simpletons, nightclub dancers and well-kept ladies, elderly women and young girls.

Could this really be happening to him?

Several days before, he'd been given the picture of a dignified-looking Bedouin man and was asked to take it to a craftsman to have his image carved into raw wax. So he did. Then a couple of days later he was asked to bring a small slab of lead. So he did. They were burning voodoo dolls to afflict their intended victims with a fever, and inscribing their images into lead to afflict them with splitting headaches. For a long time now he'd been thinking of getting out of this place before he did something foolish. He could go live for a while with Amir among the unfortunate, the outcast and the weary. There, at least, he could come and go as he pleased. On the other hand, he needed the money he was making at Raghid's. For all he knew, he might have to help a wounded sister or pay for a brother's funeral. He was so, so worried. The newspapers spoke of the dead only in terms of raw statistics. But the victims' families wanted to know their names, letter by letter.

So this world was carrying on with its modern-day madness. However, being closer to the Middle Ages than the modern age, it didn't really give a damn about the values it boasted of. No one cared about the slain except their own families. Everybody prided himself on his humanitarianism while forgetting about human beings, and loved all the peoples of the world while hating people. Statesmen were striving so hard on behalf of the masses that they'd forgotten individuals. (The state of the world proves the truth of the saying, "No one shows compassion for the twig except its own bark.")

Nasim heaved a sigh of relief when Raghid got ready to go out. But then he suddenly changed his mind, saying that he wanted to make a telephone call first and that he might pass by the sorcerer's wing. Also, he said his bulletproof vest was heavy and uncomfortable, which meant a rerun of the rituals involved in taking off his clothes.

(Damn. The humiliation of having to scrape for a living is a bitter pill to swallow.

Why did I choose the hard way? Why didn't I go to work as a sorcerer, for example? All I would have had to do was get hold of some musty books and follow the instructions inside to the letter. That way I could have relieved both my head and my pocketbook, and everybody would be pleased with me: left and right, reactionaries and at least some revolutionaries.

But it's too late for that now. I've crossed the threshold on the way to the needle's eye.)

◆　　◆　　◆

"Yallo, Nadim. What's Khalil's latest news on the Ghanamali family?"

Raghid had a special, nonchalant way of pronouncing "Hello" that turned it into "Yallo." And this "Yallo" of his scared Nadim, since it meant that he was dissatisfied with something and was going to make trouble.

"Hilal's health isn't good, and he's getting ready to leave the country. He's determined to contract out the airport to somebody else by putting it up for a public bid."

"So, we'll just make our own bid and we're sure to get it."

"He'll intervene to make sure that doesn't happen."

"Have you tried the dancer?"

"It didn't work. Hilal really is a virtuous man."

"What a bastard. You mean he doesn't like women?"

"The ones he wants, he marries in accordance with Islamic law. My spies haven't been able to hit on a single weak point that would enable us to get at him."

"Impossible. Try pride and arrogance. Send him some beauty to do the journalist number."

"I tried that. He refused to meet her."

"Let him see her. He might. . ."

"I sent her to his doctor's waiting room. She introduced herself to him and asked for an interview. He just sent her away politely."

"And Sakhr?"

"Hilal's too much for him. He's in the position of strength. People are on his side, and his word is respected. As for Sakhr, he's almost a pariah among his own people."

"Is he really trying to persuade that damned brother of his, or does he just not care about making another billion?"

"According to Khalil, he doesn't seem to care. He doesn't hate you. But he isn't willing to get into a row with his brother for your sake."

"I'll ruin the man."

Nasim "happened" to be listening to the telephone conversation. Rubbing his hands together with glee, he said, "The war of the dinosaurs has begun! I'll tell Amir about this."

As soon as the disappointing phone call had ended, Raghid rushed off to see his sorcerer.

"Please, sir. I want to bring ruin on an enemy that I used to think was my friend. There's nothing in the world that I want from you more than this one thing. I want to ruin Sakhr Ghanamali and his brother."

"That's a tall order. The lords will only fulfill it if the request is a just one. I'm nothing but an instrument."

Raghid's tears began to flow. He had the ability to weep for the most trivial reasons.

"It *is* a just request!" he insisted.

"These powers have wisdom and secrets of their own," cautioned the sorcerer. "I am blind, but they see. I am ignorant, but they know. And if they fulfill the request, they do so to the letter. I am a medium, but they are the lightning bolt that chooses where it will strike. You're asking for the ruin of a wrongdoer. And if God so wills, it will take place. But are you certain that he really is in the wrong?"

"Of course! First of all, he isn't doing a thing for our partnership. He's got the advantage of having been born in a rich country, which of course is a mere coincidence. He also has influence. As for the work, though, I'm the one who goes running around night and day getting projects carried out, overseeing them, etc., while he rakes in half the profits. And now he wants to leave me in the lurch. He isn't making the slightest effort to stand by a lifetime friend."

"Very well. I'll do it."

"I'll be waiting."

"It will take some time."

"I'll wait two or three ages if need be. What matters is for that wicked Hilal to be destroyed, and to pay Sakhr back for the way he slighted me and then stabbed me in the back."

◆   ◆   ◆

Sorcerer Watfan sat writing in black ink on a piece of red fabric: "They plotted, and We likewise plotted. Look at what became of their plotting. We destroyed them and all their people. Their houses are empty because of their wrongdoing. Everything has been destroyed by the decree of their Lord. Now nothing can be seen but their habitations. This is how we recompense a sinful people."[21]

Then he lit a fire and burned incense. When he spoke, his voice came from what seemed like a frightening cavern, and his breath was like the blowing of a cold wind: "Daha Ouf Kahl Nakir Luloud Law Yamloud Kaymal Dimsal Ahlil Idhu Ahlil Ouhlak."

He recited the words twelve times, each time beginning with the name of a different spirit and reciting the rest of it line after line in accordance with the sorcery chart which he had inherited from his ancestors: "Daha Ouf Kahil Nakir Marid Law Yamloud Kaymal Dimsal Ahlil Idhu Ahlil Ouhlaq, Ouf Kahil Fikr Muloud Law Yamloud Kayhal Dimsal Ahlil Adhu Ahlil Ouhlaq Daha

---

21. An allusion to Qur'an 27:50–51.

Kahil Nakir Millou Dimloud Daymal Dimsal Ahlil Idhu Ahlil Ouhlaq Daha Ouf Nakir Muloud Law Yamloud Kaymal Dimsal Ahlil Adhu Ahl Ouhlaq Idhu Oukahil Muloud Law Yamloud Kaymal Dimsal Ahlil Idhu Ahlil Ahlaq Daha Ouf Kahil Nakir Law Yamloud Kaymal Dimsal Ahlil Idhu Ahlil Ouhlaaq Daha Ouf Kahil Nakir Muloud Kaymal Dimsal Ahlil Idhu Ahlil Ouhlaq Daha Ouf Kahil Nakir Muloud Law Yamloud Dimsal Ahlil Idhu Ahlil Ouhlaq Daha Ouf Khil Tanakkur Muloud Law Yamloud Kaymal Ahlil Idhu Ahlil Ouhlaq Daha Ouf Kahil Nakir Muloud Law Yamloud Kaymal Dimsal Idhu Ahlil Ouhlaq Daha Ouf Kahil Nakir Muloud Law Yamloud Kaymal Dimsal Ahlil Ahlil Ouh-laq Daha Ouhlaq Daha Ouf Kahil Nakir Muloud Law Yamloud Kaymal Dim-sal Ahlil Idhu Ouhlaq Daha Ouf Kahil Muloud Law Yamloud Kaymal Dimsal Ahlil Idhu Ahlil."

Raghid sat there listening to him, his breathing accelerating as he stared at half of his face in the mirror opposite him. As the smoke from the incense ascended, he coughed, and felt the heat radiating from the burning embers beneath the incense as the sorcerer stoked the flames with exotic herbs, woods, and frankincense. Then without warning, the mirror shattered. It happened at the very moment when the sorcerer finished reciting his special supplications for "hatred, separation, illness, enmity, and the destruction of rivals and foes."

In a near panic, Raghid said, "The mirror can be replaced. Maybe the heat of the burning coals, incense, and frankincense was too much for it."

The sorcerer sat down, his energy spent as though he'd picked up a mountain and flown with it across seven seas.

"May I make another request?" Raghid asked.

"Go ahead."

"I don't want to destroy just Sakhr. I want to do the same to his friends, and to his twin brother Hilal."

"But we've already cast the spell."

"If you please, I want you to repeat it with a more potent spell. Sakhr wants to avoid any conflict with his brother."

"What day is today?"

"Wednesday."

"Fine. I'll do it now."

The smell of burning frankincense, sulfur, tar, asafetida, aloe, and myrrh filled the room. Nasim nearly coughed from the place where he had "happened" to stop behind the door. He'd been passing by and, as he always told Amir, he hadn't been meaning to spy. "But I have this irresistible urge to find out everything that's going on around me. And I always happen to find myself in the middle of the action!" The sorcerer took out a colocynth plant, then began reciting incantations and writing on the colocynth, his voice fading in and out:

"Humoush Mudaqhir Fushoush. . . . Marqoush Shaqrush Shaqhourash. . . . Humoush. . . . How heinous is murder, how profuse is the murmuring of the waters, how difficult is Izra'il, the angel of death, how confined is the grave, how difficult is the parting. 'He frowned and turned away.'[22] In like manner, may Sakhr bin Silfah Ghanamali turn away from Hilal bin Silfah Ghanamali. 'When the blind man came to him. . . . '[23] In like manner, may Sakhr bin Silfah Ghanamali be blinded to Hilal bin Silfah Ghanamali. You have been assigned responsibility for them, O Salagh, O Ibn Malakh. Cast enmity and hatred between them, between Sakhr bin Silfah Ghanamali and Hilal bin Silfah Ghanamali. Whenever they ignite the fires of war, may Iblis keep them ablaze with his wickedness. And may he prevent them from attaining what they desire just as he did to their followers before them. Indeed they are in a state of grievous doubt."

Sorcerer Watfan stopped to rest for a while. Then, after panting for quite a long time he said, "Take this colocynth plant and this red rag, and tell Nasim to bury them in the garden outside Sakhr Ghanamali's house."

At which point a terrified Nasim fled on tiptoe as fast as his legs would carry him.

"Khalil Dar' can take care of that," said Raghid.

"Fine. Will there be anything else today? Do you want the decree against this wax figurine to be carried out? Shall I burn it and cast my spells over it at some isolated, abandoned gravesite?"

"Yes. It's an image of Hilal. At least the face is his."

"I'll engrave the necessary things on it, then Nasim can bury it in a grave that no one ever visits. After that, the person whose image it is will be destroyed—provided he is a wrongdoer."

"I thank you, sir. He most certainly is. We'll bury the figurine in the grave of Lilly Spock's mother. She says she never goes there."

"And this lead plate, who is it for? You told me you wanted to cause a headache to some wicked foe."

"This is to afflict Sakhr with a headache."

---

22. Qur'an 80:1.
23. Qur'an 80:1.

The sorcerer sat down again and drew a grid on the lead plate. Then, inside the squares of the grid, he wrote numbers, cryptic symbols, and the names of particular demons and afreets. Then in the final squares he wrote the words, "Cast   down . . . the . . . head . . . of . . . Sakhr . . . bin . . . Silfah. . . ," with one word in each square. On the right end of the rectangle he drew what looked like another grid that extended outward from one side of the original one, and in it he wrote incantations and the phrase, "Destroy 21199."

Then he burned some more incense along with some asafetida and recited a vow twenty-one times. Raghid was enjoying the fiery session, burning with the anticipation of fulfilling his malevolent wishes. Then Sheikh Watfan turned to him and said, "Let Nasim bury it under a blacksmith's anvil. Then every time he strikes it, the blow will come down on Sakhr's head wherever he happens to be."

Fatigue had begun flowing through the sorcerer's veins, his growing weakness noticeable in the trembling of his voice.

Rubbing his hands together with glee, Raghid said, "Pardon me, I've taken a lot of your time today!"

"That's all right."

"Would you like me to give you a ride to the hotel? I'm going to the airport, and the hotel is on my way."

"Actually, I'm so tired, I won't be able to meet people's needs there today."

"How many times have I asked you to rest, and to let people fend for themselves? Those people exhaust you with their trivial concerns! And then there are the journalists who keep running after you to give them something for their horoscopes. You're a wealthy man, and at the peak of fame. Why don't you a rest a little?"

" . . ."

"If you'll excuse me, I have to go meet Bahriya, my relative, Bahriya Zahran."

When he heard the name, the sorcerer quaked as if an invisible whip had just stung him on the back.

In a feeble voice, he said, "You haven't brought me her mother's name so that I can determine what her rising star is."

"I discovered that they'd forged her passport. My men had no other choice in the matter after it proved impossible to get any information from her. The girl has been mute ever since the building where her family was staying collapsed before her very eyes during the bombing."

"So then, we won't be able find out what it is."

"You can read her mind."

"I'll try."

"What's your feeling about it?"

"It isn't reassuring."

"She's an unfortunate young woman. You wouldn't be able to hurt her by doing so. In any case, she can be gotten rid of at any time."

"I don't know. . ."

"Have you calculated the day we should schedule the Night of the First Billion celebration? Or rather, the Night of the Lover, as Layla Sabbak and my friends refer to it . . . lover of gold that I am!"

"Yes, I have."

"What did you conclude?"

"September 28 wouldn't be a suitable date for it, even though it's the day you prefer."

"Why?"

"The stars will be against you."

"What would the best time be, then?"

"Much sooner than that. I'll calculate it for you."

"We can make it either later or earlier. I'll do whatever you say."

"God bless you. I shall consult the stars. And perhaps the *mandal* also."[24]

"Do whatever you think is best. I hope you'll pardon me for having to leave in such a hurry. Oh, and I forgot to tell you that four days from now you're invited to a party that I'll be hosting in Bahriya's honor. I want to introduce her to people of high society."

"You know that I don't attend such events."

"I know. But I always like you to know that you're invited. See you later."

"Goodbye."

◆　　◆　　◆

Bahriya Zahran . . .

She was simply a young woman who had lost the ability to speak. So why was he so afraid of her? Why had he felt a hot iron prong going right through

---

24. Consulting the *mandal* refers to a magic practice in which a fortuneteller or a medium prophesies while contemplating a mirrorlike surface.

him when he learned of her imminent arrival? She was due to arrive in just a few hours. But what concern was she of his?

Why had a hot wind come blowing through his room, scattering his 'work documents' and turning the room upside down just at the moment when Raghid spoke her name for the first time?

Why had her picture burned his fingers? And why had she taken him back to the world of fears and anxiety after he'd been tranquil and at ease in his private paradise with the demons and sprites and with his consort, the Princess of the Jinn, at his side? Why had she plunged his world into tumult once more, just when he'd been about to forget Anbara?

He tried to reassure himself. (There's an extraordinary resemblance between her and the picture of the Princess of the Jinn, whom I chose for myself to be my beloved and companion.)

I never touch a woman unless the Princess of the Jinn has inhabited her body.

(My uncle approached the woman lying on the couch. She had been begging him to treat her for infertility. I was young at the time, maybe around ten years old, and I was checking out the sorcerer's profession after my mother had agreed to let me work as my uncle's assistant. I'd been present at the two previous sessions, during which my uncle had informed the woman that there was an afreet occupying her womb that would have to be cast out. During her third visit he sent me out after I'd brought him oil, nutmeg, incense, and sulfur. Then, surrounded by the smoke of burning incense and the prayers of supplication which he had been reciting as he felt her all over, the woman began to quake as though she really *was* possessed by an evil spirit. Continuing to massage her entire body until he reached the place where the sterility-inducing afreet resided, he wrote an upside down *nun* on her forehead. This done, the woman's voice changed as though the spirit had begun to speak through her, and she tore her dress. Then my uncle mounted the afreet that had possessed her and, with their voices getting louder and louder, the two of them began to shudder together on the couch. The afreet wept and wailed and begged, my uncle moaned and groaned as he wrestled with the afreet, and the woman quivered and quaked. When my mother walked in and saw the two of them, she burst into tears and shrieks, cursing the day she'd agreed to be his wife. He slapped her and banished her from the room, telling her never to meddle again in his rituals for casting out demons and treating infertility. As for the woman, she kept coming back to us until the afreet had been exorcised and she'd gotten pregnant. After this my uncle's fame spread far and wide, and women began coming to us in droves. Each of them was given a different treatment. However, when I got older, I noted the fact that the troublemaking demon always happened to possess beautiful women, in whose cases my uncle would be obliged to fight it off with bare hands and body.)

◆　　◆　　◆

Once again Watfan took refuge in his bath. In its warm waters he found a captivating tenderness that seemed to bestow a touch of mercy upon his aching spirit when it was being torn asunder by feelings he couldn't comprehend. Surrounded by its perfumed mists, his soul would have compassion on its own hidden depths, so full of conflicting passions and unspoken desires. He immersed himself in the hot, bluish water saturated with salts and perfumes like someone taking refuge in a sea so familiar it's come to be a trusted friend. No. He wasn't going back to that hooker on Berne Street, even if his beloved Princess of the Jinn *had* passed into her body. He'd treat himself instead. (I'd been wandering around for a long time in search of the only bookstore in Geneva that specializes in books on magic. Anbara had happened to pass by it once, and told me about it. I don't know what gave me the urge to see it. In any case, I hid my face behind a pair of dark glasses, covered my head with a kaffiyeh and put on the white, gold-embroidered silk cloak that I'd received as a gift from Sakhr Ghanamali to make myself look like some rich Arab. I walked around for a long time without finding the library, but that didn't bother me. I just needed to get out into the world of people for a while. After all, I'd grown up in a low-class, crowded neighborhood, and had ended up living between a mansion and a hotel as isolated as it was luxurious. It made me happy to see housewives scurrying about with their loaves of Swiss bread as long as baseball bats and their delectable, matronly posteriors. And the children . . . they were bursting with health and enthusiasm. It had been ages since I'd touched a child that wasn't sick. At the intersection of Berne Street and one of its side streets, I glimpsed a sidewalk café bubbling with life and friendly clamor. I headed toward it, and to my surprise, found the bookshop right nearby. I don't read French well, of course, but I do understand some, and I'm familiar with its alphabet. I also recognized the place from the crystal balls that had been placed in the display window alongside books with magical symbols on their covers.

There were also voodoo dolls and amulets for sale. I stopped to stare at the books, crystal balls, and other modern devices for use by astrologers and hypnotists. I stood there thinking about updating my professional practices with some modern technology, and perhaps buying some recent books in my field, hiring a translator, and getting a computer to help me with my astrological calculations. Then I saw the image of a woman walking along the opposite sidewalk reflected in the windowpane. She was walking in a spot where the sunlight was particularly intense, and the light surrounded her like a radiant, translucent crystal ball. My heart skipped over to the other side of the street. I no longer saw the books in front of me. Instead, I started seeing her shadow as more real than any book in existence. The woman on the opposite sidewalk called out forgotten jungles within me. So, leaving my spot in front of the magic shop, I went in pursuit of her magic. She was dazzlingly beautiful, with fair skin and a tall, willowy frame. She possessed that European charm that we Arabs love so much. We melt before the warmth of its glow, which we hypocritically describe as "cold." I decided to follow her to the ends of the world. However, when I went up to her, she asked me to follow her to her room, that is, if I had three hundred francs on me! So I withdrew, and she came after me.

"Would two hundred and fifty suit you better?" she asked.

I ran away from her again, as far away as I could get, and I didn't come back until I was certain that the Princess of the Jinn had entered that glorious body of hers.)

Leaving his tension behind in the blue waters of his bath, Watfan got out feeling almost merry, thinking about his tragedies and his wealth and how he might have a new life ahead of him after all, far from the memories both of his homeland and of the sorcerer's profession.

Then, as he looked into the steam-covered bathroom window, he was startled to find something written on it. It was as if the spirits had written him a message in code. He read the word "Palestine," and beneath it the signature of his father, Bahjat; the word "Lebanon" and under it the signatures of his two brothers Kan'an and Ghilan; and the words "the Arabs," under which there was the signature of his brother Burqan. Baffled, he wondered, Who could have written that? He was sure that no one had come in during his bath. And Nasim wouldn't have done such a thing, anyway. Nasim was afraid of him and didn't know his miserable secret. The spirits? Impossible. He of all people knew it was out of the question. His own guardian spirit was invincible . . . unless he'd begun turning against him. Impossible! Or was it? After all the times he had tampered with their territory, visited their graves and called upon them, could they have manifested themselves and defeated his afreet? He opened the bathroom door and stood there in a daze. For so long he'd been confused and uncertain. Had he begun at last to enter the phase of certitude? For so long he had thought he was dreaming when he would take the hand of his consort, the Princess of the Jinn, and go walking through the gardens of pleasure and delight. He'd considered them mere daydreams with the taste of reality for a soul that had been deprived since childhood everywhere but in his dreams. So had the dream begun to become his reality, and wakefulness a passing illusion? Was there really another world, a world he had tampered with for years without knowing whether it truly existed? Had he now become part of the world of cryptic letters and mysterious magic spells? Impossible. The only rational explanation was that, unaware of what he was doing, he'd gotten up and written his inmost thoughts on the mirror. That's right, he thought. As long as there was no other logical explanation for it, he had to be the one who'd written those things. But . . . why was it that the handwriting in each group of words was different, as if three different people had written them? Besides which, each of them was written in a script different from his own. He was sure of it. Even so, he decided he'd better bring in a handwriting specialist to analyze them before he lost his mind. He stared at the mirror again to make sure that what he thought he'd seen was really there, only to find that the steam had escaped through the bathroom's open door, and the surface of the mirror was a neutral silver once more.

A disquieting thought came to him: Bahriya Zahran was setting foot in the airport at this very moment. He could see her through the walls. He saw her clearly, and could feel her presence. And perhaps she was aware of his presence as well. Otherwise, why would she have written him this sort of a warning on the mirror?

❖   ❖   ❖

Heat burst forth from everywhere, like an unspoken, fiery message from the desert. Nadim entered the airport, driven forward in his steps by the beastly, unfamiliar heat. Heaving an anxious sigh, he stood behind the glass partition that looked out on the arrivals lobby. The plane from Cyprus had landed, and within minutes he would be seeing Bahriya Zahran. Then he would know whether it had been a mistake to bring her to Switzerland, or whether it would actually help in improving Raghid's public image among the Arab masses. His brow was moist with perspiration. Heat . . . Geneva was so hot, it was as if a desert wind had swept over it. Or was it just his imagination?

He saw an airline attendant accompanied by a young woman of towering height. She seemed extraordinarily beautiful, in which case he might benefit from her coming in more than one way.

He rushed to the reception gate. He could see Bahriya peering out from behind the glass. He wiped the sweat off his brow with his silk handkerchief. Bahriya approached. Bahriya arrived. The aroma of a forest came wafting off her hair, rivers of milk and honey flowed from her lips, sparrows came flying out of her fingertips, and in her eyes there stretched forth the horizons of a warm sea inhabited by mysteries and pearls. Her simple black dress seemed almost to vanish at her slender waist; then, as it descended, it clung to dreamily rounded hills and valleys, revealing a trim, youthful physique, as well as the marks of wounds as yet unhealed. Her arms, her chest, and all other areas of her lovely body not concealed by her dress were covered with delicate scars— miniscule wounds that looked like pores that were sweating blood. And she seemed to be far, far away. (Are these the wounds she received from the flying glass?) He reached out to shake her hand, but she made no response. Instead she seemed to be looking straight through him as if he weren't there.

The airline attendant said, "She's ill. She went mute from the shock."

(This will make good publicity. We'll take responsibility for treating this disconsolate beauty.) She walked with him toward the car where Raghid was waiting along with a number of correspondents, photographers, and journalists from magazines and news agencies. He wasn't imagining things. There was a furnace ablaze from the sun, as though the winds of his homeland were exhaling their hot breaths here in Geneva. He looked at Bahriya again, only this time she looked different to him. Instead of perceiving her as a distant presence, he felt as though she was close to him, that he knew her. In her eyes there danced the image of his mother, and in her sigh he heard the sound of his father's breathing. He was assailed by the image of the old Beirut alleyway where he'd grown up and the old house that his parents were still so attached to, and he felt deep regret when he realized that he hadn't even so much as tried to inquire about whether they were dead or alive. Were they buried beneath the rubble left by the bombing? Had they died of starvation? Damn! It was true, of course, that he'd been busy, but how could he possibly have allowed himself to be distracted from things that lived in the deepest parts of him? What torment it was for him when he woke up to the fact that he'd been drowning in trivialities and had forgotten what's truly essential! Something about Bahriya nearly drove him to distraction, to remorse, even to tears. When she tossed her exquisite hair this time, it gave off the stench of fires and gunpowder.

As Raghid received her from him, acquiescing happily to the reporters' lenses through the bulletproof windows of his car, Nadim went to his own car feeling devastated. He felt like a tree that's been hit by a fiery thunderbolt that's incinerated its leaves and branches and left nothing but its forgotten roots for one to stare at in bewildered dismay. Oh . . . how could I have forgotten? My mother . . . my father . . . my house . . . my country. Are they still alive? Or were they killed by the latest arms shipment I sent to Beirut?

It felt like summer in Beirut. He was dripping with sweat, and there was something that felt like a stone weighing so heavily on his chest that he could hardly breathe. A huge stone, like the Hubla Stone in the Ba'albek ruins. Ah, Ba'albek. How could he have forgotten it? How, how, how could this have happened to him? And what had revived his memory? What sort of magic had come over him, rending the curtains that had once separated him from his past? It was like being struck by a sword the way it used to happen in the Aladdin and Sindbad films he'd seen as a child. (I'm talking nonsense. I've got an important business engagement to get to, and here I am sitting in my car raving like a lunatic. What sort of magic just struck me with its invisible wand?)

As he turned on the ignition and then the air conditioner, it seemed that even machines had gone mad with the touch of this inexplicable magic. If not, then why was it that the air conditioner had started exhaling hot winds into his face?

❖　❖　❖

The heat burst forth from everywhere like an unspoken, fiery message from the desert.

Nasim was delighted with the heat. The aroma of a beloved land was in the air, like the scent of his mother's skin. The mysterious hot winds had come blowing through to drive out the demonic chill that emanated night and day from the mansion's walls, its paintings, its corridors and its curtains. He rushed to open the windows, and the rays of the sun poured in like a river of loving joy.

Looking out the window, he saw the car pull up and the chauffeur rush to open the door. Then he saw Raghid "put on" his cigar and reach to help Bahriya get out. She didn't take hold of the hand extended to her, and nearly stumbled.

Nasim rushed to the door to receive them.

The sun was shining from behind her, creating a partial silhouette. Her presence wafted like a soothing breeze over his heart, riddled as it was with the sufferings of life far from home, and passed over his wounds like a healing balm. Something about her presence comforted him, giving him a sense of both joy and sorrow. When she turned around and, with a look of fatigue, sat down on the seat nearest to her, light came pouring out upon him from her face (or so it seemed to him). Her dazzling features had a beauty that was strange and unfamiliar, and yet also so inviting and intimate that they reminded him of his mother and some of his sisters. Looking at her, he got a lump in his throat and nearly cried. There was something mysterious about her. It was as if she took on a new face with every passing moment. When he looked at her for the second time, he noticed her wounds as though they hadn't even been there before. She had cuts and bruises as though she had gone crawling for ten years over broken glass. When he looked at her the third time, he saw nothing but lofty, snow-covered mountain peaks. Her features picked him up and carried him away, then flung him down in a mountain village in Lebanon where the winds blew through the oak and cedar trees, and he was overcome with a kind of dizziness. Finally Raghid reprimanded him for staring at "Miss Bahriya" and told him to go make the tea and close the windows and the drapes.

As Nasim left the room, he took one last look at her and saw still another of her faces. She was casting Raghid what looked like a hateful glance, her presence like a stormy sea breaking over its shores. The fragrance of the waves filled the room, and he felt the salt water washing over his face as he drowned and drowned . . .

When he returned with the tea, he was astonished to find Raghid speaking in a tone so different from what he was accustomed to hearing, he hardly recognized his voice. As he asked Bahriya about her condition, his voice trembled as though it had been electrified by her captivating presence. Silence was her only reply. However, her hand was shaking as she took the teacup. She raised it to her lips with the help of her other hand, but it fell to the floor and shattered.

For the first time since he'd known Raghid, he didn't rant and rave over the breaking of an expensive cup. Instead, he rushed over to make sure that the hot spray hadn't burned her feet. And when she closed her eyes in what looked like a swoon, Raghid shouted, "Quick! Call my doctor and have him come right away. And tell Sheikh Watfan to get down here right now."

Nasim scurried off in a terrible fright. Meanwhile, Raghid went on thinking about this young woman who looked like a little girl when she closed her eyes, and for the first time in his life, he understood how it felt to be anxious for the welfare of another human being who wasn't his father. Feeling somewhat ill at ease, he remembered his mother whom he'd never known, his mother who had died while she was bearing him. Her loss had left him virtually mute with women when it came to matters of the heart. Yet never once had he felt the need for a truly intimate moment with a woman. He saw women as mere decorations for the world of businessmen, or means to other ends.

But with Bahriya, he felt the need for a new language, and at the same time he was aware of his illiteracy when it came to human relations.

As these thoughts went through his head, he placed his hand on her feverish forehead with a lustful craving that now lay broken on the threshold of true affection. Could this really be happening to him, Raghid Zahran?

◆　◆　◆

Meanwhile, something had happened to Nasim that left him utterly bewildered.

He had gone into Sheikh Watfan's room and found him sitting in front of his crystal ball, gazing into it as though he were actually seeing through it, as if it were nothing but a kind of magnifying glass. His eyes were exploring other places, moving beyond the walls of the room and traversing great distances like someone with ESP or the ability to engage in telepathic communication.

Then suddenly he heard him say, "I know you came to summon me to her. I witnessed the moment of her arrival at the airport. I saw her sting Nadim with the scourge of her witchcraft, paralyzing him for several minutes, and in the car I heard her reciting her silent incantations, paralyzing Raghid's mind and blinding him to what she really is. I saw the teacup shatter in her hands from the white heat of her aura, not from its falling on the floor as you two imagined. And I saw Raghid sending you to me. . ."

Nasim left the room without uttering a word about what he had seen, heard, or felt.

Trying to reassure himself, he thought, perhaps he's just been snooping around for information on her arrival. But why would he declare his rejection of this poor, wounded Lebanese girl and put his magic to work against her before he's even laid eyes on her? Is he afraid she'll remind him of something in his homeland that he wants to forget?

◆   ◆   ◆

"Ahimoush Mudaqhir Ahimoush Madaqhir Jamrush Jamrush Qashqoush Qashqoush Tahish Tahish Qannash Maharqannash Maharsi'i Si'i."

As the sorcerer recited, he held in one hand a knife on which he had written the magical combinations, "4311919441111119" and "1111611hh," and in the other a bat wrapped in a rag to which he had tied three dove feathers, three peppers, and three coriander leaves. He then slit the bat's neck and placed it together with its "wrapping" inside a clay jug. He rang the bell for Nasim and asked him to put the entire mixture in the oven and bake it until it had burned, then bring it back to him. When Nasim brought it back, the sorcerer enveloped the container once again in clouds of incense and cast a spell over it. Then he removed from it an amount the size of a grain of wheat and asked Nasim to slip it into Bahriya's food.

"I can't do that," he replied.

"But I'm ordering you," said Watfan.

Intent on his refusal, Nasim said apologetically, "I'm afraid some harm might come to her and I'd get in trouble with the Swiss police."

Then, as he headed out of the room he added, "Whatever you want to do, do it yourself."

"No harm with come to her," said the sorcerer. "This is a love potion. If she takes it, her hostility toward us will leave her."

"But she isn't hostile. She's just a sick young woman who's been devastated by the war. Why don't you leave her alone?"

"Because she won't leave us alone. She's been planted here by a powerful foe of ours, and she's going to bring about the destruction of everyone around her, including the Pasha and me."

"I feel quite comfortable with her myself. The poor girl just got here yesterday, and she's exhausted. Leave her alone."

And with that Nasim left the room feeling almost afraid for Sheikh Watfan. (He seems to be suffering from both delusions of grandeur and paranoia. I don't know what it is about poor Bahriya that provokes him so.)

◆   ◆   ◆

How am I supposed to slip the love potion into her food myself when I'm afraid even to go into her room? And how can I tell Nasim that? Who would believe that I'm afraid of that crazy little girl, who claims to have lost the ability to speak but who really hasn't? How can I tell them that I don't dare slip a love potion into her food in hopes that she might love me and stop tormenting me the way she's been doing ever since she got here? Raghid left me alone with her yesterday so that I could recite incantations over her to make her nightmares go away and to make her stop screaming out at night and waking both of us up. With those shrieks of hers, she plants fears and anxiety in our lives. But we didn't wake Nasim up. Apparently he didn't hear our cries coming from the servants' wing on the first floor, since otherwise he would have been sure to come running. In any case, after the doctor sedated her and left the room, I sat down in front of her. What a beauty she is. Praise be to the Creator! She looks so meek when she's asleep. And there's such a resemblance between her and my consort, the Princess of the Jinn, you'd think she'd taken up residence in a human body. Then all of a sudden she opened her eyes and stared into my face. And without knowing why, I was overcome with a deep sorrow. I began reciting incantations to restore speech to this extraordinary beauty, and as I recited I began to feel my powers giving out and the spirits withdrawing from me. I didn't feel strong the way I normally do at such times. Instead I had a growing awareness of who I really am. As I went on reciting, I nearly forgot that she was sitting in front of me. All I was conscious of was how miserable and alone I was: the greedy descendant of an impoverished family of sorcerers who had always been above reproach. How many times I tried to pursue a different destiny for myself, the way my brothers did, but I failed. For so long I practiced sorcery against my will, all the while writing poetry on the sly and riding the winds into darkness and oblivion. What a coward I am. I was afraid of my uncle, afraid of Beirut. And I've been so alone since they burned everything up. All they left me were the old family books that I'd refused to have anything to do with before then. They burned everything they laid their hands on. They destroyed everyone I'd loved and everyone I'd hated, leaving me nothing but some yellowed leaves that had belonged to my ancestors. So what could I have done but resort to them in the end? And now, as I try to bring healing to this puzzling creature, what do I have to aid me but those same aged books that I read later on? I read them, I learned what was in them and I carried out their teachings to the letter, without knowing whether I really loved them or whether I was convinced of their validity. I didn't sift the good from the bad, or the reasonable from the ridiculous. Instead, I carried them away just as they were. I preserved them just as they were. I had no other choice. After all, they'd left me nothing else, and no power with which to examine them critically. I was spent, depleted, like a drowning man who doesn't dare question the hand that rescues him. Instead, he simply does what he's told. And I did what I was told, with their demons opposing me constantly.

I went on reciting my incantations to restore speech to this extraordinary beauty. Then suddenly the ground shook beneath us. The candle went out, the place went dark, and I felt as though I'd fallen into a deep well. At the same time, I heard the voice of the afreet that was living inside her, imitating a masculine voice that I didn't recognize. Claiming to be my father, it recounted the story of how he died in Palestine when an artillery piece exploded in his hands as he was loading it. Then I heard the voice of my brother Ghilan telling me how he was murdered on a riverbank along with some of his buddies, how he suffered and bled alone, and how the Israelis attacked him while he was down. Then her voice changed as though she were possessed by countless numbers of afreets, and I heard the voice of Kan'an howling in pain as the tank smashed him to a pulp inside the car he was driving. This was followed by the voice of Burqan telling me about his death, how he was murdered by his closest friends for fear that he would betray them to the enemy even though he had no intention of doing such a thing. He told me about the excruciating pain caused by the bullet that lodged in his abdomen, and the relief brought by the one that went in through his ear.

Then she seemed to catch on fire in the darkness. She took on my mother's face as she sobbed and burned, going up in flames all over again before my very eyes. So I attacked her, cast spells over her, and called upon the kings of the jinn, binding her with their magic and coating her body with special ointments and medicines. Next time I'll have to wash her in birds' blood and cast a spell over her with incense so that her afreets with their myriad voices and faces will stop making trouble. That's right. I'll ask Nasim to bring some she-camel's blood and birds' blood so that I can perform the rituals for casting the evil spirit out of her.

I left the room covered with ointments and perspiration. As I washed myself off, I wondered, who is it that wants to destroy me? Which spirit is it that bears some grudge against me and sent me this living corpse that speaks with a thousand and one tongues? First they sent Khalil to do the job. And now they've sent a more potent magic in the form of a body that's in total surrender to them. But maybe she's out of her mind, in which case it's best that I treat her for insanity. On the other hand, if she's just insane, then who is it that revealed my secrets to her and told her of my inner torment? Or were those voices coming out of my own mouth as I fell under the spell of that deadly, dark-light gaze of hers? Have my psychic perceptions been stripped of their protection from the past that I've fled from? And why is all this happening to me now, since her arrival?

Who is this Bahriya exactly? A human being or a jinni? A friend or a foe? Why is she tormenting me this way? And why did I sense the danger she posed the moment I first heard her name and saw her picture in that Beirut newspaper as if I'd known her for ages?

Nasim will have to bring me camel's blood and birds' blood. Then I'll try the spells for casting out demons. I'll also try a treatment for madness. I'll try everything I have to defend myself against her. If I don't, she'll burn me up with her witchcraft. She'll doom me to spend the rest of my days wandering aimlessly through the land of the jinn with no power to help myself or anyone else, helpless to free myself from women's grip and go out into the world of people for all eternity. I'm not going to let this ravishing, unknown human being annihilate me.

On second thought, it might be better to get hold of the camel and bird blood without Nasim knowing about it. I'll ask Raghid directly about it, since Nasim doesn't believe in me—the fool. He hasn't noticed that since she got here, she's possessed him with a little demon and has been using him as her slave. She's dangerous. Dangerous. I'll persuade Raghid of the necessity of having amulets planted under his skin to protect him from her if she toys with him and strips him of the ones he's got sewn into his clothes. I'll make sure he understands that in Moroccan sorcery, they can protect a man from dying even if he's received an otherwise fatal bullet wound. Besides which, they're no larger than a pistachio and it won't be painful having one planted under the skin. And if he's a sissy when it comes to pain, then let him have that sterilized Swiss doctor of his implant it after giving him anesthesia. I'll go talk to him about it right now.)

◆   ◆   ◆

The heat continued to burst forth from everywhere like an unspoken, fiery message from the desert. The Geneva media couldn't seem to find anything to talk about but the heat wave that had hit this summer of 1982, registering record highs the likes of which the country hadn't seen for a quarter of a century. The nightclub was packed, and the dancer, dripping with perspiration, was writhing in exquisite, primeval, snakelike gyrations. For all he knew she was old and decrepit, the priestess of frenzied, erotic love for untold ages, possessing something that surpassed earthly time. Raghid sat staring at her without seeing her.

His eyes were filled with the image of Bahriya, with her broken, melancholy beauty and her glaring wounds. His thoughts were occupied with her eloquent muteness, and her terrified screams by night as she traversed her nightmares alone. The doctor was unable to offer her anything but sedatives and sleeping pills, and Sheikh Watfan didn't know what to do but recite his incantations, offer up his sacrificial victims, cover her resplendent body with blood surrounded by clouds of incense, and feel his way with uncertainty through the darkness of fears and angst. Oh, if only she would recover and speak! He no longer knew exactly what he wanted from her. He knew he wanted her to stop being so distant and unapproachable, so inscrutable, so sorrowful and childlike. He wanted to find an opening in her spirit through which he could reach her. He didn't know how to take possession of her, nor did he even know if he wanted to possess her the way he had everything else throughout his lifetime. On the other hand, perhaps his shameless anxiety over her was nothing less than the supreme lust to possess—to possess her in particular: Bahriya, the Bahriya of pure, unadulterated simplicity. There was something about her that went beyond her dazzling beauty, and which had planted turmoil in his spirit ever since she arrived. It was a "something" which he couldn't name, yet it was having an effect on virtually everyone who laid eyes on her: Khalil, Nadim, Lilly, Kafa, Nasim. . . . One by one, they and everyone else had been drawn by curiosity to come congratulate her on her safe arrival, and once in her presence, every one of them had experienced something akin to an electric shock. Was she really bewitched as Sheikh Watfan insisted? Was she possessed by a demonic spirit that had come to destroy him? And if so, then what had made Raghid grow so attached to her that he couldn't bear the idea of sending her away despite his belief in magic and his confidence in Watfan? Was this also an effect of her witchcraft?

The dancer continued her graceful, snakelike writhing. Nadim watched her contentedly despite the fact that when in "high society," he always insisted that he liked ballet and didn't care for belly dancing. The guests gave her an intoxicated applause and the celebration was on. However, the guest of honor wouldn't be attending. Raghid felt somewhat bitter about it. He'd wanted to introduce her to people, not—as he'd hoped at first—so that the magazines would write about him on their society pages, lauding his nobility and the kind reception he'd given to his wounded Lebanese relative whose family had been exterminated by the war. Rather, he'd come simply to enjoy the feel of her presence by his side, even if she did happen to be a time bomb. He'd originally brought her out of Lebanon so that people would sing his praises and say, "He may not be Lebanese, but he takes care of his family wherever they are!" And now he'd nearly forgotten the reason that had led him to bring her to Switzerland in the first place. In any case, the press had applauded him the day he received her in the airport, and a picture of the two of them together had appeared in some magazines. He hadn't gotten out of his armored car for the photograph for security reasons. Even so, the pictures had turned out well through the car window. And now some other magazines would be publishing photos from the present celebration, and he'd be sure to remind them of the occasion for the event. After all, he mustn't forget his political interests. And the second billion he intended to amass would be sufficient to bring him back to the "correct" path of cool decorum. So let him forget about Bahriya and go back to worrying about his own affairs. . . . He took a small tape recorder out of his pocket and pressed the "play" and "record" buttons to record an order. As he placed the microphone to his mouth, the dancer was reaching a fever's pitch, as if she were participating in a *zar*,[25] with a corresponding wild intensi-

---

25. A *zar* is an event connected with the folk tradition of Egypt in which Muslim women gather for the purpose of calling upon occult powers, casting out evil spirits, and so forth. The event involves various rites, including frenzied dancing to which allusion is made here.

fication in the music. That's the way he was all day long, filling a tape with whatever orders came to mind and having Nadim carry them out. And Lilly wasn't bad either. She was the one who had taken charge of organizing this occasion, and everything was smashing: the well-known Arab belly dancer whom she'd brought from her home country, and the big name singer who had been singing in Paris and played sick for one night so that she could fly to Geneva specially for this occasion. That, of course, was only after Layla had made clear to her that Raghid Bey would compensate her for the money she would have made that night in her Paris nightclub, including the special tips she was accustomed to receiving from admirers who would slip money into her bosom.

Lilly had brought in a team of workers specially to polish all the gold and silverware before the party, and the mansion looked like a blazing mass of silver-studded golden incandescence. The best thing about Lilly was that she worked fast and never left any loose ends. Now that he'd managed to take her away from Amir, he'd have to have her once, just once. He only liked young women, but necessity sometimes imposes its own requirements. And in this case her body would be nothing but a battlefield in which he intended to register another victory over Amir. He would plant his banners in the same hills and valleys where Amir had gone roaming for so long, kissing them as one kisses the land he loves. He'd teach him that nothing is sacred, and that Satan himself is master of all. It's simply one's point of reference that differs.

Besides which, she didn't seem all that bad as a female, either. It was true, of course, that the real reason for his interest in her was that she'd once been Amir's sweetheart. But she also wasn't bad judged purely on her own merits. In fact, she was quite attractive. Amir's taste in women was better than his taste in politics. Her mother had died and he'd forgotten to offer her his condolences. Now he regretted it. He'd like to have seen a strong woman like her in pain. After all, there was nothing he enjoyed so much as the pleasure of watching other people suffer. It was true that he was alone and loved by no one. But this, at least, shielded him from the anguish that loved ones bring when they get sick or die. It's tragic to love a mere mortal. Fortunately, this hadn't happened to him yet except in relation to himself—that is, until Bahriya came along. He couldn't describe the unfamiliar feeling he had toward her as love. But she'd planted a kind of trepidation under his skin, like the special amulets that he'd had implanted in his flesh that very morning based on his sorcerer's advice.

The dancer's body was wet with perspiration, and she looked especially alluring, as if while she danced she'd performed magical rites that stripped ten years off her age.

A number of his guests thronged around her. One of them, a potential partner for a water drainage project that he had in mind for a particular Arab country, was looking quite pleased. Another of them was his present partner in dealings with oil tankers. The third was Saqr Ghanamali. He'd have to take note of who her admirers were, since this was information he might be able to make use of in a deal here or there. Then suddenly Saqr withdrew and went back to where he'd been seated near Coco. Perhaps he'd noticed that the dancer was old enough to be his mother.

She went back to the center of the floor after being asked to do another number. And as she danced this time, Saqr didn't even glance at her. It was obvious that he was quite taken by Khalil's wife, which was something else Raghid could make use of in his attempts to secure the airport contract, that is, if Sheikh Sakhr were to die suddenly or be killed in some accident. . . . Yes, indeed, he did seem infatuated with Kafa, who had been given the nickname Coco by the others in attendance. She had objected at first because, as she pointed out, Coco Chanel is "skinny and ugly." But the others insisted that she had Coco Chanel's brains and elegance. And thus the name was baptized in a bottle of champagne. Khalil had been listening to these goings on and hadn't appeared terribly pleased to have his wife transformed from Kafa to Coco. The dimwit. He appeared to be the stubborn, stupid type, which was unfortunate, since it meant he lacked the qualifications to fill Nadim's shoes later on. He thought back to a similar scene he had witnessed about fifteen years earlier, when Dunya had been christened Dado, the star of high society. But she'd been looking washed out lately. She'd lost her quick wit and charm. Maybe she'd fallen in love with some fellow young enough to be her son. No matter. Whoever he happened to be, she'd pay the price and he'd oblige. She'd come to life again for a while, then be forgotten. Or do you suppose she'd worn herself out for good? As for this Coco, she really was quite beautiful. She seemed to sparkle with euphoria in the gold dress that he'd given her especially for this occasion. He'd had it sent to her hotel as part of a plan to raise the level of elegance among his employees' wives—the pretty ones, at least. The plan served a number of purposes. At worst, he wanted to be able to boast that his employees' wives were better dressed than the wives of other people's staff.

Khalil was included among his personnel even though officially he was working for Saqr. And based on his express instructions, Nadim had been the first one to introduce him to people. He'd wanted to do a kind of "mini-experiment" at Nadim's place before taking the risk of inviting Khalil and his wife to his own home. And now Coco was passing one test after another with flying colors. She'd set the gold dress on fire with a red rose. Then she'd put gold hairspray on her hair and highlighted her already bewitching eyes with gold eye makeup. He wondered, how do you suppose she'd feel if she knew that she'd become part of the game, a battleground where men vie to prove their masculinity and the virility of wealth and status? She might enjoy it, but of course, without understanding the ideology of the game. She's got just enough brains to doll herself up and to be in a state of constant bliss over the way men admire her. She's content, but a bit of a harebrain. It's obvious that Khalil knows it all too well, and he looks worried. As far as Raghid was concerned, this made her all the more alluring. Yes. He was definitely going to try her out, even if only once, the way the proprietor of a restaurant tests the food before letting it be served to the clientele. He wasn't going to content himself with Nadim's report on the matter, despite the latter's assurances that she'd be able to wear out even a young stud like Saqr in a single week. Looking rather fainthearted, he'd even come begging for a dose of Sheikh Watfan's special potion, explaining that after the Herculean effort he'd made to carry out the assignment, it looked now as if she was expecting him to try again! But Raghid wanted to try her himself first, availing himself of Sheikh Watfan's experience in such matters and even the prescription that he knew was contraindicated by his high blood pressure. Damn this condition of his. Then, realizing he'd forgotten to take his medicine, he took a pill stealthily out of his pocket. He didn't want anyone to notice that he was ill. After all, he had to convince everyone that he was going to live forever. Otherwise, all his deals would be sure to slip out of his hands, in which case—alas!—he wouldn't be able to amass his second billion! He looked to make certain that the pill was on the sealed part of the paper. He was suspicious of everyone and was afraid someone might come along and replace his medicine with poison. There was someone who wanted to kill him, but he wasn't going to make it easy for whoever it happened to be. Instead, he tightened security measures more every day, and he didn't even trust Nasim anymore. As for his guests, they didn't know that on their way in they'd passed through a walkway whose walls were equipped with an invisible arms-detection device, and that as they were admiring the gold objets d'art on one side of the corridor, they were being monitored by an employee seated behind the velvet curtains on the opposite wall.

When the dance ended, everyone clapped except Khalil. (Nothing pleases that ill-bred jerk!) As for Saqr, he was applauding Coco's beauty, and not once did he take his eyes off her well-rounded curves. Damn! The dancing and the loud music were over and now he would have to deliver a speech in which he addressed everyone without saying anything in particular to anyone. At the same time, he would have to have his ears tuned to pick up all the whispered words that he wasn't supposed to hear.

"Where is the guest of honor?"

"She suffered a relapse, and the doctor had to inject her with large amounts of Valium."

He wasn't lying. However, what he didn't tell them was that after the doctor left, she was treated by his sorcerer with bat and camel blood. (Watfan covered her half-naked body with blood while he recited his incantations, trembling in fear of the afreet that said it had possessed her while Nasim trembled with rage. I mean, you'd think we were raping his sister! He might even have hit Watfan if I hadn't rushed to send him out of the room. That boy doesn't believe in magic, and he doesn't understand a thing about the mysterious powers that control this universe. Instead he assumes that "capital" is the key to everything. . . .)

Noticing how intoxicated Saqr was with Coco's beauty, Raghid went over to him and, taking him by the arm, led him aside with the intention of asking for his help with the airport contract. It was an unspoken assumption at gatherings such as this that Coco was his property, and that without his approval Saqr wouldn't get so much as a nibble at her. Such are the customs of the world of businessmen! The two men walked toward the balcony, with Saqr thinking about Coco, and Raghid about the airport.

No sooner had they taken a few steps away than there gathered around her a new circle of admirers, each of whom Raghid had something to gain from. (She's a real treasure, this woman. She reminds me of the old Dunya. As for Lilly, well, that's another matter. It's obvious that she'd refuse to be a pawn or plaything, since she has aspirations to be one of the players herself. She's a male trapped in a female's body.) It bothered Raghid that Saqr was so tall. He didn't like walking beside people who were taller than he was, so he suggested that they sit down for a while. Once they'd found a seat, he asked Saqr why his father hadn't come to the party.

"He's got a bad headache," Saqr replied.

Meanwhile, a new group of fans had surrounded the renowned singer. Khalil had only seen her in pictures thus far, so when he got a closer look at her, he was shocked to find that she looked like a mummy coated with white paint with a wig of red straw on its head. So he got as far away from her as he could. Then his eyes met Dunya's. Something about this woman made him feel drawn to her. There was something that made her stand out. At this party, as at all the others he'd been to, all the women looked nearly alike to him. He still could hardly tell them apart. It was as if all rich men's wives had a single face and a single hairdo, both of them dictated by prevailing fashions. As if the plastic surgeon they all went to for their facelifts only knew how to come out with a single result. And they all went around with the same expression: an affected look of utter bliss and goodwill, and the ability to pretend that they were listening to others with pleasure while inwardly wandering around through their clothes closets, and comparing. . . .

But Dunya had seemed different to him from the first time they met. And every succeeding encounter had confirmed this impression. This particular evening she was looking melancholy and distant. At the moment she was having a conversation with Layla, and a cloud of mutual dislike seemed to hang over the two women as they spoke. When Khalil walked up to them, Layla hurriedly withdrew. She was a fiery, intense woman, and perhaps she didn't want witnesses to the conversation that had been taking place. Dunya looked pale and fatigued. Yet as she peered intently into his face, she radiated tenderness.

"How are you?" she asked.

"The same as you."

He felt as though he might fall in love with her if she looked at him one more time with that unaffected warmth of hers. Kafa had accused him, among other things, of not being able to resist the look of a mature, tender woman. And perhaps there was some truth to this accusation, at least.

"You look unhappy," he told her.

"Well, you're not exactly the picture of bliss yourself!"

She'd brought his sorrows to the surface. Women can be so wicked! One word and they've switched places with you! They know how to interrogate the judge and the public prosecutor as they sit forlornly in the witness stand!

"This isn't your world, is it?" she asked.

"No."

"And it isn't mine, either," she said with a sigh. "You can still pull out, though. As for me, I'm stuck."

"Pulling out wouldn't be easy. I mean, if I did, where would I go?"

"You could go back to Beirut when the war's over."

"But I didn't come here to get away from the war."

"How's that?"

"I had to leave the country for other reasons. I ran away from what you might call 'the war of repression.'"

"In Beirut?"

"That's right. We were afraid that Lebanon was losing its Arab identity. But to reaffirm it, some people decided to resort to repressive practices—the way most other Arabs have done!"

"Of course, it isn't just Lebanon's Arab identity that's in the balance anymore. The Arab identity of Arabs everywhere is being put to the test. And the people most able to do something about it haven't lifted a finger."

"It really is shameful. And we don't dare talk about it anymore. We're more likely to be killed by our friends than by our enemies."

"Did you know that the people who tried to kill Amir Nealy weren't his avowed enemies, but his so-called friends?"

"Yes, I know."

"The dispute between him and them was over the matter of 'freedom.' He'd dared to criticize their terrorist activities, not as their opponent, but out of love for them and their cause. He said they were liberating their homeland all right, but from what? From freedom itself. So they tried to liberate him from his life, so to speak."

"I know."

"In fact, his enemies decided to allow his son to come visit him."

"It's nothing but a liberal-looking ploy aimed at creating the illusion of democracy and making us think that they deal fairly with people."

"But they didn't try to kill him or his son."

"They just keep stoking the fires of whatever disputes exist between us so as to make us do their dirty work for them. But even if everything we've built falls apart, and even if it becomes clear at some point that everything we've done so far was wrong, they're still not the alternative we're looking for."

"But how can we demand that others stand with us when we don't even do that for each other?"

"We? I didn't think you got involved in that sort of thing!"

"And I didn't, either. But . . ."

"We're organizing a protest against the Israeli invasion of Lebanon and against the indifference being shown by most Arabs. Would you like to participate?"

"I don't dare. I wish . . . I'll try."

"Good. If I can't contact you, then get in touch with Amir Nealy. I'll give you his number."

"I have it."

"How's that?"

"As I've mentioned, we were friends before I took a different path in life. I have his number. In fact, I have his home address, too. And I've gone there more than once without daring to go in. I think Nasim saw me one day."

Then with bitter irony she added, "Don't you know that I used to be a freedom fighter for women's liberation? And that I was a fantastic painter? And . . . and . . ."

Swaying back and forth and caressing some rich Arab's chest, the singer began to croon a love song.

Khalil was revolted by this type of repetitive, singsong begging. However, he and Dunya carried on with their conversation in whispers despite the loud clamor of those around them. Then a troupe of the women got up and, forming a circle around the singer, proceeded to sway from side to side with quivering hips and bosoms, vying with the dancer for the admiration of the males in attendance. In the lead was Coco, who outdid the professional dancer, taking her place as the object of the onlookers' lustful gasps and stares. Khalil looked on as his wife engaged in her favorite sport. Meanwhile Raghid watched her in delight, and Saqr devoured her with his eyes, all the while excitedly rubbing his nose. (He must have sneaked a snort of cocaine out on the balcony. Who knows? Maybe Raghid offered it to him before he lit up his big cigar.)

Ignoring his wife's disgusting behavior, Khalil said to Dunya, "And what happened to all that after you married?"

"I thought it was all over. But . . ."

"Where are the women who shared your political sentiments?"

"Some of them went on to devote themselves to having children, or to getting rich. And some of them kept on with the struggle. Layla, for instance. She remained true to the cause for some time. I don't know what changed her later on. Now she's trying to get rich and make a slave out of herself—like me. The strange thing is, she started doing that just as I was starting to try to be like her!"

"Were you two having an argument a little while ago?"

"Of sorts. I asked her about Amir. The mere mention of his name gets a rise out of her now."

"And your other women friends?"

"My husband managed to wreck the small circle of friends I had left. Most of their husbands have started working for Raghid, and fear for their livelihoods keeps most of them from persevering. Both my husband and Raghid make it clear that they don't encourage any sort of liberal tendencies, and they use the husbands to keep the wives quiet. As a result, the circle I had around me has grown smaller and smaller."

"I know what you mean. It happens to men also to some extent."

"I didn't think I'd change. Back when I did paintings of naked men, the critics launched an all-out attack on me, and Amir was the only person who took up for me. He said, 'Why do we applaud a male artist who does a painting of a naked woman, and ostracize a female artist who does a painting of a naked man? It's the same principle in both cases, and what matters is that it's art. Judge her on the basis of whether her work is art or not, nothing more.' For a long time Amir encouraged me."

Just then they were intruded upon again by the intrusion of the singer's voice.

They noted with disgust that she was trying to imitate a particular Arabic dialect in a cheap ploy to extract donations from her well-to-do listeners. And the trick worked—naked as it was—as if her own nakedness helped to make it go over on her audience. And thus began a 'benevolence contest' to see who could stuff the most into her scantily clad bosom.

Khalil and Dunya exchanged looks of chagrin.

"And you?" she asked him. "What's your story?"

"Do you want the short version or the long version?"

"The long version."

"Well, when I was a little boy, my father always taught me to tell the truth, and nothing but the truth. So I did. And, that's all!"

"All right now, let me hear the short version!"

"Once I spoke the truth to my buddies. I said, 'The slogans you use call for revolution, that is, for joy, love, self-sacrifice, and peace. But the names you choose for yourselves do nothing but strike terror in people's hearts. You, for example—why are you Father of Horrors? And another one calls himself Father of Skulls. Then there's the Spider, Lover of Death, The Boulder, and Father of Terror. What are we, anyway? A gang in league with the Marquis de Sade? Why won't you let me call myself Father of the Saint, Father of Joy, Father of Tenderness, Father of the Sun or something like that? Haven't you noticed that we've brought about the deaths of frightful numbers of the poor and innocent, and that never once have we killed an actual, declared revolutionary target? We've got to rethink the whole concept of liberation terrorism.'"

"What else?"

"One time I took my identity card and scratched out the section that says 'Religion,' since I'd decided that religion is a personal matter between me and my Maker. Well, after that I started getting beaten at *all* the checkpoints. I was beaten by Muslims and Christians alike. Even the 'progressives' who tend to support secularism used to beat me at their checkpoints, then detain me and subject me to interrogation!"

"Go on."

"You may already know the rest of the story from the newspapers. But these are jokes that I've paid for with broken ribs and months-long stints in prison. I'll tell you the rest at the next dinner party."

Just then Raghid caught them in the criminal act of laughing.

Like someone issuing an order rather than an invitation, he said to Khalil, "Your wife is a top-notch dancer. So why don't you sing for us?"

The tone of his voice concealed an unspoken desire to humiliate. Grabbing him by the arm, Raghid said loudly, "He's got a beautiful voice, and he's going to sing something for us!" Without knowing how, poor Khalil found himself in the middle of a group of guests who started pushing him toward the center of the room, while scores of women with the same face screamed in voices spattered with bloodred lipstick, "Sing for us! Sing for us!" He looked over at Nasim, who was serving drinks to the guests. As their eyes met, he felt the warmth of friendship, like an unseen artery pumping blood back into his face, which was white with fright and embarrassment. One of the women wrapped a long scarf around her hips in preparation to dance, while the professional dancer approached him purportedly to contribute to the success of his number. The applause began. Then, singing the way he used to as a little boy when he was afraid of the dark, and later when he had to face people who frightened him or were trying to crush him, he belted out with his throaty, rustic voice, "O darkness of the prison, descend upon us! We cherish the darkness, for the darkness can only be followed by the dawn . . ."

Suddenly the entire place was enveloped in baffled silence. The dancer froze, and looks of searing, venomous reproach came pouring in upon him. The whole thing had happened in a matter of seconds, but Raghid rushed to save the party. Laughing and clapping for Khalil, he said, "What an imaginative sense of humor you've got!" Soon he was joined by the rest in applause, laughter, dancing and merriment, with everyone singing whatever struck his fancy. And before long everyone had forgotten all about Khalil and his song—everyone, that is, except Raghid, who shot him a look that Dunya translated for him: "He's saying that he'll settle accounts with you later on. But don't be afraid of him. He can't stand up against the truth. He'll just have to pay more to buy you off, that's all."

It was as if Khalil's "joke" had put life back into the party. Either that, or it had aroused unspoken fears, which people hurriedly crushed with all the more raucous celebration and wild dancing. The singer announced that she possessed a "key" which she considered her artistic capital, as it were. She said she could perform songs from the Gulf, Libya, Sudan, Egypt, Lebanon, Iraq, and elsewhere, since her voice, as she put it proudly, was "a musical Arab League" where everyone could find what he was looking for. Someone asked for a song from the Gulf, and she hastened to fulfill the golden request, her voice backed up by hips that quivered to the beat of the music and the audience's gasps of approval.

Then all of a sudden a hush began to fall over the place, and people's gazes were drawn toward the staircase leading up to the second floor. A scantily clad young woman was descending the stairs, her body covered with blood and partially healed wounds.

Her beauty was both luminous and grim, and she looked as though she were wearing scores of dresses rather than just one. Her long hair was black as coal, wild and unruly like waves of time undulating in the night. Her face was free of makeup and forced smiles, devoid—like Nature herself—of expressions of good or evil. Yet even so it was bursting with life, despite the mesmerized look in her eyes. Her body was like a statue of exquisite beauty immortalizing the essence of youth, hotheaded and impetuous yet without its usual strife and tumult. It was a statue that had trod through jungles of fire and horror and passed through seven levels of hell.

Some of them murmured, "Is this one of Raghid's nice surprises?"

Raghid cried, "Bahriya, what are you doing here!"

She didn't seem to have heard him. Instead, she passed him by without seeing him or anyone else: regal in her nakedness, clad in her wounds as she went her solitary way.

Everyone there was left in a bewildered daze. She was so beautiful that some of them forgot all about her wounds and the horrific sight of the blood that covered her body. There was something about her that aroused in some of the men the desire to possess and ravish, bringing out their primitive natures as club-carrying savages running through prehistoric forests. In others, she aroused feelings of grief and remorse. In her eyes there was something that reminded some of the women of their longing for tenderness and lost innocence, whereas for others she was a reminder of forgotten passions.

In an attempt to turn the scene into a joke, Raghid said, "I present to you my relative, Bahriya Zahran, clothed in war attire just as she was when she arrived from Beirut. She wanted to attend the celebration being held in her honor wearing her national costume!"

No one laughed. No one breathed. Meanwhile, Bahriya continued her solemn march toward the balcony like a butterfly in search of fresh air. And before descending the stairs to the garden, she turned in their direction and cast them a collective stare full of reproach and contempt, like someone contemplating a beast with multiple faces and bodies. Or so it seemed to them. Then her eyes glazed over again and she walked away until she vanished into the darkness.

His heart filled with anguish, Nasim took off running after her like a madman who's just seen his deceased mother leave her grave and go walking through the streets. When he finally caught up with her, she looked at him, then through him.

Taking off his butler's jacket, he placed it gently around her bare shoulders. And as he did so, he thought he saw her smile at him ever so slightly.

Everyone in attendance was paralyzed by a heavy silence, even after Dunya rushed out to her and was seen leading her back into the mansion through another door.

As the guests withdrew one after another, Khalil noticed that the flowers adorning Kafa's head and bosom had withered and dried up, as had the flowers on the other women's heads and in the men's coat lapels. As for the guard dogs, they took off howling in what sounded like bitter human sobs.

◆   ◆   ◆

The following day the sorcerer decided: I'll treat her . . . I'll bring her a special treatment for madness.

Bahriya's appearing naked and covered with blood had been a source of chagrin to Raghid who, as he had expected, had come to him furious after the party.

The sorcerer then summoned Nasim, who came in grumbling.

He said to him, "Bring me an ounce of camel's eye, an ounce of almonds, an ounce of pine nuts, aromatic oil, a kohl stone, dry dung, and . . ."

"Pardon me, sir," he replied, "It won't be easy to find camels' eyes here in Geneva. Are you in dire need of them?"

"According to my books, this is what the treatment for madness requires."

"Madness? Who's mad?"

"Bahriya."

"She isn't mad. She's just an unfortunate girl who's suffered a breakdown. After all, her family was buried before her very eyes. All she needs is some peace and quiet. Don't your books say anything about that?"

"Maybe. I'm not sure."

"Why don't you get some rest yourself, sir? Yesterday I heard you speaking in many different voices. I happened to be passing by your room as I dusted the statues. You provoked the poor girl and drove her to run away half-naked. She was so drugged up, she wasn't aware of what you'd done to her."

"I wasn't the person speaking. She was—or rather, the demons that have possessed her and caused her to go insane. At least, that's how the books explain her condition."

"What else do the books advise you to do?"

"We have to shave her head down the middle so that we can apply the medicine, which I'll prepare from the ingredients that I just dictated to you. We'll put a few drops of it in her ears as well. And you'll help me."

"I'm going to help you shave her hair off?"

"Of course! She's dangerous, insane, destructive."

Replying with frightening calm, Nasim said, "Listen, Sheikh Watfan. If you or anyone else so much as touches a hair on her head, I'll inform the police. Remember that you're in Switzerland, not in the land of the jinn. If anyone so much as touches that poor girl, I'll kill him."

Nasim left the room trembling with rage. (What is it about this devastated young woman that arouses such lunacy? And why has Raghid been so agitated ever since she got here? Why is he suddenly afraid of dying? And why do he and others imagine this wounded girl to be some sort of ingenious secret agent on behalf of evil spirits? They took her away from her homeland and brought her here a voiceless captive. So what is it that these fiends want from her?)

The sorcerer was more convinced than ever that Bahriya had been possessed by the most powerful of the jinn kings, and that this same spirit had taken control of Nasim to put him to use as a guard over her.

A tremor went coursing through his body. He was afraid of her. And he was afraid of Nasim. Yet he didn't hate her. On the contrary, he longed to be united with her, and wished only that she would cease tormenting him, causing his memory to speak out, reading his thoughts. So who might slip a love potion for him into her food?

◆   ◆   ◆

The heat continued to burst forth from everywhere, like a fiery message from the desert.

There was something about Bahriya that refused to leave Khalil.

There was something about her gruesome stroll through the midst of the dinner party at Raghid's house that had brought him to his senses, despite the "forgetting powder" that Saqr had been stuffing up his nose. Something about her bleeding, her dignity, and her silent, proud wound had reminded him of his children, of his homeland and of his previous life, which had been a time of big dreams and lofty ambitions. Grieved to see her being held captive this way, he decided: I'll look for another job. I'll try to get my life back on track with Kafa, my partner in misery.

Something about Bahriya brought his children so urgently to mind that the morning after the dinner party, he went to see them, managing to meet them in the school courtyard between classes.

The heat was beastly, just as it had been ever since Bahriya's arrival. On his way there in the taxi, the radio announcer bemoaned the "canicule" that had suddenly swept over Geneva with unaccustomed desertlike winds. As he was

approached by Rami and Fadi clad in sports clothes that revealed their delicate, fragile frames, he found himself imagining them being burned up by explosives, while his heart wept for Widad.

He didn't ask the two boys about their mother. She hadn't visited them for
quite some time, and they appeared to be in a state of forlorn serenity bordering on indifference.

"Is the food here good?" Khalil asked them.

"Yes."

"Are your studies well organized?"

"Yes."

"Do you both have friends?"

"Yes."

"Do you go on outings and play football?"

"Yes."

"So are the two of you happy here in Geneva?"

"No."

"What do you want, then?"

"We want to go back to Beirut!"

"Why's that?"

Neither of them said a word. However, Rami threw himself into Khalil's
arms, while Fadi walked some distance away, kicking the gravel as he went.

After his dismal visit to the children, Khalil didn't go back to the hotel.
The moment he opened his eyes on the morning after the party, he had
slipped out of the hotel room without his wife noticing. He decided he
needed to be alone if he wanted to get a clear look at his predicament. He
didn't tell Kafa that his boss had granted him two days' leave while he took
care of a newly arrived shipment of Far Eastern beauties. If he had, she would
have scheduled all his free time for him, making him spend hours in front of
fancy store display windows on Rhone Street while she gazed at furs, jewelry
and pricey clothes, oohing and aahing and planning.

He needed some time alone. So he left his boys' school and headed for the
train station. From there he went to the Cornavin Station, then headed down
Alp Street until he reached the lakeshore on quai du Mont-Blanc. Once there,
he went into Brunswick Park and sat down on one of its benches, where he
crowned his misery with a cigarette brimming with tar and nicotine. He stared
out into the busy street a few steps below him, and at the lake that lay beyond

the opposite sidewalk. But he didn't see a thing. All he could see was Beirut in flames, which went darting across his field of vision in scenes of the sort he'd grown accustomed to seeing every night on television. (Did the plan require that Israel invade us when we were in this sorry state: some of us fugitives, others dead, or repressed, or in prison? We gave up everything for the cause. Even freedom and democracy came to be secondary concerns. And now we've lost our freedom and we haven't recovered our land. In fact, we've lost even more of it. I was forced to leave to get away from the terrorism of "friends," and now the enemy comes in with his own brand of terrorism while I'm gone. The mistake began on the day we agreed to give up democracy so as to give priority to "the requirements of liberation." What we failed to notice was that a population of slaves can't liberate their own land or anyone else's.)

He was still living in Beirut, not in Geneva. Even the new electronic watch that his wife had given him couldn't force him to relocate in time or space. He sat staring at the numbers that jumped every second to show the new time, but all he could see was one time repeating itself over and over: 12:30. He was still there. Every bomb that exploded in Beirut went off in his head, and the houses being razed there collapsed in his eyes. That magical square box commonly known as the television carried him back to Beirut like a time machine whenever he stepped inside it through its glass screen. Just then he realized that someone was speaking to him. He looked up. It was a Japanese-looking young man accompanied by a lady friend. Saying something in Japanese, the young man reached out to hand him a camera as he and his girlfriend pointed to the button he was supposed to press. He understood the body language, at least: they wanted him to take their picture. So he took the camera to the sound of their grateful, delighted laughter.

Two young people, perhaps on their honeymoon. Framing them inside the small square window, he was surprised to find flowers flanking them on either side and a lovely fountain behind them. It was as if he were taking in the sights around him for the first time. He pressed the button, whereupon the woman sprang nimbly over to him to take the camera back, happily murmuring what he took to be a "Thank you!" Within moments they had vanished into a cloud of bliss. (No doubt they have a house to go back to. And in the safety of their home they'll recall the happy moments they spent overseas. As for me. . . .)

Khalil plunged anew into his sorrow. He hadn't really seen the flowers before. Nor the fountain. Nor the towering trees or the lush garden with its exquisite statues. And he would never have his picture taken the way those two young people had done, since he, unlike them, was a homeless wanderer, not a tourist. He didn't know whether he'd ever return to his homeland or not. And if he did, he didn't know whether his neighbors and friends would be alive for him to show them the pictures he'd taken in Geneva, boring them to tears with happy descriptions of the occasion for each photograph and relishing the memory of the blissful moments he'd captured on film. After all, he happened to be living through the most miserable, angst-filled moments of his entire life just now. When he was in prison he thought he'd reached the depths of wretchedness: with his daily march from his cell up some stairs to the interrogation room, then down corridors with soundproof walls that muffled the cries of the tortured. It had never occurred to him that he could be perfectly free and in good health, sitting in a park as lush as paradise itself with some gorgeous woman taking a sunbath right in front of him, and at the same time be racked with grief. His heart was about to break with a reality so horrific he hadn't dared even to contemplate it before: that the Israelis had surrounded Beirut and might occupy it at any time. And if they did, would they prevent him and others from coming home? Would they only allow those already there to remain inside, refusing reentry to those who had fled? Hadn't something similar happened in Palestine before? Would he end up as a homeless refugee? Would he be denied the opportunity to return to his own country? He felt a red-hot skewer going right through his gut, the way he used to feel under the blows of the torturer. Yes. The horror of horrors that had haunted him for the past several days was simply this: the fear of being deprived of the right to return to his country of origin, and of being turned into a captive who, like Bahriya, had been struck dumb by the shock.

He topped off his misery with another cigarette and tried to flee from the terrifying thought that hurled him into a black, bottomless pit, leaving him to fall deeper and deeper without ever reaching the blessed bottom where at long last his skull would be mercifully crushed to pieces, delivering him from his endless torment. Might he actually find himself a refugee? He'd been trying to escape death. But wouldn't death there have been easier to bear than the slow death he was dying here? Wouldn't death have been easier to endure than the cup of humiliation that he now had to drink from every day, one drop at a time?

A nauseous sensation assaulted him in his stomach and an ulceration in his nostrils. It was that damned cocaine that Saqr forced him to share with him. He was going to wreck his health and demolish his stomach for a handful of money that he'd end up spending on Kafa's favorite type of red shoes, his forlorn existence in the hotel, and a safe place for his children who, once the initial excitement of having new things had worn off, had become as forlorn as he was.

He looked around, trying in vain to regain a sense of familiarity. But it was as if the sun that shone down on him was a sun he'd never seen before. He looked at his hand, but without any sense of recognition. He pictured his wife's face, and it looked like the face of a total stranger. Even his past life seemed so far away it might as well have belonged to some other man. Standing on the brink of psychosis, he cast a cold, unfeeling glance about him. (I don't know anyone. No one has ever touched me. Not a soul has ever come near me. I'm alone. Alone. I've never known the warmth of friendship. I've never shared with anyone in planting a rose or drinking in music over glasses of wine. I've never. . . .)

He grabbed hold of the wooden bench, which was coated with green paint. To his right there were red, white, and yellow flowers planted in the shape of a butterfly. (I'm not here. I've left the present and fallen into a trap of pain and fear, the fear of becoming a refugee without a country to call home. For so long I prided myself on the fact that every cozy house on the face of the earth was "home" to me. For so long I declared that I was calling for Arab unity as a small step toward cosmic unity. And now here I am, trembling like a homesick little boy, pining away for the uneven cobblestones leading up to the front doorstep of our house. I remember how my grandma was buried under one of them for "good luck," after which my dad tripped over it and broke his hand.)

He tried in vain to recall the color of the chairs in the hotel lobby. He tried to remember the color of the bathroom wall, the way their room smelled, the texture of the towels, the color of the walls in Nadim's house, the color of his car, the scent of the velvet curtains in Raghid's mansion and what the maitre d' in the Mövenpick Restaurant looked like. But his senses couldn't pick up a thing. It was as if he'd been floating around this whole time in a vacuum of misery, curled up inside the womb of his grief . . . as if he'd never even set foot in Geneva, never visited any of the museums whose treasures he'd always wished he could see, never gone to the Petit Palais Museum to see the Picasso exhibit there, never gone into a single bookstore except to buy a newspaper. As for the Nacomme Naville bookstore, he'd just passed in front of it rather than going in as he'd always dreamed of doing in hopes of learning how to arrange his own bookshop some day. It was as if he rejected the mere fact of his being here. Yet he was here. He was taking cocaine with Saqr. He was going to soirées with Kafa. (I'm living like a margin in time's notebook. I exist both outside life here and outside my own country, deprived of both the culture of my land of exile and the chance to belong to my homeland.)

So what good were all his sighs and tears doing him? As long as it was impossible to run away and go back to Beirut, why not try to organize his life a bit? Hadn't he made up his mind that morning to get his life back on track? Why not try, for example, to move out of the hotel into a small flat? And why not have the boys live with them rather than staying in a boarding school like rich folks' orphans? Why not be a bit more positive?

For some reason, he was assailed again by the image of Bahriya, clad in nothing but her wounds, strolling through Raghid's soirée like the Princess of the Suffering, trailing her sorrows behind her like the train of her royal robe. He felt an overpowering affection toward her. She was as close to his heart as his wife was distant. In her presence there was a telegram of sorts from Beirut, written in blood, wounds, and silence. It was as if she represented the entire city, and as if everyone who left it was like her somehow: naked, clothed in nothing but wounds and mute afflictions, cast out into a vast, empty expanse to be torn to pieces by people in search of the best way to make use of a new corpse!

He trembled in weakness and defeat. He'd never get used to these European summers that felt icy cold one minute and hot as blazes the next. Something about the warm winds that had been blowing took him back to the summers and springs back home. What had come over him? For a long time he'd had the yen to travel, thinking of it as a window that might open onto a dream. But now. . . .

(I've come to say goodbye to you," she told me. "I'm going with my family to Europe."

"Lucky you!"

"And you, what are you going to do during the vacation?"

"I'll go to my village."

Vivienne, a pleasantly plump thirteen-year-old, was my first love. But I was filled with an inexplicable feeling of resentment toward her when I found out that she was going out to see the world while I only had enough money for a ticket back to my village.

I said to her, "I'll say goodbye to you, but it will be our last farewell. I don't want to see you anymore."

I hadn't even sprouted whiskers yet, but I decided to be firm and resolute like a man. She wept bitter tears, and I said nothing.

"If I didn't go with my family, could we go on seeing each other?"

"No. It's all over between us."

"Why?"

"I don't know."

"Do you feel class hatred toward me?"

"Who taught you that cliché?"

"My dad. And he was right. He said you'd never be able to love me, or any other girl from my class for that matter. And he advised me to get away from you."

"Maybe he's right. Goodbye, Vivienne."

"Au revoir."

That night I went home with a big map. I lay it out on the bed the way I used to dream of doing with Vivienne's body, and began reading the names of the cities that I'd heard so many inviting stories about. The city names seemed sort of like the names of women: delectable and alluring—London, Vienna, Paris, Geneva, Zurich, Bangkok, Leningrad, Sofia, Stockholm, Honolulu . . . and every one of them sent me flying through worlds of unspeakable delight. From that time onward, meditating on maps satisfied my dreams and longings. When I opened my bookshop, I set aside an entire shelf for books on tourism and descriptions of all the lands in God's vast world.

And now here I am sitting in Geneva with Saqr, who's about to take me to some or all of those very cities that once were so inviting to me. But instead of excitement and happy anticipation, I feel dread washing over me. And why? Because a refugee can't be a tourist?)

◆　◆　◆

Coco woke up that morning still filled with the exhilaration of the previous evening's party. She'd been the star of the evening, which Khalil had ruined with his tasteless song, "O darkness of the prison . . ." and which Bahriya had spoiled the rest of the way with her rash, unseemly behavior.

She could hear her husband shaving in the bathroom. She didn't feel like seeing him this morning, so she closed her eyes and pretended still to be asleep. She wanted to be alone and think about her future. Then without knowing why, she thought about Bahriya. She hadn't seen anything in her but the wounds that marred her beauty so badly, and her impoliteness toward the noble people who'd shown her so much kindness. As far as she was concerned, Bahriya's behavior the night before was proof of the fact that she was an ill-bred girl who wasn't any relation of the great altruist, Pasha Raghid. As she listened with her eyes closed to the irritating rustle of Khalil's clothes as he got dressed, she swore to herself: I'm not going to let Beirut mar my beauty, drive me out of my senses, or ruin my happiness anymore. I'm going to live in this heaven on earth and enjoy my life to the fullest. I won't let my children become a hindrance to my freedom, and I won't let Widad's memory lacerate my mind the way that bomb lacerated Bahriya's face. I've suffered enough for several lifetimes, thank you! And if my fool of a husband decides to go back to Beirut, I'm not going with him. I'll never go back to Beirut until Beirut goes back to the way it used to be. I'm not going to deprive myself of any pleasure that comes my way.)

There are days when you wake up with the feeling that your whole body is bursting with life and with a yen for the unknown. That's the way Kafa woke up on this particular morning after a long night's sleep. She'd drifted off again after Khalil's departure and dreamed of forbidden delights. When she left the hotel she was accosted by the mysterious heat and by the extraordinary beauty of the lake, the trees, and the lofty mountain peaks. She passed by two elderly ladies chatting outside a lovely, ancient-looking church. And in the church garden she saw two sparrows making bird love in full sight of the statue of an angel. After making circles around his lady bird, the male would puff up his feathers, then mount her in an impassioned embrace while the angel looked on without embarrassment and as the sun bathed them in its blessing. Kafa paused for a few moments to watch them, then took a seat in a nearby café and ordered firewater rather than morning coffee.

Downing it in one gulp, her senses were suddenly ignited with the desires of the five lean years she'd just been through, and at the same moment, her eyes met those of a young Italian man sitting at the other end of the coffee shop. He was handsome and sophisticated-looking, like the type of man that appears in ads for high-class cigarettes. She recalled the usual sequence of

events: a look, a smile, a greeting, a conversation, an appointment, a rendezvous, a . . . and she was ablaze with unspoken longings, being blown to
and fro by the winds of a feverish storm.

When she looked over in his direction a second time and didn't find him in
his seat, she felt a twinge of disappointment. But then to her surprise she found
him standing beside her, and saying something in a language she didn't understand. He pointed toward the empty seat at her table. She smiled. He sat
down. Then, looking at her amorously, he said something else. She realized by
this time that he was speaking in Italian, and that he was flirting with her. Her
fires blazed brighter. He reached out and gently touched her hair. As he spoke,
she understood and didn't understand, and nodded her head in agreement.

He paid the tab, then took her by the hand. She stood up with him, and he
stepped back to make room for her to go out ahead of him. It reminded her of
the sparrow that had been hovering around his lady bird in the church courtyard. He said something else, and again she nodded her head in agreement,
the bird's dance fanning the flames of her passion. She spread her wings and
tried to fly away to some far off place, but he placed his arm around her shoulder, lowering his wing over her trembling body.

He led her by the hand to a hotel not far from the coffee shop on quai du
Mont-Blanc, and she followed him in unquestioning surrender. When they
found themselves inside the hotel room, she gazed at him with longing and
curiosity. A young man radiant with well-being several years her junior, perhaps in his early twenties, he looked to her eyes like a bird with superb wings
that must be able to fly long, long distances. And when he touched her lips
lightly with his in a kiss of invitation, she took off and went soaring with him
to the land of delight and bliss. As they flew, she imagined the angel statue
gazing down on them with a look of dispassionate approval the way it had
done with the two love-smitten sparrows in the courtyard. Oh, how she'd
missed this sensation, caustic yet invigorating, this intercontinental flight,
soaring above tropical forests with the warm rain soaking their faces, and with
the mouths of volcanoes pouring forth their molten contents as they writhed
and rolled about, each of them clutching the other's hand for fear of not coming out alive. His voice would come to her across the ages, calling, "Amore
mio, Amore. . ." They may have been the only Italian words she understood.
Then off they took once more. "Amore mio!"

Then she felt that fierce cosmic outpouring that she hadn't known for so long, while multicolored fireworks exploded inside her head. And in what felt like a moment of truth she said to herself: This is the only reality there is! Everything else is a fake, a cheap imitation, or a product of self-deception. Everything, that is, except this feeling, the kind of feeling that digs its fingernails into my whole being. Everything except this singular moment that repeats itself without repeating itself. With her eyes closed she whispered, "Amore . . . amore . . . amore mio!" Khalil was always trying to convince her of everything else, anything else. But she knew there was no acceptable substitute for that one, irreplaceable moment.

She opened her eyes in search of her bird with the splendid plumage, ready for another flight around Planet Earth. But to her surprise, she found him getting dressed and counting out some money, which he left for her beside the bed. And then he was gone!

Cascades of ice-cold water washed over her, then came pouring out of her eyes. Shivering from cold and loneliness, she quickly put her clothes back on.

Ever so quietly, she picked up the Italian currency that the young man had left for her, folded it up, and placed it inside her bra the way her grandma had always done with her money. Then she rushed out of the room.

As she stepped into the street, a sudden wind blew up like a small storm. She felt like a confused, lost bird being tossed to and fro by a gale after losing its sense of direction and getting separated from its flock. She let the wind fill her sail and began walking whichever direction it happened to blow.

Another stranger approached her. Another handsome man. Another bird. She was still thirsty and hungry for that intercontinental flight that she'd been deprived of for five long years. So when her new suitor hovered about her and said something to her, she nodded in agreement, ablaze with the longing to fly. He drew her into an embrace right in front of Brunswick Park, and she responded with a passion that astounded even her. She rested her head on his shoulder as she accompanied him to his house or his hotel or his cave, and as they walked along she thought she could feel someone staring right through her. She looked in the direction of the park and cast a quick sweeping glance around her, but didn't see anyone she knew. So back she went to her suitor-bird, caressing his wings and dreaming of the rhythm of volcanoes and earthquakes.

She thought of Nadim, and decided to help him polish up his rusty wings. She couldn't blame him. After all, with a woman of ashes like Dunya, what husband wouldn't turn into a continent of ice? And with women as revolting as a land strewn with cadavers and spattered with blood—with women, that is, like Bahriya—who would be in the mood to imbibe in intoxicating delights?

◆   ◆   ◆

Khalil sat in the park for quite some time, planning the rest of his life. He'd decided not to give up. He thought of everyone he knew in all of Geneva and decided to knock on the door of everyone he thought of, even if he ended up getting thrown out. After all, that would still be better than slipping further into the slough of drug addiction with Saqr.

As he sat there, another group of Japanese tourists came by wanting their pictures taken, and women clad in bathing suits exposed their tender-skinned bodies to the delectable warmth of sunshine heretofore unknown in Geneva summers. (I'm not a tourist. And this warmth will just go on paining me. It feels like the warm breaths of my mother coming across the continents from far, far away and a time gone by.

In order to enjoy being a tourist I'd need a country to go home to, a place that I could leave knowing that I'd be coming back. But I don't know whether Israel will allow me to go back or not. All this is happening to me and to others in full sight of the "civilized" world, just as it did to the Palestinians. And nobody really gives a damn.

We've lost Lebanon, and we still haven't gotten Palestine back. But, why am I so pessimistic? After all, maybe the Arabs are planning to come to Lebanon's defense, since Lebanon was "Arab" the way they wanted it to be and it paid the price for being that way on behalf of all the Arabs together. Maybe they've got a secret plan in the works and are going to strike without warning. That's right. There's no way Israel can occupy an Arab capital like Beirut without having one hundred fifty million Arabs to contend with.

But what a pessimist I am. Would Israel actual commit such an outrage against my people? No. They wouldn't dare go into Beirut. In any case, oh heart of mine, enough of this searching for reasons to be miserable. Be positive. Come back to the land of reality. Look for a house. And for another job, one that will keep you in one piece until you can get back home. And enjoy the heaven on earth you happen to be walking around in.)

Khalil raised his head and looked again at the sidewalk and the lake as if he were seeing them for the first time. Waves of humanity continued coming along in steady succession, complete with beauty, health, wealth and pampered dogs.

And that woman laying her head on the shoulder of the handsome Western-looking fellow, she looked like Kafa. She lifted her head, laughed, and tossed her hair back. My God! he thought. It *is* Kafa! Kafa herself, with another stranger. For all he knew, she'd be slipping into some hotel room with him before long, the way she had the day he saw her with Nadim. Khalil looked at her as if he didn't recognize her. And he didn't feel a thing. Not jealousy, not anger, not regret. Nothing but a cold, dead sensation as if he'd been drugged and was rotting on the inside. After all, he figured, the entire world was betraying him, so why should it matter to him that she was doing it, too? He found himself muttering the words of Mutanabbi, "The despicable man is easily scorned, and wounds cause no pain to the dead." When Kafa looked over toward the park, he hid his face behind his newspaper. He didn't want her to know he'd seen her.

◆　◆　◆

Khalil woke up after a night's sleep full of nightmares. He'd seen Bahriya bleeding and sorcerer Watfan stabbing her with a knife of gold. Then he'd seen Dunya trying to come between them as his two boys screamed and held onto the hem of her dress.

Before opening his eyes, he reached out for a cigarette. As he lit it, he was surprised to see Kafa putting on her clothes and getting ready to go out. He didn't say anything. Then she rushed for the door as if she were running away from something and said, "I'm going to buy a dress for the tea party this afternoon. See you later."

Was she really going out just to buy a dress? Would she come straight back to the hotel, or would she go somewhere else? And what business was it of his, anyway? If she was "polluted" now, then so was he, so who was he to judge her? Had her body become public property? Everything was now fair game, a potential sacrifice on the altar of Saqr's cocaine (or "snow" as he liked to call it, or "forgetting powder," or "stardust," or any of the other names people had invented for that cursed poison that had begun destroying his stomach, his nerves and his nostrils despite the fact that he'd only taken it a few times).

The telephone rang. It was Saqr, high as a kite over the arrival of a certain famous Western actress to spend two nights with him in Switzerland. Khalil was the one who had contacted her to extend the invitation, not believing that she could possibly agree. In any case, Saqr wouldn't be needing him today or tomorrow. That didn't mean, of course, that "Secretary Khalil" was free to do as he liked. No, he'd have to stay glued to the telephone, since Saqr might change his mind at any moment. The actress's acceptance of the invitation quite astounded Khalil, since he hadn't believed that a rich, famous, gorgeous actress like her would do "that" for money. He'd felt embarrassed as he penned the letter to her a few days earlier. At the same time, though, he didn't dare challenge Saqr on the matter. And now here she was. So, everything in these evil days carried a price tag, it seemed. Everything. Even he—poor guy—had been bought off and had to stick close to the phone. (Would you enslave men whose mothers gave birth to them as free?)[26]

Khalil didn't voice what was on his mind. Instead he just said meekly, "Fine."

As he said it, it seemed as though his voice had started sounding like Nadim's. In any case, he jumped out of bed, threw on his clothes, and left the hotel without breakfast or a shave.

He bought the local newspapers *La Suisse* and *Geneva Tribune*, then betook himself to the Mediterranean Restaurant across the street from Cornavin Station. First he read the Lebanon news, which caused a conflagration to break out on top of the Nescafé *au lait* he'd been gulping down and made the little boy living inside him cry. From there he went straight to the classified ads page to look at houses for sale or rent.

There were ads directed toward the wealthy for the sale of deluxe flats for foreigners in neighborhoods where noncitizens were allowed to own real estate. Skipping those, he went on to look for something more modest, such as furnished flats in the center of Geneva. He was determined not to pay any more fees to that rich kids' boarding school. He wasn't going to go on abandoning his boys to a life of spoiled orphans. Instead, they'd all live together under one roof. He'd try to enroll them in one of the official schools in

---

26. This is a quotation from Caliph Umar Ibn Al-Khattab (d. 23 A.H.). Tradition has it that during the time when Amr Ibn al-'As was governor of Egypt, his son participated in a horse race with a certain Bedouin man, who came in first. Taking this defeat as an affront to his dignity, the governor's son took out a whip and delivered a lashing to the Bedouin. The Bedouin, angered at this violation of his rights, betook himself to the caliph, Umar Ibn al-Khattab in Mecca, complaining of the treatment to which he had been subjected by the governor's son. The caliph thereafter invited Amr Ibn al-'As, his son, and the Bedouin to honor him with a visit during the following pilgrimage season, which they did. After the parties concerned had presented their accounts of the incident, the caliph spoke to the governor's son in the Bedouin's defense, challenging him with the question quoted in the text.

Geneva, which Amir had told him were free of charge yet better than the private schools. And Kafa would go back to being a mother and housewife rather than continue on her way toward whoredom. He put checks beside the telephone numbers for the houses he considered reasonable and headed for the central post office. Then he stepped inside a booth for local calls and started trying his luck: This one's for rent. No answer. This one answers, but they say it's been rented out. Many of them simply got rid of him because his accent in French made it clear that he was a foreigner. Irritated, he left the booth and went for a walk down Michel Rosier Street. Then he came back to the telephone for another try, only to be rebuffed, or to get no answer. So he went out for another walk, came back, was rebuffed again, went out for another walk, came back, got no response, and so on for most of his day of nightmares. Then at last, a certain landlady agreed to make an appointment with him at 513 Delice Street.

◆   ◆   ◆

He forced Kafa to go with him that afternoon.

The taxi dropped them off in front of 513 Delice Street, which was located in a neighborhood quite some distance away from the tourist districts which Kafa liked to haunt.

Bewildered, she asked him, "What's brought us all the way out here? What kind of surprise have you got for me?"

As they got out he told her, "We're going to rent a furnished flat here."

"Here? In this wretched neighborhood? As if we weren't in Geneva?"

Even so, she acquiesced and came along with him without further argument, though she shot him a derisive look in the process.

They were received by a Madame Vom Halerhon, who arrived at the door panting like someone who doesn't have time enough even to breathe. She didn't invite them to sit down, but instead spent all her time answering the telephone, which kept ringing so much it hardly gave them a chance to say a word. It was as if everyone in the city wanted the flat. As she busily made appointments, Khalil was reminded of what he'd heard about the housing crisis in Geneva. Then at last she picked up her keys and they followed her into an ancient-looking elevator to go up to the flat, which was on the top floor. To Kafa the flat was a miserable, dank, mildewed place like their house in Beirut.

"Do you have children?" she asked them.

"Two boys, but they're in boarding school."

Then Madame Vom Halerhon announced that she wanted three months' rent in advance, and that she was willing to rent it to them simply because they happened to have come. She'd inherited a number of flats in various capital cities, and whenever another of her spinster aunts died, she inherited another estate, and she no longer had enough time even to take care of burial ceremonies or the proper transfer of her aunts' fortunes. Khalil agreed to her conditions, anxious to get his children out of the school and to get himself out from under the burden of working for Saqr and paying the exorbitant hotel bills, which were bound to turn him into a slave to the Ghanamali clan and Raghid Zahran until the end of time. Ignoring the look of contempt and refusal in his wife's eyes, he said he'd rent the flat immediately, determined to settle the matter without delay.

They went back down to Madame Vom Halerhom's flat, and she rushed off to get the papers to be signed. Then she got busy answering the telephone again. Another would-be renter was calling, and she informed him that the flat had just been rented out just as Khalil had been told so many times that same morning. Hearing what she'd just said made him all the more determined to hold onto this house.

"It's uninhabitable!" Said Kafa. "We couldn't possibly live here!"

"It's also impossible to go on working for Saqr or Raghid Zahran. We've got no choice but to find some modest place to make a start from."

The landlady came back with the papers and asked Khalil for his work permit and residence card.

"I don't have them yet," he replied. "I should be getting them in about another week."

"Sorry," she said, "it's against the law to rent a flat to someone who doesn't have these documents."

"But where's a person to go until he can arrange a suitable job?"

"To a hotel, of course! Or to the so-called service apartments, which are similar to hotels."

Kafa sighed with vindictive glee like someone who's just emerged from a nightmare. Khalil sighed, too, his heart bloodied like a mouse that's just been caught in the sharp teeth of a trap.

Actually, he'd known all along that he'd probably find himself in this predicament. But he'd tried, anyway. He hadn't known what else to do. He was struggling against his fate, but in vain. So while Kafa spent her time surrendering to her destiny, enjoying it to the hilt, he was feeling defeated and miserable. But he wouldn't . . .

He'd try to look for another job, for a job that wasn't degrading. He'd try to start all over again, as if he'd never met Nadim or worked for Saqr, and as though Kafa had never grown accustomed to the hedonistic pleasures of wealth that she'd missed out on ever since she left her family, and which she'd regained since meeting up with the Zahran and Ghafir clans.

He'd go searching. The important thing was for Saqr to go on being too distracted by Gina Sofia, that famous actress, to notice what he was up to.

He needed some time to catch his breath. To start with, he'd seek refuge again with Amir and anyone else he knew in Geneva: Najib, the bank director who used to frequent his bookshop before he was transferred to the bank's Geneva branch, and his college friend Badi', who was working for the United Nations now.

He'd knock on all the other doors he could think of before he let Saqr treat him to another handful of snow that would do nothing but rob him of his senses, or what remained of them. He'd start the next morning. And he'd call both men the minute he got back to the hotel.

❖   ❖   ❖

The sky was threatening to break forth with a hot summer rain of the sort that Geneva wasn't accustomed to. Kafa was looking stunning in her translucent raincoat and her super-elegant attire, so much so she could have passed as a millionaire's wife.

The bank director, Mr. Najib, welcomed them with a big smile, inviting them to sit down and ordering them coffee. He offered Khalil a cigarette, then confessed that he remembered his face, but couldn't recall exactly where they had met.

"In the bookshop. I was the owner of the Liberty Bookshop. At present, though, I'm homeless."

Not appearing to be very pleased with this piece of information, Mr. Najib cropped off the end of his cigar with the malice of someone cutting off the head of an enemy. He'd invited them to sit down, but that was the end of it. He'd always taken care to stay away from people like Khalil—destitute folks who'd had to leave home for various reasons, and who were always coming to him for help. Their numbers had increased dramatically this summer since the

Israeli invasion of Lebanon. The man's wife had misled him with her stylish clothes and attractive appearance. Khalil had looked to him at first like one of the many formerly poor folks who'd gotten rich during the war years. These were the types whose names would appear in the press as leaders of revolutionary organizations, and who would turn up later asking him to open secret personal accounts for them where they could deposit their massive fortunes. However, Khalil's obvious lack of confidence made him nervous. Homeless? Fine. But what he wanted to know was whether this was a rich homeless person or a poor one.

"Would you like to deposit your savings with us?"

"Well, sir, your kind reception encourages me to tell you about our situation. The fact is, I have no savings. At present I'm looking for a job so that I can obtain residency here, rent a flat, and bring my children home from the boarding school where they've been living."

His voice trembling, Khalil felt humiliation and anger rising from somewhere deep inside him. Here he was abasing himself, baring his soul to someone who obviously wasn't the man he had known before.

As for Mr. Najib, the expression on his face changed without warning. He looked at the two of them as if he'd never seen them before, then turned away as if they weren't even there. Then he remembered an important engagement that had slipped his mind. He didn't help Kafa on with her coat, as protocol would require him to, even though he'd remembered to help her take it off when she walked in the door looking like a woman of means. Instead, he nearly threw it in her face. Both Khalil and Kafa felt as though he were sweeping them out of his office like so much dirt.

"We'll discuss your situation at a later date. I'd forgotten that I have a board meeting now. Call my secretary for an appointment."

Her voice quivering with indignation, Kafa said to him, "We're in no hurry. My husband works at present as the secretary to Ghanamali's son. He got the job through a recommendation from Raghid Zahran."

Startled, Mr. Najib paused in front of the door and said, "Ghanamali? Zahran? Well, what's the problem, then? There must have been some misunderstanding. Come, have a seat again! I can surely spare a few minutes!"

Kafa turned to look for Khalil. But he was already standing in front of the elevator, his body trembling from the humiliating blow he'd received as if a whip had come down on his back. So, this was the way it felt to be a foreigner.

Kafa wasn't surprised when he began singing, "My country, my country, whose youth shall never fade. . ." But the other people on the elevator were slightly taken aback!

◆   ◆   ◆

Mr. Badi' welcomed Khalil warmly when he called. In fact, he told him how much he'd missed him and insisted on inviting him and his wife for lunch.

Khalil tried to persuade him to let him make a short visit to his office to discuss a private matter with him. He'd decided to try a more direct approach this time and to go alone in the hope that even if he was thrown out again, he wouldn't have to face the same sort of humiliation he'd been exposed to half an hour earlier. However, insisting on rolling out the red carpet, Badi' said he'd come by for them at the hotel at around noon.

(So then, bonds of friendship between people haven't died after all. That bank director wouldn't give me the time of day, but Badi' welcomes me with open arms. That's life, I guess. There really are people who take an interest in you simply because you're a human being, not because of what they can use you for.)

A classy car, a pale-looking wife, and a fair-sized potbelly that added to the well-to-do look Badi' had taken on in Geneva.

Khalil sat beside Badi' in the front seat, while his wife Nada sat beside Kafa in the back—an arrangement contrary to European customs, which pleased Khalil. He was determined to be straight with Badi' and speak to him "man to man" before he got the wrong impression from their polished appearance and the posh hotel where they were staying.

The ladies began the conversation—with complaints, of course. Kafa complained about how awful life in Beirut was, and Nada complained about life in Geneva! And why? Because, as she put it, "the ions in Geneva are negative, and they cause headaches and disease. It's been documented in the scientific literature." Nada then waxed eloquent on the subject, listing the titles of the books that set forth the disadvantages of living in Geneva, which to Kafa was still heaven on earth. Nada really did look sick and miserable, though. She'd broken out in a cold sweat, and she looked out at the gorgeous scenery on either side of the road with utter distaste.

Thinking to change the tone of the conversation, Khalil said, "Perhaps you miss Beirut."

"I hate both Geneva and Beirut. I've asked my husband if we could move anywhere else in the whole world besides here . . . or there."

"We own a lovely house here, and the children are in a boarding school. But Nada hates Geneva and is determined to leave it. She wants me to apply for a transfer."

"Any place in the world would be better than this hellhole."

Kafa was nonplussed, and Khalil was at a loss as to how to continue the conversation. There was genuine grief in Nada's voice, and her complaints about life in Geneva didn't let up for a moment. She seemed really to have a problem. And here was Khalil, bringing his problem to his "settled" friends in Geneva.

"We're on our way to Montreux now," explained Badi'. "We'll pass through Lausanne, then have lunch either in Montreux or Vevey. All these towns are in incredibly beautiful areas around Lac Léman—like dream worlds."

"It's time for the news broadcast," replied Khalil. "Would you mind if we listened to it?"

"Actually, we've decided to boycott the Beirut news."

"Can that be done?"

"Our families are in Tripoli, not in Beirut. And the people of Beirut deserve what they're getting. They brought it on themselves."

Too upset to hold his tongue, Khalil said, "Regardless of the mistakes that have been made by some of the resistance leaders in Lebanon, we can't just gloat over their troubles now or wash our hands of responsibility for what's going on."

"You, a southerner, talk this way? Your own family members are the ones who've suffered all this time from the growing Palestinian presence in Lebanon. And they're the ones who saw the atrocities in Sidon about two months back, just weeks before the Israeli occupation!"

"Perhaps so. But that will never make us welcome Israel as some sort of savior. Rejection of the offenses committed by some—not all—Palestinians doesn't justify support for Israel. And never once did we ask Israel for a helping hand against the Palestinian Authority. Southern Lebanon will remain just that—southern Lebanon. It will never turn into North Galilee, as Israel would like it to."

Kafa sighed audibly.

Khalil went on, "The people of south Lebanon know how to distinguish between their enemies and their friends. And their rejection of whatever human rights violations have been committed by Palestinian fighters will never blind them to who their real enemy is."

(That's my husband for you! Once he starts in on politics, you can't shut him up. Perhaps he's forgotten why we're here.)

Badi' said, "I'm fed up with everything that's going on. And I'll never go back to Lebanon. Whether on the pretext of 'Westernizing' it or 'Arabizing' it, it's been destroyed, and that's that. So I've made a promise to myself not to listen to the news. Lebanon's going to see a hundred-year war. As for me, I've only got a few years to live on this planet, and I intend to enjoy them."

Then Nada said unexpectedly, "All you care about is your own enjoyment. You don't even think about your children or your family."

Khalil was taken aback by her hostile tone of voice. And Kafa, who'd learned in the Baytmouni household always to hide family frictions when in the presence of others, didn't know what to make of it. There then ensued a cryptic conversation between Nada and Badi', with Nada ladling out accusations and Badi' humoring her in an attempt to dodge her wrath until Kafa almost envied Nada for having such a meek husband.

At last they reached Montreux, and Khalil still hadn't had a chance to explain his problem. When they'd been seated around a table overlooking Lac Léman with its sparkling blue waters, Khalil decided it was time to broach the subject.

"We're looking for a house," he began.

"Don't try," interrupted Nada. "Houses are hard to come by in Geneva."

"Besides," Badi' added, "you'll need residency and a work permit before anybody will agree to rent to you. And these things are quite problematic here."

Of course, this was exactly what Khalil had wanted to ask of Badi'. He needed a residency card, that is, a respectable job. And he planned to ask him for one straight out, and right now.

But then along came the waiter and spoiled his chance.

Fifteen more minutes went by while Badi' and Nada argued over what kind of wine they wanted, with Nada commenting on Badi's bad taste in this department. When it came to choosing what kind of fish to order, Nada said she liked trout while Badi' preferred sole. When at long last they'd solved the food predicament and the time had come for him to lay out his own dilemma, Nada said suddenly, "Our problem is that we can't stand Geneva anymore. My psychiatrist has advised me to leave the city. But Badi' insists on staying, and he's destroying me in the process."

"Excuse me," said Badi', "I'll be back in just a moment."

Then he hurriedly withdrew before Nada could object.

Khalil gazed out at the lovely lake and the white skiffs that seemed to sprout forth from the water's surface, with green mountains framing the fabulous scene along the horizon. But as he remembered lovely Qar'oun Lake in his homeland and the Litani River, which Israel insisted on swallowing up, he was overcome with a deep sadness.

"You live in paradise," Kafa said to Nada. "There's nothing I'd love more than to own a home here in Geneva. And I'd stay here forever."

"Pardon me," said Nada tensely. "Badi' is late getting back. I'm going to check on him."

And off she went.

Khalil and Kafa exchanged puzzled looks, but neither of them said a word. Before long Nada came back, looking as though all the blood had drained out of her face, her brow moist with cold sweat.

"I didn't find him. He isn't there," she said, sounding like someone who's a bit touched in the head.

"Who?"

"Badi'."

"What's wrong with him?"

"I didn't find him in the phone booth."

"Maybe he's in the bathroom. We aren't in Beirut, so you don't have to worry about him being kidnapped!"

Nada didn't laugh at the joke.

Speaking to Khalil, she said, "Would you please go check on him in the men's room?"

Not knowing quite what to make of her odd request, he got up and left the table.

Meanwhile, Kafa began devouring the delectable food the waiter had brought.

When Khalil got back he said matter-of-factly, "I didn't find him in the men's room. Maybe he went to buy some cigarettes."

Nada seemed agitated and angry. She urged Khalil to eat his food, which he did. He felt as though something he didn't understand was going on around him, that there was an unspoken anxiety and instability. And this was the "stable" friend he'd sought out for help in calming his own storms!

Then suddenly, looking at her Cartier sports watch, Nada said, "It's been twenty minutes and he's still not back."

Khalil didn't understand why she was counting the minutes. As for Kafa, she'd withdrawn into her usual indifference to others and their problems.

Then, getting up hurriedly, Nada announced, "We've got to go look for him."

So, abandoning his plate of mouth-watering food with a heavy heart, Khalil got up and went with her. They left the restaurant and Nada walked toward the luxurious Grand Hotel on the other side of the street. Then suddenly the missing person appeared and said to Khalil apologetically, "Sorry. I went to get my cigarettes."

"You're lying. You were coming from the hotel, not from the car."

"There weren't any cigarettes left in the car, so I went into the hotel to buy some more."

"You're lying. You're wrecking my life with your lies. You went to call her on the telephone!"

"Be quiet, will you? We've got guests. I invited them for your sake, to lighten up the atmosphere. I'm doing the impossible to please you."

"I will not be quiet! I'll expose you in front of them, and in front of the whole world!"

Thereupon Nada burst into tears right in the middle of the street. Badi' walked with her to the car, cursing women in general and her in particular. Khalil stood dazed in the middle of the sidewalk, like someone who's just been dropped into the middle of a play in which he doesn't know his part.

So he topped off his confusion with a cigarette. Meanwhile, Badi' came back to apologize again, then headed back toward the restaurant to pay the bill and bring Kafa with him.

When they were all in the car again, his host made an attempt to gloss over what had just happened, saying, "We'll continue on our way now to Vevey. The road that leads there is quite scenic."

Meanwhile, Nada burst into tears again. "I want to go home," she announced. "You went and called her. I know you did!"

"Well, Nada," he replied, "You're the one who went barging into her workplace, hit her, and caused her a big scandal. And now you want me not to ask how she is!"

"You promised not to talk to her anymore."

"I promised you that before you went to where she works and hit her and caused her and me a scandal."

"Well, she deserves it. Why is she stealing my husband from me?"

"She isn't stealing me. We're friends, nothing more."

"That's what I used to believe, until the detective brought me a schedule of the times you'd gone to visit her."

Looking over at Khalil in a plea for sympathy, he said, "Imagine. She hired a private eye to follow me around, and she spent a fortune to do it."

"I spent it out of my own money. And in any case, I discovered that you were cheating on me all by myself. I figured it out by intuition."

At this point the row heated up to a fever's pitch, and Badi' decided to enlist Khalil and Kafa as arbiters. He and Nada would take them home with them, and each of them would tell the story from his or her point of view!

This was just what he needed!

One hour, two hours, three hours in a beautiful house, with Nada talking and weeping and Badi' defending himself and talking and weeping, and Kafa gazing at the beautiful place with a lump of envy in her throat, and Khalil reeling with amazement at the revelations they'd just heard.

When Badi' offered to give them a ride back to the hotel rather than their taking a taxi, Khalil thought to himself: Here's my chance at last! After working for him all day as a marriage counselor, I can tell him about my situation when we're in the car. However, Nada insisted on accompanying her husband, most likely to keep him from passing by to see her rival as he was wont to do whenever he found an excuse to leave the house. Consequently, they went on with their argument all the way to the hotel. As they parted, Khalil had a bitter taste in his mouth, bitter like the degradation of life in exile. The minute he got back, he rushed over to the television to catch the latest news broadcast from home. Home was still going up in flames, and the Arabs still hadn't intervened. As his country slowly turned to ashes, everyone else was carrying on with his own battles—be they marital, political, or ideological—and his indifference to the plights of others. Before he went to sleep, he sang softly, "My country, my country, my country, to thee belong my spirit and my heart. . ."

Pretending not to hear him, Kafa shut her eyes and conjured the image of the handsome Italian, while his words, "Amore mio!" escorted her to the land of clandestine delights.

Everything about Khalil's world was gloomy, in her opinion. He reminded her of the armed vigilantes back home, whom she hated one and all and whom she wished nothing but ill. Once more she conjured the image of her Italian man, immersing herself in the warmth of his voice as her memory brought it back to her consciousness: Amore . . . Amore mio! And she decided once again: There's no reality in this entire universe except for physical love!

◆   ◆   ◆

"When should the Night of the First Billion be? Lilly is insisting that we set a date so that she can send out invitations and prepare for the banquet."

Sorcerer Watfan answered uncertainly, "I don't know what's been happening to the *mandal.* Whenever I try to do the calculations for 28 September or any other day in that month, some magical power throws water and oil in my face. You want it to be the night of 28 September. But the stars are against it."

"What do the lords say?"

"I've made my calculations according to the stars and the magic charts. I specified the name of the last Arab month on the basis of the new moon, then I took its letter. The day 28 September has the letter *ghayn* on an alphabetical foundation. Then I determined the station of the moon, and I took its letter. Then I went back to the mother's letter, that is, the first initial of your deceased mother, to the number of letters in your name."

"Fine, sir, I believe you. You can spare me the details. But just tell me, when?"

"As soon as possible."

"Why?"

"I don't know. This has never happened to me before. Do you remember the day Ahmad Ghanamali, Sakhr's younger brother, asked me whether next year would bring a change in the head of state?"

"Yes, I do."

"Well, when he asked the question, it was the twenty-fourth of Shawwal, and the moon at that time was at the Rasha station. And what we had to know was whether the Supreme Book for Jupiter and Saturn carried such a change. You'll recall that we took the letter for the twenty-fourth day, and it turned out to be *khâ.* The letter for the station according to the chart was *ghayn,* and the fortune letter was *bâ*, which falls within the first third of the period of the sign of Leo. The letter for the name was *mîm* from Ahmad, because the question was asked during the final third of Shawwal, where the four mothers were in the following order: *khâ, ghayn, bâ, mîm*. By referring back to the chart the answer was: The head of state of a given land will be changed, the change will be more dramatic than in other countries, and destruction is coming to said country without doubt. The answer consists of fifty-six letters, and once this answer becomes clear, we need to answer the second question, namely: Is the answer which was obtained with regard to this matter a predetermined certainty, or does it depend on other events?"

"I beg of you, sir. . . . You're the astrologer, not I. Just tell me when . . ."

"I was trying to explain it to you. I don't know what's going on. Whenever I try delaying the date for the celebration till the fall, I get a strange sort of warning."

"What does the warning say?"

"It says that the person holding the celebration won't attend."

"What does that mean?"

"Maybe you're destined to travel somewhere. There's no escaping one's destiny."

"Travel? I'm not planning to go anywhere."

"I don't know. But all my calculations indicate that haste is in order, Pasha."

"Well, they say that haste makes waste. That's always been my motto. And it's also my motto now with regard to beginning to amass my second billion before celebrating the first one."

"May God bless you in your honest gain, and strengthen you to do good."

"Thank you, sir. Things shall be as you have advised. We'll celebrate the Night of the First Billion as soon as the preparations can be completed."

◆ ◆ ◆

In vain Dunya tried to drive Bahriya's image out of her mind. In vain she tried to leave her and go fleeing back to the faraway, untamed lands of slumber. Or do you suppose it was just the unusual heat that was keeping her awake?

She tossed and turned, tormented and fitful.

Since Bahriya's arrival, she hadn't gotten even a bad night's sleep, still less a good one. (Every night the worries and fears come rushing into my head, then they shatter like a huge crystal goblet that someone has smashed in the middle of my skull.)

Bahriya. She thought of her descending the staircase, so bloodied it was as if her pores were bleeding and her body covered with wounds. She'd smelled of fire as she crossed the room. Not a single newspaper had written about the horrific event: about the young woman whose body had been painted with the blood of camels and bats, who'd been tortured in the name of kindness, whose freedom had been denied under the pretext of providing her with care and protection, and who'd been brought to Geneva to be exploited by a man who claimed to be her relative. And it was that damned husband of hers, Nadim, who was responsible for it all. Besides which, everyone in attendance that night belonged to Raghid's mafia, which meant that not one of them would dare speak a word of truth in a voice louder than a whisper. (Isn't what's going on here a shorthand of what's happening in Beirut right now, where most events are enveloped in either silence or heartless gossip? And the rare folks for whom the truth breaks through the silence, aren't they like me: oppressed, afraid, and full of remorse?)

She heard a voice calling to her. It was her painting. This ghostly whisper had become quite familiar to her by now. From the time she came face to face with Bahriya's wounds, her painting hadn't allowed her a single night's sleep. Every night she called out to her, complaining of her condition, reproaching her for what she'd done to both of them, and calling her to account for the way she had destroyed the young woman she'd once been, then broken the bond she'd once had with her children. Her daughter was counting the days until she could finish school, master Arabic, and go back to Lebanon. And her son . . . she'd lost him in some sense. He'd become a stranger to her.

"Dunya, are you asleep?" whispered the tormenting voice again.

She put her fingers in her ears, but the voice only grew louder.

"Dunya! Are you drunk and drowsy as usual?"

(Yes. I'm drunk as usual. But I'm not asleep. When I followed Bahriya out to the garden and persuaded her to come back into the mansion with me through the other entrance, she looked into my face. Her lower lip trembled as if she were about to cry, or as if she wanted to say something. And her eyes had a caustic, searching quality that went straight through me. Somewhere deep inside her I saw a stern, irresistible force that seemed to reproach me for I'm not sure what. Even so, an overwhelming tenderness for her welled up from deep inside me, as if the cruel blow she'd just dealt me released wellsprings of emotion that had been buried and forgotten beneath the rubble of my busy life. I found myself saying to Nasim, "This isn't fair. What's happening to this girl is wrong. And all of us are implicated in it." And I haven't had one moment of peace since.)

Once again the voice called out, "Dunya! Are you still fast asleep?"

She got up and went into the living room, where she turned on a wall lamp. She looked at her painting, but found no one inside it. Instead, it had turned into nothing but an empty frame. She sat down on the chair across from it, too stunned by the surprise to think straight. When she looked up again, she found the girl who had once graced the painting seated in the chair across from her. She was lovely, slender, vivacious. And she'd wiped the tear off her cheek.

It pained Dunya to see herself as she'd been years before, sitting right in front of her, with her bouncy youth, her undyed hair, her direct way of looking at others without a trace of flattery or dishonesty, her slender frame, and her special way of placing her forefinger and her thumb on her chin whenever she was about to mock something ridiculous or make an important decision.

Speaking to Dunya again, she said, "How long are you going to go on trying to avoid making a decision?"

"I'm not doing anything of the sort. It's just that I'm helpless!"

"Why!"

"I don't know."

"I'll tell you why, then."

"Don't say another word to me. I know everything that can possibly be said to a woman like me. So just save your breath, and save mine too. I'm doing all I can. And that's all I can tell you."

"Fine. But if you don't do anything, I'm going to leave this painting and never come back. And after that you won't find me when you need me most. I'll abandon you and leave you all on your own, and there won't be a thing you can do about it. And that's all I can tell *you*."

The painting girl then reached up and turned off the lamp, leaving Dunya awash in darkness. Then she began falling down a flight of unlit steps. She kept falling and falling, trying to scream for help, but helpless to get any sound to come out of her mouth. It was as if she'd lost her voice just the way Bahriya had lost hers.

After falling for what seemed like ages, she felt a hand shaking her. Opening her eyes, she found the maid waking her up. The maid eyed Dunya with derision for sleeping in the living room chair with a half-empty bottle of booze beside her.

"Go back to your room, ma'am," she said collusively, "before somebody wakes up and finds you here."

She got up with a migraine headache about to split her head in two. These migraines were unbearable. She'd have to go see a doctor. Every day she said the same thing to herself. Then she would swallow several aspirins and call Picasso to take him to his hairdresser. From there they would head for the health club where she would fling her flaccid body onto various and sundry massage machines, distracting herself from examining her life by reducing the size of her derriere.

No sooner had she gone into the bathroom than she heard the sound of things breaking. She buried her head under the stream of cold water, with every crash adding to her pain. She was sure no one else was up yet since it was still only sunrise, which meant that it wasn't time for anybody to be smashing things. But the sounds kept growing louder and louder, and she decided they must be coming from her son's bedroom. So, ever so quietly, she tiptoed to his door and opened it. After all, she could be imagining things, in which case she might be scolded for waking him up.

But she hadn't been imagining things. When she opened the door, she was astonished to find her son Bahir demolishing his special collection of robots, which for so long he'd considered almost family.

He didn't see her.

And for the first time she noticed that he'd grown taller than she was. It was as if he'd grown up while she was looking the other way. Besides which, he wore punk clothes complete with bracelets made of black leather and silver nails, and he had a wild, hysterical-looking, orange and blue hairdo to match. When she called out his name, he acted as though he didn't recognize her. His only reply was to light a joint of marijuana, which he sat puffing away on right in front of her as if he didn't see her. When she sat down across from him, he put his feet up in her face so that all she could see were the nails that protruded from the bottoms of his punk shoes.

When she looked into his face, she discovered that it was covered with bluish bruises and a still-bleeding wound near his eye. She clapped her hand over her mouth and fled to her room in tears. (My God! What have I done to myself and my family? Did I get Bahir away from Beirut just so he could be killed here in some punk war that's even more meaningless than the one going on at home? What have I done to him and his sister? What have I done to myself?)

◆   ◆   ◆

When Amir opened the door and saw her, Dunya was amazed to find that he didn't seem surprised to see her.

"Hi, Dunya," he said matter-of-factly, as though he'd just seen her the day before.

Embarrassed, she replied, "You remember me! It's as if you've been expecting me."

"I was sure you'd come around. Only you're a bit late—like around fifteen years late!"

They both laughed. He hadn't lost his captivating sense of humor. A feeling of warm, comforting familiarity swept over her, the way one feels upon returning to a house he lived in during a happy time of his life.

Then he added, "When you called and asked for my address so that you could visit me some day, I knew you'd be coming right away. After all, I knew you already had my address, and that you'd passed by on numerous occasions without coming in. That's why I kicked out all my visitors and put on my best face for you. I even took off my glasses and put on a smile!"

More laughter.

"Has it been fifteen years?" she asked. "No. We met up a month ago—or was it years ago? At Raghid's house."

"But that night you weren't yourself, and neither was I."

"He proposed that you put out a magazine at his expense, and you refused."

"I already knew enough to make me hate him. But life had civilized me, so to speak, so I went to hear what he had to say. It's better for a person to know what's going on around him even if he has no intention of being a part of it."

"Then you withdrew in a hurry the minute we arrived."

"He'd taken me on a tour of the mansion. He wanted me to see the golden pool of wanton consumption, and the statue. He was trying to defeat and humiliate me. So he insisted that I read my deceased father's signature on the base of the statue, and the date he'd completed it."

"But why did you get angry? I don't remember you as being a Nasser fan."

"I may have my gripes against the undemocratic practices of his government and the extent to which he was implicated in them. But whatever evil we might speak about him, he remains a symbol of Arab unity and struggle for political reform. He's a hell of a lot more honorable than Raghid Zahran and his like, who brag of their intelligence and criticize him for his humanity. Pardon me. I realize your husband works for him, so maybe . . ."

"Don't apologize. With people like Raghid, it's hard to know whether you love them or hate them even if you happen to be sharing the same bed!"

"You haven't changed much. You still call a spade a spade."

"I'm not happy about it."

"Something else hurt me about that encounter also, namely, that he didn't humiliate me as a supporter of Arab unity, but as a human being. He treats a statue done by my father as though it were some woman he's taken as a prisoner of war. As if he were trying to desecrate the creativity of my father, my ancestors, artists I love—you included—and my homeland all at once. Then he made fun of my father's naming me Prince, since he was a poor man, and so am I."

"I was a nationalist artist. But unfortunately, I succumbed under pressure."

"Why did you stop painting? We stood by you, but then you turned your back on us, on your art, and on yourself."

"Please, don't say that. It hurts me."

"But this is why you came. You came for me to refresh your memory, for me to tell you that you were real, that you were genuine, and that you made a mistake when you bartered away your creativity for gold."

"Once upon a time . . ."

"I'll never forget your first exhibit, and the opening night. I'll never forget the looks on the faces of those prudish critics as they went walking around among your paintings. All they could see was the nude men you'd drawn. All they could see was male nudity depicted by a woman without even the benefit of a fig leaf."

"I was bold."

"They were stupefied. They scourged you in their critiques. They scalped you and treated your brain with various medicaments and what not, American Indian style. When they figured they'd shrunk your head sufficiently, they hung it on the doors of the conservative newspapers. Then they tied you up with horses' tails and went dragging you through the city's clubs and coffee shops to make you a public example. What! A woman who draws nude men? That's not allowed!"

"And you came along and defended me. You stood by me and made clear to them that I paint to convey the spirit, not physical nudity. The way Michelangelo did when he depicted the spirit of indomitable youth in his statue of David, copies of which are scattered throughout the courtyards of Florence while the original is preserved behind bulletproof glass in the Florence museum. You asked them if they were demanding that we distribute swimsuits to cover the bodies of all the nude statues in cities that have an appreciation for art. You asked them if they were planning to build a factory to make underwear for all the statues and paintings in Rome, Moscow, Paris, and London, not to mention museums and streets throughout the rest of the world."

"I was asking them to judge you as a human being who paints, not as a female who had done a painting of a male. They were accustomed to having men draw naked women, something that's been done throughout history. But they'd never thought of the other possibility, that is, the idea of a woman doing the same thing of men. So when you did it, they went crazy. They took no account of your art as such, either negatively or positively. The mere fact that you, a woman, would dare do a painting of a nude man, they considered an attack on their rights. They didn't notice that you were simply exercising a common right, or, at the very least, committing an error common to both men and women."

"Those were sweet times."

"That's what you say now. Have you forgotten how much they frightened you? Isn't it on account of them that you fled into marriage? That's when I suspect."

"Perhaps. I don't remember anymore."

"Do you do any painting now?"

"A few things, the types of things that my present society approves of. I do decorations for the stained glass windows of the winter flower garden: a swan here, a carnation there. A duck here, a pond there."

"And what else?"

"Sometimes I draw pictures on silk pillows for the rooms in our house . . . insipid decorative designs that make the guests happy."

"Damn! You use to be on fire with rebellion!"

"I draw designs for needlepoint projects, then I fill them in color by color—pictures of happy families going out on a hunt, or beside the Christmas tree."

"Damn! You used to be a real artist . . ."

She burst into tears. He went over to her, kissed her on the forehead and took her gently in his arms. Then suddenly he let her go, saying, "I'm going to leave you alone now. Try to cry a little, and think a lot. I'm going out to buy some newspapers, and then I'll be back."

"It's too late."

"Certainly not. Otherwise you wouldn't be here."

"It's too late."

"It could be that you're making your first true beginning."

"It's too late. I've been polluted."

"We're all polluted. No one would dare condemn you."

"You haven't gotten your hands dirty."

"I've defiled myself with hatred and jealousy."

"Over Layla?"

"Yes."

"The fool. She wants to switch places with me. Or rather, let's say she wants to switch places with my husband."

"That's right," Amir agreed, "and that's the main problem."

"I've tried to get her to talk about it."

"And what did she say?"

"She just got angry. She refused. And then she started avoiding me."

"She got angry? There's hope, then."

"No, there isn't," Dunya insisted. "Once a person has swum in that golden pool, she'll never be the same again."

"Yes, there is, Dunya!"

"You're known for your optimism. But there's no hope either for me or for her. We've been immersed in the polluted water. We've gone swimming in the pool of gold. And there's no healing for us."

Just then someone knocked on the door, and in walked Nasim, looking as though he'd lost his senses.

Not noticing Dunya, he shouted, "Please, Amir! Raghid and that charlatan, Watfan, they're going to kill Bahriya!"

Then he turned and saw Dunya.

"Oh, pardon me!" he said, striking his head with his hand. "I didn't know you had company."

"Don't worry. She won't say a word."

"But . . ."

"Whatever it is you saw, whatever it is that's happened, she's one of us. And she isn't going anywhere."

"What's the story, Nasim?" Dunya interjected. "I swear myself to secrecy."

Certain that he could never fully trust a woman of Dunya's ilk, he said, "I tell you what, Ma'am. I'll keep my mouth shut if you'll do the same. I won't tell anybody I saw you here if you won't say anything about this."

"It's a deal. Go ahead and put it in those terms if that makes you feel better. Now, what happened?"

"Bahriya. . . . The sorcerer wants to have her head shaved so that he can cover it with dogs' dung and camels' eyes and all the rest of those revolting medicines of his so as to treat her for madness. Those two are going to drive her mad for sure this way!"

"It's my damned fault. I'm the one who called Nadim's attention to her picture in that Beirut newspaper. I was taken by the similarity between her name and Raghid Zahran's. And it's Nadim's fault for deciding to bring her here."

"Why did he do that?" asked Nasim. "I still can't figure it out. Is she really Zahran's relative?"

"My husband wanted to polish up Raghid's image in the press: Look at the wealthy altruist who lends a helping hand to a tragedy-stricken Lebanese girl! etcetera, etcetera. People just love moving, melodramatic situations like this. No one, of course, asked him what role he might have played in what befell her. That is, no one asked whether the bomb that destroyed her house and killed her family was among the weapons that he sells to both of the warring sides."

"You know quite a bit."

"I know enough to protect her. And I'm not going to let anyone touch that poor girl, even if means bringing down the temple on my own head and everybody else's."

"There's something about her that drives Raghid and Watfan crazy. I'm afraid they might do something."

"I'm going to be spending most of my time these days with Layla at Raghid's mansion helping with preparations for the Night of the First Billion bash. I'll speak to him if necessary."

"The sorcerer claims that she's possessed. So he goes to her room and talks to the 'demon.' In the process, he torments Bahriya, thinking that he's tormenting the demon. The poor thing has had a nervous breakdown, and she's gone temporarily mute from shock. What she needs is medical treatment in a calm environment. Once I heard the sorcerer's voice coming from her room, and he was talking to himself in all sorts of different voices. Bahriya wasn't the person speaking. He spends most of his time with her, and doesn't even go to the hotel anymore. He's obsessed with her."

"And Raghid? What's his attitude?"

"He's obsessed with her, too, in his own way. But he doesn't know the first thing about gentleness or affection. So he tries to shower her with gold, but it only terrifies her. As far as she's concerned, there's no difference between a gold ingot and a rock or some dirt. He's obsessed with her. In fact, there isn't a man that sees her who doesn't go out of his head."

"That's rather obvious from the way you're acting!" said Amir jokingly.

"All right," Nasim replied, "I'm included! I admit, I'm madly in love with her myself. But what I want is for her to get well, not to be destroyed!"

"Me, too," said Dunya. "This girl means something to me. It isn't pity that I feel toward her. It's a sense of responsibility. And I won't let a soul bring harm to her. If anyone tries, I'll keep her in my own home and treat her there until it's possible to send her home. Meanwhile, things may settle down. For all we know, we might discover that some of her family members are still alive. And she might regain her ability to speak."

Speaking to Nasim, Amir asked, "Are you sure she wasn't mute to begin with?"

"Apparently, nobody knows anything about her for certain. But the doctor says that there's no physical basis for her muteness, and that it was caused by psychological shock. Raghid's sent somebody to make inquiries about her there."

"He's sent somebody to that hellhole? Who in his right mind would go to Beirut now?"

"He'll pay. He'll find somebody poor enough and hungry enough to go. She's aroused his curiosity, his hatred and his love all at once."

"I'll be seeing you, Amir," said Dunya. "I've got an engagement to keep."

"Will you be joining us for the demonstration? It's in protest against the Israeli invasion of Lebanon and the bombing of Beirut. We'll head out from Molare Square in the center of Old Geneva. We've got a permit from the authorities, and it will be peaceful, as you know."

Then he added, "By the way, I've invited Khalil and his family to spend the day with me in Annecy on Sunday. Nothing fancy. Could you join us?"

"I'll be there no matter what it takes."

Amir squeezed her hand in farewell and kissed her again on the forehead.

Then he whispered sweetly, "I'll be waiting for a call from you so that we can agree on the details."

She nodded in agreement, then shook hands with Nasim, who stood there looking like a bewildered child. When she was gone, Amir said to hem, "You're still young. Time will show you things about human nature that may surprise you. It will also teach you tenderness and forgiveness. Remember, Nasim: tenderness and forgiveness."

"But I've seen her coming out of Raghid's bedroom so many times!"

"Perhaps that's what brought her back to us. Our most serious mistakes may be the only ones that can show us who we really are."

"And Madame Layla. Do you think she'll take the same path?"

"No, I don't," replied Amir. "She wouldn't agree to let her femininity be cheapened that way. But unfortunately, she's agreed to let her humanity be cheapened just the way some males do. In that little head of hers she's got the mind of a man."

"Did you invite her to participate in the demonstration?"

"No. She wouldn't come. She has the virtue of sticking tenaciously to her mistakes. In that sense she's like me. Our stances are totally opposed, but our approaches are basically the same. We've lost Layla."

With the petulance of youth, Nasim shot back, "She's the loser, not you or us!"

"I'm still not sure of that."

Changing the subject, which he knew to be a painful one for Amir, Nasim said, "And your son, when will he be coming?"

"Any time now. They've granted him the visa he needs and the authorities have given him permission to leave. I suppose he's waiting to get the marks from his final exams."

"Will he be with us at the demonstration?"

"I don't know. The fact is, I don't really know my son. I haven't seen him for four years, and as you know, our letters are all censured, so we only write to each other about trivialities. For ten years I've been in exile, even from the hearts of my children. I only see them rarely, and in the meantime they're like hostages back home."

"And Bassam, where is he?"

"I don't know. He didn't come home last night. He's been falling deeper and deeper into the whiskey bottle, and one of these days he isn't going to know how to crawl out anymore."

"And his thesis?"

"It's a lie. He left Beirut in 1975 as soon as the war broke out. And he wasn't young when he did it. Even so, he decided to go back to school, as if that were a way of avoiding having to make any decisions. Then he waited, and waited, and waited. He's basically an onlooker, not a player. He's put his life on hold indefinitely, it seems. He ran away for fear of being shot to death, and now here he is committing suicide by drinking himself a little closer to death every night."

"It's the waiting that will kill him."

"He isn't corrupt, though. He isn't one of those people who left the country for fear of getting caught in the fray, yet with a plan to join up later with the winner, whichever side it happened to be. Deep inside him there's a miniature Hamlet of sorts. He really is unable to make any decision."

"Poor guy," said Nasim, "For me, things are too clear."

"Young people are always that way. That's why they're more liable than others to make stupid mistakes. But then life surprises them when they come face to face with others—and with themselves."

"What do you mean?"

"I don't mean to put a damper on your enthusiasm, but remember that black and white aren't the only two colors on this planet. 'Love not your beloved with your whole heart, lest one day he be your foe.' "[27]

"That will never happen to me. I'd never change my position!"

"The world itself is changing. So in order to remain constant yourself, you've got to move like the needle of a compass. It's the only thing that can change positions without betraying itself. In fact, it has to do so sometimes in order for its direction to remain constant."

"But do you think this 'needle of the compass wisdom' calls for inviting Dunya and Kafa on the same outing? Don't you know that Kafa has become 'Miss Coco,' and that she's a rising star in the world of Nadim and his bunch? How can you invite a spy to spend the weekend with you? She'll blow Dunya's

---

27. A saying of the Prophet Muhammad.

secret to Nadim. And Dunya herself might turn against us and give away Khalil's secret."

"Dunya wouldn't betray us again. I know human nature well enough to be certain of that."

"So, can I trust her now?"

"Yes, but not too much. I trust her myself. On the other hand, I wouldn't mind if some secrets got out and the cards were reshuffled. This is the time for scandalous revelations."

"Could I ask her to do me a favor, for example?"

"What have you got in mind?"

"To steal Bahriya's passport from Nadim!"

"Why? Are you planning to kidnap her?"

"We might have to rescue her from that loony sorcerer. Who knows?"

"I'll broach the subject with her on Sunday. But if she does manage to get hold of it, I'll keep it with me. I don't trust the foolhardiness of youth! And you seem in love."

"I'm more than 'in love' and less."

"What do you mean?"

"What I mean is that what I desire is her well-being, but not necessarily to be united with her. There's something about her that reminds me of my sisters and my mother."

"That means that your love for her is real."

"I don't know, exactly. All I know is that I'd be willing to die to make her happy, whether with me or without me."

"Is she that beautiful?"

"She certainly is. But her beauty is the least significant thing about her. There's a light that radiates from her presence. It's as if she gives off electrically charged particles that awaken long-forgotten times somewhere deep inside you, times of wonderful freedom."

"You mean that she's bewitched, then?"

"What I mean is that she releases the magic that's been lying dormant in others. It's as though she's a storehouse of energy that brings out the true nature of everyone who comes in contact with her, then pushes things to their logical extreme, to a point of crisis. Sometimes she seems to be aware of everything going on around her, and other times she's like some inhuman, indifferent force, like Nature."

"I think I understand what you're saying. Every one of you sees her differently. Khalil, for example, sees in her an omen of the fate that might be awaiting his children and consequently, he's spent the last two days looking for a way out of his predicament."

"Has he found anything?"

"I don't know yet."

"It was a terrifying sight, her coming down to the party covered with blood. But nobody there really cares what happens to her. Besides, they believe in the sorcerer, and they're even afraid of him."

"And Raghid, isn't he too smart to fall for what that crazy magician of his says?"

"When he's with Watfan, he's just like a little boy. Bahriya has captured his heart, yet as time goes by, he's almost started to believe what Sheikh Watfan says about her rather than listening to his Swiss physician."

"And Sheikh Watfan?"

"There are times when he wants to gain her favor, and he tries to force me to slip some sort of 'love potion' into her food. Then at other times he seems to be convinced that she's out of her mind. But now he's decided that she's possessed by powerful spirits that are planning his destruction. As a result, he's started to hate her and be afraid of her, and that's what makes him liable to do something rash. I beg you, don't forget to see about our getting her passport!"

"I promise to do something about it."

"Could you ask Khalil to help, too?"

"And what could the poor guy do?"

"Well, it can't hurt to knock on all the doors I can think of."

"Khalil will be leaving any day now with Saqr. Layla's gotten the visas. That is, he'll be leaving unless he manages to find another job."

"I hope he does. But has he gotten a work permit from Saqr? If he did, that would make a lot of things easier."

"He came to see me briefly day before yesterday. It seems that all 'foxy Layla' has arranged for is visas for him and for his family. This way he remains at the mercy of the Ghanamali clan, who can have him and his family deported the minute they decide they don't like the way they're acting! He's been entertaining hopes of making contact with a couple of friends he used to know in Beirut. He didn't give me any more details, though, since he was busy looking for all the places in the Qur'an where the words 'astrologers' and 'magicians' are mentioned. He's doing it for Hilal Ghanamali, who wants to know whether he should consult Sheikh Watfan about his illness or not!"

"Our country is going up in flames, and still there are people busying themselves with finding out about angels, and whether magic is permitted in Islam! Nobody really gives a damn about what's happening to us. The only people who came out to protest the Israeli invasion of Lebanon were Arabs from the occupied territories."

"Nasim, no matter what happens, don't lose confidence in your people. They may go on being paralyzed and unfeeling for a period of time, but they won't die, and they won't lose their roots."

Nasim retreated into a grudging silence. He knew that Amir wouldn't allow anyone to cast doubts on his people, and that faith in the Arab nation was the foundation for everything he did. And this was the secret behind his optimism!

◆   ◆   ◆

Oh, what a long reach a single lie can have!

Khalil was astounded at how Saqr could revel in an untruth.

As he bade farewell to his uncle Hilal, he said, "I'm going to London to matriculate. I've decided to complete my education!"

Falling for the fib, Hilal said, "God bless you. So you've decided to be true to your heritage. Our family never had any good-for-nothings until my poor brother was corrupted by Europe."

Just then Sakhr walked in looking agitated, having heard the last words his brother said.

"I won't allow you so speak about me in such terms in front of one of my own children!" he bellowed.

"I learned today of your harem, and the suite you've rented for them in the hotel, and the sand you've been using to cover up the carpet. This is preposterous, brother! 'If you're tried for your disobediences, then take refuge in submission . . . ' Besides which, this is the holy month of Ramadan!"

"I took my family away from the house to make you more comfortable, and now you come around spying on me?"

"I wasn't spying on you. It's gotten past the point where I'd need a spy to know what you're up to. All I have to do is buy a newspaper. Here, read this."

He handed Sakhr a Swiss newspaper. In it he saw a picture of a Geneva hotel manager, then pictures of the women in his harem cooking in the posh hotel's bathrooms, as well as of his children playing in the streets on the eve of some Geneva holiday.

Hilal said angrily, "Read. You may be color-blind and not be able to enjoy the pictures to the fullest, but the words are printed in black on white."

With feigned indifference Sakhr replied, "You know her yourself, brother. It's that foreign journalist Charlotte Barnes, who's on my tail for money. She's already written one book on wealthy Arabs. She's a professional in this area, and now she's aiming to write a sequel to the first book."

"Regardless of her motives, if she hadn't found a weakness in you, she couldn't have exposed it. I don't care about her intentions. What I'm concerned about is the shame she's brought on us in the face of our fellow countrymen and other people all over the world."

"Don't worry. People in our country don't read Swiss newspapers."

"You're mistaken, brother. They read, they understand, and they get angry and resentful. And there's sure to be someone who will take the news back and translate it for them. They won't forgive us for engaging in practices like these when both the Lebanese and the Palestinians are being slaughtered, and when freedom fighters of other nationalities are dying alongside them while we spend the month of Ramadan frolicking in Swiss hotels."

"Perish the thought! We haven't been taking our ease during Ramadan. The women are cooking national foods in the hotel bathrooms in preparation for the pre-fast meal at dawn. We suffer and fast for long, long days, and we're certain to receive a reward for it. Haven't you noticed that the sun doesn't go down until 9:00 P.M.?"

"Why do you spend money to turn Geneva into a place like your home country, making us a laughingstock to strangers, rather than spending it to turn our own country into a utopia like Geneva? Why do your children go dancing in the streets in celebration of Swiss holidays, frittering away their money, spray-painting the faces of passersby and going into fits of euphoric hysteria? Why don't we all go back home and celebrate our own holidays?"

"Because we come from countries where there is no room for celebration or freedom. Our holidays are nothing but rites of mourning, visits to gravesites and social obligations that suffocate us so badly that we need another vacation afterward just to recover from them!"

"Our holidays are this way because that's how we've made them. It doesn't hurt a person to remember his death, since it can help him to live his life as though he were going to die tomorrow. There's a wisdom in visiting graves which spoils nothing but the most trifling pleasures."

"Well, I happen to like trifling pleasures. And I also love my country. But I suffocate there. Its women suffocate me, its men suffocate me, and so do its traditions. I may be wrong, but that doesn't mean my country is right."

Trembling with rage, Hilal shouted in his brother's face, "I swear to God, I'm leaving this place, and I'm never coming back! I came here to recover, but being here is only making me more ill. I can't take your shameful ways anymore."

Then, his hand still shaking, he handed Khalil the newspaper and commanded him, "Read to them, and translate. Talk to them about 'His Grace' the well-known hotel manager, who as a Jew makes no attempt to hide his connections with Israel. And he contributes to it with our money! They kill Arabs in Beirut with the money we throw away here. Read to them what the hotel maids say about our filth and our children, and about their contempt for our passive women drowning in sloth and gold. I commend your wife for picking her children up off the streets of Marbella, St. Tropez, and Nice and taking them back to their own country, where she's put them in school."

"The school to which you refer was built by Raghid. Keep that in mind when you think of denying us the airport contract. The cement needed for the project has been estimated at 50 million cubic meters. Who besides us could manage that?"

More enraged than ever, Hilal shouted, "May God cover your face with shame! You've made us a laughingstock to strangers and friends alike. And now you want to make even more money so that you can spend it on your moral depravity and showy lifestyle! So help me God, I won't let another piaster so much as touch your hand until you've mended your ways. And I won't stay one more minute in this squalid house."

Then suddenly Khalil said, "Sheikh Hilal, you asked me to search for the expression, 'Astrologers lie even when they speak the truth' in the Qur'an. I did look for it, but I didn't find it. The words 'astrologers' and 'astrology' aren't found in the Qur'an, either. However, the terms 'magic' and 'magician' are mentioned frequently. The word 'magic' is found in twenty-three different verses, while the word 'magician' is found in thirteen verses. In addition, derivatives of the same root appear in many chapters of the Qur'an. Here is a chart I drew up of the results, sir, which I hope you'll consider a farewell gift from me."

Everyone was astounded as Khalil reached out and handed a piece of paper to Hilal containing a precise record of what the man had once requested, then forgotten about.

"You're not so bad, after all," said Hilal.

Khalil took the insult in silence.

Then Hilal added, "I'm sorry I had such a low opinion of you, and of your countrymen."

His head bowed despondently, Khalil still said nothing.

(It's true. We do a lousy job of putting ourselves across to others. We ruin our reputation without help from anybody else. At the same time, there are Arabs who seem better than they are because they've mastered the game of living double lives. What good would it do to say anything now that neighbors have slaughtered neighbors in my country, while others of us have sold themselves for a handful of sins?)

Sheikh Sakhr was the first one to catch his breath. Then, taking advantage of his brother's silence, he said, "Please don't go. We'll consult Sheikh Watfan concerning your illness."

"You all are my illness! And I am going. I didn't get a good look at those verses so as to be able to decide whether they rule out the existence of magic, or curse it, or what. But one thing certain is that I'm leaving."

Saqr winked at Khalil as if to say, "Follow me," and the two of them left the room. As Khalil followed him out, he muttered apologetically, "Excuse me" to the other two men.

Once they were safely out in the corridor Saqr said to him, "Did you actually believe that we were going to register me in the university? The only thing we're going for is to enjoy the seven wonders of the world. As long as my uncle is leaving, we can put off our trip and I'll take you around Switzerland first."

"Whatever you say."

"No, I've changed my mind. Let's go!"

"Whatever you say."

(For years and years we've been waiting for them to release us. Meanwhile, they go on plastering bank notes over our eyes so that we won't see what they're doing, and stuffing them into our mouths so that we won't be able to speak. For years and years they've been talking about "the Arab identity of Lebanon" rather than "the Arab identity of the Arabs," and about "Arabizing Lebanon" whose people have paid with their blood to affirm this very identity. So what about the "Arab identity" of the rest of the Arabs?)

What a long reach a single lie can have. What power it has, and how numerous its followers! As for the truthfulness that his father had afflicted him with, it was a forgotten martyr with neither grave nor headstone.

They got into the car, and as they drove off they passed by the spot where Khalil had buried the "rag" under orders from Raghid, who in turn had been doing the bidding of his sorcerer. He couldn't believe that he'd actually stolen through the darkness and committed such a despicable act, like a dog digging in the ground in search of a buried bone. Whenever he snorted that magical white powder, he found he was capable of anything but shame.

So then, they wouldn't be leaving right away, and they might never leave at all. Saqr had changed his mind without paying any attention to Khalil's wishes. After all, what was he but a plaything that Saqr's father had bought for him from Raghid Ltd.?

Saqr said to him, "I won't be needing you this weekend. I remembered an unfinished symphony that I intend to finish myself."

Then he laughed that laugh of his, lost somewhere between playfulness, merriment, and death. Khalil had managed to avoid the mandatory daily fix, so his senses were alert and steady, and Saqr's laugh sent a chill up his spine.

Then Saqr added, "As for our friend the chauffeur, I'll be needing him on the weekend. Tell him so."

Khalil conveyed the message to the Swiss driver, who replied with a long string of words delivered with the utmost courtesy. Dumbfounded, Saqr said to Khalil, "He refuses! Instead, he insists on taking his vacation. He says he wants to spend it with his family. He says he's got his own things to do over the weekend. He has the audacity to claim his freedom despite his social status! And he does it in the name of his 'humanity'! The bastard. I'm going to fire him right now!"

"You can't do that without giving him proper notice. There are legal procedures you have to follow here. You also have to pay him certain forms of compensation. It's true that he's just a driver. But there are people to protect him here. He's a Swiss citizen."

"Who could protect him from me?"

"The law. The labor union. The government authorities. It's true that tourists love Switzerland, but the system is designed to serve its own people, not the tourists."

"You sound like a preacher. You're insufferable. Here, take another snort."

◆ ◆ ◆

When Khalil left the room, Hilal opened the carefully folded paper that miserable Lebanese had left with him, and read carefully everything he had written. It was entitled, "Magic in the Qur'an," and contained a chart with the headings, "Word," "Verse," "Verse number," "Chapter," and "Chapter number."

Sheikh Hilal read all the verses that Khalil had recorded from the Holy Qur'an. He read them meticulously and, since he'd memorized the Qur'an as a boy, each verse triggered in his memory the contents of the entire chapter in which it appeared. Then he sat for a long time with his face buried in his hands. Sheikh Sakhr sat opposite him, holding his breath. As he sat there, a rush of deep tenderness toward his brother welled up in his childlike heart, tinged with remorse over their quarrel.

At last Hilal broke the silence and said, "I'll leave without seeing your sorcerer."

"As you wish, brother. But please don't stay angry."

"When I read the word of God, my soul feels at peace. But I'm angry with myself. I was unfair to that poor Lebanese man. I treated him harshly."

"Never mind. It's part of his job to put up with our mistakes."

"But we all have to stand before God together in the end. I misunderstood his circumstances and his behavior. Saqr is the one who's in the wrong, not Khalil."

Without knowing exactly why, Sheikh Sakhr remained silent, making no attempt to defend his son.

Hilal took his checkbook out of his pocket, wrote some words on a check and signed it. Then he placed the check in a small envelope. Along with the small fortune that he'd just given to Khalil, he placed a card containing his home address on which he wrote, "I'm sorry, son. We all make mistakes sometimes. And if you should find all doors closed in your face, remember that mine is open to you."

Sealing the envelope, he wrote Khalil's name on it and gave it to his brother, saying, "This is for Khalil. Don't forget."

Whereupon Sakhr placed it on the desk in the study, and forgot about it the moment it left his hand.

❖   ❖   ❖

Khalil stopped in front of the shelf where envelopes were displayed in a large Placette department store. He needed a single envelope in which he could deposit his Lebanese identity cards, both his own and his children's. He was afraid they might get lost among the chaotic piles of things in the hotel room, including Kafa's gold stockings and the untold numbers of red shoes that seemed to be multiplying like rabbits.

He found the size he wanted being sold in packets of one hundred. So, since he only needed one, he decided to try negotiating with the sales clerk about the matter. He explained to her what he needed in a French that, although it was quite good, was inevitably tainted with a slight foreign accent. She refused to discuss it with him. Then she took to insulting him, going on about backward foreigners who can't comprehend the idea of a supermarket where everything is sold exactly as it is and for the price on the label. He stood there listening to her tirade like a guilty, lazy schoolboy and imagined himself wearing a dunce cap complete with donkey's ears. Her diatribe was interrupted by the arrival of another young man who was clearly a native. He looked to be of modest means and happened to want the same thing that Khalil did: a single envelope. But before she could pound him with a single line of the same lecture, he began shouting in protest and cursing the Placette stores, which were supposed to be serving the common people but instead were exploiting them. So, he said, he'd decided to expose her right in front of everybody, denouncing both her and the establishment she was working for. Then he proceeded to complain to the manager and the police.

The sales clerk tried to reason with him, but he just carried on with his verbal assault in French's Argot dialect. In the end the sales clerk gave in to him after one of her supervisors—a guard who was obviously posing as a customer—gave her permission with a nod of the head.

Thinking that what was permissible for this Swiss man ought to be permissible for him, Khalil went back and asked the clerk for the same thing. However, this time she really lost her temper, repeating what she'd said to him the first time and totally ignoring what had just taken place with the Swiss customer.

The humiliation of being a foreigner felt like a knife blade going straight through him. He had enough money on him to buy all the envelopes in the store. Yet he couldn't buy respect or equal treatment, whereas the other man could probably get what was due him without having more than a single franc in his pocket.

God damn the degradation of being a stranger in a strange land. Isn't a person's homeland the place where no one can humiliate or degrade him? You can be poor and live in your own country with a modicum of dignity, at least. But it's impossible anywhere else—unless, of course, you belong to the jet set. After all, money travels first class just about wherever it goes.

Then Khalil was gripped all over again by that tenacious, miserable fear: would Israel forbid him to go back home? When he left the department store, he went to Jean-Jacques Rousseau Island, about ten minutes' walk away in the center of the Rhone River. The place was nearly deserted, and the canicule wind was stinging people's faces with that mysterious fire that it always carried with it. Then, right in front of Rousseau's statue he shouted at the top of his lungs, "God damn you, Begin! I hope some day you're afflicted with the same grief and misery you've caused us!"

The park guard paid no attention to him, and the white swans just went on swinging gracefully to and fro over the surface of the lake. The statue was the only creature that appeared so much as to bat an eyelid. It may even have gotten a tear in its eye. Or was it perspiring from the heat? He left the park singing, "We the young possess tomorrow" in a mournful, broken voice that sounded like the rusty strings on some ancient, forgotten lute.

When he got back to the hotel, he found a message from Saqr: "We'll be leaving day after tomorrow in the early morning."

The new development sent him plummeting into an abyss of misery and shame. So then, he'd be leaving after all, after having failed to find any alternative. These were orders. This was the indignity of life as a foreigner. Some people would have considered him lucky to have somebody willing to support him in return for the pleasure of insulting and degrading him. He would chaperone Saqr on his trip, pampering him like a spoiled little boy. And Kafa would go to work for Raghid on Layla's team in preparation for the Night of the First Billion. Meanwhile, she might find herself enough free time to flee from her confusion and sorrow into the world of bodily pleasures. As for him, his confusion and sorrow had shut down his body's ability to experience any pleasure.

It was as if he carried all his bodily organs around inside his tormented, exhausted head. First he'd been denied his dignity at home, and now he'd been denied it away from home.

Then without knowing why, he thought of Bahriya, a foreigner like him. What could she possibly do for herself now that she'd fallen into the golden spider's trap and lived inside its terrifying lair? How was she to confront the degradation of living as a foreigner without a voice, and with a lacerated body, wounded memory, and broken spirit? And wasn't he on his way to becoming like her—he and the rest of his people, a people of captives destined for little more than oppression, fragmentation, and humiliation?

◆   ◆   ◆

It was a blistering evening, and Geneva was exhaling desertlike breaths known as the canicule.

It was a house that had been tailor-made for her. From the very beginning she'd sensed that Nadim was a man of refined taste, and now her intuition was confirmed.

Everything about the place suited Kafa Baytmouni, from the musical doorbell to the telephone with the special ring and the voice of the maid, "Lillian" as she said, "Oui, Madame Coco!"

When Nadim called and arranged to meet her at an unknown address, she thought she was on her way to another hotel. But instead she found herself in front of a brilliantly luxurious residence, complete with an entranceway lined with mirrors and equipped with video cameras for visitors' security. As for the interior, it was a shell fit for a pearl like her. He was waiting for her at the door, and gave her the secret code to open it so that she could come back whenever she chose.

He said to her, "This is my secret, private flat. Consider it home."

And what a deluxe, fabulously elegant home it was, complete with velvet armchairs, silk cushions, and a plush white carpet as thick as a grass lawn. There was a staircase leading up to two bedrooms, one of which was a veritable lovers' oasis. The curtains danced coquettishly in tango with the round bed in the center of the room, which rotated at the touch of an electric switch, and on the ceiling there was a huge mirror in which she could admire her beauty, which seemed to her more stunning than ever.

Her passions set on fire by the rich splendor of the place, she fell upon

Nadim's rusty body, kissing away the ashes and dust with her lips and sweeping out the corners with her hair. As for him, he pulsated and soared along with her, while the sound of the background music was lost beneath her ecstatic groans. As they continued on their passionate, enchanted flight, Nadim spread his wings like an eagle to bear her aloft toward uncharted heights. (Sheikh Watfan's potions really do work. What's happening to me is incredible! I haven't had this kind of a high for a long, long time. Kafa thinks I'm a real stud now, and for some reason that pleases me!)

She got up and went to the bathroom to see how she looked. On the way there she passed through a small room on the order of a walk-in closet. She'd always dreamed of having a room like this leading into the bathroom, fitted out with mirrors and designed to hold nothing but elegant dresses. As for the bathroom itself, it was a woman's paradise, with a magnifying mirror for her to look at her face in like some sort of beautician's microscope, a hair dryer, a scale, the works. So to hell with Khalil, who'd never provided her with a suitable "milieu." She wasn't going to leave this miniature heaven for anything or anyone. She'd stay right here in this flat with its owner, be it Nadim or anybody else, for that matter.

Her discovery of the clothes closet inflamed her desires anew, especially as she imagined it brimming with evening dresses and with hundreds of pairs of red high-heeled shoes. She washed her face and redid her eyes with the makeup she'd found beside the bathroom mirror, then went back to get Nadim's wings ready for another takeoff. Before long she found him flying with her again from one summit to another. And with every new peak, she was ready for more.

Then suddenly Nadim felt as though his heart was about to burst. (Everything has its limits, even Sheikh Watfan's medicines . . . everything, that is, except for this woman's appetite.)

Fortunately, he was saved by the ringing of the telephone, which he took advantage of as an opportunity to recover his serious demeanor. He rushed to get dressed and escape from her clutches, claiming that he had to attend to some unexpected business.

With feigned innocence he asked her, "Would you mind if my guest came to visit me here? He's a prominent Arab, and he has some business which can't be postponed."

Stretching out under the ceiling mirror, she unfurled the banners of her blue eyes atop her fair-skinned peaks and said, "He's quite welcome, either here or downstairs . . ."

Then she laughed at her own joke.

But Nadim didn't laugh. This, quite simply, was what he'd been planning on, either now or later. And he'd known that she would welcome it. The best type of call girl is one who finds enjoyment in her work and as a result, gives the same to her clientele. Attractive hostesses are a must for millionaires and would-be billionaires in the world of business.

◆   ◆   ◆

It was a blistering dawn, and Geneva was exhaling desertlike breaths.

Looking fatigued, Bassam said to Amir, "I've come to say goodbye."

Amir had gotten up in the wee hours of the morning to meet Khalil and his family and Dunya in front of the station where they were to take a bus to Annecy to spend the day. But before he left the house, he was surprised by the arrival of Bassam with the smell of alcohol on his breath.

Instead of apologizing the way he normally did, he said resolutely, "I've come to say goodbye."

Trying to defuse the situation until Bassam could calm down, Amir said, "I thought you'd be going with us to Annecy."

"I'm not going anywhere with you anymore, Amir. And I won't be marching in your demonstration. I'm getting out of your life forever. And I'm going to get you and everything you stand for out of my bloodstream."

"What's happened all of a sudden?"

"I'm scared. And I'm getting more so by the day."

"But you're not doing anything."

"I've decided to do something. I'm going to run away to Canada or Australia. I'll forget all about my past, and about this place."

As he said it, he pointed to the map of the Arab world, the sole decoration on Amir's otherwise bare walls. Then, striking Amir's statueless pedestal, he went on, "I'll forget all about the sculpture your father did which you dream of getting back some day, and which you've prepared this pedestal for. I'll forget all about these inglorious demonstrations of yours . . . and your books, and your pioneers, and your intellectual circles. None of it does any good."

"And running away, does that do any good?"

Bassam withdrew into a resentful silence.

Amir whispered in resignation, "As you wish, brother. After all these years of thinking, it's your right to make some decision. And I'm glad you've finally done that, regardless of what the decision happens to be."

He reached out and shook Bassam's hand in sorrowful affection. Then Bassam hurled his huge corpselike frame into one of the only two chairs in the house, while Amir left and headed for the bus station at the corner of Talberg and Alp Streets.

Once Amir was gone, Bassam got up and gathered his meager possessions into a suitcase. Ever since he'd left Lebanon, he'd been carrying two suitcases: a black one, which he kept locked, that held some of his slightly more elegant clothes for special occasions, and a gray one that held the rest of his things. The day after his departure, he'd opened up the gray suitcase and hung its contents in the hotel closet. However, he'd left the black one closed, thinking to himself: I'll be going home soon, so why open this one too and be up to my ears in chaos? Then the years passed without his opening the black suitcase even once. Instead, he just took it with him wherever he went. And the strange thing was that customs officials had never once asked him to open it. It was as if it were imaginary or invisible to everyone but him. So he went on not opening it, as if the reality of his exile would come popping out of it like a jack-in-the-box and he would have no choice but to acknowledge it as his irreversible destiny.

Opening a wardrobe against the wall, Bassam took out the black suitcase that had remained shut for such a long time, and the gray one in which he began packing his few things with grief-laden sluggishness.

(There's nothing in this black suitcase anymore except a load of trouble. I can't remember what clothes are inside it. And even if I could, they wouldn't fit around this corpse of mine, which has doubled in size as if I'd gotten fat on worry. So why do I carry it around with me, insisting on not opening it until I go back to Beirut? When the Arabs left Andalusia they carried their house keys with them. Then their houses were lost and the keys were all they had left, so they hung them on the walls of their houses in exile. Am I going to hang my suitcase on the wall in my next home as a fugitive? Are the things I packed inside it so long ago still the way they were, lying there motionless as grave clothes? Or have they been consumed by maggots as though they were a dead body? And what a dead body they are: the lifeless remains of my entire past, the life of glitter and fame that I lived in a time long gone.

How did they manage to besiege me, turning me into a creature ruled by terror: afraid of my fingers lest they write the truth, and afraid of my head lest it think—so afraid that I drug it every night by dealing it a blow with the ax of liquor, nausea, and headaches?

I've been under siege from the very beginning, since 1967, when my book *Critique of Fundamentalist Thought* came out. They dragged me to court and hanged me on the columns of the newspaper, so to speak. Then trials went out of style and assassinations came back into vogue as the preferred method of torture. After a while we had so many people stepping on us, we didn't even know anymore whose boots we had to lick if we wanted to stay alive. As for me, I'm a man with the body of a bull and the heart of a little child. I'm a coward. I'm afraid of being tortured, or killed, or humiliated. That's what happened to some men. And it would have happened to a lot more of them if they'd admitted how they really felt. Amir is a rare breed: He isn't scared off by death. But I'm not like that. At first I said to myself, I'll run away on the pretext of finishing my Ph.D. and wait for things to calm down in Beirut. So I left this black suitcase closed. The mere act of opening it would have been a tacit acknowledgment that I'd resigned myself to life in exile as a final solution. And I was just as helpless to do that as I was to go back, with the chains around people's freedoms there multiplying along with the slogans used to justify them. At the same time, I can't march in Amir Nealy's protest demonstration. And the closer we come to the date of the march, the further I slip into the neck of some bottle that can keep me numb.

Put quite simply, I'm a man who doesn't want to die at someone else's hands. Lawyer that I am, I love to do battle by pitting one argument against another, but I'm not cut out for guerrilla warfare. Begin's soldiers are laying siege to Beirut to swallow up the lunatics who've been fighting each other for years and exterminating everything around them: enemies, friends, children, logic . . .

I want to escape, and to forget: f-o-r-g-e-t. I want to die of old age somewhere on this planet . . . anywhere.)

Bassam buried his face in his hands for a while, then took out his pack of cigarettes only to find it empty. He remembered that Amir had discovered a place that sold cigarettes on Sunday, only it didn't open until 9:00 A.M. So he went walking through the house like a shade, waiting for nine o'clock to arrive. With a lump of misery in his throat, he recalled how Amir used to go out every Sunday morning to buy him his newspapers and his cigarettes while he went on with his drunken slumber. He had a feeling he was going to miss Amir. But he was tired of being afraid, tired of not taking a step backward or forward. It seemed that in these rotten times no matter what step you took, it got you into trouble. So he'd made up his mind to get out of the whole Arab chess game. He'd turn himself into a kangaroo in Australia, an iceberg in Canada, or a bear at the North Pole. All that mattered was to get out of the maze.

At last it turned nine o'clock. He'd finished off the cigarette butts in all the ashtrays in the house, and he was going to suffocate if he didn't smoke a whole cigarette. It was usually Amir who went out to get him his newspapers and cigarettes while he slept off his last bout of drinking. Today it was his turn. He left the house. But no sooner had he gone a few steps than he was approached by a man on a motorcycle. It was as if the man had been waiting for him and was trying to run him over. Bassam stopped on the sidewalk, waiting for the cycle to pass. The other man stopped, too. The streets were empty. Not even a pedestrian in sight. The man on the motorbike pulled out a revolver. Taken aback, Bassam felt as though he were watching a third rate flick. He saw the revolver being pointed at him, but he was too astonished to scream. He wanted to say something, but couldn't. Everything happened with lightning speed. He saw something flash before his eyes, but he didn't feel himself fall to the ground. Nor did he feel the blood seeping slowly from a hole in his forehead and another in his cheek. And no one heard the sound of the shot, since the revolver was equipped with a silencer.

Then the Middle Eastern-looking man took off on his motorcycle.

❖　❖　❖

The party arrived in a captivatingly beautiful park, and Dunya stretched out on the verdant lawn, overflowing with contentment. She felt as though her hair had turned into green grass that went creeping down into the heart of the soil. And the members of her body felt like arteries connecting her to the poor and simple folk who filled the place. After all, these were the people to whom she had belonged in her days as the girl in that old self-portrait of hers. Kafa lay in repose like a beautiful feline that has mastered the art of making sudden, vicious attacks. She was looking at Amir, the man she hated, with a new eye: only not the eye of humanitarian goodwill, but of womanly desire.

(This is a man that I'm seeing for the first time. I spent seven years hating him and feeling jealous of my husband's love for him. And now, two hours after our first encounter, I'm falling under the influence of his extraordinary, spontaneous physical attraction. There's a special, intimate something about him that makes me want to possess him. It's something that Nadim hasn't got. And neither does Khalil, or even Roberto, that good-looking Italian fellow who's so fun to play with. It's something that gives me the urge to shatter all the confidence and tranquility that he's so full of. I used to imagine him as being some odious old man who spoke nothing but literary Arabic and never talked about anything but philosophy. And now here he is in front of me, as simple as the soil, as fresh as the flowers, as natural as this untamed, unassuming lake. So as a male, he's not bad! He's the type I'd like to try out. An hour or so ago he looked so funny, with Rami and Fadi jumping on top of him like little puppies and him rolling around with them in the grass. So in spite of the fact that I'm sleepy, and in spite of the fact that I detest sitting in public parks with ordinary working-class folks and riding in buses like the one that brought us here instead of in fancy cars like Nadim's—in spite of everything, I find Amir attractive as a man. It's no wonder Dunya is trying to get to him by coming with us today.) Just then Amir got up and said, "I'm going to buy some sandwiches for lunch."

Kafa shivered with disgust. Now that she'd gotten used to being served meals fit for a queen complete with table service of gold, she despised men who offered her sandwiches for lunch.

"I'll go with you," said Khalil.

"No, you stay right where you are."

"But . . ."

"Sandwiches are cheap in public parks. Luxuries may be exorbitant here, but necessities are all reasonably priced. Besides, I'm not that poor!"

Irritated by Amir's poor taste in boasting of how little his hospitality was costing, Coco decided to strike him off her list of potential lovers.

"I'll go with you," Khalil insisted.

He didn't want to stay alone with Kafa. The beauty of their natural surroundings had brought his grief to the surface and he didn't want to say anything hurtful to her. He also didn't want to have to look at Dunya, who seemed to be bursting with an almost hysterical elation that made him nervous, as though she might come undone any minute.

So off they went. Meanwhile, Kafa turned over on the grass and stared up into the translucent blueness of the Annecy sky, judiciously avoiding any conversation with Dunya. She couldn't wait to see the look on Nadim's face when she told him that Dunya was now out to make herself into the new Layla in Amir's life!

The two men walked along in silence until Khalil asked, "How do you find her?"

"She's not a malicious woman. On the contrary, she's worth your making some extra effort to bring her into the fold."

"You mean she's worth my turning myself into a carbon copy of Nadim and licking Raghid's boots?"

"I didn't ask you to change."

"Then how will I change her?"

"What's needed isn't to change her, but to raise her consciousness. It's obvious that she's full of life. So let her discover that a person can be honorable, happy and enthused with life all at the same time."

"I've begun to doubt it myself!"

They both laughed, then fell silent again until they reached a large, forested amusement park. Rami was riding a horse and Fadi was driving a spaceship on a merry-go-round that spun them round and round, the sound of the children's shouts rising and falling with the movement of the big wheel.

They stopped to watch them.

(I know Kafa was in the arms of that European stranger in a bed somewhere. I was on my way to Amir's house and kept on going. I didn't tell him the details when I got there, and he didn't ask. But then I started shaking and I shouted, "I'm losing everything—my country, my wife, my children, my health! Everything's falling apart, and I don't even know anymore where to start if I want to fix the damage."

Bassam, the perceptive type who can see when other tormented souls need to be alone with Amir, said, "I'm going to work on my thesis."

The mere mention of his thesis had gotten to be something of a joke, since it was clear by now that it was nothing more than a Hamletesque ploy, an excuse to flee from making decisions. But we didn't laugh.

Then, as if he sensed what was going on in my head, Amir said to me, "Why not accept my invitation to spend Sunday with me? I've tried more than once to persuade you to spend a day away from things with your family. I'll take you all on an outing, to the town of Annecy. We'll go there by bus. It's an hour's drive through fabulous scenery. Then you come to a beautiful lake, as beautiful as Lake Geneva, but open to the general public rather than just tourists and the elite. It's got a rustic beauty without any artificial attractions to bring in tourists. On Sunday it's packed with working-class folks, including Arab immigrants. What do you say we bring your boys out of that golden prison of theirs for a while? Layla can take care of the visas in one hour. Don't forget that you're Ghanamali's secretary!"

"What's the use? What good would it do?"

"None, really. But it would please me for you to accept my invitation, and I'd like to get to know Kafa. I want to see her through my own eyes for once. I want to be able to form an impression of her without being influenced by all your disappointments and Nasim's dinner party stories."

The electrically powered merry-go-round came to a halt. The two children, ready for another spin, stayed in their places. They caught sight of their father but said nothing to him. Born during wartime, each of them was preoccupied with a world of innocent delights the likes of which he'd never known in Beirut.

Like an echo, Amir's voice sounded again in Khalil's ear. (None. But it would please me for you to accept my invitation, and I'd like to get to know Kafa.)

But so many things had changed since that morning. He'd become convinced that Kafa was bored, and that she was trying to amuse herself with Amir, although he wasn't playing along. Even the presence of Fadi and Rami didn't seem to matter much to her. She was looking for a different climate. Dunya, on the other hand, knew how to enjoy life's simple pleasures, like the sun, the birds, and the flowers, regardless of whether they happened to be made of gold.

The bus they'd gotten on at the station that morning certainly wasn't made of gold. Even so, Dunya had been as delighted as a little girl when it took off on time. Nor did it stream along noiselessly like Nadim's car. Yet she seemed perfectly happy, listening contentedly to the boys' loud raucous as they jumped into Amir's lap with children-loving Europeans looking on in approval. And when they crossed the Swiss-French border without border officials humiliating them the way they do to Arab citizens crossing the borders between Arab countries—borders that are supposedly imaginary—she expressed appreciation for the respect shown for ordinary citizens in these countries, including the poor. She seemed to understand clearly—as she had earlier in her life—what Amir was talking about in his books. It was as if she'd been aware of the tragedy being suffered in the Arab world, but hadn't found any way to deal with it but to resort to the traditional solution, namely, to seek refuge in wealth. A thread of clarity born of concrete experience was beginning to find its way into her consciousness. As for Kafa, she yawned. She didn't understand a thing except that she didn't want to go back to life in the rough.

Dunya went jumping with Khalil's two boys over Annecy's hanging bridges, which she said were like the pictures she'd seen of Venice. She didn't purse her lips in disdain, asking to be taken in a taxi the way Kafa used to do in Beirut lest the filth in the streets soil her elegant attire, or for fear of the armed vigilantes, some of whom had been known to expose women to more than mere verbal flirtation, and that in broad daylight. When they reached the park, which overlooked a gorgeous lake, Dunya seemed no less thrilled with it than she had been with Lac Léman, despite the simplicity of the location, its residents and even its tourists. It was as if when she married Nadim, she'd made the mistake of equating poverty with backwardness. It hadn't occurred to her that it wasn't necessary to make everyone in the world rich, so much as to turn one's country into a place that wasn't backward, that is, a place where people can live with dignity whether they're rich or poor. Amir wanted Kafa to make the same discovery that Dunya was making. However, she seemed to have removed herself from everything going on around her, as though she were putting up with her present affliction only because she knew Khalil would be leaving the next day!

Khalil could feel his admiration for Amir growing by leaps and bounds. Here was a man who had mastered the art of action, not just the art of words. It was as if by inviting them to Annecy, this lovely but unadorned spot, he'd wanted to put Kafa and Dunya to the test, to reveal what each of them carried around on the inside. Were they in search of true happiness, or just its outward trappings? Would they reject Annecy simply because it had no five-star hotels, and would they be bored by the trip simply because the mode of transportation had been a bus rather than a Cadillac?

As the two men stood in front of the concession stand, Khalil said, "Kafa has failed your test. But Dunya's passing it with flying colors."

"She's passing it almost too well," Amir replied, "so well it worries me. It's as if she's just experiencing a backlash against all she's been through. But when the bubble breaks, I don't know how she'll handle it."

"What do you mean?"

"I mean, she's too happy for a person in her right mind. It's as if she's taking vengeance on her past, but hasn't started doing anything to correct it. She's elated like a teenager defying authority. But what's going to happen after today's trip and the demonstrations are over? If she goes back to being her old self, Nadim won't let her go on being his wife. So the question is: will she able to stand on her own two feet again?"

"Why wouldn't she be able to?"

"Nobody can just cancel out eighteen years of her life with a stroke of the pen, or by some rational decision, even if she's convinced that those years were nothing but a lie. After all, the lie manages to get under your skin over such a long period, eating away at your strength and your potential for change. And if you try to start all over again, you might not be able to take a new path. It's in this sense that we pay for our mistakes. Merely turning away from a mistake doesn't cancel it out."

"So then, you're saying that we'll lose Dunya."

"I don't know. All I'm saying is that she's too happy right now because she doesn't see the possibility of failure. And that's not an encouraging sign."

"You two were whispering something to each other a while ago. Does she have a clear idea of what's she's going to do?"

"We were talking about Bahriya. I asked her if she could confiscate Bahriya's passport from Nadim, since Nasim is afraid that crazy sorcerer might do something to hurt her. He's thinking of subjecting her to torture under the pretext of torturing the demon that he claims she's possessed by. He wants to treat her 'insanity' by shaving her head. That sort of thing. So we're agreed that if we could gain possession of her passport, it would make it easier to get her back home. Nasim is also going to contact his family and ask them to inquire about what's become of her relatives."

"Did she agree to do it?"

"Yes, she did. So enthusiastically, in fact, that it worries me. I'm not comfortable with behavior that seems so impulsive."

When they got back with the sandwiches and drinks, they found Kafa fluttering her feet like a little girl and Dunya sleeping peacefully on the grass. She looked lovely, like a gentle bird, curled up on the grass as though she had found repose in Nature's womb and in the company of the simple folk all around her.

Looking over at Kafa, Amir whispered, "I don't know exactly what this woman has done to herself and to you, but she certainly isn't malicious. She may be lost or confused, but she's worth your concern."

Before their return that evening, they went for a ride in a crowded boat. Dunya, radiating sweetness and warmth, looked as happy and comfortable as if she were surrounded by her own family. Kafa glanced at her watch from time to time, counting the hours till Khalil and Saqr would be on their way and praying that Saqr wouldn't change his mind again! And every now and then she would fan herself with her handkerchief in a silent complaint against the canicule heat that had assaulted the region. She would have preferred to spend her day in some luxurious, air-conditioned place. But such was the taste of the man she'd had the misfortune to marry!

◆ ◆ ◆

When they'd all settled into the bus for the trip back to Geneva, Kafa went to sleep out of boredom, fleeing from the callused hands that surrounded her to her dreams and the sound of a whispered, "Amore mio!" The boys slept from exhaustion, their tender cheeks burned by Europe's summer sun.

Speaking to Amir, Dunya said gratefully, "This has been one of the happiest days of my life. I don't know how, but I was happy and relaxed, not trying to prove anything to anybody, and not envying anybody for his wealth. I apologize for the way I've neglected and forgotten you in the past."

He motioned with his finger for her to be quiet. He didn't want her to release the charge of consciousness she'd just received. If that happened, she might relieve herself of the resulting tension and lapse back into forgetfulness. He wanted these bright moments to arouse her curiosity. But with her usual fiery impetuosity, she said, "I never believed before that someone could be poor and happy at the same time"!

"It's possible if he lives in a country whose people are made rich by the way their needs are cared for."

And Khalil interjected, "And that can never happen unless people work to change the way things are."

The expression on Dunya's face changed suddenly from delight to irritation. Khalil and Amir looked at each other as if to say: We've just ruined the in-direct lesson! Damn it all. Was it really necessary for each of us add a conclud-ing didactic remark?

Laughing, Amir whispered in French, "Just chalk it up to habits of the profession!"

Amir saw his guests off at the bus station and let Dunya rely on herself by taking a taxi at least. Then he headed home on foot. For some reason Dunya had reminded him on this outing of his perfidious sweetheart, Layla. At one time Layla had been confused like Dunya, standing at a crossroads. But now it looked as though she wasn't confused anymore. He'd lost her forever. Khalil still had a chance to win over Kafa, that lovely woman on the verge of going bad. Khalil's problem with Kafa was that he didn't know how to speak to her in her own language or help her discover the goodness in herself. He was gauche and blunt, the kind who says the truth even it he gets his head cut off for it. Which was also what made Amir so fond of him.

He kept on walking, burning with longing for his children and family after this day of loud romping with Khalil's two little boys. There was something about Rami that reminded him of his own son when he was small, and whom he hadn't seen as a young man except in pictures. When he left him he was Rami's age.

When he arrived at his flat, he was surprised to find the police waiting for him at the door, along with the neighbors and the press. A camera flashed in his eyes, and he covered his face with his hands.

What had happened? Unlike usual, he'd left home early, at 6:30 A.M. So what could possibly have happened? And how could a pleasant day like the one he'd just spent end with the arrival of police, reporters, neighbors, and some of his students?

Someone had shot Bassam with a silencer-equipped revolver at nine that morning, the time Amir normally left home every Sunday. But Bassam rarely left the house on Sundays. So why had he gone out today? To be killed in his place?

After hours of the usual nerve-racking red tape, Amir found himself alone with a painful fact: they had killed Bassam by mistake. He, not Bassam, was the person they'd been after. They'd been lying in wait outside the door, and shot at the head that happened to appear at the time when Amir normally came out. Only the head that appeared this time happened to belong to Bassam—

Bassam, who had fled from his country in terror, then put his life in cold storage for eight years, waiting like Hamlet for things to work themselves out for fear of dying for no reason. And as a result, he'd died for no reason. Never once had he done anything to be punished for. Preparing one's thesis was the one thing which none of the warring factions would have penalized anybody for. Meanwhile, Amir had kept writing and writing like someone inviting death upon himself, living and speaking the truth no matter what it cost him. The first time they'd tried to kill him, they'd aimed at the right man and missed. This time they didn't miss, but they'd aimed at the wrong man.

Amir decided to ask his son not to come. After all, what if he came to visit him, and . . .

He knew that his death would be necessary in order for those rare voices that still called for democracy to be silenced. Consequently, they were bound to kill him sooner or later. But when would they make their next attempt? In any case, he wasn't going to worry about such trivial details. He'd continue doing as he had been, come what may.

But he was truly grieved over Bassam. He'd given him refuge in his home in hopes of bringing him out of his indecision. Little had he known that he was bringing him out of chronic indecision into indubitable certainty and handing him a death sentence, one that would be carried out on the very day that Bassam had decided to save his head by emigrating.

He'd continued to be afraid of dying for no reason until this very fear drove him to his own demise. And he died in vain. He died a death devoid of any value or meaning. He could have been still alive in Beirut, leading an effective, fruitful life. But coincidence—equipped as if with a silencer—is a soundless, cruel joke.

When Kafa got off the bus, she heaved a sigh of relief, promising herself never again to set foot in a means of public transport. Never, even if it meant having to part with her two little boys, the ones she was kissing goodbye as Khalil pulled them along toward the Cornavin Station to take them by train back to the College de Lamare. She didn't plan to go with them to the school. Instead, she'd decided she needed to rush back to the posh hotel room where she could run her fingers over the velvet wallpaper and reassure herself that she really had left the nightmare of potential poverty behind. She'd made up her mind: either Khalil would have to come to his senses and join up with the class of people that really knew how to live, or he would lose her. And he wouldn't be able to threaten her with depriving her of her children. He'd already deprived her of Widad, and her broken heart couldn't be broken again. In any case, they'd grow up and go far away from her if they were going to be raised under their father's care and influence. All these thoughts flashed through her mind with a kind of womanly guile as she kissed Fadi and Rami. And she told herself: I'll get myself used to saying goodbye to them. That way Khalil will never be able to blackmail me with them.

Khalil left with the boys and didn't ask Kafa to come along. He needed some time alone after this scandalous day.

With a growing sense of pain deep inside him, he bid Rami and Fadi farewell. He'd never dreamed that one day he would find himself leaving one of his children in a boarding school. And where? In Geneva, Switzerland, of all places. He noticed that as they parted, both boys clung to his neck a few moments longer than usual.

After he got back on the train, he closed his eyes, picturing Kafa in her boredom and disgust over what had been—to him, at least—the ideal holiday. She'd started off her morning with an attempt to flirt with Amir and get his attention. He'd known exactly what she was up to. Then she'd suddenly gotten tired of him and isolated herself from the whole group. And she hadn't said a word to Dunya, who was too caught up in her own frenzied euphoria to notice. It was a euphoria that he hoped would take root and last. It was obvious that Kafa had left his world for good. She had looked with revulsion at the people in the park—laborers, middle-class folks, and poor, ordinary faces, rough hands that knew the feel of life's harshness, Arab immigrants and simple French folks. She'd been dying to get out of the place. So after a day like this, how would he ever get her to understand that the world she despised was the world he belonged to?

When he reached the loathsome hotel, he found Kafa waiting for him with a look of spiteful glee in her eyes as she handed him a message that read, "Come immediately. Saqr."

Saqr received him in the library with a face he'd never seen before. It was a stern face, and in his eyes there was a cold, caustic look that reminded him of Raghid Zahran.

He asked Khalil contemptuously, "Didn't I give you orders to stay beside the telephone? Have you forgotten that you're my employee? Don't you understand that I am your master and that you must obey your master at all times without question?"

It wasn't so much the words that pained Khalil as Saqr's way of uttering them. The expression on his face was so harsh, he hardly seemed to take account of Khalil as a human being.

He was taken off guard by Saqr's new countenance, since he had thought of him as no more than a little boy dressed up as a dissolute drug addict. Little had he known that on the inside he concealed a petty dictator.

Khalil averted his gaze from Saqr to the wall, then the window, then the desk. As his glance fell on the desk, he was surprised to find an envelope with his name on it. Without batting an eyelid, he picked it up and opened it to find the check from Hilal and his note of apology. Astonished, he decided in a flash, I'll hide this check from Kafa. It will pay for our tickets home. He tried to show the check to Saqr, but Saqr paid no attention. Instead, he went on in the same venomous tone of voice, "I've been waiting for you for an hour. We'll be on our way immediately."

Khalil opened his mouth to say something about saying goodbye to his children. He wanted to get out of going some way or another. Saqr's "other face" frightened him, and he realized that the trap he was falling into might be more perilous than he had imagined. But then Saqr delivered his final blow, saying, "If you don't have your passport with you, we'll pass by the hotel to get it. You won't need to bring any clothes. Everything's ready. And I'll never let you sabotage the timing of either my play or my work again. Bear in mind that I'm the man who will manage Sakhr Ghanamali's business if he should fall ill or retire. We may play together now and then. But don't you forget for a moment that I'm the boss."

◆　◆　◆

Bahriya sat in the mansion living room, her eyes glued to the television screen as Beirut went up in flames before her very eyes.

From the time she arrived, she had imposed the Beirut news on Raghid's mansion. And since no request she made of Raghid would be refused, she sat nonstop next to the small screen, stalking the ghost of Beirut that lived inside it.

This development pleased Nasim, who took all the more diligently to polishing the silver and gold tableware that filled the huge sitting room, his gaze fixed all the while on the television and news of his country. He no longer had to make excuses to go to his room or to the kitchen in order to be sure not to miss a single broadcast, regardless of what station it was on or what language it was in. All he had to do now was to press the right buttons at the right time, provided Raghid wasn't around. The first time Bahriya saw him doing this, she eyed him with a look of friendly collusion. Then before long she'd learned to do it herself, which suggested that she wasn't as paralyzed or as ill as she seemed. She didn't let a single news broadcast go by, whether it was in French, Italian, or German. Whenever she picked up a new station, the two of them would exchange a glance that was like a gleam of understanding radiating from her eyes and being poured into his heart.

One day they were staring at scenes of the bombing, and although Nasim couldn't understand a word of the German, he recognized the location. It was the neighborhood where his family lived. The explosions came in steady succession, and the last shell he saw go off seemed to pound the very building where his family lived. Would he ever see his brothers and sisters alive again? His hand fell to his side and the golden pitcher that he'd been shining to keep himself looking busy slipped out of his grip and onto the floor. It just so happened that at the very moment the pitcher went rolling, Raghid walked into the room. He reprimanded him sternly, cursing the television along with Beirut and its news. He didn't dare scold Bahriya, so he said to Nasim everything he wanted her to hear, including a lecture on the necessity of forgetting a country on the verge of collapse and being grateful for the blessings God had granted them away from home—being grateful, that is, for him, of course. (Who else?)

Nasim left the sitting room without actually leaving it, carrying on with his work in the dining room where he could see and hear without being seen by Raghid. He couldn't help hovering around Bahriya like her guard dog. And he didn't know why. It was as if a message from home were tattooed into her strong, youthful, pain-racked body. Or was he simply falling under the power of her dazzling beauty the way Raghid was?

Raghid took out a box covered with crimson velvet and opened it. Inside it there glittered a gold necklace inlaid with diamonds, and a bracelet, a ring, and a pair of earrings. Bahriya looked apathetically at the set of jewelry, then turned her gaze back toward the television screen.

Raghid was filled with rage and the passion to possess. Struggling to keep his voice calm despite the way she had insulted him—which was something he wasn't accustomed to in his dealings with women—he said to her, "It's made of pure gold and rare diamonds, the work of a world-renowned jeweler."

She remained silent, her face not betraying so much as a flicker of acknowledgment. He picked up the gold necklace and put it around her neck. She didn't welcome the gesture, nor did she resist it. Instead she remained frozen in place like a statue of extraordinary beauty as he took her tender hand in his and placed the precious ring on her finger, fixed the two earrings in her ears, stroked her radiant, youthful cheeks, and placed his bracelet around her wrist. She remained calm, distant, and impassive. She cast a fleeting glance at her hands, but her face remained expressionless.

Raghid got up angrily and went to his room. An hour later Nasim knocked on the door.

"Go to hell, whoever you are!" he growled.

'Excuse me," said Nasim, "it has to do with Miss Bahriya."

"Come in."

Nasim entered with a worried look on his face.

"What about Miss Bahriya?"

"Her skin is swollen and it's obvious that she's in pain."

They went down together to the parlor.

At first glance Bahriya looked just as she had when he left her an hour earlier. She was sitting in the same position, and her eyes still had the same glassy look. However, there was now a reddish swelling on her neck where the earrings touched her collarbone, and severe redness on her ears and cheeks. The same symptoms appeared on her right hand around the bracelet and on the fingers of her left hand around the ring. Nasim had never seen anything like it before. Too alarmed to be cautious in his words, he asked, "Is this poisoning?"

"Shut up, you moron, and call the doctor!" Raghid screamed, "and Sheikh Watfan!"

While Nasim was summoning the other two men Raghid paced the parlor, consumed by a hate-filled sorrow and an overwhelming desire to win Bahriya's favor. For the first time in his life he'd given a woman something more valuable that costume jewelry. And for the first time in his life he hadn't heard so much as a word of thanks. On the contrary, his gesture had been received with an indifference bordering on contempt. He'd never given a woman genuine gold before. After all, most women didn't deserve the metal most dear to his heart. And now Bahriya, the only female he had ever given his precious gold to, was rejecting it with her silence, and with messages of refusal written upon her skin in swollen, crimson eloquence.

The doctor came as Raghid had requested. And Sheikh Watfan booted

Nasim out of his room, saying he wasn't up to dealing with Bahriya's demon at the moment!

After removing the small fortune she was wearing, the doctor examined her and said, "It's a condition known as articaria. It's nothing serious."

"What do you mean?"

"She has an allergy to gold. She can't tolerate having it touch her skin. Some people have allergies to nylon, dust, feathers, and so on. And this girl has an allergy to gold. The only treatment is to remove her jewelry, and to have her take a dose of this medicine until the symptoms have disappeared."

Raghid picked up the medicine, put on his reading glasses and asked in astonishment, "Atarax? This is a powerful sedative. They gave it to me before I was anesthetized for my kidney transplant operation. I keep a careful eye on the medications I take, and I don't forget a name."

"That's right. It's given sometimes prior to anesthesia, only in larger amounts."

"And is gold such a foreign body to Bahriya that she has to be anesthetized before it's implanted? What a strange creature."

"Pardon me," said the doctor, "I don't understand."

"Oh, nothing. I don't understand, either."

◆　◆　◆

When the doctor was gone, Raghid called for Nasim and politely offered him a cigar. (What does he want from me now? Bahriya's eye after he got Sirri Al-Din's kidney?)

"What did you want, sir?"

"I wanted to ask you . . . I mean, I don't understand Bahriya, and you may understand her better than I do. She's closer to you. What I mean to say is, she's been forced out of her home, and lived with her family in deprivation in spite of the fact that she's of noble birth, being my relative and all. You can understand her the way you'd understand your sister."

"In a way, I suppose. So what did you want?"

What is it that would make her happy? I mean, what would make your sister happy if she were in her place?"

"To go back home, of course."

"I can't send Bahriya back to Beirut now. But what could I do in the meantime?"

"Nothing. Just leave her in peace."

"But I'm trying to make her feel happy. And whenever I do, something happens that I don't know how to explain."

"For example?"

"Yesterday, for example, I took her on an outing in the helicopter to Gstaad and we had lunch in one of its most luxurious restaurants—the one in the Grand Hotel. I ordered lobster for her, the most expensive food they had, and she turned up her nose at it. Then when the waiter brought out the utensils used specially for eating it, gimlets, scissors, lancets, and the like—all of them of pure silver—she burst into tears as if she were terrified."

"Maybe the poor girl had never seen such things before except in some hospital emergency room in Beirut when she went there carrying a bleeding child or somebody wounded and in pain."

"That's possible, but . . ."

"What?"

"Then I gave her that black Mercedes, and instead of being delighted and giving me a kiss, she burst into tears and started running her hands over the trunk and trying to open it."

"Perhaps the dismembered corpse of her father or her sweetheart was brought back to her in the trunk of a black Mercedes. Or maybe her mother was killed when a booby-trapped car exploded, or . . ."

"That's enough. I don't want to hear any more out of the Beirut dictionary of woes."

"But this is what's really happening to us, every day."

"I'll have to ship more arms to all the warring factions in Beirut. Maybe that way I can kill them all off and destroy that city of malcontents. I'd be doing a favor for myself and you all, too."

"Will there be anything else, sir?"

"No. Is Sheikh Watfan in his room?"

"Yes."

"I'll go see him. It makes me feel better to talk to him. But having a conversation with you is unbearable."

When Raghid went upstairs to see his sorcerer, Nasim sneaked in to see Bahriya. Kneeling in front of her, he took her swollen, defiant hand in his and stroked it tenderly. She surrendered it to him, gazing at him with eyes that had turned from murky glass balls into rays of gentle spring sunshine. The blank stare gone, he sensed that she could see him clearly, reading his inmost thoughts. So why not tell her out loud, "I love you?" He didn't dare. When he was with her, his heart soared back and forth between elation and sorrow. Then suddenly her hair smelled of fire, and he remembered his family in Beirut under siege.

As he crept toward the telephone, he thought to himself: After that "personal consultation" he called me in for today, Raghid wouldn't give me a tongue-lashing even if he caught me trying to call Beirut.

He dialed to get an outside line, then dialed the Beirut international code, 961, followed by the number of his house. And for the very first time, the miracle happened and the telephone actually rang. He couldn't believe his ears. Since the beginning of the invasion, he'd been doing everything he could to contact Beirut, but without success. Whenever he was able to get away from Raghid and that sorcerer of his, he'd spent hours in post office phone booths trying to get through, but to no avail. And now Beirut was answering on the very first try. He wouldn't forget to ask his sister to inquire about Bahriya. He'd tell her what little he himself knew about her, in hopes that. . . . The phone rang, but no one answered. Then, just as he was thinking of hanging up, he heard his sister's voice. His heart was racing as if he were a sparrow in a hurricane. He couldn't remember exactly what he'd said to her, or what she'd said to him. All he knew was that the receiver had nearly fallen out of his hand when he heard the devastating news that his brother Fawwaz had been injured while fighting the Israelis in the Khalda area. Not only that, but his other brother, Hani, had blown himself up in a suicide operation at one of the entrances to Beirut under siege. Fawwaz hadn't been well trained when he took up arms. He and other Lebanese had been fighting side by side with some of the Palestinian young lions when he was wounded. However, he wasn't in critical condition.

Just then Raghid reached out and pressed a button to cut off the call.

"Who gave you the right to use somebody else's telephone to make a long-distance call?" he shrieked. "This is a private home, not a hostel for the indigent and the ill-bred!"

Nasim looked at him in a daze, without hearing a single word.

"Yes," affirmed Raghid, "I'm a tightwad with the poor and a spendthrift with the rich, and that's my prerogative. Go ahead and hate me if you don't like it. I give presents when I want to whomever I want, and my present to you today isn't a telephone call. Instead, you'll find your present in your room. It's something to remind you not to go sneaking over to Amir's house, thinking that there might be some things that get by me. Go to your room now, and you'll find your present."

By this time Nasim had plunged headlong into an abyss of such bewilderment and wretchedness, he didn't hear a word Raghid said. Even so, he had the urge to kill him simply to get him out of his way so that he could run to his room and be alone.

When he went in, he hardly noticed the statue that Raghid had left for him on the bed. Instead, he picked it up and put it on the floor, then lay down and closed his eyes.

He didn't understand that Raghid wanted to put him in his place by giving him a copy of the Freedom Fighter statue that Amir's father had sculpted for Gamal Abdul Nasser, or that Raghid prided himself on having amassed his first million by making a business out of it. In fact, he didn't see the statue until the next morning.

◆　　◆　　◆

Bahriya of the impossible . . .

She slips through my fingers like a handful of colored sand that I try in vain to steal from time's shores. She slips away like one's lifetime, like health, like youth, like all the things that I can't buy with my millions. I circle her fortress, hedged about by silence and otherworldly indifference. I search for a way into that securely sealed edifice to shake its foundations, but I find none. My augers of gold are of no use against her marble silence.

This is the only woman I've ever felt at such a loss with. It's as if every time I seek out her impossible love, I touch death. Everything about her puts the taste of failure in my mouth. That's right, failure. In her presence there's something that confirms that I'm a failed human being. If I don't learn to hate her, she'll destroy me, upsetting my golden world, balanced atop the pinhead of a lifetime ridden with angst.

Maybe my sorcerer is right. Maybe she really is bewitched, an instrument of my foes. Maybe Nadim was plotting to do me harm by bringing her here. Every since she arrived, I've been unable even to desire another woman. I haven't touched a female since she came, woman or child, and she's been my sole preoccupation.

Perhaps the time has come to break her spell over me. If I let her gain power over my spirit, she'll destroy me.

Sheikh Watfan is right. I don't want to cause trouble now, but once the Night of the First Billion is over I need to think of a way to get rid of her. I'll marry her off or kill her or have her die in a car accident . . .

But the childlike dream that I've been clinging to ever since she came will be broken. It's a dream I haven't known the likes of since I was a young man. And Bahriya is the only female that's been able to remind me that once upon a time I was an adolescent with dreams.

I've dreamed of her walking alongside me on the Night of the First Billion, her hand in mine. I was hoping to crown her myself, then take her with me to my hell, an illusory, unattainable jewel.

It's a dream that will just have to be buried in the body of some other luscious woman. I'll find a new one that I can have pass through my bedroom and then go her way.

◆　◆　◆

"Welcome, Sheikh Sakhr! It's been a long time since you last honored us with a visit."

"My brother Hilal was staying with me, as you know. Then we had a disagreement before he left, and I've been ill. I've still got a splitting headache."

"Sorry to hear that."

"Thank you for you invitation to the Night of the First Billion celebration. I'll be coming, of course."

"It would honor me for you to attend."

"I spoke with Saqr. He's doing some sightseeing outside the country at the time, but he'll come back specially to attend the party."

"I've prepared a room for him in my house. He'll be my guest."

"He seems to be quite taken by Khalil's wife—that old woman. You know he doesn't keep anything from me."

"Coco? She's not that old. She's twenty-nine or thirty. And she's pretty."

"Yes, she is. Blue-eyed. I saw her once at Nadim's house."

"She's here right now. She's been helping Mrs. Spock with the preparations for the party. Would you like to see her?"

"Not now. I personally prefer your relative, Bahriya. I came to give her my greetings. By the way, the other guests . . . where will they be spending the night?"

"There's a luxury hotel nearby, and I've rented the entire place for them. What do you think?"

"Good idea."

"It was Mrs. Spock's idea."

"And how is Miss Bahriya's health?"

"Poor thing. She's still suffering from shock."

"She's lovely. A young, innocent girl."

"I've never laid eyes on anyone more beautiful. Of course, no relative of mine could be anything but beautiful."

"Have you thought of getting her married to someone? That could help toward her recovery."

As Sheikh Sakhr spoke the words, his fingers fiddled nervously with the beads of his exquisite turquoise rosary.

Ignoring the hint, Raghid said, "Do you think so? It hadn't occurred to me. After all, she's still sick. She rarely leaves her room. And she spends all her time staring at the television and following the news from Beirut. When she sees scenes of fire and destruction, she doesn't cry or utter a word. Instead, she just trembles all over in spite of the medications prescribed by the doctor and Sheikh Watfan's incantations."

"Such a beauty, and so unfortunate. She doesn't deserve all this suffering. It's too bad what's been happening to Lebanon. Did you know that my summer mansion there has been robbed? And bombed, too."

Feigning ignorance of the matter, Raghid said, "Robbed? Who would dare lay a hand on the property of Sheikh Sakhr!"

"You see? Nothing's sacred there anymore. Like you, I was shocked when I heard the news. In fact, I couldn't believe it."

"That's right. It's incredible."

"Anyway, getting back to Bahriya . . ."

"How about getting back to the airport? It's been a long time since we discussed business concerns. It takes money to get married, as you're aware."

"I'm not poor."

"But you will be, if you go along with Hilal."

"That's true. His position is unreasonable."

With a look of pleasure and relief on his face, Raghid went on, "This airport would make you twenty thousand dollars of net profit without your having to do anything but secure the clan's agreement. In addition, I'm now holding five million dollars for you. It's your share of the profits from our arms-sales enterprise. Business is booming these days. And that's sure to cover the expenses for a wedding straight out of the Arabian Nights, complete with a young bride of legendary beauty."

"May I see Bahriya?"

"Certainly. And you can touch her as well. We'll announce the engagement on the Night of the First Billion if you wish. Her dowry will be agreement to go through with the project—the airport project, of course."

Sakhr looked as though he'd made up his mind.

"Very well," he said. "I'll contact my agent by telex. It would be marvelous to have the engagement announced on the Night of the First Billion, surrounded by friends and loved ones."

"They'll envy you. No one has ever seen a human being so beautiful. Or even a genie. Just ask Sheikh Watfan!"

They both laughed.

"But please, couldn't I just visit her now to make sure she's all right?"

"Of course. I'll come with you."

Dunya saw them going upstairs and had a feeling they were on their way to see Bahriya. Or might they be going to see the sorcerer? She winked at Nasim, who didn't need to be alerted, since he just "happened" to be dusting the statues near where the two men had been talking, and had heard everything.

After they'd gone upstairs, he said to her, "Don't worry. He won't even let him touch her hand. That way he can set his passions on fire all the more. And he wouldn't dare hurt her before the Night of the First Billion. He wouldn't want to do anything to spoil that day."

By the time Sheikh Sakhr left the Zahran mansion, his rosary had found its way into Raghid's pocket, and from there into his collection of pilfered prayer beads.

Ever since Bahriya's arrival she'd been haunting him, even in his dreams-turned-nightmares. He hadn't filched a single rosary, and several times he'd forgotten to take his blood pressure medicine. His nocturnal raids on the refrigerator had seen a notable increase, and his diabetes had been getting worse. He had to get her out of his life. So, he figured, let that be the price he'd pay for the airport deal. No matter what happened, the important thing was for her to depart from that shady, mysterious place somewhere deep inside him—a place he knew nothing about, since he'd been too busy with his gold to pay it any attention.

Besides which, his sorcerer would be delighted to learn that he'd decided to go back to his old womanizing and get out from under the curse of Bahriya's evil spell.

◆　◆　◆

Coco leaned gently toward the large golden clock as she reflected on a new location for it. As Raghid was on his way back to his room after seeing Sakhr off, he looked over at her and saw her as a marble statue picking up a vessel of gold. He wished he could take her to bed with him. On the other hand, it might be nice for her to stay right where she was so that he could have her at that very moment: on top of the plush carpet, at the feet of his golden statues, and accompanied by the golden tick-tock, tick-tock of immortal time. But that wasn't possible just now, in full view of Layla and her team of lady workers. On the other hand, why not? No. Not in front of Dunya, who'd been giving him rather nasty looks these days. She must be jealous of Coco. Or do you suppose she was jealous of Bahriya? He'd probably never know with a hard-to-read woman like her. In any case, there was no good reason to stir up a commotion among the women just now. With the Night of the First Billion just a few days off, he couldn't do without any of them. But . . . maybe she could come back that night after all of the rest of them had gone. She was certainly delectable. And his lifetime was slipping away. Besides which, Bahriya was an impossible dream. Just then Dunya approached him with a storm brewing in her eyes. What does she want from me now? He wondered. I don't have time to waste with her. And I don't want us to get into an argument. Once the Night of the First Billion is over, I'll have accounts to settle with everybody while I'm busy amassing my second billion. But not now.

"What do you say we take Bahriya in as our guest after the Night of the First Billion?" Dunya asked him. "My daughter could keep her company, and that might help her. She's near her age, and their spending time together could help her regain her health little by little. She might even regain her ability to speak."

"We'll see," he said. "Everything in its time."

Then he walked off, nearly fleeing from her, and his heart filled with resentment. (So she wants to meddle in my affairs? That's people for you. After you've sated them and filled their pockets with gold, they turn feisty on you. Nadim's gotten lazy and he's started making lots of mistakes. It was a mistake to bring Bahriya. Everything she touches, she sets on fire. She's about to un-nerve my sorcerer, who used to be a paragon of levelheadedness. And she fills my sleep with nightmares and turns people against me. Nasim's turned into an upstart, and Khalil had the audacity to ruin our whole evening with that song, "O darkness of the prison!" when we were celebrating her arrival. And now, if Sakhr doesn't manage to persuade his people to give me the airport contract, her coming will have been a waste of time and nerves without having brought any return even on the publicity front. She's totally unpredictable. No one knows what's going on in her head, and I don't dare take her to public places anymore. All the time and money I've spent on her have gone down the drain. Meanwhile, Dunya's gone back to championing women's causes. We thought we were through with all that when we bought off the husbands of the other women in her circle and the magazine that used to publish all sorts of non-sense for them. If Sakhr doesn't bring me the signature I need, then I won't know how to get rid of her. It might not be a bad idea to let Dunya take re-sponsibility for her, after all. But no. Nadim will find another way to get into Sakhr's world. However, my relationship with Nadim these days isn't quite what it used to be, not since that argument we got into over his bringing Bahriya here. He rushed into it before making sufficient inquiries. Anyway, I'm not going to let worries ruin my life. I'll distract myself from it all by settling accounts with Khalil, if not tonight, then some other time. And I'll enjoy it with lovely Coco. But I'll ask my sorcerer for some help. I've been told she might wear me out.)

❖   ❖   ❖

"I adjure you, O Unqoud, by the truth of faith and promises and black beasts of burden, by the Torah sent down to the Jews, by the power of the world of the unseen and the Name by which water comes forth from the great rock, Ha Li'aknas, li'klis, Aktouna, Altouna, Ah, Ah, tawakkal, O Unqoud, I adjure you to summon Kafa the daughter of Anisa and Raghid son of Suha, I adjure you in the name of Shamlak, Tulaz, Hasakik, and Taykal. Respond, O Unqoud, with Kafa and Raghid. Be present, O ye subject spirits and come to me from the mountains, from the sands, from the barren valleys, from the clouds and from everywhere. Tounis Mutakanis, Sharbouniya Marbouniya, by the truth of these names you must bring Kafa daughter of Anisa to Raghid son of Suha."

◆ ◆ ◆

He had to admit, her body was little more than a barricade behind which he could hide from Bahriya, and a battleground between him and Khalil: the hills of her rounded bosom, the plains of sand fine as silk that stretched out level beyond the foothills, the forest, the multicolored, moist, warm grottos, the torrid underground streams, and the never-ending departure for a nearby destination.

Coco now adorned the center of his bed, a feast of delight. She had made herself up with womanly mastery: knowing how he loved gold, she'd chosen a golden paint for her lips and encircled her blue eyes with gilded shadows till they looked like a pair of exquisite turquoise stones in a dazzling piece of jewelry. She'd brushed her cheeks with a golden pink powder, and the nightgown she wore was a diaphanous veil of his favorite metal, its hardness now transformed into the downy softness of an enchanted dream.

She seemed aglow, different. All of them came the first time aflame with exhilaration and energy, frightening him with their passionate appetites for life and affluence. And time after time, the initial glitter would fade. Then they all started to seem the same, and boring. It was as if, in their womanly wisdom, they understood that they really had no place in this golden corner of the world except as decorations, or as battlegrounds. They knew they weren't the center of men's lives, but mere playthings, and that when a man gives a fur coat to his wife, he isn't really giving it to her, but to himself, as a visible sign of his "purchasing power" for her to carry around on her shoulders. In fact, no gift is intended to give pleasure to the woman, since in essence it's nothing but the man's way of showing off his prosperity and power. So, was Coco too smart to be a mere plaything, or would she be content to go along with the game?

(Go ahead, man. Don't be afraid of her body. After all, it's as fragile as a balloon. It has no spiritual substance supporting it from the inside, and no mind to give it continuity. Prick a hole in it like a little boy playing with a balloon, and all the false appearances of pride and conceit will come seeping out never to return. Then it will shrivel up on the bed like a many-colored rag, just another empty balloon.) Raghid looked over at her again. And this time he saw her as nothing but an inflated balloon with the air gradually leaking out of it until its features looked so ridiculous they made him want to laugh.

Coco tried to help him take off his silk robe, though for some reason he didn't feel like removing it. He wondered why women wouldn't let him march into battle and plant his banners of victory over other men without having to perform these boring, tiresome theatrics time and time again: undressing, flirtation, drinking a few toasts to each other, turning off the lights, groaning and sighing, and all the rest.

And then there were the revolting questions and the customary conversation:

"Was I good?"

"Of course, my sweet."

"Am I better than the others?"

"Absolutely."

'Do you love me?"

"Forever."

"Have you ever enjoyed yourself so much before?"

"Oh, never. It's as if I'd never had another woman before you!"

He stepped into her fields, then proceeded leisurely with his hunting exhibition without really intending to excite her. But there was a face hovering in the darkness of the room, which came between him and her. The face of Bahriya appeared to him, alien and distant, charged with an inexplicable pain and an impenetrable secrecy. There swept over him a burning desire to contain her, to make love to the impossible. He'd grown weary of playthings. He was bored with his eunuchs' wives. Remembering Khalil as he sang, "O darkness of the prison," a feeling of bitter hatred went flowing out toward his limbs. With that he regained his fighting spirit and carried on with his journey toward the hills.

Then suddenly the telephone rang. (What imbecile would dare disturb me at this hour? It must be something serious, since hardly anyone knows the number to this room.)

He picked up the receiver. The voice on the other end was muffled, indistinct, as if it were coming from another planet. And whoever it was wanted to speak with Kafa.

"Wrong number," he said.

As he hung up, he felt a frigid rain pouring down over him from the bed's silk canopy. So then, someone had been spying on his private life, and was announcing the fact to him in hopes of frightening him.

"Who was that?" asked Kafa with intoxicated nonchalance.

"Somebody who was asking for you, Coco."

"For me? That's ridiculous."

"Who knows that you're here?"

"Nobody."

"Your husband?"

"Certainly not. Besides, he's out of the country."

"In any case, Khalil wouldn't know my telephone number here."

Frightened, she asked, "Are you sure?"

"Of course! But somebody asked for you."

"Was it a man or a woman?"

"The voice wasn't clear."

"Maybe it was Dunya. She's the jealous type."

"Did you tell her anything?"

"I told you, I didn't tell anyone. But maybe she figured it out by intuition and decided to try to disturb us."

"Does Saqr know that you're here?"

"I haven't seen him. I swear to you. You know he's on a trip with my husband, and that I spend all my time here with Lilly. We've been working night and day getting ready for the Night of the First Billion party."

"Is Khalil outside of Geneva?"

"You know he is!"

"The call came from inside Switzerland. I didn't hear the clicks that come with international calls."

"You see?"

"Who knows that you're here?"

"Nobody. I swear to you."

"Who brought you here?"

"A taxi. Ask your guards."

"All right. Get dressed and leave, quickly. I need to think."

As she hurriedly put on her clothes, trembling with fear and humiliation, he rang the bell for Nasim, then went personally to the door to ask him to get the car ready for the guest.

Seeing her off in a rush, he gave her a small package wrapped in gold paper, which she slipped into her handbag. Then she hurried downstairs to wait for the chauffeur to take her away in one of Raghid's opulent cars.

With Nasim standing nearby waiting with her, she felt a bit embarrassed. (All right . . . why should his being here bother me? He's nothing but a butler. And he wouldn't dare tell Khalil or anyone else.)

When she was gone, Nasim went back to his room rubbing his hands playfully with a handkerchief that he had placed a short while earlier over the telephone receiver while he called Raghid's room. He'd truly loved Khalil ever since the night he heard him sing, "O darkness of the prison!" surrounded by those brutes and prison keepers. A man like him doesn't deserve to have his wife cheat on him with a bastard like Raghid!

Suspicions would hover around the few individuals who knew Raghid's bedroom telephone number, and he was among them.

But Raghid wouldn't be sure who it was. And he wouldn't do it again. He'd promised himself not to interfere with the base dealings going on around him. Otherwise he might not get out of this lions' den alive. With one of his brothers dead and the other wounded, his poor family wouldn't be able to bear the shock of losing him, too. He might be willing to die for Bahriya, but not for a woman like Coco. And he mustn't forget it again. Instead, he needed to hurry up and get out of this hellhole. His urge to strangle Raghid with his bare hands had come back, and the Freedom Fighter statue that Raghid had given him whispered in his ear every night before he went to sleep, "Kill him! Kill him before the Night of the First Billion. Kill him. Don't let him enjoy any more crimes. Remember Sirri Al-Din. Remember your brother, who was willing to blow himself up on the walls of Beirut rather than let Israel trample them underfoot. Remember that Raghid has devoted his entire existence to ensuring the prosperity of the enemy and opening the way for them to invade other Arab capitals as well."

◆　◆　◆

The morning heaved a warm, fervent sigh, like a fiery, wordless message from some other land. Nasim walked into the sorcerer's room, bringing him his morning tea. The room was dark and stifling, and the peculiar smells of incense and the sorcerer's potions, having nested in the corners of the room, had begun filtering through the cracks in the door into the corridor until they'd nearly taken it over. Like dark, invisible creatures whose odors create suffocating climates laden with secrecy and curses, they seemed to be charging toward the door leading into Bahriya's suite on the same floor.

Nasim headed over toward the curtains and drew them open to let in the sun, which hadn't disappeared from the Geneva sky since Bahriya's arrival. But no sooner had he done so than Sheikh Watfan shrieked at him from his bed in a panic-stricken voice, "Who asked you to open the curtains and let in the light? Draw them shut again, and now!"

Nasim stared at the sorcerer questioningly, nonplussed to see him avoiding the spot where the sunlight had shone in and covering his face with his hand as he looked the other way. (My God, how Sheikh Watfan has changed. His face is gaunt, and his beard has gotten long and shaggy. The light in his eyes has faded into a couple of red puddles as though he hasn't slept for days, his hair is frosted with gray, and he's suddenly gotten lots of wrinkles in his face as though he'd aged several years all at once. I've been so angry about the way he acts toward Bahriya, I'd started to avoid looking at him. First he wanted to slip that love potion into her food. Then he tried to force me to help him torture her and shave her head to treat her alleged "insanity" and exorcise the imaginary afreet that's possessed her and which harbors enmity toward him and Raghid. This is the first time I've looked into his face since Bahriya arrived, and if it weren't for his bizarre eyes, the left one green and the right one brown, I wouldn't have recognized him. What do you suppose is going on in that barbaric, secret world of his inhabited by jinn, afreets and hatred? What's going on inside that head of his, as closed as a sealed chest full of vile insects? He seems to be harboring some tremendous evil. But toward whom? Toward poor Bahriya?)

Laboring to keep his voice sounding normal, Nasim said to Sheikh Watfan, "You have a letter."

"Put it beside the tea. Don't come near me."

Nasim was amazed at Watfan's hostile behavior, and at the fearful tone in his trembling voice. (Does he think that I'm also possessed by an afreet that intends to destroy him? Along with his delusions of grandeur, has he started suffering from paranoia, too? Before coming here, I never would have believed that in this day and age—the age of Israel's occupation of both Palestine and Lebanon—there are still people who resort to magicians for help. And if I hadn't seen that Sheikh Watfan's clients include the wealthy and the powerful and even political leaders of all different persuasions, I wouldn't have believed that this sort of nonsense still goes on, or that at the moment when my brother was blowing himself up in an Israeli tank, one of the Arab leaders was consulting a sorcerer, sitting here as meekly as a little child in his presence.)

His voice quivering, Nasim said, "The journalist has called you several times since early this morning."

"I've given you orders to tell him that I'm away."

"I did. He didn't believe me. He knows you're here. Nothing gets past those damned journalists, as you know. He said he'd call again at noon, and that he hopes you'll speak to him. They can't go on forging the horoscope, and they're paying you an exorbitant sum for the service. He says you don't have the right to end the contract unilaterally without giving them sufficient notice."

"Leave me alone. The tea will get cold."

"Would you like me to serve it to you in bed?"

"I told you not to come near me. Get out."

By this time Nasim's eyes had gotten used to the darkness, and he could see that the sorcerer had taken red powder and drawn a five-pointed star around his bed.

"Don't step across the red line," the sorcerer said, "and bring me a liter of pure white alcohol."

As Nasim obeyed orders and left the room, he could smell the odor of isopropyl alcohol, and he saw the sorcerer rubbing his hands vigorously with it. (So then, he's begun cleaning his hands in vain with alcohol. He's been using up more than a liter a day, so much that I thought he was drinking it, or getting ready to burn some animal sacrifice in it. My God, how he's changed. He's stopped smoking the water pipe with cherry tobacco the way he used to, or asking me to make him green tea while he chants merry songs to the jinn kings with his beautiful voice. He's even stopped fiddling with the beads on his long rosary like a hermit the way he used to. He doesn't dye his hands with henna anymore. And . . . and . . . oh, how he's changed!)

Once Nasim had left the room, Sheikh Watfan got out of bed. Looking like a towering ghost with a body as thin as a rail wrapped in a white, frightening-looking shroud, he rushed over to draw the curtains all the way shut. He'd come to hate and fear the daytime. He hated for anyone to see him in bright light or to see himself in the mirror. Mirrors had come to be a source of terror for him, ever since Bahriya had chased him all the way inside his bathroom mirror, then set fire to the chambers inside all the mirrors in the world. (One night I woke up terrified. I'd dreamed that I was walking toward Bahriya's room while her afreet called to me with all sorts of different voices—the voices of old people, young children, men, animals, ogres, birds and vipers. It was calling out to me and challenging me. I opened Bahriya's door and went in, and in the darkness I saw her clearly as a human corpse. The corpse was fast asleep, but the afreet living inside it was moving around, working to destroy me. The moment I came up beside her, she opened her enormous eyes without moving. And what should I discover but that her eyes were mirrors. They had neither pupils nor whites. Instead, the afreet had planted two lustrous mirrors in the sockets where her eyes would have been. When I looked into them, I saw myself as two men whose heads were on fire.

I screamed with fright, and fled from this appalling witchcraft of hers back to my room. I locked the door and drew a star around my bed with magic powder, then reinforced its potency by reciting some incantations to make it into an invisible wall that would protect me from harm. Then I sat in bed, took a mirror in my hand, and looked into it. And what should I find but that my face really was on fire, and it appeared as nothing but a mask floating in space. As I stared at it, I felt pained. I howled like a jackal so that I wouldn't wake anyone up, and hoping that Nasim and Raghid wouldn't recognize my voice and think I'd lost my mind. Since that night, I haven't been able to look into a mirror without seeing my face as a flaming mask floating in empty space. Oh, the tea's gotten cold. But never mind. I haven't got any appetite for either food or drink these days. For all I know, the afreet that's possessed Nasim to use him as Bahriya's protector has received orders to poison me. So I don't dare eat anymore unless I'm with Raghid, and after he's taken a few bites. Actually, I can't stand anybody's company anymore, including Raghid's. However, I have no choice but to sit with him at meal times, otherwise I'd starve to death. God, how I hate to be with people anymore—I, the man who used to insist on going to the hotel to meet people's needs—and to meet with those kindhearted, rabble-rousing journalists.)

The sorcerer washed his hands with soap and water for the tenth time that morning without knowing why. Then he rearranged his sorcery utensils and wiped the imaginary dust off them for the thousandth time since the previous night. He didn't know what had come over him all of a sudden. He'd started to feel the need to restore order to the chaos all around him, and he'd done just that for the millionth time since Bahriya's arrival. He no longer did anything but wash his hands, stay in his room far from light and people, and engage in the bizarre, futile tidying up of the already tidy. Since the arrival of that possessed woman, he'd stopped paying visits to the pretty hookers on Berne Street whose bodies the jinn bride used to clothe herself in. He no longer felt a desire for any female but Bahriya. He'd even forgotten Anbara, who'd been erased by Bahriya from his memory. What he had to do first was to cast out the powerful enemy spirit that had taken over her body to do him harm. When he massaged her towering, youthful body with ointments, bats' blood and camels' blood, and chanted his incantations, he used to tremble from faintness like someone in passionate love. The words that had once done his bidding had now begun to slip out of his grasp. He'd begun stuttering when he was with her, and even in her absence he had to exert a tremendous effort to keep himself from it when he was talking to Nasim or Raghid. How had her cry of distress found its way into his bosom, taking it over and turning him into a mass of contradictions and fears? She had erased his present life and sent him back into a distant but painful past. (It's as though that past is alive, as though I'm living it even now with my brothers and sisters and my parents, complete with the salty fragrance of Beirut. I feel as though I'm falling little by little into other ages and times, and burning. The voices that come to me from those times are more vivid than my present, which is dried and preserved like a piece of jerky and surrounded by images of my face as it goes up in flames in the mirror. It's as if the happy time I lived with the spirits was an illusion that's now begun to fade. As if poor Bahriya is possessed by one of the afreets from Beirut that used to plot against our family so long ago. I don't know. I don't know anything anymore except that ever since Bahriya came here, I've been exiled to other lives that I lived in the past. And the dead past has come to be more alive than my own life.)

The sorcerer turned on a dim lamp and cautiously picked up the letter. Who knows? Maybe her afreet had gone from writing messages on mirrors to writing them on paper. Anything was possible. He turned it over fearfully and opened it. Inside he found a bank statement containing information about the balance in his account. After reading the numbers over and over without understanding a thing, he finally realized that what they meant was that he was rich. He possessed a fortune in six figures. But now he'd forgotten why he'd wanted to amass it, or why his primary concern had once been to own the largest amount possible. Why? He couldn't remember anymore. He felt hungry, frightened and alone. And what frightened him even more was that everything that was happening to him with Bahriya seemed like a repetition, as though it had all happened to him some time before. It was a story whose tragic ending he already knew, and although he couldn't remember the details, he was vaguely aware of them, like someone who tries to remember a dream or a previous life. And the certainty that he had lived through all this before in some sense just accelerated his hopeless fall into the trap of loneliness and isolation. He'd become a lone wolf. He avoided people now, whereas he'd previously sought them out even against Raghid's wishes, and he was besieged by nightmares from a world of the inscrutable and the absurd. He wasn't certain anymore where dreams ended and where reality began, or when he'd stepped into his mirror nightmare and when he had left it. (I once overcame fear with power, and I was perfectly content among my subjects, that is, until Anbara came back into my life. She caused me grief, but she didn't threaten my authority in the kingdom of jinn and humans that I ruled. And now everything is falling apart because of Bahriya. I'm being eaten away on the inside, as though vicious, wild ants were consuming me night and day. Ah, this damned heat that came with her, it's like a poisoned wind blowing in from another world. I'm suffocating . . .)

He picked up a white rag and wiped the sweat off his brow, only to find to his dismay that it was the color of blood! (Have I really begun sweating blood? Or is she playing games with my senses?)

Then he picked up the mirror again. He looked into it, but this time he didn't see himself at all, as if he'd been cancelled out of existence. Instead, all he saw was a large question mark drawn inside it.

He rang the bell for Nasim. When Nasim came in a few minutes later, the sorcerer was still staring at the question mark in horror.

"Take this mirror," he told Nasim, "and look into it."

Baffled, Nasim carried out the sorcerer's order. He looked into the mirror, and all he saw was his miserable-looking face and the tracks of the tears he had shed furtively since his brother's death.

"What do you see?" the sorcerer asked him.

"My face, of course," he said matter-of-factly.

"Don't you see anything else?"

"Of course not."

Taking the mirror back, the sorcerer looked into it again, only to find that the question mark was still there. In fact, there were now so many of them that they nearly covered its mercurial, deceitful surface. Then they began wiggling and swarming like tiny worms preparing to consume his corpse.

He dismissed Nasim with a wave of the hand, and didn't utter a word for the rest of the day. However, he made a voodoo doll of Bahriya, after which he poked pins into it, cast spells over it and burned it in his censer. And even though it made him feel as though he were being burned along with it, he repeated the process again, and again, and again.

◆ ◆ ◆

Nasim walked into Bahriya's room carrying a breakfast tray. Ever since her arrival, he'd spoken to her without knowing whether she heard him or not, whether she was listening or not. And he was tender toward her as if she were his little girl or his mother. When she turned over in bed, he could smell the salty fragrance of the hot summer sea. In fact, it was a fragrance that he could always smell in her room, in her fiery presence, like a city under siege. He opened the curtains and the light came pouring in. As though she welcomed the light, she turned her face toward it so that she could drink it in. Then she turned toward Nasim and looked into his face. As she looked at him she yawned, and it seemed that she'd begun to trust him.

"Good morning," he said.

"Good . . . morning . . ."

Had she really spoken, or was he just imagining it? He didn't know. When he heard the words, he'd been pulling the table up to the bed and arranging the silverware with his back turned to her.

"A million good mornings," he said, his heart filled with affection for her.

She smiled. She really was smiling, and he wasn't imagining it. But no, he wasn't entirely sure. Yet in the moment it took for her to smile—or even to seem to smile—several suns rose, seeds sprouted forth out of scorched soil and warm rain poured down tenderly upon it, causing it to fill with trees. The trees were filled with buds, then blossoms, springs gushed forth and birds began to sing. As he arranged the dishes and silverware, he said to her, "Did you speak, or didn't you? Did you smile, or didn't you? It makes no difference, really. Blessings upon you, you poor little girl. May God protect you from all those villains, you majestic lady. One doctor goes, another comes, and both of them shoot you full of drugs. They keep you asleep day and night as if they were afraid of what might happen if you woke up. But in spite of the way they drug you up all the time, I feel as though you're as alive and as calm as a mine ready to go off. There's something about you that spurs me to action . . . incites me to murder . . . and drives me to tears!"

She got out of bed. Her wounds had healed, and as she walked over to the sink to wash her face, she looked to him to be strong and full of stamina, a goddess sculpted not out of marble, but out of flint. She emitted live sparks, and held within her the charm of Aphrodite, the resoluteness of Zenobia, the sorrows of Electra, the wisdom of Athena and the impetuosity of Cleopatra. He looked out the window and imagined that she was sprinting through the forest the way she did every night. He thought he'd caught a glimpse of her in the thicket. Or was she really in the bathroom? When she came back, the glassy, absent look in her eyes was gone. Instead, she fixed her gaze intently on his face. It was then that he remembered that he was exhausted, with hair that hadn't been combed since who knows when, and that he probably looked like an old man of thirty.

With youthful impulsiveness, he said to her, "I'm twenty-five years old, but I look like an old man because I'm already head of a family. I've got nine brothers and sisters, and I'm their sole provider. Or rather, I used to have nine, but then one of them was killed in battle. We poor folks age fast, and with us, every night is a celebration of the Feast of the Billion Victims and Martyrs."

She stared at him in silence.

He continued, "I don't know why it is that I chatter away to you like this. You're the only person I open my heart to and talk to honestly about my misery without feeling ashamed. Are you really sick? Or do you put on silence as a clever way of getting away from your persecutors? Is your name really 'Bahriya,' or is it 'Hurriya'?[28] Are you like me, someone who was cast out of house and home and driven here by fate? All I know for sure is that you aren't Raghid's relative, and that I'll do everything in my power to protect you from them, not to protect them from you. Do you really stay in bed at night, or do you go out to be with the animals and plants that Nature has placed in your care? At dawn, I always imagine that I see you merging with the forest mist. But with you being drugged up like this, I'm amazed sometimes that you can even get up and move around. Eat, precious. Gobble down your food. You've got to get your health back in a hurry so that you can leave this inferno, whether with me or without me. And watch out for them. Raghid dreams of robbing you of what he knows could never be his, and I'm afraid his love for you might turn into hate. After all, hatred is just love that's clothed itself in a frown, or in bitterness and resentment. The sorcerer is also crazy over you, in both love and hate. So beware of him. He might be dreaming of killing you. As for me, I dream of setting you free. And I'm dreaming in practical terms. I think I've managed to get your passport away from them, which will make it possible for you to leave. Do you hear me?"

28. This is a play on words: the name Bahriya means "of the sea," while *hurriya* means "freedom."

She didn't reply or even look up at him, but just went on drinking her tea in silence. Then Nasim remembered that he'd been in her room for a long time. If Raghid noticed, he might threaten to fire him the way he had on a previous occasion.

In farewell he whispered, "I leave you in God's care, you poor little princess. Listen. I forgot to let you know the results of your lab tests. There's nothing biologically wrong with you. That's what I heard the doctor telling Raghid. So that means that there's no physical cause for you not to be able to speak. You're definitely not mute, in case you'd like to know. And there's nothing they can do to you now, since they're all preoccupied with the Night of the First Billion celebration. Did you know that Raghid has scheduled it to coincide with your birthday? Is it really your birthday? If so, how could the birthdate of the oppressor and the oppressed be the same? Or the birthdays of the knife and the stab victim? Have you got a surprise up your sleeve for that night like the one you gave us at your welcome reception? Anyway . . .

"If the night of the party really is on your birthday, then may that night be blessed on your account. And as long as you're silent like this, not responding and perhaps not even hearing, I'll tell you that I love you a billion times. I don't want anything in return for this love except for you to accept what I have to give. And a penniless fellow like me can't do anything except to sacrifice his life for you."

Then he added as he left the room, "But I hope that won't be necessary. I don't think they'd dare try to hurt you, not now at least. That's what Dunya has told me."

As he shut the door, he thought he heard her say something sweet, like the scent of a spring breeze. He was always imagining her speaking to him through her tightly sealed lips. As he returned to the kitchen, he was nearly intoxicated with her. Meanwhile, Raghid was calling him on the intercom and cursing him in several languages. He didn't respond. Instead, he just sat pondering the sound that came pouring out of the intercom like a river of filth, refusing to depart from the land of his Bahriya-begotten bliss.

◆   ◆   ◆

How she detested the heat that had descended upon Geneva, digging its claws into it like a beast of prey.

Kafa had woken up with a troubled spirit, and blamed the heat for her state of mind. From the time her husband left on his trip, she hadn't left Nadim's luxurious flat, and she no longer went back to the hotel except to get some of her clothes. She'd been content until she discovered that the gift Raghid had given her was a fake, just like the ring she'd stolen from Dunya. The day after her failed night with Raghid she was dying to see the gift he'd given her. However, what should she find but that it was an exact replica of Dunya's ring, which she still had in her possession: counterfeit diamond, glass, worthless! She couldn't believe her eyes. She took it to the jeweler, who said about it the same thing he'd said about the first ring.

She felt thoroughly crushed. Then she started having nightmares. She dreamed that the sorcerer was delivering her to Raghid, whose face was bizarre. Instead of being elongated horizontally like most people's, his eyes went up and down, and they were slit down to his cheeks. His teeth were black and broken off, and his hair was nothing but straw.

The sorcerer whispered to her, "Don't tell him what he looks like. He doesn't know that he's dead."

Then he took her by the hand and lay her down inside a coffin, saying that he was going to tell her a bedtime story.

He closed her eyes with his hand and said, "Once upon a time there was a ghost . . . there was a ghost . . . This ghost used to give people gifts, but they were all nothing but an illusion."

She had breakfast, and what upset her even more was that Nadim didn't pass by as he usually did every morning. She looked out at the lake, and instead of seeming beautiful to her, it looked like a huge blue washbasin full of dirty laundry. Then when she touched the doorknob to leave the room, she got an electric shock, and for the first time she understood what used to happen to Khalil.

She'd lost her desire to work with Lilly on getting ready for the Night of the First Billion, and felt a vague sort of anxiety, like someone whose heaven on earth has turned into a bog of quicksand. She quickly put on her clothes, having decided to go out and buy a new silk dress to drown her sorrows in. As she was waiting for the elevator, she looked out the window, and the buildings that she'd thought were straight up and down seemed to be leaning slightly toward the mountains.

There awoke in her spirit an unnamed angst, a feeling she hadn't known while she was caught up in the exhilaration of her old certainty, and in the confidence that at long last she'd found the refined, urbane people with whom she belonged. She wasn't sure of anything anymore. Or at least, she was sure of only one thing, namely, that her love of riches, ease, diamonds and silk surpassed her love for anything else in the world, and that a rich impostor was better than a poor fool, or a poor imposter, for that matter. She intended to avoid pain as much as possible. She wanted to live happily, and she no longer found happiness anywhere but near wealth. She'd grown accustomed to the touch of the elderly masseuse who came every day to massage her comely physique lest she get flabby and obese from years of being holed up in the mildewed bomb shelters of Beirut. She'd also gotten used to her Chinese acupuncturist, who planted his needles in the key points on her body to deliver her from the periodic headaches that had begun afflicting her of late, as well as the eating binges she'd grown susceptible to in Geneva, adding several extra kilos to her weight. It was true, of course, that Nadim and his cronies were delighted with his development, since to them it was both a qualitative and a quantitative addition to her charms. However, she was concerned to hold onto the kind of svelte figure one likes to see in cocktail lounges and dinner parties, that is, in places other than darkened, locked bedrooms. When she got to the door, she was surprised to meet up with Nadim and a guest, whose Rolls Royce bespoke wealth and status. At the sight of them she forgot all about Raghid's ring and her fears, and her heart raced in anticipation of the new prey about to come to her lair for the express purpose of admiring her. How she loved hearing words of admiration, and what a womanly effort she always made to merit them.

She shook the guest's hand with the blueness of her eyes, and unsheathed the weapon of her long lashes. His voice trembled as he greeted her. Nadim had picked up on the vibrations of mutual admiration, and rather than regretting having made the introduction, he decided to make the most of the situation.

"Madame Coco," he said, "Might you join us for dinner? This is a guest of the Pasha's. He received an invitation to attend the Night of the First Billion and decided to arrive early to spend a short holiday in Switzerland."

"How nice . . ."

No one knew for certain what was "nice." However, they parted knowing that Coco would be spending the evening with Mr. Adel with the consent and approval of all three.

At the Maximum nightclub, Adel dazzled her with his magnanimity. She slipped a cigarette between her lips, and for the first time it gave her a thrill. She remembered how for so long she had loathed the smell of her husband's cigarettes, and had even launched an all out campaign against his smoking. After all, the smoke of poverty and wretchedness is suffocating, but the smoke of ease and opulence is like a breath of fresh air. Then Adel surprised her by taking out a thousand-franc bill, lighting the end of it with his cigarette lighter, then offering it to her for her to light her cigarette. Even Nadim was astounded by the sight. As for her, she nearly lost her senses, not knowing whether to put out the fire with her hands and rescue the bill with tears in her eyes, or to enjoy the scene that she'd seen so many times in films and wished she were the heroine. It was an unforgettable moment, in her opinion. She distended her bosom the way she'd seen actresses do in the movies, then exhaled the smoke of her cigarette in a sigh so deep, it was as though she were emptying out the last cell in her lungs and heart. Her eyes rained down blue passion upon Adel, who made no attempt to conceal his infatuation with her. So Nadim decided to himself: it's time for Adel and me to talk some business.

However, by this time things were out of his hands. Coco was behaving like a woman truly in love, as though her fidelity to the lie she was acting out surpassed even her love for treachery, and now Adel had been infected with her ardor. Meanwhile, Nadim felt a growing desire to win her back, snatching her out of the arms of the men to whom he had offered her. (Here's a woman who's corrupt to the core. She practices vice so wholeheartedly, she doesn't even notice what she's doing, and social settings set her ablaze all the more. Am I going to end up falling in love with a woman this shallow—a woman on fire and capable of sending me up in flames with her?)

Determined to roil the waters between the two lovebirds, he asked her, "Have you gotten any news from Khalil and Saqr since they left on their trip?"

"Khalil? Saqr?" she replied simply, "Who are they?"

Whereupon she proceeded to bury her face in the chest of a blissful, glowing Adel. And for the first time, Nadim felt something akin to jealousy, though at the same time there was something deep inside him that refused to be drawn into such a senseless rivalry. In a flash, all of his emotions toward her were transformed into feelings of bitter resentment toward his passionless wife, Dunya. He would never understand women. And he never had understood them, despite his reputation as a connoisseur of the fairer sex.

(The first woman I ever loved committed suicide when her family refused to let her marry me because I was poor. And now the second woman I loved—and married—is about to commit suicide because I'm not poor anymore. As for Coco, she says that because she loves me, she loves all men on earth. And she proves it in action with every man I introduce to her. I'll never understand women.)

Just then he was surrounded by a flock of dancers with colorful plumage dangling from their heads and posteriors like the soft tails of some sort of peculiar animal, and he ogled them as if he were seeing them for the first time in his life. (They've ruined my life from the very start. They've robbed me of my freedom with their lust for wealth. They're the ones who command social respect for their position as "women of means" while I obey their every whim.)

He thought of his elderly mother—that gentle woman who had endured both his father's cruelty and the cruelty of life in Beirut, that blameless, chaste woman who'd born the vicissitudes of fate with patience and restraint. As he thought of her, a forgotten dagger stirred deep within him and caused him a twinge of pain.

As if he sensed what Nadim was feeling, Adel waited until Coco had absented herself to go the ladies room, then said, "Let's talk some business, friend," which they proceeded to do against a background of uproarious merrymaking.

◆   ◆   ◆

When Raghid saw the picture of Bassam's lifeless body in the newspaper along with a photo of Amir concealing his face from the photographers' lenses, his heart was filled with a sweet relief that had the delectable taste of revenge.

But when, several days later, he saw a picture of Dunya in the same newspaper marching in a protest demonstration next to Amir, he picked up his magnifying glass and drew it near the newspaper to make certain it was really her that had committed such a heinous act. And his heart wasn't filled with relief, but with anxiety. (This heat is about to suffocate me, and I'm allergic to air-conditioning. Dunya's behavior comes as no surprise to me, since I've been watching her change lately. But this is a dangerous sign.)

This was a woman who had come to know plenty of secrets over their years of contact with each other, and she had no right to act as though she were her own agent—since that, quite simply, would mean going over to the enemy camp. Her punishment would have to be that meted out to a spy who commits treason.

But her death now (even in a supposed car accident, for example, as in the case of Sirri Al-Din) would be bound to arouse suspicion, especially coming just days before the Night of the First Billion. So he'd have to wait a bit. And until the definitive solution became feasible, he'd have to take some tranquilizers. He hurriedly summoned his assistant Nadim who, as Dunya's husband, was responsible for his wife's recent tendency to "stray." He'd been devoting too much time to Coco and forgetting to keep an eye on Dunya, with the result that she'd begun posing a danger to him personally. Besides which, she didn't even care about appearances anymore. So now she was marching publicly in Amir's demonstration, and in the first row to boot, cheering for Lebanon and booing Israel as if she were trying to go back to the way she'd been before. Fool that she was, she didn't realize that once someone passes through his mansion and steps into his life, she'll never be the same again, even if she leaves. For a person like her, there was no hope of survival.

He'd repeat his instructions to that damned, negligent Nadim now.

When his spies had brought him videotaped scenes from the demonstration, he'd studied the demonstrators' faces and had determined to hurt all those he knew, especially his butler, Nasim. But the blow he received from seeing Dunya was the most painful. She looked hysterically happy as she walked down the street with her hand in Amir's, cheering for her country against its executioners.

Consequently, his tone of voice was deadly serious when he summoned Nadim to show him a film which, as he put it, would be "of concern" to him. As he sat waiting for him in his gold-lined, octopus-shaped pool, his lips foamed with the lust for revenge, then dried like bitter salt.

◆　◆　◆

The heat continued to invade both her waking hours and her sleep, like an unspoken, fiery message from the desert.

Dunya was still undecided. Did she love these canicule winds, or hate them? And she was equally ambivalent about everything that had happened to her over the past several weeks.

She felt lost. She'd left her old morass, but hadn't found a new "vessel" to contain her. She spent her days in contradictions, sometimes playing the revolutionary, and other times rushing off to the hairdresser to play the society lady. In the morning she might march in a protest demonstration, cheering for Lebanon, the Arabs and the laboring class, and in the evening find herself at a cocktail party with her people's executioners. And all the while she would be wondering in horror, do you suppose my picture will appear in tomorrow's newspaper? Will they see me on the evening news arm in arm with Amir Nealy at the head of the demonstration? Is that hostile, mocking look on my daughter's face a sign of her contempt for my inconsistent behavior?

And now here she was in her fancy car, being driven by the chauffeur back to the villa after another useless day of traveling back and forth between the poles and the equator. (Oh, I'm so exhausted. All I want is to throw my body into a lukewarm soak bath and rinse off another day's accumulation of confusion and fatigue.)

In the morning she was surprised by a telephone call from the private investigator whom she'd employed for so long to spy on Nadim—since the days when her love for him, or at least her desire to possess him, was breathing its last. Those were the days when she'd paid secret visits to Sheikh Watfan to wage war on her husband's virility and to keep him away from other women. She went to see him in his office.

("Your husband is cheating on you."

"I don't care anymore."

"You didn't give me instructions to stop following him. I've got information that will be of interest to you. And I haven't shared any of it with you without verifying it first."

"I don't care anymore."

"He's been cheating on you with an attractive Lebanese woman named Kafa. She's married to a man by the name of Khalil Dar who recently left the country."

"I don't care anymore."

"He takes her out to public places, sometimes in the company of others, and all of them men of wealth and influence."

"I don't care anymore."

"She's now left the hotel in which she's registered and has begun spending all her time in a flat owned by your husband."

"I don't care anymore. Stop following him, and I'll pay you all the fees I owe you for services rendered.")

But would she continue not to care in the future? Might she not regret this some day and rebel against Nadim's ways? She'd grown accustomed to her constantly vacillating moods, and to her periodic plunges into abysses of despair.

She contemplated the lovely path leading up to her house as the car rolled her along gracefully toward the villa. Was she really capable of doing without all this luxury? Or, come winter, would she go marching in a leftist demonstration decked out in a mink coat?

Was she really able to bear responsibility for her actions?

(This is the first time I've ever betrayed the common interests that my husband and I share. It's the first time I've done something that could cause us a direct material loss and get us into big trouble with the big, dangerous boss, Raghid. The private investigator was talking about my husband's infidelity to me, but I've been planning an infidelity to him by stealing Bahriya's passport out of his desk drawer. Something about her reminds me of my youth and the way I look in the self-portrait that I painted once upon a time. Something about her overpowers me. She plays on my heartstrings as a mother and as a human being, and even as a priestess in some unnamed temple who has no choice but to obey. So I went back home. When I got there I was relieved to find Nadim rushing off and saying to me roughly, "Raghid wants to see me about a serious matter."

I opened the study door and stole the passport. My fingers trembled as I did it. How can I entertain hopes of going back to painting with a hand that shakes like this? In any case, I took the passport to Amir as I'd promised him I would. Nadim won't notice it's gone for a long time, and if he does, he's certain not to suspect me, since I've never been known to do anything like this before.)

Exhausted, she was dying to get into a lukewarm, multicolored, perfumed bubble bath. She asked the chauffeur to speed up a bit, and at the top of the hill she glimpsed her jewel of a house. Was she really willing to give up everything in a desperate attempt to reclaim herself? And was there that much left of her self to reclaim? Then suddenly she heard the screeching of brakes followed by the sound of another car colliding with hers. The force of the collision sent her lunging forward. After the initial shock was over, the chauffeur asked her if she was all right. She assured him that she was, and she wasn't lying. The chauffeur got out and went to speak calmly with the driver of the other car. No one had been hurt, with no damage to anything but the cars' fancy metal frames. Dunya opened the car door, slipped out calmly and walked toward the house. A day like the one she'd just had could only end with a collision of some sort. And fortunately, its only victims had been a couple of automobiles.

But she'd hardly been walking for several minutes before she started feeling her high heels cutting into the flesh of her feet. She'd forgotten how to walk. She'd forgotten what grass smelled like. She'd forgotten how to avoid cars running into each other. And every time a car came up from behind and passed her, she paused on the sidewalk and trembled. So how did she expect to be able to go out alone all over again into the rough and tumble of life when she didn't even know how to stand on her own two feet anymore? What a day it had been. Her husband had called in the afternoon telling her to have dinner ready for some guests. She detected a malicious tone in his voice that she'd never heard before. She told him she wouldn't be able to do it. He insisted. She gave in, but asked him to postpone the engagement until the next day. Then she left the house again and instructed the chauffeur to head for a large bookstore, where she bought herself a new set of oil painting supplies.

(Oh, I'm so tired. I can't walk another step, even though the house is just a few steps away.) She thought again of the perfumed bubble bath to rinse away her day and clear her head. So she took off her shoes and left them on the ground, then kept on walking until she reached her destination. She opened the door with her key. As she walked in, she saw Nadim sitting in the entrance and staring at her in gloating, derisive silence. Neither of them spoke to the other. She went to her room with a run in her stockings. When she went into her bathroom, she was aghast to find the bathtub full of bloody water and the dead body of her dog Picasso floating in the middle. His head had been partially severed from his body, and his eyes were wide open with a look of teary, black dismay.

She screamed in horror, then came running out of the bathroom wailing with grief. Her son Bahir passed by her as she came out, but paid no attention to her. Instead, he just went on half dancing, half walking toward his room, and stroking his gaudily dyed hair. Within moments loud punk music was competing with her muffled screams. As for Nadim, she didn't find him where he'd been sitting when she came in. But she kept pointing toward the bathroom, her shrieks barely audible as though they were coming out of a head that had been half severed from its body, like the head of her dog Picasso. Then she fainted and collapsed on the floor of the entranceway.

When she came to, she found herself in her bed.

She could hear her daughter saying indifferently, "I just got here. Dad said you were sick, so I came to check on you."

"Sick!" Dunya screamed in agony. "I am not sick! But your father slit my dog's throat and threw him into the bathtub. I knew he'd get back at me for marching in that demonstration!"

As Dunya pointed a trembling hand toward her bathroom, her daughter went inside and turned on the light. Dunya could hear her walking around, then pulling back the shower curtain. When she came out she said tepidly, "There aren't any dead bodies or slaughtered dogs in your bathroom. Are you sure you haven't been drinking too much?"

So then, Nadim had taken advantage of the time she was unconscious to clean up the mess and teach her a lesson. He'd prepared everything for the sole purpose of frightening her. This was a message of warning, and she couldn't deny that her body was quaking with fright. She'd understood every word written in it, and she'd read between the lines as well.

"You're imagining things," her daughter assured her.

"All right then, where's Picasso?"

Her daughter left the room for a while, and when she came back she said apathetically, "I didn't find him in the house. Maybe he ran away. I've got some homework to do now."

With barely enough strength to stand up, Dunya got out of bed and headed for the bathroom. The bathtub was clean. There was no sign of blood, or of Picasso! So what was there for her to do but take refuge in the company of her only friend—the bottle?

◆   ◆   ◆

"Madame Spock, Mr. Amir Nealy is asking for you again."

"Didn't I tell you to say I'm not here?"

"I told him that yesterday, and he's asked for you ten times this morning."

"Just tell him the same thing every time: She's not here."

"He'll know I'm lying."

"That's the whole point."

"Okay."

"In any case, you won't have to lie anymore today. I'm going to the hairdresser's, then to the mansion."

(I don't want him to knock on the door of my heart with his voice, like someone knocking on a coffin whose occupant is still dying. There's a tiny part of me that still misses those times with Amir. It's an obscure, secret spot deep inside me that still hasn't been reached by the armies of reason. It's still disobedient, raising the banners of longing for that old allegiance, like a spot that moves about in that vast expanse between the pillow and slumber, and in never-ending nightmares where he embraces me and draws me into that old hell of his like a make-believe certainty. I reject him with everything that I am, and I miss him with every part of me that I've renounced!)

In the elegant hair salon, Layla observed herself in disbelief. There were no fewer than three people waiting on her hand and foot. There was a man styling her hair, a woman trimming her fingernails, and another woman occupied with her toenails. And all of them were in direct physical contact with her. (I used to be bothered by intimate situations connected with commercial purposes, even if they were devoid of all sexual content. I'd feel annoyed it the hairdresser got up next to my body to comb my hair. After all, he was a complete stranger, someone I didn't know and whose perfume or body odor I might not be able to stand. It would have embarrassed me to let some other woman trim my nails as long as I wasn't ill or incapacitated. Yet here I am today, stretched out like a dressed up corpse with these three people gathered around me. I feel a strange numbness all over, and a kind of poisonous apathy flowing through my veins. I look at them, and nothing matters to me. I look at my face in the mirror, and the face that looks back at me is like that of a stranger, as though I were seeing it for the first time. And I nearly ask it, "Have we met before, Madame Lilly?")

Alberto asked her something about the color of her hair. She told him what he needed to know. A bell rang indicating that another customer's time under the hair dryer was finished, and two women who'd been "mortal friends" exchanged a hug, pretending to be delighted over their unexpected encounter at the hairdresser's. Joseph sang as he combed a client's hair against the sounds of music blasting in the background and the whining of the telephone, while another client got into an argument with herself over something or other and still another headed upstairs to the suntanning room. And all the while Layla sat relaxing in this atmosphere which for so long she had despised and mocked. She'd grown weary of being friends with losers, and for once she wanted to make an alliance with a winner. (I used to have a special knack for unwittingly siding with the underdog. It was as if I were the lady friend of goodhearted, gifted and genuine folks who also happened to be down-and-outers financially, socially, politically, and, basically, in every way that has

anything to do with earthly life. Never in my entire career have I fallen in love
with a winner, or even been attracted to one. When Amin and Nubal had a
falling out I sided with Amin, then Nubal started making a profit and turned
into a millionaire. When Talal and Ghassan came to loggerheads, I stood by
Ghassan. Then Talal [of course] started making it in life and became a big
businessman while Amin went back to his village and Ghassan to the mental
institution he'd been in. My entire history is one big victory for my defeats,
and I'm sick of it. So this time I'm going to side with Raghid, the man on the
top, not with Amir, the one I love but who also happens to be a marked man
who's more or less living on borrowed time. Tomorrow, when Amir is killed,
his wife will sit in mourning surrounded by her children and friends while
everyone ignores me. Even though I've been his companion in exile, defeat,
and struggle, I would only dare approach his grave in secret. How could I have
allowed myself to fall for the lies in his world? His comrades will be the first to
declare their contempt for my relationship with him. They'll destroy themselves with their double standards, while I fall into the abyss separating their
words from their deeds. They encourage me to rebel against tradition, and
when I do they pronounce their blessing upon my madness. But if my man
dies, they'll cast me out of their midst, since I'm not even a widow. No matter
how much men may differ in their ideas, their passions, or their ideologies,
their world is unspeakably cruel wherever you go. They're all in agreement on
one thing: unspoken contempt for the woman. The proletariat may have
found someone to defend them, but all women have found are those who are
ready to use women's suffering to defend the male proletariat. So if the revolution should succeed, the men will reap its fruits while the women are sent back
into hiding. Even the "revolutionization of women" is a pretense. Everything's
a pretense. And the simple solution is for me to work like a man and to love
like a man. A man only loves a woman in his spare time, that is, when he isn't
busy building his own future. So that's the way I'll be, too. I haven't got time either to love Amir or to hate him. I'm building a prosperous future by men's
standards, and if they don't like what I'm doing, then they're really only condemning themselves and their own standards. I'm tired. Tired. I'm always giving. I was taught that my calling as a woman is to give. But then something
went slightly amiss. I noticed that nobody really loved me as a female. My
family doesn't love me. Instead, they're just anxious to close my social file by
getting me classified as married. My friends only love me to the extent that

they can make use of me. My country doesn't love me since its laws don't grant me equality with men, and I have to pay a kind of social protection money before the law will soften its heart toward me and grant me so much as a passport. I left my country and fell for Amir, who was synonymous with everything I'd left behind. I used to march in every demonstration that he organized in the streets of exile, without knowing who it was for or against what. After all, I myself was a walking demonstration, protesting inwardly against a world devoted to oppressing me. In Amir I found another homeland, a homeland distilled into a man, a bridge back to a time that I'd once burned, then abandoned. But I'm aware that Amir doesn't belong to me. Even my mother's loyalty wasn't to me, but to her reputation. My homeland isn't mine, and neither is my daughter. The only thing a woman can own in this world is her bank account. My country welcomes the woman who's been abroad and comes home rich and influential, but it spurns her if she happens to be poor and fallen. Male society has taught me that the only reality is money. So what fault is it of mine if I've learned the lesson well? Men have taught me that love is weakness and that for a woman, the mind is nothing but an adornment. So what fault is it of mine if I've started making myself up in the way they like so much?)

She was jolted out of her reverie by Alberto, who was asking her, "Madame Lilly, shall I use hairspray on your hair?"

"Definitely. Make it as stiff as a mannequin's. I don't want a single hair to budge without my telling it to."

On her way to her appointment, the car she was riding in passed the cemetery where her mother lay with her blue Bedouin tattoo. (I haven't visited her grave yet. And I'm not going to. Standing beside her tomb would just make me aware of how fragile I am. Mama was secure in her own world. There wasn't even a crack in her armor. She belonged "there" with every ounce of her being.) Then without knowing why, she remembered that Frederic, the Swiss boyfriend that her daughter was sharing a flat with, lived near the grandmother's grave. In fact, the flat's balcony practically overlooked it. And without knowing why, she wished they lived in some other neighborhood, far out of sight and far from her sighs.

❖　❖　❖

Kafa had discovered for the first time what a pleasure it is to capture the affections of a rich, influential man. Not only because loving someone wealthy made life's difficulties easier, because it made the feverish canicule winds come blowing into the car as a cool, air-conditioned breeze, and because all her wishes were being fulfilled, but also because possessing a powerful man was tantamount to possessing the scepter in his hand. The chauffeur became more polite, and his bow more respectful. The maid Lillian began to say, "At your service, Madame!" with more enthusiasm, and the concierge performed services as if he were grateful for her having requested them of him. The businessmen who came to her flat—Nadim's flat, that is—to meet with Mr. Adel would kiss her hand whenever they came in or went out, vying with each other for her pleasure and approval. Adel seemed delighted with her, and had signed whatever contracts Nadim had offered him and virtually moved into Nadim's flat from the hotel where he had been staying. Coco rarely visited her hotel, contenting herself with a periodic telephone call to see whether anyone had asked for her. Khalil hadn't done so even once since he left on his trip, which she considered sufficient justification for the opulent life she was leading in Nadim's flat with Adel. It never occurred to her that he may have called without leaving his name, or that he might be imprisoned with Saqr inside a bottle of white madness powder. After all, she didn't like to worry her pretty little head.

She bathed Adel in a sunny, blue-skied look of gratitude. He had escorted her on a visit to her children in the College de Lemare so that she wouldn't find the trip tiresome. How kind and sweet of him. Everything about him was different from her boor of a husband Khalil. In fact, she'd come to measure a man's admirability by how much he differed from her life partner, or rather, her partner in the miserable part of her life.

The driver stopped the car. It didn't bother her that Adel waited for her in the car and didn't seem terribly anxious to meet her boys. She entered the front courtyard facing the school cafeteria, then paused under a tree to wait in the shade until her children came out. She noticed that a large number of the pupils in this prestigious school were Arab children. Soon her two boys passed by in a raucous festival of children without noticing her. One of the children was calling to a little girl walking beside Rami, "Widad! Widad!"

The name pierced her heart like a knife. If her daughter had still been alive, she would have been about the same age as this little girl or a bit older. She couldn't remember Widad without her heart blazing with resentment toward Khalil. She held him responsible in some sense for their daughter's death—him and other troublemakers like him. But he was the most responsible of all because he'd refused to get Widad out of Beirut before anything could happen to her. And when he did finally leave, he only did so because he personally was in danger. He didn't leave to rescue his children or his wife. Rather, his enemies had decided to kill him and had actually started to do it.

Widad looked around to see who was calling, then darted away like a little sparrow. Rami turned with her and glimpsed his mother, whereupon he and Fadi came over to where she was standing.

Before kissing them or hugging them or even saying hello, she asked them, "Widad . . . who is this Widad?"

They replied nonchalantly, "Her dad owns the big house over there. His name is Wahib Wahib."

She gasped.

"Do you know her?" asked Fadi casually.

"No. But I know her father." (He's a leader of the so-called progressives in our country. His tongue never stops wagging about the virtues of revolution and the people's misery. And here is his daughter Widad living in the safety of his mansion, which simple, foolish folks like me don't even know exists. God, how I hate them. And I hate their moronic "executive organs" like Khalil, the father of these two boys.)

She suddenly felt alienated from her two little boys simply because their father happened to be Khalil. And there flashed in her head a thought that had always been there in the back of her mind, if not consciously. (If they grow up in his care, they'll turn out like him. And if we parted, there's no way he'd let me raise them. Sooner or later I'll have to say goodbye to them and get used to them entering the barbaric men's world in Beirut.) Clouds of grief suddenly started gathering in her heart, mingled with her constant bitterness toward Khalil. Meanwhile, Widad Wahib had disappeared behind the trees that surrounded her "proletariat" father's mansion. As Kafa enclosed her boys in an embrace, they quickly drew away lest they suffer the embarrassment of being seen by their buddies, and she was filled with indignation all over again. (My daughter Widad gets killed by the remains of shells from a battle between the followers and allies of the man who owns this mansion. Meanwhile, his daughter Widad lives here in peace because my stupid husband refuses to understand. How many times did I tell him that they were just exploiting us, only to have him give me another lecture, saying, "There are charlatans on both sides, right and left. But that doesn't change the real issue, the issue of the people. And it doesn't cancel out the existence of genuine progressives who really do sacrifice their lives for others." So just let that damned Khalil lead me to some of them. Then I'll lead him to Wahib's mansion and to the countless numbers of others like it in some of the loveliest spots on the globe. Wahib? His slogan is: "Revolution until we reach the mansion!" Not, as he claims, "Revolution until we reach victory!")[29]

"On the weekend we're going to the mountains on the telepherique!" said Fadi.

"I love field trips!" added Rami.

With an unexpected rush of affection toward them she asked, "Do you know that a telepherique is?"

Looking at her reproachfully the way children do when adults betray their ignorance, they replied, "Of course! We've seen it on television and in pictures. And Farid told us about it, too."

"Who is Farid?"

"He's our schoolmate. He's ridden on it before, and he got really scared. But he's coming with us anyway."

"Why?"

"Because he likes to get scared."

"And you two?"

"We don't know. When are you going to take us to Annecy again? Where's dad?"

"He's on a business trip. And when he comes back we'll take you there."

"I have a class now. I'm going."

"Me too."

An abbreviated hug, a quick kiss, and off scampered the two little boys before they had a chance to notice the look of offense on their mother's face at the mention of Annecy. (I'll never set foot again in that uncivilized town until they've built a decent hotel there—a five-star one, that is. Nobody's going to force me to do what I don't want to ever again. Crazy? Maybe I am. Who wouldn't be after living through the past seven years in Beirut? I'm going to take life by storm armed with nothing but my passions. I'm going to exercise absolute freedom in life the way the armed vigilantes do in murder. And if they find my life offensive, then they're more offensive and more harmful to people

---

29. The Arabic contains a play on the words *qasr* (mansion) and *nasr* (victory).

than I am. What I'm doing is the woman's equivalent of what they do with weapons. I'm giving free rein to my instincts. . . .)

She cast a parting glance at the Wahib mansion and went back to the car. When she saw Adel, she forgot all about her anger in a split second, and focused her existence on straightening his tie. (Oh, how awful! It's slightly askew. And the handkerchief in your breast pocket is wrinkled!)

◆ ◆ ◆

He'd been charmed by this infernally beautiful young girl, Bahriya. His heart had been stolen away.

From the moment Sheikh Sakhr saw her, he forgot the sorrows of his past. He forgot his son's death several years earlier, killed while flying in his private helicopter. And he forgot about his other son, who'd come back to him several months earlier from a trip to the Far East as an ascetic Buddhist. He no longer touched either meat or women, and he walked around barefoot with his lean body wrapped in a yellow robe. Carrying his own music and his own world around with him, he secluded himself in his private suite for several weeks, then left again for the Far East to settle there and become a servant in some pagan temple.

Driven by the heat, the sheikh had issued orders for a beautiful tent to be set up in the mansion courtyard. He was now seated in the middle of the tent with his barber dying his hair black and suggesting that he also dye his copious chest hair, or at least the part that showed when he left his shirt partially unbuttoned. There was nothing he wouldn't have done in hopes of Bahriya seeing him as young and handsome.

She'd caused him to forget his anger at the Arab-language newspapers that had learned of the Night of the First Billion celebration even before he received his invitation, then published the news item in a provocative way. He'd been expecting a reproachful call from Sheikh Hilal forbidding him to attend. One newspaper had mentioned that three hundred millionaires, including several billionaires, had accepted Raghid Zahran's invitation to celebrate the fabulous Night of the First Billion, and that most members of the Imperial Hawks Club, among whom were a fair number of wealthy Arabs, had also received invitations to the legendary celebration. It went on to note that the personal fortunes of the scores of Arab millionaires who would be attending added up to a total of more than one hundred billion dollars. The same cursed newspaper listed some of the names, and didn't forget his.

Let them write whatever they please. The only thing that mattered to him was to be pleasing in the eyes of Bahriya, Bahriya with her extraordinary fairness, alluring as a fairy tale sorceress, tranquil as a desert sunset, lithe and slender as a palm tree from his homeland.

Her relative Raghid wanted the airport deal as her dowry. All right. He'd send that clever Lebanese fellow Khalil to speak to his brother Hilal in an attempt to persuade him to agree. He'd send him as soon as he returned from his trip with Saqr. He'd make clear to him that obtaining a signature of this nature would bring in a fortune sufficient to assure him a future as a prominent businessman.

There was only one cloud of sorrow which Bahriya's image couldn't dissipate, namely, his grief over the death of his she-camel. She'd given up the ghost all of a sudden, shriveling up like a tiny dark patch of desert surrounded by vast rings of hostile greenery.

(Why did she die in spite of the heat? Do you suppose it reminded her of home, too?)

◆　◆　◆

Layla woke up terrified. The doorbell was ringing insistently. She'd been sleeping alone ever since the death of her mother, and her daughter Mariame had moved in with Frederic, her Swiss fiancé, for a prenuptial trial run after the manner of some Swiss young people, among whom she'd been raised and whose world and values she'd adopted as her own.

She looked at her wristwatch. It was past midnight. She looked through the peephole in the door and saw the face of Amir. She was slightly startled. He'd never intruded upon her at night before, even in the early days of their love affair. And it wasn't like him to visit someone without calling first. So what had come over him? She opened the door and, sounding almost panicky, said, "Hi, Amir. Has something happened?"

"I came for us to talk."

She didn't like anyone to catch her feeling afraid. So, concealing her fright with sarcasm, she said, "Talk? Now? In the middle of the night? I thought you were some vampire that had left his coffin and then lost his way to the blood bank."

He didn't laugh.

"You're angry. And drunk."

"That I am," he replied.

He didn't tell her that he felt that the way he'd been acting toward her had become like that of Bassam toward life in general, waiting and waiting and never taking action, or that he'd decided to move at the same moment when the thought had come to him.

"What's happened?" she asked.

"You know."

"No, I don't. Don't tell me it's the invitation."

"How dare you send me an invitation to the Night of the First Billion?"

"You returned it to me after writing on it, 'as if I'd never kissed her lips . . . as if I'd never reached her, nor she me.' What's that nonsense supposed to mean? I'm the one who should be angry!"

"You know what I think of Raghid and the billion that he's squeezed out of the Arab people's blood through wars, unrest and oppression."

"I know you bear a grudge against him because he amassed his first million using the statue your father sculpted."

"I don't deny that."

"The people you ought to hold a grudge against are the spineless idiots who bend the knee to every new ruler that comes along, the ones who would be willing to buy his statue out of fear, then decorate their offices with it while they're seething on the inside."

"I despise them, too."

"And your anger should be directed against the ruler himself, who terrorizes them so much that they don't dare say what they really think."

"That's true."

"In other words, you should hate Abdul Nasser, whose enemies feared him so much that they bought copies of his statue against their wills."

"The man wasn't a terrorist. Maybe his followers were the corrupt ones."

"All Raghid did was to use people's fear and turn it to a profit."

"Rather than being true to his calling as a citizen and as a human being by exposing the corrupt individuals in the government of the righteous ruler who was fighting on so many fronts, he couldn't possibly be aware of everything going around him."

"And why couldn't he?"

"Because he was only human."

"But you elevate him to superhuman status."

"He was a symbol of Arab unity and struggle. We do elevate him above the status of someone like Raghid Zahran and people of his ilk, but not above other honorable people struggling for what's right."

"Well, both Abdul Nasser and Raghid Zahran are responsible for untold numbers of victims."

"Even if what you say is true, Raghid Zahran is a man of evil intentions, and can't even be compared to Abdul Nasser. The mere act of comparing them is unacceptable. The difference between the two men is qualitative, not quantitative."

"But it seems that's why you came here in the middle of the night—to make comparisons between Abdul Nasser and Raghid!"

"On the contrary. I consider it wrong even to utter both their names in the same breath. There's nothing in common between them, and I don't even think it's possible to compare them."

"Why did you come, then?"

"I came to get acquainted with Ms. Lilly Spock. I make myself the butt of all my friends' jokes when I defend Layla Sabbak. They tell me you've turned into an entirely new creature. So I decided to come get to know her and save myself. I've come in shock and disbelief over the way you've been behaving. How could you not march with us in the demonstration against the invasion of Lebanon? So you don't want me as your lover. That's understandable. But why is it that you're washing your hands of your own people?"

"You're drunk, in love, and defeated."

"That I am. But that doesn't nullify the question I'm asking: Why didn't you participate in the demonstration? Are you turning your back on our country? What's happened to you?"

"Just as other people have told you, I've turned into a different creature."

"I got that feeling when I found out you'd been willing to sell the Palestinian piaster to Raghid. A smart woman like you wouldn't be ignorant of the ramifications of what she'd done."

"You mean, because it was a gift from you?"

"Because that piaster is worth too much to be given to someone as despicable as Raghid. I gave it to you at a time when I still thought you were capable of grasping the significance of such a gift."

"If I've received a gift, I have the right to do with it as I please. It's my right to sell it, too. And that's what happened."

"Why? Why did you lose certainty?"

"Because those who talk with such certainty about the cause don't practice what they preach. Instead, they rely on fools like me to do it for them, and they even expect me to die for the cause as a penniless martyr. Meanwhile, they live the way Raghid lives, and murder the way he murders. They even tried to murder you. Then they whitewash their barbarity with moralistic platitudes, and try to justify their insatiable lust for sadistic preying on others with empty philosophizing. I'm sick of the way they use us."

"But . . ."

"You know it's true. You also know that most of the funds that are earmarked for the masses go into the pockets of political leaders who fritter away their fortunes the way Raghid does his. But instead of exposing them, you cover up for their shameful ways under the pretext of keeping up morale, the tactical necessities of battle, strategy, and other verbal fabrications."

"You can't hate Palestine just because some scoundrel has exploited certain slogans related to Palestine to make himself rich. The fact remains that there are two million homeless Arabs who were expelled from their land and saw it occupied by organizations that cherish the hope that all Arabs will meet the same fate. You go straight from naming individual errors to making sweeping generalizations."

"That's because a mistake spreads quickly. We began working for freedom, then before we knew it we'd turned into gangs that fight and kill each other. We called for democracy, then we started putting guns to each other's heads before asking for each other's opinions and booby-trapping voting booths if we didn't like the way the voting was going."

"There have been mistakes."

"Plenty of mistakes. And terrible ones. And they pile up on top of each other until they've turned from a handful of sand into a dam."

"If we're going to act, there's no way to avoid making mistakes."

"But we're not getting any closer to correcting them. In fact, we're headed 99.99 percent in the opposite direction."

"All peoples, when . . ."

Interrupting him, she said, "The people who tried to kill you weren't your enemies, but your friends, and only because of some opinion you'd expressed about oppressive, undemocratic practices. Instead of opening some sort of dialogue with you, they just got more stubborn and arrogant."

"Mistakes made by individuals don't mean that you have to stop believing in the same principles they do. All they mean is that those who've gotten completely off track need to be expelled, others need their hands slapped, and then we continue on our way."

"Principles aren't phantoms that go wandering around in our heads. They're fleshed out through human beings, and as a result they take on the same contours as those people's behavior and actions."

"But you . . ."

"But I'm influenced by the words of the poet Al-Bayyati, 'Go to hell, you little terrorist, for you think and speak after the manner of the thieves, murderers and liars whom you intend to kill, and whose authority you aim to wrest away from them.' "

"You're insulting me."

"I'm not talking about you personally. But you've fallen into the idolatry of habit. Your patriotism is nothing but a habit. Your good morals are also just another miserable habit. You're a man who's been petrified inside the statue of a freedom fighter. As for me, I've decided to broaden my options."

"Layla . . ."

"You're dead. You've died and that's that. In other words, sooner or later they'll succeed in killing you. And like anybody on his way to becoming a martyr, you experience your death daily and you feed off your coming glory. As for me, I'm an earthling, a mere human being."

"Layla . . ."

"I'm not Layla Al-Amiriya. Maybe I made a huge mistake when I chose exile over living in my own country. But that's all in the past. And now I've found a new home country."

"You've decided to join the jet set?"

"That's right. The rules of the game are clear with them, at least. And the game has well-established traditions. Besides which, when the wealthy make a mistake, they can find someone to make up excuses for them more easily than the poor can. I won't be poor and alone. Poverty and loneliness together are unbearable."

"But with us you weren't alone."

"With you my loneliness was exposed. I discovered what a contradiction we'd been covering up, and what terrorism we'd been practicing in the name of freedom."

"All right, well, I've begun to understand what my friends have been saying about you."

"Have you accomplished your mission?"

"Not completely. Aren't you ashamed to be celebrating the Night of the First Billion when Israel is besieging an Arab capital and could invade it at any moment?"

"If it does, that will be a happy day for its residents. They'll be rid of terrorism, they'll enjoy some measure of stability, and they might even learn to practice democracy. Besides, what's happening isn't a surprise to anyone but you freedom fighters, since you were too busy blowing each other's heads off to notice what was on the horizon."

"Shut up!" he shouted in her face.

Without batting an eyelid, she replied, "So this is your way of having a dialogue?"

"I never dreamed that my beloved would turn traitor some day. How can you go parroting this sort of unrealistic, imperialistic nonsense? No one can deny that mistakes have been made by the resistance in Lebanon, and that the people responsible for them ought to be punished. But no one can deny the processions of genuine martyrs, both Palestinian and Lebanese. Whatever tragedies we may have brought upon ourselves, nobody has the right to blur the distinction between patriotism and grand treason, or come to play the role of the returning Mahdi. No matter how many mistakes we've made, they can never be made into a justification for treason. That's something I'll never tolerate, Lilly Spock!"

"What a shortsighted fool you are!"

"Right. That's what I was when I came here to talk to you. I didn't know you'd become such a dyed-in-the-wool traitor. You, not poor Bahriya, are the one whose head ought to be shaved, like every traitor to her country who co-operates with the occupier."

"So have you fallen in love with her, too? I can't blame you. She's got a body that would win her the Miss World Pageant. And then there's that mysterious face of hers and the silence that makes her all the more captivating. Even women have begun falling at her feet. Dunya Ghafir, for example, never showed signs of being susceptible to falling in love with another woman until now!"

"You should be ashamed of yourself, woman. She feels compassion for her the way she would for her own daughter. But you've become like 'them.' You've started to think that all human emotions have to revolve around one of two things: sex or money."

"I tried something else, and I failed."

"That was a mistake."

"Making mistakes is the only thing I'm good at. I loved the wrong man at the wrong time."

"And now you're trying to fix it with a mistake that's a hell of a lot worse—a mistake by the name of Raghid Zahran."

"He's a civilized man. And he's invited me to a civilized celebration."

"He's invited me to crush me and humiliate me. And you've invited lots of other poor, honorable people for the sole purpose of giving him the pleasure of being malicious and hateful and satisfying his thirst for revenge."

"Not at all. It's just a social nicety."

"You commit all your outrages behind a mask, and then you invent nice-sounding names for them to make them look acceptable."

"I hear your son's coming for a visit."

"That's right! So do you intend to send him an invitation as a social nicety extended to the younger generation?"

"It's not a bad idea. I'll do it. Raghid Zahran would be delighted to meet Mutlaq Nealy, grandson of the famous sculptor, Mufid Nealy."

"God, are you ever contemptible! You were on your way to becoming a great woman. And instead you've ended up as a petty executioner. Haven't you thought even for a second of passing by and offering your condolences on Bassam's death?"

"You know I don't perform that sort of silly ritual. And who would I offer condolences to as long as Bassam isn't going to be there?"

Amir was still trembling with humiliation. And for the first time he found himself wishing another person dead: Raghid.

In a broken voice she said, "Listen. I'm exhausted. Getting ready for the party is taking all my time and energy. Could we postpone our debate till some other time?"

"If you go on working on the Night of the First Billion, we won't be seeing each other again."

"Don't say that. We'll stay friends."

With betrayal, there's no peaceful coexistence.

"We'll stay friends."

"In keeping with the principles of the successful businesswoman? Gain every friendship you can. You never know when you might need it! No, it's all over."

"Maybe I exaggerated in some of the things I said. And maybe you did, too."

"After the Night of the First Billion, you'll be Lilly Spock for good as far as I'm concerned. And Layla Sabbak will die. If you don't withdraw from what you've gotten yourself into before then, it'll be all over."

"We'll stay friends."

"I told you, friendship and betrayal can't coexist."

"I haven't betrayed you. I'm up to my ears in work, just the way a man gets to be."

"You haven't betrayed me? Who would care from now on, anyway? When you've sold your soul to the devil, it doesn't really matter that much what you do with your body."

Imitating him in a mocking tone, she said, " 'When you've sold your soul to the devil, you don't care about your body!' Good grief! You all are so wild about words and catchy phrases, they've gotten to be a habit with you. But they haven't improved people's lives one iota. On the contrary, they're paving the way for a new brand of terrorism under the umbrella of your slogans. So I've decided that I'm going to try to free myself from you—and everybody like you—even if I'm late in doing it. Has 'fighting for freedom' come to mean schools closing, people being kidnapped and humiliated and having their eyes blindfolded as they're carted off to prisons located right in the middle of residential neighborhoods? Criminals among you are granted amnesty for political reasons while the innocent are punished, likewise for political reasons. You were in a race to see who could be defeated the fastest—you who invited Israel to invade Lebanon with your disunity and your tyrannical grip over the majority of the populace. The reason for all your troubles is your inability to rise to the demands of democracy. You practice terrorism amongst yourselves, and we detest you for it, regardless of the slogans you use to cover up your lack of organization. I agree with the thinker who said, 'Revolutionaries are politicians who couldn't get seats in parliament.' "

"I told you not to start generalizing. This is what's happened. However, the solution isn't to turn our backs on 'the revolutionaries,' but to punish the guilty ones among them."

"Very well then, allow me to express my disappointment in some leftists, and some revolutionaries. But I'll be careful not to generalize! How you sang freedom's praises. But when a revolution adopts undemocratic methods, it severs its connection with intellectuals and lends support to terrorists and to cowards who take advantage of others' misery and helplessness to make themselves look like heroes. To hell with them all, whatever they call themselves and whatever slogans they spout. To hell with anyone who crushes people in the name of law and order and practices oppression in the name of liberty . . ."

"And you," he interrupted, "what do you understand 'freedom' to mean?"

"The freedom that everyone on this planet is looking for," she answered hurriedly, "the freedom not to be killed if you hold a dissenting opinion."

"Does that include the freedom to commit treason? What is all this nebulous talk? If we don't learn how to have a dialogue with each other, we'll never get anywhere. "

By this time they'd both grown weary, howling at each other like a couple of cats fighting under a tree by night on some darkened sidewalk.

Her composure thoroughly shattered, she screeched, "I'll exercise every freedom in the book, including the freedom to be a whore if I want!"

"All right then, go ahead and burn in gold's fire. Be a sardine in the polluted seas dedicated to the world of sharks who need to prove their financial prowess and virility. In the world of wealth, women are nothing but decorations and means to other ends. Either that, or they leave it with honor."

"It seems you're just possessive of my body and are trying to hide your jealousy behind patriotic slogans."

"There's no way I'd ever sink that low, even if there are moments when my jealousy over you as a female causes me pain. There's no way I'd betray the martyrs, both young and old, who are dying at this very moment in south Lebanon and on the outskirts of Beirut to defend Arab honor . . ."

Interrupting him, she shouted, "The real Arab martyrs are freedom of thought, democracy and secularism, and everyone who falls, falls because these have died."

"If we grant for the sake of argument that what you say is true, then do you suggest that we all turn into traitors?"

"Never again will I defend someone who's been wronged and who waits for the moment when I liberate him to kill both me and those who've been causing his suffering."

"Aren't you ashamed of your new friends' 'abject wealth'? Don't you ever feel nostalgic for the obscene poverty of the friends of yesterday?"

"Why are you dodging the issue? The revolutionary forces have . . ."

Taking his turn to interrupt, he screamed, "*Some* revolutionary forces."

"All right. *Some* 'revolutionary' forces have instituted virtual dictatorships, suppressing freedom of expression as 'reactionary.' The only time they defend freedom of expression is when they're the ones being hurt, and when they do, it's only their own freedom that they talk about."

"You didn't used to be so definitive and harsh in your opinions."

Well, as they say, anyone who doesn't become a progressive by the age of twenty has no heart, and anyone who stays a progressive till the age of forty has no brain."

"So now you've started inventing sayings tailored to suit your purposes, you snob!"

"All right. So I'm a snob. As for you, you come to the defense of a handful of traitors, morons, repressed neurotics, and megalomaniacs as a way of sublimating your repressed sex drive. You try to promote democracy by means of terrorism, and to spread freedom by practicing oppression. All the tragedies that have come upon our homeland happen in the name of Palestine when in reality, they have nothing to do with each other. Who do the Arabs hate more, Israel, or each other? Which would the Palestinians like to have more—Beirut, Haifa, or both of them together? Israel hasn't caused the Arabs nearly as much harm as they've caused to themselves. You're hopeless."

Amir felt hot blood rising suddenly to his head. At the same time, he felt his eyes clouding over, his chest getting tight and his breathing accelerating, while the left side of his chest was pierced by a sharp pain. He tried to say something, but all he could do was whisper, "Shut up, you turncoat."

She continued viciously, 'You're always talking about history. You're a fool. If the Arabs conclude a peace treaty some day with Israel, historians and thinkers like you will make Anwar Sadat into a champion of peace, and if they don't, your Nasser will remain the hero. Everything is headed for collapse for the simple reason that you all are more enamored with destroying each other than you are with defeating the ones you call your enemies. You're your own enemy. Your fingers fight amongst themselves. You're all through."

By this time Amir was about to gag on the betrayal of the one woman he had ever truly loved. He felt as though something deep inside was about to explode—his sick heart, to be exact. Then he heard Bassam's voice. ("Slap her. I tell you, slap her!") His left shoulder and arm were nearly paralyzed with pain, but without knowing exactly how, he suddenly raised his left hand and gave her a resounding slap. Both of them froze for a long moment, each of them gaping at the other. Amir turned and headed for the door.

And as she closed the door behind him he thought he heard her say, "Thank you."

◆ ◆ ◆

Although he didn't know why, the conversation today in Amir's house seemed disjointed to Nasim. It rose and fell, with people's voices fading in and out, and all he heard was snippets of ideas.

When people gathered at Amir's house, they usually expressed their self-criticism with the burning passion of one in pain, not with the coolness of someone gloating over others' mistakes. After all, all of them were true "sons of the cause," having been "guests" at one time or another in some Israeli or Arab prison by reason of their political convictions. He noticed that since Israel's invasion of Lebanon, they'd lost the jocular spirit that they'd always had before. The Zionist aggression against the Lebanese and Palestinian peoples had been a defeat for the entire Arab nation.

He heard someone saying, "When slogans are separated from the reality of people's everyday lives, they become like bills without a gold reserve to back them up. They turn into worthless pieces of paper. I expect a sharp response from the younger generation.

Young people will be taken in by reactionary ideologies and distance themselves from progressive thought, even if only temporarily. Regional loyalties will grow stronger, and they'll withdraw more and more into their own concerns."

"And now we have an added responsibility to reinstill principles of Arab unity."

"We'll lose the battle again as long as freedom of expression—the basic condition for intellectual growth—is forbidden to us."

"Let's admit where we've gone wrong. In situations where we've managed to take over power, we've engaged in a similar kind of prohibition. It's as if all we did was switch seats with yesterday's rulers and preserved the institutions devoted to keeping people oppressed. We weren't exercising democracy for everyone, or freedom of the press. And everybody whose ideas we didn't like, we would accuse of treason or of being an agent for the enemy and either chuck him in prison or deport him. And we didn't treat each other any better. I've met up with my former enemies in coffee shops overseas. Both they and I had been accused of disloyalty. What's happened makes no sense, and keeping quiet about it is a crime, since it will just lead to further tragedies."

"A kind of neo-feudalism has grown up inside some of our progressive organizations."

"We have to protect our revolutions from turning into suicidal explosions or blind violence that consumes itself, since that just provides a ready excuse for the enemy, who'll jump at the first opportunity to invade."

"What do you think, Nasim?" Amir asked.

He remained silent at first. He wasn't very fond of theoretical discussions, and like most people in their twenties, was anxious to leap straight into action.

Finally he said, "I'm thinking of going back to Beirut and fighting the Zionist enemy. I don't see any other enemy who deserves to be given priority. And I don't see that the road to Palestine has to pass through Beirut, Tripoli or anywhere else. The way there is a straight line that begins with the electrically charged barbed wire that Israel put up a few years ago after swallowing up part of Lebanese territory."

Someone else replied, "And what about Israel from the inside? What about the Palestinians who've allied themselves with Israel?"

Another voice spoke, saying, "But we've made it easier for them to do just that. We've given them every reason to think of throwing themselves into the arms of the enemy. Our mistakes are responsible, too."

"Does that justify the way the people of East Beirut have been dancing around and rejoicing these days, gloating over the misfortunes of West Beirut and saying, 'You all invited the Palestinians to come in while we refused, so pay your dues now!'? Aren't the dues for being Arab supposed to be shared by all?"

"It would be easy to accuse everybody of treason. But what we want to do here is to admit our own mistakes, mistakes that have led some people to react in ways that, to the outsider at least, look like cold-blooded betrayal. This, of course, isn't to deny the existence of a few real traitors, as happens in all countries and all ages."

"Our purpose tonight is to disclose, not to justify. So let's go on focusing on our mistakes."

The word "focusing" fell like a curtain inside Nasim's head. He no longer heard a thing but a jumble of voices.

Someone was saying, "People used to blame Lebanon for its nonchalance, saying it acted as coquettish as a harlot. And now it's the country that's proving its seriousness."

Nasim sank, then floated to the surface again.

He heard another voice saying, "There are some progressives who actually help reactionaries get the upper hand."

"The Arab experience is just getting more futile and ironic."

"The phase we're going through is just a passing one. In the future we'll . . ."

"Arabs are falling into confusion and fear. There's a plan to alienate them from their defeats, their history . . ."

Once more he sank, then floated to the surface.

(What's come over me? Is it because I'm so afraid of what might happen to Bahriya on account of the sorcerer's madness and Raghid's despair? Is it my grief over my martyred brother? Is it the sadness that I'm picking up on so strongly from Amir? Is it because I miss poor Bassam, who died for no reason but that he fled from dying?)

As he pondered the people around him, he was assailed by a succession of faces: the eternally vindictive Raghid, Nadim with his undying opportunism, Dunya, the sorcerer, Layla. . . . As Amir had said to him once, all of them were like abilities and potentials that had lost their way. And he, would he find his way? What kind of future awaited him? What home country, with the war captives of his own country being scattered among the continents of the world? And Bahriya. . . .

He tried to break out of his reverie by connecting with his surroundings. He loved Amir's house. Sitting on the floor surrounded by its rustic pillows and cushions, he felt relatively peaceful and comfortable. He gazed at the map of the Arab world on the white wall opposite him. What a contrast it was to the gold-framed paintings of remote, strange places in Raghid's house, which was as stuffy as an abandoned museum belonging to some alien civilization. (At night, when the moonlight is reflected off the broad waterway that separates Raghid's mansion from his servants' quarters, the water looks bloody rather than silver. It's as if it were a moat surrounding a fortress straight out of the Middle Ages, filled with bloodied cadavers. I'm a prisoner inside the castle, cut off from my people who are in some faraway place. The gate leading onto the bridge that connects us to the servants' building is securely locked, and I feel as though I'm under siege: surrounded by suffocating walls covered with paintings that have nothing to do either with my heritage or my temperament; flanked on one side by a sorcerer and on the other by an executioner; hemmed in by my fear for Bahriya and by the electrified iron barriers that stand between me and the fellow workers that I wish I could spend the evening with; imprisoned by my family's poverty and need. Surrounded, surrounded . . .) He noticed that everything in Amir's house was in stark contrast to Raghid's castle. (Even the pedestal for the statue here is empty, whereas in the mansion there are two statues: the original sculpture beside the golden swimming pool to crush the Arab people as a whole, and a copy of it in my room to crush me personally.)

As if he sensed how distracted Nasim was feeling, Amir whispered to him, "What's wrong?"

"Maybe I forgot to tell you . . . Raghid gave me a replica of the Freedom Fighter statue to put me in my place. Would you like to have it here on top of this pedestal?"

"No. This pedestal is waiting for the original, the one that my father sculpted once upon a time. We're in the business of being patient. Being patient and working. There's something else worrying you. What is it? Bahriya?"

Nasim nodded his head without saying anything. (The morning after she arrived, I took food into her room. She was still drugged and asleep. I opened the curtains, and the sun seemed to shine out of that exquisite body of hers. Wondering what her secret was, I came up to her and looked at her hands, since hands always bear telltale signs of one's profession. I noticed her wide, untrimmed fingernails. Without waking her up, I took one of her hands into mine. It was rough and dry, like the hands of working-class folks. It betrayed her identity as a working girl, someone who knows the meaning of toil and misery. I felt as though she was close to my heart, and I thought of my mother's hands, which must have been the same way when she was a young woman.)

Amir continued, "Her passport is in my possession. Did I tell you?"

Without replying, Nasim said suddenly, "Miss Coco was a guest in Raghid's bed recently. But I spoiled their night together. She doesn't deserve a man like Khalil."

"Khalil doesn't deserve anything that's happening to him. I'm worried about him on this sudden trip he's taken with Saqr."

"Do you think he knows about Bassam's death?"

"I don't know. I haven't seen him since the day it happened. Saqr's really got him hemmed in on all sides. Of course, that's one of the basic principles of gaining control over another person."

"Or another country. By the way, it looks as though our sorcerer is on his way to losing his mind. If it weren't for the way he's isolated himself, he'd give himself away."

"Don't be so hard on him," said Amir. "We don't know exactly what happened to him in Beirut. Khalil tells me he saw him once with a brother of his at a meeting of some political organization, and he seemed reticent, timid and weak. He said he'd changed a lot, and that if it weren't for the color of his eyes, he wouldn't have recognized him. It isn't every day that you see a man with one green eye and one brown one."

"I read in some newspaper that he claims to have changed the color of one of his eyes to green by his own magical power—as his first miracle."

"That isn't true. I asked a doctor about it once, and he told me that there are people who are born that way. It's quite rare, but it can happen. According to Khalil, his eyes were the same way when he saw him several years back . . . before he went from being a failed would-be revolutionary to being a wealthy, influential sorcerer."

"Wealth . . . revolution . . . have you ever noticed that they're spelled with the same letters?"[30]

"There are times when everything seems like everything else. But what matters is how you apply things. The alphabet contains a finite number of letters, but the words that can be formed from them are endless."

"Bahriya, *hurriya*—freedom—I wonder which of them is her real name."

"So we're back to Bahriya. You're really in love, son."

"And you . . . what do you think of her, seeing as how you're never seen her?"

"I look at her without illusions. She's nothing but a penniless working girl who no doubt is smarter and more alert than she seems. As for everyone around her, they're acting like raving lunatics, and they're bound to drive her crazy, too."

"She's the one who's driving *us* crazy!"

---

30. The Arabic word for "revolution" is *thawrah*, while the Arabic word for "wealth" is *tharwah*.

"You all are in a race, it seems. But you, stay off the track, and show concern for her welfare without being too passionate about it."

"I will, I promise. Are you going to give me her passport?"

"I'll keep it for the two of you, or for her, until such time as it's needed. The important thing is for Nadim not to notice that it's gone. Otherwise, he'll do something to get back at Dunya."

Someone came out of the kitchen carrying a tray of coffee cups and a large, long-handled coffee pot and started serving the others. This was the signal for side conversations to end and for group discussion to resume.

Turning on the television, one of them said, "It's time for the news."

They all fell silent, their eyes glued to the news broadcaster as she transmitted the latest events in Lebanon: the people of Beirut were being starved out, and their water and electricity had been cut off. As Nasim thought of his family and his wounded brother, he buried his face in his hands, consumed with grief.

A few minutes later he whispered to Khalil, "I've got to go. Otherwise I'll be gobbled up by my golden spider."

Amir accompanied him to the door.

"And how's the spider doing? No doubt he's happy about the upcoming Night of the First Billion."

"Actually, he's a brokenhearted lover. He claims that he's scheduled the celebration to coincide with Bahriya's birthday."

"He's a fraud."

"He's a lunatic at large who could hurt somebody. He's so in love with himself, he gets off on the sound of his own voice, even when he burps."

Neither of them laughed.

As he went down the stairs, Nasim asked, "Did you find a manuscript among Bassam's papers?"

"The only thing I found was a blank notebook. All he wrote was terrified silence."

"Who knows? Maybe he was writing with invisible ink. I don't think he was a liar. We've got to discover his language."

In a mocking impersonation of Raghid, Amir said, "Don't worry. Trust me, and everything will be all right!"

Nasim left without laughing. The words reminded him of the death of Sirri al-Din. (We've totally lost our sense of humor.)

The First City

At one time I imagined that Saqr and I really were going to the capitals of Europe, where we'd get to see the museums and treasures that I'd dreamed for so long of seeing but couldn't because I was so poor.

And now here I am in some city, but I don't know its name.

From the moment we left, I realized that our trip would be completely different from what I'd expected, and that it would be a journey not to civilization, but to hell.

I realized it from the moment I found myself taking off in a crowded private airplane surrounded by Saqr's entourage, people I didn't know and whose faces looked so much alike I couldn't tell them apart. All the women had the same face, and so did the men except for a beard or moustache here and there.

In the middle of the cabin I saw a life-size statue of a naked woman. The mere sight of it made me shudder. It looked like an idol being taken away by its worshippers, and I'd been forced to come along. Saqr noticed how upset and confused I was, sitting with these people who looked so much alike it was as if they were all wearing the same mask. So he treated me to a snort of snow, even though I hadn't recovered yet from the one he'd forced on me before takeoff. I'd made the mistake of telling him that I was afraid of riding in a cramped private airplane. And when I told him, he didn't laugh that wild laugh of his, lost somewhere between a gasp of futility, a merry chortle and a death rattle. Strange, the way he's changed. In the twinkling of an eye, he's been transformed from a little boy into an executioner. It's as if, once he was assured that he'd taken possession of my soul, he could dispense with playing the lovable little boy and show his true colors. No sooner had I started to get over the hot explosion that had gone off in my head than Saqr winked at one of his lady friends while pointing at me.

She came up to me in a friendly way, smooth as a viper. Then she stuck out her tongue, and what should I find but that she really did have a snake's tongue, forks and all. I was so alarmed, I screamed. I looked at the other people around me but they paid no attention, as if they hadn't seen her tongue. Then her dress was peeled back to reveal one delectable breast, then another. However, each time she quickly covered it up again, like a cloud that parts to reveal the moon only to obscure it once more. The howling of voracious, forgotten wolves was awakened in my blood, and I surrendered. She drew me into her arms, and I responded by embracing her with a hunger as old as history. But to my amazement I found that her body had turned into a mass of barbed wire in the shape of a woman. Whenever she drew me to her, her pointed extremities dug themselves into my flesh. Even so, she went on embracing me more and more passionately until I screamed and pushed her away. Some of the other passengers watched me and laughed, while others clung to their own woman-shaped bundles of wire.

When we got to the hotel, Saqr told me I looked tired and that I'd have to have another pill to liven me up. He takes pleasure in destroying me. I fell half-unconscious in the adjoining room. When I came to, I looked at the damned watch Kafa had given me and was horrified to find that instead of showing the time, it was writing out my telephone number in Beirut. I was so terrified, I fled from the room and went back to where the other people were. Then the bell-boy wheeled in the meal cart, but I discovered to my dismay that it was the operating table from the makeshift emergency room that we'd set up in our neighborhood in Beirut, and I couldn't eat. Saqr pressed me to have something and so did his friends, who since the beginning of the trip had made badgering me one of their favorite pastimes. I told them I hated the metal carts that are wheeled into people's room in fancy hotels, since they look suspiciously like the tables used for operations and autopsies. Then they had themselves a long laugh at my expense. I looked back at my electronic watch only to find that instead of indicating the time, it was showing my Beirut telephone number again. I decided to take advantage of the opportunity—that is, the opportunity to call my family. So I did, at midnight in front of a nightclub. And it was there that I discovered that we were in Athens.

So I asked them, "Are we going to see the Acropolis and the museum?"

But they just had another long laugh and dragged me with them to a nightclub in the Plaque quarter. When we got there, I was amazed to find that the entire place had been reserved for Saqr, his friends and his guests. We were then joined by still more faces that looked exactly like those of the entourage on the airplane. There was food and drink, there were dishes being shattered here and there amid the din and clamor, there were hookers, and there was dancing and singing, bouzouki and ouzo. I'd started to feel tired, so I pretended they weren't there for a while, then left.

I went walking down a narrow, steep street that was deserted and rather dark. A refreshing night breeze was blowing, which helped me regain a bit of my sobriety. As I stumbled down the street's ancient-looking cobblestone sidewalks, I began looking at shop display windows. I looked at my watch again, which was still showing the same number.

Then I came unexpectedly upon a long, rickety staircase leading down to an underground shop. In its small display window someone had placed the Israeli flag. I noticed that the shop's goods consisted of Lebanese artifacts and ruins, now covered with a thick layer of dust: the pillars at Baalbek, the ruins of Sidon, the mosques in Tripoli, the amphitheaters in Jubayl, the contents of the Beirut museum, and basically everything that I'd seen and revered in my childhood. In the relative darkness, they looked as though they were shrouded in the dusty web of a spider that had either fainted or gone to sleep, while a small rat scurried frantically round and round among the ruins behind the windowpane. When I squatted down and stared at it, it stopped in its tracks in front of me and stared right back. Its nostrils were twitching, and a kind of sadness seemed to come pouring out of its melancholy eyes.

I felt as though I were looking into a mirror. I cried, and it cried, too. When I took out my handkerchief to wipe my face, it did the same, then turned its back to me and went away. After this I walked for a long time. I went down a street that began to get wider, and once again there were cars vying with me for a share of the crowded pavement. Then I found myself in a huge plaza, which I figured must be El Sintagma, when I saw lights flashing the name "Meridien," the hotel where we had been staying. I was familiar with such landmarks from the days when I'd gone traveling through books and maps. And now here I was, traveling as a homeless wayfarer through the land of humiliation.

When I went into the hotel I was surprised to find the attendant at the reception desk giving me a key. I was led up to my room by the lift operator, who noticed that I was staggering as I walked. He turned on the room light for me and closed the door behind him when he left.

I didn't know how to use the cursed telephone with my head spinning the way it was. I asked for one number after another and heard voices speaking in languages I didn't understand until finally someone spoke to me in English. So in French I said that I wanted Beirut and I read the number from the face of my watch. After a few moments, or maybe ages, I'm not sure, the telephone rang on the other end and I heard the voice of someone in my family. I cried like a baby until I began to sob. My uncle's wife sobbed along with me as she told me that her son and the son of one of my other uncles had died fighting in our village in south Lebanon. One of them had gotten it into his head to fight the Israelis single-handedly, so they fired a tank shell at him that destroyed both him and his house. All the other one did was surrender, but they killed him, too. After crying for a long time, I fell into a deep abyss and flung myself onto the bed in tears the way I used to do in secret when I was a little boy. I don't know how much time passed, but at some point Saqr's people woke me up and stood around my bed like the angels of death that cast the damned into hell. They were all giggling at me with fearsome-looking, three-tined iron forks in their hands.

Then Saqr said with a laugh, "Hey, rat, we've been looking all over for you. We even informed the police that you were missing. And here you are sleeping in my bed! How did you get here?"

"I don't know. I went for a walk, and this is where I ended up."

Then all of a sudden I got a severe stomachache, and felt a kind of ulceration in my nostrils. I asked them to get me a doctor, and was surprised to find that it was already sunrise. But instead of bringing breakfast, they brought a bottle of whiskey and forced me to drink half of it right then and there while their red eyes encircled me with cruel, derisive cackles. I had an urge to weep equaled only by the deep shame that I felt in the face of such humiliation. It was the same feeling I used to get when I was being tortured in the cold, bare prisons that I'd once spent time in. And when I remembered the deaths of my two cousins and the demolition of that old house that I'd loved for so many years, I broke down. I felt loathing for the people around me. Saqr picked up on the spark of hatred that had just flashed through my soul, and he seemed pleased by it. The look on his face reminded me of Raghid when he was indulging in the pleasure of hating people.

Meanwhile, they carried on with their frenzied celebration, going back and forth among the various rooms in the place, which opened onto each other. There were so many look-alike faces, I didn't know anymore whether they were switching places or whether they just changed clothes. People came and people went. I wondered, do you suppose they work in shifts to make Saqr happy?

In spite of myself, I began staring out at the Acropolis, which could be seen if one looked straight out the window. I remembered my longing to see the Agora, the location of one of the first democracies on Planet Earth, where

Socrates, Plato, and Aristotle used to roam about among the people debating and discussing. Was I actually in Athens, the cradle of Greek civilization, without getting to see anything but a periodic snort, deadly embraces, the shattering of plates in underground nightclubs, and the antiquities of my homeland being sold at auction?

Then suddenly I heard myself screaming, "I want to go to the Agora!"

All of them burst out laughing, while Saqr said contemptuously, "You're no good for anything anymore. But you're not a bad clown sometimes."

It was either evening or morning, I'm not sure. All I knew for certain was that we were in the same nightclub that we'd been in before, and that the barbed wire woman was trying to torture me again by taking me into her arms. I kept trying to get away from her while everyone else laughed in derision.

I walked for a long time. I went down the same narrow, empty, half-dark street and was accosted by the same black, nocturnal breeze. I stumbled along the aged, cobblestone sidewalks like someone who's walking down a path that he went down in a dream the night before. When I found my way to the shop, there was an Israeli flag in the display window and a sign indicating that it sold Israeli cultural artifacts. But when I went inside, I found that what was being sold were artifacts from my own country. The beautiful, enormous column from Baalbek with that frieze that had captivated me for so long wasn't there anymore. Maybe it had been bought by some connoisseur of objets d'art. The rat was still there making the rounds among the fortresses, the churches, the mosques, and the museums so dear to my heart, and when it saw me it stopped in its tracks again inside the shop display window.

I asked it, "How did they manage to shrink all these antiquities? A single column in Baalbek used to rise so high it looked as though it were piercing the sun, and the Sidon fortress on the sea used to extend over the entire horizon. How could this have happened to us?"

Placing its paw on its cheek the way I had my hand on mine, it said, "When they're uprooted from their own land, they shrivel up and get smaller."

"That's true."

"It happens to people, too."

"That's true."

"Whoever leaves his homeland becomes less of a person."

"You're right."

"As they say, 'A stone that stays in place is too heavy to move.' "

"Right."

"How did you know?"

"How could I not know, now that I've turned from a man into a rat?"

The Second City

Judging from the way this man loves to show himself off, he must have been born under the sign of the peacock! He's been trying to occupy my soul little by little, and he must be succeeding, since his interest in me is on the wane. He's also decided what my definitive role in life will be: trip jester.

At first I thought of him as a spoiled little boy. Then I discovered that when he's still getting acquainted with someone, his desire to possess and control turns him into a kid who creates the illusion of warmth and familiarity, if not friendship. But with every new piece of my soul that he manages to take over, he starts paying a little less attention to me, like a broken toy, or like so much refuse. He treats me with seriousness mingled with banter, with cocaine, with enticements and with the threat of poverty. And now I find that I've become one of his servants—I who in a moment of stupidity once dreamed of reforming him, pitching all the whiskey bottles out of the study and replacing them with books to educate him with! But instead he just goes on peeling off one mask after another, and every time he does it he takes me off guard all over again. The contact I've had with his outer world has made clear what influence this junior Ghanamali wields in virtually all spheres. In every city we go to, he has a circle of admirers who imagine him to be a successful businessman, a second circle composed of suppliers whose allegiance he's bought, and a third circle of night companions. He's got the capacity of an elephant to hold up under the drug that's begun destroying my stomach, killing my senses and degrading my soul. I've stopped telling the truth. In fact, I've stopped saying anything. I've turned into a rat in a shop that sells my country's antiquities as it goes up in smoke. At the same time, I'm dying one of the most hideous deaths one can imagine as an addict and as a pimp, and witnessing the birth of a new Nero whose modern-day madness may surpass even the decadence of the aging Raghid.

As the private airplane took off with us to who knows where, Saqr noticed that I was distracted. A gleam of anxiety flashed in his eyes, like a hunter who notices that one of the wild stallions he's been getting ready to break in has gotten away. As for me, I could feel anger rising inside me, so I aimed it at the end of my cigarette, and lit it.

"Smoking isn't permitted during takeoff," said Saqr.

I ignored him.

Someone else said to me jokingly, "Do you recognize me, or are you always drugged up and drunk?"

The face of my father flashed through my mind. It was like the blow of an ax that split me in two as I recalled with bitterness his advice to me, which I no longer followed: "Son, never speak anything but the truth."

"Recognize you?" I said to the other peacock. "Of course not. When people live away from home, nobody remembers or recognizes anybody else, even if they're brothers."

And they all burst out laughing, in spite of the air turbulence we'd just encountered and which scared me to death.

"He's insufferable," said Saqr. "Give him a snort."

And for the first time I took it with a feeling that I needed it. It was a passing sensation, but it worried me, like a secret that's donned a mask in an attempt to pass hurriedly into oblivion.

Then I joined in the congeniality, the warmth and the delirious bedlam that surrounded me on all sides.

When the barbed wire woman with the adder's tongue came up to me, I screamed with fright. I was also approached by a young, innocent-looking woman with translucent skin, so translucent, in fact, that her nerves and bones looked as though they were encased inside a body of glass.

Then suddenly I noticed insects scampering about under her skin and swarming over my eyes. And in the place where her heart should have been I saw a time bomb. I could even hear it ticking.

"A bomb!" I shrieked. "A time bomb!"

And before I could explain to them where I'd seen it, everyone got up in a panic and started rushing around the airplane.

"Where did you plant it, you bastard?"

My head was spinning like a wave being twirled about by a hurricane. Not quite comprehending what he'd asked me, I said, "I've forgotten."

Saqr vilified me in the filthiest possible terms, and we scattered like rats, with everyone looking for something though I didn't know what.

"Look for it with us!" Saqr screamed at me.

"What is it that you want me to look for?" I asked.

"For the bomb, you numbskull!"

So I sprang into action, looking for the bomb. But what bomb? I wondered. Who said there was a bomb on the airplane?

As they searched, I saw them making circles around the naked golden statue like some prehistoric tribe circumambulating its idol. I ran off to search in the comers of the plane. As I scurried back and forth like a madman between Saqr's bedroom, his study and his bathroom, I gasped at all the gold I saw. The water faucet was solid gold, and the bathtub was made of gold and silver inlaid with precious stones. The sauna room looked like something straight out of a fairy tale, like a jewelry box large enough to hold a man. So, I thought, these things really do happen, whereas I used to think they only existed in novels and in journalists' imaginations. A single gold faucet would have paid my children's tuition through graduate school, and the price of the gold toilet would have armed my entire village. I burst out laughing at the old-fashioned, ridiculous notions going through my head. After all, why should I want to educate my children? All they have to do is take some stardust. One snort, and all their sorrows will dissipate like a mound of sand in the wind.

People will have to be recruited into the "Mandatory Numbing Corps." I'll think of a way to fix things on Planet Earth in light of my latest discoveries. Anybody for a golden water faucet? A golden toilet? A flying city of gold that can take you to summer, winter or whatever season you choose? As Saqr says, the seasons are only the lot of the poor. As for the wealthy, they choose the season they prefer for every day of the year depending on their mood. A bathtub inlaid with precious stones lest the bather slip and fall? Oh, my head is going to explode. Where are you, Saqr, damn you? Bring me another snort.

Another snort. . . . I'm going to send out an SOS. I'll light a match and let it burn all the way down. With the charcoal that's left I'll write "SOS" on my cigarette. I'll pour the perfume out of this bottle onto the marble floor and put the message inside it, then fill the bathtub with a stormy sea so that I can throw the bottle into it. Do you suppose anybody will rush to my rescue? I need a snort.

I went running around like a chicken with its head cut off, screaming, "Please! Give me a fix! I'm going to die of the cold!"

Then sure enough, a hand reached out quickly to stuff my nose with that snowy white powder, and I was on fire again.

When I looked out the airplane window, for some reason I recalled the bee trapped inside the Coke bottle at that sidewalk café and its futile attempts to escape from its prison. I remembered how its wings broke again and again in its desperate struggle to fly out once more into freedom's expanse. Release the ships from their seas! Release me! Oh, freedom!

The Third City

In the airport, a limousine with drawn curtains transported me, Saqr, and several other members of his entourage to an official room of some sort without us having to pass through the routine procedures normally required of passengers. So then, I thought, these things happen even in European airports, and not just in Beirut. Or are we not in Europe after all? I didn't know anymore.

Saqr and some of his companions went into the office of someone who, from the looks of his pretty secretary, must have been some sort of VIP. It was also evident from the huge waiting room outside the office. Saqr ordered me to stay outside as if I were some dispensable servant who just happened to be tagging along.

I sat down in a leather armchair that was so soft you would have thought it was upholstered with human skin. And for some reason I thought of Kafa, that pathetic fool whom I hadn't called even once since leaving Geneva. After all, I knew she was cheating on me, and it hurt. I also knew what had driven her to it, which was something that filled me with such shame I didn't like to think about it. My wife was now an adulteress, and I was on my way to becoming a drug addict. My stomach was starting to hurt, my nostrils were ulcerating, I'd begun getting painful cramps in my abdomen, and I didn't know how to tell the truth anymore.

(Kafa, wherever you are, however you are, your sins are forgiven, 0 poor, lost woman. You and I were like a couple of feathers being blown about by the wind. So by what right do I condemn you? Both of us are polluted, devastated, gone astray. May the Fates protect our poor little boys, and may they protect our memories from thoughts of our third child, Widad . . .

Then I fell into a lightless abyss of sorrow. This was the dreaded moment of coming down. And I didn't have a speck of stardust on me. I was standing on the threshold of addiction. (You're a goner, Khalil.)

I began to shake slightly as I leafed through one of the old newspapers that lay piled up in the waiting room. I was coming apart. The siege was too much for me. One circle was being encompassed by another, then another, then another, both in my home country and elsewhere, with the concentric rings extending out to infinity. And now I'd been broken and wanted a fix. If I didn't get it, my hand would start shaking all the more violently as I tried to hold the newspaper steady. Or do you suppose I was imagining it, exaggerating things in my mind?

Then suddenly I got sober.

Was this Amir's picture in the old newspaper I was reading, or was I hallucinating?

Was this him trying to shield his face from the photographers' lenses? And was this really Bassam's body on the pavement, his head awash in blood? I could hardly make out the words as black dots leaped about before my eyes and insects swarmed between the lines. Even so, I read. And . . .

Then I saw my own face where Bassam's face had been . . . Bassam, who had fled from his first death to his final one, which had been useless, useless, useless . . . Damn you, Kafa!

Damn you, Khalil.

She's the one who . . .

But you agreed . . .

She . . . You . . .

With every passing moment, I gained a greater appreciation for Saqr's gifts of perception, including his ability to read minds for the purpose of humiliating those around him.

How did he manage to pick up on what was going on in my head from the moment he came out of his office in the airport without even looking at my face? And why did he suddenly decide to bring me closer to him after such a long time of degrading me and keeping me at a distance?

"I have a personal visit to make," he announced, "and only Khalil will come with me."

Or was it just a coincidence?

She was young, pretty and fair, and her hair was decorated with a wilted rose. She was shivering in her bed and weeping.

Introducing her to me, Saqr said, "My one and only true love, Helga."

As he spoke, the screaming of a newborn baby could be heard coming from the adjacent room.

"She had him three days ago," explained a friend of Helga's, "and he cries constantly. And so will we until the doctor gets here."

"I acknowledge that he's my son," Saqr said, "and I'll take care of him. He won't cry again from this moment onward, and we don't need a doctor!"

As she puffed away on a joint, Helga's friend said, "He needs a shot of morphine."

"Why!" I screamed in spontaneous horror. "An injection of morphine for a three-day-old baby?"

Noticing with displeasure that I'd recovered some of my capacity for normal reactions, Saqr said with haughty defiance, "Helga prefers morphine. And she can take more of it before getting woozy than most people can!"

Appearing to be a teenager like Helga, the friend went on, "Her son was born addicted. We didn't know that it could be passed from mother to child. But . . ."

"I'll marry you some day, Helga!" Saqr cried with delight. "You're my kind of woman, the kind that has children like me. This little addict is truly my son!"

Taking me by the hand, the friend led me to another room. I was sober, although I was pretending to be high after having succeeded in tricking Saqr into thinking I'd swallowed the last dose of poison when I really hadn't.

"Are you rich, too?" she asked me.

"No, I'm poor."

"Aren't you an Arab?"

"Yes, I am."

"Aren't all Arabs rich?"

"There are other Arabs besides the rich ones. And I'm one of those."

Then we took leave of Helga, with Saqr having promised her to come back that evening. Once we were in the car and I'd topped off my misery with a cigarette, he said, "We've got to get out of this city now."

"Why?"

"Because she's a minor. And that could mean prison for me."

"But you promised to marry her."

"I didn't promise her a thing. And you didn't hear a thing!"

"I convinced her that I wanted to write an illustrated version of our love story to immortalize it, so to speak, so she gave me the pictures we'd had taken of us together, and some little cards that I'd written to her on various occasions."

"As long as there's no physical evidence, why should we leave?"

"Because I still don't trust you. Every now and then something in you wakes up, something I don't like. And I'm afraid it might do a number on me in court. When it comes to minor girls, there's no playing around in this country."

Then he stared over at me with his piercing eyes.

"I'll never trust you," he said, "Your innocent looks fooled me at first."

I almost replied, "The feeling's mutual."

But just as I started moving my lips to speak, he shouted at me, "Take your cigarette out of your mouth when you address me! I'm sick of that country bumpkin look of yours, with a fag stuck to your lips and moving along with the inflections in your filthy, mean voice when you talk."

I didn't say anything for fear I might blow up.

I turned my face toward the car window and started pondering the streets that I'd once dreamed of coming to see, and which I was now traversing from inside my transparent coffin. I closed my lips tightly over my cigarette, letting the ashes fall onto my clothes rather than flicking them into the ashtray. And I didn't take it out of my mouth until it had burned down to my lips.

The Fourth City

I awoke after a deep sleep. And no sooner had I opened my eyes than I realized that Saqr had declared cold war against me.

In front of me on the wall, someone had hung a huge color poster showing a patch of green grass beneath which was written: "Erythroxylon Coca," the plant from which cocaine is extracted.

In vain Saqr tried to understand what was behind my fierce rejection of any further attempts to drug me. I no longer tried to get out of it secretly for fear of losing my source of livelihood the way I'd done at first. Instead I simply began to refuse. It was a mystery he was at a loss to comprehend: What had happened between the moment when I'd been looking around imploringly for another snort after he left me behind like a rat in the secretary's office, and the moment when—not more than half an hour later—he left the VIP's office to find me and my entire spiritual aura cursing him with a thick silence and an unmitigated hatred, part of which was directed against myself?

He interrogated me again the next morning, this time directly. I glared at him with my cigarette planted firmly in my mouth, and we sat there in silence for a long time like a couple of rapacious wolves. When the ashes began falling on my clothes, I said, "Nothing," with the cigarette still in my mouth.

I resumed my silence until the hot embers at the end of the cigarette started to burn my lips. Then I said, "Nothing!" again before throwing it away.

He'd regained his interest in me, or rather, in gaining control over me. He was showing himself to be a master at psychological warfare. How wrong I'd been when I imagined him to be less crafty than I knew him to be now. His father, Sheikh Sakhr, was nothing but a harmless adolescent by comparison.

I began staring again at the "Erythroxylon Coca" poster. In my blood there was a stifled cry whispering its name. I remembered another white wall that resembled this one, only with a different poster in the center of it, namely, the wall in Amir's house covered with a map of the Arab world. In it I saw what looked like a map of my own life. But all I found with Saqr was a poster of cursed "coke."

I jumped out of bed and buried my almost painful tremors under the spray of a cold shower. I looked at the electronic watch that my wife had given me in her attempt to civilize and modernize me, only to find that the same thing was happening to it that had happened to my previous one, whose hands had clung to Beirut time. Or at least, almost the same. Taking on a life of its own, its face had begun showing everything but the time. And on this particular day, instead of flashing the time one second after another, it alternately flashed the names of my two sons, Fadi and Rami. It was as if it had been hooked up to my bloodstream.

It would have been nearly impossible to try contacting them. I didn't know what time it was either where I was or where they were. Besides which, Saqr had tapped the telephones of everyone in his entourage. And, small town boy that I am, I don't know how to say what I'm feeling when I know I'm being spied on, not even my feelings for my own kids. So I decided to try some other time.

I was amazed that nobody had come knocking on my door. But then I realized that Saqr's plan to humiliate me might call for neglecting me, leaving me completely alone, like a frightened rat with no cash in its pocket, no passport, and no snort just when it had started getting used to it. I didn't know exactly what time it was, or even whether it was morning or evening. When I opened the window I discovered that I was on the twentieth or thirtieth floor of a hotel that might have been in any European or American capital. And I wondered: Am I capable of giving up this poison all on my own, by an act of the will? Or have I reached the point where I need to be treated by a physician? Have I crossed the threshold? Have I set off down the river of no return?

Saqr had forgotten just one thing in this prison of mine. He'd forgotten to put the TV out of commission. And it was the one thing I really craved . . .

By the time the others came back some hours later, I'd satisfied my thirst by listening to all the news broadcasts my fingers could bring onto the screen. I'd seen Jean Jacque Bayrou, Francine Bouchi, Annette Léman, and Miriella Calame, along with other female and male announcers that had become familiar to me over the course of the grief-laden summer. So then, I concluded, we're somewhere near Switzerland, since I'm able to pick up Swiss broadcasts. Or have we come all the way back to Switzerland itself? In the broadcasters' voices I detected a note of sympathy with what was happening to my country. But what good was that? Tomorrow they'd forget, or be forced to put it out of their minds. Sympathy won't bring back a lost homeland.

And so it was that Saqr's entourage caught me in the act of watching television. And Beirut was going up in flames.

Then one of the folks with the look-alike faces asked me, "Do you like watching war films? Turn off that stupid video!"

"I'm watching the news on television, not a video," I replied. "It's Beirut going up in flames."

"Going up in flames? Why?"

"The Israeli invasion. Haven't you heard about it?"

"No, I haven't."

"There's a war going on in Lebanon."

"Really? I don't believe it. And even if it's true, it makes no difference to me."

"But . . ."

"We haven't got any mansions in Lebanon. My father's quite careful that way. And we've always had a preference for Europe, anyway."

"You're lucky," Saqr said to him. "My dad built a mansion in the West Market instead of in the West!"

"Let's not talk about Beirut. Let's get ready to go to the market."

(I understood him to mean the "white meat" market, and "dark meat," too.) Then he added, "Arab hookers will go to bed rich and happy tonight!"

I said to Saqr, "I've got a headache. Can I stay here?"

"No," he replied, "We'll treat it with some snow, with stardust, with Miss Erythroxylon Coca."

"Thanks, but I don't need her."

"The most charming thing about you is your moodiness. You're a real clown, especially when you take the part of the freedom fighter concerned for his homeland. At our next stop, I'll introduce you to someone who'll be of interest to you. He's a nationalist poet like you. Perhaps you used to struggle to exhibit his books in the infamous display window of that dogma-peddling bookshop of yours near the Beirut Arab University. You'll get a good look at him this time. You'll see him as he really is."

I was dumbfounded. How could he have found out all this about me?

Then he added, "I've made some inquiries about you! Did you really think I was just some naive little boy whose job was to teach you how to ski and swim and fish and peel cucumbers?"

I sat observing him, my cigarette quivering in my mouth.

Then suddenly he shouted at me, "When I speak to you, douse your cigarette out of respect, you insolent moron!"

Before I had a chance to slap him, I noticed that he was red in the face, and I realized that he must have swallowed an inordinate number of his upper pills. So I kept quiet, too exhausted and disgusted to say a word. Then we were saved by the arrival of a new group of people, some of whom had come to "receive a blessing" from the gifts they knew he'd brought.

I now knew that Saqr had a circle of addicts that gathered themselves around him in every city he went to. Well-to-do and young, they loved to congregate around piles of that white snow that burns the nostrils, the head, the heart and the stomach, as well as causing ulcers in the latter two. Or at least, that's what had nearly happened to me. But what really astounded me was that in every city we passed through, there was also a contingent of businessmen that came around. When he was with them, he would put on a face similar to the one I'd caught a glimpse of long before with Raghid, then forgotten about. I'd seen it when the two of them walked together out to the balcony at one of Raghid's soirées. It was the night of "O darkness of the prison, descend. . . !" It seemed that Saqr was the "favorite" in every flesh market we passed through in Western cities, and that—spendthrift and wastrel that he was—he was considered the champion and protector of these disgusting, haremlike places. However, they weren't his sole concern as I'd imagined at first. Perhaps the most dangerous thing about Saqr is his ability to make use of the element of surprise. He can transform himself with the speed of lightning from a dove to a hawk.

After some of his guests had left, he asked me to accompany him to his private suite.

I'd managed to go forty-eight hours without taking any of his various and sundry stardust poisons. Consequently, my head had cleared and I could see with relative clarity, albeit a clarity clouded somewhat by that weak part of me that still longed for an infernal snort. No sooner had Saqr shut the door behind him after getting to his suite than he collapsed onto the bed, groaning in agony. Then he had a bout of cramping in his thighs and began writhing, moaning and trembling as though he'd been stung, or as though he were being scourged. I checked his pulse. It was so fast, I was afraid he might die. I looked into his frightening-looking eyes, and his pupils were dilated like those of a cat in the darkness. Then came an attack of nausea, and he tried in vain to sleep. He was in pain for hours, yet he refused to let me inform anyone in his entourage of what had come over him. So when they kept pressing me to let them see him, I claimed that he had a "lady friend" visiting him. He even refused to let me contact a doctor. When I suggested the idea, he was suddenly gripped by a strange fear: that the doctor would murder him, or that his friends would send him to a sanitarium. He didn't want to see any of his buddies, since they were plotting to kill him so that he wouldn't become ruler of his country, which—unless they did away with him—was inevitable for a great man like him, despite the fact that he wasn't related to the ruling family! He was a Napoleon incognito, concealing his talents and gifts lest he be put to death on their account. His father, Sheikh Sakhr, was envious of him as well, and was seeking his destruction. Everyone was in league against him, and he wanted me to keep quiet about it, promising to reward me richly if I wouldn't betray him and carry out their wicked designs! So I swore myself to secrecy. Meanwhile, he went on thrashing about in agony, cursing and threatening all the people who were conspiring to bring him down—great man that he was— until he was mercifully overtaken by sleep.

I sat staring at him for a while. He was a wreck of a young man. In him I saw what I myself was bound to look like some day if he managed to take over my spirit and bring me into subjection to his terrifying, frigid rule. I was delighted that he'd gone to sleep. This would be the first night since our journey began that I'd get to be alone with myself—or with what remained of it.

I was torn apart inside by the deaths of my cousins.

I missed my children . . . my homeland.

And I wondered what Kafa was doing with herself. Unfortunately, I knew.

And Bahriya. What were they doing to her? I wasn't certain.

And Beirut. They'd done what they'd done to us so as to make it easier to do what they were doing to her. They were all fools, innocent and guilty alike.

I pounced on the television and turned it on. The broadcaster appeared on the screen, stared me in the face for a while, then said, "Go to sleep, poor guy. You've missed the news. But Beirut was on fire tonight, too."

"Please, couldn't you do a rerun of the news for my sake?"

"Sorry, friend. I'd be fired if I did that."

"Please . . . try."

"I can't. But, what are you doing here? Why don't you go to Beirut?"

"Are you really talking to me? Does this happen to everybody who watches the news?"

"Actually, it does. But they just don't notice. They don't listen well. Pardon me. I don't mean to meddle in your affairs. But what are you doing here?"

"I don't know, friend. I don't know anything anymore."

"Remember. How did it all begin?"

"We were having some sort of argument amongst ourselves. And then along came the enemy and gobbled us all up."

"I think you're oversimplifying matters. I mean, I'm the international news broadcaster. And I see a connection between what's been happening to you all, and what certain powerful countries want."

"The seeds of corruption were already there to begin with. If our hearts weren't already full of holes, no one would have found any way to get to us."

"You're feeling sad. Go and get some sleep."

"No. Please, stay where you are. I need to talk to somebody who's sober."

"I can't stay any longer. I've got to go."

"Don't leave me alone. There are a lot of things I want to confide in you."

"Come on in if you'd like. Step inside the box and we'll talk till morning. Or even until time for the next broadcast."

All right. I'll do that. Give me your hand. Thanks . . ."

"Your hand is cold."

"So is yours."

The Fifth City

After that unbearable night of paroxysms and distress, how could Saqr wake up his old tyrannical self?

I didn't know.

It was as if he hadn't spent the night in torment, being scourged by the residual effects of his drug, swallowing tranquilizers and bawling like a baby right in front of me.

When he got up the next morning, he was more of a bully than ever, as if he wanted to humiliate me in return for my having been witness to his disgraceful condition of the day before. Or was this how the drug worked? After quaking the whole night before in terror of a certain attempt on his life, and of the envy-inspired plot being spun against him in the darkness by those nearest and dearest to him, including his father, he'd gotten up today acting like Napoleon at the pinnacle of his success. He swallowed some of his multicolored tablets, snorted and sneezed, and got high on his own glory. Then off he flew, and we flew off with him, only in his airplane.

He'd started cultivating our friendship anew so as to be able to humiliate me:

"Are you still on strike against joy powder? Why are you afraid of being drugged? Do you think you were really sober before? And do you folks in Beirut imagine that you've been awake all these years? Do you think that your people, the people you boast about along with your teacher Amir Nealy, are awake? Here they are invading your homeland, and nobody has so much as raised his voice in protest or waved a ruler in Israel's face. Everybody's drugged. But there's a blessing to be found with the poets and writers of literature who are going to turn your defeat into victory. Who's the victor? Of course, it's whichever side the genius collects cash from, or whichever side rewards him with prestige and influence, literary prizes, or a bribe in the form of translations of his work into other languages. The payoffs might take any number of forms, but the price ends up being the same, more or less. It all runs like clockwork inside the drug machine, and the tiny "screw" that tries to turn in the opposite direction will break. You're bound to break, too, if you don't adjust to the narcotics machine that's been set up 'from the ocean to the Gulf,' to use the phrase you all like so much."

"You've got quite a bit in common with Raghid Zahran," I told him. "I mean, your views are a lot alike."

"We've both discovered that lately. My dad isn't fit to manage his business affairs anymore, and there's a need for some new blood to keep the work moving ahead and to help us clinch the airport deal."

"Your uncle, Sheikh Hilal, rejects the idea."

"My uncle is a disaster standing in the way of development and civiliza-tion. But it won't be difficult to get him out of the way once I've inherited my dad's business."

"Does that mean you're going to murder him?"

"No. Some 'progressive forces' will take care of that for me. Then the lead-ership of the organization concerned will release a statement condemning the crime and denying involvement in it, and promising to bring legal action against the 'unruly elements' so as to punish the offender. Then the days will pass, and the numbed state people are in will make them forget. Across from the airport I'll build my late uncle Hilal a mosque with his name on it on behalf of his departed spirit. Numbness, you fool. That's what the lives of millions of people have been based on for hundreds of years. So why not go to sleep with them? You'd bring some relief both to them and to yourself. Here, take a snort. You're unbearable when you're sober."

I turned away from him and lit a cigarette.

He snatched it out of my mouth. Then he brought the ashtray up to my eye and nearly put out the cigarette in my pupil.

In a cold voice he said, "Today you'll see your sophisticated geniuses on a 'drug gig.' And they'll join with you in what you mistakenly consider to be worldly vanities, you tiresome dolt!"

Then he clapped his hands, thereby announcing that the conversation had come to an end and that his entourage should approach. Music! Dancing! And soon the airplane had turned into a huge box swarming with rats. There was a frightened rat cowering somewhere inside me, too. What sort of terrible dis-appointment was Saqr leading me toward?

Just then he turned toward me, as if the drug awakened some of his senses at certain rare moments to the point where he could read my thoughts.

He said, "Didn't I promise you I'd take you to see the seven wonders of the world?"

So then, Saqr hadn't been lying when he said that in one of the European cities that we'd be visiting, he would take me to a poetry festival devoted to the victory of Palestine and Lebanon. And he hadn't been lying when he said that our poet, Irsheed Nu'aymaqi, would be one of the orators at the festival, and that he'd be spending an evening with us.

Yet I still didn't believe him when we were on our way to the activities building where the festival was to be held in "City Number Five." Irsheed, widely renowned for his "politically committed" poetry—could he be a friend of someone like Saqr? What could the two of them possibly have in common, when the first had devoted his poetry to the revolution and to the cause of the poor, while the other had devoted his life to destroying both?

While we were in the car, Saqr said suddenly, "My dad and my uncle both contribute to the organization that funds Irsheed, you idiot. Didn't you know that nationalist poets have expenses to pay, too? Wives, mistresses, alimony, fancy silk clothes, hotel bills, bars, hospitals. Did you think they went around barefoot, bearing the cross of humanity and being creative free of charge? Gone are the days of roving bards and vagabond poets, you dimwit. We're living in the summer of A.D. 1982, not the year A.D. 82. Won't you ever catch on?"

I didn't understand him or believe him until we got to the big building. We went in with him pulling me by the hand. Meanwhile, we were being followed by an entourage which was devoid of women except for a number of educated call girls who'd managed to publish something once upon a time in some little known newspaper, and who had made literary names for themselves based on their bodily qualifications.

Fearing that I might be seen with Saqr by some thinker or author that I held in high regard, I said, "I've changed my mind about going to the poetry reading."

"But we've got to go," he insisted. "Irsheed will be delighted that I made it, and you'll be glad you went."

So we went, and what I'd been afraid would happen, happened. To my surprise, I saw Munir Nawadimi, an Arab thinker known for advocating Arab nationalism. I tried to look the other way, but he apparently recognized me anyway, and started walking in my direction with open arms. I felt ashamed and humiliated to think that he had seen me with Saqr.

"Hello, hello, friend!" he shouted, still coming toward me with outstretched arms which, once he'd gotten closer, he enclosed around Saqr! My lower jaw dropped to my shoes, and I just stood there in a daze. When Saqr introduced me to him, he shook my hand with a solemnity that made me wonder whether he remembered me or not . . . me, the one who had laid out his books along with those of Amir, Irsheed and others in my bookshop display window. He'd even paid me a visit at the shop once or twice.

We came to a large room that opened out onto four huge halls. In the first one there was a woman singing in an exquisite, melancholy voice, and whose massive body was reminiscent of a cadaver. As for her thousands of listeners, they were sitting without chairs, as if their bodies had been transformed into stony seats. It was as though they had been there for ages, sobbing and shrieking, their moans mingling with hers until one could hardly tell which was which. Her crooning had such a hypnotic effect that whenever she waved her handkerchief, the handkerchiefs of the audience would respond in kind, their tears streaming out the door. At the entrance to this hall there hung a sign written in ancient script that read, "Music Room."

In the second hall I heard the sounds of drums and cymbals, and I saw thousands of men in brightly colored costumes spinning around in circles and repeating a single phrase. Every now and then one of them would tear his garment and fall to the floor unconscious. Meanwhile, the others continued on their way to the star of oblivion. On the door to this hall there hung a sign that read, "Dervish Room."

In the third hall I saw men and women seated around a huge table in the center of the room on which there lay stacks of papers and articles, with their chairs facing away from the table and toward the walls. Every one of them was talking to himself or to the wall facing him in a whisper or a shout. Others were beating on the walls, and some of them had drawn pictures of windows, mountains, caves, mansions or tents on the portion of wall in front of them. Not one of them was speaking or paying the least attention to anyone else. On the door to this hall the sign read, "Professors' Room."

Then we came to the fourth hall, which was the Festival Room. When we went in, it was teaming with several thousand Arabs who were bellowing and shouting, braying like donkeys as though they were trying to free themselves from their lives in exile by exhaling it in deep sighs. I was flooded with a sense of relief. Despite the interest that Nawadimi had taken in me, nobody here would take notice of the shameful fact that I'd come with Saqr. He must have thought I was somebody else. In any case, no one would recognize me here. In exile, nobody recognizes or remembers anybody else even if he happens to have been his bosom buddy, someone whose coffee cups he's drunk out of and whose books he's displayed in his shop window. It's true. In life away from home, no one knows anything but how to worry about where his next day's sustenance will come from.

Saqr introduced me to some of his local bootlickers, who were rolling out the red carpet for me in my capacity as a "journalist friend." They seated us in one of the front rows, after which Irsheed came along to extend a personal welcome to Saqr. I regretted having displayed his books alongside Amir's writings. Well, I said to myself, maybe the poor man doesn't know what sort of a character Saqr really is. Maybe he thinks he's just some young enthusiast that he might be able to win over.

Words. Words. Speeches. Lyric poems. Rhetorical passion and linguistic catharsis. Shipments of eloquence packed up and delivered specially for expatriate Arabs. Onward toward oblivion, brothers! Cheering and clapping! Loud clamor! Rapturous delight like what we used to feel during the Umm Kulthoum concerts of yesteryear! Release for our pent-up nationalist sentiments! Applause in atonement for taking part in the fighting. After all, reconciliation is the supreme achievement—but only with your enemies, not your friends! Innocent folks and knaves. Goodhearted, naive masses. Sorcerers and snake charmers the likes of Irsheed serenading "Lady Suffering," then making her dance for the masses like a circus elephant.

Frenzied hours went by interspersed with messages from various political leaders, including some who had had a hand in the invasion of Lebanon. It was the chasm between such people's stated goals and their actual behavior that had caused the sense of alienation that had grown up of late on the part of both the general public and certain murderous freedom fighters.

Intelligent and creative man that he was, Irsheed knew the role he was expected to play in the game, and he was content with it. But why wasn't he ashamed the way my father had been when he had to face me as a child in 1948, the way both my father and I were in 1967, and the way I was now as I had to face my own children in this ignominious summer of 1982? Dates, dates . . . Words were raining down on my head, mingled with the pages of a calendar as black as a list of obituaries. Meanwhile, Irsheed went on reciting his poems, his gargantuan, bushy moustache twitching with delight as he was inundated by shouts from the audience calling for more so that the whole "shipment" could be unloaded. When it was over, everyone would go back to his lair in the world of exile, clinging once again to his sorrows, his woman, his humiliation or his loneliness. So let poetry come pouring forth from Irsheed's mouth and let the applause resound! Let the thousands of wounded and homeless seek refuge in houses of verse, be it rhymed or prose, to live along the shores of the *kamil* or *basit* meter. One of them might rest his head on the *rajaz* meter, while another makes his bed out of antithesis, wrapping himself in a blanket of paronomasia and feeding the children of rhymed prose.[31] Long live poetry and the poetic counterinvasion! Numb yourselves, boys, and return to your niches in the land of exile!

I felt as though I was about to suffocate.

My whole life began passing before my eyes—the trivial life I had dedicated to honesty and truth. A life that had been betrayed by people who claimed to be speaking on its behalf, but who then exploited it for their own purposes.

Feeling fatigued, I suddenly realized that Irsheed and others of his ilk had been basically living on top of my shoulders and the shoulders of others like me. We'd been racing along, running after our daily bread, and they'd been going along for the ride without lifting a finger. Some of them were writing real poetry and suffering for it.

But I'd been suffering a torturer's lashes and enduring dungeons and caves, while they were saying nothing about all they knew. Instead, they would write things that posed no danger of inciting the wrath of their master, who was seated along with them atop my head. I thought of my maimed little girl, Widad. But before my tears could remember their way back to their dried-out aqueducts, the party was over and we were surrounded by "stars." Since I'd come as Saqr's friend, Irsheed singled me out as a recipient of the text of the poem he'd recited. Many others followed his lead, giving me poems that they'd penned while living as expatriates. They were full of rhymed, metered longings for the homeland, condemnations of the Israeli invasion that had been cooked up on the spot, or cleverly written cliches designed to keep their thousands of listeners shouting for four hours and more, cheering for Palestine, Lebanon, and the like. They'd done their part for the Almighty. So now,

---

31. There are several plays on words in this passage that do not translate easily into English. "Houses of verse" (*buyut al-shi'r*) is a pun on the phrase "houses of hair" (*buyut al-sha'r*), a term used to refer to the camel-hair tents of the Bedouin, and is thus an allusion to the notion of an Arab's return to his roots after the wearying, uprooting experience of living as a foreigner. The pun is extended in the reference to "shores of the *kamil* or *basit* meter," where the Arabic word for "meter" (*bahr*) is the same as that for "sea," while *kamil* and *basit* are literary terms referring to specific meters of Arabic lyric poetry.

it was off to the pubs. They bombarded me with verses most of which were hardly distinguishable from each other. Their words had lost their meaning and significance, but the next day they were sure to be applauded by partisan newspapers. They'd done their part toward achieving glory and fame, and woe be to me and to penniless folks the likes of me who didn't know what had been going on behind the scenes.

After the poetry reading, it was time for the behind-the-scenes action to begin. Casting off the last vestiges of their utilitarian nightmare and the tell-tale signs of their crime, they unloaded their poems and other papers onto me and gathered around Saqr. We went out to cars that stood waiting to take us to every bar and pub along the route leading from the festival hall to the hotel, as if each of them were some sort of mandatory way station. One of them had to have a snort, while another needed a shot of morphine. This brother wouldn't smoke anything but marijuana, while another preferred alcohol. However, none of them would have turned down an offer of women, although some preferred them on the manly side, so to speak. In any case, our hotel suite had provisions for all this and more. After all, we'd rented an entire floor just for Saqr, his entourage, and the freedom-fighter geniuses that had come along as his guests.

Saqr breathed a sigh of relief when he settled into his room in the Wonderland Suite, with its velvety walls, ceiling and carpet, all of them an imperial purple. Saqr stretched out on his bed, while Irsheed engaged in a bit of artistic "spontaneity," removing some of his clothes and taking a dip in the bathtub next to the bed into which one descended by going down a three-stepped ladder to bathe surrounded by opulence, pomp and admirers. I left the Wonderland Suite laden with piles of poems and speeches and went to my room. As I stood out on the balcony and breathed in the fresh air, I was chilled to the bone, despite the sweltering weather and the hot canicule winds that continued to sweep over the continent. I started shivering from the cold, feeling naked and alone in history's vast expanse. Then I sat down on the floor of the balcony, piled the poems and speeches in front of me, then lit a match to them and began warming myself by the fire.

My head as inert as a stone and my thoughts dead, I sat there for a long time feeling so scattered, not a vessel in the world could have contained me. I felt like a little boy in my mother's arms again, her old, familiar scent filling the air, and I wept silently and without tears.

When I went back into my room, I saw the red light on the telephone blinking. I picked up the receiver and heard a woman who worked at the hotel saying that the Wonderland Suite had called for me and wanted me to call back as soon as I returned to my room.

I didn't call. I wanted to go back to the time before I'd known them. If only I'd never seen them, never known them, never seen the other face of my homeland's nightmares—outside my homeland.

The Sixth City

In Saqr's honor, Irsheed accompanied us to the sixth city, a European capital whose museums and libraries I'd dreamed of visiting one day.

Saqr gave himself a snort, which he also shared with Irsheed. And for the first time, he didn't try to force me to take one along with him.

So then, I thought to myself as I sat drinking my tea in silence, nobody's heart is completely devoid of mercy!

The tea was bitter, and so was my mouth. The deaths of my two cousins were bitter, too, both the one who'd died as a martyr and the one who'd been murdered. What am I doing here? I wondered. The tea descended heavily into my stomach. Then there was a series of mysterious explosions inside my bloodstream. A volcano sprouted inside my head, and my heart started pounding against the walls of my chest as if it were trying to escape.

Irsheed and Saqr burst out laughing. "Did you like the taste of the cocaine in the tea?" they asked.

I don't know how I managed to keep quiet.

"We slipped it in when you weren't looking. Perhaps you prefer it that way! How do you like it?"

Then Irsheed added, "You'll love the Arab circus that they put on in this city. People come in droves to see it every day. You really shouldn't miss it."

We went into the Arab circus along with a huge procession. I hadn't realized that we Arabs had talents in this area too. I'd gone to see an American circus in Beirut once, and a Russian one in some other city. But I didn't know that the Arabs had one of their own. My head felt like a hot air balloon that was about to fly away. If I'd had a rope on hand, I would have used it to tie it down. Damn those two! They were sure to have spiked the tea with a huge amount of the drug. Even so, they'd never be implicated in my murder. I had hours of torment ahead of me before its effect wore off, and days of pain before the possibility of addiction departed from my body. Addiction? Addiction to what? I couldn't concentrate anymore. I was overjoyed to find someone offering me a seat. Meanwhile, the lights were being dimmed and the show was getting under way over a land area so huge, it looked as though it would nearly have covered two continents from shore to shore.

It was quite an inventive show. Something different was going on in each corner of the huge circus, and you could choose what you wanted to see. But then images of things started to get mixed up in my head, with some of them juxtaposed on top of others. I tried to focus on the scenes around me, but it was no use. I'd faint, then come to, float to the surface, then start to sink again. Saqr had fallen asleep and was snoring away with his head on Irsheed's shoulder. Meanwhile, Irsheed was writing a poem in the dark, dictating it to himself out loud as if he got a charge out of hearing his own voice. And since he had his eyes closed, he wasn't seeing a bit of the circus. I wondered why he'd even come with us. So that people would see him here and talk about how he was doing his patriotic duty as a nationalist poet? Perhaps. In any case, it was none of my business. And as long as I'm here, I figured, I might as well try to concentrate on what's going on around me.

In one corner I saw a number of men riding bicycles. Only before getting on, they'd fixed the cycles to the ground and put holes in their tires. They sat there peddling away, some more energetically, some less so. However, not one of them moved an inch forward. It was as if entire ages were passing by as I sat there watching them. Whenever any of them grew old and fell off, his place was taken by his children and his grandchildren. And if any of the younger ones tried to take off and go somewhere on his bicycle, he'd be stopped by men carrying whips, who would first try to convince him of the virtues of fixing it to the ground. If the rebel soul refused to be convinced, they would force him to follow in the footsteps of his ancestors: He wasn't to change his location or look up at the planets and stars. Instead, he was to fix his cycle to the ground, puncture its tires, and get on. Then with the utmost resolve and enthusiasm, he would proceed to pedal away until he'd grown old and decrepit. And when he died and his skeleton had fallen to the ground in a pile of ashes, his sons and grandsons would take his place.

In another corner I saw a gargantuan machine being serviced by millions of circus performers. Upon closer inspection I could see that it was an ancient

Arabic clock, perhaps the one that Haroun Al-Rashid gave once upon a time to Charlemagne, to the amazement of the Western world. However, something peculiar was happening. The millions of folks servicing the clock were scurrying chaotically back and forth among the various parts of the machine, bumping into each other, tripping over each other's feet and falling to the ground, some of them dead and others unconscious. They were arguing and beating on each other with hinges, and some of them were even stuffing one another's heads in between its toothed cylinders. Each of the survivors did his work differently from the others depending on the orders he'd received from his workshop supervisor. As for the workshop supervisors, who made no attempt to conceal their mutual hatred, they exchanged curses and insults through a team of men specially assigned to this task. Sometimes the altercations between the insult teams would get so loud they sounded like the howling of wolves. Whenever the howling intensified, the workshop supervisors would start handing out gold to their respective wolves. I forced myself to look away from this chaotic, planless clock management. Everything that one person managed to accomplish was soon cancelled out by the work of somebody else until the cogwheels no longer fit together properly and were about to be ruined. I looked back at the clock, and was astonished to find that sometimes its hands moved backward, and at other times they stopped altogether. If they moved forward even for so much as a second, a great furor would ensue, complete with the arrival of delegates from outside the circus bearing plans and recommendations and sending experts around to repair the defective parts. Not long after this the hands of the clock would grind to a halt, then resume their backward revolutions.

Strange, this circus. And a bit pathetic, too. I'd never seen the likes of it anywhere else in the world.

When I looked in still another corner, I saw twenty-two men imprisoned in a cage, in one corner of which there lay an enormous, grotesque-looking hyena. The prisoners were arguing among themselves over who would be the leader of the cage. Every ten years or so the hyena would wake up, pounce on the prisoners and devour one of them, then go back to sleep to digest its victim so as to have all the more strength when it came time to devour its next prey. In the meantime, the prisoners went on fighting over who would be the leader of the cage. Anyone who withdrew from the conflict and tried to draw the others' attention to the hyena was subjected to ostracism and ridicule. If he dared oppose them in what was little more than a natural reaction to an unnatural situation, they would come back at him with provocations and insults in hopes of making him forget about the hyena. If he cried, "Hyena!" they would manage once again to put him on the defensive. And if that didn't work, they'd persuade some other hyena to come around and stuff its head in through the bars at one corner of the cage until its claws could wound the offending party, who would bleed until a pool of blood had formed on the cage floor. As the act came to an end, I saw the prisoners standing in what looked like a bloody marsh and carrying on with their altercation over who would be their leader. One man had nearly been devoured by the hyena, another was bleeding, and a third was trapped in one corner of the cage while a hyena outside the cage wounded him through the bars.

I'd never seen anything like it before. When I looked around me, I found Saqr carrying on with his snoring, Irsheed still getting high off his poetry, and Saqr's entourage carrying on with their regular daily activities, yawning, and casting an occasional bored glance at the circus program. When I glanced around at the rest of the audience, I found that most of them were either asleep or busy with their own affairs: One was shaving his beard, and all he cared about was finding a place to drive a nail so that he could have a place to hang his mirror. When he happened to drive his nail into a neighbor's chair, a quarrel broke out, and soon the two men were engaged in mortal combat without any interference by the police, who stood around acting like tourist guides and not lifting a finger to prevent assaults, snoring and the like.

While the first man was getting his beard shaved, another man's wife was giving birth, a third was carrying his ill mother to the village sorcerer, a fourth was singing a ditty, a fifth was delivering a lecture on the evils of birth control pills, and a sixth was selling household electrical appliances. I was sitting in the midst of a world of common, everyday clutter, petty conspiracies and disputes, food and drink, humble joys and sorrows and fragile dreams.

What a circus. And the spectators were a more curious sight than the performers themselves. Besides which, I noticed that the circus performance area was rotating ever so slowly in such a way that the audience could see everything without having to crane their necks or even so much as turn their heads—which might, God forbid, wake them out of their slumber. It was easy to see that for a spectator at this sort of circus, sleep was the ideal state to be in.

Before me now was a large group of performers inside a cage with a roof of solid iron. The performers were all fast asleep, and ever so gradually, the cage roof was descending.

And in a flash I realized: If the roof keeps coming down at the same slow but steady rate, it's going to pulverize everyone in the cage. It was happening so slowly that it was nearly imperceptible at first glance, but it could easily have been verified by the simplest scientific measurement.

Some of the performers were waking up and trying in vain to alert the others to the danger of the descending roof. They would listen, then go on yawning and snoring, moving just enough to turn over and go back to sleep. And if anyone insisted on waking up the others, he would be mocked for his pessimism and told to go back to sleep.

Then without knowing why, I shouted out a warning. My shout coincided with that of one of the men in the cage. For some time I hadn't been living by my peasant father's advice, the advice I'd paid so dearly for trying to live by before: "Son, never speak anything but the truth, no matter what." As it turned out, none of the men in the cage even heard me. However, a policeman came along and, in a whispered threat, said, "It's against circus rules to disturb the peace. If I hear another peep out of you, I'll throw you out into the street. And you won't be able to come back again."

It was then that I realized that the circus police did have a job to do after all, though at first I'd thought all they did was stand around. It appeared now that the actions considered to be crimes here weren't things like murder or disturbing public order, but rather, waking people out of their slumber and speaking the truth in too loud a voice. What a peculiar circus indeed. Never in my life had I laid eyes on anything more curious. Even so, it wasn't long before I stole over to one of the men in the cage before any of the police could take notice of me. I woke the man up and whispered in his ear, "The cage roof is about to crush you all, sir. Why don't you try to remove one of the bars of the cage so that you can escape? If you all work together, you could manage it without any difficulty."

Smiling wryly at my naivete, he said, "Don't worry, son. Nothing will happen to us unless it's been foreordained."

Most of the other men in the cage nodded their heads in agreement and returned to their blissful slumber.

By this time the policeman had seen me and, grabbing me by the neck and dragging me back to my seat, he said, "It's forbidden to speak with the performers. If you hadn't come with Saqr Pasha and the brilliant Irsheed, I'd kick you out."

Next I saw a group of women performers with their children inside a cage, all of them preoccupied with familiar daily activities. One was having her hair styled, another was taking a bath, a third was cooking, and a fourth was washing her children's clothes. An elderly woman was preparing a meal and another was hanging laundry on lines stretched between the bars of the cage, which had been designed originally to keep circus animals from escaping. In the middle of the cage there was a large barrel containing the "water of life," and in the sand that covered the cage floor there was a fuse that was slowly but steadily burning down. Tracking it with my eyes, I saw that it was attached to a bundle of dynamite set to explode as soon as the fire reached it.

Making my way stealthily over to the women, I asked the one nearest to me, "Don't you see the explosives?"

"And what do you want me to do about them?" she replied.

"Pour water over them."

"We're only allowed to use the women's 'water of life' for certain purposes."

"Fine. I haven't got time to discuss taboos with you. A policeman might come along any minute and throw me out. But why don't you all put out the fuse by stepping on it? Your feet are just as strong as men's, at least when you're afraid and it's a matter of life and death."

"Afraid? Of what?"

"Of the explosion."

"What explosion?" she asked, still zealously engrossed in cleaning the cage floor.

"The burning fuse. The dynamite . . ."

"We aren't used to dealing with such things. We're just married ladies with good hearts who don't get involved in things that are none of our concern. So why are you meddling in other people's business?"

"Everything that's happening here is my business. And it's your business just as much as it is mine. Don't you understand?"

"Go back to the bleachers where people in the audience belong, or I'll call the police!"

"You're going to call the police to protect your right to commit suicide and to kill your children out of sheer stupidity? Talk about a bizarre circus!"

Then I fell into a swoon. It may have lasted years, or centuries, or moments. I don't know. But when I came to again, the Arab circus in that European capital was still going strong and was still packed to capacity just as it had been when I fainted. The performers were still doing their acts, and whenever any of them fell ill or dead, they were replaced by a new team. After all, the circus women were breeding like rabbits, so to speak, so there was no lack of people to take charge when the need arose.

Before me now there was an enormous cage that held entire villages whose poverty-stricken inhabitants were screaming with hunger. Just outside the bars of the cage there sat a number of well-to-do folks dressed in costumes that appeared to date back at least to the days of the Ottoman Empire. They sat at tables laden with mounds of food which they were devouring nonstop. The well-to-do folks were also enclosed in a cage, which had bars of electrified silver and a door of solid gold. As they carried on with their rites of gluttony, their rings set with precious stones became soiled with oil, fat, and meat broth, and none of them took the slightest notice of the hungry people in the neighboring cage. Meanwhile, outside there stood men dressed like revolutionaries who were brandishing clubs, axes, scythes, and gargantuan knives like the ones mounted on guillotines.

"Death to the traitors!" they shouted. "Deliverance for the impoverished, toiling masses!"

The poor folks in the cage cheered as the revolutionaries who had come to save them shook the golden door with what seemed like the force of an earthquake. I felt such sympathy for them, I nearly shouted for joy when the door came crashing down and the rebels made their way inside. Meanwhile, the destitute folks kept shouting and applauding from behind the iron bars of their cage despite their hunger and diseases, and I would have joined them if I hadn't been afraid of being kicked out by the policeman. The rebels put to death the corpulent, cadaverous bodies, which had consumed so much over the centuries it was difficult even to extricate them from their chairs. Then they flung them to the ground and began mutilating them while the poor shouted, "Feed us first, and then take your revenge!"

However, the rebels paid no attention. In fact, they were so busy putting on their victims' fancy silk clothes, they seemed to have forgotten all about the people they came to rescue. Then after they'd donned their new attire, they sat down and, as if they'd fallen under a magic spell the moment they came in contact with the chairs around the table, they began devouring the repast before them even more greedily than their predecessors. After all, they'd been hungrier that much longer than those who'd been at the table before them. They became so engrossed in eating and adorning themselves with costly jewelry that they disregarded everything and everyone else, including the needy, whose cries no longer even reached their ears. It was as if they were shouting on a wavelength that their would-be rescuers weren't able to pick up anymore, having turned from revolutionaries into nouveaux riches. As for me, I sat there dumbfounded as I watched things go back to exactly the way they'd been before. All that had happened was that one rich man had now been replaced by another who had once been poor. Meanwhile, some of them went to work repairing the ancient gold door that they had torn down on their way in. And the game carried on as before.

The last act left me utterly speechless. I hadn't seen anything more "splendid" in the entire circus. So I decided to go smoke a cigarette and rest for a while before watching more of the program. But as I was on my way out the door, I saw a man falling off a high wooden platform into a pool of water that had been drawn onto the ground like a kind of blue mirage. When he landed, his body was dashed against the solid marble surface, leaving nothing of him but his red, imported swimsuit. I saw another man on his way up the ladder to the same platform to do what his friend had just done.

"Stop!" I yelled, thinking that he hadn't seen what had happened.

"Didn't you see what happened to your buddy? What you see on the ground below isn't water, but a mirage. The pool is nothing but a drawing."

"Don't waste my time, Khalil," he said angrily. "What business is that of mine? He didn't belong to my religion!"

"This has nothing to do with religion. Don't you see that all of you are jumping to your deaths? What happened to him will happen to you, too."

"Why? What connection is there between what happened to him and what will happen to me?"

"It's the same jump and the same ground, you idiot."

"I'll take charge of things and settle accounts for myself."

"Death alone will end up taking charge of you and everybody else. Suicide isn't a victory. Why don't you discuss the problem and agree on what you'll do to oppose the one who created this mirage trap for you to fall into?"

"Get out of our way, you moron. Can't you see that you're holding things up?"

Just then I was surprised to see a long line of men fighting and jostling each other to get up the ladder and jump.

So I went back to minding my own business. Nonplussed, I left the main tent and went walking around the circus grounds smoking a cigarette.

As I was passing by a small tent, I heard whispering. I came closer and looked inside, and saw a number of children playing on the sly with some scientific equipment.

"We're going to emigrate now," said one of them. "Why don't you come with us? If we don't escape from the circus, they'll kill us. They're going to force us to start playing those backward games of theirs. Either we go along with it or we'll be killed when we grow up."

And his companions voiced their agreement.

Then the little boy they were trying to persuade said, "We've got to stay and teach our families about the things we learned while they were playing those tricks of theirs. We've got to help them."

"But they refuse to be helped. You know very well that every child who refuses to take part in the games when he gets older is either killed or banished. So come on, let's emigrate. God's earth is full of wide open spaces. And there are plenty of countries that would welcome our knowledge and inventions."

"You all go on without me. As terrible as it is, I can't bear to live far away from the circus. So you all get going."

The young boy then buried his face in a pipe that he'd been clinging to, while the others slipped away without saying another word. And when he was sure they'd gone, he began to sob.

I came up to him and said, "Pardon me, friend, but I heard what just happened."

"Are you from the police?"

"Do I look like it?"

"I don't think so."

"Very good. In fact, they hate me."

"They hate anybody who doesn't either participate in the performers' games or stay asleep."

"Do you and your friends play some sort of game?"

"We're scientists. Inventors. But no one trusts us because they think we're just children. And we seem to be, since our muscles don't grow. There's something about this circus that transforms intellectual activity into a bodily defect that robs whoever has it of his strength and stamina, with the result that it becomes easier either to exterminate him or to bring him back to the straight path."

"You mean, you aren't a child, then. You just look like one."

"Something like that. It would be hard to explain right now."

"What's your invention?"

"It's very simple. I've discovered a liquid that, if someone drinks it, causes a change in his cells such that he can penetrate the time barrier. More specifically, the person's chromosomes undergo successive reorganizations at a speed greater than that of light, with the result that they can freely move back and forth through time. Are you following me?"

"Not exactly."

"Any sort of transfer that occurs faster than light will cause you to break through the time barrier, making you able to travel from one age to another. If you're able to control it, you'll be able to travel to any area you choose. I've managed to do it myself. And the formula is incredibly simple. Let me explain."

"I'm not going to understand a thing."

"You might get so you can understand more if you give it a try. Would you like to?"

He handed me a glass with horizontal, numbered lines on it containing a colorless solution that was as luminous as a dawn horizon.

"All right, I'll try, little friend, "I said apprehensively.

"Fine. Which age would you like to go to?"

"I want to be an Arab prince in Spain during the days of the Arabs' greatness and conquests. That is, to the time before this circus opened."

"Very well. Drink the solution down to this mark. Don't drink a single drop more or less. You'll remain in that era for sixty seconds. One minute, neither more nor less. Then after it's over, we'll continue our conversation."

So I did as the little boy told me. And great was my amazement when I found myself clad in the garments of an Arab prince and walking down streets filled with signs of a thriving civilization, of goodness and blessing, with people bustling all about me in the most contented rhythm. But the astonishment I felt at my clothes, the era to which I'd escaped so suddenly, and the sight of the palaces and mosques around me was nothing compared to my astonishment at the inward sensation that I experienced: of the earth being solid beneath my feet, of not being fearful, subservient, beleaguered or oppressed. I was free, free, free. It was a feeling I'd never known before, and in light of it everything else took on a new dimension: the blueness of the sky, the flowers, the sun, children's laughter, the flight of the sparrows, the greenness of the trees. Everything had a new, different flavor. A river of calm, solidity, resoluteness, and self-confidence came pouring forth from deep inside me. Oh, how marvelous it is to feel one's humanity and one's liberty, far from phobias, guilt complexes, or having to play either the murderer or the victim. I was in such bliss, I nearly swooned for joy.

Then suddenly I was back in the circus tent, and what should I find there but the little boy hanging by the neck from a guard's whip.

"How did you get in here?" the guard shouted at me. "Get out of here and go back to your seat." (So then, the little boy-man hadn't been lying.)

When I went back to where I'd been sitting, the show was over. Saqr was getting ready to leave, and Irsheed was exclaiming ecstatically, "I've produced an exquisite poem! The Arab people will be intoxicated by it. Wouldn't you like to have exclusive rights to it, Khalil? You could publish it in your magazine!"

Someone in Saqr's entourage said, "We've got to get out of here fast, before the next show starts. The circus performances never completely stop, really, and it wouldn't be in our interest to disturb the peace."

The Seventh City

After the moment of exhilaration that I'd experienced as an Arab prince in Andalusian Spain, I lost my tolerance for anything that might debase or humiliate me, regardless of the reasons or justifications for it, be they "tactical," "strategic," family-related, goal-related, or any other newfangled terms from the obscene language of degradation. It's a language we've lived with for so long—sometimes in the name of tolerance, and other times in the name of prudence—we've stopped noticing how ugly it is.

Now that I'd known the taste of freedom, if even for a few seconds, the taste of death itself now seemed a small burden to bear if I were deprived of it again.

Everything had changed since that moment when I stood at the top of the world as a ruler with strength and liberty, free of feeling of guilt, shame, or cowardice.

Restore to me that moment of freedom, and you can have whatever remains of my fleeting life!

I didn't explain anything to Saqr, or even to Irsheed, who took leave of us without us being any the poorer for it. They would never have believed me if I'd told them what had happened to me at the Arab circus. In fact, they denied that we'd been to any circus at all. They claimed that I'd fainted as a result of the drug they'd slipped into my tea, and that I'd hallucinated so badly they were afraid I might die and cause them a lot of trouble.

And now we were in London. From the airport we went straight to a jewelry store where Saqr bought two extravagant necklaces of diamond and exquisitely blue turquoise.

"Doesn't the color of turquoise remind you of your lovely wife Coco's eyes?" he asked me.

I didn't reply.

We were in London, the hours were slipping away, and we still hadn't set foot in the British Museum, the Tate Gallery, or any of the other places that I'd dreamed of seeing. With Saqr, the only thing I saw were his favorite obscenities, while he carefully avoided any contact with the country's civilized side. We saw nothing but our suite in the luxury hotel overlooking Hyde Park, his country mansion in the suburb of Wentworth, his entourage of chatterboxes and businessmen, and the *maysir*[32] table in Crockford in the Mayfair district.

It was ludicrous to be in London without seeing any of its sights but a *maysir* table. I'd heard that the Playboy Club had closed its doors. Yet now what should I find but that scores of "Playboy" clubs filled the tourist district of the city, most of them devoted to pleasing wealthy Arabs. I'd begun to be anxious for the Night of the First Billion to happen, since that would mean our return to Switzerland, getting my passport back, and being set free from Saqr and his drug.

Saqr was winning tonight at the gambling table. He'd lost, of course, when he tried to force me to take a snort of snow while he sat and looked on. It brought back memories of the blazing, feverish outburst that always accompanied a fix and the sense of degradation that followed on its heels. However, he won at the *maysir* table. And he won, and he won, and he won. He asked me to exchange piles of chips of various colors and shapes, and I came back bearing a fortune that would have sufficed to cover tuition for my boys and for all

---

32. *Maysir* is an ancient Arabian game of chance that involves gambling for stakes of slaughtered and quartered camels by the use of headless, featherless arrows.

the kids in our neighborhood all the way through college graduation. As we left the casino, the chauffeur came out with us, staggering under the weight of a case full of bills. I'd never seen anything like it before. Saqr seemed indifferent to the money he'd just won, and bid farewell to his entourage like someone dismissing so many servants. Then he told me that we'd be going on a visit that would add the crowning touch to the night's conquests.

At first the visit seemed a pleasant enough task—a friendly visit to a Lebanese family living in London. However, it wouldn't have been possible for Saqr to engage in such a "virtuous" act. So I took a seat and waited to see what would happen next. The husband was middle-aged, and his wife wasn't without a certain beauty. I thought to myself: Like a lot of younger men, maybe Saqr is attracted at times to more "mature" women. Or do you suppose he's thinking of some sort of business deal with the husband? The house was elegant, as was everything in it. But what would have brought Saqr here in particular? And why was he presenting one of his two costly necklaces to the wife, who blushed with pleasure as he placed it around her neck? Then there entered a young girl of extraordinary, coquettish beauty. Her eyes were ablaze with a green flame of the sort that only illumines the eyes of young women at the moment when they cross the threshold that leads beyond childhood. Her beauty was also discernible in her pristine, blossoming physique, which was visible for all to behold through the nominal, translucent garment that hung from her shoulders by a couple of delicate strings.

No, I thought to myself. Not possible . . . she's still just a little girl. She may be no more than fourteen years old!

She shook our hands, then kissed her mother with childlike sweetness, announcing that she was on her way to bed.

When she'd left the room, her father carried on with a litany of complaints: conditions in Beirut going from bad to worse, no liquidity, etc. As a result, he might have to move out of his posh villa with its exorbitant rent, since he didn't have enough to buy it and thereby avoid the degradation of being a tenant and of not having his own home even in middle age. The woman appeared stronger and more self-possessed than her husband.

"How much is the owner asking for the house?" Saqr asked the man calmly.

"Half a million sterling pounds. A fantastic sum."

"Well, perhaps you could manage it. After all, you're an old friend of my father's."

"How? I couldn't borrow the money, since I wouldn't be able to repay it as long as conditions in Beirut stay the way they are. My assets there aren't worth a thing anymore."

"I've been thinking about your daughter. Would you allow me. . . ?"

The man's face lit up. It was obvious that he was anxious to become related by marriage to the Ghanamali clan. As for the worldly-wise mother, she looked less sanguine.

"Certainly," said the father. "It would be an honor for me to. . ."

Interrupting him, Saqr said, "I wasn't talking about marriage. I was speaking of something else. Some night. . . . Tonight, for example."

The father began to tremble, while Saqr got out his checkbook and wrote out a check for the half-million pounds. As he tore it out of the checkbook and placed it on the table, he said in a cold hiss, "What would you think of going out with the Mrs. for the evening?"

The man said nothing, while the mother got up and took the check. After scrutinizing it carefully, she folded it up and slipped it inside her bra. Then she turned to her husband and said, "Come on. We'll be late for the party. Don't forget the house key. The maid's on vacation."

After they'd left, Saqr looked upstairs, took a snort, then laughed that hysterical laugh lost somewhere between a gasp of delight and a death rattle. As for me, I went out to the car and sat in the front seat beside the chauffeur. Neither of us said a word. Some time later—whether long or short, I don't remember—Saqr came out, too.

Speaking to me as if I were a whale or a pack animal, he said, "It looks as though we'll be coming back to this house often, Khalil. Virgins have a charm that doesn't necessarily fade after the first night. Virginity isn't just a membrane, it's an idea. The membrane might go, but the challenge of the idea remains. And you just have to come back."

I didn't say anything.

On our way back to the hotel, the car took us over the Waterloo Bridge, which spans the Thames River. As we were going over the bridge, Saqr asked the chauffeur to stop. Then he got out of the car with the suitcase full of money in his hand, and started walking toward the edge of the bridge. At first I thought he was going to jump. But then what should he do but take the money out of the suitcase and scatter it in the wind, letting it fall into the river! A fortune which would have sufficed to banish misery from the lives of hundreds of poor people, and he took pleasure in throwing it away. As I looked at him in the dim light of the street lamp, I was at an utter loss for words, my nerves a twined rope of crazed tension. I got out of the car as he screamed sarcastically, "Didn't you know that gambling is forbidden in Islam? So I'm casting the profits from it to the wind!"

I don't know what came over me, but I found myself pouncing on top of him and putting my hands around his neck. As I did it, I could feel my muscles pouring forth rivers of misery, ignominy, bitterness, and rage, feelings I couldn't contain anymore now that I'd had that taste of freedom.

I started squeezing and squeezing until his eyes bugged out, which only increased my desire to torture him to death, just the way he had been doing to all the rest of us. I remember the chauffeur trying in vain to pull me off him, after which I lost consciousness of everything.

When I came to, I found myself in the hotel. I was tied up, and the chauffeur was sitting beside me and apologizing for having had to hit me on the head with a screwdriver to keep me from killing Saqr. He seemed to be worried about me and even to sympathize with me, as if I'd done something he wished he could have. As for Saqr, he'd decided that we'd have to leave right away so as to get to Geneva in time for the Night of the First Billion. And he didn't say a word about the incident in which I'd nearly strangled him on a riverbank, only to be prevented from it by his driver.

On the plane on our way back, he snorted a larger amount of snow than usual, laughing and joking with his entourage and ignoring me entirely.

As I sat there suspended between heaven and earth, I decided: I'll never work with this man again. I won't stand for the taste of degradation in my mouth even it means dying of starvation. He plans to turn me into some sort of groveling hit man, and I don't want that. I won't do it, even if I perish with my children on the Mont-Blanc Bridge.

Then I began to sing, "O darkness of the prison, descend . . ."

"What's with him?" asked the woman with the barbed wire body.

"He's crazy," Saqr replied.

"How come?"

"I don't know. He's just crazy like all the people who are fighting with each other in Beirut. They're criminals by nature. The only thing they care about is waging war on their neighbors."

"Who's fighting in Beirut?"

"Everybody. There's a war going on there."

"There's a war in Beirut? With whom?"

"With Israel. And city residents are running away like rats. A freight ship with a capacity to transport five hundred sheep now transports a couple of thousand fleeing people."

"I hadn't heard about it. All I know is that Beirut is a city full of gangs that stand for just about everything you can think of, and that it isn't safe to work in its nightclubs anymore. But I hadn't heard about the war."

"Neither had I," said a woman nearby.

Then all the look-alike members of Saqr's entourage chimed in, "And neither had we!"

One of them asked me, "And what's that got to do with you? Is Lebanon an Arab country?"

I continued singing, 'O darkness of the prison, descend. We love the darkness, for the night is followed by . . ."

◆　◆　◆

"Hello. Raghid Pasha? This is Saqr Pasha. I'm speaking to you from my car. I just left the Geneva airport, and I'm quite keen to attend your Night of the First Billion in my capacity as a businessman."

"As long as you're this close by, why don't you come, then? Coco is here waiting for you."

"Coco? I've brought her a gift that will go perfectly with those blue eyes of hers."

"Is that what you called to tell me?"

"Actually, I called to inform you that I've spent the first payment you made me, and that I'm in need of another payment from you, especially in view of the fact that I've met some more people who can help open up the airport deal for us. It's a deal I plan to wrap up myself, without my father's help."

"Come right away. You'll be able to see your father tomorrow at the Night of the first Billion. And the time you have here won't weigh on your hands. Thanks to Coco, it will pass without your even noticing it. She's told me how impressed she is with your good looks. Besides which, she likes younger men."

"Fine. I'll be there right away. For the sake of Coco's eyes! First I'll pass by another lady friend that's been missing me, and then I'll come see you two. But be forewarned: the commission that I intend to charge for the airport deal will be twice what my father usually asks. The junior Sheikh Ghanamali's rates are high, but his deals are sure to go through."

"We'll discuss the details later. And now, trust me, and everything will be all right. Meanwhile, Coco is waiting for you."

Then Saqr laughed his whimsical, macabre laugh and ordered his chauffeur to head first for the lady friend's house, then for Raghid's mansion. And all the while, the Ghanamali mansion was right within view! He simply didn't miss his father. In fact, he didn't miss anything but enough money to relieve him of having to beg for the Ghanamali clan's approval until such time as he inherited his father's business—or part of it.

As for Khalil, he listened to the telephone conversation without batting an eyelid. He didn't feel as though the two other men were talking about a woman of concern to him, namely, his wife. (When I conjure an image of Coco with her painted face, her body wrapped in silk and velvet, and her shameless, flashy charm, I feel as though I don't even know her. In vain I try to recover the image of that sweet, blue-eyed student who used to frequent my bookshop with such impassioned diffidence. She was most definitely another woman—and she died the day Widad was killed.) He glanced out the car window in order to avoid having to look at Saqr, but it only made him feel more distressed. Dark clouds filled the atmosphere with dank gloom. And in the distance, beyond the horizon, he thought he saw what looked like a naked flash of lightning approaching on tiptoe. Stripped of its usual thundery garb, it was like a telegram written in silence and light against the darkened sky.

◆   ◆   ◆

(Tomorrow is the Night of the First Billion. Tomorrow I'll be crowned as one of those kings of the planet who control the destinies of men and peoples. Tomorrow I'll fulfill my dream, and my father—the only human being I ever truly loved—won't be there to see me. And neither will any of the rest of my family, whom I lost track of one after another in the excitement of my rise to the top. If any of them tried to bring me back into the fold now, I'd be so taken off guard, I wouldn't know what to do. It's in this sense that Bahriya seems like my true relative: wild and untamed, vicious and wounded, without a memory. She's so dazzlingly beautiful, no one can lay eyes on her without being stupefied, without losing his senses. Even Sheikh Watfan nearly goes out of his mind around her. There's something about her that reminds me of gold. The desire to possess her makes people lose their balance, the way she nearly did with me, and forget about everything but her. Gold is magical, eternal, different from all other metals. And she's a female like other females, but different. She's recalcitrant, a rebel. Her silence is a wall like the kind that they build around gold to keep it from being stolen away. I might end up being the only person who deserves her. After all, Sheikh Sakhr will never understand her, since as far as he's concerned, she's nothing but one more dazzlingly beautiful female. On the other hand, isn't that all she is to me, too? If she were homely, or old, would I see her as being like gold? Isn't she made all more attractive by her inexplicable illness and her melancholy isolation? And will I have to choose soon between her and the airport deal? Doesn't she seem like an impossible woman, standing on the thread of indifference that separates death from sorrow? Wouldn't it be preposterous to try to possess the world of calamity and secret revolutions that she is? And the very preposterousness of it, isn't that exactly what makes the thought so enticing?

But why don't I just content myself with what's possible—that is, with a second billion dollars and the airport—and leave it to others to butt their heads up against that granite-hard heart of hers? Damn her. Ever since she arrived, my feelings toward her have vacillated between hatred and revulsion, and longing and wild passion. It's as if, like others, I'm "madly in hate with her," so to speak. She's brought anxiety and worry into my life. Confusion. And nightmares.)

He set about eating his daily magic egg. He broke it, and out came a crying baby boy. After sprinkling salt and seasonings into the boy's eyes, he hurriedly devoured him. Then he slowly chewed up the chickpeas on which his sorcerer had written cryptic symbols designed to neutralize the "evil eye," put on his bulletproof shirt despite the protective charms which had been planted under his skin, and got ready to go on a tour of the mansion and the garden to oversee the preparations being made for the Night of the First Billion. Nadim had just called him at his bedroom number, which meant that it had to be about something vital. And sure enough, he'd been bearing "good tidings" concerning the ruin of the enemy. In an excited tone he said, "It looks like Sheikh Watfan's magic really can do wonders. In punishment for Sheikh Sakhr's lack of cooperation on the airport deal, one of his sons has been killed."

As if he'd lost his only potential partner, Raghid said irritably, "Which son? Who? Saqr? He spoke to me just a little while ago."

"No. a young boy."

"Where?"

"In his home country. It's his son by his paternal cousin, the one who took her children back home to be educated in the school that we built."

"And when did he die?"

"I don't know yet. I just got the message from one of our agents, and then communications were cut off. I'll give you the rest of the details as soon as they come in."

"Don't tell anyone that you've informed me of the matter."

"Why are you telling me to keep it a secret? You know I'm accustomed to keeping things confidential."

"There have been some small mistakes . . . lately."

"If you're referring to Dunya's meddling in affairs that don't concern her, then rest assured that I've disciplined her. I killed her dog and made her think she's going crazy. And I've got a few more surprises for her up my sleeve. She's started to come apart from the inside. I'll tell you the details later. But when you see Dunya today, she'll have come to her senses."

"I haven't seen her yet today. But the minute I set eyes on her, I'll know whether the discipline has been sufficient, or whether she needs another dose. In the latter case, I'll let you know so that you can deliver her a few more blows in good time. But the important thing now is for you to get me more details about the death of Sakhr's son."

"Everything will be just the way you want it to be with regard to Sakhr's son, and Dunya."

"Discipline her. And don't worry. Trust me, and everything will be all right."

He hung up the receiver and, having decided against going out, took off his bulletproof shirt. He was filled with excitement. So then, Sheikh Watfan's magic had worked! He really was what people said he was, and he deserved all consideration and respect. And to think that to please Bahriya, he'd nearly dismissed the man! This sheikh was a treasure house of knowledge and abilities. Poor man—he'd been neglecting him of late, or nearly so, since Bahriya had cast her gloomy spell over his heart.

So he went to see him. He had to knock a number of times before the sheikh gave him permission to come in. And when he entered, he was surprised to find him gathering up some of his belongings into a small bag. He was also astonished to see the signs of illness and even old age that had suddenly begun to appear on the sorcerer's face in the preceding weeks.

"Where are you going, sir? Are you ill?"

"To the hotel, until the party is over."

"Why?"

"I don't like a lot of noise and uproar. And I don't want to disturb your guests."

"On the contrary, they'd be delighted to have you here. In fact, most of them are anxious to see you."

"All right then, I'll be frank with you. As long as Bahriya is here, I won't set foot in this place again."

Raghid fell silent. He didn't like anyone to speak to him in such a tone of voice, even if the person happened to be his favorite sorcerer. When Bahriya arrived, he had housed both of them on the same floor, with the left wing reserved for Sheikh Watfan and the right wing for Bahriya. It hadn't occurred to him that her staying on the same floor with the sorcerer would be upsetting to him. The house was a massive fortress with plenty of room for everyone in it. But Bahriya's presence seemed unduly upsetting to his sorcerer. Or was he right to be so disturbed?

"She's possessed by demons, and you won't allow me to cast them out of her."

"I've told you that I don't want trouble before the party is over. Something about the woman moves people to defend her, to do her bidding, to feel compassion for her. But it's just a superficial compassion that's a veneer for a wild lust to possess. She's turned Dunya against me, and Nasim, and Khalil. Even Nadim has been making mistakes in his work since she arrived. In fact, it was a mistake even to bring her here."

"Don't you see? What you're saying proves my point. The demons that occupy her body have tremendous power. They can put on any face they choose, so that to one person she seems like a mother, to another a sister, and to still another, a sweetheart. She speaks in all languages and in any voice she chooses. She speaks to you with the language of the heart and of the mind and of the body. She utters whatever sweet or wicked words will destroy you. She speaks in the name of the past in order to kill you with regret or sorrow, in the name of the present to overwhelm you with the torments of unfulfilled desires, and in the name of the future to fill you with weakness and dread. Yet it would be impossible to get rid of her, just as it would be to get rid of one's homeland. After all, sometimes she disguises herself behind the mask of the homeland, too. Don't you see what she's done to the weather in Geneva? Haven't you seen the sky today?"

"I promise to get rid of her. Once the celebration is over, we'll send her back to Beirut or marry her off so that she'll leave and go to some other household. Besides, the poor girl might die in a car accident, or commit suicide. What do you say to that?"

"There won't be any rest or peace for me as long as she's both alive and demon-possessed, in other words, as long as she's in rebellion. From the time she arrived, she's been heating up the winds, and today you can see black, ominous clouds gathering in the sky that forebode some perilous evil. It's consistent with what the *mandal* has been saying as well."

"After the Night of the First Billion, you shall have what you wish. I'll bring you everything you've requested: the skewers, the chains . . ."

"We'll torture the demon that lives inside her until it departs from her dead body."

"As you wish."

"We'll dismiss Nasim so that he won't to able to meddle in things he doesn't understand."

"As you wish."

"We'll inflict a grievous punishment upon the demon to force it out of her. Otherwise, she's destined to be a source of harm to you."

"As you wish. Trust me, and everything will be all right. In any case, I came to thank you. We've succeeded in ruining the enemy. What's happened will make him so miserable, he'll resort to numbing himself out with women the way he's been in the habit of doing before, and as a result, he'll be in need of a few more million dollars. He's fallen into our trap."

As if he hadn't been listening to what Raghid was saying, Sheikh Watfan went on like someone with a touch of madness, "I won't come back until she's been bound with chains to the walls of her room. I won't leave her demons at large. I won't let them poison my spiritual outflows, planting white flies in them and garbling their electrified winds . . . setting fire to my face, and planting her helpers inside my mirror so that they can torment me inside my kingdom . . ."

Raghid had made up his mind to avoid any sort of argument or scandal before the Night of the First Billion. After all, what would his guests say about a beautiful young woman bound with chains to the wall like some torture victim out of the Middle Ages? And what would the police say?

Once the party was over, he would move her residence elsewhere. He would marry her to Sheikh Sakhr or keep her as a captive mistress. Now, however, he couldn't afford any scandals. So let the sorcerer go to his hotel. After all, he was bound to feel forlorn there, too. He always ended up coming back. There was some special bond between the two men, as if neither of them could live without the other's care.

◆ ◆ ◆

When the sorcerer left the house, Raghid felt a bit frightened. Without knowing why, he took it as a bad omen, as if his protective amulets had left him. He contemplated the dark clouds and the sweltering moisture they emitted like satanic breaths, and in the distance he thought he glimpsed a flash of lightning that glistened like a sword. Bahriya evil? Perhaps. After all, she'd been tearing his world apart. His sorcerer had abandoned him, Dunya had begun defying him, Nasim was rebelling against him, Geneva's climate was changing, and obscure voices had started coming over his telephone receivers, turning women's bodies into the ashes of a spent cigarette before his very eyes. The voice that he'd heard that night asking for Kafa hadn't been human! Maybe it was her demons taking over the machinery around him. Whatever it was had even neutralized the surveillance and arms-detection device at the mansion entrance. And perhaps it was her spiritual emanations that had worked havoc on the security alarm on his golden pool two days earlier, causing its sirens to go off at night due to what the repairman claimed was an unexpected malfunction.

◆ ◆ ◆

Dunya woke up as usual to a blow of the headache ax. It was almost noon. During the previous night she had made a decision to set things right with her son Bahir. Whenever she was in the process of gulping down a bottle of firewater by night, she would make a series of resolutions. Then the resolutions would get lost the next day between her headaches, her frantic rushing to and fro, and her disappointments. Her headache was about to get the better of her. However, she got hold of herself and started heading toward Bahir's room even before washing her face, fixing her hair, or opening the curtains. She remembered an old song that she'd been fond of in her younger days, "Now or Never." I'll talk to him honestly about everything now, she thought. Otherwise I'll never be able to. The gulf between us is getting wider and wider. Besides, his father is busier than I am, and hardly takes any notice of him. It's as if he's forgotten that we have two children.

She opened the door to his room. He had his back to her, and was sitting as usual with his feet up on his desk. He didn't turn around when she came in, as if he hadn't heard her. Standing in the doorway, she said all the things she'd been wanting to about how sorry she was for neglecting him, and her regret, and how busy she'd been making money for him and his sister. As she spoke, she felt that her lame words couldn't possibly justify the way things had been. On the contrary, as she tried to apologize to him she was all the more aware of the magnitude of her crime. As for him, he didn't utter a word of pardon or even turn in her direction. Instead, he remained in the same position and began rocking to and fro in his chair in a nonchalant, rhythmic motion, causing the blood to rise to her headache-racked head.

"Haven't you got any manners?" she screamed. "When I'm speaking to you, you could at least look at me!"

It was only when he turned and looked at her with a look of astonishment on his face that she noticed the headphones plugged into his ears and the two delicate wires dangling onto his chest from his Walkman, which had rendered him safely oblivious to all sounds coming in from the outside world!

So then, he hadn't heard a single word of the confession she had just bled forth before the securely bolted doors to his inner world. When the maid saw her returning tearfully to her bedroom, she avoided her, pretending to be busy cleaning the elegant marble floor from which she had just taken up the carpet.

(A world of opulent isolation. Prisons graced with the most elegant décor. That's what we've made our house into.) Without knowing why, she sought refuge in her painting. But as she devoured it with her eyes, she was astonished to find that a knife had been thrust into the canvas right at the site of the young woman's chest. Upon closer inspection, she saw that the knife was her letter opener. Collapsing onto the chair in front of the picture, she shouted to her daughter, who was in the process of trying to leave the house without having to face her mother.

"Come here, you little beast!"

The girl come up to her mother and the two of them exchanged hateful looks. Then, casting an indifferent glance at the painting, she said, "Are you going to accuse me of doing that, too? First it's my dad who's the criminal, and then it's me!"

"Who did it, then?"

"You, of course, Mrs. Dunya Thabit!"

"Would I rip my own painting to shreds?"

"When you get drunk, you give up your identity as Madame Ghafir, and you're possessed by delusions of grandeur. When that happens, you go back to being 'Dunya Thabit, the forgotten painter.' It was definitely you who did it, when the two women who live inside you were fighting it out after you downed your bottle of firewater last night. And it was definitely you who took your dog away somewhere, then accused us of killing him. We've all got enough worries of our own, so why don't you just leave us alone with ours? I'd also advise you to see a psychiatrist. I told my boyfriend about the condition you've been in, and that's what he thinks you should do, too."

Then she nonchalantly left the house. (How cruel young people can be, especially one's own children!)

Then suddenly she heard a voice speaking to her: "But you've never been a friend to her. So why do you expect her to treat you like one?"

Had the voice come from inside her, or had the painting started talking to her in the daytime as well? And which was it now anyway—daytime or nighttime? It was hard to tell with the dark clouds that had invaded the sky, filling the atmosphere with a dusky opacity. Oh, she didn't know anymore. She didn't know who had done this to the painting. She didn't know anything. So she asked the painting itself, and a voice—she didn't know whose—answered her, saying, "It doesn't matter. After all, other people can't really threaten us unless we're already coming apart on the inside." All she knew was that she had to rush over to Raghid's mansion. The Night of the First Billion was the very next day, and she had to hurry. Was this really the voice of the young woman in the painting speaking to her, her own voice, or some other voice deliberately playing tricks on her senses? She didn't know. But she had to get going, and fast. What good was it doing to shut herself up in the house in a futile attempt to do a painting when her fingers trembled over the canvas like a little child caught in a storm? Whenever she tried to paint now, her thoughts would get scattered, and suddenly she would realize: I can't do it anymore!

She walked up to the painting, but didn't remove the knife. Perhaps leaving the wound as it was would make her mummified heart start beating again. Then she heard a voice from behind her.

"It doesn't hurt," said the voice, "but I'm worried about you."

Dunya turned around and, to her consternation, saw the young woman from the painting sitting on the same seat where she herself had been sitting moments earlier. Now that she had left the frame, it was entirely empty except for a rip at the place where her chest had been.

Then she continued in a whisper, "Blows from the outside don't hurt or wound me. But beware of weakening yourself. If they succeed in shaking you from the inside, it's all over for both of us. You're the only danger that threatens me."

◆　◆　◆

Kafa woke up intoxicated with life's wine. She opened the curtains, but took no notice of the thick, dark clouds that covered the sky like a black cloak. She hadn't found Adel by her side. She'd gotten used to having him around. However, his absence didn't bother her. After all, before her she had the Night of the First Billion, where she would glitter like a princess of the night, sashaying proudly over admiring eyes. She was too busy getting ready for the big event to think about Adel or the clouds or her children or Khalil, or anything else for that matter. She had so many things to do: She had to make sure that the hairdresser had found the right combs for her hairdo, and this evening the shoe salesman would have to get her transparent, golden party shoes ready. She'd be like a piece of gold jewelry adorning the night. She also had to buy those silk ribbons to wear around her waist. And since she'd bought her shawl during the day, she'd have to try it on at night to make sure that the color wasn't the type that looks washed out after dark. She had so many responsibilities and worries! And after doing all this, she'd have to rush off to Raghid's house to help Lilly get the place ready for the three hundred or more millionaires that she'd be meeting the next day. Ah . . . her heart was so aflutter with excitement, it seemed to have risen to her throat, nearly causing her to choke.

No sooner had she entered the mansion than she met up with Nasim, who had never seen her in anything but high spirits.

So he asked her, "How are your two boys since the accident?"

"What accident?"

"Are you serious?"

"Are *you* serious? What's happened to my boys?"

"Where have you been living, anyway?"

She didn't dare say. But she remembered that it had been days since she'd set foot in the hotel. And the school had no other address for her.

"What's wrong with Fadi and Rami?"

"I read the name of one of them in the newspapers. There was a malfunction on the telepherique on some school field trip and it fell, causing deaths and injuries. It was on all the television channels."

"I don't believe it."

"Well, that's your business. Pardon me."

Enraged, he hurriedly withdrew. (Is this a mother? Do she and my poor mother have anything in common? Thank God Khalil's coming back today. Otherwise it would be my duty to go check on those kids myself. Is this a mother?)

She telephoned the hotel. The receptionist told her, "You have several messages from College de Lemare, and also from the Hospital Pardinienne."

"Could you please tell me what the messages say now?"

"All right. Here's a message from the school. Just a minute . . . It says, 'Please contact the administration concerning an important matter related to your son.' "

She hung up and called the school. They said things to her and she said things to them. She claimed that she'd been out of the country. They didn't claim anything. Instead they simply told her, "Rami is in the hospital. He was injured on a school trip. The telepherique broke down, and there was an accident. Some children were killed, and others were injured."

Were her son's wounds serious? The secretary didn't know. However, she said his name wasn't among the fatalities. She'd have to ask the hospital. Here was the number. And her other son? She didn't find his name among either the dead or the wounded, which meant that he was back in school. He was apparently riding in another car when the accident occurred. In any case, the school would pay for Rami's treatment, since tuition fees automatically included a certain amount of money for accident insurance.

She called the hospital. The line was busy.

She paced around the telephone like an anxious tiger. She needed someone to stand by her. Anyone—her neighbor, some woman passing by in the street—she wasn't used to coping with disaster alone. And she wasn't accustomed to the secretary's calm, neutral way of informing people of the catastrophes that had befallen them.

She remembered shouting at the secretary over the phone, "How could there be an accident on the telepherique? We're in Switzerland!"

Unruffled, the other woman replied, "Accidents happen everywhere. And people get injured in Switzerland, too."

There was just one self-evident fact that had slipped Kafa's mind, namely, that even here, people could die, and that as long as he was human, her son wasn't entirely safe even here in Switzerland.

Meanwhile, Layla was pacing and forth in the next room, and the hospital line was still busy. Kafa went to her and informed her of what had happened.

"All right," she replied coolly in French, "If your son is in critical condition, you can have today off. But I'll need you tomorrow. There's a lot of work to be done tomorrow morning. Call the hospital again and let me know."

Then she quickly left the room.

◆　◆　◆

Raghid decided to go to his golden pool to invite the Freedom Fighter statue to the Night of the First Billion. And while he was at it, he'd make use of the opportunity to thank it for his first million.

Like a jailkeeper, he opened up his golden cage with a key that never left his possession. As he was going in he had a thought: Why not move the statue to the mansion's main hall so that it can attend the party? But no. Its presence would be upsetting to most of his guests. So he decided to keep it where it was. Then the two of them could celebrate together after all the guests were gone. They could play "heads and tails" with the piaster. They'd throw it up in the air, and if it landed on the floor with the side bearing the name of Palestine facing upward, the statue would win the bet. However, if the side bearing the coin's value in Hebrew, English, and Arabic faced upward, then Raghid would win his second billion.

"Pasha . . ."

He turned around in a near panic.

"The guests will start arriving at the hotel today," Layla said. "The 'yellow millionaire' called, and I told him you were out of town. I said you'd be coming back tomorrow in time for the party, and that if you returned before then, you'd contact him."

"Very good. What a capable woman you are! I'll be the one to choose the time we meet. I've got to see the 'red millionaire' first. I prefer making deals

with him. He's up-to-date in his way of thinking, and decisive. He doesn't hes-
itate to use the knife on anyone who would dare ruin our deals."

(I've come to prefer dealing with him to people like Sheikh Sakhr and that
disaster of a twin brother of his, Hilal. Men the likes of Hilal could make me a
poor man again, with no more than a few million dollars to my name. As for
Saqr, he's an addict, and couldn't be depended on in the long run. However, he
might help ensure the airport deal as he claims to be able to. Since I gave him
that huge advance before he left on his trip, his father will have to pay it back
if Saqr doesn't come through.)

"Has Dunya arrived?" Raghid asked Layla.

"She just walked in."

"Is she helping you?"

"A bit. Her nerves are shot, and I think she needs to spend some time in a
mental institution. But she'll be able to finish her assignments during the few
hours remaining before the party."

"And how about Coco?"

"She'd be superb if it weren't for the fact that she found out this morning
about the accident her son was in. I kept it from her as long as I could."

"She doesn't read the newspapers, she doesn't watch television, and my informer tells me that as usual, she spent all last night out with Adel in some
disco. Beside which, she hasn't gone by her hotel. So how could she have
found out about it?"

"I don't know. Maybe she asked about the boys at their school."

"Or maybe Nasim told her. I'm going to settle accounts with that son of a
bitch the day after tomorrow—after the Night of the First Billion."

"In any case," Layla reassured him, "Coco will come through on all her duties from now to the end of the party. Her son's injuries aren't serious. At least
that's what they told her when she called the hospital."

"Take good care of Coco. The guests love her, and Saqr has a thing for her.
And I might be needing him in the coming weeks."

"I'm planning to put Sheikh Saqr in the room next to hers."

"That was foresightful of you."

"And as long as Sheikh Watfan is gone, why not honor the 'red millionaire'
by putting him up in Watfan's suite?"

"Excellent idea. But . . . the place is full of his magic paraphernalia."

"The 'red one' won't be arriving before tomorrow evening. We'll put everything into a big chest and store it in the basement, then return everything to its place after the party is over. What do you say to that, Pasha?"

"Fine. Do whatever you think is appropriate."

"Excuse me, Pasha, but I need a cash payment from you. I've used up the first payment you gave me, and the bank won't honor my checks anymore since my balance has run out. I borrowed two million dollars from the bank director as a special favor from him, and checks still have to be sent to the restaurants. You wouldn't want them to ruin the party for us by sending out inquiries about bad checks with my signature on them."

He had a long laugh over what she had said, which brought him some comic relief, but only increased her distress.

"It'll be a Night of the First Billion joke—food on credit and bad checks! Don't worry about a thing. Tabulate your accounts and put them away in a safe place, then tomorrow morning you'll be a rich woman. I'll reimburse you for your expenses and pay you for your services at dawn tomorrow—that is, in less than twenty-four hours. After all, I'm generous with those who serve me well. Don't worry, Lilly. Trust me, and everything will be just as you've been hoping."

"So then, Pasha, I'll go to bed tonight a poor woman in debt?"

"It will be the last night you have to spend with debt and poverty. The payment will take place at daybreak tomorrow, in this very room. You and I will have morning coffee together to review the final arrangements, and you'll get the first really big check you've ever collected in your life. I just want to take a final look at the names of the people who've been invited and at the seating plan for the dinner table, since there have been some modifications."

Worried, Layla said, "In that case, I may have to make modifications in the garden arrangements. These clouds look as though they might bring in a storm. And the weatherman on television says the same thing."

As they walked back to the mansion from the octopus-shaped pool of gold, Raghid's dog happened to pass by, at which point it howled and took off running. Nobody liked him, and he knew it. Even his dogs detested him.

As they walked back to the mansion entrance, Nasim came up to them and informed them that Saqr had arrived.

"When?"

"A few minutes go. I took him to his room. He said he was exhausted and needed to rest."

Whispering in Lilly's ear, Raghid said, "That means he needs a 'snort.' "

Then, turning to Nasim, he said, "Tell me, Nasim, did Khalil come back with him?"

"Yes, he did. Then he took off for the hospital to see his son."

"And who told him his son was in the hospital?"

"I did. I thought he already knew about the accident."

"Damn you. You've gotten to be a blabbermouth. You've started slipping up like the rest of them. You all used to be as dependable as Swiss watches. What's gotten into you since . . ."

He nearly went on to stay, "since Bahriya came," but thought better of it.

Nasim took off for the kitchen in a hurry, with all of his hatred and bitterness toward Raghid rekindled. Raghid, Sirri Al-Din's murderer—how could he possibly not inform a father that his little boy has been injured?

Lilly said, "I'll claim that my secretary forgot to send the telex."

"But Khalil begged me to let him know personally if anything happened to his family. That crazy hick will be furious, and I don't want any extra crazies running around on the Night of the First Billion."

"We'll say that you delegated that responsibility to me. I asked my secretary to take care of it, and she didn't. And she'll be punished by being fired."

"This thing isn't worth losing your secretary over. I expect he'll be satisfied with an apology from you."

"I was planning to get rid of her anyway. She's got a big mouth and can't keep anything confidential. Besides, I saw a picture of her in the newspaper marching alongside Dunya and Amir."

"I admire your decisiveness. I think we'll do a sifting operation once the celebration is over."

"I'm at your service."

"Nadim, for example. He's started to make me nervous."

"His wife is dangerous. Dunya."

"Are you jealous of her, Lilly?" Raghid asked playfully. "After all, she stayed by Amir's side throughout the whole demonstration. And after it as well. Then she didn't come back from his house until after midnight."

"Me? Jealous of her? That poor, idiotic drunk? She's on her way to self-destruction, and then to the insane asylum. Besides, I don't get jealous of women. There's no sort of female competition between me and them. My field of operation is the same as men's."

"Nadim ought to be worried about you as a rival. By the way, what do you think of Khalil?"

"For what purpose?"

"For the purpose of getting him ready to take on some of Nadim's responsibilities."

"I don't think he'd be fit for it in the long run. He's basically corrupt, since he's got the stupid urge to say what he imagines to be the 'truth.' It's true, of course, that he lived all his life in Beirut. But his small-town roots still determine the way he behaves. He lacks flexibility. Besides which, he's got the potential to become a dangerous man."

"What do you mean?"

"I mean, he'd be hard to tame."

"That's just the type I like. After all, all men are for sale. Every one of them has his price."

"However, this one happens to be a senseless man who will never set a price for himself. He prefers holding onto old mistakes rather than discovering a new life."

"I think he's one of those people who sell themselves for free. At first they appear to be unyielding. But, then all of a sudden, they collapse before your very eyes when they see you wielding your power. In fact, they themselves are in love with power, but they conceal it behind a thin veneer of principles."

"He seems bullheaded, and the type who doesn't keep his back covered. Do you remember how he sang, 'O darkness of the prison, descend'? That was really obnoxious."

"I'll conduct some mental plastic surgery on him. As for his stubbornness, that may be just the thing I find so attractive about him."

"You know your men better than anyone else does. But it seems to me that he isn't worth all this trouble, and that his unpredictability might cause problems. He's confused, as if he were thinking about the meaning of his life—or dreaming of immortality."

Picking up a gold figurine in the shape of an apple, Raghid said, "I'll teach him that this is immortality. I'll put it in his hand and tell him to hold onto it. This alone endures. Human beings die, from kings to vagabonds. But gold always remains, eternally revered."

Just then Coco walked in, her pretty face betraying signs of fatigue.

"How's the boy?" asked Raghid.

Then, before she could reply, he asked. "Have you seen Khalil?"

"No. Is he back?"

"Nasim told him the news the minute he arrived, and he made a dash for the hospital."

Matter-of-factly, Coco said, "It amazes me that he would carry on with his trip without giving a damn what was happening to his son."

"It seems that life's pleasures can make one forget a lot of things," replied Raghid knowingly.

She sensed that he was reproaching her. All right then. So she was a criminal. But that didn't change the fact that her husband was becoming a criminal like her. And at least she, unlike him, didn't go around bragging about her principles!

Her face clouded over with grief, as if she herself had just now remembered that her son was in the hospital.

"Coco," interrupted Raghid, "There's a surprise waiting for you in your room."

"A happy one?"

"Of course. Do I keep any other kind in my quiver? Don't worry. Trust me, and everything will be just fine."

"So what is it, this happy surprise?"

"A dress for tomorrow evening's party."

Quickly drying her tears, she rushed toward the room that Lilly had assigned to her and Khalil for the Night of the First Billion, and possibly for tonight as well if, as was likely, the requirements of work made it necessary.

"Do you see what I mean?" said Lilly. "This is a woman who's malleable. It only takes a little to make her feel joy or sorrow. She isn't like her husband. She's more likely than he is to cooperate with us."

"But what's the use of that? She's stupid."

"You'd be hard pressed to find an intelligent person who would also be easy to tame, unless he consciously chose to follow your path."

"You mean to say, I'd be hard-pressed to find someone else like you?"

"Exactly," she replied, and they both burst out laughing.

Their laughter faded out gradually when Nadim suddenly came into the room. His aristocratic savoir-faire gone, he seemed like a mountain goat running scared through a thunderstorm.

Without greeting Lilly or even looking her way, he said to Raghid, "I've got to speak with you alone."

Withdrawing in overdone politeness, Lilly said, "Pardon me, I have things to do."

Sensing how terrified Nadim was, Raghid replied, "Come, let's go to the study."

On their way they passed by Nasim.

"Bring us coffee in the study . . . right away," Raghid told him.

They also ran into a distraught-looking Dunya, whose eyes seemed to emit sparks of madness.

She and Raghid exchanged a cold handshake, after which she greeted Nadim meanly, saying, "You certainly left the house early this morning—but not so early you couldn't find time to commit a murder first."

"I'm not the one who did that. You are. I saw you sleepwalking with your letter opener in your hand, and I didn't dare go near you. You've turned into two different women that are constantly at each other's throats. And before that you got rid of Picasso, then accused me of doing it."

"You're a liar."

Yet she said it lamely, as if his accusation had found fertile ground somewhere deep inside her. (Maybe I did it when I was drunk. Maybe I really *do* want to get rid of that bewitched, worrisome painting. God! I can't tell the difference anymore between reality and illusion, or between dreams and what I've actually done. Things have started overlapping in my mind, and I'm in torment.)

"Beginning forty-eight hours from now you two can carry on with your family dispute at home," said Raghid in an authoritative tone of voice. "But until the Night of the First Billion is over, I forbid you to have even so much as a conversation with each other."

◆　◆　◆

Once they were alone in the study, Nadim heaved a deep sigh, then collapsed in his chair, wiping his sweat-drenched brow.

"You've already told me the good news of Sheikh Sakhr's son dying," Raghid said anxiously. "Saqr is here, but we won't inform him that one of his brothers has been killed. Of course, even if he knew he might not give a damn. Besides which, he's busy taking his white fix. So what's on your mind?"

"It's a catastrophe . . . a catastrophe."

"What's happened?"

"The school . . . the school we built has collapsed. Sheikh Sakhr's son died under the piles of resulting debris, and scores of other children along with him."

"What? The school collapsed?"

Both men fell silent for a long, long time. When Nadim had caught his breath he repeated his story, adding, "If it hadn't been for the summer vacation, hundreds would have been killed. Sakhr's son and his classmates were in the library that we donated for summer reading."

"I don't believe it."

Nadim went back to wiping his profusely sweating brow.

Then, in a mournful tone he said, "It collapsed without warning after a sandstorm. Thanks to graft, the construction materials were bad. It looks as though your engineer went a bit too far this time. However, there's no denying your own responsibility in the matter."

Raghid unsheathed a cigar and lit it without saying a word, then sat there in silence for quite a while. In the meantime, Nadim gulped down a glass of firewater which no one had offered him. It was the first time he had broken the rules of "protocol" in the Pasha's presence.

After a long silence between the two men, Nasim walked in with the coffee.

Raghid took a sip and said, "The coffee's cold. Have you been standing outside the door eavesdropping, the way you usually do?"

Too startled to reply, Nasim took refuge in silence.

"Do you actually think I don't notice everything that goes on? You and I have some accounts to settle after the Night of the First Billion. And the first person who'll have to answer for you is the one who brought you here and put in a good word for you."

As he spoke, he looked over at Nadim with such unfeigned hatred, as if he blamed him for everything that had gone wrong on Planet Earth since the days of Adam.

Meanwhile, Nasim made a beeline for the door.

"And now, what to do?" asked Nadim. "Should we cancel the Night of the First Billion to keep Sheikh Sakhr from turning it into a scandal?"

Raghid said nothing for quite some time. Then, with the finality of someone issuing an irrevocable decree, he said, "Canceling the Night of the First Billion is out of the question. I've invited most of the true rulers of the Earth, that is, the money kings who control the world's affairs with their purse strings. And some of them have arrived."

"Untold numbers of children have died."

"They die every day and everywhere for one reason or another."

"It's a catastrophe. We're finished. Their families are in a state of grief and shock, and that's sure to be followed by a state of rage. We're finished."

"It's a problem that has to be dealt with, that's all."

"Sakhr and Hilal will never keep quiet about this, and neither will their clan. They'll destroy our business everywhere. We're finished."

Raghid fell silent again. As he sat absorbed in thought with his facial muscles alternately tensing and relaxing, Nadim imagined that inside this powerful man there was a computer with red, blue, and white lights flashing as it carried out complex arithmetic operations, yet without anything appearing on the screen to indicate the result. Then at long last, in a calm, neutral voice that told him virtually nothing, the computer said, "Go to your room and rest. I'll call for you later on. Don't say a thing to Dunya or to anyone else. And be sure not to inform Saqr."

"They'll find out anyway. The collapse of a school that we built and the deaths of scores of children can't possibly remain a secret. It'll be in the newspapers, and everybody will be talking about it. And the Interpol might even step in to arrest the person responsible."

"Don't breathe a word to anyone. And let me handle it. And most important of all, don't worry. Trust me and everything will be just as you've hoped!"

◆   ◆   ◆

Kafa gazed at the shoulderless dress that Raghid had given her with its golden translucence, and she forgot all her worries. She even forgot about Khalil, who had rushed off to the hospital to check on his little boy without bothering to see her, shake her hand, or ask her how she was.

She put on the costly silk, which revealed special charms in her neck that she'd never noticed before. Nor did she notice the stealthy glances Saqr sent her way, staring at her through the curtains from the balcony that extended the length of both her room and his. She threw herself onto the bed, intoxicated with her own beauty. Yet as the minutes passed, the effect of the exquisite dress began to wear off, like some mild narcotic that starts to lose its initial effect as one grows accustomed to it. Once again she was accosted by the image of her son Rami lying in the hospital. She had reassured herself that his wounds were minor. Yet even so, the thought of him brought her back face to face with the nightmare: the possibility of losing him here in a foreign land. (He's fine. So just forget about the accident.) But . . . every disaster or near disaster reminded her of Widad, and whenever that happened she was overwhelmed with sorrow all over again. (Never again do I want to lay eyes on anything that will bring me grief. I can't take it anymore. I grieved enough in Beirut for several lifetimes, and I shed enough tears for several tribes of women.

I lived alone with my fears while my husband sat in prison, reveling in the luxury of his imagined greatness. I'm tired of being tired. I'm tired of everything. I'm not as stupid as I seem to be, or as stupid as people around me would like to believe. Of course, it doesn't bother me what they think, since I've chosen my path and that's that. My new slogan is, "Look out for Number One!" Whether I die young or live to a ripe old age, I want to live a lifetime's worth of pleasures. How things have changed since my name was changed from "Kafa" to "Coco." From now on I want to move about with the freedom of the beautiful women that appear on the pages of fashion magazines. If I catch a glimpse of someone who's wounded, I'll turn my face away and look across the street or into the display window of the first jewelry store I come to. Is it evil for me to avoid pain and not to help the wounded? Perhaps. But I'm no more evil than the person who wounded him, or than the stupidity that may have caused him to get hurt. People pass judgment only on those who are happy. But when it comes to those who bring misery both to themselves and to others—people like my husband, for example—you find poets and thinkers making up slogans for them and whitewashing the wounds that they cause. They even manage to delude the simpleminded into thinking that a wound is more beautiful than a smile. If only I hadn't had children. In this barbaric world of ours, a child is nothing but sorrow in the making. But what's past is past. The important thing now is to forget, and to get away from anything and everything that might cause me grief. Adel is planning to go away after the Night of the First Billion celebration. He's promised to buy Nadim's flat and let me live in it on condition that I remain faithful to him during his absences. And I accepted his condition. However, I won't be faithful to him. After all, if I did that, I wouldn't be faithful to who I am. The only reality I'll be faithful to is my own desires and whims, be they great or small.)

Saqr continued to stare at Kafa. His body was trembling, perhaps on account of the huge number of uppers he'd swallowed, and he kept rubbing the cocaine into his nostrils to keep himself from sneezing.

Then suddenly she got up off the bed, gripped by an unexpected idea. It was so compelling that it took possession of her, making her forget everything else: She'd try on the dress that she'd prepared herself for the Night of the First Billion, then she'd wear the one she looked most beautiful in. The more lovers she took on, the less inclined she was to submit to Raghid or anyone else. It was as if a woman she hadn't known before had begun coming to life deep inside her. And her fingernails had grown longer, too. It was as if she hadn't really discovered herself yet, a self that had been buried by Beirut for seven long years under mounds of corpses strewn here and there, booby-trapped cars, refuse, howling and random gunfire, sometimes in celebration, other times in mourning, sometimes on the way to the hospital and other times on the way to the graveyard.

No sooner had she stood in front of the mirror for the second time than she saw a hand reaching out through the curtains that hung across the door leading onto the balcony. The hand was holding onto a box covered with purple velvet, and inside of which there glittered a necklace of exquisite beauty. Set with blue stones, it glistened and sparkled as though a special sort of life raged inside its shiny gold frame.

She turned around, half-bewitched. Her senses and even her sorrows numbed, she no longer saw anything but the waves that swelled in the seas of turquoise before her. A necklace like this on her neck would bring out the blueness of her eyes. As the hand moved the necklace toward her, she could see nothing else, mesmerized by its splendor and by her lust to possess it. When at last she looked up at the face of the person holding it, she was startled to find a horrifying devil's face that looked like a mask. Before she could scream, a powerful hand had been clamped over her mouth, and a familiar voice that she couldn't quite identify whispered, "Don't scream. I've come to give you this necklace. I mean you no harm, and I don't want to frighten you. But I have my own way of doing things, including giving gifts . . ."

By this time he could tell that she had calmed down somewhat, since her features had relaxed under his hand. He released her, saying, "Turn around and look in the mirror. And see how Cartier created this necklace especially for eyes like yours."

"Cartier?" The mere mention of the name sedated her. And she nearly gasped with delight as she saw the delicate necklace being placed upon her neck, like an opulent base for a statue of exquisite beauty.

A few moments later she grew frightened again, which he sensed from the way she covered her nearly bare breast with her hands.

In a commanding tone he said, "Put on your coat."

Bewildered, she put it on.

"Put something on your head," he added. "Wrap it in your shawl."

So she did, feeling all the while as though she were stepping into an absurd dream. Meanwhile, the clouds around her were growing thicker and thicker, the room seemed to be getting gradually darker, and a sinister shadow was descending from the ceiling, pouring forth from the sultry heat of a day that had seemed charged with electricity.

She could feel hidden storehouses of violent passion welling up inside her, as if mysterious currents were stealing into her from this unidentified demon, opening doors deep in her soul that until now had been shut tight.

Then suddenly, without either of them uttering a word and without his removing her coat or the cover on her head, he flung himself onto the bed and drew her along with him, like an island being carried away by enchanted waves. Within moments the waves had begun invading her grottos and washing over her mosses in a loud fury. The island surrendered to the gales, sinking one moment, floating the next, while the devil's mask came and went before her eyes. She wanted to express her gratitude for being able to touch the bottom of the sea with its extraordinary, caustic light. Then, without knowing why, she slapped him.

She slapped him so hard, in fact, that she sent his mask flying and hurt her hand in the process. And who should she find her assailant to be but Saqr, that young, handsome, well-to-do fellow who for so long she'd fantasized about whenever she ran her hands over her body. She slapped him again, cackling like a lunatic, and was astonished to find that her ferocity only made his seas rage all more tempestuously. He slapped her back, and she was on fire with passion. The harmony between them in their mutual, intoxicated savagery was something to behold indeed. And before long the waves had immersed the island once again, filling in its caverns and its dry wells. It was a mystery-filled sea voyage mingled with pain, and with the delights of discovering the maritime side of hell. She was at the bottom of the sea on the rim of a watery, molten volcano about to erupt and shake the sea from its foundations. Saqr was awed by this extraordinary creature. Never before had his aggression been greeted with this sort of fierce, unaffected welcome.

Then the door opened, and who should peer inside but Khalil!

When she saw him she screamed, "Help! He's raping me!"

Seeing her rapidly changing states, Saqr's admiration for her increased all the more. Her voice had come out sounding muffled and, as if he hadn't seen or heard a thing, Khalil shut the door behind him, headed toward an armchair, sat down, and turned his back to them.

Saqr jumped to his feet, carefully put his mask back on, and straightened his clothes. Kafa sat up on the edge of the bed, still wearing her summer coat and with her head still wrapped in her shawl. She didn't feel embarrassed or flustered. In fact, all she felt was the urge to get out of the room, though a few tears came flowing out of her pretty eyes, perhaps out of respect for the gravity of the moment. Then she left, slamming the door behind her.

With a chill in his voice, Saqr said to Khalil, "How much do you want for your wife? I want her for myself. Set the price and let me know."

He'd been planning to leave the room the same way he'd come in, that is, via the balcony. However, for some reason he changed his mind and, after taking off his mask, went out through the main door carrying it in his hand. Khalil didn't look at him or utter a word. It had been a shock for him to see his wife in the very act of betraying him. He'd known about it, of course, but when he came face to face with the reality of it, he lost his voice and was filled with a host of nebulous, hard-to-define emotions.

◆　◆　◆

When Kafa left the room she met up in the hallway with Layla and Dunya, who were in the process of arranging a lace sheet at the base of a statue that they had moved to a new location.

Then, without knowing why she said tearfully, "Saqr just raped me."

The other two women looked at her incredulously.

"No one's raped you," replied Layla nonchalantly. "Saqr is asleep in his room. You must have been dreaming. Your son's accident has shaken you up, which is only natural."

However, just then the door to her room opened again, and who should walk out but Saqr, who proceeded to slip stealthily into the adjoining room.

He didn't see the women standing at the end of the corridor or the looks of astonishment on their faces.

After he had disappeared behind the door, Layla continued cruelly, "Your nerves are just on edge. No one raped you. Isn't that right, Dunya?"

Dunya remained silent.

"That's a lovely necklace, Coco," she added. "But this isn't the time to be wearing it. Hurry up now and change your clothes, then come back and help us. There's a lot of work to be done."

◆   ◆   ◆

Kafa went back to her room and changed her clothes with trembling hands. She wished Khalil would say something to her—anything. That way they could have a fight, at least. However, he didn't even look her way. Instead, he just sat there with his head in his hands. She nearly asked him about Rami's health, but then she remembered that he was all right and that his wounds were minor.

"Khalil," she called out to him.

He made no reply. (That's it. I don't give a damn what happens to anybody. "Look out for Number One!" I'll live for myself, and myself alone. I won't allow pain to eat me up on the inside, and I'll silence any and all voices inside me that would keep me from being happy. Tomorrow is the Night of the First Billion. I'll be meeting at least three hundred millionaires, and I plan to dazzle them all. The doors to life have opened up before me.)

Then she left the room, saying to herself, "Maybe he's dead, too!"

◆   ◆   ◆

After the encounter with Raghid that had warned of an approaching storm, Nadim took refuge in his temporary quarters in the mansion, contemplating the torrid black clouds that likewise augured a storm to come. Dunya came in after him and, thinking he was asleep, began shaking him to wake him up. However, he wasn't asleep, but had shut his eyes the moment she walked in to avoid having to say anything to her. The stones from the collapsed school were raining down on his head, and the resounding scandal that was about to become common knowledge felt like a guillotine blade being brought down on his neck again and again and again.

"Nadim . . . get up. Something horrible has happened," she said, still shaking him.

"So you know about it, too?" he asked. "How's that?"

"I saw him leaving her room."

"Who are you talking about?"

"And you, what are you talking about?"

"Why did you wake me up?"

"He raped Kafa. Saqr raped Kafa. And Khalil, he might . . ."

Interrupting her angrily, he said, "Trivialities! That's all woman think about. What do I care whether he raped her or not? Besides, why would he have to rape her when she's been flirting with him right in front of her husband and everybody else from the first time they met?"

"I don't know why. But he did."

"Maybe they enjoyed making a theatrical production out of it. And now, leave me alone."

"But he really did rape her. Layla refuses to testify, and you pretend not to care and not to know that I know about your relationship with her."

"That's not true."

"You're lying."

"Our whole life is one big lie," he said in desperation. "And now you refuse to accept this little one? My relationship with her, Saqr's relationship with her . . . it's all trivialities. So overlook them, the way you usually do."

"I can't anymore. Your killing Picasso won't frighten me, and your stabbing my painting won't change me."

"I swear I didn't do either of the things you're accusing me of. You went sleepwalking and stabbed your picture. And as for Picasso, I don't know a thing about him. Maybe he ran away. Or maybe he got run over by a car."

"You're not going to be able to delude me into thinking I'm crazy. And you won't find a single mental institution willing to put me away."

"Please, Dunya, leave me alone about Coco. And about your painting, and your dog, and your art, and all your other petty concerns."

"If these are petty concerns, then what do you consider to be serious? In any case, I'll testify to the truth of what I saw. Saqr raped Coco with her consent. I want everyone to know that you aren't her only lover. And that's my revenge against the two of you."

(She was shocked to hear herself saying what she was saying. What had happened to change her so? And why had her emotions started running out of control all over again? Her behavior was erratic, and she couldn't seem to bring it under control.)

"Raghid will be angry," Nadim threatened her.

"I don't care."

"I'm the one who'll pay the price."

"He wouldn't dare. He wouldn't dare hurt an ant. And if he tried, I'd threaten him myself."

Sounding hopeless, he said, "I hope not. Ants aside, I hope he wouldn't dare hurt me, at least."

"What's wrong?" she asked him, sounding a bit concerned.

He buried his face in his hands.

"What's happened? Tell me. Whatever it is, we've lived together a long time—the years of our youth, our whole lives. And we won't get a chance to relive them. Nobody's going to hand them to us on a platter for us to start over. In other words, we're stuck with each other. So what's happened?"

"Are you my friend?"

"I don't know. But I'll try to be, if not for your sake, then for my own. I'm definitely not your sweetheart anymore. But we've got our children in common, which means that whatever misfortunes come our way will affect both of us together for some time to come. Tell me, what's happened?"

"Dunya . . . I think I'm going to find myself in a huge fix. I'll tell you a secret. But don't tell a soul. And if anybody tells you about it, pretend you didn't know a thing."

"That's enough suspense, please. What's happened?"

"Raghid is going to want to stay on Saqr's good side more than ever before, since there's going to be a war between him and the senior Ghanamali."

"Why's that?"

"Because Abdullah, one of Sheikh Sakhr's sons, was killed yesterday. He was his son by his Arab wife, Sita. I think she was his paternal cousin, or some relation of his at least, which is bound to complicate matters that much more."

"And what does that have to do with us? Another of his sons died earlier when his private helicopter crashed. And before that . . ."

"But . . ." he interrupted, "Abdullah died along with scores of other boys when their school collapsed on top of them . . . the school that Raghid built, or rather, that *we* built."

She said nothing for a while. Then, in a terrified whisper, she said, "But you're not responsible. Raghid is . . . either Raghid, or his head engineer. And that has nothing to do with us."

"For sure. But I'm scared."

"Why?"

"I don't know exactly. I just am. In situations like this, there has to be a scapegoat. The big dinosaurs might start fighting, and some of them may get wounded. When that happens, they always end up trampling some of their assistants underfoot and offering the rest of them up as scapegoats."

"Don't be afraid."

As she said the words, she herself was trembling with fright. She had lived in the society of dinosaurs long enough to understand exactly what her husband meant.

She thought of leaving the room before she could be scolded by Layla, who was always complaining that she was the only one who ever did anything to get ready for the Night of the First Billion.

How Layla had changed, and how merciless and domineering she'd become. And perhaps now her chance had come to clip Nadim's wings and take his place.

Catastrophes always begin with a small mistake. When she'd invited Layla to that dinner party way back when, she'd done it in part because she felt sorry for her, the way one invites some down and out divorcee in her forties so that she can entertain the old men. But then she'd met Raghid, and snared him. And now here she was, threatening Dunya's livelihood and even her safety.

Of course, there's no such thing as safety—or a true woman friend—in shark-infested waters.

Still quaking in her boots, she repeated, "Don't be afraid, Nadim."

Did she really feel sympathy for him? Or was she inwardly glad to see him suffering? She didn't know for certain. All she knew was that she was terrified. She was like someone who's been riding inside a Rolls Royce with gold-plated handles through a modern zoo of the type where the animals are allowed to roam freely, and who knows the rules of the game: Keep the windows closed. Don't speed so as not to provoke the animals. And don't stop. Then suddenly she finds herself alone in the jungle, without a car and without anyone to come to her aid, including the gunmen whose job was to kill any animal that threatened someone's life. Suddenly all the rules of the game are invalidated, the rules that once determined everything from what paths the wild animals followed to when they were sedated, thereby ensuring the safety of the passengers riding through the zoo.

Now she would have to cope once more with the chaotic, untamed way things really are. And until such time as the jungle was restored to some semblance of order, she would have to protect herself from the very moment she'd dreamed of for so long; the moment of her freedom.

◆   ◆   ◆

Raghid was on his way to his car when Layla caught up with him, intending to speak to him about money. She began the conversation by playing the spy in hopes of inspiring his confidence and reminding him of how much he needed her.

"There have been some problems," she whispered. "Saqr has raped Coco."

"That's all I need."

"I've forbidden her to talk about it. I made it clear to her that no one will believe her and that I won't testify on her behalf."

"Who saw them besides you?"

"Nobody but Dunya. But I'll make sure she doesn't get out of line."

"And Khalil?"

"He may have seen them, too. It seems that I caught a glimpse of somebody . . . I'm not sure. I was working at the time. But I don't think he was back yet. After all, if he had been, he would have come by and said hello."

"He must not have been here, then. If he had seen them, he would never have kept quiet about it. You know how he is. And now, listen, Layla. I've got urgent business to attend to. So you take charge of everything. Be my partner in bearing my burdens, and you won't regret it."

She nearly asked him for money right then. She had decided to insist on it. After all, she couldn't wait until the next day. She was a woman prone to doubts and fears, and she knew quite well that signing bad checks could mean scandal and prison. It was true, of course, that Raghid would be paying her at dawn on the following day as he had promised her. However, she was being cautious, and planned to be paid now based on the principle of the thing. Like a magic spell, the phrase, "Be my partner" numbed her for a moment—long enough, that is, for Raghid to leave her behind with nothing but the memory of his words, "You seat the guests around the dinner table however you like. I have urgent business to see to, and you're the only person I can count on . . ."

As Layla was thinking about whether she liked the name Layla Zahran and deciding that it wasn't bad as long as it meant becoming one of the world's wealthiest widows, Raghid was dismissing his chauffeur and driving off in his car without his bodyguards.

He had no choice but to engage in some risky behavior if he was going to escape from the catastrophe of the school's collapse and Abdullah's demise. Besides, he wasn't going to let trivial details like these spoil the celebration of his first billion, and of his second billion to come.

◆ ◆ ◆

With tears streaming down his face, Raghid walked into the room where Sakhr sat surrounded by fellow mourners.

"What is this disaster that I've heard about, brother Sakhr?" he wailed. "I've come to console you. . . !"

Screaming as if he'd just been stung, he replied, "There'll be no consolation for me until I've handed you over to a court of law! You'll spend the rest of your life behind bars. You caused my son Abdullah to die under the remains of that school of yours, and scores of other children along with him."

"Calm down, my friend. May God grant you patience to endure what's befallen you."

Then, addressing the others gathered round, Raghid said, "Leave the two of us alone for a while."

So they left the room, nearly falling over themselves to get out the door. None of them had the least desire to be witness to an altercation between "the two billionaires," since the well-to-do can be quite unpredictable, and when they are, it's the witness who pays, since without his knowing how it happened, one of them might suddenly transfer him from the witness stand to the prisoner's dock. And everyone in attendance knew this all too well.

"How dare you come to my house after murdering my son and ruining my reputation back home!" Sakhr thundered. "You've destroyed me, God damn you!"

Continuing his lamentation, Raghid said, "And how could I not come to the house of my beloved friend and brother in his time of affliction?"

"Haven't you figured out either from Nadim or from your own common sense that I intend to bring you to justice? You'll be tried there in Lebanon. And if you don't go voluntarily, I'll abduct you and carry you to the courtroom with my own two hands."

"I don't blame you, brother. If I were in your place, I'd do even more than that. However, Nadim hasn't told me anything. Poor man, his conscience is tormenting him. He's so quiet, it's as if he's been struck dumb. And he's so eaten up with regret, he's been sweating like a horse, as if that's the only way he can let it out."

"What do you mean?"

"Well, Nadim, damn the guy, he's the cause of the whole disaster. He'd pulled the wool over both your eyes and mine. Hasn't the news reached you? Haven't your assistants told you about Nadim's crime?"

"What?"

"He came to me to confess. It was all his game. And the engineer was in on it, too."

"If what you're saying is true, I'll kill him with my own two hands."

"There's no need for you to sully your lily-white hands on his account. I've persuaded him to turn himself in and confess to his crime. As for the engineer, I'll punish him myself once he's finished with our next major project: the tourist complex."

"My God! I though you were the culprit!"

"Shame on you, brother! Have you forgotten about our friendship? Is such a thing possible? The minute I heard the news, I came running. In fact, I was so beside myself, I came without my bodyguard or my chauffeur. And now I have to be on my way to make sure that Nadim turns himself in. May justice take its course without either of our spotless reputations being besmirched."

Sakhr escorted him to the door in disbelief. He knew that Raghid wouldn't take a single step without both his chauffeur and his bodyguard. And as he looked outside, he was astonished to find Nadim's car waiting in front of the door, empty, with the motor still running and the door open. At the sight of it, his goodheartedness got the better of him, and before he knew it he was embracing Raghid as he wept, saying, "May God curse Satan, friend! And please forgive my brother Hilal, who planted such suspicions in my heart!"

As they observed the scene through the window, the people who had been gathered at Sheikh Sakhr's house saw the two giants embracing: one billionaire pressing the other to his bosom. So they turned their faces away in fear, not wanting to be called forth as witnesses either to a battle or to a truce between the two men.

"Bahriya is in need of rest," said Raghid. "Would you be willing to host her in your house for a couple of nights—tonight and tomorrow night—until everything is over? She won't be able to attend the Night of the First Billion, and there's no justification for her coming anyway as long as you're not going to be there. I tried to cancel the party in mourning for Abdullah, but Madame Spock has informed me that half of the guests have already arrived, and it isn't in keeping with Arab hospitality to send one's guests away. Of course, we'll cut out anything that smacks of gaiety, being certain to keep it an austere affair. So could you possibly take Bahriya in for these two nights?"

"She's your relative, which means that she's mine as well. And my house is yours."

"And your son is mine, may he rest in peace."

Whereupon Raghid began to weep again, saying, "I'll send Bahriya to you this evening. Will you be inconvenienced by visits from her doctor?"

"Who would deprive an unfortunate girl of treatment? May God heal her and cause her to enjoy perfect health! I'll consider her to be a sacred trust while she's with me."

"If I weren't certain of that, I wouldn't have committed her to your care."

"And Sheikh Watfan, will he be attending? Or will all the commotion disturb him as well?"

"He left the house this morning and went to the hotel."

"He's a man of integrity. I'll go to see him there tomorrow. And I may invite him to attend this evening's gathering at my house."

"Do you plan to return home to attend the funeral?"

"I can't. My doctor won't allow me. My ulcer has been bleeding, and I may have to have an operation if it doesn't respond to medication and to Sheikh Watfan's incantations."

"Farewell, friend. And pardon me for this untimely visit."

"If you had done anything else, I would have gone on suspecting you and holding a grudge against you. And I would have done something to avenge my son's death."

As Raghid drove away, a diabolical smile filled his tear-drenched face. Whether he laughed or cried, he did it with such sincerity, he'd come to believe his own lies.

◆　◆　◆

Something about this stifled, stifling day was causing things to burst at the seams.

Layla couldn't identify the source of the vague distress that had overtaken her, digging its savage, metallic claws into her heart.

Perhaps she was just exhausted. After all, she'd been organizing a veritable army of servants and wine servers who would have to be present the following day, playing their roles to perfection in costumes that she had rented herself and whose fitting she had overseen. She'd seen to every last detail having to do with the celebration, from the decor and protocol to the arrival times for the private airplanes that would be bringing in a variety of imported fruits and other foods from all over the world so that all four seasons would be represented at the banquet table. In addition, she was responsible for coordinating the musicians who would be gracing the occasion, making certain that their performances were scheduled such that no one would end up stealing the limelight from anyone else, in which case an altercation might break out between them right in front of the audience. She also had to reserve parking spaces for VIP's who had never walked a step in their lives. After all, every step means something, and if any of them made an unstudied move on the billionaires' chessboard, there might be a drop in the price of certain currencies on the stock market. Her job even included putting up with the rudeness of the electrician who had set up the microphone to announce the names of the people in the audience.

The Night of the First Billion would have to bear the imprint of the billions on behalf of which it was being hosted, from the bathroom towels with the date of the great occasion hand-embroidered on them with gold thread, to the doorstep attendants whose job was to wipe off the soles of the guests' shoes before they entered the mansion on near-bended knee.

However, the angst she felt was too immense, too all-encompassing to be explained by such details, numerous though they were. Its outlines were as distinct as those of a tombstone, and as blurry as the outward edges of the horizon. It was an angst with a somber, muffled hue that left a bitter taste between her teeth, which were clamped as tightly shut as the jaws of a time-stiffened corpse.

Was it on account of the black clouds that had been multiplying since morning like the hosts of some unnamed enemy, and the catacomb-like dankness that had settled over people's hearts? Was it because of the flashes that looked like some sort of veiled lightning? No sooner had she glimpsed it than it disappeared, setting her soul aflame with vague, unspoken fears as if she were deciphering hostile messages by telepathy. But no . . . she was a practical woman, and she knew that even this unnatural canicule heat wave would have to end eventually with a wild thunderstorm. So, was the source of her anxiety the thunderless lightning that gave way once more to darkness as soon as it appeared? Why did she feel as though the sky had grown dark for her personally, and that the clouds had gathered to terrorize her alone?

Why didn't she just admit to herself that she was afraid of Raghid—afraid that, now that she had signed those bad checks, he would double-cross her the way he had so many others? On the other hand, she'd known ahead of time that the profession of "businessman" would involve daily gambles of this sort, and when she chose this path for herself, she had tacitly accepted the inevitable element of risk that goes with any large profit. (I've learned from experience that time is a traitor. I don't even trust "heart time" anymore. I can remember men that I really did love at the moment when I told them so. Yet now I can hardly recall their full names. I can remember men whose chests I lay my head on, mistakenly imagining that I'd reached my port of destination, so to speak. Yet the time came when yesterday's friend became today's enemy, and the heart of my beloved had turned into a hornets' nest. The men I'm thinking of weren't without some degree of integrity and virtue, yet I never fully trusted any of them. So how could I trust a man the likes of Raghid? How could I have signed those checks? What if he tells me tomorrow, "I'm not going to pay you. You do whatever you can for yourself"? Yet why would he do that to me? On the other hand, why wouldn't he?)

When Raghid returned, Lilly ran after him, having decided not to wait until the next day. He would have to pay now. She wouldn't be able to sleep if he didn't. She would tell him that it was a matter of principle. Then let come what may.

When he saw her, he came up to her saying, "Lilly! How good it is that you're here. I was afraid you might have gone to the hotel. I want to speak with you."

"And I want to speak with you, too."

"Lilly, you must help me. Nadim has been involved in a huge embezzlement operation—a construction-materials fraud. As a consequence, the school that we built collapsed, killing Sheikh Sakhr's son Abdullah along with scores of other children. Abdullah was his son by his wife and relative, Sita."

"That's quite distressing. And it comes at a bad time."

"I'll persuade Nadim to confess and turn himself in to the police."

"That's better for everyone. And this way you can help him later on."

"That's exactly what I intend to do. And now, I want you to take Bahriya to Sheikh Sakhr's mansion. All the commotion around here is harmful for her. And I don't want her to come downstairs naked and doped up the way she did at that other party. You remember it, no doubt."

"Besides which, she can keep the bereaved father company."

"She'll distract him from his worries until the Night of the First Billion is over and we're able to attend to him ourselves. I've managed to calm him down a bit. But he's bound to be furious after he's spoken to Hilal, others in his clan and the families of the other victims. He's got a good heart, but he's easily swayed. So take her to him."

"It's an excellent idea. But I hope she won't disturb him. As you know, Bahriya is dangerous in a hard-to-explain sort of way. Otherwise, your own invincible sorcerer wouldn't hate to have her around."

"She's half-drugged all the time at present, and I'll tell the doctor to make certain she stays that way. She seems to leave disaster in her wake wherever she goes, to the point where her mere presence somewhere I take to be a bad omen. Curses on the person who brought her here. I don't want her at the Night of the First Billion. There's no telling what calamities she's got in store for us on that ill-fated night of her birthday—that is, assuming that the date on her passport is correct."

"Well, when would you like me to take her?"

"As soon as possible. Oh, pardon me. There's Khalil, and I want to speak with him. There's an operation that he needs to take over for Nadim."

Then he left her as quickly as he had alighted upon her, heading toward Khalil with a half-smile on his face. He'd said everything he had to say to her. But she hadn't said everything she had to say to him. Very well, then. She'd postpone it till evening. And before it was time for the banks to open the following morning, the "big check" would be on its way to them. Then she'd become wealthy by a mere stroke of Raghid's pen. With it she would cover the bad checks she had been signing only a few minutes earlier. And once that was done, she would still have a huge surplus of francs for herself, since the prices she had quoted on her invoices were three times the actual value of the merchandise she had purchased. She wasn't stealing, exactly. She was just collecting for services rendered . . . in her own way.

She never intended to offer another service free of charge. Never. In fact, she wasn't even going to shake someone's hand without demanding something concrete in return.

(For so long I've given without taking account of what I should receive. Then I discovered that I was nothing but a fool who was going to die alone and poor. I may still die this way, but I'll die alone and rich, at least.)

◆   ◆   ◆

Raghid shook Khalil's hand with a warmth that seemed out of character for a man of his type. (What do you suppose he wants from me now? I leave the room to look for Nasim, and I get Raghid instead. What luck.)

"Welcome back. I didn't see you at noon."

"I just got here a little while ago. I was at the hospital."

"And how is he?"

"Fine. But he's suffering from his bruises."

"Don't worry. Children mend quickly. Have you seen Coco?"

"No, not since I got back. (I'm not going to tell him that I happened to see her in bed with Saqr presenting me with a welcome that they'd prepared specially for me!)

"She's here somewhere. She might be resting in her room, or helping the other ladies with the work. In any case, I'd like to speak with you. Come with me to the study. There's an extra job that I'd like to assign to you, and which will make you an additional sum beyond anything you've dreamed of. It's a job that Nadim was supposed to have taken, but due to unforeseen circumstances which will make him unable to work for a period of time, it won't be possible for him to take it on."

As he spoke, he was studying Khalil's weary looking face.

When they got to the door of the study, Khalil asked him bluntly, "What exactly do you want from me?"

Changing his mind about how to approach the situation, he replied, "First I want you to sleep until dinner time. You look like death warmed over! Have you seen your face in the mirror?"

"I don't know how I look. But I know how I feel."

"Fine. Go to sleep, and we'll talk this evening after dinner. Trust me and everything will be all right."

From long experience in dealing with men, the worldly Raghid realized that at this moment the doors to Khalil's lusts were shut tight.

As to whether they were shut temporarily out of exhaustion or for good, he couldn't tell yet. He would have to let the fingers of rest massage his nerves, which were as taut as the quills of a porcupine. Then he'd try again after dinner. The catastrophe of the school's collapse had to be dealt with quickly. And at the same time, it wouldn't do for him to let Nadim's absence ruin all the other deals that he had been heading up.

And Khalil might be interested in some of them.

◆   ◆   ◆

"Good evening, Bahriya, O soul most precious to me in all the world! You may hear me, or you may not. You may love someone, or you may not. But if my life is worth anything, it's yours."

Nasim brought in a tray with afternoon tea on it, speaking to her out loud without expecting any response. Ever since her arrival, he'd talked to her and pampered her without expecting anything in return.

Gazing into her opaque, enigmatic face he whispered, "I've heard that they plan to move you to the mansion of Sheikh Sakhr Ghanamali. I can't go into the details now. But don't worry. No one would dare do anything to hurt you, and I'll protect you any way I can. But beware of them anyway. Here. This is Amir Nealy's address. He's a good person who's concerned for you as much as I am. Keep it in a safe place."

Her hard-to-read features registered no change, and she said nothing.

Then, as if he were talking to himself he went on, "I don't know whether you hear me or not, or whether you understand me or not. But I'm determined to try to help you. Here is some money for taxi fare if you have to escape. I'm sorry, this is all I've got."

He slipped the address and the bill into her hand, then took a good look at her before leaving the room. She looked radiant, having recovered her health after a period of rest and good nutrition the likes of which she appeared not to have had since she was a child. And treatment as well. She seemed so extraordinarily strong and alive, one would never have guessed that the sorcerer who sat withering away in the opposite wing had spent every night since she came sticking pins into a voodoo doll representing her and burning her photograph. He had even mounted an image of her engraved into a lead plate on a blacksmith's hammer so that the demon that lived inside her would be afflicted with a headache every time the smith struck the anvil. Or that he had worked night and day as a kind of traffic policeman for the spirits that he wanted either to cast out of her or to send into her. Nasim chuckled with delight at the thought, and went into raptures when she bathed him in what looked like a smile.

Before leaving the room he pleaded, "Go back to sleep. Don't say that you're well now. Don't speak to anybody. They're preparing you for a feast that won't be to our liking. And from now on don't take the drugs they give you. When they're not looking, get rid of them. Keep yourself sober during the days to come."

It seemed to him that she knew what was being prepared for her, and that she possessed an inner firmness and determination of which they knew nothing—she who for so long had suffered a torment the true nature of which she had divulged to no one. It was as if she knew that the cycle of sorrows is constantly beginning anew. The name of the lover-torturer might change from Raghid to Sakhr to something else, and that of the sorcerer from Watfan to Hamdan. The name of the mansion might change as well. But the same war goes on being fought. Bahriya went on being just as afflicted and just as composed as ever. And the sorcerer went on being tormented and mad with hate-filled passion for her.

Could this go on like a never-ending nightmare? Would there be no peace for this war-torn captive?

◆   ◆   ◆

Nasim hovered around the mansion's front door pretending to be cleaning the entranceway until he caught sight of Layla escorting Bahriya to a luxurious car that had pulled up in front of the house. Raghid hadn't come down to bid her farewell. (Do you suppose he's also suffering over having to part with her? Is pain found everywhere—albeit only for a fleeting moment—even in the hearts of executioners, murderers, and torturers?) The sky had grown dark with layer upon layer of clouds that went darting about like stray spirits. Bahriya lifted her gaze toward the mansion in what seemed like a look of farewell, then looked up at the clouds and sighed. As she did so, Nasim thought he saw the first clearly discernible flash of lightning strike down directly behind the mansion, like a gigantic sword that nearly split the house in two. Then—or so it seemed to him—the opaque, glassy look in her eyes cleared away, and she cast Layla a deadly glance of the sort people speak of when they say, "If looks could kill. . ." With a shiver he said to himself, "If they could . . . Layla would disintegrate into a pile of ashes."

But instead she urged Bahriya into the car, then took her lightweight travel bag from Nasim and got in herself.

As the car pulled away, he thought he saw Bahriya blessing him with a look of goodwill and affection. Or did he just imagine it? In any case, his heart nearly flew out of his chest. In that sweet, tear-filled moment, he felt the need to talk to a friend. He looked behind him and saw Dunya. He had never trusted her and never would, despite Amir's instructions to the contrary. He decided to take Khalil's coffee to him. He had escorted him to his room without their exchanging more than a few brief words, but he felt the need to open his heart to him: Bahriya, his two brothers. . . . If he didn't talk to someone, his youthful intensity confined under pressure inside the trappings of "prudence" was liable to explode.

❖   ❖   ❖

"Oh camel driver, greet my mother. / Tell her what's happened, and complain to her of my sorrows."

Alone in the room that Layla had reserved for him and Kafa on the occasion of the Night of the First Billion, Khalil hummed a song to a tune that he'd learned long ago from his grandmother. Where was she now? And his family? Beirut? He'd moved from one hell to another. In the first one he used to return from prison to his family and at least find them at home. But here in Switzerland, he'd come back to find his son in the hospital. And what a reunion with his wife! (As Nasim received me, he asked, "How's Rami? I knew he would be all right. And your wife? I think she's still in the big reception hall helping count the gold table service and preparing the table for the Night of the First Billion."

He said it almost apologetically, since he knew that she hadn't visited the boy in the hospital. He led me to this room through the golden spider's web, then rushed off, announcing that he'd bring me some coffee as soon as he was able. Then when I walked in, what should I find but Saqr—whom I could hardly believe I'd finally gotten rid of—possessing my wife.)

"Oh camel driver, greet my mother. / Tell her what's happened, and complain to her of my sorrows."

He hurt whenever he breathed. That damned white powder had made his nose bleed, and had nearly destroyed him. And now here he was, fleeing from one nightmare to another: from the nightmares of Beirut to those of life as a foreigner, from Saqr's delirious nightmares to Raghid's, from the nightmare of

Widad's death to the nightmare of Rami's bruises . . . and the nightmare of co-caine, a voyage of terror. Insects had sprouted under his skin and he'd seen them scampering over his fingers. He'd stared at his own hands as if they were some creature he'd never seen before. He'd walked the thin line between mad-ness and sanity in the darkness of a soul filled with diabolical enigmas. And now he'd come back to Switzerland, only to have Raghid collar him as if he looked upon him as a new human sacrifice to be offered up in gold's temple. He didn't know exactly which sword he intended to slaughter him with, or to which billion he'd be presented as an offering—the second one? Or the third? Based on things Raghid had said to him, he gathered that this was what had happened in a certain sense to Nadim, and he didn't intend to let it happen to him, too. In fact, he didn't even know why he had come back *here* now that he'd made up his mind to go back *there*—to his home country. If Rami was destined to die, then let it be in his own country, not on some telepherique in a foreign land suspended somewhere between heaven and earth.

Just then he looked out the window and saw Lilly grasping Bahriya by the arm and helping her into the car. She seemed to be doing it stealthily, like someone carrying a baby away with the intention of abandoning it in front of someone's door in the darkness. They were followed out to the car by Nasim, who had a bag in his hand. Something about the look on his face indicated that he wished he could speak to Bahriya. However, Lilly kept them apart. Everything happened in a flash, after which Nasim beat a quick retreat to the mansion. Or had he just imagined the whole thing? He felt terribly distraught. What were they doing to Bahriya? Where were they taking her? And why? He lay down on his bed and closed his eyes. No, he hadn't just imagined it, just as he hadn't been imagining things when he saw Kafa riding in a car next to Nadim one day, or when he saw her slip into a hotel with some Italian man the day he left on his trip, or when he called the hotel once during his trip to ask for her only to be told that she wasn't in, even though it was 3:00 in the morn-ing! He hadn't really cared all that much when any of these things had hap-pened. Nor had he gotten sufficiently angry when he saw Saqr and his wife making passionate love or when Saqr asked him how much he wanted for her. So why should he be overtaken now by a feverish, angst-filled rage at the sight of Bahriya being carted away on the sly? Hadn't Raghid chosen the date for the Night of the First Billion based on the fact that it was her birthday, at least according to her passport?

What had happened? Had he suddenly become outraged on her behalf?

And why? What concern was she of his? For all he knew, they'd just taken her to some beauty salon to get her ready for the next night's party. Or did Raghid want to get rid of her? (What concern is this of mine? After all, I'm the one who feels nothing but pity when I see my wife flitting from one man to another and committing acts of foolishness the seriousness of which I can only begin to calculate. Kafa blames me for not being as jealous as I ought to be. And she's right—I'm not. There's no more room in my heart for jealousy. More specifically, there's no more room in my heart for jealousy over a woman. From the time they brought such dishonor on the body of my homeland, I haven't been able to find a place in my spirit for passion, womanly caprices, or the desire to lay claim to the territory of a female body. And since I got a taste of freedom and dignity during those moments that I spent as an Arab prince in Andalusian Spain, I've been obsessed with the idea of making that experience last. Am I mad? Perhaps. I'm a fool for Beirut, a fool for Lebanon, a fool for the homeland—not Layla's fool. I'm madly, deliriously concerned for my homeland's shores, meadows, and mountains, and for people whom I love without knowing their names or their faces. Nothing in my body throbs for sex now that I've seen the human race being exterminated in my own land. Kafa says I'm crazy. And if this is what it means to be crazy, then that's what I am. Besides, why should her behavior bother me as long as it doesn't bother her? Because of my dignity? Her being a fool doesn't detract from my dignity any more than it does hers. And now Saqr wants to pay me a fee in return for my giving her up to him, as if her body were a piece of deluxe real estate. Well, they can both go to hell. I'm not about to be distracted by her body from all the other bodies that are being dishonored, burned and maimed back home. She wants me to say to her, and mean it, "Your body is my homeland and my dignity." And she claims that this would be love! I wish I were able to love in that way: filling the horizon with her body till I couldn't see beyond it, distracting myself with its borders and contours from my own and all other borders, resting from the battle. But . . .)

Nasim brought the coffee in without knocking. He seemed to have deliberately forgotten to pour it into the cup as an excuse to come into the room.

"They're taking Bahriya away," he said anxiously.

"So I see."

"Layla really has turned into Madame Spock. She's even got the face of a prison warden. But I managed to slip Amir's address into Bahriya's hand. I told her to call him if anything went wrong. What an idiot I am. I forgot she was mute. Or do you suppose she isn't, really? She seemed to understand what I was saying. And she closed her hand around the address as if she'd been expecting me to give it to her. Maybe she's just pretending not to be able to talk so as to avoid having to deal with the people in this place."

"I hate this place, too. What sort of cursed wind blew us here, anyway? I can't believe I'm actually going to have to spend two nights here. I wish I could wake up and find myself in my bed in Beirut, even if bombs were raining down on top of me."

"This is war. And Bahriya is one of its captives."

"What hurts is that she's been robbed of her freedom to choose, and she's helpless to defend herself. They've taken her to the Ghanamali residence."

"I'll speak to Layla about it if you like."

"She'll just throw you out."

"She wouldn't be able to do that so easily. She's going to have to cooperate with me from now on. Raghid is still dreaming that I'll join up with him."

"Instead of Nadim?"

"Something like that. How did you know?"

"I was afraid something like this might happen. It's a trap. Not a single man has ever worked with him but that he's ended up either behind bars, out of his mind, or disappeared."

"Even if he refused to get his hands dirty?"

"Listen, Khalil. You're like a brother to me, and I don't know what I'd do without you. Whenever I'm on the verge of collapsing I think of you and sing, 'O darkness of the prison, descend. . . !' and 'My country, my country.' It really does give me strength. I don't want you to end up like Nadim. You're going to be hearing some unpleasant news the details of which I can't go into right at the moment. I'll let you know more about it when I manage to come see you again. But Nadim's going to pay for what's happened."

"I won't do what Nadim did. I won't do anything . . ."

"It's possible that the poor guy didn't do anything."

Khalil thought back on that unforgettable scene: his wife in the car beside Nadim. All right then, he didn't care enough about it to kill the man. But he also wasn't going to send him a thank you note. He was at least irritated. Kafa was a fool, and whatever Nadim did, he shouldn't have. So now, he wasn't going to care whether he got help or not. He wouldn't plot evil against him, but neither did he intend to stand by him in his time of need.

He told Nasim, "There's nothing that would move me to make any sacrifices for the man. I'll listen to Raghid's offer, then I'll do what I think suits my own interests—even though I may know ahead of time what I intend to do."

"There isn't any kind of work with Raghid that would suit a conscientious person like you. Judge for yourself. But beware of his treachery. His plan is always the same, namely, to offer up his men as scapegoats, or to put his assistants at loggerheads until one of them destroys the other. He wants to make you into an instrument of Nadim's destruction. Then he'll wash his hands of both of you."

"Well, thanks all the same. Beirut is on fire. The Israelis are destroying us under siege and for all you and I know, our families are dead. And here we are, sinking into a morass of gold. It's as if there's a plan to get us out of our country, then distract us till we've forgotten it."

"Well, don't let anything distract you from Raghid's perfidy."

"My little boy laid up in the hospital distracts me from everything else."

As Nasim took leave of Khalil, he felt frustrated. He had intended to speak to him about a number of things, including the story of Raghid and his wife, and that ill-fated night, and how he'd had to risk making a mysterious telephone call to get her out of Raghid's bed.

He didn't know why he hadn't told Khalil about it. Maybe he felt sorry for the man. He wasn't about to say to someone who'd just gotten back from a visit to his little boy in the hospital, "Your wife has been cheating on you." Besides, he felt genuine affection for Khalil, and sensed that he was exhausted and withdrawn and in no mood for such a revelation.

Defeated, he quietly shut the door behind him. But hardly had he taken a few steps before Khalil overtook him. Placing his hand on Nasim's shoulder, he said, "I'm really sorry. I understand you quite well, and I thank you. It's just that I'm in such torment, I've gotten cantankerous."

Grasping his arm affectionately, Nasim said, "I understand. And I'm not in any better shape than you are. My brother has been killed. He blew himself up in a suicide operation against the Israeli soldiers who are besieging Beirut."

"I envy him."

"And my other brother is wounded."

"I envy him."

"And you, what's your family's news?"

"I envy my cousin, who died fighting against the Israelis when they stormed his village. And I'm sorry for another cousin of mine, who didn't resist them and was killed also."

"Have you seen the news?"

"They've been dropping leaflets into West Beirut urging the residents to flee. People are tired. And some of them are running away."

"I don't see anything anymore. Saqr, Raghid and others like them drown you in money, misery and in worries that have as much substance as so many soap bubbles to distract you from what's happening in your homeland—and in your own soul."

◆   ◆   ◆

Khalil went back to the room and lay down exhausted on the bed, which was still in disarray from Kafa and Saqr's struggle. His chest was tight, as taut as an artery about to burst, and he felt oppressed by the hot, dark, moisture-laden clouds that seemed to come pouring out of the sky and into his bloodstream. He tried to think about the whirlwind he found himself in, having made a rather impulsive decision to leave before taking account of all the details. But images kept getting confused in his head until he wasn't fully aware of anything anymore. Had he really been asleep? He didn't know. Then suddenly he found Kafa beside him. Her lovely face was close to his, and a blue radiance poured out of her eyes in a river of warmth.

He was bowled over when she said to him simply, "I missed you! On the day of Rami's accident I needed you so much!"

(Is she deranged? I understood from Rami that she didn't even visit him.)

In reply he asked her, "Are you all right?"

"No. And you?"

"Neither am I."

Then, as if he hadn't witnessed her sado-masochistic frenzy as she and Saqr betrayed him with obvious pleasure, she said, "And something else has happened, something awful. I've got to tell you about it."

"What's that?"

Without hesitating, she surprised him again by informing him as if he didn't already know about it, "Saqr put on a mask and gave me a necklace. And then he raped me."

As she said it, tears came streaming out of her eyes.

"Incredible!" he replied sarcastically, and nearly burst out laughing in spite of all his worries. Was it possible for a woman to be such an accomplished liar?

"You don't believe me, either?" she continued. "He did it at noon today. I thought you saw him. He broke into the room . . ."

He lit a cigarette and eyed her with interest.

"How?" he asked.

"He's living in the room next door, and he came in through this balcony door."

"I don't believe it!" (I thought you both had lead roles in those violent theatrics!) He nearly told her what he was thinking. However, he was so nonplussed by her extraordinary capacity for sincere lying, he didn't say a word.

"I don't blame you," she went on. "Even the people who saw it refused to believe it. Lilly insists that I'm imagining things, and Dunya refuses to testify against him, saying she needs time to think it over."

"They saw him?" Khalil asked mockingly.

"I screamed for help, then he took off the minute someone came into the room."

(Wives' tales. The only thing they think about is sex and countersex and keeping one's husband in the dark until the very end. So then, you started dreaming of being raped. And when it finally happened, you enjoyed it so much you took even Saqr off guard. And now he wants you. This is your punishment. Little do you know what a punishment it is to be wanted by Saqr. And I'm not going to tell you a thing about it. You'll find out for yourself when he gives you your first fix of madness powder.) Without saying a word, he sat pondering her necklace, the necklace Saqr had bought for her one day in some city they'd gone to. He'd been with him at the time, but it didn't occur to him that it would find its way onto his own wife's neck.

"I swear that's what happened!" she continued. "Lilly will deny it and so will Dunya, but it's the truth."

He decided to say something meaningful to her, even if she happened to consider it a catastrophe and started crying again.

"Listen, Kafa," he said, "I've decided to stop working for Saqr, and I ask you please to postpone this nonsense. My head's too full of other things, including our little boy lying in the hospital, and our other one trapped in a boarding school. Living abroad has torn us apart even more than the bombs in Beirut. We've got to take some time out to rethink things. The currents have been sweeping us away and landing each of us in different kinds of predicaments. I'm going to try to sleep for a while, so leave me alone and go back to your lady friends. I mean, you all have a lot of work to do."

"You don't believe me, either! What a hellhole this is!"

With his cigarette still in his mouth and with ashes beginning to fall onto his chest, he replied, "Remember, Coco, that you did everything you could to make it happen. You flirted with the man, and you kept on flirting. So why are you complaining now?"

"All right. So I'm a free agent. And when things like this happen, it has to be with the consent of both parties. But not his attacking me wearing a devil's mask! I nearly died of fright."

He said nothing. Instead, he closed his eyes and pretended to be asleep in hopes that she would leave the room. He didn't want to talk to her about it anymore.

"Ugh . . . ugh . . . ugh. Oh camel driver, greet my mother, tell her what has happened and complain to her of my sorrows!"

◆   ◆   ◆

Sheikh Watfan paced around in a frenzy, preparing his incense and incantations. The dark clouds that had gathered looked to him like ashen, diabolical specters that had come from Bahriya's islands to deal him a final, feverish blow. He was ill. His body was ablaze with a bout of influenza that was in reality no more than a shroud behind which he could be incinerated by the magical powers of Bahriya's demons. Before long they would scourge him with lightning, screaming at him with a voice that other people would mistakenly imagine to be thunder and reducing him to ashes—that is, unless he uttered the proper incantations and called upon his helpers to come against them with his counter-magic. And this was what he intended to do now: "O Naila, O Haila, O Daughter of Kings fearless in battle, on behalf of your straying band and your eight sisters, mount your camel, beat your drum at the door of the small house, and be present at my council tonight. In the names of your father Zahalif and your mother Zurbouna, O Sikhoun O Mayharoun, O Mahdaroun, O Flower of the Branches, I have believed in your Lord, so lend me your ear with haste before I speak. Shalhoub Malhoub Anoukh Azraheesh Raseen Umm Assahabeen, and for the sake of Haytaloush the Greatest, your moonlit face and your green birthmarks, answer me and be present by the truth of the words, 'For every message is a limit of time'[33] with urgency, with urgency, make haste, make haste, at this hour, at this hour . . .

---

33. Qur'an 6:67.

". . . .

"Hayloukh Hayloukh, Shamloukh Shamloukh, Baroukh Baroukh, Yaloukha Yaloukha, Imlash Imlash, Shamhal Shamhal, Yattit Yattit, Karou Karou, Tahish Tahish, Imeeqaqish, Shamahloush, Nahish, Anoukh Anoukh . . .

"Respond, O Master Tarish by the truth of these names, by the authority of Haqalqash, Hahalqash, O Hayalish. Respond, O Tarish, for otherwise, the words I have recited to you will consume Bahriya, daughter of Bahriya, daughter of the jinn, urgently, with haste, at this hour.

"Tabshi, Sadrus, Gheekou Batou, Bahatoursh, Larsh, Abdash . . .

"Bayhauser, Hayser, Shamshoun, Bahauser, every smell by Aydakh, Hawdan, Announ . . .

"Dawda Day Karkar Dayan Lukh, Ha' Seen Yah Wameeta Lukh Lukh Wamshia'na, Lukh. Respond, O Tarish, and you, O Amer . . . Amesh, Hurmaqush, Shamsours, Ajoubah, Ahdaleesh, Klamsh, Shahesh, Kalamarsh. Respond, O Za'zou' by the sanctity of these names and their authority over you. I command you to respond and to take command of Bahriya, daughter of Bahriya, daughter of the jinn, lest she be guided by the truth of the names left written on the olive leaves after they were consumed by fire and suspended from the Power. By the truth of the name which begins with "Aal" and ends with "el," that is, the "el" of Shala' Ya'ou Boubay Yaha Youh Waha Aha Bayh Batkafah Batakafel Bas'a Kas'a Mimyal, who are obedient to you O Al Jall Ziryal, whose name no spirit has heard and disobeyed but that it was struck with lightning and burned: Respond, O Za'zou,' and do not delay in carrying out what I have commanded you. In the twinkling of an eye, in the name of Ahyasher Ahya Adonai Sabaoth El Shaddai, with urgency, with urgency, with haste, with haste, at this hour, at this hour. . ."

His voice growing faint, the sorcerer's strength began to fail and he raved. (I have so much work to do, so much. . . . Her magical power is dangerous. I'm helpless before her. These incantations do no good against her demons. I'm in need of numerous magical plants. I also need to be able to recite my formulas over her directly, with sound and flame, and to roast her demons on a spit over a hellfire. Otherwise she'll defeat me. She's stealing my voice right out of my throat, and drawing my spirit out of me one breath at a time. I'm dying slowly, but I know she'll have victory over me in the end. She takes the words off my tongue so that I've started stuttering and stammering. She's destroying me with fever and illness. She's destroying me.)

Still ranting, the sorcerer got up from where he'd been sitting with his censer. He'd turned into a mass of suffering and explosive will power trapped inside a body: I'll fight her. I'll confront her and fight her face to face. If I don't, she'll annihilate me.

Like a wild animal caged and bleeding, he paced around his private hotel suite, stumbling over the opulent furniture and collapsing onto his knees like someone being scourged by invisible whips, his face aflame with agony.

(I don't have the strength to stay away from her. It's as if my punishment is to love the dagger that she thrusts into my ashes. I detest her, that destructive, evil, satanic being. Yet even so, I long to be united with her, and to know her affection and her unattainable love.)

The sorcerer felt as though he were writhing about inside a fiery crucible filled with his blazing passions for her. And he heard a voice come from deep inside him, saying, "You're weakening before her. She's defeating you. Go back to her and wage war on her demons. Otherwise you're certain to perish." When he took a look at himself in the mirror, it confirmed the truth of what he had heard. He saw his face blazing with a pale, bluish flame that sometimes glowed bright red, and other times orange, violet and deep blue—a fire with the ruthlessness of a rainbow rising over a land that's just been struck by an earthquake. As he stood there looking at himself, his face took on the features of his grandfather, then his father, then his brother. And all of them were on fire.

The telephone rang. It was that journalist again. Those damned reporters. How could they have found out where he was when he'd only been here a matter of minutes? Or had it been hours? He didn't know what time it was. All he knew was that the sun hadn't set since his parting with Bahriya.

"I told you I wasn't here!" he screamed, his voice bristling with claws and talons. "And I meant it! If you harass me again, I'll zap you with a headache. And a nosebleed!"

He hung up and resumed pacing around his luxurious cage. (How will I be able to wait for two nights with this fever eating me up? How can I wait until the Night of the First Billion is over before I go back to Raghid's mansion and wrestle her demons one last time? Then it will be her fire pitted against mine. How can I, with her roasting me over her fire from afar, and with me unable to penetrate her schemes?)

He sat down in front of his crystal ball and gathered his vast hidden powers, calling them forth one and all from their unknown hiding places in the uttermost reaches of the soul and summoning his spiritual forces from their cosmic orbits. After sending them forth like soldiers in the direction of Raghid's mansion, he closed his eyes, concentrating his powers on that particular spot on this star lost among millions of heavenly bodies. Then he muttered in a soundless voice, "Death . . . death . . . ruin."

It had become easy for him to move inanimate objects in the room with his eyes. He simply focused on them that energy which all human beings possess, though without knowing how to train it or put it to use. He had mastered the art in recent days thanks to his isolation and the disintegration of the outward shell of his body.

He wanted to shake Bahriya up as she sat in that castle of gold. He wanted to make her quake in her bed or go flying through the room and bleed onto the walls and ceiling. ("Death . . . death . . . ruin.")

The telephone again. The universes of the black stars came tumbling down out of their fiery orbits, and he was assailed again by a headache . . . and terror. He looked fearfully at the telephone like someone who's just awakened out of a coma, then rushed to the bathroom and carefully washed his hands. He needed some alcohol. And what was this chaos in the room? He distracted himself from everything else by tidying it up again. Someone knocked vigorously on the door several times. Panic-stricken, he broke into a cold sweat and hid in his bed, covering his head with the sheets the way he used to do as a little boy. Terrified, he had no intention of opening the door.

But then he heard a familiar-sounding voice. It was Sheikh Sakhr, saying, "Please open the door, Sheikh Watfan. Please. I need you."

Half-dazed, he got up and opened the door. Sakhr collapsed into the first chair he came to and wailed, "My son Abdullah! They've killed him!"

It seemed to Sheikh Watfan that he had heard the news before, but he wasn't certain where or when. He needed some alcohol to wash his hands with.

"I need some rubbing alcohol . . . right away," he mumbled.

Meanwhile, Sheikh Sakhr cried, "Raghid came to me claiming that he was innocent in the matter, and I believed him. Then my brother Hilal spoke to me. He said I was a stupid ass to believe him. So I've come to ask you to reveal the truth to me. I want to know who was responsible for my son's death so that I can kill him. Was it Raghid, or Nadim, or just the engineer?"

Like water trickling down a pane of glass, the names glided over the surface of Sheikh Watfan's memory without leaving so much as a fingerprint or any other trace but the water itself. Who was Raghid? Who was Nadim? He vaguely recalled the names, the same way he had recalled Sakhr's voice, and just as he had found his face to be somewhat familiar, yet without comprehending exactly whom he was talking about or what he meant.

As Sheikh Watfan went to the bathroom to wash his hands again, he heard his guest saying in a terrified voice, "Is it really possible that Raghid would do this to me? And if he really is the culprit, then why would he bring Bahriya to my lair?"

Bahriya! Watfan heard the name loud and clear. As he went on slowly rinsing his hands, he saw his face on fire in the mirror. Bahriya. . . .

In an audible, almost trembling voice he said, "Bahriya. Did you say Bahriya?"

Then he came back into the room as Sheikh Sakhr went on with his grievances. However, all he heard was the name, "Bahriya."

"That's right," said Sheikh Sakhr. "He's planning to have me host Bahriya in my house both tonight and tomorrow night, that is, until the Night of the First Billion is over. So I ask you please to come with me, to reveal the name of my son's murderer and to prepare some medication for the pains in my stomach. Please. Oh, my God! You look feverish and sick yourself!"

So then, was Bahriya in the care of this man whom he knew, yet didn't know? He would definitely go with him, whoever he was. He would do battle with her on any turf she happened to choose. He would go to the uttermost reaches of hell to wage war on her. In fact, he no longer remembered having any other mission in life.

"I will go with you," he replied calmly.

Overjoyed, Sakhr cried, "I knew you wouldn't let me down!" (So then, she's sent me one of her messengers. This is the final duel. I won't back away from the challenge, and I won't allow her to distort my perceptions. I've got to remember my incantations well so as to be able to summon my helpers. And I've got to prepare my incense and the plants that carry my voice to them wherever they happen to be.)

In a cold tone of voice Sheikh Watfan told Sakhr, "But I have my conditions."

"All the money and gold you desire will be yours."

"I don't want anything of that nature. Write down my requests, and I want all of them to be available before sunset tomorrow."

Sheikh Sakhr walked around the room in search of a pen and a piece of paper. He eventually happened upon a piece of paper bearing the hotel emblem and address, which reminded him of where he was and the time he was living in. It was as if electrically charged ions emanating from Sheikh Watfan had removed him temporarily to other universes. He mumbled in silent admiration, "What an astounding sorcerer. There's no limit to his powers, even when he's burning up with influenza. But this damned weather is going to be the death of all of us."

Watfan said to him, "Write down these medicaments." Then he proceeded to dictate to Sakhr. However, he didn't tell him that the materials he was requesting weren't for the purpose of identifying his son's murderer, but rather to destroy Bahriya: pepper, mustard seed, watercress, wolf bile, a piece of black wool, the heart of a red heifer, gall oak, honey with the top foam removed, saffron, white cumin, black cumin, oriental frankincense, European garlic, myrrh, oriental wormwood, aloe, camel dung, a dirhem of mastic, onion seeds, an ounce of *ladansaj*, an ounce of *kharanfash*, an ounce of *dirbal*, an ounce of gyrfalcon, medicinal powder, green *barnuf* leaves, kohl, almonds, a camel's eye, Sudanese natron, *madghah*, and two dirhems of *ghandazout*. I also need ink of verdigris and vermilion, leucoma and camphor and green arsenic. And I need rubbing alcohol, several liters of alcohol."

"Most of these materials will be in your hands by this evening—in fact, all of them. And my men will take responsibility for moving all the equipment you have here. The important thing is for you to show me who killed my son. My twin brother Hilal considers the practice of sorcery to be a kind of blasphemy. However, I have absolute confidence in you. I have a feeling deep down that he's right in his belief that Raghid is the real culprit and that Nadim is nothing but a scapegoat. But I hope you'll accept my hospitality and come with me immediately. We have to be on our way right now so that we'll get there before Bahriya arrives. Please. . . . You're in need of medical attention. You really do have quite a fever, and you sound as though you've got influenza."

The name Bahriya fell into the waters of his soul like a blazing meteorite.

"I don't need any medical attention," he replied. "I know what's causing my suffering, and I'll treat myself. But I will come with you."

◆   ◆   ◆

Nasim rapped on the door.

"Go away, whoever you are!" screamed Saqr.

Without his realizing it, his hand clung to his gold dagger. After all, he knew he was a great man, and that someone might try to murder him during his fitful sleep.

He had swallowed several sleeping pills, which cast him into a miserable, nightmarish slumber.

"Dinner is served, sir. They're waiting for you."

"Go to hell. I'm not hungry. I'm going to sleep."

"Thank you."

Nasim walked away feeling thoroughly revolted. He'd just seen Beirut under siege on television, with pamphlets being rained down on its residents asking them to leave and caravans of cars fleeing the city. He imagined himself in a car on the other side of the street, coming back to the hell of Beirut rather than staying in the hell of "here."

Saqr had resumed his nightmare-ridden sleep. His thigh muscles were twitching and his whole body was going through intense convulsions left behind by his drug in body and in spirit. He started feeling nauseous again. (Damn them. Why did they wake me up? Don't they know what a precious commodity sleep has gotten to be since I started going on white flights? Why can't there be pleasure without pain? And why do women usually not understand this? But Coco, she's a rare exception, worth taking good care of.) And now he was in pain. These were the cursed moments of coming down. He turned on the light and swallowed another pill, then looked at the picture of his sweetheart, the one who never left him. She had a plant's body and her name was written under her picture: Erythroxylon Coca. Oh, my darling Coca! Won't you allow me to sleep for just a while after raping Coco?

He'd had no other choice. He had to have the wife whenever the husband concerned was obstinate and refractory. This is what he'd decided in the very beginning, even before he'd tasted of Coco's honey. He'd never come across a mule as stubborn as Khalil, and this might help to tame him. But he wasn't going to let him loose for any price until he'd raped his spirit, too. He wouldn't leave him alone until he was nothing but a limp rag. And until then, he'd go on "loving" him. He needed to destroy people to keep them from touching his spirit with love or affection. His was a world that had no room for anyone but men that he had bought or sold according to the dictates of his will alone. And Khalil still had some will left . . . a private spot in his soul where he curled up now and then like a snail inside its shell. And Sakhr wanted it for himself.

He intended to ravish it by whatever means he could. He was going to open it up, if not with money, then through his body. He wouldn't be able to rest until he had vanquished Khalil's rebellion.

He'd come back from their trip more thirsty than ever to take possession of that pristine, countryside spring, and he was going to do it.

But Coco had taken him by surprise. She was a woman who'd been made for a man like him.

◆　　◆　　◆

(This is the last dinner I'll have before my coronation tomorrow night—the Night of the First Billion. My heart is beating so fast, it feels like a train speeding through wildernesses of glory and fame. I—the friendless, fainthearted, dumpy Raghid—have conquered!) It was a peaceful dinner after a long, long day that had exhausted all of them.

It was peaceful, that is, in appearance, what with the soft velvet of the tablecloth, the gold of the eating utensils and the silence of the butlers and maids, who served the food as if they were dancing the ballet without music.

But a volcano was seething inside every one of them, with the stillness and tension of a hand ready to strike with a dagger.

Kafa and Nadim didn't make eye contact the way they had a few weeks earlier. He was staring at his plate, speechless and distant, too preoccupied to pay attention either to her or to his food. He pondered the papers that Raghid had brought with him to the room, then set them aside on a chair like a revolver to threaten him with. (I know what those papers are. They're documents he could use to get me convicted of embezzlement. If I refuse to go to Lebanon and confess to a crime I didn't commit, do you suppose he intends to use them to put me in prison here in Switzerland, where there would be no way to get out of it? I'll have to make a choice between being a scapegoat for Raghid and his engineer in return for the possibility of Raghid's getting me out of prison based on some pardon to be issued once people have forgotten and Sakhr has forgiven, or a guaranteed prison term here of at least ten years with no hope of escape or manipulating the authorities. I know the scenario, because I saw Raghid play it out with his former assistant. In fact, I helped him carry it out and was even the one who suggested it. And now here I am, falling live into the furnace I helped to build. Do you suppose he'll do the same thing with me, or force me to write a confession so that he can knock me off later and make it look like a suicide? There's nothing he wouldn't do. Nobody knows that better than I. God, how I detest him—that insatiable monster. I despise him. I wish he were dead. I wish I could kill him. I wish I could get up right now and strangle him. I wish. . . .)

Raghid choked on some water and coughed, and everyone respectfully stopped chewing. And when he sprinkled salt on his specially prepared food—which was salt-free in view of his high blood pressure—Layla felt a rush of vindictive delight. (He'll bite the dust in no time if he goes on devouring his food like a glutton, pouring on the salt, and sneaking to the refrigerator after dinner to eat all the things that are bad for his health. After he marries me, I might not need to kill him in order to become the world's richest widow instead of the world's biggest debtor, which is what I am tonight. But if he tries to double-cross me, I won't beg him on bended knee to rescue me from the consequences of writing bad checks. Instead, I'll just kill him. I'll kill him. I won't go to sleep tonight until he's written me a check to cover me at the bank. And if he tries to get out of it by going to bed himself, I'll come after him and wake him up. Tomorrow he won't have any time for me. His guests will start coming around in the early morning to cut deals with him. Not one of them has really come to celebrate the Night of the First Billion. Instead, they're attending it the way they might go to a conference for the exchange of mutual interests to develop their billions into trillions. I'll speak to him tonight before he goes to bed. I won't go to sleep as long as I'm at his mercy. And I won't let him live if he decides to . . .)

The lightning flashed through the windows. Everyone held their breath in anticipation of the thunder to come, while Khalil wished it would start pouring down rain. But nothing happened at all.

The atmosphere was stifling. Stifling. A tomblike dampness seemed to have settled on people's chests, and a subtle, feverish heat flowed through the room. Meanwhile, the distant lightning held out its niggardly promise of rain and of the drumbeats of thunder that hadn't been heard even once on this long, oppressive day.

With an air of indifference Raghid asked Nasim, "Did you invite Saqr to the dinner table?"

"Yes, I did," he replied.

"What did he say?"

"He said, 'Go to hell.' "

Shooting Nasim a venomous look, he muttered, "Watch your language."

Detecting the glimmer of a collusive smile in Khalil's eyes, Nasim said nothing more. (God, how I hate him, that beast drinking firewater and using Sirri Al-Din's kidney. He's also drinking the blood of my slain brother. And for all I know, he may have collected a commission on my other brother's wounds from some arms deal with the enemy. After all, he ships instruments of destruction indiscriminately to anybody who'll buy them. I hate him. I hate his sorcerer. I hate what they're doing to captive Bahriya, and to me, and to Khalil, and to stupid Kafa, and to that hysterical Dunya. I'll never forgive him for murdering Sirri Al-Din, or for turning the lives of people in torment into a pastime by watching them on videotape as if they only existed for his entertainment, or for the sadistic pleasure he takes in seeing other people being oppressed and defeated, or his lust to destroy Amir, or his degrading treatment of the Freedom Fighter statue. I'm from a generation that never knew Abdel Nasser. So I tend to feel confused when I hear all the conflicting testimonies as to what he was and what he did. But I love the artistic work that Mufid Nealy, Amir's father, did. And in the statue he sculpted I really do see the Freedom Fighter, regardless of whether or not Abdel Nasser was a perfect expression of that ideal. I detest Raghid so much, I'd dearly love to murder him. I'd be delighted to see him dead because he. . . .) He was roused out of his reverie by a stern rebuke from Layla.

"I told you to pour water for Professor Khalil! Can't you see that his glass is empty?"

As he poured the water for Khalil, he noticed that he looked depressed and had no appetite. The waiter took away one plate after another without his having taken more than a few small bites. Raghid, meanwhile, had succeeded in consuming all of his diet meal. He'd also done his share toward sweeping away every delicacy that passed over the table, including the chicken, the fish, and the fatty red meats. Nasim looked over at him with vindictive glee. (He's sure to have indigestion tonight. He'll be in so much pain he won't be able to sleep, and then tomorrow he'll be ill and have to miss out on the Night of the First Billion.)

Kafa's immoderation was second to none but Raghid's. However, it was an immoderation that placed a rose in bloom on each of her youthful cheeks and contributed to the development of her already exquisite curvature. Her blue eyes seemed to overflow with happiness, but also with disappointment at everyone else's gloomy lack of enthusiasm. (Tomorrow is the Night of the First Billion. Tomorrow I'll be meeting scores, even hundreds of millionaires. It's my chance to get out of Beirut forever. Tomorrow I'll establish my glory, and I'll be able to announce publicly—rather than just to myself—that Adel, Nadim, Saqr, Khalil and Raghid are all just different names for a single man, and that it makes no difference to me if he changes bodies, names, masks and styles as long as he can take care of me and provide me with leisure, money, security and pleasure. As for my wounded little boy, I'll forget about him, since he'll forget me anyway in a few years when his father pushes him into some militia in preparation for having him killed. Besides which, I have to forget him in order not to remember Widad, Beirut, the shattered glass, the hunger, sleeping on the floors of cockroach and mice infested bomb shelters filled with the sound of people coughing and the anticipation of the next assault by armed vigilantes. Oh Lord of my soul! From here on out I'm looking out for Number One! I'll never let another person commandeer my life. If Khalil doesn't like the way I'm acting, then to hell with him. If my sisters and brothers-in-law don't approve of my life, then let them forget my name. And if Raghid tries to rein me in in the name of the friendship between him and my father, I'll kill him—that stingy, ugly old man who gave me a ring with a phony diamond in it just the way he did to Dunya, then threw me out of his bed like some sort of pack animal. I'll choose my own men. And if Raghid dares to use me to entertain some guest of his, I'll murder him for trying to take without giving, just the way the armed vigilantes in Beirut do! I'll entertain whoever I please. And I'll be a slave to my passions alone. I'll tell Raghid straight out that he's just one more man in my life. And the fact is, he's so old and decrepit, he doesn't appeal to me as a lover or even as a boss. My God, when I was in Beirut, I didn't know that I was capable of such things. With Saqr I discovered my ability to enjoy giving and receiving pain—and maybe to kill as well.)

Silence continued to rein at the table. However, they could hear the sound of hot winds blowing, warning of a change in the weather.

Meanwhile, the flashes of lightning continued in close succession, like the approach of giant, mythical birds, their beaks laden with thunder.

Layla said, "If only the rain would hold off until after tomorrow night. We've prepared a special session in the garden. It's designed to be an "Arab paradise," with an artificial river of honey that recirculates electronically, and alongside it another one of milk. It's sure to impress our guests."

No one replied. Everyone was lost in his own thoughts. It was as if they were listening to the tidings and warnings being brought to them on the wind. As if the distant lightning had touched the keys to their souls, bringing forth in a fiery display what had been buried deep inside them.

Raghid, by contrast, seemed oblivious both to the weather and to his guests, as well as to the longings cherished by some of them to kill him or at least to see him dead. He was preoccupied with own greatness and the extraordinary appetite with which he was crowning the eve of the Night of the First Billion. Dunya noticed her husband's misery and Raghid's elation. (I wish I could see him dead, that Raghid. He's destroyed both my life and Nadim's. He's destroyed my art. He's devastated me from the inside to the point where I don't even know who I am or what I want anymore. In his bed tainted with illness and old age, he sucked me dry like a leech, deluding me into believing that he was bestowing a great honor upon me by touching me with his "blessed" hand, when in fact it was like the hand of Midas, who couldn't touch anything or anyone without turning it into a statue of gold. And maybe I've turned into a gold statue that doesn't know what it's doing at night. Maybe I really *was* the person who put a knife through my painting. Maybe I really have neglected Nadim, causing him to abandon my body with its constant headaches and lack of desire. Maybe it's all my fault that both my life and my family have fallen apart. And maybe it's time I forgot all about Amir, Bahriya, art, critics, and men of letters and tried instead to repair my shattered life and family. Raghid's the one who's done it all to us. And now he wants to ruin my husband. At the same time, I'm not confident that I'd be able to manage without him. I may not love Nadim, but I've gotten used to my life with him and to my dislike of him. I don't know anymore how I'd start over, or where I'd start if I tried. I tried with Amir and his world, and I failed. I tried not to care about Bahriya, and I failed. I tried to leave Nadim, and I failed. I may be dead with him, but I'd die without him. And I won't allow Raghid to suck him in now that he's spit me out. I'll kill him. I'll expose him. I'll bring the mansion down on myself, on him and on all his cronies. I'll reveal every secret I know. I'll go to him at night and speak to him. I'll tell him that I'm going to put a knife through him just the way my husband did to my painting and my dog under orders from him—or the way I did myself, for all I know—and that after all that's happened, I'm now capable of murdering him. I'll say, "I'm going to kill you.")

When the delectable repast had come to an end, Raghid didn't take his medicines as he normally did. He was feeling so invincible, he was sure that nothing, not even illness, could touch him. (Even if Sakhr thought of killing me in revenge or turned my disgruntled sorcerer completely against me, or if the two of them convinced Bahriya to join their side, I wouldn't give a damn. I'm too crafty for them.) When he rose from the table, everyone else followed suit with the exception of Khalil, who was too absorbed in his own thoughts to notice what anybody else was doing. He wasn't thinking about murdering Raghid, or even about his dying. He was simply thinking about his own life. His little boy would be leaving the hospital in two more days. So why not take his family back home? (Widad was killed in Beirut. However, Rami was nearly killed here in Switzerland, suspended between heaven and earth. We all die sooner or later, one way or another. But not all deaths are the same. If Saqr died from an overdose of cocaine, it wouldn't be the same as the death of Nasim's brother, or the deaths of my two cousins as martyrs. It isn't true that no matter how much the causes may vary, all death is the same. For me to stay here would be a kind of death, which is why I have to get completely out of here. Have I lost my chance to get rich, the chance of a lifetime? Perhaps. But even if I have, I'm leaving here and going someplace far away.)

Noticing his failure to keep up with the "chorus," Khalil hurriedly got up, thereby making the gesture unanimous. Once everyone had risen, they all prepared to retire to their respective quarters for the night, with most of them holding back words that they would have liked to speak to Raghid, either with their lips or with a dagger. Meanwhile, the winds blew, striking against the walls of the mansion, blistering winds that opened one of the windows and sent glasses, candelabras, and silverware flying off the table as if some mysterious witchcraft had tampered with them. But Raghid paid no attention to the resulting clutter or to the lightning, which appeared to be getting closer and brighter. Everyone fell silent for a moment as they prepared to take leave of the banquet hall—after its master, of course. Unsheathing his huge cigar, Raghid said, "Nadim . . . I want to speak with you. Why don't you come with me to the pool?"

Nadim and Dunya exchanged what looked like a farewell glance. Raghid picked up the incriminating documents and handed them to Nadim. Then Nadim walked away with him looking like someone being led away to his death. As he climbed the stairs leading to the garden, then the pool, he looked like someone mounting the gallows, carrying the papers that proved his embezzlement operation like someone bearing his own writ of execution.

Raghid turned to the others and, doing his best to sound cheerful, said, "Good night! See you tomorrow, at the Night of the First Billion!"

After some effort, Raghid managed to open the door leading into the golden pool, which was as heavily reinforced as that of a bank safe. Meanwhile, Nadim wiped his profusely sweating brow.

Once the two men were alone, Raghid told Nadim straightaway, "You'll be going to prison in my place."

Nadim didn't look surprised. This was what he had been expecting. In fact, he'd been anxious to hear Raghid say it so that he could be freed at last from his questions and uncertainty. So then, he wasn't planning to murder him and leave a confession beside the body—a supposed confession that he'd been coerced into writing prior to his supposed suicide.

And as long as Raghid was planning to keep him alive, there was hope of deliverance.

"But I haven't done anything," he protested. "I had nothing to do with the school deal or tampering with the building materials. Your engineer went a bit too far this time. And you know it. The engineer is to blame, and you're sure to have known about it. As for me, I'm innocent of the whole thing."

"I know that you're innocent of this deal in particular. However, you're not innocent of others. And I have evidence . . ."

Raghid pointed to the papers showing the manipulation of accounts, embezzlement, and breach of trust that Nadim had engaged in and said, "If you refuse to go to prison in my place with regard to the school, you'll end up behind bars anyway here in Switzerland on account of these . . ."

"But the engineer . . . why doesn't he take the rap? At least he has a direct connection with the deal."

"I can't let him go to prison now. He's completing that tourist complex for us in another Arab country at the moment, and hundreds of thousands of dollars are at stake."

"As for me, I'm dispensable, right? And for that reason I go to jail for a crime I didn't commit?"

"Instead of going there for a crime you did commit."

"That isn't fair."

"It's best for everyone. You'll admit to the crime, you'll confess that you and the engineer's assistant were accomplices in the fraud, and you'll go to prison. But after that I'll be able to help you. I'll get you out after you've done a year's time or less, once people have forgotten about the accident. I'll hold your profits from other projects that haven't been affected by this shakeup, and I'll support your family and your children. No one will become homeless or go bankrupt."

"Can't you find some other scapegoat? Why should I be imprisoned for something I didn't do?"

"Otherwise, you'd be imprisoned for something you did do. I've simply replaced one crime with another and arranged a better location to be behind bars."

"But when I did what I did, I admitted it to you. I was already in financial straits, then suddenly my expenses skyrocketed in an incredible way. Life with your wealthy associates is exorbitant. At the time, even the most trivial luxuries seemed like necessities: fur coats, fancy cars, the villa, a chalet in St. Tropez, another chalet in Gstaad. With the rich, all these things seem as necessary as bread is to the poor. Then, as you'll remember, my elderly parents' house was destroyed in the first Lebanese war. So when they asked me to help them rebuild, I couldn't say no, especially since I already felt guilty over the fact that the bomb that burned their house up was of the same type that I myself ship to Beirut. They refused to leave the old house and swore they'd live in a tent if I couldn't rebuild it just where it had been. So I did the embezzling and rebuilt it in the same dangerous neighborhood, knowing full well that it would just be demolished all over again. So I weakened. I made a mistake. But later on I offered to pay back what I'd taken, and you rejected the suggestion. Do you remember? You told me to consider the money a gift from one friend to another."

"And now you abandon our friendship when I need you most? Help me, and I'll help you. That's surely better than your going to prison in Switzerland, where I can't pull any strings for you. Here, justice will take its course and you won't leave prison until you've served your full sentence. There, on the other hand, if you went to prison in my stead I'd be free to help both you and myself, and it would be almost as if nothing had changed. Your second week in prison you'd be transferred to a luxurious, private wing in the prison hospital where everything you asked for would be there for the taking. You could consider it a period of rest. Meanwhile, I'd work toward getting a pardon issued for you. In fact, Sakhr himself would do that. He's got a good heart. Besides, he's going to become my in-law. I'm planning to give Bahriya to him in marriage, and he wouldn't refuse anything I asked of him."

Nadim remained silent for a long time while Raghid tapped the incriminating documents with his fingers. He knew the rules of the game all too well.

He'd fallen into the golden web of the worldly-wise spider. True, he didn't trust him. But to openly declare enmity against him would mean perishing for certain. He had no choice. He'd sold his soul to the devil and signed the agreement in gold ink. And now it was time for him to offer up his blood.

"Isn't there any other way?"

"I've examined all the possibilities, and I haven't found anything that would cause less harm to either your interests or mine. Once news of the collapsed school gets out, everyone will be talking about it. So I'm going to ask you and Dunya to leave here early tomorrow morning and go back to your own house. I'll be in touch with you after I've arranged for you to turn yourself in."

"And the rush arms deal? Who's going to take that over for me?"

"Khalil."

Nadim remembered having glimpsed Khalil walking down the street one day as Coco caressed him in his car. Their eyes had even met for a second. Khalil knew what was going on but had chosen to ignore it. And now he was sure not to lift a finger to help him. On the contrary, he'd be filled with vindictive delight no matter how indifferent he pretended to be. No, Khalil wouldn't help him. And he wouldn't believe him if he told him that he'd been nothing more than a test tube employed by Raghid to discover Coco. Like a wine taster of sorts, he was required to make reports to his boss on this woman or that—excluding the virgins, of course. Nobody would help him. He was alone. Dunya hated him, and Raghid had done his part to make certain she went on hating him. His children couldn't care less about him. Nasim had no respect for him. Khalil despised him, Lilly wanted to replace him, and the two of them would probably just divide his corpse between them. After all, a wounded shark is devoured by the others.

He had to admit it: he was a goner.

He'd been loyal to Raghid, but in doing so he'd been loyal to treachery. So he was finished.

In a decisive tone, Raghid said, "Tomorrow I'll turn you over to Sheikh Sakhr. He'll take responsibility for repatriating you to face a fair trial. My guests will learn of the two events in close succession, if not at the same time: the news of the school's collapse, and of your breakdown and confession. This way, people will gradually stop talking about it and before very long, the dust will settle. After I explained your extenuating circumstances to Sakhr, he promised to go easy on you."

"So then, you'd arranged for everything even before consulting me?"

"I knew you wouldn't refuse a request from me. Isn't that so?"

". . ."

"And that you'd prove that you're my only man when the going gets rough. No one could take your place."

". . ."

"When you come back, you'll find your position vacant and waiting for you to fill it again. This is just a passing cloud. It's one of those ordeals you have to pass through on the way to becoming rich."

". . ."

"Don't worry about a thing. Depend on me and you'll be safe. Trust me, and everything will be all right."

Raghid got up and poured himself a large glass of firewater.

Nadim realized that the issue was settled as far as Raghid was concerned, and that he was celebrating the happy ending.

Raghid's shadow was reflected in the golden pool, and his image in the water looked like that of a man of gold emerging from some diabolical myth. Nadim felt a vicious urge to drown him, to strangle him underwater. (What if the families of the victims tear me limb from limb in the airport before the trial? What if they kill me in revenge? The matter of an entire school collapsing couldn't possibly be passed over as simply as Raghid would like to make me believe. So regardless of the details, he's sending me to my death.) Then, as if he sensed what Nadim was thinking, Raghid laughed arrogantly and said, "Don't wish you could kill me. Even if I die, you'll be going to prison. These papers aren't confidential. Layla, for example, knows about them in her capacity as a lawyer. It's in your best interest—and hers, and everyone's—for me to stay alive. My death would mean prison for both of you. This is always my first line of self-protection."

He could feel Nadim's loathing for him, and it was a sensation that gave him such exquisite pleasure, he suddenly regained his vitality and merriment.

For him, there was nothing like the ecstatic rush that he got from a dose of mutual hatred. He looked over at the statue as if he wanted to get a rise out of it and said, "To you!"

Whereupon he proceeded to drink a toast.

Meanwhile Nadim rose from his seat speechless and devastated, gazing around him at the golden cocoon with a volcano of bitterness and regret blazing inside him.

◆　◆　◆

Early on the morning of the Night of the First Billion, everyone who had spent the night in the fortress of gold was roused to the sound of a scream of unmitigated terror. And the first scream was soon followed by others.

Nadim, who hadn't been asleep to begin with, heard the panic-stricken cry ring out through the mansion without being able to make out any particular words. However, he recognized in it the voice of Saqr approaching from a distance.

Doors opened. Lights were turned on. Feet went scurrying to and fro. A single minute, and everyone in the house had gathered, one after another, in the large hall downstairs. Meanwhile, Saqr continued to scream with fright. His face flushed and his veins protruding, he said, "Raghid! Raghid's body . . . in the pool! I came downstairs to look for something to eat, since I'd gone to bed early the day before without any lunch or dinner. I saw the lights on at the pool, so I headed in that direction. And I found his dead body. I found him floating on the surface of the pool."

No one moved. All they did was stand there shivering with cold after a night of lightning and thunder in which none of them had slept a wink. The night's rains had poured down, pounding on the windows and sending away the message of heat.

Pointing in the direction of the pool of gold, Saqr continued, "He's there. Murdered. Strangled. I saw his corpse with my own two eyes. It's frightening . . . frightening."

It was obvious that Saqr had taken a hefty dose of "white flight powder." Trembling and speaking in a plaintive, mournful voice, he seemed like a scared, pampered little boy who'd just seen a dead body for the first time.

"Maybe you just imagined it," Khalil said. "As you know, a person can have hallucinations. And you know very well what I mean."

"He's there. Come and see for yourselves."

In the middle of the vast, gilt hall that housed the extraordinary pool, Raghid's lifeless body floated on top of the water, his features distended and blue, his lips hardened into what looked like a malicious grin, and a sardonic stare in his open eyes. He was still wearing the clothes that they'd seen him in at dinner the evening before. His corpse looked as though it were floating in a womb filled with golden water, and the room looked like a huge coffin of gold.

Layla stared at him blankly, like someone with a touch of madness. Then she looked around at the others: Kafa . . . Khalil . . . Dunya . . . Nadim . . . Nasim . . . Saqr.

In a frenzied calm, she said, "All right now, who murdered him?"

With sarcasm and hatred in his voice, Nasim said, "And why do you speak to us as though you were the police inspector in some mystery novel? Why should one of us be the murderer, and not you, for example?"

Looking at Nadim she said, "There are no secrets. And it's obvious that Nadim did it. We all saw him coming here with Raghid after dinner."

All eyes were fixed on Nadim. Looking pale, he glanced this way and that like someone searching for something he's lost.

"You murdered him, and I know why," she went on mercilessly. "You left everything as it was and fled from the scene of the crime: the lights still on, the door open . . ."

Nadim collapsed onto a chair, trembling and whispering as if he were talking to himself, "But he was alive when I left him. I may have wished I could kill him yesterday. But I didn't do it."

"You're under no obligation to say a word to her," said Dunya.

"Well, he certainly didn't commit suicide," said Layla conclusively. "There's been a crime, and I'm going to call the police, and an ambulance."

"Let's all get out of this place," moaned Saqr. "Come on to the other hall."

With stern coldness Layla said, "Don't touch anything. Don't obstruct the course of the investigation or ruin the evidence with your fingerprints."

Speaking to her husband, Dunya said, "Get up out of that chair and get your arms off the armrests. They'll find your fingerprints on it."

"They'll find them everywhere anyway," he replied tearfully. "I really was with him here yesterday. But I didn't murder him. I swear to you all, I didn't murder him."

◆　◆　◆

Nasim telephoned Amir.

"Good morning!"

"What's gotten into you? You wake me up at 5:00 A.M. to tell me good morning?"

"May he rest in peace. Raghid's left us at last."

"What?"

"It appears that Nadim murdered him. At long last, the bear kills its captor."

"Are you sure?"

"Almost. We're waiting for the police to get here, and the ambulance, and the Red Cross, and the Green Cross, and maybe the Mafia."

"You're too happy."

"The only thing that puts a damper on my delight is that I didn't kill him myself."

"And what makes you so sure you didn't?"

Nasim didn't appreciate the joke. In fact, it struck terror in his heart.

He said goodbye to Amir, hung up, and sat engrossed in fearful ruminations.

Would they notice that he'd replaced one statue with another? And would Layla or someone else notice that the Palestinian piaster had disappeared? Would he be accused of committing the murder in order to steal the piaster and the statue?

(But I didn't kill him!

I found him dead when I went to the golden pool before going to bed. It was nearly 2:00 A.M., and I noticed that the lights were on beside the pool. So I went by to investigate. OK, I admit, I was intending to eavesdrop the way I usually do. But I didn't commit any crime greater than that except for the fact that I was drunk—I, who hardly ever touch alcohol. When I do, I wake up the next morning miserable and repentant. I didn't hear any voices, so I took a step closer. When I did, I saw him floating on top of the golden water, a mass of lifeless filth dressed in fancy, drenched clothes. When I saw him looking so dead I was overjoyed, and the word "murdered" flashed into my mind. The thought of it pleased me, since somebody else had done it. I noticed that the door to the Freedom Fighter statue's cage was open. Do you suppose the statue came out and killed him? I wondered. I cursed Sheikh Watfan for infecting me with the habit of thinking such scary, absurd thoughts. But was it absurd?

On the other hand, I thought, maybe it's the booze working on my brain waves. I went back to my room feeling terrified. I was shaking in my boots. The minutes passed by slowly, and I didn't hear a sound except for the howling of the storm winds laden with rain that came pouring down like tears. Gradually I regained some of my courage. So then, no one had discovered the body yet. And it wouldn't happen until early the next morning with the arrival of the wine tasters, the maids, and the chef. Then I decided to do something that had been a longtime dream of mine, though I don't know where I got up the nerve to carry it out. Do you suppose it was on account of the liquor that had taken over my brain? Or in spite of it? I don't know. In any case, I picked up the replica of the Freedom Fighter statue that Raghid had given me to "put me in my place" and carried it to the golden chamber where the pool is. Sweating like crazy and with the rain pounding on the windows around the pool, I removed the original statue from its pedestal and put the replica in its place. And when I saw the Palestinian piaster, I decided to make my gift to Amir complete: After wiping my fingerprints off the faked statue and its base (I'd seen enough police shows on television to know at least this much), I went back to my room and deposited the original sculpture where the copy had been. The maids wouldn't notice the difference. Then I put the piaster inside a jar of Nescafé and covered it up with coffee. It was a moment of temporary insanity. The sight of him dead just like any other earthling had flooded me with the exhilaration of discovery. I knew now that even bloodthirsty tyrants like him are "murderable," and that their dead bodies look just as wretched as anybody else's. The blood that comes out of their veins is red, not blue, and when they're killed, their faces turn blue just like that of anyone else when he dies. A thrill mixed with a feeling of horror coursed through my whole body, and I was filled with daring, if only for a few fleeting moments.

I didn't sleep. Instead, I wretched, and an unexpected headache came over me. Regretting what I'd done, I started to shake. What if I were accused of killing him myself? It was as if I'd done the murderer a favor by personally transporting some of the evidence of the crime to my room. I thought of returning everything to its place, but then I thought I heard something or somebody move. There was someone coming down, then going up again. I locked my door. What if the murderer had come back because he'd forgotten something, for example? And why shouldn't he kill me if I saw him and recognized him? And why wouldn't I recognize whoever it was when the only people in the house that night besides me were Khalil and his wife, Nadim and his wife, Saqr and Layla? Besides which, the door leading to the bridge separating us from Raghid's staff quarters was locked. But my elation over his death muted my fears, shrouding them in a haze of tender affection.

Did Nadim kill Raghid? He must have.

But if only he'd done it a lot sooner. A *lot* sooner.

Khalil couldn't have done it. At the time of Raghid's death he was still being pampered and corrupted, and hadn't yet reached the stage of abject humiliation.

As for Layla, she stands to lose from his death. He was coming to depend on her more and more without realizing it. Or had there been something going on between the two of them that I wasn't aware of?

Kafa, on the other hand, is the delicate type. She wouldn't be capable of murder anywhere but in bed.

And *I* didn't do it.

So if it wasn't Nadim that killed him, then who was it?

Saqr certainly didn't do it. After all, he still doesn't know about the collapse of the school and his brother's death, since when his father called him yesterday he was so drugged up, he refused to answer the phone. Or do you suppose he called his dad after everyone else had gone to bed and his instinct for revenge was awakened?

Bahriya couldn't have done it. And oh, what blessed good fortune it was that took her away from the mansion last night, since otherwise the police would inundate her with questions, and the sorcerer would accuse her of doing it. On the other hand, her being far from the scene of the crime might not exempt her from the accusation if Sheikh Watfan insists that she's the culprit, mysterious person that she is. Besides, he would have quite a number of witnesses to confirm her eccentricity. After all, anyone who would attend a celebration being held in her honor naked and covered with blood—a stunt sure to strike terror in all the other guests' hearts—could also be accused of making her way from one mansion to another to commit a murder. After all, the witnesses wouldn't know what's really been happening between her and the sorcerer behind closed doors.

Or might Sheikh Sakhr have sent someone to murder him in revenge? He might have made an appointment to meet with him beside the golden pool, then come and killed him himself. Or he may have sent someone to do it for him. Wouldn't that explain Raghid's having left the armored door open?

If Nadim isn't the one who murdered Raghid, then it's clear at least that he was waiting for someone to come. And it was this "someone" who had an appointment to meet with him, then killed him. Maybe Raghid had summoned the person. So who was it, if not Nadim?

But the murderer has to be someone here in the mansion. After all, how could Sheikh Sakhr or Bahriya have come in without being seen by the guards? And how would either of them have made it past the electrically charged fences and the armored doors? However, a professional hit man sent by Sakhr might have managed such a thing by deactivating the electric fence around the garden, slipping into the swimming pool area where Raghid was waiting for his guest, and finishing the job in a hurry.

What this means is that any man of influence who knew Raghid could have arranged a nighttime rendezvous with him at the pool on the pretext of wrapping up some enticing deal, then sent someone to murder him to protect some sort of commercial interest. The person might have wanted to have the profits from the deal all to himself and to be rid of Raghid as a competitor. The "red millionaire," for example, might have done it after finding some way to have the airport deal all to himself. And then there's the "yellow millionaire"—and any of the other millionaires who've been waiting for the sun to rise on this day so that the celebration could begin. And if the murderer is clever—which no doubt he is—he might have postponed his arrival, made arrangements for his meeting with Raghid by phone before his private plane touched down at Geneva airport, then committed the crime by remote control by sending his professional killer to finish the job before he arrived.

The only person not in the mansion last night who could have done it without having to cut the electrical wires on the garden wall is Sheikh Watfan. After all, he could have hypnotized the guards with those frightening eyes of his, shut off the alarms, and pressed the necessary buttons with a mere glance. I'd noticed lately that if I came into his room unexpectedly, I'd find him levitating objects by looking at them. But the minute I walked in, he'd let them drop. It seemed that the sicker and more emaciated he got, the more his terrifying, ominous strength increased. It was as if it were feeding off his body, or as if some malign spirit really did live inside him, sucking up his vital powers. But why would he have killed Raghid? Because he was bitter toward him on account of Bahriya? Because Raghid hadn't given him permission to shave her head and subject her to torture in order to drive the demons out of her? But if so, then why would he come all the way from his hotel to murder him when he could have done so on any other occasion? Why couldn't he just have slipped some poison into one of the potions that Raghid accepted so willingly from his hand? Or had relations between the two of them soured of late because of Bahriya, causing Raghid to stop trusting anyone, even his sorcerer? Yet even if they had, why would the sorcerer kill him by strangulation the way some ordinary human being would have done, when he could just as easily have sent aches, pains, and illness into his body?)

Nasim's head was about to explode with these thoughts. At the same time, he was filled with remorse over having switched the two sculptures and stolen the piaster in his fit of youthful madness. Based on these two pieces of evidence, they might pin a murder charge on him for no reason except that he was a penniless butler who couldn't afford to hire himself a lawyer. If that happened, it would be welcome news to everyone but Khalil and Amir. However, he knew for a certainty that he hadn't killed him himself, not being given to sleepwalking. So who did kill him, then? Once again he began thinking of all the people who had spent the night in the mansion and who for that reason would have found it easiest to commit the murder. Then, overcome by a sudden headache, he took his head in his hands.

(It looks like I've been reading too many whodunits. I'm not the one to decide who killed him, like Inspector Poirot in some Agatha Christie novel. All that matters this time is for me get out of here in one piece.)

He got up and washed his face in cold water, then rushed to put on his clothes.

(Damned booze! If it hadn't been for the bottle of wine left over from their dinner that I took to my room and drank, I would never have been audacious or hotheaded enough to switch those two statues and steal the piaster. Am I going to be accused of murder just because I pilfered a few swigs of firewater? And will I pay for it with my life, while the real killer goes on swimming around in a sea of liquor and vice? No doubt that's what will happen. It's only the poor who pay for their sins on this planet of ours.)

◆　◆　◆

With a touch of malice in her voice Dunya said to Layla, "May I go up to my room to change out of my nightclothes?"

"What business is that of hers?" interjected Khalil. "She's under as much suspicion as any of the rest of us here. And I'm going up to change my clothes, too."

Then he left the room. Layla didn't utter a word. The only one making any noise was Saqr, who was balling like a baby and shrieking like a maniac, "I want my father! I want to go back to my father's house! Let me go!"

And although Layla said nothing in reply and hadn't done a thing to prevent him from leaving, he stayed seated in his chair as if he were bound to it by invisible chains.

"They'll murder me, too!" he wailed. "There are people who hate the great and the rich. Let me go! I may be the one they really meant to kill. They must have meant to murder me, not him!"

Dunya went into her room and took some documents out of her purse, the ones that Raghid had used to threaten her husband the previous night. Then she rushed with them to the bathroom, took out the gold cigarette lighter, and proceeded to burn them one page at a time. The toilet flushed, sweeping away the remains. She waited a few moments to make sure that no scrap of paper or specks of black dust remained on the water's surface, then flushed it once again.

She washed the fine black dust off her hands, then checked to make certain that none of it remained under her fingernails.

(So then, did Nadim kill him? He came back to our room at around midnight sobbing like a little boy. He didn't tell me he'd killed him. Instead, he told me about how Raghid was going to throw him in prison for a crime he didn't commit after forcing him to admit responsibility for the collapsed school. At the time, I hated both of them. But I was also afraid. In fact, I was filled with dread. A vague sort of angst welled up from deep inside me, and I felt the need to plan out my life and how I might leave Nadim, that is, if I ever had guts enough to do it. I couldn't bear the thought of continuing to let Raghid plan things for me. That only complicates matters. I was about to break, and I was certain to break if I had to part with Nadim, the person I'd lived with, hated with, slipped and fallen with for so many years.

Maybe all I wanted to do was to hurt Raghid, not to help Nadim. I don't know, exactly. But I couldn't sleep after hearing the story Nadim had told me. So then, Nadim would go back to Lebanon to be imprisoned there, and Raghid would carry on with his games forever. There would always be someone to go to prison in his place so that he could live by stealing others' freedom . . . and someone to die in his place so that he could live by stealing another's kidney, or heart, or eye. . . . I was defeated, and enraged.

I tossed and turned in bed for at least an hour.

Then at around 1:00 A.M. I told Nadim, "I'm going to talk to him."

He was so devastated, he didn't say yes or no. I went to Raghid's bedroom, a place I knew well, and knocked on the door. I kept knocking for quite a while, but no one answered. When I tried turning the knob, I was amazed to find that the door was unlocked. However, I didn't find him in the room. I went down to the parlor. No one. I saw the lights on through the windows around the golden pool. I thought for a moment of begging him to leave us in peace and telling him to take every dollar we'd saved up with his help. Then on my way there I imagined myself killing him, strangling him in the pool of gold, holding his head under the water while golden bubbles rose to the surface until his strength had given out and he'd faded away in my grip—stinking, slimy creature that he was. But when I got there, what should I find but his body floating on top of the water, strangled. So, someone else had already fulfilled my fantasy. I was so flabbergasted, I couldn't move for a moment or so. Then I saw the documents condemning my husband lying on the table. When I saw them, I felt as though I began glowing with fright, and that an unusual strength started flowing through my veins. I quickly fingered through them, and when I saw Nadim's signature and the tables showing the falsified accounts and embezzlement, I realized what they were. Then I picked them up and took them back to the room.

I said to Nadim, "So, you killed him."

After a long silence, he said, "I wish I'd dared. I wished I could strangle him in the pool of gold, then hold his head under the water and watch the golden bubbles rise to the surface until his strength gave out. . . . But I didn't do it."

"But he's been murdered," I told him. "I saw him floating dead in the pool."

"Incredible," he said. "Impossible. People like him don't die. He was just making fun of you. Maybe he saw you coming and wanted to play a trick on you, so he dove into the water real quick."

"With all his clothes on? Does that make any sense?"

"Well then, you're just scared and imagining things."

"Come with me and see for yourself."

"I'm exhausted," he said.

I backed off. After all, I thought, maybe he really *has* been murdered. And what if we were found there? They'd accuse us of killing him together!

I didn't tell Nadim anything about the papers. I was too petrified. Instead I just lay in bed trembling without saying a word until Saqr's scream rang out. When I heard it I felt relieved. The waiting had been crueler than the certainty.

So then, he'd killed him but hadn't told me. And now here I was removing evidence of the crime, which made me his accomplice. Ever since the beginning of our life together he's gotten me into trouble, and now it's too late to pull out. Why did I intervene after I'd decided to get out of this hell we share together? I don't know. I don't know. I don't know anything anymore.)

◆ ◆ ◆

Nadim washed his face in the guest bathroom just off the main parlor. As he dried his face, he sobbed into the towel. And instead of changing his clothes, he stayed in his pajamas and put on his robe over them.

So then, Dunya had killed him.

(What have I done to her and to myself?

She killed him without realizing it, just the way she stabbed her painting without knowing it. First she accused her daughter of doing it, and then decided that I had to be the culprit, and that I'd done it under orders from Raghid. It's true that Raghid asked me to repatriate her, so to speak. But I contented myself with killing her dog Picasso. As for the other, I didn't do it. I didn't put a knife through her painting. And I don't think our son did it, either. After all, that would have meant leaving the killing field on the video game screen and Intelevision tapes for the screen of real life.

She's the one who did it without realizing what she was doing. I'm going to testify against the poor woman. I've already destroyed her and myself. Life seemed like a big game to me: whoever doesn't take his share by force loses his right to it, and to a fitting tomb as well. All I was doing was taking what I believed to be my due, and I encouraged Dunya to help me. How could we have sunk so low?

Yes. When I was with him yesterday, I had the urge to strangle him in the pool of gold, then dunk his head under the water and watch the golden bubbles rise to the surface until his strength gave out and he slowly expired in my hands.

But I didn't do it. I didn't do it.

All the evidence points to me. So would Dunya save me by confessing, or abandon me to life imprisonment? Did she kill him so that I'd be accused of the crime? Is this her way of getting back at me? On the other hand, maybe she killed him during one of her nervous fits and really doesn't remember it, just the way she did to her painting.

Or what if she's innocent? If so, then the murderer is on the loose right here in the mansion. Who is it? Khalil? He wouldn't have had anything to gain from it.

Nasim? Possibly. He hates us all. And ever since Sirri Al-Din died, he's avoided looking me in the face.

Layla? If they'd been married she might have done it. But as things stand now, she won't inherit anything but debts.

Saqr? He's the most likely suspect. He's constantly under the effect of cocaine or some other kind of madness powder. So did he kill him in revenge for his brother's death? Did he find out about it, then decide to act on the basis of tribal codes in a world ruled by nothing but the law of the jungle? Did that shrewd Hilal convince his brother Sakhr that my confession is nothing but a farce that won't be believed by anybody, and push him to take revenge? Did they send a hired hit man to do the job?

I'm the primary suspect. But I didn't do it, and I know that nobody will believe me. The real murderer knows that, too. And this might have encouraged him to carry out his plan.)

◆   ◆   ◆

Kafa put on her clothes in a panic. Despite the gold and the opulent furniture that filled the room, it looked to her eyes like a place of misery and torment. So then, she'd lost out on her chance at the Night of the First Billion, and the dawn of the same day had destroyed her dreams with news of crime and murder.

She didn't look at Khalil, who was also getting dressed in a hurry. Neither of them said a word to the other. Was this what went on in the mansions she'd dreamed of for so long?

On this bed Saqr had raped her. She also happened to have enjoyed it, but that was her business, and hers alone. From the outside, however, it had been obvious that he raped her. So why were her husband, Dunya and Layla all refusing to stand by her in the matter? She wasn't asking them to lie. All she was asking of Layla and Dunya was to "speak the truth," as Khalil liked to say. But they'd refused.

(But, why am I so angry? Hasn't the issue of speaking the truth been my main bone of contention with Khalil? Do I really want people to speak the truth? Or do I only want them to speak the truth when it's to my advantage?

So then, Khalil killed him. Or at least, he's the most likely suspect. Besides Khalil, I'm the only one who knows that Raghid was still alive when Nadim left the pool last night. I know it because he spoke to me afterward over this very receiver. He told me that he'd just informed Nadim that he would be dispensing with his services for committing a breach of trust and for causing the collapse of some school. Then he asked me if Khalil was asleep, and promised to give him an extra assignment that had been Nadim's, saying that it would make us a lot of money. I was so excited, I thanked him and told him that Khalil was taking a bath but that I'd call him anyway, and he said to do that. If I'd told him that he was on his deathbed, I think he still would have told me to call him. Then he gave him instructions to meet him at the golden pool.

Khalil went down to see him after midnight, maybe around 1:00 A.M., though I don't recall exactly. All I remember is that I got scared because the storm started raging all of a sudden and I was all by myself. I thought of going across the balcony to take refuge in Saqr's body, but I didn't dare. Besides, Khalil wasn't gone very long. Either that, or it just seemed that way because I fell asleep. I remember that vaguely. When he got back I was half-asleep, and I asked him what they talked about, what Raghid had offered him, how much the monthly salary would be, whether it would come in cash, through commissions, etc. And he just answered me calmly, "He made me an offer, and then I killed him."

I laughed at the joke, but grudgingly. I'd decided there was no need for an argument over a bad joke after a day as exhausting as the one we'd just been through, not to mention the fact that it would be followed by the night of the party. Besides, I needed my beauty rest, so I decided just to be quiet and go to sleep.

But my sleep was restless. I dreamed that all the people in the mansion were raping me. They were wearing devil's masks on their heads and they took turns with me, one after another. Even Layla had a man's body in the dream. Then I woke up to the sound of Saqr's scream. I didn't believe that Khalil meant what he said until I saw Raghid's dead body floating on top of a bed of watery gold.

If only we'd stayed in Beirut. The death, the bombing, the terror, any and all of it was better than this crime. As the wife of an imprisoned murderer, I won't be invited to any more parties. He's destroyed my social life for good. If only he'd waited till after divorcing me to murder him. All he thinks about is himself. Oh, what's going to happen to me and the boys? I used to think of Ghanamali as someone I could count on if things got rough. But would he have me now that I've become a murderer's wife? Who would think of inviting me to his mansion now? And who will support me? Will Khalil be sentenced to death? Do they apply the death penalty in Switzerland? I've asked about nearly everything in this wonderful country except . . . that.

I never imagined that we'd end up being so humiliated. But now I might become a murderer's widow.

I won't testify against him, since I might be accused of withholding information. I'll keep my mouth shut. I'll say that I was asleep and that I don't know a thing. I don't want to know, and I don't want to believe it. And if he claims that he told me about what he did right after returning from the scene of the crime, I'll tell them he's a liar, a liar. Who would believe a murderer anyway? And who would disbelieve these innocent, teary blue eyes of mine? Damn that Khalil. I'd just barely stepped out onto the stage to be crowned one of the stars of the Night of the First Billion when he brought everything down on his head and mine. And in the process, he ruined my future as an international socialite. I'll never forgive him for this. The fool—he's kicked wealth and success in the teeth and ruined my whole life.

◆   ◆   ◆

(Yes, I killed him. And I'm proud of it. I'll say so in court, too. When the judge calls me forward and asks me, "Why did you murder him, Khalil Dar?" I'll tell him the truth. I'll say, "I murdered him because he took a commission on the bomb that killed my little girl. All the children in our neighborhood who've died were killed by bombs the price of which he poured as gold into his pool. I killed him because he asked me to share in his filthy business and his filthy commissions. First he threw me into the quicksand of Saqr's drugs and prostituted my wife. Then he called me away from weeping over my little boy after midnight to have me join in his dirty work and dive with him into the morass of shipping arms to people on both sides of the fighting in Beirut. He was proud of the fact that the war that's been raging in Lebanon for the past eight years made up the greater part of his first billion dollars, and he was counting on it continuing to amass his second billion. As for the construction projects he was engaged in, he was planning to phase them out gradually. After all, if something you've built caves in and causes death and destruction the way the school did, you've got yourself in a real predicament. But arms sales are just the opposite, since, as he put it, "the more destruction and wreckage you cause, the more money you make.")

Khalil got dressed quickly, left the room without saying a word to Kafa, then sat down in the hallway like a forgotten statue. After he'd been sitting there for some time, Nasim came up to him carrying a cup of coffee and drew him out of his petrified condition. Khalil gulped it down in dejected silence while Nasim waited without saying anything.

Then he said warmly, "Come on, brother, let's get some fresh air at the door."

"Have the police arrived?"

"Yes, and the doctor, too. They're at the pool now. They've got the mansion surrounded, and they've forbidden anyone to leave the place."

Khalil walked toward the door with Nasim, and when they'd gotten some distance away from Layla's stupor and Saqr's shrieks, he said matter-of-factly, "I killed him."

"And I didn't hear you say a thing."

"I killed him."

"Who among us wouldn't have loved to kill him? Who among us hadn't dreamed of it, and maybe even tried to do it? But Nadim is the one who did it. He looks overwhelmed, and I think he's going to confess."

"I'm the one who killed him, Nasim."

"Do you mean what you're saying?"

"Yesterday after Nadim left the pool, he called my room and ordered me to come down to see him. When I got there, he instructed me to take over some of Nadim's assignments, specifically, deals involving arms shipments back home. He speaks of Lebanon as if it were a chessboard made for gambling on. He forgets that there are human beings suffering and dying there, and that you and I, your brothers and sisters, my cousins and the rest of our families are among them. He wants me to take over the shipment operations. He's offering me a high commission—one percent—and the first shipment is worth $10 million. In other words, I'd make one hundred thousand dollars off the first shipment alone. And if the first deadly dispatch doesn't kill off more than twenty thousand people, then I will have made five dollars off every victim— like my little girl Widad, for example.

"When I heard what he'd said, a kind of temporary insanity came over me. I didn't say a thing. As for him, he didn't look at me, and he didn't even seem concerned about what I might say. That's how confident he was that I'd agree to it. But I'd made up my mind to strangle him in the pool of gold, then dunk his head under the water and watch the golden bubbles rise to the surface until his strength gave out and he slowly expired in my hands—stinking, slimy creature that he was. It was a dream that I'd cherished for a long time, and at that moment I decided to fulfill it.

"He turned his back to me and drank another glass of firewater. Seeming quite pleased about the long-anticipated 'night of celebration,' he told me that it was past midnight, which meant that the 'day of the first billion' had begun. Unlike usual, he was drinking too much in celebration of the fact. But I kept quiet. Then suddenly he coughed and fell on his knees in front of me, and the glass he'd been holding rolled out of his hand and broke. He doubled over and grabbed his chest as if someone had stabbed him in the stomach. He looked at me as though he were asking for help and tried to say something, but all I heard was a rattle in his throat. Then he collapsed at the edge of the pool and fell into the translucent golden water. He gave me another imploring look and reached out his hand. I thought: a man like him carries the seeds of his own death inside him. Now the seeds have matured and are ready for picking. I stood staring at him and at the golden shimmer as it danced over his body. He was thrashing about, and there was a look of severe pain on his face. Unable to swim and shivering in his tight clothes and suffocating necktie, he looked panic-stricken and exhausted, impotent and laughable, like a tiny chick in the middle of a huge, infernal, golden egg. He reached out to me again . . .

"I don't know what took possession of me, but I didn't extend my hand to pull him out of the water. Instead, I put my right hand in my right pocket and my left hand in my left pocket and nearly started whistling for joy. I left him to drown. I enjoyed the sight of him suffering and flailing about, enjoyed the sound of his golden death rattle as it grew fainter and fainter. I just stood there and watched him die without lifting a finger to rescue him. I didn't do a thing. Instead I started singing in a low voice, 'O darkness of the prison, descend . . . ' while he looked at me one last time as if he were begging me on bended knee. But I'd decided to condemn him to death. And when his body went limp, I stood there looking at the place where he'd drowned with my hands still in my pockets and with a feeling of total disbelief flooding over me. I hadn't known I was capable of such violence—a violence as frigid as the glitter of his pool of gold. The violence that even Beirut itself hadn't been able to release in my soul came pouring out with all the cruelty of that pool's golden water. I knew now that I, too, was capable of murder. As I contemplated Raghid's watery golden death, I felt caught somewhere between pleasure and indifference. Meanwhile, twin gleams of terror and gold flashed in the pools of his dimming eyes. It was surprising, even astounding.

"I went to my room, and when my wife asked me what Raghid and I had agreed on and how much he was going to pay, I told her that he wasn't going to be paying anything from now on or shipping any more arms to anybody, because I'd killed him. And she didn't believe me."

"I believe you," whispered Nasim, "and I beg you: Don't say a thing. That despicable man doesn't deserve to have somebody else die just because he did!"

"But I feel a sort of remorse now. I've never killed anybody in my life. For years I call for democracy and dialogue and justice, and then I end up being as bloodthirsty as some petty-minded terrorist."

"Don't say anything now."

"Why not? Do you want to be a character in some detective novel where the police go on investigating until they drive you to distraction along with everybody else staying here?"

"Brother Khalil, I'm telling you, be quiet! Please! Don't say anything, at least not until the investigation is over."

"I used to be a pacifist, and now I've ended up as a murderer. My sole ambition in life was to be an honorable freedom fighter. Now that the exhilaration of revenge is gone, I realize that I'm just a murderer. And I feel sorry now."

"You didn't murder him, though. You didn't push him into the pool, and you didn't ask him to guzzle down that damned booze like a jolly fool. He was killed by greed. He was killed by his excitement over the Night of the First Billion. He was killed by the huge, gluttonous meal that he ate last night, his elation over ruining Nadim, and his malicious glee over the death of Sakhr's son."

"Even if I didn't kill him with my own two hands, I still killed him in a certain sense. Even if I'm not answerable before the law for plucking out his corrupt spirit, I'm still answerable to myself for the corrupt act of killing him."

"The corruption of letting him live would have been greater than that of killing him. There isn't a soul among us that hasn't wanted to kill him at one time or another. So calm down, brother. One time he killed one of his poverty-stricken workers by hitting him on the head with a gold ingot. And for another gold ingot, his shrewd lawyer arranged to have him acquitted."

"Every time I think back to yesterday, I feel as though I'm staring into the river of hell. But unlike Orpheus,[34] I won't be able to climb out of it. I'm drowning in remorse. How could I have done it?"

"How could we all have kept from doing it before now?"

"I regret it."

"I'm proud of you. Calm down, and don't say a thing to anyone. Now, let me check out what's going on."

◆　◆　◆

It was nearly daybreak, and Sheikh Watfan was unable to get out of bed. (All night long Bahriya bound me with invisible shackles. She scourged me with lightning and set her demons loose to steal the winds from the four directions, then hurl them against my windows mingled with the tears people have shed in earthquakes, tornadoes, famines, and plagues. She's done things this way to delude me into thinking that what's happening is just another storm, and that my feverish, tormented sleep is just an ordinary human slumber.

But from the time I saw one of her demons occupying Sheikh Sakhr's body and coming to the hotel to invite me to his home, I knew that this would be the final battle.

When I saw that smile on her face as she waited for me in her room guarded by three cat spirits, I was certain of it. It was a half-smile that wouldn't be visible to anyone but me. I'm the only person who can see past it to her demon's black teeth. The demon that possessed Sheikh Sakhr in an attempt to deceive me said, "She'd only been in the room a few minutes when Abdullah's cats came and started rubbing up against her. After you've identified my son's murderer, I urge you to treat this innocent young woman as well."

But of course I didn't believe him. She was caressing her guard cats and watching television like some ordinary earthling. When I came in she turned to look at me, and her demon shot me a derisive grin. At the same time, her body trembled as if it knew what unthinkable torment I have in store for it in order to deliver it from its demon.)

Sheikh Watfan tried to get out of bed, but the fever had consumed all his

---

34. According to Greek myth, Orpheus descended into hell to fetch his wife Eurydice. As the two of them were riding in a boat down the river of death, Orpheus violated the gods' condition that he not look back at his wife's face until they had returned to the world of the living. As a consequence, she was sent back to hell, and he lost her forever.

strength. (I have to go to her before dawn breaks. The spirits that I want to summon only respond in the dark). He tried again, but still wasn't able. (When I got here from the hotel, I knew she'd set the stage for the battle to her own advantage. She's made it similar to our previous battleground—although I don't recall exactly where that was. She's to the left of the main hall and I'm to the right, and the hallway that leads from one room to the other is narrow and dark. Ever since I got here a few hours ago, I've been trying to summon my assistants, and whenever the butler brings in another of the medicaments I requested, I recite an incantation over it with my censer lit. When I sat down at my crystal ball—something my ancestors didn't use, but whose secrets I've mastered myself—I was able to see her just as she is and to do a thorough study of her room. After all, I've developed the ability to read what's written on a folded piece of paper simply by touching it. So what surprise is it that I should be able to conjure her image with my psychic powers inside this glass ball? And why do you suppose Sheikh Sakhr was so taken aback when he came to invite me to go see her and I told him that I already saw her clearly inside the crystal ball? When the spirit possessing him didn't believe me, I gave him a detailed description of her room, including the white bed that one gets into by climbing up three steps and the translucent curtains that hang down from the bed's wooden canopy in seven tiers. I also told him that not all the tiers were hanging down at the moment. Only four of the seven were hanging down, and they were tied on either side with pink ribbons. There's also a huge, exquisite chandelier hanging from the ceiling in one corner of the room rather than in the center as one usually finds. (His interior decorator has fine taste indeed.) As for the wall behind the bed, it's covered with the same type of translucent curtains, which descend from a wooden tiara inlaid with shells and gold. Directly beneath the chandelier there's an armchair facing the television. Bahriya isn't in bed, but sitting in the armchair watching TV. It's a room that truly befits the Princess of the Demons. Sakhr's spirit pretended to be amazed. So, speaking to him as an ordinary person and ignoring the fact that he was possessed, I said, "You consider it a normal thing to see images of people on another continent on the television screen. So why are you so astounded to see her image here when she's just in the next room?"

He said, "Television has broadcast stations, and there's an antenna that picks up the image and conveys it to the viewer."

"Well," I told him, "human beings and spirits have their own 'broadcast stations.' And I've found the antenna that picks up their images. It's inside me, in fact. I direct it invisibly wherever I choose just the way people do with electrical currents and sound waves, and I can pick up any image I want to."

When he saw the power of my sorcery, a look of genuine amazement appeared on his face. And I challenged him. I told him that if he gave me a few minutes to focus my powers, set up my receiving screen and get tuned into the vibrations coming from a particular person, I could give him a description of everything in that person's room.

Appearing frightened, he drew me by the hand and said, "I want you to concern yourself now with my son's murderer, and we'll do all these experiments later."

But I insisted on the challenge, saying, "I'll describe to you her room and her clothes as well!"

He objected strenuously. So I walked along with him while he said over and over, "Come to greet her now, and you can do that later on."

I went with him to see her, and the room was exactly as I had seen it in my crystal ball. Like my room, it was on the first floor with a window overlooking the garden, which was planted in wild roses. The rose bushes were more than a meter high, and came up as far as the windowsill. Then, just a few moments after I'd come to a halt, one of the cats "barked" in a mysterious, satanic sort of cat voice, and fled by jumping out the window. Then the second ran away, followed by the third. The reason was that I'd sent a painful electric shock through their demons. When Bahriya found that her protectors had abandoned her from the first few moments after my arrival, she looked over at me, pretending to be terrified and pouring molten sulfur onto my face. I nearly screamed in pain, but instead I directed my gaze away from her adorable, odious face and focused it instead on the chain that held up the chandelier. I poured forth all the power in my spirit to split it apart, but it was harder than steel. Even though I'd been accustomed of late to breaking mirrors and windows with a mere glance, I encountered tremendous resistance in that bewitched chandelier chain. By the time it finally came down, my heart was beating like mad and getting bigger and bigger until it was about to burst. But with phenomenal speed, Bahriya's demon swept her out of the way with the agility of millions of cats, and the chandelier shattered on top of the chair. The demon escaped unharmed, and Sakhr shrieked in alarm.

When I came out of the room, I left him kneeling at the feet of Her Majesty to make certain she was all right. I went back to my own room panic-stricken

and shaken. She'd won the first round. She'd assaulted me with fire and succeeded in burning me, and I'd failed to return the blow. So I sat there preparing
myself to burn her with my magic and summoning my assistants from the ends
of the earth: from its east and its west, from its belly, from its winds, from its seas
and from its outer space. When Sheikh Sakhr came to invite me to dinner and
reassure me (!) of Bahriya's well-being, I shouted at him, "Leave me alone to do
my work!" So he went away, muttering something meaningless like, "I'm confident that you'll reveal the identity of my son's murderer by dawn. Good night.")

The first traces of dawn had begun appearing in the sky, and dread came
creeping into Sheikh Watfan's heart. (If I don't gain victory over her before it
gets light, I'm finished. I don't have enough strength left to wait another night.
How could this blistering storm of hers have laid me up in bed with my censer
out of reach? And how could she have bound me and tormented me all night
long? She even came into my room and stared into my face, with its mask of
unconsciousness, fever, and delirium. If it hadn't been for Maymoun the Black
One who frightened her off in a hurry, she would have poured my four liters of
alcohol onto my bed. Then she rushed out of the room, leaving me to bear my
agony. Once she was gone, she broke the locks on my spirit and assaulted me
with the voices of my father, my brothers, my sisters, and my mother, which
she'd released from the chambers of my memory. My mother went up in
flames all over again right before my very eyes, and I could even smell the odor
of gasoline and charred flesh. She howled, and I wept. I saw the deaths of my
brothers Ghilan, Burqan, and Kan'an repeating themselves, and their blood
stained my face. I saw my sister Wad'a in flames while my uncle and all my
nieces and nephews screamed as I cried. My father fell down wounded and
began to die, while I was bound by invisible chains, too weak to do a thing. I
was being rent asunder. Then I knew what a hideous end she had in store for
me: I was doomed to burn to death in my torment, and the sentence would be
carried out by the loved ones whom I'd fled from for so long to the land of spirits and oblivion. She would turn me back into a mere earthling, capable of
being tortured and annihilated, then leave me to die in defeat.)

The sorcerer finally got out of bed despite the fever racking his body, and
despite the fire that he'd seen raging in his head when he looked in the mirror.
Then, with a supernatural strength coursing through his body, he picked up
the containers of alcohol and started heading in the direction of Bahriya's
room. Everyone in the mansion was asleep and the door to her room was
open, as if it were daring him to walk in. The moment he stepped inside, he

felt as though he'd lost his sight. Like someone afflicted with night-blindness, he moved forward and poured the alcohol onto the bed and the curtains suspended over it. The fire that resulted broke out with such tremendous speed, it was as if it were a burning force that had long remained hidden, and now at last had made itself visible. He could feel himself being incinerated like so much firewood. And his failure to flee caused him no surprise, as if he had known for a long time that this was his inevitable fate. He looked for Bahriya in hopes of closing his eyes on the sight of her face going up in flames the way his was. But he was in so much pain, all he could see was thick darkness.

He didn't cry out.

Before he faded away, he heard a scream that didn't sound human, but more like the howling of a wolf.

(Was that her voice, or mine?)

Sheikh Sakhr heard the scream as well. However, it didn't wake him up, since he hadn't been asleep to begin with.

What with the lightning flashing, the rains assailing the mansion like watery warhorses wailing in sorrow, and his heart weeping over Abdullah's demise, he hadn't shut his eyelids once all night.

He heard the scream.

It hadn't been a human voice, and at first he thought he was imagining things. But then he smelled fire. When he went downstairs, he saw everyone that had spent the night in the mansion rushing toward Bahriya's room.

It was a bizarre sight, with the sorcerer a blazing mass kneeling near what was more like an oven than a bed, and with very little smoke, as if he were being smelted inside an unseen crucible. A strange fire the likes of which he'd never seen before, it simply went out all by itself. Or was it thanks to his engineer, who had promised to have "fireproof carpet" laid in the mansion?

When the firemen and the ambulance arrived, it turned out that there hadn't really been any reason for them to come. However, after examining the bedroom, they informed him that they had found the remains of a single male corpse. So then, where was Bahriya? Had she managed to escape through the window or the door? Or had she not been in the room when the fire broke out? And what had the sorcerer been doing there?

◆ ◆ ◆

The dawn before the Night of the First Billion.

The telephone rang in the large parlor of Raghid Zahran's mansion. Most of the mansion's guests had changed their clothes, then met in the parlor to wait for a word from the investigator. Nasim started with fright when he heard it, as did everyone else. Their nerves were on edge as they anticipated what the police and the forensic doctor would do with them once they'd finished their work at the golden pool.

Still behaving as though she were the widow of the deceased—or at least, the only one among them above suspicion—Layla lifted the receiver. Most of the time she listened, and the rest of the time she uttered curt phrases like, "Yes," "When?" "What happened to him?" "And she, where did she go?" "Hasn't anyone seen her?" and "All right, I'll inform Saqr."

Then, sounding as dispassionate as a radio announcer reading off news of no concern to her, she said to Saqr, "A lightning bolt struck the room where Bahriya was staying in your father's mansion. The room caught on fire and Sheikh Watfan was burned to death. But they haven't found a trace of Bahriya. Your father wants you to come to him as soon as you wake up."

"Why didn't you tell him I wasn't asleep?!" Saqr screamed at her, "How am I supposed to go to him when the police have forbidden us to leave this place? And why didn't you tell him that Raghid's been found murdered?"

She made no reply, and the news she had relayed descended like a second bolt of lightning on everyone in the room. They were all bewildered to hear of the sorcerer's having been in Sheikh Sakhr's mansion, not to mention his dying in Bahriya's room. Khalil and Nasim felt anxious for Bahriya, while Dunya marveled over the realization that Sheikh Watfan was mortal like everybody else. Nadim wished Bahriya had been killed too so that he could get out of the predicament of having brought her to Switzerland, especially in view of the fact that her papers were forged and she wasn't really Raghid's heiress. Kafa regretted not having consulted Sheikh Watfan concerning some of her personal affairs before his death. And as for Layla, she kept repeating over and over like someone who's lost her senses, "Bahriya killed both of them. Bahriya is the murderer. Everywhere she goes, she passes through like a fire that leaves death and destruction in its wake."

Nasim nearly replied, explaining to her that Raghid was the one with a monopoly on the death industry, that sorcerer Watfan had been a man more dangerous to himself than to anyone else and that his death by fire had come as no surprise, whereas Bahriya had just been one more of the two men's victims. But then he remembered the predicament he may have gotten himself into with the statue and the piaster and the possibility of being accused of killing Raghid if Khalil changed his mind and didn't confess. So he kept quiet. As for Khalil, he plunged once again into his sorrow and regret: How could I have turned into a murderer? How could they have finally made me into a killer?

◆　◆　◆

The dawn before the Night of the First Billion.

The sun peeked out through an opening in the gloomy black clouds, and the light of day emerged through a dreary rain. Meanwhile, the lightning in the distance continued to dispatch its thunderless signals, and the mansion guests waited for the police either to tell them something or to interrogate them. All that mattered now was to find their way out of the ice chest of anticipation.

When the result came, it came with the force of a thunderbolt. An official dressed in civilian clothes emerged and said to them matter-of-factly, "You may go now. The doctor has examined the corpse, and it appears that the man died not of drowning, but of a heart attack. The body shows no signs of having been assaulted in any way, and it's clear that when he suffered the attack, he was standing at the edge of the pool, causing him to fall in the water. If any of you would like to leave Geneva before the autopsy is completed and the initial report is finalized, please inform us."

This was what the police inspector had to say, and no one else uttered a word. Then he added, "Write down your names and addresses on this piece of paper. However, I don't expect that we'll detain you in Geneva for more than forty-eight hours, which is how long it will take for the death certificate to be released. It's all just a matter of formalities."

None of them budged except for Saqr, who, in a sudden fit of madness screamed, "I killed him! I'm the murderer!"

"There is no crime, and consequently there is no murderer," replied the inspector.

"I killed him!" Saqr screamed on. "I assure you of it! And here's the weapon!"

Whereupon he took out his dagger.

Everyone was taken by surprise. The police inspector approached him and he fled to his room sobbing. Kafa gasped, not having known about his addiction, and the policeman followed him, muttering some cliché that policemen often repeat at such times. Khalil heard him say, "Whenever there's a crime, all sorts of people volunteer to play the criminal. I'll never understand it." And he nearly burst out laughing, but he didn't find enough air in his lungs.

◆ ◆ ◆

The morning before the Night of the First Billion.

With the announcement that Raghid had died a natural death, it was if the beads in a necklace had suddenly broken apart. Once the police had made the announcement and released them from their terror, not one of them so much as spoke to anyone else. The only exception was the look of affection mingled with astonishment and joy that passed between Khalil and Nasim. No one commented on the police's discovery of the drugs in Saqr's room, or the medical examination he was obliged to submit to, or the doctor's decision to transfer him immediately to a treatment center before he died from the huge doses he'd taken earlier in the morning.

Layla was the first to leave the place. She didn't gather up her things and she didn't offer Khalil, Kafa, or Nasim a ride in her car. In fact, she took off in such a hurry that she nearly ran down one of the cameramen who had arrived on the scene. She wondered how they'd gotten wind of events so quickly. As she drove away, she saw one of the millionaire guests who'd come to sniff out the news. He was standing in front of his car with his brawny chauffeur and motioning to her to stop, but she ignored him. She was too preoccupied with the catastrophe that was about to befall her. (So then, the bank manager will hear the news the minute the bank opens its doors in a little less than an hour. And I'll become an outlaw for writing bad checks.)

And none of the others was far behind her. No less anxious than she was to escape this "castle of death," they rushed to pack their things and flee from the nightmare. No one said a word to anyone else, and those who had cars didn't even have the courtesy to offer the pedestrians a lift to the nearest bus stop or station. It was as if all any of them wanted was to get alone as fast as possible to congratulate himself on escaping from the accusation of murdering a man that he would have loved to liquidate, and to ponder the state of affairs that had come about since Sheikh Watfan's demise and Bahriya's disappearance.

As Nadim drove through the mansion garden with his wife, he passed Khalil and Kafa, but instead of stopping he sped off as if he hadn't seen them.

"I told you to get us a taxi!" Kafa told Khalil reproachfully.

"All that matters is for us to get out of this damned place," he replied, "I'll carry you on my back if I have to. I'll buy you the train and the station. Just let us get through this gate."

The minute they came out they were surrounded by journalists. Khalil covered his head with his shirt and went rushing through the gauntlet, while Kafa stopped and surrendered happily to their camera lenses, then started answering their questions in her capacity as the daughter of Mr. Baytmouni, friend of the late Raghid and guest of honor at the Night of the First Billion on account of which she had been assigned a private room in the mansion. She answered all the questions in the greatest detail, her blue eyes and her eyelashes glistening with tears. When another contingent of reporters approached, she took out her handbag and adjusted her makeup in preparation for more photographs.

When Khalil was about to turn the corner, he looked back at her and saw her smiling warmly at one of the photographers. Then he went on alone to the train station.

There he met up with Nasim, who was sitting quietly with his big suitcase. Nasim didn't ask him about Kafa, and when the train arrived the two of them got on together and sat side by side without exchanging a word until Khalil started preparing to get off.

"Where to?" Nasim asked.

"To the hospital. And you?"

"To Amir's house."

"I'll join you there later."

◆　◆　◆

The morning before the Night of the First Billion.

What sort of wind had blown this treacherous, lovable, loathsome sweetheart his way?

Amir opened the door and found her standing there. She had come to him just the way he'd dreamed of her doing: her eyes full of tears and her hair unkempt. She'd come too late, of course. Even so, her coming had been necessary to assuage his wounded pride. And to give him the strength to bury her in the recesses of his memory.

(He embalms her. He lays her as a splendidly beautiful Cleopatra in a golden sarcophagus in the heart of the pyramid. He perfumes her. He adorns her with jewels. He kisses her lifeless lips and says to her, "I love you, I hate you, I love you, I hate you." Then he bids her farewell. He leaves the chamber and closes the door gently, being careful not to make any noise inside his head, which is where he first erected the pyramid dedicated to her immortality.) Still in his nightclothes, he was taken by surprise.

"Pardon me," he said, "I was expecting someone else."

"I won't be staying long. I'm in need of a million Swiss francs. If I can't round up that amount, I'll go to prison."

"A million francs?" he repeated. "You know I'm poor."

"Couldn't you borrow it from the fund you keep for helping your friends?"

"Embezzle it, you mean?"

"I'll try to return it quickly. But I don't suppose that will be easy from now on."

"What happened? Let me guess."

"I gambled, and I lost."

"Raghid got you into a fix the way he does with most of his assistants. Didn't he?"

She nodded silently.

Then she murmured, "He didn't mean to. He died suddenly of a heart attack. In any case, what difference does it make? I'm in the same fix either way—bad checks written for food that nobody's going to eat, and caviar that'll just get thrown back into the sea. And when the bank opens in less than an hour, I'll drop dead. I'm a goner."

"I'm sorry. I'd like to help you, but I can't dip into money that belongs to the poor to pay for the wastefulness of the rich. I'm not going to deprive the guys of help with their university tuition and medical care to pay for the Night of the First Billion dinner on behalf of the late Raghid. Why don't you go to Sheikh Sakhr or somebody else of his breed?"

"I can't do that again."

"Sorry, Layla. Really sorry."

Before taking leave of him, she stepped up to him and planted an unexpected kiss on his left cheek. He remembered having slapped her on the left cheek once. But before he could say anything, she was gone.

After she left he went on standing there in a daze, his thirst for revenge gone. For so long he'd dreamed of this moment, hoped for it, waited for it. But when it finally came, he'd taken no pleasure in it. He didn't gloat and he didn't grieve. Instead, he was overcome by a vague sense of emptiness.

Not grief, not joy, not vindictive glee. Just emptiness. Emptiness. Emptiness. An emptiness with the taste of "absence" that one inevitably grows accustomed to after having lived with someone for a long time—the way one grows accustomed to one's hand, after which it's cut off!

As Nasim approached Amir's house, he thought he saw Layla driving by and burying her head in the steering wheel. When he looked in her direction to make certain that it was her, she sped away. He thought to himself: It's as if she's looking for an accident as a way of committing suicide!

And when he saw the melancholy look on Amir's face, he knew for certain that the morning's visitor had been Layla. He didn't say anything to Amir about her. Let her go to hell, he thought. He'd never liked her—or Dunya or Kafa, for that matter. That type of woman didn't appeal to him. If it weren't for the existence of women like his mother and Bahriya, he would have ended up hating the whole lot of them.

He set his big suitcase aside and flung himself onto the only chair in the house. Amir sat down opposite him on a couch and said, "What a morning it's been. Two hours ago you called me to tell me he'd been murdered, and I heard from . . ." (he nearly said, "Layla," but caught himself in time and continued), "I heard that he died of a heart attack."

"Khalil told me that he killed him. The poor guy imagines that he killed him because he was with him when he had the heart attack and he didn't help him, but let him drown. And I for my part was afraid we might both be suspected of murdering him if they knew what I'd done when I discovered the body."

"And what is it that you did? What is this madness that came over the two of you last night?"

"It's the weather."

Nasim got up and opened his suitcase. Then he took out the Freedom Fighter statue and placed it on top of the empty pedestal that had been waiting for it for so long, saying, "This is the original statue, the one that your father sculpted. When I discovered Raghid's dead body, I also discovered that the door to the cage where Raghid kept the statue was open. So as fast as I could, I replaced it with the copy that Raghid had given me to humiliate and defeat me."

A spark of elation appeared in Amir's eye, then turned into a dry tear. He wanted to say something to Nasim but he couldn't find the words. It was as if the alphabet were thirty-four colored fish that had migrated out of the waters of his heart, leaving him nothing but the sound of the wind in his throat. So he contented himself with a muffled gasp.

Nasim continued, "And this is another gift, to you from the castle of death."

"What's that? A jar of Nescafé? You really have lost your marbles!"

As he spoke, Nasim was rummaging through the jar's contents, which he'd poured out onto the table.

He took the piaster out from under the heap of coffee granules, cleaned it off by blowing on it and said, "And this also has come back to us."

"You risked your life for a piaster, you fool?"

"For a piaster? Not exactly. And you know that."

They both fell into a long silence. Then Nasim said, "A fire broke out in the Ghanamali mansion and killed Sheikh Watfan."

"I know."

"How did you find about it?"

Amir smiled a mysterious smile, then said tersely, "News has been traveling fast this morning."

"And Bahriya has disappeared."

" . . ."

"I don't know exactly what's become of her."

" . . ."

"I'm thinking of going to offer my condolences to Sheikh Sakhr with regard to his son. I'm also thinking of applying to work for him as a butler. Bahriya might reappear, or I might be able to find out something about what's happened to her. Maybe he's holding her prisoner, for example, and is using the alleged fire as an excuse to hide her away."

When at last Amir spoke, he did so with a confident, somewhat mysterious smile on his lips. Stressing every word as if he were uttering it for the last time, he said calmly, "Bahriya is fine. I'm not worried about her. So don't you worry, either."

"What do you mean? Did she come here?"

Amir made no reply. With youthful impetuosity, Nasim pressed, "Please tell me, why aren't you worried about her?"

" . . ."

"I gave her your name and address. Are you hiding something from me?"

" . . ."

"Is she in a safe place?"

"I told you not to worry, man."

"Are you hiding something from me? I am worried about her."

"And I'm worried about you. I've told you, and I repeat: Bahriya is fine, and I'm not worried about her. So put your mind at rest. And now, tell me: What are you going to do with yourself?"

"I don't know yet. I haven't had a chance to think. But I suppose I'll go back home."

"You're not going back there until you've finished your thesis. Your country needs educated people, too—not just fighters."

"Don't forget that I've lost my job."

"We'll find you something for the short time you have left before you graduate from the university."

"Maybe . . ."

"I'd been hoping to invite you to come live with me. But I don't want you to end up like Bassam. I'm a marked man, and at the stage we've reached now, I'm bound to be killed—either I or someone else who, like me, is still convinced that there's no salvation for us without democracy and freedom of thought. In any case, you're exhausted now. We'll talk later on about this and a lot of other things. Get up now and go to bed."

"I forgot to tell you about what happened to our friend Saqr today."

"He's of no concern to me. But tell me, where's Khalil?"

"He went to see his little boy in the hospital. He'll join us in a while."

"And his wife?"

"I don't know. She wasn't with him when we met at the station."

Nasim stood up unsteadily and nearly fell.

"My God!" he said, "I really *am* tired!"

Amir didn't hear him. He was too busy running his hands over the Freedom Fighter statue, his father's signature, and the line that had been erased from it. His mind somewhere else, it was as if he had slipped through the hole in the antique Palestinian piaster into some distant tunnel.

◆   ◆   ◆

Morning on the day of the Night of the First Billion.

Exhausted, the two of them returned to the house like a couple of skiffs demolished by a storm of golden flames and cast onto some unknown shore as debris, black dust, and the tattered remains of sails.

As they sat at the window gazing down at Geneva in the valley below, the city looked detached and indifferent, and the lake was so still, it looked as though some mad artist had drawn it onto the surface of the earth. So then, Dunya thought to herself, he didn't kill him. So then, thought Nadim as he eyed her unaffectionately, she didn't kill him.

As Nadim ran his hands over his head, Dunya thought she saw puffs of ashes come flying out of his hair, his eyelashes and the wrinkles in his cheeks.

(How we've aged. In our mad rush to save time and make the most of every moment, we've frittered our lives away. We never paused even for a moment to ask: Why? Where are we headed? What now?)

"Strange, this telephone," said Nadim. "Even with all the rich folks that live in Geneva, not a soul has called to ask me about what happened to Raghid, or what will happen to me."

Dunya whispered, "I cut off all telephone calls to the house. I cut the telephone cord, that quotidian thread of madness."

"Why?"

"So that I could talk to you. So that we could have a conversation with each other. That hasn't happened to us for a long time. We talk, but we don't communicate."

(Here I am running in the race. Nadim runs. Raghid runs. Everyone I know is racing toward an electrically charged mountain of gold. From the top of the mountain there ascends a flame that's just barely visible, but which has the power to strike one down like lightning. We rush and we pant and we extol the name of King Midas. Every one of us would strike a blow against his nearest and dearest if he got the chance. Everyone who falls, we trample under foot and carry on with the race. Without even stopping for a breath, Nadim gives me orders: "We're having five guests for an intimate dinner. Be sure to invite such-and-such a dancer. We'll be having one guest for dinner, and be sure to bring in so-and-so the poetess, since he's wild about her singing and dancing." "Change your dress." "Cut your hair." "Wear the fur coat, the diamond ring, the gold necklace." "Hurry up." "Yes, sir," I say. And I hurry up. I long for the chance to sit with him for a moment so that we could have a real conversation. "Please, couldn't we exchange a kiss along the way? Can't I tell you something about my heart, my spirit, my confusion?" "Gold!" he shouts at me. "That's all there is! It's a race, so hurry."

So I hurry. And he hurries.

He doesn't notice that the winner in this race is rewarded by being murdered. His prize is illness, loneliness, and homelessness.)

"Please, Nadim. There are things that we have to make decisions about together, like civilized people, without arguing."

"All right, what do you want?"

"I want us to get out of the rat race we've been living in ever since we got married."

"And move to Australia, buy a farm, raise poultry, and live off the crops we plant? You're a fool. Don't you know what problems I face?"

"Can't we have a single conversation, for once, without you getting sarcastic and insulting me?"

"It'll be hard, but I'll try."

"There's a serious matter I'd like to tell you about."

"What's that?"

"I've stolen something for your sake."

"What did you steal?"

"The documents that implicate you. I stole those papers. I went down to talk to him, to plead with him to leave you alone. Either that, or to threaten him, or maybe to kill him. I don't know exactly. But in any case, I found him dead, so I didn't plead or threaten. And when I found the papers, I picked them up and brought them back with me."

"And where are they now?"

"I destroyed them. There. Before the police arrived."

Neither of them said anything more for quite some time.

Then he said, "I thank you. You really are a noble lady after all."

Then he added, a bit nastily, "Isn't that what you wanted to hear? All right now, what do you want in return?"

"For us both to come safely out of the fire of gold."

"It's no use, Dunya. This whole escapade of yours was useless. Do you really think Raghid was that stupid? Do you think those papers were the only copy? He was a clever old fox. The originals have to be somewhere, in the hands of some lawyer—both they and others. And justice was supposed to take its course the minute he died or was killed. He was certain that there was somebody who wanted to kill him, and that whoever it was might actually do it. He always went out of his way to make sure we knew that his death wouldn't be the end of our troubles, but the start of them. He was sure he'd be killed, and he'd arranged everything on that basis. It had never occurred to him—or to any of us—that he might die naturally just the way millions of other people do every year. He thought his death would be special and memorable, not something ordinary."

"And the result?"

"The result is that you performed a superfluous service. There's another document somewhere that implicates me in the embezzlement. There's no way out of going to prison, unless I go to work for somebody powerful who can protect me."

"You mean, for another Raghid?"

"Exactly."

"Why don't you wait a while? Maybe it was the only copy."

"But maybe it wasn't. And if it wasn't, then no one will ever hire me again. If I fall, the knives aimed at my jugular vein will multiply like rabbits. You know that's the byword of the world we live in. However, if I were working for another 'strong man,' another Raghid, then I'd have a chance to bargain with the lawyer before the case reached the Swiss judicial system which, once you're in it, there's no way out of."

"And what if the case did reach the courts? We could just pay the amount you embezzled and your sentence would be lightened."

"Pay? Are you out of your mind? I'm not about to give up a single franc or dollar of my fortune. Besides which, if I went to prison, I'd lose my reputation as a top-notch businessman, in which case no other billionaire would hire me and we'd be back to point zero."

"And what if we were? We could go back to Beirut, rebuild your parents' house, and rebuild our lives along with it."

"Now? When we're both forty-five years old? Have you forgotten that in Beirut also, people despise the poor? In spite of everything that's happened, they still live by the maxim, 'If you've got a piaster, you're worth a piaster.' Even if I had to choose, I'd take prison over poverty. But I'm not obliged to make that sort of choice. And we're not going to leave our life of wealth for the hell of poverty, death, bombing, and homelessness."

"But we're already living in hell."

"Speak for yourself."

"I personally prefer our losing our wealth and your going to prison if that's what it takes to get out from under this yoke."

"I'm indebted to you for your enlightened thoughts. And now, let me fix the telephone cord and rebuild my bridges to the world of people. Isolation on a morning like this is a crime."

"It's our chance to break free."

"It's still the day of the Night of the First Billion as far as I'm concerned. Half the well-to-do people in the world are here in Geneva, opportunities abound, and you've chosen today of all days to isolate me from the outside world. Are you trying to destroy me? You're a crazy, loud-mouthed alcoholic. You're not fit to be a wife to somebody like me."

"A woman like Coco would make you a good wife," she replied derisively.

"I thank you for pointing that out to me," he said seriously, "and I just might do something about it. You'd stay to take care of the children, and she could take care of the business. Lots of people have done that sort of thing, but I didn't see the wisdom in it till now. The first wife always gets old and worn out while her husband is reaching the top, and as a result he needs a new, fresh woman who has the strength to keep pace with him."

Once more she had the sensation of her self being gelatinous and ill-defined. She went groping from one container to another without knowing exactly what she wanted. One word would drive her to hate him and ask for a divorce, and another would hurl her into a state of jealousy and the desire to possess.

(I've lost my sense of inner reality. My feelings are so fickle, I don't trust them anymore.)

Her emotions rapidly took on one hue after another, shifting back and forth between different rhythms and cadences. Suddenly she was overcome by an urgent impulse to monopolize his attention, and at any price. And she found herself saying, "I want a divorce. Today."

"Sorry," he replied indifferently, "I haven't got time for such trivial details. What I've got to do now is get on my feet again. And instead of helping me, you try to tear me down."

"I'm trying to save myself from your tearing us both down together. You're married to the rat race, not to me, so either way, the divorce is over and done with. I've given you a chance to save yourself, for us to save ourselves. I stole those papers for your sake, and I expressed my willingness to live in poverty if you'd do the same. Being in prison is better than living a life without a speck of light."

"Be quiet now. The children have woken up, and we don't want to confuse their lives with our craziness."

"Their lives are already in a shambles. They aren't Arabs anymore, and they'll never become Europeans. Don't you understand?"

"Maybe it would have been better if I'd contacted Sheikh Sakhr and arranged to go back to work for him. After all, someone your already know is a better bet than someone you don't."

"You don't have a solid reality anymore, either. You've become a parasitic plant that needs to cling to a plant that's bigger."

"I'll explain things to him and he'll believe me. I'll tell him that Raghid lied to him and forced me to play the scapegoat, the evidence being the divine retribution that's been wrought on my behalf. I'll prove to him that I had nothing to do with the school fiasco. He's a compassionate man, and in his heart of hearts he may already be convinced that Raghid was the culprit."

"Our children don't have any roots, and you don't either. You're parasitic creatures floating in air saturated with gold dust, trying to rob other people of their achievements and blessings."

"I think this is a good time for it. I'll trick him into thinking that I've gotten a lot of offers but that I prefer to go back to working for him."

"We'll never enjoy a democracy that we don't deserve. We'll never enjoy a freedom that we haven't paid for. Living in Switzerland won't turn us into Swiss citizens no matter how rich we are. We'll never enjoy a happy life anywhere."

"I'll get in touch with Coco, marvelous Coco, who's fit to be the wife of a man like me, always determined to succeed. The fact that the two sheikhs—Sakhr and Saqr—are taken by her is no secret. There isn't a man who's seen her but that she's knocked him off his feet. And when Saqr gets out of his treatment center, I might need her."

"Are you listening to what I'm saying?"

"Do you hear what I said?"

"Do you hear what I said?"

"You're not having a conversation with me."

"I'll go meet Sheikh Sakhr. Now that Raghid's gone, I've got to hold onto him—or to somebody who's his equivalent financially. If I'm not back early, be glad, since that means I succeeded in my mission. Raghid I has died. Long live Raghid II."

"I'm going out to buy a brush and some oil paints. I'm going back to drawing and painting. Now that everything's fallen apart, I've got to hold onto the only thing that's left."

"That's right—I'll go to Sheikh Sakhr to offer my condolences and test the waters with him, so to speak."

"I'll go to the paint supply store."

"Would you like to go with me?"

"Would you like to go with me?"

"Go with you? I'm busy. What did you say, Dunya? Where is it you wanted me to go with you?"

"And you, what did you say? Where did you want me to go with you? Oh . . . let's try."

"Try to do what?"

"To see if each of us can hear the other's voice when he says something. Let's try to rebuild our lives. Let's try . . ."

"You're drunk. This evening you'll be sober, and then we'll talk. Or tomorrow morning."

"This time I'm not drunk."

"What is it that were you drinking from that bottle the whole time we were in the car and ever since we arrived, then? And without breakfast at that? Listen, Dunya. I know that I made a mistake when I brought you that damned painting in a rare moment of sentimental weakness. But we also pay for mistakes like that. And it's worn me out these past few weeks. Let me be frank with you: Maybe you were gifted as an artist in the past, and maybe not. But don't you understand that like everything else, talent gets rusty if we don't use it? Don't you understand that you can't cancel out two decades of your life with a mere decision, or go back to a point in the past that you loved? The seeds of talent die if we don't give them the proper care. You can't return to the past. It's gone. So if you want to escape, you've got no choice but to escape forward, not backward. You'll never be able to get the girl in the painting back again, because you killed her."

"I'll try. At least I'll try. As for you, you refuse to try anything."

"I got past the experimental phase of my life a long time ago. And I know what it means to be nearly fifty years old. It means no turning back. Nobody starts over at this age."

"A person can start over at any age. He can try, at least. And I'm going to try."

"Pep talks. Theories. Speechology. We are what we do. And the rest is nothing but rationalizations. Have you gone back to visit Amir and his gang?"

"Yes, I have. I have, and will again."

"What do you see in a poor fool like him?"

"A point of light."

◆   ◆   ◆

It was the Night of the First Billion.

But instead of enjoying himself, he found himself a near-prisoner. It was the Night of the First Billion, and Saqr's first night in the addiction treatment center, without cocaine and without his devil's mask.

They had found the drugs in his private guest room in Raghid's mansion, and he was to be punished by being reformed. Not even a million men like his father would do him any good here.

But he'd killed Raghid. He'd killed him in self-defense because he'd been jealous of him. So why wouldn't anyone believe him?

Why did they persecute him and despise him and not notice how great he was? It was true, of course, that he'd concealed from everyone how dangerous he really was. However, he'd thought it was too obvious to miss.

Why were they persecuting and tormenting him? Why did they claim that he'd invented all these ideas because of the white girl, his beloved drug, which, according to them, was what had turned him into such a wreck? What wreck? Couldn't they see his coming immortality and his present glory?

And why had Khalil turned his back on him, refusing to say that the drugs belonged to him? Wasn't that what his employees were supposed to do—go to prison and be tortured in his place? Why wasn't anybody doing his job? He would have rewarded him handsomely. But that son of a bitch had refused and abandoned him instead.

Someday he'd leave this place, and he'd cut off all Khalil's sources of income in Europe. He'd stalk him. He'd buy every establishment he went to work in so that he could dismiss him from it. He wouldn't be able to escape from his revenge. His revenge. His revenge against . . . against whom? He'd forgotten . . . forgotten. All he remembered was that they were torturing him, persecuting him, tying him down. He wanted to tear something apart, anything: the pillow, the wall, the window, the clouds, his face, his neck. Insects were crawling under his skin, and hundreds of black bugs were attacking his eyes. "Help! Help!" he screamed.

The nurse inserted her sharp needle into his arm and filled his ulcerous nostrils with a moisturizing cream.

"I don't want cream!" he screamed, "I want flying powder! I want white dust, happiness dust! Let me fly away. Don't tie me down to earth. I don't recognize it. I don't know its people or its problems or anything about it. Ever since I was born, my father has taken me flying far away from everything. I want to go on living my own way. And fly, fly. Help, Coco! Save me, and I'll punish you by murdering you. And you'll enjoy it, you—the only sane woman in the world!"

❖   ❖   ❖

It was the Night of the First Billion.

And Dunya was getting drunk alone. Her two children avoided coming near her, then left the house. Nadim hadn't returned since morning, which meant that he'd managed to arrange something with Sheikh Sakhr or some other man of means.

"And Coco's started to get cheeky. She called and asked for him, then left her telephone number—the number of my husband's own flat. And she didn't even go to the trouble of saying hello to me or asking how I was. She was so oblivious to social decency, she treated me as if I didn't exist. Or like a handful of ashes. A past that's over and done with. I'd sure like to see her when *she* turns into a handful of ashes.)

She tried to do some drawing in the afternoon, but she wasn't able. Her hand was shaking and her inner self was running scared into deep, dark passageways. So she dismissed the maid and was happy to see her children leave the house. Then she switched on the television and sat devouring food like a glutton, oblivious to the world. As she watched the afternoon news she heard that Layla Sabbak had died in a peculiar car accident in which she ran headlong into a large truck while driving at top speed down the wrong lane. And she didn't give a second thought to the question posed by the news announcer: Could it have been a suicide, as the truck driver suspects?

When she heard the news, she didn't gloat or feel happy. Instead, she just felt indifferent, as if the space inside her was so crowded with emotions, there was no room left for any more. She got up and went to bed, slept a few hours, then woke up with the thought of painting still plaguing her. I'll try again, she thought, and if I fail, then it will mean Nadim was right.

So she tried again, and her failure in post-sleep sobriety was undeniable. She felt like someone searching for a jewel in a forest that he hasn't visited for a long, long time, or who's only visited it in some half-forgotten dream.

(So, I've come full circle. I'm back to where I started. But I feel more frustrated than ever. It's as if, instead of ending up back where I started, the circle has started to close in on me. As if I've spiraled around once or twice until I reached the center of the circle, then started spinning round and round like some lunatic in a fit of delirium. I'm going to see Amir.)

She poured another glass of firewater and downed it in one gulp.

(No . . . I'm not going to see Amir. After all, I already know everything he could say to me. I've memorized all the encouraging words that might be spoken on an occasion such as this. For example, he might tell me that I'm being too hard on myself when I compare myself to the young woman that I was way back when. He'll tell me that we look upon our youth in the same way that we do those who've died, that is, with the eye of unconditional approval. We erase everything negative we've seen in the past and take nothing but the good points into account. Words, words. But the only reality is: I'm miserable.)

When Dunya had drained the bottle, she got up as usual to inspect herself in her painting. She was astonished to find that the young woman in the picture had disappeared entirely, as if she'd left for good.

It Sheikh Watfan had been alive, she would have accused him and Nadim of perpetrating this crafty feat of wizardry.

When she turned on the light and came up close to the painting, she noticed that the picture of the young woman was still just the way it had been, but that a dense, ashen mist now covered the painting, obscuring it from view.

Dumbfounded, she collapsed onto her chair for a few minutes, trembling with shock. She waited for the girl in the painting to speak to her as she usually did. But she seemed far, far away, somewhere beyond those light years of darkness and dense fog.

She got up and ran her fingers over the painting, only to find to her astonishment that there was a layer of grayish-white paint covering it. It was as if someone had painted on a layer of fog beneath which the girl had almost vanished completely.

(Might I have done this while I was asleep?)

She trembled with anguish as a terrifying thought flashed through her mind with the certitude that comes at the moment of clear vision: Perhaps I'm seeing the girl in the painting for the last time, and tomorrow morning the fog will swallow her up forever.

However, she didn't have to wait till the next morning, because when she looked into the painting again, she didn't see anyone. The young woman had disappeared entirely. And what she left behind wasn't the whiteness of the canvas before it's been painted on, but a color somewhere between white and gray. It looked like the dirty, off-white hue that's left by a little boy after he's scribbled with his pencils in his school notebook, then tried to correct his error with an eraser.

She gulped with fright. (So then, nothing can erase our sins after all. And it's impossible to break through the time barrier, since the bridges we burn behind us can't be rebuilt.)

❖   ❖   ❖

Khalil didn't feel as though the nightmare of the Night of the First Billion was over until the moment when Rami pointed with his broken, plaster-covered hand toward dry land, shouting, "Beirut! Beirut!" The days that had passed between the Geneva airport and Larnaca, followed by the search for a boat to take them to Beirut, had seemed to him like one long, long night. That bandaged, childlike hand had been like the white arrow on street signs that indicates the direction of traffic. Overcome by seasickness, Fadi lay limp as a rag on the deck, his head resting on the knee of a woman he didn't know but whose heart went out to him in motherly affection. And she in turn was resting her head on the knee of another woman who, like her, lay prostrate on the deck of the small livestock freight vessel as it was tossed to and fro by the waves. People were piled on top of one another, possibly on their way to being slaughtered like the animals that normally would have been transported on the same boat. A few days earlier, a ship fleeing from Beirut had burned up with all its passengers in this very spot. That's what one of the people on board was saying, at least. And on the open sea they spotted another ship heading from Beirut to Cyprus. Khalil gazed at it without envy.

(Where is there to escape to? I ran away like them once. Like them, I rode in the opposite direction and went scurrying toward the world's other shore. But I didn't get out of the cycle of nightmares. Instead, I was like someone swinging back and forth between one nightmare and another.)

Rami cried with delight again, still pointing toward Beirut with that living, white arrow of his.

Khalil's heart pulsated with warmth, and he felt a renewed sense of dignity. Here, he wouldn't be a refugee, a homeless wanderer. Never again would he beg for a job, a residence card or an entry visa . . . not to mention a number of other things he'd never do again. And if he found his house destroyed, he'd live in a tent in the same spot until he'd rebuilt it. Here was the beginning, not on a chair in a sidewalk café in some European capital, or in Raghid's morass of depravity.

As the ship approached land, he was filled with joy and excitement. It let down anchor, followed by an eternity of waiting, pushing and shoving to get off, tears, and more pushing and shoving.

Questions. Answers. Entry. Taxi. He enjoyed bargaining over the fare even though he had more than enough money to pay for it. He'd used the gift from Sheikh Hilal to pay for the trip back, and he was glowing with delight as he looked around at the streets of his homeland, bathed in sunshine and full of fa-miliar-looking faces. That is, until the critical moment arrived: the Israeli checkpoint.

He could hardly believe that this was really happening to him.

For the first time in his life he was stopping at an Israeli checkpoint in his own land. (Here where we fought among ourselves, I see this Israeli check-point replacing us all.) Before this there had been one local checkpoint after another. And after every battle there would be a reshuffling of the fighters manning the checkpoints, along with the slogans and the pictures of political leaders—so similar one could hardly tell them apart—that adorned their bar-rels. And now they were gone, one and all. The Israeli checkpoint had been set up as if it were the finale to the whole drama. The finale? No, no, no!

It was the first time he'd seen an Israeli soldier. The soldier manning the checkpoint looked like any other young man his age. It was possible that if he'd met up with the same person in Geneva or stepped on his toe in Larnaca, he would have apologized politely and lit his cigarette for him. At this mo-ment, however, he was seized by a painful question: What is this man doing here?

Once he was sure what kind of a checkpoint it was, he was overwhelmed by feelings of humiliation and rage. The Israeli soldiers had contented them-selves with taking a string so thin it was nearly invisible and stretching it across the road.

No wooden beams. No barrels. Nothing but a dirty, white, thin string stretched from one side of the road to the other. And behind this string there stood veritable caravans of cars, with hundreds of them heading out of Beirut. Khalil felt as though the thin string that the Israelis had tied across the street as a roadblock was being tightened around his neck with jagged cutting edges and was about to choke him until he could no longer speak. The taxi driver an-swered the soldier's questions, and his hand gave the soldier the passports as if it had been disconnected from his head and the rest of his body. His chest tightened and a sharp pain erupted from somewhere deep inside him, as if someone had just plunged a dagger into his waist. Meanwhile, because a blockade had been imposed on the Beirut residents who had held out against the invaders, the soldier searched the car to make sure it contained no food or water.

(I see 170,000,000 Arabs lined up single file in the desert. And I'm among them. We're all standing motionless in front of a cotton string as thin as the one before us now, which is as flimsy as the threads that people use to sew buttons on with. We get into a fight among ourselves over how to cut the string. Some of the orators in our midst theorize about the proper way to cut it, including when and where it ought to be cut—toward the right end, toward the left end, or in the middle. And if anyone tries to go ahead and cut it, some of the enemy agents that have been planted among us pick a fight with him so that he'll get lost in the sea of disputes. With everyone shouting at once, we start fighting one another and cutting off one another's heads, but nobody cuts the string. During the periodic lulls in the fighting, someone comes along and runs his hands over the string in preparation to conduct a strategic study on the subject, while someone else delivers an eloquent sermon that starts with the words, "O string, O string. . ." Then some of the people in the crowd lift the speaker onto their shoulders shouting, "Down with the string! Down with the string!"

This group passes by another one that happens to be shouting something different. As a result, people start shooting—not at the string, but at each other—until it's turned into an outright battle. Meanwhile, the string stays just as it is—a thin string, nothing more. "The theories are many, but the string is one.")

Everyone in the taxi was silent. Rami and Fadi were holding their breath, and they were nearing the house. Eyes were fixed on the windows. The saw the after effects of fire and crashes and the remains of barricades in the streets, streets that had been filled with carnage for the sake of religious identity over seven long years of civil war hysteria. "Civil?" Is this really what "civil" people do to each other, not to mention fellow countrymen?

For the first time in a long time Khalil thought back to the moment when they opened fire on him in the graveyard without killing him, and he almost felt as though he'd done a foolish thing by coming back to Beirut. But no. Never again would a Lebanese—or any Arab—fight against another in Beirut. After all that had happened, it wasn't possible. Or was it? No. Yes . . .

(Now the thin string cuts across the streets of another Arab capital, and no one has lifted a finger to prevent it. So, will it go on making its way across more and more cities, turning into a huge spider's web where we flail about in our torment? What sort of fate am I condemning my children to by bringing them back here? And what sort of homeland am I bringing them back to? All this devastation—the inward devastation made visible through the devastation of buildings and bodies—can it be undone? Didn't I make a terrible mistake when I brought my children back from Geneva? As long as Kafa was determined to leave me anyway, I could have looked for a job in some honorable, if humble profession and stayed far away from both the tragedy here and its extensions there in the form of people like Sakhr, Saqr, and Raghid. So why did I come back?)

Khalil was on the verge of drowning in a shadowy abyss of remorse as the car rolled along, the atmosphere charged with confusion.

(What should I do when it seems that every step I take causes some sort of harm? And if it was a sin to run away, then isn't coming back now a fatal error?)

Then suddenly he caught sight of a peculiar spectacle.

Above all the wreckage and in the space between the demolished houses, he saw a multicolored kite soaring up into the air and gleaming in the sunshine as if it were made of gold. Dangling from it there was a white string with the flavor not of humiliation, but of joy. It was something strange, yet familiar, sprinting along over the face of death like a baby boy who's emerged alive from the womb of a dying mother. Khalil gasped like a woman in labor at the moment when she collapses like an animal being slaughtered for sacrifice.

As he stared at the kite, a shot rang out. The driver said, "Don't worry. There aren't any snipers around here."

(I see them. They're coming together. They're firing at the colored kite. No matter what it costs them, they want to shoot it down as it flies over this vast, scorched land.)

However, it went on flying, while Khalil went on following it with his eyes until his neck started to hurt. When he looked back down at the scorched ground, he thought he saw Bahriya running about among the ruins of the houses. She ran with the speed of fire and with the sweetness of that multicolored paper aircraft. As she ran, Sheikh Watfan came scurrying along behind her, his body in flames. Or did he just imagine it?